Luftwaffe Letters

About the author:

Edward Thorpe was dance critic of the *Evening Standard* and has written extensively elsewhere, for *The Guardian*, the *New York Times* and the *Los Angeles Times*. He has published five books on dance as well as a successful novel, *The Night I Caught the Santa Fe Chief*, which is currently being developed as a film.

Praise for *The Night I Caught the Santa Fe Chief*:

'Some of the best scenic writing ever met in a thriller. People real, too' – *Sunday Telegraph*

By the same author:

FICTION
The Night I Caught the Santa Fe Chief

NON-FICTION
The Other Hollywood
Chandlertown
The Colourful World of Ballet (with Clement Crisp)
Ballet Genius (with Gillian Freeman)
Isadora: The Making of a Ballet
Black Dance

BIOGRAPHY
Kenneth MacMillan: The Man and the Ballets

Edward Thorpe

Luftwaffe Letters

ARCADIA BOOKS

Arcadia Books Ltd
15–16 Nassau Street
London W1W 7AB

www.arcadiabooks.co.uk

First published in the United Kingdom 2006
Copyright © Edward Thorpe 2006

A catalogue record for this book is available from the British Library.

ISBN 1-900850-97-4

Typeset in Bembo by Basement Press, London
Printed in Finland by WS Bookwell

Arcadia Books distributors are as follows:

in the UK and elsewhere in Europe:
Turnaround Publishers Services
Unit 3, Olympia Trading Estate
Coburg Road
London N22 6TZ

in the USA and Canada:
Independent Publishers Group
814 N. Franklin St.
Chicago, IL 60610

in Australia:
Tower Books
PO Box 213
Brookvale, NSW 2100

in New Zealand:
Addenda
Box 78224
Grey Lynn
Auckland

in South Africa:
Quartet Sales and Marketing
PO Box 1218
Northcliffe
Johannesburg 2115

Arcadia Books: *Sunday Times* Small Publisher of the Year 2002/03

Author's note

This story is set against the historical background of World War II and many of the characters who appear (e.g. Göring, Goebbels, Himmler, Heydrich and his wife Lina, Kesselring, Milch, Galland, Mölders, etc.) were, of course, prominent, even distinguished, figures in that conflict.

The leading characters in the book are, however, entirely fictitious, as is Jagdgeschwader JG233. All other units of the Luftwaffe mentioned did exist and I have endeavoured to be as accurate as possible in all references to them, to the engagements in which they fought, the victories they achieved, the defeats they sustained, the aircraft they operated and the bases from which they flew.

On all relevant occasions I have used German terminology, not only because the story is told from the German point of view but also because there is rarely a direct translation into English. Even so, the provision of a glossary should prove helpful.

The organisation of the Luftwaffe

The administrative and operational organisation of the Luftwaffe was highly complex so that for the purposes of this story the following explanation is reduced to basic essentials.

The chief tactical operational unit of the Luftwaffe was the Geschwader which corresponded, loosely, to the Royal Air Force Wing or United States Army Air Force Group.

Most Geschwader were usually composed of three front-line Gruppen (Gruppe=RAF/USAAF Squadron) together with a fourth training Gruppe which, during the war, was often pressed into operational service. Fighter and bomber Gruppen usually had three Staffeln (Staffel=RAF/USAAF Flight). There was no regular subdivision of Staffeln but fighters usually operated in pairs (Rotte) or two pairs (Schwarm).

The operational role of each Geschwader was designated by a prefix, e.g. Jagdgeschwader (JG) Fighter Wing; Kampfgeschwader (KG) Bomber Wing; Stukageschwader (SG) Dive-bomber Wing, etc. (Stuka was a contraction of Sturzkampfflugzeug, literally falling-battle-flying machine, and applied to all dive-bombers irrespective of design.) It was customary to use Arabic and Roman numerals to determine each level; thus the abbreviation 1.II/JG3 would indicate 1st Staffel II Gruppe 3 Jagdgeschwader.

As the war progressed the distribution of the Gruppen comprising a Geschwader became extremely fluid: they could even be assigned to different theatres of war and operate different types of aircraft. In addition there were Gruppe formed for special duties, e.g. Ground Support, Night Fighting, High Level Reconnaissance and Experimental Operations.

The upper echelons of command, the several Luftflotte (Air Fleet), were established territorially, both within Germany and in various theatres of war and constituted self-contained air forces comprising fighters, bombers, transport and communications units, etc., under the command of a General Oberst or higher (Air Chief Marshal). The fighter force was represented at Luftwaffe HQ by a General der Jäger (Director of Fighters).

The Luftwaffe system of promotion was not linked to a command appointment but it was commonplace for a Staffel to be commanded by a Hauptmann (Captain) or Oberleutnant (First Lieutenant). There is no direct equivalent of ranks between the Luftwaffe, RAF and USAAF but the accompanying table is an approximation.

Ranks of the Luftwaffe

Luftwaffe	Royal Air Force	US Army Air Force
Generalfeldmarschall	Marshal of the Royal Air Force	General (Five Star)
Generaloberst	Air Chief Marshal	General (Four Star)
General der Flieger	Air Marshal	Lieutenant General
Generalleutnant	Air Vice Marshal	Major General
Generalmajor	Air Commodore	Brigadier General
Oberst	Group Captain	Colonel
Oberstleutnant	Wing Commander	Lieutenant Colonel
Major	Squadron Leader	Major
Hauptmann	Flight Lieutenant	Captain
Oberleutnant	Flying Officer	First Lieutenant
Leutnant	Pilot Officer	Lieutenant
Stabsfeldwebel	Warrant Officer	Warrant Officer
Oberfeldwebel	Flight Sergeant	Master Sergeant
Feldwebel	Sergeant	Technical Sergeant
Unterfeldwebel	--------	--------
Unteroffizier	Corporal	Staff Sergeant
Hauptgefreiter	--------	Sergeant
Obergefreiter	Leading Aircraftman	Corporal
Gefreiter	Aircraftman First Class	Private First Class
Flieger	Aircraftman Second Class	Private

Note: The officer in command of a Staffel was referred to as Staffelkapitan irrespective of rank.

A brief glossary

Abwehr: Counter-intelligence
Ausland SD (Sichheitsdienst): Foreign Intelligence Security Service
Bodo: Luftwaffe slang for base
Dicke Hund: literally, 'fat dog'; Luftwaffe slang for enemy bomber
Erprobungsstelle: research or test centre
Horrido!: fighter pilots' victory shout
Katschmarek: protective wingman
OKW (Oberkommando der Wehrmacht): High Command Armed Forces
RLM (Reichsluftfahrtministerium): State Ministry of Aviation
RSHA (Rasse-und Siedlungshauptamt): Central Office for Race Resettlement
Rustsätz: field conversion set
Schirmütze: peaked cap
Technisches Ampt: Technical Office of RLM
Tuchrock: service tunic

For Andy Johnson

Book One

War

From: Leutnant Peter von Vorzik
III Gruppe JG233
Jagdflieger HQ
To: Countess von Vorzik
Schloss Adlersee
Bavaria

1st September 1939

My Dear Mother and Father,

I have only a few minutes to write this. I have just come from the Briefing Room and we shall be taking off in half an hour.

After the years of waiting, the months of uncertainty, the Führer has at last decided that the Fatherland will strike back at our enemies. I am honoured to be in the vanguard of our vengeance.

Had I the time I would write at length to thank you both for providing me with everything in life. Without your love, understanding and guidance I would not now be able to help Greater Germany in her fight for freedom. If I do not return please know that I did everything in my power to be worthy of our name. Give Edith a kiss for me and when you speak or write to Christian give him salutations from his brother.

Ever your loving son,

Peter

Leutnant Peter von Vorzik
Journal entry

2nd September 1939

I doubt if I shall be able to write this journal on a daily basis but after the momentous events of yesterday I feel the need to put down my thoughts and impressions while they are fresh in my mind. If, one day, I become a father, my children might find these jottings of some interest.

A week ago it became evident that the Polish crisis was moving to its climax. We left our comfortable quarters at Brieg and moved to a bleak, temporary airfield close to the border where we were held on permanent standby. Tension was high. The newspapers and radio told us the Poles had mobilised a million men and Polish divisions were massing on the German border. Our sense of outrage at the harassment of German residents in Poland was equal to the feeling of frustration at doing nothing about it. When we were summoned to the Briefing Room at 03.00 hrs yesterday morning and the Führer's orders to strike in defence of Germany were read out there was a wave of cheering that took a minute or two to subside despite the Staffelkapitan's appeals for silence. I was still trembling with excitement as I scribbled a brief letter home.

Take-off was difficult because of a ground mist. Our Messerschmitt Me109Es (we have nicknamed them Emils) are always tricky at take-off anyway (there is a tendency for the port wing not to lift at indicated flying speed) so I was specially careful about procedure and when I finally eased the stick back the little fighter lifted off smoothly and seemed almost to float into the air. I was glad to see that my Katschmarek, Oberfeldwebel Kurt Schneckel, had also made it safely and had taken up station slightly above and behind me. Together we joined the rest of the Staffel, led by Staffelkapitan Zwemmer.

The western sky was still dark with one or two stars just visible but as the sun came up the eastern horizon was flooded with golden light. Our Staffel was joined by others from the Gruppe as we climbed steadily to 4,000 m. I felt tremendously exhilarated, just like when I made my first schoolboy flight in a glider.

Below, and to starboard, was a Gruppe of Junkers Ju87b Stukas to which we had been assigned as protective cover. They were to attack road and rail junctions in the vicinity of Lodz. When their attack was completed and they were safely on the return flight, we were to make free-ranging attacks on whatever targets we found – trains, convoys, troop concentrations, canal traffic and so on.

At 3,000 m there were small puffs of cumulus cloud obscuring the plain. Some minutes before we reached Lodz columns of black smoke extended through the cloud: the first wave of Stukas had found their targets. I saw the leading Ju87s of the Gruppe below us peel off and begin their dive. The first one had not assumed its full dive-angle before the second followed, then the next and the next, like the slow unfolding of a fan. It was fascinating to watch and I had to remind myself that this was the most dangerous part of the mission when we could most expect to be attacked by defending fighters. I made a mental note how easy it is to disregard the first rule of combat: *Never Relax Vigilance* – I could almost hear the gruff voice of my old instructor at the Kriegschule making us repeat the phrase.

The columns of smoke began to spread out in a grey pall through which single Stukas were starting to emerge, climbing back to operational height and reassembling. When the Gruppe was once again in position – none seemed to be missing – and were heading back to base our Staffel was given the order to break formation. We split into three Schwarme of four aircraft each.

Our Schwarm, led by Zwemmer, dived beneath the cloud level. Below, the plain was divided into big rectangular fields from which the grain had been harvested and there were lines of conical haystacks that reminded me of clowns' hats. We flew due west, following a road that was cluttered with farm carts and a few motor vehicles. Zwemmer gave the order to change course so that we were flying directly over railway tracks that ran parallel to the road. Less than a minute later we saw a feather of smoke from a locomotive but even as we approached there was a sudden ball of flame followed by billowing black smoke: some other pilots had beaten us to the target.

Within seconds the train was visible in detail. Although the remains of the locomotive still appeared to be moving I could see tiny figures jumping from the carriages and running across the stubble field. Then we saw the planes that had made the attack: Henschel Hs 123s, small obsolete biplanes, doing duty now as ground-attack aircraft. We watched as they turned to make a low strafing run with their machineguns, flying in line ahead at almost treetop level. Suddenly, the leading aircraft reared up and hung on its tail, then the nose dropped sharply and the aircraft plunged the few metres into the field. I saw the spout of earth as the propeller chewed into the ground, the wings crumpled and there was a flash of flame that swept through the aircraft as if it was made of paper. Even as I watched I was wondering why. Why? Engine failure? No, the stall was too sudden, too violent. A hit from a hidden gun emplacement? The field was flat and empty apart from the blazing train which had come to a halt. Then I saw the obvious answer: a flight of six PZL 11 fighters, of the Polish Air Force, coming in at an acute angle to the Henschels. I recognised the enemy aircraft from the photographs, silhouettes and models we have been studying these past weeks: large monoplanes with high gull-wings, fixed undercarriages and radial engines.

Zwemmer gave the order to attack. We were perfectly positioned above and behind the Polish aircraft and as I switched on the Revi reflector gunsight I was filled with anguish and anger at the loss of the Henschel. It was a bitter moment to accept, the first aircraft I had seen destroyed, a German one. Then, in imagination, I heard my Kriegschule instructor again: "Emotion is no help to marksmanship." In combat, rage, hate, fear are as dangerous as the enemy, diffusing concentration, slowing reflexes.

Following Zwemmer's orders I eased the stick over to port, gave the Emil a touch of rudder and brought the gunsight graticule onto the extreme starboard PZL. At nearly 400 kph I calculated that I was travelling at nearly twice the speed of the target and I had to be careful not to overshoot. I needed only a small angle of deflection while allowing for the fall in trajectory. When the PZL was a mere 200 m away I pressed the firing button and gave a three-second burst from all four guns, two cannon in the wings and two machineguns mounted on top of the engine-cowling – my first shots in anger!

At such close range the wingspan of the PZL filled the gunsight; I could see the red-and-white quartered squares of the Polish insignia on each wing tip. The 20mm cannon shells exploded along the length of the fuselage like a row of sparks. Almost immediately oily black smoke came from the engine cowling and the PZL began to spin, leaving a dark spiral on the landscape. I pulled back sharply on the stick and went into a steep climb, aware that I could be in the gunsights of another PZL. I was unable to see my victim hit the ground but I was certain I could claim my first kill. Near the cloudbase, mindful of Zwemmer's order to reform as Rotte,

I did a half-roll, diving down at the moment of inversion, searching the sky above and below not only for other PZLs but also for my Katschmarek. Then, on the radio transmitter, I heard Kurt's voice: "Stay on course, sir, I'm right with you." And there he was, sliding into view, behind and above on my port quarter. Good old Kurt! Amazing how he had kept track of me during that brief combat.

With fuel running low we turned back to base. After a few minutes flying we came across a Panzer division advancing across the plain, the tanks followed by motorised infantry and then, slowly and laboriously, horse-drawn gun-carriages and columns of marching troops. Exhilarated by my kill and by the feeling that I was part of that implacable force, I wanted to land my Emil alongside those marching men and get out and embrace my brothers-in-arms.

Back at base Kurt confirmed the destruction of my PZL, and Zwemmer claimed another one.

From: Edith von Vorzik
Schloss Adlersee
Bavaria
To: Leutnant Peter von Vorzik
III Gruppe JG233

5th September 1939

My Dear Peter,

Father has asked me to write to you on behalf of us all. We were tremendously proud and pleased to have your brief note. It said very little but it meant so much. Of course, we are terribly anxious for further news. According to the radio everything seems to be going splendidly but we know that there have been casualties. We pray for you every day and mother has a candle constantly burning for you in her room. I was terribly worried when France and Britain declared war on us but father says that it is nothing but a face-saving formality and the war will be over within the month.

Peter, I have some bad news, mother is very ill indeed. She collapsed at Mass last Sunday (3rd) and the doctor says she is suffering from a pernicious blood disease for which there is no cure and which will make her weaker and weaker. She probably has not long to live. It might be some months, it might only be weeks. Is there any chance of your getting leave? I wanted to send you a telegram, or try and reach you by phone but father would not hear of it. He says you have a task to perform and nothing must interfere with that, but if you could possibly get home for a few days I know it would be the best tonic that mother could have. I did telephone Christian in Berlin and he is coming soon but you know it is you that mother most wants to see.

Meanwhile, take great care of yourself. We hear of the Luftwaffe's great victories but there is constant anxiety for your safety on the part of

Your ever loving sister,

Edith

PS Since mother's illness father has become terribly morose. I dread every meal when we sit in silence (mother eats in her room). E.

From: Leutnant Peter von Vorzik
III Gruppe JG233
Jagdflieger HQ
To: Edith von Vorzik
Schloss Adlersee
Bavaria

12th September 1939

My Dear Edith,

I was very pleased to receive your letter but of course terribly upset to know mother is so ill. She has always seemed delicate but I assumed that beneath her natural pallor she was quite healthy. Did you know? Did she confide in you about her weakness? Is there really no hope? Has she seen any other doctors or specialists? If not then I think she should – do try and persuade father that we cannot just accept one verdict.

I hope to get leave very soon. After our swift victories it seems likely that the Staffel will be withdrawn to rest and re-equip, then I can have a few days at home.

I realise things must be rather depressing for you – we will have a long talk when I see you. I am enclosing a note for mother. Give father my affectionate greetings.

Ever your loving brother,

Peter

PS You may congratulate me on my first victory!

To: Countess Elisabeth von Vorzik

My Dearest Mother,
You can imagine how distressed I was to hear from Edith that you have been unwell. I pray and hope that by now the doctor's tonics are having some effect and that you are regaining your strength.

Our victories in Poland have been overwhelming and that means I shall soon be home on leave. Perhaps by the time I see you you will have recovered completely and we can play some music together and enjoy this beautiful autumn weather. Until then, God bless you and make you well.

Ever your loving son,
Peter

From: SS-Standartenführer Christian von Vorzik
RSHA Prinz Albertstraße
Berlin
To: Leutnant Peter von Vorzik
III Gruppe JG233
Jagdflieger HQ

17th September 1939

Dear Peter,
I received your greetings via Edith and when I telephoned Adlersee last night she told me that in a recent letter you said that you had gained your first victory. Congratulations. I also understand that you expect to go on leave soon. Your presence at Adlersee will be very welcome. Apparently mother is very weak and nothing can be done; it is just a matter of time.

On your way to or from Adlersee perhaps you could stop off for a day or two in Berlin? There is much we have to talk about. I still think it would be very advantageous for you to transfer from the Luftwaffe to the SS. It could easily be arranged through my office. I am myself expecting immediate advancement with an appointment to Obergruppenführer Reinhard Heydrich's staff. I will tell you all the details when we meet. Remember, the SS has within its ranks some of the finest blue blood in the country – you would be in good company. You can always telephone me here. Anticipating an early reunion,

Your affectionate brother,
Christian
Heil Hitler!

From: Leutnant Peter von Vorzik
III Gruppe JG233
Brieg
To: SS-Standartenführer Christian von Vorzik
RSHA Prinz Albertstraße
Berlin

21st September 1939

Dear Christian,

I was very pleased to have your letter. We have been pulled back from the front and I will go on leave to Adlersee tomorrow. I will certainly stop off in Berlin on my way back and look forward to seeing you.

I must congratulate you, too, on your new appointment and thank you for the offer of transferring to the SS but, you know, flying is what I have always wanted to do more than anything and I would not be happy in any other organisation – however eminent.

Affectionate greetings,
Peter

Leutnant Peter von Vorzik
Journal entry

25th September 1939

Withdrawal of fighter units from Poland began on September 17th. After the 3rd there was virtually no opposition from the Polish Air Force, most of which had been destroyed on the ground. Our Staffel lost no aircraft through enemy action but three were badly damaged in careless landings. Continuous attacks are being made on the Warsaw garrison by our bombers and the capitulation of the city is expected hourly. Our campaign in Poland is virtually complete.

I decided to visit Christian on my way to Adlersee because I was fortunate to obtain a lift to Berlin on a communications aircraft. Christian sent a staff car to meet me at Templehof, a big Mercedes with an immaculate young Unterscharführer as chauffeur who clicked his heels and greeted me with, "Heil Hitler."

Berlin seemed strange in the black out, the streets were thronging with people, everyone, it seemed, in uniform, and a great mood of excitement, almost gaiety. Our victory has been stupendous, greater than anyone dared to anticipate and France and Britain have been powerless to affect the outcome. The Führer was right when he called them effete and degenerate.

I stayed at the same small hotel, the Goldener Spinne, that I used to use when I was at the Kriegschule. I rather suspect it has become something of a bordello! At least, there were a lot of young Wehrmacht and Luftwaffe officers in the bar with women of questionable character. Anyway, it is comfortable and relatively inexpensive and centrally situated just off the Kurfürstendamm.

I was both surprised and impressed by Christian's huge new apartment on several floors of a large new building close to the SDHQ. When I entered the marble-floored vestibule there were two SS men on guard. A manservant in a white jacket came forward and ushered me upstairs into the main salon. Inside I was unprepared for such a brilliant gathering. The room was long and high, lit by chandeliers and wall sconces. The rest of the furnishings were hidden by the throng of people but there were two ornate mirrors on opposite walls and I glimpsed a large console table on which was an elaborate display of fruit and flowers.

Most of the men in the room were in SS dress uniform but a few were in white tie and tails and all the women wore full-length evening dresses. I felt terribly out of place even though I was wearing my best walking-out uniform. A waiter offered me champagne from a tray and then Christian came forward to greet me, shaking my hand so vigorously I spilt some of the champagne on the rose-pink carpet which, I saw, had a border of swastikas. The champagne glass had a swastika etched on it with the SS rune on the other side.

Christian looked quite magnificent in his full SS officer's evening dress. He is nigh on two metres tall (several centimeters taller than me) with pale blond hair and I felt very underdressed and out of place in his presence and reproached him for not warning me it was such a formal reception. He replied that, on the contrary, with one exception, I was the star guest, the only person there who had been in action at the front. I asked him who was the star guest he referred to but he only smiled and said that it was a double celebration, one for the SS and one for him. Apparently the Reichsführer SS had just approved the formation of a new organisation, the Reichssicherheithauptampt, which brought together various divisional organisations and unified all aspects of state security. Christian said it was a great step forward for the SS. As for himself, he had been promoted to Gruppenführer and appointed to Heydrich's personal staff.

I raised my glass and congratulated him. Christian insisted that I meet the Heydrichs. "He is brilliant, she is charming," he said. He led the way across the room to a group of SS officers surrounding one woman and broke into their conversation without ceremony, introducing me to Reinhard Heydrich and his wife, Lina. I was unsure whether Party protocol or social politeness dictated how I should respond. I followed Christian's lead and spoke first to Heydrich. He smiled at me. He was nearly as tall as Christian, also with fine fair hair brushed close to his scalp, alert blue eyes and an aquiline nose. The smile had a sardonic quality.

"My dear Leutnant," he said, "Christian has told us about your valiant performance in Poland. The Reich is very proud of its young airmen." I thought the tone seemed slightly mocking to match the smile and I felt myself beginning to blush. How absurd! How gauche! I was annoyed with myself – and Christian, too, for telling everyone about my one easy victory. I said that Christian had exaggerated, that I had had but one success and there had been little opposition. Heydrich said that there would be further opportunities for me to increase my score. Frau Heydrich caught my eye. "I hope you are not going to confine your conversation to the war, Herr Leutnant," she said, extending her hand. I took it in mine, bowed low over it and clicked my heels. Her blond hair, slightly darker than her husband's, was swept up on top of her head exposing her regular features. She wore pearl-studded earrings and her long silver dress had a spray of pink silk roses on one shoulder. She was, indeed, a very attractive woman. She asked me how long I was staying in Berlin and I replied that it was just for a day or so before I went home to Bavaria.

"I love Bavaria," she said. "We lived there for a few years, of course. I was sorry when we moved here."

I said I didn't know Berlin very well, only having visited it a few times, once as a boy with my parents, and then on two or three short leaves while training at the Werneuchen Kriegschule.

"Well, I enjoy the theatre and opera," Frau Heydrich said, then glancing at her husband and the other SS officers and lowering her voice a little, she went on, "But I am so bored by the society. Endless parties and receptions and always the same people. It's nice to see a new face." Her eyes looked directly into mine and I felt myself blushing again. I did not want to flirt with the wife of an important Obergruppenführer and Frau Heydrich's manner was distinctly flirtatious.

A young woman edged between us, saying, "Lina, who is this handsome young airman you are keeping to yourself?"

Frau Heydrich introduced the young woman as Fräulein Mathilde Zugmann. Briefly I took her outstretched hand encased in a long white kid glove, and clicked my heels again but did not bow. Fräulein Zugmann had dark, wavy hair framing her face; her eyes were dark, too, her nose small and her mouth large but the disproportion was somehow pleasing. Her emerald dress left her shoulders bare except for narrow straps and the low neckline was accentuated by a diamond clip. "My dear, Berlin is simply full of attractive men. The war has made it the most romantic city in Germany." She was speaking to Frau Heydrich but kept her eyes on me.

"I have just been saying how boring it is," Frau Heydrich said.

"Only for the married ones, perhaps." The two women exchanged a look and they both laughed. Two waiters approached, one carrying a tray of canapés, the other more champagne. We all exchanged our glasses. I was very hungry and took a tiny vol-au-vent but both women refused the food.

Christian joined us. "I see you have already met Mathilde," he said, "I was going to introduce you to each other."

"Mathilde wastes no time," Frau Heydrich said.

"Of course not, Lina," Mathilde replied quickly. "No woman can afford to be extravagant with time, even though some of us have more of it than others."

Frau Heydrich did not seem put out by the implication of the remark. "We none of us know how much time we have," she said, "It's what we do with it that counts."

One of the waiters came across and whispered in Christian's ear. He excused himself, saying that an important guest had arrived.

"I thought we had met the most important guest," Frau Heydrich said, looking at me. I was becoming weary of her flattery and somewhat

11

surprised at the forwardness of these women. Only a few weeks before Hitler's own newspaper, the *Völkischer Beobachter*, had carried a long article criticising women who, by wearing makeup and indulging in flirtatious behaviour, degraded the dignity of German womanhood. Apparently it did not apply to the wives and friends of senior Party officials.

Christian appeared through the main doors of the salon with an SS officer at his side and it was some moments before I recognised who it was as the general conversation dwindled into silence. "Ladies and gentlemen," Christian said, "We are privileged to have with us the Reichsführer-SS Heinrich Himmler." There was a smattering of applause. A woman in a long red velvet dress stood behind Christian and the Reichsführer. "Who is that?" whispered Mathilde, "Frau Himmler?"

"Of course not," Frau Heydrich replied, turning away. "You'd know Marga Himmler if you saw her – size 50 knickers!" I was astonished at the open contempt with which she spoke; nor did she bother to lower her voice.

Christian and the Reichsführer moved slowly among the guests, stopping to speak briefly with various people, the woman in red a step or two behind them. When it was my turn to be introduced I stood stiffly to attention and when the Reichsführer shook hands with me I stared straight ahead as if I were on parade. I felt foolish and awkward and rather intimidated at meeting one of Germany's most important leaders. When Christian introduced the woman as Fräulein Hedwig Potthast I relaxed my stance a little and as she did not offer her hand I bowed and clicked my heels. Frau Heydrich gave a little curtsey to the Reichsführer and when he had moved out of earshot she turned to Mathilde and me and said, "Herr Himmler disapproves of me."

"How do you know?" Mathilde asked.

"My dear, he has made it very plain to Reinhard on several occasions. He even implied that Reinhard should divorce me."

Mathilde said she found it hard to believe. Frau Heydrich laughed and said the Reichsführer thought that she was "too headstrong." "I'm certainly too strong for that dry old stick," she went on, "forever issuing directives and writing letters of reproof. The only thing to do is ignore them." Heydrich moved to his wife's side; whether he had heard what she was saying or not I could not tell.

The assembly began to break up. The Heydrichs went off to dine with the Reichsführer-SS and Fräulein Potthast. Christian announced that I would be joining him, Mathilde and another young woman whom he introduced simply as Frieda. She was wearing black velvet with a white camelia in her hair and I wondered if she saw herself as Marguerite Gautier. She was strikingly beautiful, with large dark eyes and her hair arranged with the severity of a ballerina. It transpired that she was Rumanian by birth and was, in fact, a dancer at the Vienna Opera.

From: Leutnant Peter von Vorzik
Hotel Goldener Spinne, Berlin
(as from III Gruppe JG233
Brieg)
To: Fräulein Mathilde Zugmann
23 Hevelius Straße
Grunewald

22nd September 1939

Dear Mathilde,

As you see, I am taking you at your word and with your permission to write I hasten to pen this short note before I leave for Bavaria. Your presence at dinner last night made the occasion an especially enjoyable one. I hope we can repeat it in the not-too-distant future.

At the moment everything is uncertain. We expect to be moved soon, but where I do not know, I just hope it will be within easy reach of Berlin. The war situation looks very hopeful; Poland is almost ours and I expect peace will be declared in a week or so, then I will have leave on a regular basis. Perhaps next time I am in Berlin you might care to accompany me to the opera, the Ring Cycle is scheduled for the autumn season – but perhaps you would prefer something a little lighter, more romantic? *La Bohème* is also being revived.

Please keep your promise and write to me, it would be a great consolation in the life of your

Sincere admirer,
Peter

From: Edith von Vorzik
Schloss Adlersee
Bavaria
To: Leutnant Peter von Vorzik
III Gruppe JG233
Brieg

1st October 1939

My Dear Peter,

You cannot realise, I am sure, just how wonderful it was to see you for those few days. It was reassuring for all of us to know you're in good health and spirits and, of course, especially beneficial for mother who talks of you all the time. She certainly seems to have rallied a little since your visit, and even left her room for an hour or two to sit in the conservatory, but she remains terribly weak. I read to her each evening, mostly poems by Eichendorf which seem to give her spiritual comfort and then, of course, we talk about you.

Father, of course, remains very quiet and when he does talk it is always about the Russian occupation of eastern Poland. He is convinced that it is a dire threat to us and says we will end up fighting them. I find it all depressing; I had hoped that everything would be settled by now but it all looks more and more complicated.

Do you remember Franz at the farm? He has joined a Panzer regiment and says he will marry Liesl when he comes on leave. Father is concerned about the running of the farm; there are only two farmhands left now and the estate manager says the herd must be sold. But I do not want to concern you with such things.

Please write when you can, it is such a pleasure to have your letters, however short, and a wonderful tonic for mother.

Ever your loving sister,
Edith

From: Fräulein Mathilde Zugmann
23 Hevelius Straße
Grunewald
To: Leutnant Peter von Vorzik
III Gruppe JG233
Brieg

1st October 1939

Dear Peter,

You see, I am keeping my promise and writing to you!

It was a pleasant surprise to get your note so soon. Let me hasten to say that I, too, enjoyed our evening together although, I am afraid, you may have thought me a little forward. The truth is I am not used to drinking wine and I have the feeling that I probably talked too much. Please believe I am usually rather shy but it was such a convivial occasion (your brother is also a most stimulating companion) that I lost my usual reserve.

I, too, hope that you will be posted nearer to Berlin. I should love to accompany you to the opera and, in fact, *La Bohème* is my favourite work.

Did you enjoy your visit home? I do hope you found your mother in better health, she must have been so very happy to see you.

The weather here in Berlin has been beautiful; warm, still days with golden sunshine that makes the autumn leaves look so beautiful. I have been taking long walks by the lake in the early evening; everything is so peaceful and still it is difficult to believe that there is a war happening anywhere.

Lina (Heydrich) and I met for coffee last week. She is full of scandalous gossip about members of the Party and is very indiscreet but also very funny! I do not know whether to believe her tales but she swears they are all true. She asked to be remembered to you when I wrote.

Mother is calling me to lunch so I must stop now. Please let me know how you are and what is happening to you. I hope we meet again soon.

Yours affectionately,
Mathilde

From: Leutnant Peter von Vorzik
III Gruppe JG233
Brieg
To: Edith von Vorzik
Schloss Adlersee
Bavaria

7th October 1939

My Dear Edith,

Thank you for your welcome letter. I am pleased to hear that mother seems a little better but I must say it was a terrible shock to see how ill she looked and I fear the doctor must be right, it is only a matter of a short while before we lose her. I do think you should tell father that she must have a nurse, it is too much for you to run the house and look after her as well. I shall write and tell him so, too.

There are constant rumours that the Gruppe is about to be moved. Some say it is to the western front but nothing is definite. Until you hear from me keep writing to this address. Next time I come on leave I might bring my Katschmarek, Kurt, with me. He comes from Hamburg and has never been to Bavaria. He is a fine fellow with a great sense of humour. I know you would like him.

I did not get a chance to tell you that when I was in Berlin Christian introduced me to a charming young woman, Mathilde Zugmann. We had dinner together and I was very taken with her. She lives with her mother in Grunewald and we have corresponded. I would like you to meet her, too – perhaps I should invite her to Adlersee sometime although, on second thoughts, this might not be a good idea with mother so unwell.

Things are very quiet at the moment, with just a little activity from British aircraft over Heligoland which keeps us all alert; with winter approaching I think it will remain quiet. Perhaps the war will be over by Christmas; in any case I look forward to more leave and spending the holiday with you.

Please give my regards to everyone at the farm,

Your loving brother,
Peter

From: Leutnant Peter von Vorzik
III Gruppe JG233
Brieg
To: Count Christian von Vorzik
Schloss Adlersee
Bavaria

7th October 1939

My Dear Father,

Just a short letter to accompany the one I have written to Edith. We have been kept busy re-equipping and carrying out exercises so letterwriting is an activity that has to be snatched at odd moments.

I need not tell you how grieved I was to see mother looking so frail; it must be a constant worry for you. It also places a heavy burden on Edith who already bears such a big responsibility with the housekeeping. Do you really need to keep open so many rooms? Of course I know you like the library as your own "retreat" but the main drawing room, the billiards room and the music room could all be closed for the winter, together with several of the guest rooms. I also think it is imperative that you employ a nurse to help Edith tend to mother's needs, even if it is only during the day. Edith, too, is not so strong and I noticed how tired she seemed. Household economies (such as closing the rooms I have mentioned, burning less fuel and less wages to pay on the farm) would cover the cost of nursing.

I also think we could sell the horses. Neither Christian nor I have much opportunity to ride, except on our brief leaves, and it seems an unnecessary expense to keep them now. Actually, Christian took me riding in the Tiergarten when I passed through Berlin – the SS have their own stables. I am sure he could arrange for the RSHA to buy our animals now that he is on Heydrich's staff.

Edith tells me you are not eating very much; do keep up your strength, it is even more imperative that you remain in good health while mother is so weak. I must go now to attend a lecture on tactics employed by the French Air Force; perhaps we shall be encountering them soon.

Ever your loving son,
Peter

Edward Thorpe

Leutnant Peter von Vorzik
Journal entry

20th October 1939

I have not been able to write this journal for nearly a month as we have been kept busy with a series of navigational flights, testing new equipment and with night flying training, although I cannot think that our Emils will ever be used for night interception. What little spare time I have had has been used for writing letters home.

Rumours persist that the Gruppe is being moved and that the whole Jagdgeschwader will go to the western front. The speculation has gained credence because we have received several lectures on the formation, training, tactics and equipment of the French *armée de l'air* and the British Royal Air Force. We have spent many hours looking at photographs, silhouettes and models of French and British aircraft and learning by heart performance characteristics and offensive and defensive armament. Only the British Spitfire is considered any real threat to our Me109s; the Hurricane and the French Dewoitine and Morane-Saulnier fighters have inferior speed, manoeuvrability and fire-power. Even so, one Nachtrichten Offizier who came to lecture us emphasised that, in brief skirmishes over the Franco-German border, the French and British pilots have shown great determination in pressing home attacks in spite of poor equipment and combat training. No one, he said, could make an assumption of superiority; the complacent pilot would be a dead pilot. Everyone is anxious to get to grips with the French and British but there is little activity on the western front and the war is now referred to as the "Sitzkrieg."

Leutnant Peter von Vorzik
Journal entry

27th October 1939

Quite unexpectedly several of the Staffel were granted a 48-hour pass. I immediately telephoned Christian to see if he could arrange tickets for the opera which he did (apparently the SS have their own box). I also telephoned Mathilde who cancelled a previous arrangement in order to join us. (Christian came with Frieda). Of course I would have preferred to spend the evening with Mathilde *à deux* but we sat at the back of the

18

box at the opera and held hands except for those emotional moments when Mathilde was dabbing at her eyes. *La Bohème* does affect the emotions somewhat and I had a lump in my throat, too, during Mimi's death scene.

After dinner, which Christian ordered at a restaurant favoured by the SS (I would have preferred something a little more *intime*) he put the staff car at our disposal and, I told the chauffeur (the same very formal Unterscharführer) to drive very slowly to Grunewald. I commented to Mathilde on the exquisite fragrance she was wearing and she said it was Je Reviens, adding that now we were at war with France it would be difficult to get. The chauffeur had placed a thick chenille rug over our knees and under it I squeezed her hand. When the car stopped at the house I leant towards her and swiftly kissed her cheek before the chauffeur opened the door. I stayed in the car while he escorted her to the front door.

The next morning we had coffee together on the Ku'damm. Before we met I searched the department stores and managed to find a large bottle of Je Reviens. When I gave it to her she turned towards me on the banquette and kissed me on the mouth. I wanted very much to take her in my arms but it was not the time or place. I did ask her if there were any other young men in her life and she said no, none that mattered. Mathilde came to the bahnhof to see me off on the journey back to base. She put her face up to be kissed and I drew her close to me. I could feel her warmth through the woollen coat she was wearing and my uniform and the excitement it generated stayed with me throughout the tedious train ride and then for several hours after.

I have never been in love and I'm wondering if these tender feelings I have (though I must be honest and admit they are also of a sensual nature) and the constant thoughts of her could be interpreted as genuine emotion? My previous experience with women has been confined to a couple of encounters with the girls who used to hang around the Kriegschule. They weren't exactly prostitutes but they liked being given a "good time" which usually meant a meal in a cheap restaurant followed by drinks in some local Weinstübel or Biergarten and then perhaps a hurried moment of sex in a field near the Kriegschule. I did it merely to match the boasts of the other student pilots but afterwards I always felt rather guilty and unclean and nervous in case I caught some disease. Even to think of Mathilde in these terms seems somehow a betrayal of her apparent affection for me. I would like to talk to Kurt about it but feel too shy to broach the subject. I know he has a girlfriend back in Hamburg.

From: Leutnant Peter von Vorzik
III Gruppe JG233
Brieg
To: Gruppenführer Christian von Vorzik
RSHA Prinz Albertstraße
Berlin

28th October 1939

Dear Christian,
This is a belated note to thank you for organising the seats at the opera and for the delicious dinner afterwards. I have to confess to you what you have probably observed for yourself: I am very taken with Mathilde and she seems to respond to my tentative advances, too, which is another thing I have to thank you for.

On a more serious note I have written to father to say that I think that mother should have a nurse, at least during the day, to relieve the burden on Edith. I hope you will support me in this and write to father, too, making the same suggestion. You know how stubborn he can be over domestic matters, but he listens to you and respects your opinion and often quotes you – at least when the subject is politics!

I have also suggested that we could sell the horses which would help towards paying a nurse's wages. We both know, sadly, that it will not be for long ... Do you think the SS would be interested in buying them? Could you arrange that? They are not suited to farm work, no one seems to do much hunting or hacking in Adlersee now (except the Wiecks and father dislikes them so much he would never consent to selling to them) and I would hate to think of them slaughtered (the horses, not the Wiecks!) for dog-meat. Let me know what you think.

Ever your affectionate brother,
Peter

Leutnant Peter von Vorzik
Journal entry

8th November 1939

Yesterday we finally received orders to move – not to the west, as we had all expected and hoped, but to an airfield near Oldenburg, 40 km due south of Wilhelmshaven and Bremerhaven. Our three Staffel are making the journey separately and because of the generally poor flying weather and short daylight hours we made an overnight stop at Werneuchen. Many of our pilots had trained at the Fliegerschule there and last night I was caught up in a noisy reunion party with several of my old instructors. We reminisced about student colleagues and comic mishaps and about the girls we had known – apparently several of them still make their services available in the area for a "good time." We sang songs and drank beer and this morning both Kurt and I felt rather the worse for wear before setting out on our final leg to Oldenburg. The airfield is set in bleak and barren countryside, flat and sandy with only an occasional tree to break the visual monotony of the landscape. The Gruppe's task is to patrol the North Sea around the string of Friesian islands that stretch from the Dutch border in the west to the Danish border in the east, including the broad estuary of the River Elbe leading to Hamburg. Kurt is pleased at the posting: he feels that in carrying out coastal patrols he has a personal assignment to protect his family in Hamburg!

There have been several reports of British aircraft laying mines along the coast and generally harassing shipping and yesterday's patrol against these marauders led to our first encounter with British aircraft.

Our scheduled take-off at 07.00 hrs was delayed by bad weather. Kurt and I were placed on stand-by and we sat in the stuffy operations room playing chess. Around 10.00 hrs the heavy rain squalls diminished, the strong westerly wind veered to the north, the low grey cloud began to break up, visibility increased and Kurt and I prepared for take-off. The route we were given was due north over Wilhelmshaven, out over Wangerooge, the most easterly of the Friesian islands, then on a wide sweep of the Heligoland Bight, returning over Cuxhaven and Bremerhaven.

With the wind gusting to very nearly 50 kph and the grass of the airfield sodden with the rain, take-off was particularly difficult. New concrete runways are being prepared but so much bad weather recently has prevented their completion. Two days ago an Emil ground-looped when it struck a marshy patch on landing. Small triangular flags had been placed where the ground was particularly soft and the take-off strip was very narrow so that Kurt followed directly behind me, instead of alongside, on take-off.

An incoming Fieseler Storch communications aircraft held us up a minute or two. I held the big Daimler-Benz motor at 1,800 revs, watching the young Obergefreiter with his two Ground Control flags, one plain red for "hold", the other a green diagonal cross on a white ground for "clear". The Storch came in steeply, its elaborate system of slots and flaps allowing a slow descent and a landing run of less than 40 m. When it had taxied off the landing strip the Obergefreiter raised his green and white flag and I opened the throttle wide and released the brakes. I could feel the stickiness of the muddy ground dragging at the undercarriage; acceleration was noticeably slower than normal and it was some seconds longer than usual before the tailwheel came up and we were skimming the ground at a level attitude. At maximum revs I lifted off smoothly and held the Emil in a shallow climb until I saw Kurt 200 m away on the port beam.

Over Wilhelmshaven we climbed to 5000 m, holding that altitude as we crossed the coast. There was still quite a lot of cloud, fast-moving under a strong wind which was giving us a bumpy ride, but we had occasional views of broad stretches of sea. Even at that height it was possible to see the heaving grey-green wavetops flecked with white spume. There was a considerable amount of coastal shipping, including flotillas of fishing boats, but we were able to identify two cargo ships of around 10,000 tons whose movements we had been given at the briefing.

After twelve minutes we changed course to a bearing that brought us almost due east over the coast of Schleswig-Holstein; after another six minutes we made a 90° change of course to bring us back over the Elbe estuary. A movement on the starboard quarter caught my attention: against a bank of grey cloud I made out the silhouette of a twin-engined aircraft with a single fin and rudder. A Junkers 88? As I shouted the sighting to Kurt through the r/t I could hear the pitch of excitement in my own voice. With a touch of right rudder I slewed the Emil round and went into a shallow dive, at the same time switching on the Revi gunsight. The unidentified aircraft was flying east to west at a speed I calculated to be around 250 kph. My own speed in the dive had increased to 330 kph but

I kept the motor throttled back so as not to approach the strange aircraft too quickly. When it was just over a km away, right in front of me, I took a long look: the engine nacelles seemed too short, the fin and rudder too pointed for a Ju88. With those characteristics there was only one other type it was likely to be... Even as I positively identified the aircraft as a Bristol Blenheim I made out the red-and-blue roundels on the upper surfaces of the wings. I shouted to Kurt that I was going in to attack and almost simultaneously a stream of tracer bullets came from the bomber's dorsal turret, a lazy arc of red dots curving up towards me. But the gunner had made insufficient allowance for the fall in trajectory so that the bullets passed harmlessly underneath the Emil.

As the image of the Blenheim grew rapidly in the gunsight I was anxious not to make the same mistake as the RAF gunner. I kicked on about three degrees of left rudder to counteract a natural tendency the Emil has to slide-slip, then, when the centre of the Blenheim's fuselage lined up with the vertical graticule of the gunsight and with its mainplane just below the horizontal line, I pressed the firing button. The Emil shuddered under the recoil of the four guns and a second later the Blenheim pilot put his machine into a steep dive to starboard – a move that I had sensed almost instinctively: a turn in that direction meant heading for the English coast. But the manoeuvre pulled the bomber across the Emil's stream of fire. I closed up, intent on getting in another burst, knowing as I did so that I was presenting an unwavering target. I would have liked to get underneath the Blenheim because from that position it was completely undefended, and that was why the pilot had put the aircraft into a dive, but I knew from all those hours of studying enemy aircraft that the dorsal turret carried only a single rifle-calibre machinegun and the frontal area of the Emil presented a minimal target: it was a calculated risk.

I fired another long burst and this time the Blenheim weaved to port. Even as it slid out of the gunsight graticule a faint wisp of smoke came from the starboard engine. In order to follow him I yanked hard with both hands on the control column – at speeds above 300 kph the Emil's ailerons become very heavy and demand a lot of strength – and gave it full left rudder. The Blenheim was diving fast and once more directly ahead; for a moment its silhouette filled the gunsight again, and again I pressed the firing button. I could see the cannon shells exploding around the centre section of the bomber's fuselage and the smoke from the starboard engine was growing rapidly thicker. I kept firing until I had exhausted the ammunition and was in danger of collision, then I pulled back hard on the stick and kicked the rudder-bar to the right, putting the Emil into a fast climbing turn.

For a few moments I lost sight of the Blenheim. I levelled out of the climb but kept the Emil in a tight turn. Emerging from a bank of white cloud I saw a wavering line of black smoke and peering out of the canopy I followed it to its source. The Blenheim was about 1,000 m beneath and skimming the wavetops. The starboard engine was well alight, with orange flames curling over the upper surface of the wing. As I throttled back and watched the stricken aircraft I heard Kurt's voice over the r/t: "You got him, Peter, you got him!"

I glanced to right and left and there, on the port quarter, was Kurt's Emil about 100 m away. I felt guilty that in the excitement of the encounter I had once more forgotten all about my Katschmarek, but he was on station as if nothing had happened. Just like that first encounter with the PZLs in Poland he had fulfilled his function perfectly, protecting me from attack from any other quarter, ready to engage any opponent. "Well done, Kurt," I said, "I thought I might have lost you." "Not so easy, Herr Leutnant," he replied, returning to the formal mode of address. There was satisfaction in his voice.

I was about to tell him to dive down and finish off the Blenheim when the bomber's blazing wing suddenly dropped sharply and hit the water. Immediately the plane performed a spectacular cartwheel on its wing tip, flipped over on its back and sank within a few seconds. For several moments fragments of the burning engine scattered flames on the spray then, as they flickered out, all that was visible was an oily stain on the water, quickly teased into tentacles by the action of the waves. There was very little debris, no sign of life, no raft or dinghy. Kurt switched on his r/t again. "Horrido!" he yelled, the Luftwaffe pilot's traditional shout of triumph, but to me it sounded more like a valedictory Amen.

From: Gruppenführer Christian von Vorzik
RSHA Prinz Albertstraße
Berlin
To: Leutnant Peter von Vorzik
III Gruppe JG233
Oldenburg

9th November 1939

My Dear Peter,

I have some new information which might persuade you to change your mind about transferring to the SS. I realise that a desk-bound staff job may not appeal to you when compared to the excitement of flying but one must look to the future. Eventual promotion in the Luftwaffe will mean much the same thing, will it not? Administrative duties, staff meetings and so on. Because it is not – and never will be – such an elite organisation as the SS, promotion will be slower and (I stress this) the authority it wields within the Reich, particularly after the war is over, will never be comparable. A position in the SS will guarantee your being close to heads of state, possibly one of those who make vital decisions about the future direction of our country, an individual of real importance rather than just another high-ranking Luftwaffe officer.

The news I have which may make the idea more immediately appealing, is that the Führer has decreed that SS Brigadeführer Gottlob Berger may raise recruitment for his Verfugungstruppe, and equip them with heavy weapons. This is despite fierce opposition from the Wermacht generals but the plain facts are that in Poland the SS suffered proportionately heavier casualties than the Army. Anyway, the Führer is anxious that the SS should now develop several crack fighting regiments which will be known as the Waffen-SS. Does this not appeal to you? It would give you all the excitement you seem to crave and, later, you could be promoted to a position of real influence within the Party.

Think about it, Peter. It would please father, of course, to have both his sons in such positions of power. The future of the Third Reich is exciting; I urge you to be a part of it.

Ever your affectionate brother,
Christian
Heil Hitler!

From: Leutnant Peter von Vorzik
III Gruppe JG233
Oldenburg
To: Gruppenführer Christian von Vorzik
RSHA Prinz Albertstraße
Berlin

12th November 1939

My Dear Christian,

I have waited some days before replying to your letter in order to give your suggestion of joining the SS a great deal of thought. Thinking over all the points you make I still return to my initial and instinctive response: I love flying. It is as simple as that and although you are probably right when you say I will end up as some unimportant officer with a desk job, that does not deter me.

In any case, once the war is over (and the excitement of flying, for me, is far from being limited to combat) I might very well resign my commission in the Luftwaffe and apply for a position with Lufthansa. The civil air routes are only just beginning to be opened up and the Third Reich must continue to lead the way in the future, just as it has done in the last ten years.

So you see, my answer is, once again, thank you for the offer but no. One other thing: unlike you I am not a political animal. You love being at the very centre of things, having influence, sharing in making major decisions; my interest is much more specific, in a particular science, and my contribution to the future of the country, although less important than yours, must lie within those boundaries.

I do hope you understand,

Ever your affectionate brother,
Peter

From: *Fräulein Mathilde Zugmann*
23 Hevelius Straße
Grunewald
To: *Leutnant Peter von Vorzik*
III Gruppe JG233
Oldenburg

14th November 1939

Dear Peter,

It is several weeks since I last heard from you and now, from an unexpected quarter, I understand why! Lina phoned me yesterday to say your picture was in all the newspapers following your brilliant victory in shooting down that enemy bomber. Many congratulations!

I feel very proud to have met you and I have told all my friends that I have dined with one of the Luftwaffe's young heroes.

Of course I realise how busy you must be with all this air activity (I don't even know where you are but I am sending this note to the last address you gave me in the hope that it will be forwarded to you) but please spare a few moments to write to me when you can. I cherish the memory of the evening we spent at the opera and do so hope that you might be coming to Berlin again soon.

Once more many congratulations on your victory.

Take care of yourself,

Yours ever,
Mathilde

Leutnant Peter von Vorzik
Journal entry

22nd November 1939

Our success in shooting down the Bristol Blenheim was corroborated by fishermen who saw the aircraft hit the water and who picked up small pieces of debris. There were no survivors. Kurt and I celebrated in the mess that night with a bottle of champagne and then, to my surprise, we were both given five days' leave. I would have liked to have spent the time in Berlin (I feel remiss in not having even telephoned Mathilde to let her know where I have been posted but feel sure we could have seen each

27

other) but felt it was my duty to go to Adlersee. The long train journey to Bavaria meant that two days were cut out of the leave (there were no aircraft on which I could get a lift) but I knew it might be the last time I could see mother and the visit would please Edith.

Wondering whether I was doing the right thing I invited Kurt to accompany me. It was not an easy decision for him, either, as he felt he should go home to see his parents but as Hamburg is so close to Oldenburg he can manage to slip away at odd times, so he said yes. November, of course, is not the best time to visit Bavaria, but we were blessed with fine late autumn weather, cold and sunny with blue skies which made a pleasant change from the damp, grey days we have been having in the north.

After a tedious 9-hour train ride we were met at the station in Munich by father's chauffeur-valet Werner (he had been father's batman on the western front in 1917). Instead of the big Maybach, Werner had brought a little DKW that had been bought because of its low fuel consumption. I sat up front with Kurt in the back because it would have been ridiculous for both of us to squash together on the rear seat of the tiny car, but I could see that the arrangement offended Werner's sense of propriety.

It was after midnight when we arrived at Schloss Adlersee and as there was no moon and little illumination from the car's headlights Kurt was unprepared for the size of the house. He stood in the main hall gazing about him and shaking his head. "You never told me, Peter," he said, almost reproachfully. "Told you what?" I asked. "That you lived in such grand style," he answered. I told him the guest rooms were simpler, that father confined himself to his study and the library and that mother and Edith had their own apartments. I could see that he suddenly felt apprehensive about the visit.

Werner had laid the long dining room table for two, with cold meats, sauerkraut, potato salad, pumpernickel bread and Sachertorte. There was beer and wine and coffee percolating. Werner hovered, waiting to serve us but I told him to go to bed and I would show Kurt to his room when we had finished our meal. I wanted everything to be as informal as possible but I could see it was not going to be easy.

I was very hungry but Kurt ate very little. I could see him looking about the room, at the coat of arms over the big stone fireplace, at the rather dark family portraits on the walls, at the heavy velvet hangings. Suddenly I saw it all with his eyes and it did seem rather oppressive. Our rooms were on the same floor and he looked rather relieved when I told him we would be breakfasting by ourselves in the morning.

Meeting father was something of an ordeal. He received us both in his study after breakfast. Kurt stood at attention in front of father's desk and I thought of how I had done the same when talking to Reichsführer-SS Heinrich Himmler. Father said he was pleased to welcome "one of Peter's comrades-in-arms," a phrase which was intended, I thought, to gloss over the fact that Kurt was not an officer. I could see father looking at the Feldwebel collar-patch on Kurt's uniform. I felt uneasy in case father inquired too closely into Kurt's social background; it was a similar situation to when, in our childhood, father had disapproved of Edith and me playing with Liesl and the other farm children. After questioning us both about our encounter with the Blenheim, father picked up his pen as a sign of dismissal; we clicked our heels and withdrew.

During the rest of the morning I took Kurt on a leisurely tour of the estate. We stopped at the farm where Liesl greeted us with great affection and served us with apple juice. Her fiancé was due home that evening and they were to make plans for an early wedding. She showed us pictures of Franz in his Panzer uniform and was flushed and excited. There is a party for them at the village inn and we promised to attend.

We walked as far as the Adlersee which gleamed like pewter under the pale November sun. The trees bordering the lake were bare of leaves, but the meadows which stretched down to the water were still a bright emerald green. A dark pinewood threw indigo shadows that seemed to stretch to the horizon where the crests of the Bavarian Alps were already tipped with the first snows of winter. It seemed extraordinarily peaceful and quiet and impossible to think of war.

We did not talk very much but I asked Kurt if he had thought of marriage. He replied that he had not, although he had a girlfriend in Hamburg who, it seemed, considered the relationship more seriously than he did. "I do not want to think of marriage until I've had some promotion," he said. I said that was sensible, but it should not be long in coming if the war continued. Kurt asked if I thought it would. I said that Christian, who was in touch with a number of important Party officials, seemed to think it would – at least until the threat from France and Britain was removed. I made a mental note to recommend Kurt for promotion as soon as we returned to Oldenburg. His efficiency as my Katschmarek would suffice as a reason.

With father in attendance lunch and dinner were formal affairs and I could see that Kurt was anxious not to make some social gaffe at the table. He made no attempt to initiate conversation and his usually lively disposition was very subdued. When Werner presented dishes of food to him he took absurdly small portions and I kept urging him to take more. Edith also spoke very little and father kept his comments confined to politics. At mother's empty place at the foot of the table a bowl of flowers had been put where the table setting would have been.

After dinner I settled Edith and Kurt in the music room where they played gramophone records while I visited mother. Edith had told me that she spent most of the time in bed but for me she had made the effort to get up and sit in a chair. She looked terribly pale and fragile but also very beautiful in the soft lamplight. I sat beside her and held her hand and we talked of years gone past when Edith, Christian and I were children. It seemed to give her pleasure remembering those days in the late twenties when we had all visited the zoo in Berlin and spent winter holidays in Kitzbühel. There were also long silences when mother closed her eyes and I thought she must have fallen asleep but then she suddenly said that I must join my guest and would I send up Edith to help her into bed again.

Back in the music room I rang for Werner to bring some cognac, and Kurt and I sat sipping our drinks and listening to Brahms's Third Symphony. The big mahogany gramophone console was fitted with an automatic record changer so that we did not have to keep getting up to replace the records. When Edith returned Kurt found some Schubert songs in the music cabinet and sang some of them in a light, clear tenor while Edith accompanied him on the piano. I was surprised by Kurt's musical accomplishment and I could see that Edith, too, responded to his gentle, amiable manner – a very different Kurt to the jokey one I knew in the Staffel mess.

On the last night of our leave Kurt and I attended the party for Liesl and Franz. It was held in a big room at the side of the village inn. There was a local band dressed in brightly coloured satin shirts and a group of Tyrolean dancers with the men in felt jackets and lederhosen and the women in embroidered blouses, laced bodices and dirndl skirts. When they had finished their demonstration dances everyone took to the floor as the band played popular songs in a relentless polka tempo.

After nearly two hours, exhausted from the ceaseless stamping dances and a little dizzy from the new wine we had been drinking Kurt and I went outside for a little fresh air. After the hot, stuffy room the night seemed chilly. At the rear of the inn there was a garden with a pergola-covered path that led down to the Adlersee. At the end of the path was a wooden jetty and we sat on the rough pine boards watching the moon come up over the foothills of the Alps. The moon was not quite full, a disc flattened on one edge like a can and when I remarked on the similarity Kurt said it was the most unromantic description of the moon he had ever heard. A shooting star, low on the horizon, caught the attention of both of us and Kurt said how strange it was to think that it was a separate world that had died millions of years before we saw it, and how insignificant our own lives seemed when one contemplated the heavens. I think the wine and the evening's gaiety had made him a little sentimental.

The next day we returned to Oldenburg and I found a letter from Mathilde awaiting me. I must write to her and perhaps I can spend my next leave in Berlin.

From: Leutnant Peter von Vorzik
III Gruppe JG233
Oldenburg
To: Fräulein Mathilde Zugmann
23 Hevelius Straße
Grunewald

23rd November 1939

My Dear Mathilde,

Your letter was awaiting me when I returned from an unexpected leave which I felt compelled to spend at home as mother is so ill.

What a pleasure it was to hear from you again! I feel very guilty in not having written to you for so long. As you see we have been moved to the north-west and have been kept rather busy with patrols. Yes, we have had some successes which accounts for my picture being in the paper along with many others – how surprising that you should see it. I am afraid that it is not a very flattering portrait, it was taken just after I had graduated from Fleigerschule and I think I had drunk rather too much beer celebrating the night before!

Having just had leave, I do not know when I shall be due for another weekend pass, but I expect (if all remains quiet) that we shall be given some days off around Christmas time. Will you be staying in Berlin during the holiday? If so, I will make a point of spending a day or two in the capital – need I say how much I look forward to seeing you again?

Life here is fairly monotonous and, of course, I am not allowed to give you details of our daily routines even if they could be thought interesting. I long for us to be able to talk at length together, to find out more about you, your likes and dislikes, hopes and ambitions. All I know at present is that you wear Je Reviens and cry at *La Bohème* ...

Please continue to write when you can, the daily arrival of the post is the high point of all our lives here. I, too, promise to write to you more often if that is not presumptuous of me.

Meanwhile, every good wish from your

Sincere admirer,
Peter

From: Oberfeldwebel Kurt Schneckel
III Gruppe JG233
Oldenburg
To: Count von Vorzik
Schloss Adlersee
Bavaria

23rd November 1939

Dear Count von Vorzik,
I write to thank you for your most gracious hospitality at Schloss Adlersee last week.

It was a most enjoyable vacation and a memorable first visit to southern Germany which is, indeed, the most beautiful part of our great nation.

I feel very privileged to be flying as Katschmarek to Leutnant von Vorzik, a most gallant fighter pilot and an inspiration to everyone in the Staffel.

I do hope that Countess von Vorzik is feeling a little stronger.

Yours sincerely,
Kurt Schneckel

From: Oberfeldwebel Kurt Schneckel
III Gruppe JG233
Oldenburg
To: Fräulein Edith von Vorzik
Schloss Adlersee
Bavaria

23rd November 1939

Dear Edith,
(If I may be so presumptuous as to call you that), I must thank you
for all you did to make my stay at Schloss Adlersee such a memorable
one. I know from Peter that you are responsible for so many domestic
duties looking after that beautiful house, as well as attending to
Countess von Vorzik, so that another visitor must have been an added
burden.

My stay was not only a wonderful opportunity to relax from the
rigours of duty in idyllic surroundings, but also an opportunity to
exchange views with Peter on a more informal basis. I am sure you
know how much I admire and respect him as a pilot of great ability and
courage.

I did so enjoy our "musical evening," an hour or two when all thoughts
of war and conflict were banished.

With best wishes,

Yours very sincerely,
Kurt

From: Leutnant Peter von Vorzik
Internal memo to: Staffelkapitan Zwemmer
III Gruppe JG233
Oldenburg

24th November 1939

Sir,
I should like to put before you a recommendation to be forwarded to
General Geisler that Oberfeldwebel Kurt Schneckel should receive promotion.

In our two main encounters with enemy aircraft, which resulted in
the destruction of a Polish PZL and a British Blenheim, his performance

as my Katschmarek has been exemplary, keeping station and affording support and protection throughout two difficult situations. An acknowledgement of his outstanding ability as a pilot and his punctilious adherence to duty would, I am sure, prove a great encouragement to all members of the Staffel.

Leutnant von Vorzik

From: Staffelkapitan Zwemmer
Internal memo to: Leutnant von Vorzik
III Gruppe JG233
Oldenburg

26th November 1939

Your memorandum of November 24th and your comments therein have been noted and passed to General Geisler for consideration.

Following your successes against enemy aircraft you are hereby informed that permission has been granted for you to affix a personal insignia to your aircraft in the approved position.

F. Zwemmer
Staffelkapitan

From: Edith von Vorzik
Schloss Adlersee
Bavaria
To: Oberfeldwebel Kurt Schneckel
III Gruppe JG233
Oldenburg

29th November 1939

Dear Kurt,

It was very nice of you to write to me. I am so glad you enjoyed your short stay with us and, for our part, we were delighted to have you as our guest. As Peter's comrade please be assured you will always be welcome at Adlersee – I hope the next time you are able to come it will be for a longer stay.

I, too, enjoyed our little *moment musical*. During these rather anxious months music has been a great balm to my spirit, but I am afraid my rather inexpert pianism is not conducive to good ensemble! When I know you are coming I will spend some time practising.

> With best wishes and prayers for your safety,
> Edith

Leutnant Peter von Vorzik
Journal entry

5th December 1939

My recommendation to Staffelkapitan Zwemmer that Kurt should receive promotion has been forwarded to General Geisler. I hope that it goes through. Apart from the recognition of his flying ability, the little bit of extra money that the promotion will mean will be very welcome. I have a suspicion that his parents are poor; his father has been forced into early retirement (I think that he was manager of a shoeshop) through ill health, and Kurt said that his mother does dressmaking to help with the bills. Kurt, I know, makes an allowance to his parents from his pay.

Zwemmer has given me permission to have a personal insignia painted on my Emil. I spent yesterday afternoon watching our official Staffel painter and signwriter paint the crest on the fuselage, just under the cockpit canopy. I took as my symbol the golden leopard rampant that is part of the von Vorzik family crest and instructed the artist to endow it with wings. It looks rather splendid on a plain black shield. The Emil is already decorated with the Gruppe's emblem of a scarlet hawk on the engine cowling. The propeller-boss, like all the other aircraft in Zwemmer's Staffel, is also painted a bright red and the engine cowling itself is in the Gruppe's identification colour of bright blue, and there is a broad band of the same colour around the rear fuselage, just forward of the tail empennage. The Staffel number forward of the fuselage cross is also in red and aft of the cross is a white horizontal bar, another Gruppe identification mark. All this gaudy decoration rather defeats the regulation camouflage scheme of light and dark green zigzag markings on top of the wings and fuselage sides, with pale blue undersides.

As I was writing this Kurt knocked on the door of my little bunkroom and appeared flushed and smiling to tell me that he has been promoted to Stabsfeldwebel. Apparently Zwemmer told him that I had originated the suggestion and Kurt insisted on my accompanying him to the Staffel messroom and celebrating with a bottle of schnapps. Of course I am very pleased for him and he thoroughly deserves the promotion. He will still be flying as my Katschmarek.

From: Fräulein Mathilde Zugmann
23 Hevelius Straße
Grunewald
To: Leutnant Peter von Vorzik
III Gruppe JG233
Oldenburg

6th December 1939

Dear Peter,

I was so pleased to have your letter and to know that you are safe and well. Every time that I hear on the radio that there has been some encounter between our Luftwaffe pilots and enemy aircraft I am anxious for your safety.

Life here in Berlin goes on as usual and we are preparing for Christmas. Mother may go to visit her sister in Cologne (they are both widows and Ilse came here last year) but I shall be staying in Berlin – especially if there is a chance of your passing through.

Last week I had lunch with Lina Heydrich and she told me the most extraordinary thing. (You may already have heard the news from your brother.) Do you remember that lovely young woman who accompanied your brother the evening we first met? Her name was Frieda. Well, apparently your brother has received a directive from Herr Himmler, via Reinhard, that he must not see her any more as she is dark-haired! Lina says it is preposterous and if it was her she would take no notice. (As you may have noticed she is rather headstrong.) I understand that all high-ranking SS officers may only associate with blonde woman of Aryan descent. Frieda is Rumanian, as you know, and has no Jewish blood but being brunette is suspect! Lina says that she had to return to Vienna anyway, for the beginning of the season, but is very upset about it as she was in love with Christian. I must say I find it all rather perplexing.

Last week I went to the opera with mother to see *Der Freischütz* and enjoyed it very much though not so much as *La Bohème*. Afterwards we went backstage to meet one of the singers who is a friend of mother's. He told us that the only reason that the opera is allowed to present a work by

Puccini is because of the Führer's admiration for Mussolini. Everything else in the repertoire must be by German composers. The Christmas production will be *Hansel und Gretel*. Perhaps if you visit Berlin...?

Our lovely, warm autumn has disappeared and we have been having cold, wet days. I expect you have been having similar weather, only probably colder and wetter. Does that stop you from flying? Let me have your news when you can, I understand that you have little time to write and very little that you can write about, but a word from you is one to be cherished.

Yours ever,
Mathilde

From: Edith von Vorzik
Schloss Adlersee
Bavaria
To: Leutnant Peter von Vorzik
III Gruppe JG233
Oldenburg

12th December 1939

My Dear Peter,

We have not heard from you since you returned from leave and we are assuming that no news is good news – please do not take this as a reproof, we know how busy your days must be. It is only that you are so precious to us and an occasional word, however short, comes as a reassurance that you are well.

Christian came for four days. I cannot say that it was a happy time although of course it is always a pleasure to see him. But he seemed very preoccupied and, I might say, depressed. He had long talks with father, mostly about politics (father is very concerned about our relationship with Russia; he feels our pact with the Soviets goes against everything that we have previously been led to believe). Of course, I know very little about politics but what I have read over the last few years does seem to indicate that Russia is the greatest threat to our safety. Now we have to look upon Stalin as our ally.

Mother continues much the same; some days she seems very weak, then she rallies and appears stronger and interested in everything that is going on. She talks a lot about the past but is often confused about when things happened. She spoke yesterday about a visit from father's sister Aunt Birgit (do you remember her?) who came to stay with us when you were about twelve.

37

She had a terrible argument with father and they have not spoken since. Anyway, mother seemed to think it all took place a few days ago. I did not correct her. She often talks about things that occurred years past as if it was yesterday. She is frequently confused about what time of day it is, insisting it is late at night when it is mid-morning, and asking for her breakfast when it is the evening. I told the doctor about it when he was last here and he said it was a symptom of mother's illness, and the only thing to do is humour her. But most of the time her mind is quite sharp. She was pleased to see Christian and talked with him perfectly normally. She asks after you all the time and wonders when you are coming again, as we all do ...

Father has agreed to mother having a night nurse, which will be a great help to me, as she usually summons me at least twice during the night. The doctor is arranging it for us.

There is very little else to tell you. I think it will be a very quiet Christmas. Christian says he does not think he will be able to get away. It would be wonderful, of course, if you were able to get leave, but I realise that you cannot request it just when you want. I am sure all your Staffel are hoping to be home for the holiday.

Please give my greetings to Kurt, I hope he is well. Take care of yourself, you are precious to

Your loving sister,
Edith

Leutnant Peter von Vorzik
Journal entry

20th December 1939

Something very puzzling has happened. Five days ago the radio announced a great German naval victory in the South Atlantic: our battleship *Graf Spee* had encountered three British cruisers and put them out of action. Then, yesterday, came another radio report that the *Graf Spee* had scuttled herself outside the harbour of Montevideo and that Captain Langsdorff had committed suicide. The survivors have been interned. No more details have been given. What can have happened? Opinion in the mess is that obviously the first reports were inaccurate but why should the battleship have destroyed herself? Who can have given such an order?

To counterbalance such news there has been a wonderful victory in the air. On the 18th, Messerschmitts from three Jagdgeschwader stationed at Jever, Nordholz and Neumünster encountered an armed reconnaissance raid by twenty-four Vickers Wellington bombers of the RAF and shot down twelve of them with the loss of only two Me109s. Of course we were all terribly disappointed that our Staffel was not involved in the engagement but even so it gave us something to celebrate.

Today came the news that I have been given five days' leave over the Christmas holiday. After much wrestling with my conscience I have decided to spend the time in Berlin. In my heart I know that I should go to Adlersee and I feel very guilty about the decision. Two days of my leave would be taken up by travelling to Bavaria, even if I could get a lift on a communications flight but I know that even the briefest of visits would give pleasure to Edith and mother. The more I think about it the more selfish it seems not to go. On the other hand there is Mathilde in Berlin by herself ... I will telephone her tonight and write to Edith. Perhaps Christian will go to Adlersee.

From: Leutnant Peter von Vorzik
III Gruppe JG233
Oldenburg
To: Edith von Vorzik
Schloss Adlersee
Bavaria

20th December 1939

My Dear Edith,
This is just to say that I shall not be coming to Adlersee for Christmas. I have been granted some time off but it is really not sufficient to include the time taken to make the long journey. I hope you will not be too disappointed – I will apply for more leave on compassionate grounds early in the New Year and hope to spend more time with you, mother and father then.

I hope the arrangement with the nurse is proving satisfactory and that you have a little more time to yourself. In any case you must be careful to eat well and rest as much as possible for your good health is vital to everyone. How is father? I am sure he is still absorbed by the Russian invasion of Finland and the political and strategic effect it will have. So far the Finns have put up an amazing fight against such a mighty opponent and it reveals much about the Russian military strength – but I don't want to bore you with such questions.

I am very well but must admit to being bored myself with the comparative inactivity here. Of course there will be very little change in the situation during the winter months and we must put up with the general dreariness of life on the base and hope that everything will be better with the coming of spring. It might even be that the war will be over by then. Meanwhile, I send loving Christmas greetings to you all (I am posting some small gifts separately) and look forward to seeing you soon.

Ever your loving brother,

Peter

From: Edith von Vorzik
Schloss Adlersee
Bavaria
To: Leutnant Peter von Vorzik
III Gruppe JG233
Oldenburg

23rd December 1939

My Dearest Peter,

We received your letter today and of course we are all disappointed that we shall not see you for Christmas but quite understand that the long journey would eat into your leave time (you do not say how long you have but I'm sure it is just a day or two). We take heart from your hope of getting compassionate leave in the New Year and look forward to seeing you then. In any case there has been a heavy fall of snow and Werner says it is very difficult getting through to Munich by road. Of course the snow makes everything look very beautiful, especially at night because there is a full moon now – but then you must know that, unless the weather in the north is obscuring the moon.

There is no news worth relating. Mother seems to be the same, with periods when she seems to be in another world and times when she is perfectly lucid. The night nurse is a great help and I am able to get a complete night's rest, but she is going to her parents in Linz (she is

Austrian) for Christmas and I do not think we shall be able to get a replacement for her over that period. Mother does not like her and says she is rough when helping her into the bath; at other times she seems not to know who she is and asks me who is that woman sitting in my room.

Father remains the same, doesn't say much and when he does it is always about politics, particularly the Russians and the war in Finland. I think he is writing his memoirs, he spends all his time in his study and the library and keeps Werner busy finding books and maps.

We have a young girl (15), Gretl, from the village to help Frau Schuster in the kitchen. Frau S. says it is all getting too much for her and she will have to give up working soon (she is 65, apparently) but I have persuaded her to stay on at least until the spring. At the moment the war is making it difficult to get help but perhaps by the spring things will be different. Father, of course, objected to having to pay for more help but I argued with him (you would have been surprised to see how forceful I was!) and he realised there was no alternative. I am sure all this domestic trivia is boring for you, Peter, but there is nothing else for me to write about and you do say that you like to receive letters.

So, I hope you manage to enjoy your Christmas, whatever you do I am sure it will be a relief to get away from your base and relax for a few hours. We shall be thinking of you and I will be saying a special prayer for you at midnight mass on Christmas Eve.

Ever your loving sister,
Edith

PS I have sent a Christmas parcel separately, it includes a chocolate cake from Frau S.

Leutnant Peter von Vorzik
Journal entry

29th December 1939

I telephoned Mathilde from the base to say that I would be spending my leave in Berlin and hoped that we might see each other for some of that time. I was surprised by the warmth of her response. She would not hear of my booking into a hotel; her mother was spending the holiday with her sister, there was a spare bedroom and she was insistent that I stay with her, Mathilde, in the house. She said we would have a lovely Christmas together, she had invitations to several parties but had made no plans, no commitments.

When I arrived by train in Berlin it was bitterly cold with flurries of sleet blowing in my face as I waited in a long queue for taxis at the Bahnhof. In the early afternoon twilight the big, grey granite buildings of the city looked as forbidding as a row of fortresses. There were no lighted windows in the shops, of course, no illuminated Christmas trees, just lines of pedestrians huddled against the weather, anxious to get home before total darkness descended. It was all in great contrast to the gaiety and warmth of September.

When I finally reached Mathilde's house in Grunewald it was in glowing contrast to the gloom outside. The sitting room was comfortably furnished with a deep sofa and armchairs upholstered in plum-coloured plush, and several large pieces of well-polished furniture, a glass-fronted bookcase, a writing-desk, an oval mahogany table, all of which reflected the light from pink-shaded lamps and an open fire. In the corner stood a tall Christmas tree decorated with red satin bows, small white candles and carved and painted wooden fruit. On a low table in front of the sofa facing the fire was a red lacquer tray with coffee, Berliner cakes, a brandy decanter and two glasses.

Mathilde sat on the sofa and patted the cushions as an indication for me to sit beside her. She poured coffee and cognac and offered me the plate of cakes which I declined. We chatted for a few minutes, sipping our drinks and then, emboldened by the brandy, I leaned towards her, took her in my arms and kissed her. I had half expected her to pull away but she responded with some passion. My kisses became more ardent and then she did release herself from my embrace, patting her hair into place. "Patience, Peter," she said with a smile, "We have plenty of time."

I felt gauche at having become so passionate so quickly but ever since I had spoken to her on the telephone from Oldenburg she had been constantly in my thoughts – indeed, my fantasies. Mathilde poured more brandy and I asked if I might take off my Waffenrock, the long blue-grey tunic that we wear. Without answering she began to undo the buttons, leaning so that I could see the curve of her breasts under her dark green velvet frock. I could feel my breathing grow faster and had to make a conscious effort to control it. Mathilde asked about Christian and I said she probably had more up-to-date news of him than I had. "And what have you been doing," she asked.

"Patrol duty over the North Sea. Very boring." I sipped my brandy and wondered if even that vague information was a lapse of security.

"But you are always in some danger?"

"A little. Mostly from the weather. Our aircraft have a very short range and a navigational error could mean coming down in the sea. We have lost several aircraft like that."

"You must take care, Peter." There was real concern in her expression. I put my drink on the tray and took her in my arms again and this time she did not pull away.

Later, when Mathilde was preparing supper and I lay soaking in a bath which she had scented with verbena oil, my sense of well-being was disturbed by further feelings of guilt, knowing that Edith would be having a dismal Christmas even if Christian did decide to spend a few days at Adlersee.

Guilt feelings or not, however, the next few days were idyllic. We did some late Christmas shopping in which Mathilde's assistance was invaluable. It had been impossible to buy any suitable presents near the base and anyway I was devoid of ideas. At Mathilde's suggestion I bought mother a bed jacket of soft, lacy Angora wool; on my own initiative I bought father a newly published biography of Charlemagne, and between us we chose a small silver and amethyst brooch in the shape of a butterfly for Edith. Of course all the presents would arrive late, after Christmas, but that could not be helped. My great problem was what to buy for Mathilde. I considered jewellery but for one thing I am not yet sure of her taste (she always appears very smart) and such a present seemed perhaps a little, well, premature. Our feelings for each other have burgeoned into something I find hard to describe. I think it might be love but want to be certain, at least about my own emotions, but I have no previous experience with which to measure it. Time will tell but for the present I think it best to be wary.

When we were having coffee and cakes during the rather exhausting shopping expedition (the department stores were seething with people) I made an excuse to slip away and in some desperation settled on a rather elegant powder compact with an abstract design in black, scarlet and silver enamel which the salesgirl said was the last consignment of goods from Paris before the war broke out. One advantage was that it was very flat and even when wrapped it slipped easily into one of my tunic pockets.

The next few days, including Christmas day itself, were a round of festivities and parties given by Mathilde's friends whom I liked very much. Several of them were connected with the theatre and opera and they made attractive, amusing companions even though some of their jokes were a little risqué and their political opinions somewhat, shall I say, unorthodox. We ate foie gras and pheasant, goose and venison, and drank hock and champagne; we sang carols and danced to gramophone records and the radio broadcast that everything was quiet on the western front. Thoughts turned to peace in the New Year and we drank toasts to Hitler and the Third Reich and with each day I felt more and more that I was in love with Mathilde. As I write this I am sipping schnapps from the leather and silver hipflask, inscribed with my initials, which she gave me and the memory of Christmas morning in bed, exchanging gifts and afterwards making love comes back to me with a force I have never felt before. But is it love or just a physical infatuation? I simply cannot be sure because this is the first time I have had what I suppose one must call an *affaire* and the complex emotions it generates and the sexual urges that it provokes are new to me and in some ways frightening. At the moment it all seems wonderful and I do not want to do or say anything that might disturb the status quo.

In contrast, poor Kurt's love life has been most upsetting. Apparently, on Christmas Eve he had a furious argument with his girlfriend in Hamburg which ended in her breaking off their friendship. She broached the subject of marriage and Kurt was adamant that he did not want to consider the question yet, saying that until the war was over the idea seemed premature, which seems sensible. He says that will only probably mean waiting to the spring but of course all that is conjecture. Anyway, I have the impression that he was not all that enamoured of the girl and he views the situation with some relief. I told him I had had a wonderful leave in Berlin but did not elaborate on my affection for Mathilde. Meanwhile life at the base seems particularly dismal after the warmth and jollity of Christmas. The weather has been very bad and we have done little flying, just sitting about in the mess reading and trying to do a little studying though it is hard to concentrate on navigational exercises and theoretical combat tactics when my thoughts keep returning to Berlin.

From: Edith von Vorzik
Schloss Adlersee
Bavaria
To: Leutnant Peter von Vorzik
* *III Gruppe JG233*
Oldenburg

28th December 1939

My Dear Peter,

Your lovely Christmas presents arrived this morning and we were all so delighted with them. My brooch is really exquisite and I have been wearing it all day. It is something I will always cherish. Mother was also very pleased with her bed jacket – how clever of you to think of it, the one she has been wearing has become frayed at the cuffs and I had intended to buy her a new one (nothing so pretty as your choice) but had not had time to do so. I told her it was from you which she understood although an hour later she asked me where it had come from.

Father, too, was pleased with the book you sent him. He has asked me to thank you as he now finds it difficult to write because of the arthritis in his hands. It seems to have been exacerbated by all the writing he has been doing composing his memoirs. He now speaks into a dictaphone machine and twice a week a typist comes in from Starnberg to transcribe from the cylinders. That is about the extent of our social life!

Christmas was very quiet, of course. Christian was not able to get here, he was sent on some mission to Austria, I believe, and so the day passed more or less like any other. Midnight mass was very beautiful and the address very moving. Of course we all prayed fervently for peace and I really do believe that it will come in the New Year.

Now, my darling Peter, I must wish you every happiness and joy in the coming year and trust that God will sustain you in His safekeeping.

Please write soon,

Ever your loving sister,
Edith

PS I trust the Christmas parcel arrived safely. E.

From: Leutnant Peter von Vorzik
III Gruppe JG233
Oldenburg
To: Edith von Vorzik
Schloss Adlersee
Bavaria

2nd January 1940

My Dear Edith,

Your letter arrived this morning and the very welcome Christmas parcel was awaiting me after my return from a brief leave which I spent in Berlin.

I am pleased that you were pleased with your little present – I have to admit that I enlisted the assistance of Mathilde (you remember I spoke of her, Lina Heydrich's friend) in choosing it as my taste is not very reliable when it comes to jewellery and suchlike. She also suggested the bed jacket for mother, something that I simply would not have thought of, so you see my choice of presents was not so clever although they came with all my love and blessings.

On the other hand your parcel of good things was, I know, all your own ideas. I shared the chocolate cake with Kurt (who, incidentally, sends you New Year's greetings) but have greedily kept the tin of pâté for myself! The fur-lined gloves are wonderfully warm; I have been wearing them on patrol, they are so much better than our regulation issue. Thank you again, they are a daily reminder of your love and thoughtfulness.

I am sorry to hear that father is afflicted with arthritis which is so painful, but I am glad that he has devised a way to circumvent the problem of writing. I am sure his memoirs will be of great interest – have you read any of them? He has spoken so little of his past to us (though he has talked a lot to Christian) but his service on Ludendorff's staff during the last war will be of great documentary interest. Did you know he won his Iron Cross at the battle of Tannenberg? I did not, Christian told me.

Tell mother that I am hoping for an extended leave early in the New Year. She may not remember it for very long but perhaps the information will please her for a few minutes.

I am sorry that Christian did not get to Adlersee for the Christmas holiday. I rang his office while I was in Berlin but was told he had gone on a "special mission" (not to Austria, as you thought, but to Rumania, apparently). No doubt we shall hear about it when he returns but so much of his activity is shrouded in secrecy.

Well, my dear Edith, I have no news for you except to say that I am very fit and well and hoping, as we all do, that the war will be over in a few months. Excuse my scribble but I am writing in haste so as to catch the mail collection from the Staffel office.

All my love,

Ever your devoted brother,
Peter

From: Gruppenführer Christian von Vorzik
RSHA Prinz Albertstraße
Berlin
To: Leutnant Peter von Vorzik
III Gruppe JG233
Oldenburg

8th January 1940

Dear Peter,

I was sorry to hear that you did not manage to get to Adlersee for Christmas as I was unable to get there either, owing to a sudden order to make contact with the SD representative in our Bucharest embassy. (More of that later.) It must have been a rather sad and solemn holiday for Edith, what with mother so ill and father more and more reclusive.

I understand (via Lina Heydrich; what need has the SD for its internal security services when such gossips abound?) that you spent an enjoyable Christmas in the company of Mathilde. Well, I cannot blame you for that, she is a most attractive young woman and you deserve some relaxation from your arduous duties defending the Reich against air attack. But do try and get to Adlersee some time soon if it is possible.

For my part I cannot tell when I shall be able to go. There is much activity within the SD at present, which I cannot put into writing. Suffice it to say that my trip to Bucharest was to liaise with the SD mission who are in close contact with the Iron Guard there, although Ribbentrop and the German Ambassador are in favour of the Iron Guard's rival, General Antonescu, who they see as a future dictator of Rumania when (and if) King Carol is deposed which, from all accounts, appears increasingly

47

likely. I wish we were not so involved with these Byzantine Balkan conspiracies – or, at least, we had a consistent policy of our own. As it is, the Reichsführer-SS and von Ribbentrop seem to be pursuing opposing courses of action; as you know there is no love lost between the two. As Heydrich's personal emissary I find myself playing a diplomatic role for which I do not feel ideally cast. Perhaps when you are next on your way to Adlersee you could stop off for an overnight stay in Berlin so that I could confide in you. It would be helpful to have the opinion of someone who is not personally involved in these machinations. For the present,

All good wishes for the New Year,

Your affectionate brother,
Christian
Heil Hitler!

Leutnant Peter von Vorzik
Journal entry

28th January 1940

I have not had a chance to continue with this journal for some weeks; although there has not been much opportunity to fly due to bad weather, my days have been fully occupied and, on a purely personal level, the last day or so has been somewhat momentous so that I want to record it all in some detail.

During the first week of the New Year I was summoned to Staffelkapitan Zwemmer's office. Zwemmer makes himself available to all his pilots if we have specific complaints or personal problems but he rarely calls us in individually unless it is to deliver some reprimand and I could not think of anything I might have done or not done that would merit such an interview. But he received me cordially, offering me a cigarette from an elegant gold case, which I refused as I don't smoke. Zwemmer indicated that I should sit in the chair facing his desk. He lit a cigarette himself, inhaled and let out the smoke through his nostrils. All the while I was anxious to know why I had been summoned. Finally he spoke. "I am going on leave next week," he said, "And I am putting you in charge of the Staffel."

I was so surprised that I responded in a rather blank manner which conveyed nothing of the excitement I felt or the awareness of the honour it conveyed. "I will do my best to maintain the efficiency of the Staffel," I replied blandly. Then I added, "It is a great challenge, Kapitan, I shall endeavour to be worthy of it."

"I am sure you will," Zwemmer replied. "Of course you will liaise with the other Staffelkapitans of the Gruppe. You will assume command as from 18.00 hrs tomorrow. That is all. Good luck."

Within the next few days my enthusiasm for the role of Staffelkapitan was quickly dampened. The running of the Staffel left me little time for anything else. I was unable to relax in the mess with Kurt or any other of my comrades or even take part in what little flying there was. Situation conferences, briefings, operational reports, replacement requests, training schedules, postings in and out, requests for personal interviews, the sheer volume of paperwork and even the problem of the inadequate drainage system of the airfield kept me administratively busy from early morning to late at night and I quickly decided I wanted to remain an operational pilot as long as possible. But it was invaluable experience and an illuminating insight into the problems facing senior officers and increased my admiration for the way Zwemmer commanded the Staffel.

During my brief period of command the Staffel began taking delivery of the latest Emil subtype, the E-3, equipped with a slightly uprated engine and provision for an extra 20mm cannon mounted on top of the crankshaft and firing through the airscrew hub. The extra cannon considerably increased the fire-power of the Me109 but after initial test-firing I received several reports from the armourers that the gun had a tendency to overheat. In addition the pilots complained about vibration problems when the gun was fired in flight, all of which I included in my report to the Technisches Amt of the Reichsluftfahrtministerium and circulated to other Staffeln within the Gruppe. When Zwemmer returned from leave I was once more summoned to his office, this time to receive congratulations on my running of the Staffel. "Your report to the Technisches Amt was a model of concise, factual analysis, Herr Leutnant," he said. "I think it may not be long before you find yourself commanding your own Staffel."

"Thank you, Herr Kapitan," I said, "But to be honest I'd much rather continue flying, I'm not much good at paperwork."

"On the contrary, you have proved yourself to be very good at it. However, I think you will get your share of both in the near future. I understand that as soon as the Staffel has completed its re-equipment programme we shall be moving again. You had better start familiarising yourself with your new E-3."

I was longing to fly patrols again but severe winter weather kept us grounded for nearly two weeks. First there were gales, then a heavy fall of snow which blanketed the airfield in deep drifts. As soon as they were cleared fresh blizzards from the north covered the field again then, when the snow stopped, fierce frosts cracked the newly concreted runways. Each day the ground staff started the engines and ran them up and cleared the aerofoil surfaces of snow just in case there should be a sudden change in the weather and patrols resumed.

During the inactivity I took the opportunity to have my new Emil set up in the firing-butts in order to calibrate the armament. Twice the engine-mounted cannon overheated and jammed so after consultation with the chief armourer, a tall, taciturn man whose black groundstaff overalls were always immaculately pressed, I had the cannon removed. Once again I had my own insignia painted just beneath the cockpit and was impatient to try out my brand-new aeroplane.

Two days ago the weather was clear and bright although the temperature remained below zero. Under the winter sunlight everything looked brilliant: the snow was so dazzling that we took to wearing the tinted glass lenses in our Leitz goggles. A glittering frieze of icicles decorated the eaves of the airfield buildings and ice on the runway became an added hazard but the Staffel was cleared for flying and at last I was able to try out my factory-fresh E-3.

In my fleece-lined two-piece flying suit (the first time I had worn winter equipment) the narrow cockpit of the Emil seemed even more cramped than usual, but as I went through the familiar drill, checking the instruments and controls, I found an almost sensual pleasure in the very smell of the aircraft, an amalgam of acrid aromas, of benzine and oil, lubricants and coolants, of aluminium alloys and tungsten steel, cellulose and resin. As it was a working-up test flight I was flying alone with a strict brief to keep within map-reference coordinates. Despite the treacherous runway I managed the take-off smoothly. I held the control column forward until I could feel the aircraft straining to lift off; when I eased the stick back the clean little fighter responded instantly, soaring easily without that usual dropping of the port wing. I had scarcely cleared the airfield perimeter when I heard the ground controller calling me on the r/t. "Ground Control to Jumbo Four. Bandit in area Caesar-Kurfürst, bearing 23°. Approximate ceiling 7,000 m. Pursue and engage."

I felt a great surge of excitement as the r/t crackled into silence. The bandit was in an adjacent map-sector but flying high and on a receding course. Obviously mine was the only fighter already airborne and therefore likely to make an interception before the intruder was out of range. It was hardly the circumstances I would have chosen to meet the enemy – a new, untried aircraft, no covering Katschmarek, but I was thrilled by the knowledge that I was about to engage in solitary defence of the Reich. It was fortuitous that I had decided to make the test under conditions of total all-up weight, fully armed and fuelled.

Given time for ideal tactics I would have manoeuvred up-sun but if I was to make contact with the adversary I had to take up the pursuit on the most direct course: the long climb with the sun on my port beam would destroy any element of surprise. I opened the throttle to maximum revs and closed the radiator flaps as far as I dared without risk of engine overheating. I trimmed the variable-incidence tailplane and put the Emil into maximum rate of climb which would, I calculated, take me the best part of eight minutes to reach 7,000 m. During that time the intruder would be heading out to sea; it would be touch and go whether I would make contact before he was out of range.

"Bandit in Caesar-Ida, bearing 92°."

"Victor, Victor, message understood." The bandit had changed course to a north-westerly direction which would help me to close the distance between us.

Even in my fleece-lined suit and my heart pumping the blood through my body I felt bitterly cold. At 5,000 m I put on my oxygen mask, a difficult procedure with numbly fumbling fingers. The sky was a beautifully clear azure, cloudless as far as the milky-white horizon where the slate blue of the sea made a dark dividing line, and it was the very cloudlessness that led me directly to my prey: there, still nearly 2,000 m above, was a long vapour trail; all I had to do, Jason-like, was follow the trail until it led me to the enemy. But those wide open skies were no labyrinth; the line was direct and undeviating, dispersed a little by the winds but getting sharper the closer I got. Soon I could see the dark speck at the end of the white path. Had the enemy seen me? I doubted it; the sun was now almost directly behind me and, if it was another Blenheim, I was approaching from the aircraft's blind spot. I reasoned that it was probably just such an aircraft, the RAF had no other known aeroplane suitable for this high-altitude reconnaissance work except the bigger, slower Wellington and after the mauling they received over Wilhelmshaven last December it seemed unlikely the RAF would risk sending a lone aircraft of that type. Then I realised the obvious truth: if the enemy was leaving a vapour trail, so was I. I strained around in the cockpit and looked back: yes, there it was, another thin line of cloud forming just behind the tail. I must have been seen by the enemy, now everything depended on closing the distance between us. I opened the throttle to its fullest extent and the big Daimler-Benz motor responded with its 1000-plus horsepower. Within a few seconds I was able to confirm the intruder as a Blenheim. "Jumbo Four to Ground Control: am in contact with raider. About to engage."

My Emil was about a 150 kph faster than the Blenheim and I could see by the sudden curve of its vapour trail that the pilot had put his aircraft into a shallow dive in order to increase speed, a manoeuvre which briefly brought us to the same altitude. I adjusted the Revi gunsight and moved the selector switch for all four guns. Then I pushed the control column forward in order to dive below the Blenheim again. The range was closing rapidly and then the bomber made a steep, diving turn to starboard.

I kicked the rudder-pedals hard and used both hands to pull the control column across but I had lost the chance of coming up underneath the Blenheim's undefended belly and even as I cursed the lost opportunity I saw the orange chain of tracer bullets curling up from the dorsal turret to meet me. I was angry at myself; this was the second time I had engaged a Blenheim and I should have been able to work out a better tactical approach, despite the need to make early contact. The Blenheim's machinegun bullets bit into the Emil and I felt the little plane jerk under the impact. I pushed the stick farther forward and kicked the rudder pedals again and dived to the port side of the raider. I knew I was in danger of overshooting the target – if I lost contact now I would not have enough fuel to catch him again. I banked the Emil in a tight turn, keeping the nose up, flying near the stall. For a brief instant the Blenheim came into my sights and, allowing for a considerable degree of deflection I pressed the firing button and once again the Emil shuddered, this time under the recoil of its own four guns firing simultaneously. From the trajectory of the tracers I felt sure I had hit the bomber's port engine but there was no smoke, no flame, no bits of cowling breaking away, and then the Blenheim suddenly reversed its downward plunge, turning sharply to port so that I had to heave hard on the control column and kick the rudder pedals once more in order to keep the bomber in my sights. The raider was proving more manouvreable than I had expected.

The range had lengthened with the Blenheim's latest turn so I opened the throttle and increased the speed and angle of my following dive; I was determined to get under the bomber and attack it where it was most vulnerable. 380, 400, 420 kph, the Emil's speed rose sharply and I almost lost sight of the target; I had to stare almost vertically upwards through the top of the canopy to see the Blenheim. I knew then that I must be invisible to the bomber's crew and using all my strength, straining my arm muscles, I pulled back on the control column and the Emil's nose came up in a steep climb, the note of the Daimler-Benz motor changing from a high-pitched scream to a guttural roar.

With the Emil's nose now pointing straight at the Blenheim's under-belly I pressed the firing-button again, keeping my thumb there even when the planform of the bomber filled the gunsight, keeping the Emil on what would be a collision course.

A second after I pulled the Emil into a climbing turn to starboard the Blenheim exploded violently, hurling flaming debris in a great star-burst. The Emil bucked violently in the blast and for a moment I thought that the two aircraft might have actually collided but the Daimler-Benz kept pulling and the controls remained responsive. I kept the Emil in a tight turn, looking for my victim, anxious to check on its total destruction. A large dirty black cloud, bigger than the bomber itself, hung in the air and then, some 900 or 1,000 m below, I saw the remains of the intruder falling into the sea. The tail section had disappeared altogether; the main plane, engines and what was left of the fuselage were spinning lazily round and round like a leaf floating gently down in autumn air. I circled, watching, waiting for parachutes, checking the position, but nothing happened. The Blenheim continued to spiral down, the revolutions gradually becoming quicker. Horrido! I breathed.

There was no need to wait and confirm the bomber's destruction; I knew that I had to try and save my own aircraft. A quick glance at the fuel-gauge showed that I did not have enough benzine to get back to Oldenburg; instead I would try and make Jever, JG26's base near the coast. There was a strong smell of burning in the cockpit but there was no smoke visible from the engine cowling and the temperature gauge registered normal, as did the oil pressure. Perhaps the smell was the result of the explosion. I opened the radiator flaps and throttled back to an economical cruising speed.

"Jumbo Four to Ground Control. Jumbo Four to Ground Control. Bandit destroyed in sector Caesar-Ida. Have sustained some damage. On course one-one-oh degrees, attempting to reach Jever but fuel low, may not get beyond Wangerooge."

"Victor, Victor. Congratulations, Jumbo Four. Keep radio contact. Good luck."

After ten more minutes flying I still had not sighted the Friesian coast and a layer of cloud had formed 1,000 m below. If I went below the cloud level to check my position I would lose precious height should I run out of fuel. I looked at the gauge and, as I had dreaded, the needle was flickering on empty. I throttled back still more and pushed the control column gently forward, that way I could sustain speed in a shallow dive while keeping the engine revs to a minimum. Within another two minutes the red fuel warning light was glowing constantly and I knew the motor would soon splutter to a stop.

"Jumbo Four to Ground Control. Out of fuel. Beginning descent from 3,000 m somewhere in sector Caesar-Kurfürst. Hope I can make the coast."

"Victor, Victor. We have no confirmation of your position. Heavy cloud to 1,000 m. Rescue services alerted at Jever and Wangerooge."

Even as I switched off the r/t the Daimler-Benz began to falter. I feathered the airscrew, switched off the ignition and pushed the control column forward to maintain speed. If I was forced to ditch in the sea the plane might just float for half a minute, just long enough to scramble clear but I doubted if I could keep afloat in my heavy flying gear and I was not wearing a life-jacket. In any case, survival in the icy waters of the North Sea would only be a matter of minutes. The sea-rescue service would need to find me pretty quickly. If only I could make Wangerooge I could take a chance with a crash landing but I did not know what choice I had until I cleared that damned cloud.

With the engine stopped and the airscrew slowly revolving in the slipstream the quietness was uncanny, just a soft sighing of the wind around the cockpit-canopy and a faint rumbling from the engine as the propeller turned the crankshaft. 2,500 m, 2,000, 1,700, I was entering the cloud and it was even more strange drifting silently through the grey vapour, a ghost aeroplane, a phantom fighter. I could not allow such silly thoughts; as soon as I cleared the cloud I must be ready for an instant decision. 1,000 m, 900, for God's sake, was the cloud down to ground level? Suddenly I was through it and there, perilously close and clear, was the grey-green sea, the wavetops crested with foam. I glanced to starboard: a mere kilometre away I could see the tip of Wangerooge – I had just missed the island. The mainland was a mere four km away: could I make it or should I attempt to turn towards Wangerooge? What was the wind speed and heading? What was the rate of descent? It must be more than 1,000 m per km. The indicated airspeed of 140 kph was almost twice the speed at which the Emil would stall in a glide. I decided to risk flattening out the angle of descent by pulling up the nose, ever so gently, fighting for distance, desperate to clear that icy channel of water.

"Jumbo Four to Ground Control, Jumbo Four to Ground Control."

"Go ahead, Jumbo Four."

"Have overshot Wangerooge, am heading for coast due north of Jever. Height 700 m, might just make it."

"Victor, Victor. Keep it going, Jumbo Four, we'll soon have someone with you."

The voice was encouraging but I knew it had no bearing on my desperate gamble. Two km away I could make out the curling edges of white foam merging with the snow-covered dunes. To be so near ... The agonising slowness of my approach was like a nightmare, the coastline creeping towards me, the Emil dropping lower and lower towards the wave-crests as the speed decreased. Indicated airspeed 105 kph, 15 kph from the stall with flaps and undercarriage up, the coast still a kilometre away.

I unlatched the cockpit canopy in preparation for ditching. What was the depth of water, I wondered. Enough to cover the Emil? How ironic to drown in five metres of water! 95 kph and I lowered the flaps to hold off the stall. Half a kilometre to go, the waves directly beneath, the surface laced with circles of white foam, the altimeter registering zero, the coast just visible over the nose, would I even have height to clear the dunes? And then I was over them, missing them by millimetres, skimming the surface of a snowy field, no chance to choose a landing place, holding the nose up until the Emil was bouncing over the earth on its belly, bending the propeller blades on soft German soil, throwing up clouds of powdery snow and I wanted to laugh with relief and happiness.

Within half an hour I had been picked up by a Kübelwagen and a guard was placed by the Emil to deter the interest of a handful of bemused peasants. I was driven to Jever HQ where I made a preliminary report and received the congratulations of the men of JG26. It was not only the destruction of the Blenheim that was important but the photographic information that it had gathered. After being driven to Oldenburg I was debriefed more fully; then a bath, a brandy and another boisterous reception led by Kurt.

Yesterday evening, after supper in the mess, Staffelkapitan Zwemmer appeared at the door of my little bunkroom carrying a piece of paper. "Leutnant von Vorzik," he said, formally, "I have received a telegram from Reichsmarschall Göring who has been pleased to award you the Knight's Cross – for conspicuous bravery and determination in defence of the Third Reich."

From: Edith von Vorzik
Schloss Adlersee
Bavaria
To: Leutnant Peter von Vorzik
III Gruppe JG233
Oldenburg

2nd February 1940

Dearest Peter,
What wonderful news! How thrilled we are! I hasten to congratulate you and send you all the love and good wishes of all of us here at Adlersee – you are our own special hero! In particular it has been a great tonic to father who is anxious to know all the details of your exploit. Mother seemed to think you already had this award but I am sure she was confusing you with father.

Now of course we cannot wait for your next leave – do you know when that will be? Surely your marvellous victory should merit some reward as well as the accolade? Do let us know.

Life goes on here very uneventfully. I wanted to join a sewing circle but father will not allow me to go into the village and will not have "strangers" to the house so I have to do my little bit of war work by myself. I wish I could do something more worthwhile (there must be something I could do) but I suppose my first duty is to father and mother and running the house.

I have no other news for you except to send all my love and congratulations once more,

Edith

Leutnant Peter von Vorzik
Journal entry

4th February 1940

When I returned from an uneventful patrol yesterday I was summoned to Staffelkapitan Zwemmer's office. I knew that it was something serious from his grave expression and, speaking very quietly, he told me there had been a telephone call from Edith to say that mother had died in her sleep. The funeral was to be in four days' time. I was given immediate compassionate leave and the use of the Staffel's Bücker Jungmann, the little biplane used for general communications work. Within an hour I was airborne, having telephoned Edith to expect me sometime late that evening. Everything was fine until I reached Kassel where I refuelled at the Luftwaffe airfield, but after taking off again the weather deteriorated with heavy rain and strong gusts of wind which buffeted the little plane and gave me a most uncomfortable ride. With poor visibility and not much daylight left I decided to land at Würzburg and spend the night there. In the morning, after sleeping rough at a nearby barracks, the weather had cleared and I took off after breakfast in the officers' mess. I had to climb to over 1,000 m in order to clear the peaks of the Fränkischer Jura, then after crossing the Danube near Ingolstadt I was only 50 km from home.

I had enjoyed flying the Jungmann, the aircraft type in which I had first flown solo, but as I neared Adlersee and throttled back to land in a field near the Schloss, my heart felt heavy. Normally I would have buzzed the Schloss, using the aircraft's astonishing manoeuvrability to show off a little and announce my arrival but under the circumstances it would hardly have been appropriate. No one had heard my approach, the Hirth engine making little more noise than a car. I met Edith in the hall and she clung to me for half a minute or more, not only happy to see me but obviously anxious to relieve her feelings; there was no one else she could embrace.

Mother had been laid out in her room, looking, in death, very much as I had last seen her, asleep. Christian arrived in the evening, driven by his usual Unterscharführer in the big Mercedes. We all had a rather silent supper with father, after which Christian and I retired to the library where father wanted to hear about my pursuit of the Blenheim and to discuss the latest political news with Christian. I excused myself, saying I wanted to retire early as I was tired from the flight but actually I wanted to spend half an hour or so with Edith who I knew must be feeling lonely and depressed. I found her in the music room playing the piano with her foot on the soft pedal. We sat and talked about mother for some time, reminding each other of happy times in our childhood and while we could not but feel sad I could see how relieved Edith was just to be able to talk to someone. I told her that after the funeral I would speak to father about her having a holiday. We have friends and distant relatives scattered about southern Germany whom she could visit or, alternatively, she could go to Berlin and stay in Christian's apartment. The relative gaiety of the city, some visits to the theatre and concerts would act as a tonic for her.

Mother was buried in the family vault of the small chapel adjoining the Schloss. It was a quiet ceremony but the little church could hardly accommodate all the mourners. There were several of the older workers from the estate and surrounding farms and neighbours and villagers who were fond of mother. There were masses of beautiful flowers and wreaths and I found the occasion very moving. There was a reception in the Schloss afterwards but everyone had left before evening. I suggested to Christian that Edith might spend a week or so with him in Berlin and he promised to speak to father the following morning before we left.

The return flight was uneventful, the weather much better than on the way down. I was glad of the solitude, able to give vent to my own feelings of sadness at mother's death, buzzing gently along in the little Jungmann. On landing at Oldenburg I was greeted with the news that the Gruppe would be moving within a few days.

From: *Gruppenführer Christian von Vorzik*
RSHA Prinz Albertstraße
Berlin
To: *Leutnant Peter von Vorzik*
III Gruppe JG233
Oldenburg

10th February 1940

Dear Peter,

I hope you had a good return flight. As you suggested I spoke to father about Edith having a holiday and, of course, his initial response was a refusal. I have come to recognise his way of dealing with such questions: at first he ignores the matter entirely, talking about something completely different so that one has to reintroduce the subject once more, either then or later. The second time he usually gives a gruff "no" and once more changes the subject. But if one persists he becomes involved in a discussion that more often than not is resolved by his reluctant agreement. To win the argument or get one's way it is necessary to persist in the face of his obtuseness and, of course, to have logic or a good case to present!

Anyway, I finally got his consent to Edith's vacation. It really will not affect him, he is mostly closeted in his library all day and Werner looks after him hand and foot. I suggested that Edith comes to Berlin and stays in my apartment. She can stay as long as she wishes; the only difficulty is that once again I have been ordered to Bucharest. It seems the differences between Reichsführer-SS Himmler (and Heydrich) who support Horia Sima and the Iron Guard and von Ribbentrop's Foreign Ministry who support General Antonescu against King Carol have become more acute and splenetic; Heydrich wants me in Bucharest to monitor what is going on and report to him. As long as it is only a watching brief I can put up with the posting but as I have said to you before I am not really cut out for diplomatic game-playing. Besides, I much prefer to be here in Berlin where all the decisions are made.

I don't suppose you will be able to get leave so soon after the funeral but if you could manage a weekend and join Edith I'm sure it would make all the difference to her holiday. I shall introduce her to Lina Heydrich and one or two other women friends here but frankly I think she will be rather out of her depth in such sophisticated company. Even so it will be a welcome change from Adlersee; she really needs to get away from that stifling atmosphere. Do what you can to spend some time with her and if you have any suitable friends to introduce her to (remembering how shy she is!) please do so.

Ever your affectionate brother,
Christian
Heil Hitler!

From: Edith von Vorzik
Schloss Adlersee
Bavaria
To: Leutnant Peter von Vorzik
III Gruppe JG233
Oldenburg

11th February 1940

My Dear Peter,

I do so hope you had an uneventful journey back. I had such a feeling of desolation when I watched your little aeroplane disappearing into the distance. Although I found it very tiring looking after mother now that she has gone the house seems so very empty and time weighs very heavily. But, would you believe it! Christian has persuaded father to let me go on holiday. I shall be spending some time at his apartment in Berlin and then perhaps going on to Elise before returning home. I am so looking forward to it (I leave next week) but also a little apprehensive. This will be the first time I have travelled alone and I am sure I shall feel the gauche country cousin in the city! But Christian says he has several friends he will introduce me to although he is being sent back to Rumania and will not be there in Berlin more than a day or two after I arrive. But I shall have an official car at my disposal (how grand!) and his chauffeur (the one who drove him here) will accompany me. I do not suppose you will be able to visit Berlin but of course it would be wonderful if you could manage it. I hope to go to the theatre and the opera and do some shopping – my clothes will seem very out-of-fashion in Berlin I am afraid. Perhaps you will phone me at Christian's apartment?

Father sends his love, as does

Your sister,
Edith

Leutnant Peter von Vorzik
Journal entry

12th February 1940

The order to move came three days ago and here we are at last near the western front, at a new airfield not far from Aachen. We are close to the German-French-Belgian-Dutch borders so we have to be very careful with our navigation! Another Staffel has already made contact with fighters of the French Air Force, shooting down four of them, but we have not yet had the excitement of an engagement.

We made the flight from Oldenburg in one jump as the distance was well within the range of our Emils, the Staffel flying as three groups of four Rotte. The accommodation here is excellent and the airfield itself equipped with concrete runways – no more getting stuck in the mud. Unfortunately we are farther from Berlin, and Kurt is much farther from Hamburg.

The news came today that Reichsmarschall Göring himself will be visiting the Gruppe sometime soon, information that fills everyone with pride but also a great deal of trepidation in case the Commander-in-Chief of the Luftwaffe, the second most important man in Germany, will find something to displease him. He is said to be capable of great rages. Certainly there will be a great deal of spit and polish going on and preparations have already begun with repainting the administrative quarters.

From: Leutnant Peter von Vorzik
III Gruppe JG233
Aachen
To: Fräulein Mathilde Zugmann
23 Hevelius Straße
Grunewald

13th February 1940

My Dear Mathilde,
You must be wondering why it has been so long since you heard from me and perhaps the new address will partly explain the reason. Yes, we have moved again, this time to the western front and, while I must admit I feel excited by the expectation of more activity, of course I am disappointed to be even farther from Berlin...

Prior to our move I was suddenly summoned home to attend the funeral of my mother. Her death was not unexpected; as you know she had been in decline from an incurable ailment for some months, but of course it was a shock and a sad loss to us all.

I think it is unlikely that I will get leave in the immediate future, but I will be able to have the odd 24-hour or even 48-hour pass from time to time. Dare I hope that you could make the journey to Aachen, or even Cologne, so that we might meet? I realise it is a lot to ask but, dearest Mathilde, you are so much in my thoughts each and every day that I feel bold enough to make the selfish suggestion. Please be assured that I will understand if you are unable to make the journey, I know there are many reasons why you may not. But please write to me, your letters are a wonderful boost to the morale of

Your adoring,
Peter

From: Fräulein Mathilde Zugmann
23 Hevelius Straße
Grunewald
To: Leutnant Peter von Vorzik
III Gruppe JG233
Aachen

15th February 1940

My Dear Peter,
You cannot imagine what joy and happiness your letter brought me! Of course I have wondered (and worried) about you these last few weeks and several times I have been on the point of phoning your brother to ask for news but thought better of it, despite encouragement from Lina. She even offered to make the call but I restrained her; it did not seem proper, somehow, to let my personal concerns intrude upon his duties. Anyway, to know you are safe and well is sufficient to set my mind at rest. As for my heart, well, merely to see your writing on the envelope made it beat faster.

Yes, yes, yes! Of course I can come to Aachen or Cologne or anywhere if there is a chance to spend a few wonderful hours with you. So please let me know as soon as you are able where we can rendezvous. You may remember, I have an aunt in Cologne but, of course, it would be much better to stay in an hotel ... Why not telephone me and we can arrange something. I am in most evenings but in case I should have gone to the cinema or a concert with mother, Maria, our maid, would take a message. Better still, write me a postcard and tell me when you will be phoning and I will wait by the phone!

Life here goes on as usual, I have thought of learning to type and doing some secretarial work merely in order to do something useful, but mother is against it. Now, if there is a chance of seeing you I should be upset if I was unable to do so because I was committed to sitting in front of a typewriter! Can you make sense of my jumbled thoughts?

I was very sad to hear of your mother's death, I am sure it has been a time of great unhappiness for you, you have all my sympathy, Peter. How is your sister? I am sure she must be feeling very lonely and depressed. Was she pleased with the brooch we chose for her at Christmas?

I am anxious that you should get this letter as soon as possible so will dash to the post now and await your reply with impatience. Please let me know when we can meet as soon as you can.

With all my love and prayers for your safety,

Mathilde

PS I have dabbed a little Je Reviens on the paper to remind you of our last meeting ...

Leutnant Peter von Vorzik
Journal entry

11th March 1940

From the beginning of this month JG233 has been undergoing reformation. Two of the three Gruppen have been re-equipped with the new Messerschmitt Me110 as Zerstörergeschwader in which Reichsmarschall Göring apparently places high hopes. With their longer range the Me110s will operate as escort fighters for the Kampfgeschwader formations as well as being capable of a number of other tasks such as ground attack and reconnaissance work. Although the Zerstörergeschwader are considered to be the elite of the Luftwaffe I am glad to stay with my old Jagdstaffel; I much prefer the comparative independence of operation and greater manoeuvrability of the Emil to the unwieldy Me110 and its crew of three.

As a consequence of the changes several new pilots have been drafted into the Staffel. Some have come from other Jagdgeschwader and others straight from Fliegerschule. Staffelkapitan Zwemmer has spent much time with us as a result, flying on training operations and in the mess. He is anxious to establish the same *esprit de corps* that existed before the re-organisation and he told me, unofficially, that he had specifically requested that I should not be transferred to the Me110 units. I took that as a compliment.

It is always a difficult process getting used to new members of the Staffel and I have to confess that there are two or three pilots whom I do not personally care for. There is Jan Würling, a large red-haired man who never stops telling dirty jokes. After being buttonholed at the mess bar by him one evening both Kurt and I make a point of avoiding him. It is not that we are prudish but both of us found the endless succession of sexual stories infinitely boring. Our avoiding action seems to have gone unnoticed; Würling seems happy with any audience even if it is only the long-suffering mess orderly.

Wilfred Beckmesser is exactly the opposite: small, dark and taciturn, he is a man who appears to prefer his own company. He answers civilly enough when spoken to but does nothing to advance the conversation himself. He has been seconded from JG77 with a fine flying record, having shot down five aircraft during the Polish campaign.

Ulrich and Friedrich Schleff are brothers although they do not look alike. Ulrich is the elder, tall and lean with lank blond hair; Friedrich is several cm shorter with wiry brown hair cut close to his scalp. III Gruppe is their first operational unit and they stay mostly in each other's company, with the younger brother flying Katschmarek to the older. They have flown with Kurt and myself as a Schwarm and we have occasionally continued the association over a drink in the mess when the conversation has naturally centred on tactics.

Franz Steinitz is a typical Prussian with a hawk-like nose and short, black bristly hair. He, too, tends to be a bore, forever expounding military strategy with particular reference to the Great War and how Germany could have won it. He wears the Party badge in the lapel of his uniform and it is noticeable how other members of the Staffel suddenly find they have appointments elsewhere when he enters the mess.

Eberhardt Kroll is also straight from Fliegerschule. He is short and stocky with a round baby face and blond curls. His boyish appearance is complemented with extrovert good humour and he has been appointed Katschmarek to Beckmesser. The two make a stark contrast to each other and it is apparent that there is a distinct degree of hero-worship in Kroll's attitude to his Rotteführer.

Finally there is Erich Pfister, very much a dandy and a ladies' man, lean and swarthy with highly brilliantined hair matching his well-polished boots. He has, he says, given up a promising career in the theatre to join the Luftwaffe. His rather flashy appearance is reflected in his flying and Zwemmer had occasion to reprimand him for rolling his Emil at low altitude over the airfield in order, presumably, to impress the ground staff. It certainly did not impress his fellow pilots.

Late yesterday afternoon, after returning from a routine practice flight with Kurt, I was told Zwemmer wanted a word with me in his office. Ever since I deputised for him that time a summons to his office has set my heart beating a little faster. This time it was to give me the rather alarming information that I am to receive the Knight's Cross from the Reichsmarschall himself! Naturally, I feel rather apprehensive at the prospect. In the first place I consider the award unwarranted. The Knight's Cross in its various categories is usually awarded on a points system, so many points for each enemy aircraft shot down and the automatic bestowal of the accolade when certain totals have been reached. My three victims are a long way from equating with the Knight's Cross 1st Class, but the pursuit and destruction of the reconnaissance Blenheim was considered to be "special circumstances" and Zwemmer says that the Reichsmarschall has taken a great personal interest in the action. In the second place the personal investiture seems to exaggerate the importance of the episode; other decorated pilots in the Gruppe have victory scores running into double figures.

From: Edith von Vorzik
Schloss Adlersee
Bavaria
To: Leutnant Peter von Vorzik
III Gruppe JG233
Aachen

14th March 1940

My Dear Peter,
Here I am back at Adlersee after the most marvellous visit to Berlin. It has all been so exciting that I find it difficult to sort out my thoughts and

impressions! My only regret was that neither you nor Christian could be there at the same time but Christian's friends have been so kind, taking me sightseeing and to the theatre.

As you may have heard I met Mathilde on several occasions and found her a most charming young woman. We had two or three shopping expeditions together and although I bought only one or two things (everything seems so expensive in Berlin) we had a happy time together. She is obviously very fond of you and asked me many questions about your childhood.

I also met Lina Heydrich. I cannot say that I took to her so much, she is so very, well, outspoken on so many subjects and sometimes really quite embarrassing with her remarks. I also met her husband, Reinhard, and although he was very courteous and attentive when we went to the theatre I found him rather forbidding. I know from Christian that he (Reinhard) is a very powerful person and Christian is very proud to be on his staff. During dinner Reinhard spoke about the difficulties of the Jewish question. Apparently Dr Frank who is in charge of the Polish lands has complained about the number of Jews being sent to the new settlement at Nisko. Reichsmarschall Göring has given orders that the resettling has to stop and Reinhard says there will have to be a new solution to the problem. I have often wondered where Frau Kastner went. Do you remember her? She was the dressmaker who used to come and visit mother, such a nice woman, her husband had a jeweller's shop in Munich, he always used to look after the clocks in the house but he gave up the business some years ago.

Christian sent a note to say that he has arranged for the horses to be taken over by the RSHA and two officers will be coming shortly with a horse-box to take them away. I shall be very sad to see them go. Christian said I was not to mention it to father, he will not even know it has happened. He is well but still spends all his time in his study, he even has his meals in there sometimes so I dine in state all by myself. After Berlin everything here seems so quiet and I find time goes very slowly. Now that the weather is improving (it is so lovely to see the buds coming on the trees) I have been taking long walks by the lake.

As you can see, dear Peter, I have no news except to say again what a wonderful change it was to savour the excitement of Berlin. Keep well, write when you can,

Constantly thinking of you and praying for your safety,

Ever your loving sister,
Edith

From: Leutnant Peter von Vorzik
III Gruppe JG233
Aachen
To: Fräulein Mathilde Zugmann
23 Hevelius Straße
Grunewald

17th March 1940

My Dearest Mathilde,
How thrilled I was to receive your letter and to know that you can make the journey here to meet me. I have heard that I am to receive my Knight's Cross from Reichsmarschall Göring himself and I have to admit that I find the prospect rather unnerving. Anyway, the better news is that after the award ceremony I am getting a 48-hour pass. I have booked a room at a small hotel in Cologne, the Orpheus, in the hope that you will join me there on the 25th. Of course I understand if you would prefer to stay with your aunt but your letter indicates otherwise... I shall be counting the days – hours! – until we meet. Until then, in great haste,

Love, Peter

PS I am not sure when I shall arrive in Cologne but it does not take long by train and I should be at the Orpheus by midday. P.

Leutnant Peter von Vorzik
Journal entry

28th March 1940

Momentous days! Well, at least in personal terms. Prior to the Reichsmarschall's visit the Staffel administration buildings, the personnel block, the workshops and dispersal buildings had all been given coats of paint, including camouflage. Officially it was called "seasonal refurbishment" but everyone knew it was for the Reichsmarschall and the Staffel Oberlagermeister had indented for paint, furniture and fittings considerably in excess of general maintenance supplies.

The day before the Reichsmarschall's visit the Staffel carried out a dress rehearsal. Every conceivable Emil was lined up with precision on the dispersal area with the ground crews in line with the port wings, the pilots four paces in front, in line with the propeller bosses. The Staffel band was in attendance and an Armed Guard of Honour paraded the Staffel emblem. Staffelkapitan Zwemmer was meticulous in his briefing. First, he said, the Reichsmarschall would inspect the guard and then the aircrews, then I should be ordered forward to receive the Knight's Cross. The band would play the German anthem after which we would dismiss to the mess for a formal reception. The Reichsmarschall's Adjutant had telephoned to say that afterwards the Reichsmarschall would give an informal address to the aircrews.

The day of the Reichsmarschall's visit was bright and sunny but with a bitterly cold wind blowing across the airfield. As we were driven to the dispersal area Kurt remarked to me that he hoped the RAF would not attempt a raid during the investiture; he could imagine the Reichsmarschall and his entourage being unceremoniously scattered as we pilots scrambled to get into our aircraft. I told him he had a grotesque sense of humour.

Standing beside my Emil I became very cold and started to shiver; I wished I had had the foresight to bring my hip flask of brandy which I invariably keep in my flying suit. Of course it is strictly against regulations but several of the Staffel's pilots carry brandy or schnapps to keep out the cold at high altitudes. As my shivering grew more acute I suspected it was compounded of nerves as well as the low temperature.

At precisely 11.15 hrs a line of open black Mercedes appeared on the perimeter track. The Staffelkapitan called us to attention and by swivelling my eyes I watched the procession of cars as they slowly advanced across the bumpy grass. I could see the large figure of the Reichsmarschall seated in the back of the leading car with another member of his staff. The cars stopped 50 m away from the assembled aircraft and as the Reichsmarschall and his retinue descended Staffelkapitan Zwemmer marched forward to meet them. He gave the Hitler salute followed by the Luftwaffe salute, then shook hands with the Reichsmarschall. Amongst the senior members of his staff I recognised Generals Jeschonnek, Chief of Staff, and Kesselring, Chief of Luftflotte 2 as well as Generaloberst Frink, Kommandeur of Fliegerkorps VI. All these senior officers looked intimidatingly impressive but the Reichsmarschall eclipsed them all, not only because of his personal presence, accentuated by his size, but also because of his resplendent powder-blue uniform and matching Schirmmütze piped in silver, and the array of medals glittering in the sun. In his white-gloved hands he was carrying a Feldmarschall's baton and at his left side hung a sabre attached to the silver and black braid belt by a massive portapée. The Reichsmarschall was beaming with pleasure as he greeted the Staffelkapitan, his plump cheeks seemingly as polished as his gleaming accoutrements. The Reichsmarschall began his inspection at the furthest line of aircraft and as he began his slow progress towards me my shivering increased. I tried stiffening my legs at the back of the knees which imposed a partial rigidity on my oscillating limbs but it was not easy to sustain the stiffness and when I relaxed my aching muscles the involuntary vibrations started all the more violently. Concentrate, I thought, breathe deeply, think of the importance of the occasion, of the honour you are about to receive. For a fleeting second there flashed before my eyes the image of the Blenheim spinning slowly down into the sea: four men going to their doom, another receiving a medal and congratulations. That was war.

The Reichsmarschall was talking to the pilot of the next aircraft, Beckmesser, who was wearing his Knight's Cross; he had been through it all before. I could hear snatches of their conversation, the Reichsmarschall's voice booming, Beckmesser's quiet replies. I stared straight ahead but out of the corner of my eye I saw the blue blur of the Reichsmarschall's massive form moving slowly towards me; within seconds the illustrious leader of the Luftwaffe, President of the Reichstag, Police Chief of Prussia, the Führer's deputy, was standing facing me. The opulence of the uniform, the rows of medals, the huge breast orders, the dark red watered silk sash shimmering in the sun was an impressive sight but the pale blue eyes (matching the uniform), the plump pink cheeks, the beaming smile were reassuring and friendly. Like a proud father doting on a favourite son, the Reichsmarschall was obviously enjoying himself and I suddenly felt a great surge of pride and patriotism, thrilled to be under the command of this brilliant man.

Staffelkapitan Zwemmer took a pace forward. "Reichsmarschall," he said, "May I present Leutnant Peter von Vorzik."

"The Luftwaffe's latest hero!" the Reichsmarschall replied and his eyes became lost in folds of flesh as his smile became even broader. My eyes were focused on the face before me and I realised with a shock that it was heavily made up, giving the impression that I was looking at a waxed and painted replica. The light eyebrows had been accentuated with a dark, arched line; the sun, shining directly on to the fleshy cheeks revealed powder and rouge and the thin lips looked an unnaturally vivid pink. But, of course! Such a great man, whose every move was constantly photographed, would need to be made up so that his features would register for the camera. Even as the practical explanation dismissed the bizarre effect a group of cameramen positioned themselves around the Reichsmarschall, crouching near the ground, adjusting lenses, jostling for position to record the moment. I wondered what publications they represented, but doubtless there would be an official photograph I could send to Edith. She would be so proud – and, to be honest, so would I. If pride is a sin then it is an enjoyable one.

"A magnificent achievement, Herr Leutnant! I took great interest in the record of the action," the Reichsmarschall said. "What are your comments?"

My comments? I was confused by the question, had not expected to have to express any opinion. "It was a straightforward engagement, Herr Reichsmarschall," I replied. "Pursue and destroy. But I wish, sir," I went on boldly, "that our Emils had a greater range, then I would not have had to risk my own aircraft." I wondered if the Reichsmarschall had been expecting any criticism of our equipment.

"Yes, yes, that is something the Messerschmitt designers are considering. Of course, if you had been flying one of our new Zerstörer there would have been no problem. But, as chance would have it, you were there and you performed with the determination one expects from every Luftwaffe pilot. Always remember, Herr Leutnant, that chance often plays an important part in war."

"Yes, Herr Reichsmarschall."

"Excellent, excellent." The Reichsmarschall beamed again and as he returned to his entourage the band played a Luftwaffe march. After a minute or two during which the Reichsmarschall conversed with his senior officers, the band stopped playing and in the ensuing silence Zwemmer ordered me to step forward. I stopped in front of the Reichsmarschall as I had been instructed and gave the Luftwaffe salute. The Reichsmarschall returned the salute then held out his hand to his left side at shoulder level, palm upward. An aide, dressed in Oberleutnant uniform, hurried forward with an open black leather case containing the Knight's Cross. He lifted the decoration from its velvet pad and placed it in the Reichsmarschall's hand. Holding it delicately by its ribbon the Reichsmarschall moved forward until he was an arm's length away. "As Reichsmarschall of Greater Germany and Commander of the Luftwaffe it gives me great pleasure to award you the Knight's Cross — for conspicuous bravery in defence of the Reich," he said. Carefully he attached the medal to the small hook that had been sewn to the left breast of my Tuchrock, above the pilot's badge. Then he took two paces back and raised his right arm in the party salute. "Heil Hitler," he said. As I responded with all the surrounding officers I noticed there were tears running down the Reichsmarschall's cheeks. The band played the anthem as the Reichsmarschall and his retinue entered the waiting cars. After they had moved off Zwemmer dismissed the parade and the ground staff began manoeuvring the Emils back to their dispersal positions around the airfield perimeter.

"Thank goodness that's over," I said to Kurt as we walked back to the mess. "I was shaking like a jelly, I'd rather face a whole squadron of RAF fighters than go through that again."

"Well, at least you didn't faint," Kurt said, "I can't imagine the Reichsmarschall bending down to pin the medal on your prostrate form."

In the mess, over glasses of champagne, the Reichsmarschall talked to all the pilots in turn. When he came to me he asked if I had any other criticisms to make about the Emil, apart from its limited range.

"No, sir. It has one or two awkward characteristics but it is an exciting aircraft to fly and it gives me great confidence."

"How would you like to fly one of our new Zerstörer?"

"Well, sir, I'm sure it is a fine aircraft but frankly I prefer single-seaters. Of course I have responsibilities to my comrades in the Staffel but I enjoy having sole command of my aircraft."

The Reichsmarschall nodded slowly and pursed his lips in a way that made his wide mouth almost disappear into a tiny dot. "As an old fighter pilot myself I know exactly how you feel, Herr Leutnant. But our Zerstörergruppen will be invincible! None of our enemies has such a formidable aircraft." The Reichsmarschall turned to Zwemmer who was by his side. "I should like talk to the pilots as a group, Herr Staffelkapitan. Will you ask for their attention?"

There was a scramble to get close to the Reichsmarschall in which chairs were overturned and a lot of pushing and shoving. The

Reichsmarschall stood beaming broadly, then held up his white-gloved hands for silence. "Gentlemen," he began, "although I am talking to you informally, what I have to say is of the greatest importance. In a short while Germany will be launching a final blow at her enemies which will bring the war to a quick conclusion. My Luftwaffe will be playing a vitally important role in that offensive and the Jagdgeschwader, as the elite formations of the Luftwaffe, will be in the forefront of the attack." The Reichsmarschall looked at the eager, adulatory faces around him. His voice rose, tremulous with emotion. "I bring you this message from our beloved Führer: You, gentlemen, are the Reich's new Teutonic Knights! You are privileged to be the spearhead of the attack that will deliver Germany from her oppressors! Death to France and England! Victory to the Third Reich! Heil Hitler!"

Everyone in the room leapt to their feet, stood to attention and returned the salute with a shout. It was followed by cheers and applause and all the pilots quickly followed up with their own war cry, bawling "Horrido!" at the top of their voices while the Reichsmarschall stood beaming paternally.

From: Gruppenführer Christian von Vorzik
RSHA Embassy of the Third Reich
Bucharest
To: Leutnant Peter von Vorzik
III Gruppe JG233
Aachen

29th March 1940

My Dear Peter,

I write to you in absolute confidence and would ask you to destroy this letter when you have read it.

As you see I am back in Rumania. The situation here appears to be moving towards a crisis and I find myself in the middle of it. I have had long discussions with Horia Sima who is head of the Iron Guard here and (it is well known) is plotting to depose King Carol. In this he is opposed by General Antonescu who, it is believed, is also plotting against the king. It would seem sensible to let them work together but the trouble is that Sima, who controls the Iron Guard, is a follower of

National Socialism and Antonescu has no brief for National Socialism or Democracy. Naturally, Reichsführer-SS Himmler and SS Obergruppenführer Heydrich support Sima while, for some unaccountable reason, the Reich Foreign Minister, von Ribbentrop, is behind Antonescu. This exacerbates the ill-feeling between the SS and the Foreign Ministry and I am in the middle of it! Heydrich expects me to bring off a political success for his protégé, while maintaining an appearance of compromise and cooperation with von Ribbentrop's minions here. Apparently von R has threatened to tell the Führer himself that the SS is deliberately operating against the Foreign Ministry's policy. You see how delicate my position is? I would not bother you with all this but I have no one to confide in other than you and it helps to relieve the tension to tell someone whom I can trust.

On a more personal level I am also embroiled in another intrigue. Do you remember Frieda, the young Rumanian dancer who dined with us in Berlin? As you may have guessed we had a rather passionate liaison but I received an order from Reinhard that our relationship was disapproved of because she was dark-haired. I know it must seem somewhat extreme to you, but senior SS officers are required to consort only with women of obvious Aryan ancestry. It would not matter so much if I were not attached to Reinhard's staff but my position so close to him and to the Reichsführer-SS makes it imperative that I observe the edict. I have to confess to you (hence the need to destroy this letter) that since returning to Bucharest I have been seeing Frieda fairly frequently (she has left the Vienna Opera and is now a ballerina with the state company here). Most of our meetings are clandestine but thankfully my fellow officers in the RSHA here are less concerned with the niceties of protocol and discipline than they are in Berlin. In fact, many of them are involved with a number of local women who would scarcely receive the approval of Reinhard or Heinrich... My main concern is that I find myself becoming more and more emotionally involved while knowing that, in the circumstances, it has to be a limited *affaire*. But for the moment the relationship affords me great pleasure and, I flatter myself, is rewarding to Frieda, too.

I wonder how your friendship is progressing with Mathilde? I know you are unable to see her as frequently as I am able to be with my *amour* but, then, absence makes the heart grow fonder, does it not? I think it is very necessary for us to have the support and affection of women in these fraught times and I notice that both Reinhard and Heinrich avail themselves of extramarital female companionship.

I have heard from Edith that she enjoyed her stay in Berlin; between us we must engineer more holidays for her during the year, it must be rather depressing for her to be shut up at Adlersee without companionship of her own age – indeed without companionship of any sort. Father has really become a recluse and I wonder just what sort of progress he is making with his "memoirs". I have the feeling that he just sits and dozes and dwells in the past and that very little actually gets put down on paper. Next time I am at Adlersee (whenever that may be) I will ask him if I may read some of his manuscript.

This has become a rambling letter I am afraid, so no more of these meandering thoughts, I am sure you have no need of my lugubrious ponderings. Do not forget to burn this.

With every good wish for your safety and well-being,

Your affectionate brother,

Christian

From: General Nikolaus von Falkenhorst
Oberkommando der Wehrmacht HQ
Berlin
To: Reichsmarschall Hermann Göring
Feldmarschall Walther von Brauchitsch
General Franz Halder

8th April 1940

MEMORANDUM RE: OPERATION WESERÜEBUNG

Following our operational planning instigated on February 21st I can report that all forces are now in place and that the occupation of Denmark and Norway will begin at 04.00 hrs April 9th by order of the Führer.

von Falkenhorst

Leutnant Peter von Vorzik
Journal entry

12th April 1940

First things first. Mathilde joined me at the Orpheus and our two brief (too brief!) days together were quite idyllic. We spent most of the time in the hotel room, only going out to eat at a little restaurant around the corner and, simply to enjoy the splendour of the service, to attend Mass in the cathedral. We did take an evening stroll after dinner in order to get some fresh air but we could have been anywhere, our joy in each other's company amounting to a kind of delirium in which we were oblivious of our surroundings.

I know, now, that I am in love. There can be no other explanation for my feelings. Emotionally I am totally obsessed with Mathilde, every moment is filled with thoughts of her, her looks, her voice, her movements, even her smell which is not altogether Je Reviens. Physically, I am equally under her spell: I find it difficult to keep from caressing her and (if this is intended to be read, someday, by my children I must restrain the impulse to describe my erotic thoughts) – how can I put it? – am in a constant state of arousal. That another human being can instil such a feeling of ecstasy has come as a revelation; all one has ever read, or heard, all those stories and poems and songs suddenly have a real meaning. No wonder people have raved about the condition of being in love for so many centuries – it is a kind of madness. I realise that this must all seem so very obvious and naive to those who have experienced the condition before but when one is infected for the first time the need to talk about it, to set it down on paper. (if only I did have some talent as a poet!) is overwhelming. I did tentatively speak to Kurt and said that I thought I was in love. He looked at me and said, "Yes, Herr Leutnant, I can see you are in pain," in his ironic way, so I did not pursue the subject. I have sufficient sense, I hope, to realise that droning on about it can be extremely boring for other people. This journal is something of a safety valve for me to express my feelings, however inadequately.

The really important news is that German forces have managed to forestall a French and British invasion of Norway and Denmark by occupying those countries. Fighting continues in Norway, especially around the northern port of Narvik where the British have managed to establish a force but, from all reports, it is only a matter of time before they are destroyed. Of course, the Luftwaffe has played an important part in the campaign, particularly the transport aircraft carrying paratroops and supplies and the Kampfgeschwader formations attacking shipping and airfields. The Jagdgeschwader have also been very active, especially the new Zerstörer, their long range so important over the inhospitable terrain. Only a few Emils have been operating and we are getting reports that some have been lost entirely due to their short range; by getting into navigational difficulties they have crash-landed in remote icy areas. Apparently, the Luftwaffe forces have been formed from General Geisler's Fliegerdivision 10 which was originally created for the purpose of anti-shipping operations over the North Sea; it has been redesignated Fliegerkorps X.

Naturally, most of us in the Staffel would have liked to have been involved, especially as we have been under strict orders to avoid combat with French and British fighters over the Maginot Line, which has been most perplexing and frustrating. All that has happened have been armed reconnaissance sorties although, on the few occasions when our 109s have encountered the enemy they have proved crushingly superior. Personally, I am aching to get to grips with the enemy; Staffelkapitan Zwemmer says, cryptically, that we will all have our chance soon although I do not know where he gets his information from.

From: Fräulein Mathilde Zugmann
23 Hevelius Straße
Grunewald
To: Leutnant Peter von Vorzik
III Gruppe JG233
Aachen

12th April 1940

My Darling Peter,
That is the first time I have called you "darling" on paper, though not the first time I have wanted to. I cried when I saw your figure receding on the station platform, it was such a sad parting after our wonderful few hours together and our even more wonderful discovery of how we love each other. Oh, Peter, let me say it again! I love you, darling, I love you! I

think I have from that very first moment when me met and during these few months the realisation has become so insistent that sometimes I feel my heart will burst when I think of you.

Is it not strange that one really has this feeling in one's heart when we know all our emotions are centred in the brain? I suppose it is because the heart is the organ that responds to emotion – it misses a beat or races faster when we are frightened or excited. My love for you produces a constant ache, responding, I know, to the yearning in my brain, my mind, to be close to you. What ecstasy that closeness brought in Cologne! Your caresses, your strong arms about me, your beautiful body fused with mine ... These are moments I recall every moment of the day – and night – my darling Peter, moments that sustain me when the routine tasks seem so boring and burdensome.

The miraculous thing is that you love me in return! You really do, darling, don't you? It was not just because of those exquisite sensual moments we shared? No, of course not! I know from the look in your eyes, from your tender attentive attitude throughout our time together, that your whispered admission in the darkness was also from the heart.

How I wish this wretched war was over! Being parted from you is anguish enough but to be in a constant state of anxiety about your safety makes it doubly difficult to endure. I know that must sound weak and unpatriotic of me, that I must summon just a little part of the courage and bravery you possess, even so I find it hard to achieve and pray every night that God will protect you from all harm.

I have mentioned to mother that I have "strong feelings" about you without actually saying love, but I am sure she knows just how strong those feelings are. She smiled and kissed me and said that she could tell that I was "enamoured" from my general behaviour. She says I have been "dreamy and absent-minded and singing and humming sotto voce." How easily we give ourselves away! Lina Heydrich has also been questioning me closely – she is avid for gossip. She knew, of course, that I was going to see you and was *importunate* with her persistent questions. Of course I told her nothing, except that, yes, we shared a room, what did she expect? Anyway, she too says my general demeanour indicates I am in love so I might just as well hang a sign round my neck.

I have no real news – everything centres on you but you are the only person I can talk about it to, hence this outpouring. I went to a concert with mother, all Beethoven, *Egmont Overture*, *Third Piano Concerto*, *Seventh Symphony*, quite wonderful, the only thing that could have made it better being your presence. I must stop or I feel you may become irritated by my constant reference to your dear self – but then, when you know it is motivated by love, you couldn't be annoyed with me, could you?

Keep yourself safe, darling, you are forever in the thoughts of

Your ecstatically happy,

Loving,

Mathilde

From: Leutnant Peter von Vorzik
III Gruppe JG233
Aachen
To: Gruppenführer Christian von Vorzik
RSHA Embassy of the Third Reich
Bucharest

13th April 1940

My Dear Christian,

First let me assure you that your request concerning your letter has been carried out. I sympathise with your predicament but, of course, can offer no advice on such matters although I do realise it helps for you to "get it off your chest." I must say that it reinforces my feeling that I was right not to accede to your suggestion that I should transfer to the SS! I would be quite hopeless faced with such intrigues, diplomacy – at least in that degree – being beyond me. I trust that you are coping with the situation and fulfilling the confidence placed in you by such important leaders. I know that you find the proximity to such men, your position close to "the centre of things" the very breath of life, but for me it would be constantly unnerving. The few minutes in the presence of Reichsmarschall Göring when he decorated me with the Knight's Cross was quite enough; I am content to be a very small (but I hope efficient) cog in the machine. Anyway, I trust all is proceeding smoothly and you are managing to carry out your difficult and delicate duties to your own satisfaction, as well as pleasing your superiors.

Yes, I was rather astonished at the "edict" you refer to, finding it difficult to understand how a person's colouring can be associated with their desirability as a companion. But this — and other — precepts are probably best left to personal discussion. There are a number of things we have to consider when next we meet. I do agree with you about the dreary and isolated life that Edith now lives. She has no friends of her own, nothing to stimulate her daily routine, no sense of participating in anything. We must find some activities for her or I feel she will become prey to a state of depression and ill health.

Just when we can get together appears, at the moment, to be a distant prospect, does it not? There you are in the Balkans, here I am on the borders of France and now that spring is here everyone thinks that something is about to happen — an attack by the French and British forces, perhaps. Although, for some reason, we have been under orders not to seek combat, there has been a lot of general activity and the whole Fliegerkorps is in a state of readiness and anticipation.

You ask about Mathilde. Well, I can say that our relationship has blossomed into something very serious. Yes, I am in love (a most disquieting feeling, as you probably know) and I am sure she is in love with me. Again, it is a situation that is not helped by the war. To be separated at such a time is particularly painful, it would be so wonderful to indulge one's emotions to the full, to have frequent rendezvous with one's beloved, but all that will surely be possible in the near future. At the moment it is frustrating, disconcerting and only serves to intensify one's passionate feelings. You say in your letter that "it is necessary for us to have the support and affection of women in these fraught times" which may be so but, ironically, such "support and affection" seems to have made life more emotionally complicated for both of us! Some philosopher or poet, Goethe or Schiller, perhaps, must have provided some quotation, a summation of our predicament, if only I knew of it.

All I can offer is the sympathy and affection of your

Devoted brother,
Peter

From: Leutnant Peter von Vorzik
III Gruppe JG233
Aachen
To: Fräulein Mathilde Zugmann
23 Hevelius Straße
Grunewald

14th April 1940

My Own Darling Mathilde,
Yes, it is wonderful to be able to write the word darling! But as I write my thoughts are so jumbled, so incoherent, that I fear all the other words I write will not make much sense. I will try and put them in some sort of order.

Those few hours at the Orpheus crystallised so many thoughts and emotions that had been whirling about in my brain since, well certainly since Christmas. Quite simply, I have never been in love before, didn't recognise the symptoms, only knew that I was seriously disturbed in some strange and rather worrying way – even thought of seeing the medical officer! But now I know, darling, that it is love for you that gives me this odd feeling of weakness, of lack of appetite, of drifting about rather than making positive, controlled movements. The knowledge of what it is, however, doesn't make it easier to bear. Even so, there is a wonderful, exciting element to it all, a feeling that life is even more beautiful than it has always seemed, even more mysterious than one had ever imagined. And all because of you, my own precious Mathilde.

I have read your letter over and over again, it is like some strange elixir, some magic potion that stimulates every fibre of my being – no wonder I have lost my appetite, I feast on your letter, your words of love.

Spring is here, the birds are singing and from the air the fields and hedgerows present a green haze. Much of our flying has been merely routine but everyone feels that we are approaching a climax, that momentous things are about to happen and that must surely mean, my darling Mathilde, that we shall be together again soon, able to plan for the future ...

Do not worry about me, despite my strange feelings I am really in splendid health and excellent spirits. We have the best equipment and training and are far superior to our enemies. I am due on patrol in a short while so will conclude this with all my love.

Longing to hold you in my arms and cover you with kisses,

Peter

From: Reichsmarshall Hermann Göring
Reichsluftfahrtministerium HQ
To: Generaloberst Albert Kesselring, Luftflotte 2
(Attached Army Group B, Feldmarschall Fedor von Bock)
Generaloberst Hugo Sperrle, Luftflotte 3
(Attached Army Group A, Feldmarschall Gerd von Runstedt)
OKW HQ Munstereifel

29th April 1940

MEMORANDUM RE: CASE YELLOW (FALL GELB) MOST SECRET.

Owing to the discovery that Operation Case Yellow has been disclosed by a person or persons unknown to Colonel G.J. Sas, Dutch Military Attaché in Berlin, the Führer has decreed that the plan of attack has been postponed from May 3rd to not later than May 10th so that he may set down the full justification for Case Yellow.

Book Two

War in the West

Leutnant Peter von Vorzik
Journal entry

16th May 1940

It has begun! The war against our real enemies, France and Britain, has suddenly flared up into a major conflagration. On May 10th the Führer gave the order for our armies to attack in the west. Once again we out-manoeuvred the French and the British who were planning to attack us through Belgium and Holland by forestalling them with our own forces. Using paratroops and airborne infantry we secured the main airfields and bridges at strategic points in the Lowlands. Supported by Stukas and Zerstörer our armies had soon over run the defences of these nations and within only five days the Dutch army had been forced to surrender. There is fierce fighting still going on between Antwerp and Namur where General von Reichenau's 6th Army is engaged with British, French and Belgian troops, but the enormously strong Fort Eban Emael has been taken, according to a communique from OKW, by "a new method of attack." This refers to glider troops who landed on top of this "impregnable" fort and, with specially prepared explosives and flame-throwers, soon overcame the defenders.

Further south we are already across the borders of France and our Panzer groups are advancing with tremendous speed. The French army is in precipitate retreat and today's OKW communique says that General Heinz Guderian's XIXth Armoured Corps is already 50 km west of Sedan and racing towards Paris. Of course all units of the Luftwaffe have been flying in close support. We are with Luftflotte 3 attached to Army Group A and have been flying up to five sorties a day and are beginning to feel very tired. Even so, the tremendous superiority of our forces, both on the ground and in the air, is very exhilarating and each time we take off I feel the adrenalin flowing in my veins in anticipation of more encounters. I have already scored eight more victories over opposing fighters.

My first meeting with French fighters occurred nearly a week ago. The Gruppe was escorting a number of Dornier 17s which were to attack French airfields near Metz and Nancy. Just after we had passed over Saarbrücken, the Dorniers came under attack from a flight of twelve Dewoitine D520s. Our Staffel, flying at a height of around 4,000 m above and behind the bombers, were in a perfect position to attack the Dewoitines. By the time Zwemmer had given the order to deploy, however, the French fighters had broken formation and were pursuing the Dorniers, one of which had already peeled off with flames and smoke pouring from the port engine, so it was up to each of us to select a target from the melée. On the r/t I radioed to Kurt that I was going to pursue one of the fighters that was on the extreme starboard of the Dornier Gruppe and he followed me down in a shallow dive.

I opened fire on the Dewoitine with a short burst just as he opened fire on one of the bombers. I could see my cannon shells hit the Dewoitine's port wing and he took immediate evasive action without seeming to suffer any real damage, but at least my intervention had left the Dornier unscathed. Suddenly the air was full of aircraft; the Dorniers' close escort from another Jagdgeschwader had already joined the fight and the Dewoitines were outnumbered by three or four to one – and I was aware, for the first time, how easy it would be to become involved in a collision. Even so I managed to keep track of my original quarry, the pilot having put his aircraft into a steep climb. The Emil proved to have a considerably faster rate of climb which I knew in theory from our various lectures on enemy equipment and I managed to get in another brief burst before the Dewoitine turned steeply to port. I heaved on the control column with both hands in an effort to get inside him just as he turned away again, this time to starboard. Although I had a distinct advantage in speed, acceleration and climb, the Dewoitine proved to be very manoeuvrable and it was difficult to line him up in the gunsight. Then, in an attempt to gain speed, the French pilot put his aircraft into a dive and this was a fatal mistake for it allowed me to get in quite a long burst at a stable target. Bits flew off the Dewoitine's port wing and engine cowling and then there was a sudden flare of orange as the whole aircraft became enveloped in flames. Horrido! My first victory over a French opponent.

There was no time to exult, however. I had no idea where I was, the Dorniers were out of sight and there was no sign of Kurt who had doubtless become involved in separate combat. Through the canopy I could see Messerschmitts and Dewoitines some thousand metres above me. As I put the Emil into a steep climb in order to regain necessary height I glanced at the fuel gauge and saw it registered only a quarter full. I had to take quick bearings and start back for JG 233s forward airfield. Levelling out at 4,000 m I saw a lone Dewoitine 1,000 m below me; it was a tempting target but conscious of that low fuel register I restrained the impulse to attack, took a compass bearing of approximately 17° north-north-east and headed for home. It proved a sensible decision: as I circled the airfield waiting for a damaged Emil to land the fuel gauge was flickering on empty.

I need not have worried about leaving that tempting target. In the next few days I claimed seven more victories: four more Dewoitines, two Morane-Saulnier 406s and a twin-engined Potez 631 fighter-bomber which was attempting to carry out low-level strafing of a Panzer column. Apart from its radial engines the aircraft looks very similar to our Zerstörer and I was pleased with myself for recognising the enemy. Every member of the Staffel has recorded victories – Beckmesser's score is into double figures and we have quickly established air superiority over the whole front. Fighters of Luftflotte 2 supporting Army Group B in the north have encountered Hawker Hurricanes of the RAF. According to reports the British fighters are slower than our Emils but very manoeuvrable and sturdily built enabling them to take a lot of punishment before breaking up. They are armed with eight machineguns which, if they are brought to bear at one point, can do enormous damage. So far none of our Jagdgeschwader has met with these aircraft but we have been warned to treat them with respect if we do.

The latest communiques from OKW indicate that the French retreat is becoming a rout and without being unduly optimistic we can expect the battle to be over within a week or two. The British and Belgian forces are being forced back to the channel ports and will doubtless be surrendering within a few more days. As I write news has come through that the Gruppe will be moving to another forward airfield recently abandoned by the French Air Force. Such is the rate of advance of our ground forces we can scarcely keep up. The French radio today announced that the newly appointed British Prime Minister, Winston Churchill, has flown to Paris to confer with the French Premier Reynaud. Much good it will do them! Another communique just issued by the OKW says that Guderian's armoured columns are now 60 km beyond Sedan and there is no defendable countryside between there and Paris. Victory will soon be ours!

From: Gruppenführer Christian von Vorzik
RSHA Prinz Albertstraße
Berlin
To: Leutnant Peter von Vorzik
III Gruppe JG233
Luftflotte 3

19th May 1940

My Dear Peter,

As you see I have been recalled to Berlin which, in some ways, is a great relief. On a personal level, as you will understand, I have regrets.

Our offensive in the west has proceeded with such success and at such a pace, however, that for political reasons (which I will explain to you when we meet) my presence at Reinhard's side is considered to be of immediate importance.

You, of course, are in the thick of the action and no doubt are finding it all tremendously stimulating, athough I hope you are conducting yourself with prudence; here in Berlin we have to consider the long-term consequences of our military successes. To this end I have had several meetings with Reinhard, his brilliant young aide Walter Schellenberg and Dr Franz Six who will be responsible for directing the activities of the RSHA in London after England's capitulation which will be brought about, one way or another, within the next two or three months.

If only you had agreed to join the SS, dear Peter, you would now be in a position of some authority with almost unlimited prospects within the unfolding political scene in Europe ... However I know you are adamant in wishing to stay in the Luftwaffe and this is no attempt on my part to try and dissuade you from your chosen course. By the way, there is a young man on my own staff, Walter Schleff, who comes of good Prussian stock, who would make an ideal escort for Edith when she next comes to Berlin. I think we should make a point of organising little holiday breaks for her every two or three months. She is simply stagnating in Adlersee and if that continues she will easily become an old maid. Father does not need her, he relies entirely on Werner and practically ignores Edith's existence. Berlin is swarming with eligible young men and we have a duty as her brothers to see that she meets some of them. When is your next leave? I imagine after all the activity you have been involved in that you will be due for a rest period soon.

So much is happening so quickly that it is difficult to keep pace with developments. I look forward to our meeting soon so that we may plan our own futures in the Greater Germany that is emerging.

Until then, my best wishes for your continued safety and success,

Ever your affectionate brother,
Christian
Heil Hitler!

From: OKW HQ Army Group A
Charleville
To: General Heinz Guderian and General Georg-Hans Reinhardt

24th May 1940, 11.42

By order of the Führer all further advance along the Aa canal line between Dunkerque and St Omer will stop pending further infantry support and in order to conserve Panzer forces.

Signed
Field Marshal Gerd von Runstedt

From: *Edith von Vorzik*
Schloss Adlersee
Bavaria
To: *Leutnant Peter von Vorzik*
III Gruppe JG233
Luftflotte 3

28th May 1940

My Dear Peter,

Such wonderful news from the western front (we have just heard on the radio that King Leopold of the Belgians has surrendered to our forces early this morning) but of course we are constantly anxious for you knowing that you are in the thick of the battle and that some of our planes have been shot down. The candle that mother lit in her room and before which she used to pray for your safety is replenished daily and, like her, I offer up my prayers for you. It does seem that the war will soon be over and we shall all be together again.

I feel so helpless here, as I have said before. Everyone in the village seems to be making some contribution to the war effort but every suggestion that I have made has been vetoed by father. I suggested that some of the women could come here and we could have a sewing circle; I suggested that we could have a produce sale; I suggested that I could organise a small concert in aid of the Women's League, but he would not agree to any of it. But now the news makes all those suggestions rather redundant.

Father hardly ever emerges from his study now. He listens to the radio constantly, has all his meals in there, is attended by Werner all the time and has given up his daily walk. I seldom see him except when I present the household accounts. He pores over them for hours and questions everything, including Werner's wages! Next time that Christian is here I want him to talk to father who objects to almost every expenditure – coal for the boiler, household cleaning materials, everything. It is very difficult for me having to argue over every little item.

Frau Schuster has made you a chocolate torte which I am sending separately. I said that you were moving about so much that it would be stale by the time it reached you, if it ever did, but she was anxious to send you something (you have always been her favourite, as you know).

Christian telephoned last night and during the conversation he said that he would be organising another visit to Berlin for me. Of course I should enjoy that very much but it seems not so long ago that I was there and I know father will say no, no, no! But Christian says he will not accept a refusal and is prepared to argue – even insist on my behalf. I should certainly love to stroll down the Unter den Linden and Kurfürstendamm in this beautiful late spring weather. The gardens here are full of flowers, the cherry trees and laburnum have been wonderful and bird song wakens me every morning. I cannot help comparing the idyllic scene here with the terrible things we hear about on the radio and the pictures in the newspapers. Of course I know the French are our enemy but I keep thinking how awful it must be to have tanks crushing you to death, and aeroplanes dropping bombs on you.

It may be some time before this letter catches up with you – like the cake! – and it could even be that you are given leave before that. Christian says you must surely be given a rest period soon. I do hope so, dearest Peter. In the meantime my prayers for your safety continue.

Ever your loving sister,
Edith

Leutnant Peter von Vorzik
Journal entry

1st June 1940

Something of a respite from the hectic life we have led these last two weeks. Sorties and patrols from dawn to dusk, furious encounters with the enemy (I have yet to meet any aircraft of the RAF) grabbing meals when we can, uneasy sleeps disturbed by constant noise, frequently moving from one primitive and inadequate airfield abandoned by the French to another – I feel physically and mentally tired. I have also had my first taste of fear. In all my early encounters, with the brief engagements in Poland, with the pursuit of the Blenheims, with those first recent fights with the French, I was never conscious of being frightened, but yesterday's encounter gave me a horrifying glimpse of what warfare means.

Kurt and I were flying on patrol as a Schwarm with the Schleff brothers when we sighted twelve Morane-Saulnier 406s about 500 m below us on the port beam. We turned to attack and obviously surprised them. I got one with my first burst and Kurt accounted for another. Friedrich Schleff claimed a third and his brother Ulrich claimed two, also sustaining some damage to his own fuselage without, luckily, affecting anything but the main structure; the French cannon shell could so easily have severed one of the cables actuating the rudder and elevators. After these losses the 406s broke off the engagement and turned west. We did not pursue as, once again, our limited range would have endangered our own safe return to base.

Satisfying and successful though this encounter was there was a moment that has stayed in my mind ever since. During the melée, just after I had destroyed my 406 and was repositioning myself to find another target a 406 passed close to me with flames bursting from the engine cowling and enveloping the cockpit. (I think it was one of Ulrich's victims from what he said at the debriefing.) For an instant I could see the pilot's face, his mouth open in a scream and in that split second I was aware of the agony of such a death, how the pilot must long for the oblivion of the final impact. The image was so graphic it has stayed with me and, for the first time, made me think in a different way about the meaning, the horror of war. I have to confess that until now it has generated a sort of excitement in my blood, an aggressiveness that must be there in the temperament of every fighter pilot. But until now I have ignored the reality of it, what it means to destroy another human being even though that person is the enemy of one's country. I don't for one moment question the rightness of our cause, the necessity to fight, but now I am grimly aware of just what happens when I press that firing button. It hasn't deterred me in any way, hasn't unnerved me, only made me all the more implacable in an engagement: it's him or me and I will do everything in my power to avoid that sort of death. I have wondered if other pilots have had similar thoughts. I am sure they have but it is not the sort of subject one can discuss easily – even with Kurt. One's feelings could so easily be misunderstood although I am sure fear is not only a natural reaction to the circumstances of combat but also a very necessary part of one's fighting temperament. Without it one would be foolhardy and that is not a quality that makes for a consistently successful fighter pilot.

For the moment, though, it has made me reconsider my intention of asking Mathilde to marry me. After our ecstatic time together in Cologne when we both declared our love for each other I had resolved to propose to her during my next leave. Now the idea seems somewhat precipitate. Mathilde could so easily find herself a widow a few days after marriage and I have no wish to burden her with that. At the moment our relationship is wonderful; I am thankful for that and marriage can wait until the war is over which it surely will be in a few weeks' time.

Incidentally, I asked Ulrich Schleff if he was by any chance related to the Walter Schleff that Christian mentioned in his letter but he (Ulrich) said no, he doesn't think so.

From: Fräulein Mathilde Zugmann
23 Hevelius Straße
Grunewald
To: Leutnant Peter von Vorzik
III Gruppe JG233
Aachen

2nd June 1940

Darling Peter,

As you see I am sending this to the last address you gave me. It is such a long time since I heard from you but I tell myself that no news is good news and I know you must be involved in the terrible battles that are going on. I had thought of trying to get in touch with your brother via Lina Heydrich and her husband's office just to find out if he had any news of you but then I thought that such an inquiry might seem improper considering the illustrious people involved.

So, my darling Peter, here I am, desperate for news of you (I also thought of phoning your sister but rejected that idea, too, as being intrusive) and wondering every moment of the day what is happening to you. Of course the news is wonderful, mother and I sit by the radio for hours listening to all the reports but, exciting though it is, every time there are details of aerial engagements my heart misses a beat thinking of you. Well, I won't express my fears, only say again that you are in my waking thoughts every moment of the day. In dreams, too.

We have just heard on the radio that the Luftwaffe has sunk three British destroyers at Dunkirk. I wondered, darling, if you were involved in that operation? I long to see you again, I wait for the post every day hoping to hear you are coming to Berlin. Nothing else has any meaning.

I go shopping with mother, play a little music on the gramophone, but all my thoughts are centred on you, I cannot concentrate on anything else. Oh, Peter darling, I am sure these outpourings are probably irritating to you but you cannot know how it feels to love someone so much and not know where they are, what is happening to them. Forgive me, then, for writing in this manner when I realise what you want is letters full of interesting news that help to take your mind off all your own anxieties.

Please, darling, write to me when you can, just the briefest postcard will do to let me know everything is all right and that you still love me as much as ever. My body aches to feel your arms around me once more.

Forever in my thoughts and prayers,

Always your adoring,
Mathilde

Leutnant Peter von Vorzik
Journal entry

14th June 1940

Paris has fallen! General von Kuchler's 18th Army entered the undefended city this morning and the German flag has been hoisted on the Eiffel Tower. According to the latest OKW communique the French government has fled to Bordeaux. Surrender can only be a matter of days – maybe hours – away. The British have been both clever and lucky to get so many of their soldiers back across the English Channel. Of course, their powerful navy was largely instrumental in achieving this successful withdrawal but apparently they used scores, even hundreds, of small boats, yachts and pleasure craft, to evacuate the troops from the beaches. Bad weather hampered our bombers in destroying this strange flotilla but there are rumours in the mess that for some unaccountable reason the advance of our Panzer forces was halted just when they were about to overwhelm the British, French and Belgian units, thus allowing them to organise a rearguard action while the majority escaped. If this is true then no doubt there will be reprimands and sackings amongst the General Staff except that another rumour (where do these tales originate, I wonder?) suggests that the order to halt came from the Führer himself. Difficult to believe and, if true, even more difficult to understand.

Four days ago, the Italians declared war on the French and British. While it is nice to have an ally in the south I cannot help thinking, somewhat cynically perhaps, that Mussolini waited to see how the war was going before deciding to support us. The feeling in the mess is that his forces, particularly his air force, will not be much help. Much of their equipment is obsolete but of course their strategic position in the North African colonies is important and they have a big navy that will be a threat to the British Mediterranean Fleet.

On the very same day that Italy entered the war, OKW issued a communique announcing that the British have at last been driven out of Narvik; the Norwegian campaign is finally over and we now control the whole coastline from the Arctic circle to the Bay of Biscay. Our navy, particularly the U-boats, will now be able to operate from numerous new bases to attack the British convoys coming across the Atlantic. All these factors point to a rapid conclusion of the war.

Today we have been withdrawn from the front-line as JG233 is only 30% operational. This is due to losses and the difficulty of regular maintenance while flying constant sorties. We have lost Erich Pfister from the Staffel, posted as missing. The normally taciturn Beckmesser remarked that Pfister was probably having the time of his life in some French brothel. It was a callous remark but Pfister has never been very popular.

We expect to be granted leave but at the moment things are in such a state of flux owing to the rapidity of the French collapse that Zwemmer says that Luftflotte 3 HQ is still trying to catch up with events and sort out who is where! I have decided to spend all my leave in Berlin. I think I deserve a vacation near Mathilde (a letter from her arrived this morning, together with one from Edith and a cake from Frau Schuster; the mail, too, has not been able to keep up with us) and there is little reason to go to Adlersee even if I could get a lift in a transport. From what Christian and Edith say in their letters, father would grant me a 15-minute audience and then forget I was there and in any case Edith might well come to Berlin herself.

While writing this, Zwemmer came to announce that the Staffel is granted fourteen days' leave from tomorrow. I queued for over an hour to telephone from the only line open for personal use and then had great difficulty in making connections to Berlin which was very frustrating but now (it is late evening) everything is arranged. I was able to contact Christian who readily agreed to my staying in his large apartment near Prinz Albertstraße. It has two guest rooms and Mathilde can join me there. The domestic staff are perfectly discreet. My second call was to Mathilde who was rather emotional. She said she was shedding tears at the sound of my voice and I, in turn, found myself trembling at the sound of hers. She said that I could stay with her in Grunewald but I would feel somewhat inhibited with her mother in residence although she is an understanding woman. At Christian's apartment it will be like staying at an hotel without paying the bill! It is also much more central to the life of the city and, besides, Christian and I have much to discuss.

The last few weeks seem, now, to have been a feverish dream, the immediate future a vision of paradise.

From: Leutnant Peter von Vorzik
en route to Berlin
To: Edith von Vorzik
Schloss Adlersee
Bavaria

15th June 1940

My Dear Edith,

Forgive the wobbly scrawl but I am seated in a Ju52 squashed between comrades and equipment while flying to Berlin. Apart from the cramped circumstances it is proving to be a very bumpy flight.

Yes, I am on leave, safe and well after a few hectic weeks. I shall probably telephone you before you receive this but as I find I so often put the phone down having forgotten to mention several things that I intended to, I want to make sure that I thanked you for your letter and for the cake, thank Frau Schuster for me please. It arrived just before I was leaving so I shared it around the mess, otherwise I would have eaten it all myself with just a slice or two for Kurt who always shares his delicacies from home with me (very often some fishy speciality from Hamburg!).

I am sure you will understand that I will be spending all my leave in Berlin. I need to relax and although Adlersee would be a haven of peace I also look forward to the stimulus of a big city after so many days spent on bleak airfields. Also, and I have to admit this is the most important reason, I want to be near Mathilde. It will be no surprise to you, dear Edith, when I tell you that we are in love. It is a disturbing emotional state to be in, believe me, as I sincerely hope you will soon find out for yourself. The war, of course, adds all sorts of practical complications and the need to make the most of opportunities to be together is paramount. It would be nice if you could manage to come to Berlin too; perhaps Christian and I can arrange it. We shall see.

The light is blinking to tell us that we shall soon be landing. Until we speak or meet,

Ever your loving brother,

Peter

From: Gruppenführer Christian von Vorzik
116 Kaiserstraße
Berlin
To: Leutnant Peter von Vorzik
To await arrival

15th June 1940

My Dear Peter,

Welcome back to Berlin! You come as one of the Reich's glorious young warrior heroes and I have given orders to my staff that they are to serve you accordingly. Just ask for whatever you want.

I have arranged for a car to collect Mathilde from Grunewald and she should be waiting at the apartment to greet you. I must apologise for not being there myself. At the moment we have an enormous amount of work to get through. You may recall that I mentioned in a previous letter that I am working with Walter Schellenberg and Dr Six on the programme for the RSHA after the British capitulation. Reinhard's office is also closely concerned with the ever-growing problem of Jewish resettlement. Before the French collapse, Franz Rademacher, head of the Jewish Desk at the Foreign Ministry, proposed that France should cede Madagascar to Germany and we should set up a large ghetto there for four million Jews. This proposal has now been given to Obersturmbannführer Eichmann who is liaising with Reinhard's office. I will not bother you further with all this, I tell you only to explain why I cannot greet you in person. I shall, however, be taking a few days off while you are here and I have arranged several parties, dinners and soirées to celebrate your triumphant return from the battle.

Until we meet,

Salutations from your proud brother,

Christian

Heil Hitler!

Leutnant Peter von Vorzik
Journal entry

23rd June 1940

My leave here in Berlin is proving more hectic and exhausting than I had anticipated – perhaps I should have gone to Adlersee after all. But it is a different sort of weariness to that which I felt during the recent campaign. My tiredness now comes from a social whirl and constant physical contact and release with darling Mathilde. The ecstasy we discovered in Cologne has been repeated – even more intense, if possible. Nothing is more lovely than waking late in the morning, excitement regenerated by the presence of my dearest one by my side and then, an hour or so later, ringing for the maid to bring us breakfast in bed. Such luxury!

Usually we go for a gentle stroll, do some window-shopping, have a light lunch in a café and then back to the apartment for a siesta where, inevitably, we become physically entwined again. We cannot enter a café or restaurant or bar without total strangers offering us drinks or the proprietors refusing to give us a bill. It is all the fault of my uniform, of course, but I have no civilian clothes here. I find it all rather embarrassing, people even ask me to recount how I won my Knight's Cross! Mathilde says she is immensely proud when we receive such attention but I really wish we could be left in peace to enjoy each other's company.

I have been reconsidering my decision to postpone asking Mathilde to marry me. The war is virtually over and I cannot think that it is sensible to ignore the depth and intensity of our love. It seems, now, the right thing to do to acknowledge our feelings by taking the obvious and proper course. I have spoken to Christian about this at length and he agrees with me. He says at least we should announce our engagement during this leave and wants to give a huge party (there have already been several large ones!) for the occasion. Even while writing this I have decided to make the formal proposition this evening. We are due to have dinner with the Heydrichs and some other members of his staff; perhaps I will propose to Mathilde while we are dressing – I will make sure that a bottle of champagne is put on ice in my room.

The second night of my leave Mathilde and I had a quiet dinner with Christian and his girlfriend. She was an attractive blonde who seemed somehow familiar. It was a moment or two before I realised it was the Rumanian dancer, Frieda, (I learned her surname is Vopescu) whom Christian had been seeing clandestinely in Bucharest. He told me afterwards that she has dyed her hair blonde and Heydrich's office has furnished her with papers proving an impeccable Aryan ancestry. I find it all rather ridiculous but apparently such things are taken very seriously amongst senior Party members. Christian also said that Herr Himmler has been making a tremendous fuss because Reich Minister for Propaganda Josef Goebbels has been conducting a fairly open affair with a Slavic actress. Goebbels is able to ignore Himmler's protests because his (Goebbels') position vis-à-vis the Führer is impregnable. Apparently he (G) is a great favourite at court (as Christian puts it) and he has many affairs with women although, in various newspapers and magazines, he and his family are held up as perfect examples to all the citizens of Greater Germany. All this gossip and tittle-tattle which appears to be the mainspring of almost every conversation here in Berlin seems unworthy of men leading the country. I said this to Christian and he agreed with me but he also said that throughout history all great men have had their sexual peccadilloes, from Alexander the Great to Napoleon. He even hinted that certain Party members were involved in homosexual practices although in the SS such activities are punishable by death. These conversations leave me feeling like a naive country bumpkin. Anyway, I'm glad for Christian's sake that Frieda has been made persona grata. She certainly seems a charming young woman. She has left the theatre in Bucharest and taken up a position with the Berlin Opera – I believe Heydrich's office "arranged" that for her, too. How glad I am that I remained in the Luftwaffe where things are relatively straightforward!

Later

As we were dressing, over a glass of champagne, I proposed to Mathilde. She fell into my arms and clung to me, crying. I said I hoped I hadn't upset her but through her tears she said I had made her the happiest woman alive. Really, women are strange creatures! But she recovered and

I could tell that she was tremendously happy – for the rest of the evening she simply sparkled. She looked ravishing in a cream silk dress with diamond earrings and pendant that had been her grandmother's. My decision to propose had been so impulsive that I had had no time to buy a ring but that will be something pleasurable for us to do together in the next day or so. (My leave is passing so quickly. I have barely six days left.)

I had told Christian of my intention and he had organised a reception and supper party for us. The Heydrichs were there as well as some officers and aides from his entourage including Walter Schleff whom Christian had mentioned as a possible escort for Edith. And then, surprise! As we were gathered talking and drinking, who should arrive but Edith herself! Christian, of course, had arranged it. He had sent a car all the way to Adlersee for her, giving the chauffeur a letter to give to Werner to hand to father. A *fait accompli*!

Christian had telephoned Edith telling her to have her bags packed and be ready to leave. She was very nervous at being so secretive but Christian had been insistent. He says he thinks father is rapidly becoming senile and has little apprehension of what is really happening. He added that he, Christian, is to all intents and purposes, now the head of the family which I suppose is true. Certainly he is in a position of power and authority within the Reich while father remains just a *pater familias*.

The evening was one of tremendous gaiety although I would have preferred to have had Mathilde to myself. We dined at a private room at the Adlon and then went on to a cabaret at the Olympia on the Ku'damm. It was an enjoyable show, especially a burlesque apache dance with the man dressed as a ridiculous bowler-hatted Englishman and the woman as a French prostitute. At dinner and at our cabaret table Edith had been placed next to Schleff; the next day she told me she found him opinionated and overbearing. So much for Christian's matchmaking.

Although Edith no doubt finds Berlin very stimulating after her quiet and almost solitary existence at Adlersee I can see that she feels somewhat *de trop* at times – I had the same feeling at that first introduction to Christian's circle. She is visibly shocked at some of the sophisticated stories and conversations of Lina Heydrich and her friends but perhaps it is as well that she should be exposed to such society; as Christian says, she is only stagnating at Adlersee and we must see to it that she finds a suitable husband. As neither of us is resident in the south we must concentrate our efforts in Berlin. Christian, of course, is the one to guide that process, he is more or less permanently there and able to organise matters.

My night with Mathilde after the engagement party was one of utter joyous delirium. Both of us had had rather too much champagne which lent a sort of dream-like quality to our lovemaking – but not so as to diminish our ardour! Afterwards I lay awake with Mathilde sleeping with her head on my chest, thinking about the practicalities of our marriage plans. I have to obtain permission from the Gruppe Commander but that is only a formality. Then, where should it take place? Ordinarily, it would be in the chapel at Adlersee but the war makes a difference and in any case Mathilde might want it to be in Berlin. Then, where should we live? We must find a small apartment somewhere. Mathilde says her mother might move from the house at Grunewald and join her sister in Cologne, apparently she has been talking about it for some time – but I would not want to feel we had pushed her out of her home. Anyway, there is no hurry; I do not even know where I will be stationed in the coming months, so much will depend on the military and political situation as it develops.

Christian says there are all sorts of problems attendant on the recent course of the war. The most pressing seems to be the situation of the Jews; Heydrich says there are various plans to deal with these people but, personally, I cannot see that there is any problem but I keep my mouth shut when the subject is discussed. At the moment I am concentrating on my own problems which are not really problems at all, just domestic questions that have to be resolved. What is certain is that I have never been so happy.

The day after our engagement party I received notification of my new posting. JG233 is being refitted and reformed at an airfield near Paderborn in Nordrhein-Westfalen. The Gruppe is awaiting the delivery of new aircraft and my leave has been extended for a few days (Mathilde cried with happiness when I told her) and I am to rejoin the Staffel on July 5th. I have told Mathilde I would rather she did not come to the station with me; she is bound to cry and I could not bear it. Much better that our farewells should be in private rather than amongst the milling crowds on the railway platform.

The day after the party we went looking for an engagement ring. Together we chose a square-cut emerald surrounded by small diamonds. Mathilde said it was far too expensive but I could see she loved it the moment the jeweller brought out the tray and I insisted. It certainly does look very beautiful without being ostentatious. Edith and Lina both gave their approval and I was secretly amused to see how Mathilde places her hands in such a way that the ring is noticeable. But it is an indication of how she is happy with our engagement and I love her for it.

4th July

This is the last day of my leave. Tonight will be passionate but fraught with the awareness of our last few hours together until who knows? I dread tomorrow's departure.

From: Adolf Hitler
HQ Obersalzburg
To: Reichsmarschall Göring; General Franz Halder;
Gr. Admiral Erich Raeder:
Directive No. 16

16th July 1940

TOP SECRET
Since England, despite her militarily hopeless situation, still shows no sign of willingness to come to terms, I have decided to prepare a landing operation against England, and if necessary to carry it out. The aim of the operation is to eliminate the English homeland as a base for the carrying on of the war against Germany and, if it should become necessary, to occupy it completely. The code name for the assault will be Sea Lion.

Adolf Hitler

Leutnant Peter von Vorzik
Journal entry

20th July 1940

So much has happened since I last put pen to paper over two weeks ago. Of course Mathilde came to the station with me, she wanted, she said, for us to be together until the last possible moment and I could not dissuade her. In any case our farewell was going to be an anguished one wherever it took place, I would just have preferred it to have been more private than the station platform.

I rejoined the Staffel at Paderborn and four days later the Gruppe flew to a new posting in northern France, just north of the Seine near Rouen.

It is an old French airfield which has been hurriedly improved with new quarters and a dispersal area although the runway is still grass. We are attached to Luftflotte 3 under Generalfeldmarshall Hugo Sperrle. I have managed to telephone Mathilde twice although connections to Berlin are erratic and the whole process is one to try one's patience. There are two phones for general personnel and of course there is always a long queue. When I have managed to make a connection our conversation is always rather stilted; it is curious how I store up things to say and then, with the phone in my hand, it all goes out of mind and I waste precious seconds with banal generalities and even with what seem like long silences. I am conscious that all my endearments can be overheard. One's most passionate thoughts and feelings are best expressed in letters, anyway. Even so, these brief moments of voice contact are fine for morale.

We have now been re-equipped with the latest Emils, the Me109E-4. It has a revised cockpit canopy which incorporates some armour plating behind the head (very reassuring!) a bulletproof windscreen (so it is claimed) and the armament has now been standardised with two MG17 machineguns mounted on top of the engine cowling and two 20mm MG FF wing-mounted cannon with improved rate of fire. The camouflage scheme has also been changed: the light and dark green splinter pattern remains on the top surfaces but the fuselage sides are now light grey with dark grey mottling and light grey undersurfaces. The engine cowling retains the bright blue of the Gruppe's identification colour. These last two weeks we have been kept busy working with the new aircraft and perfecting combat techniques. Our radio radius is still limited to about 50 km and the overall range of the Emil remains at about 500 km at a cruising speed of around 240 kph according to height and conditions.

Last night the Führer gave a most wonderful and inspiring speech in the Reichstag. He was generous in his references to the defeated French with whom we have now completed an armistice (there was an enjoyable irony in the signing of it as the Führer ordained that it should be in the very same railway coach in the forest of Compiègne where we Germans had surrendered to Marshal Foch in 1918) and who are now represented by the old Marshal Pétain. The Führer also made it plain that he was ready to offer similar generous terms to the British but we have heard on the radio today that they have rejected the offer of peace. Zwemmer says that we shall soon be fighting the last offensive of the war when we attack the British mainland. Their army has already been defeated and the RAF is weak in numbers and equipment. Of course they have a big navy but that will not avail them much in this final battle. I have always had an admiration for the British and their achievements but I am afraid they are now going to pay the price for their obstinacy.

From: *Gruppenführer Christian von Vorzik*
RSHA Prinz Albertstraße
Berlin
To: *Leutnant Peter von Vorzik*
III Gruppe JG233
Luftflotte 3
Northern France

25th July 1940

My Dear Peter,

I trust you are well now that you have rejoined your Staffel. It was such a pleasure to have you with us here in Berlin and I know that Mathilde misses you very much – as do one or two other ladies who, I am sure you are aware, are also your admirers! But you have made a splendid choice and I am confident that you and Mathilde will have a happy future together.

My main reason for writing is this: at a celebratory dinner at Savarin's the other night I was talking to Dr Robert Ley and from what he was saying – he stutters and, being an alcoholic, was somewhat the worse for drink so it was not easy to grasp the information – his Labour Front intends to make a survey of womens' contribution to the war effort and to begin compulsory service in transport, factories, hospitals and on the land. Of course my thoughts were instantly centred on Edith and while it would not be difficult to obtain immunity for her from such service on various grounds, I think it would be best if she were to prepare herself for some form of national duty that she would find amenable. She has herself suggested making some such contribution on several occasions. In any case, as we have previously agreed, she is stagnating at Adlersee and we must find a suitable partner for her and provide for her married future.

To this end I have had a preliminary talk with a friend of mine (you may have met him when you were here?) Brigadeführer Walter Stahlecker

101

who has fallen out with Heydrich and has been transferred to the Foreign Ministry; he is anxious to return to the RSHA and is therefore ready to listen to any personal request of mine. He is prepared to find a place for Edith in the Information Department of the Ministry, but she will first have to take a course of typing and shorthand. She is fluent in French and her English is quite good and that will be an advantage in translating foreign periodicals and documents. I have not told her about this but I will telephone her tonight and send her a letter with all the relevant information. Initially she can stay with me and then I can find her a small apartment somewhere near the Auswartiges Amt where she will be working.

All this is for the best. Her leaving Adlersee will not affect father; as it is, he is scarcely aware of her existence. He can retain his own quarters and we can close up the rest of the house for the time being.

Let me know what you think.

Ever your affectionate brother,
Christian
Heil Hitler!

From: Edith von Vorzik
Schloss Adlersee
Bavaria
To: Leutnant Peter von Vorzik
III Gruppe JG233
Luftflotte 3
Northern France

27th July 1940

Dearest Peter,

I am writing to you full of excitement and trepidation! As you probably know, Christian has arranged for me to leave Adlersee and take up clerical work in Berlin. It really is a tremendous change for me, there could hardly be a greater contrast in my style of living here in tranquillity in Adlersee and the noise and bustle of Berlin. Of course, in the last few months I have had some experience of life in the city which is undeniably stimulating in small doses, but whether I shall be able to withstand it day after day for months on end I do not know. Christian, however, is most reassuring. First, he says, I must resolve to make an effort to rally my abilities as he, you and all other Germans are doing at a time that demands sacrifices from us all and, secondly, although I am a female who has led a rather sheltered life I must remember who I am and take pride in the family name and what it stands for. That is true of course and listening to his voice on the telephone inspires me with courage and fortitude but then, when I am alone, I begin to have awful doubts about what he calls my "abilities." What I am really afraid of is being incompetent and letting other people down through lack of training. You know I have very few "abilities" that can be put to helping the country in its great struggle. I can sew a little, play the piano a little and do the household accounts. I can't even drive a motor vehicle.

Christian says when I have learnt typing and shorthand I shall be able to make translations of interesting and important documents at the Information Office. He says I am intelligent and will soon fall into the routine and even enjoy the work which, he says, often deals with secret information. That certainly makes it all sound exciting. I must admit, too, that I have wanted to feel that I am making some contribution to the war effort even though it now seems as if I shall be coming in at the end of it all.

Enough about me and my worries. Dear Peter, as always you are continually in my thoughts, especially since there have been so many reports in the last few days about aerial activity over the English Channel and I feel sure you have been involved. Christian says we are about to embark on the last phase of the war and that the Luftwaffe will be the main element in defeating the British. How I long for the war to finish and not to have the constant anxiety about your safety.

I realise, of course, that things will never be the same again here at Adlersee. With mother gone and father now something of a recluse, Christian's career keeping him in the capital and you, too, probably living there when peace comes, those days we all enjoyed as a family unit are over. I have always thought, secretly, that I might marry and bring up my family here and I suppose that is still a possibility although its realisation seems, at the moment, a long way off. We have never talked about these things and now is not the time but when we meet perhaps we can all consider our future plans with regard to Adlersee. Had you contemplated bringing Mathilde here and starting a family? There would be room for all of us and I think it would be marvellous to have all the rooms in use again, at the moment it seems so gloomy.

Let us look forward to happier, brighter days ahead!

Ever your loving sister,
Edith

PS Frau S will be leaving when I go to Berlin next week but Gretl is staying to help Werner with the household duties. He says he can manage the cooking and in any case father only likes plain fare. I suspect they will be living on sausages and sauerkraut! E.

From: Leutnant Peter von Vorzik
III Gruppe JG233
Northern France
To: Edith von Vorzik
Schloss Adlersee
Bavaria

2nd August 1940

My Dear Edith,

I was delighted to receive your letter and have your reaction to the arrangements Christian has made for you (yes, he had told me his plans) and I think you will be able to manage it all with your customary aplomb. You probably underestimate your "abilities", not realising just how much you have undertaken in supervising the smooth running of Adlersee, looking after mother during her illness, coping with father in his difficult moods and handling the various aspects of the estate. Incidentally, Christian did not tell me who will be managing those affairs; I take it that Klinger will be staying on as estate manager? Also, who will be paying the wages to the farm hands, Werner and Gretl? Father cannot be relied on to sign cheques any more, but I am sure Christian has made suitable arrangements for such things.

Of course Berlin will be a big contrast to life at Adlersee but I think you will soon become accustomed to the pace of life there and enjoy what the city has to offer – opera, concerts and theatre. I am sure you will also be stimulated by the social scene and I know Mathilde will be only too pleased to take you under her wing and help you settle in. Christian, too, will be there to make life easy for you and deal with any problems that you encounter. Apart from making your contribution to the national war effort it will be a marvellous educational experience for you, both Christian and I feel that life in Adlersee is really rather stultifying for a young woman. For my part I am delighted that my dear sister and my darling wife-to-be will be living so close together and I shall not feel torn between having to decide whether to stay in Berlin or make the journey to Adlersee during my leaves!

I may not be able to write again for a few weeks, we are now expecting to be very occupied in the immediate future since the British have so stubbornly and foolishly refused the Führer's offer of peace. Yes, there is going to be one last big battle – it has already begun and when that is over we can all get together and resolve some of the questions you raise in your letter. I should certainly like to think that my children will be growing up where we both spent such an idyllic childhood.

Keep saying your prayers for me, I shall have need of them during the coming weeks.

Ever your loving brother,

Peter

From: Fräulein Mathilde Zugmann
23 Hevelius Straße
Grunewald
To: Leutnant Peter von Vorzik
III Gruppe JG233
Luftflotte 3
Northern France

2nd August 1940

My Darling Peter,

When your train drew out of the station I made a vow that when I wrote to you I would not burden you with tales of how desperately I miss you... But I have to say that, so that if I refrain from writing how miserable I feel, how every waking moment is filled with thoughts of you, you will not assume that I am not thinking of you. Oh, what a tangle I have made in trying to explain my dilemma, but I am sure you can make sense of it!

I hear from Christian that Edith is coming to live and work in Berlin. It will be marvellous for me to have her here, to have another person to talk to about you, I am sure we shall be a great support to each other and of course I will do everything I can to help her settle in. It will be a big change from her regular way of life and Christian says she is rather nervous at the prospect of it all but in her quiet, unassuming way she is so intelligent that I am sure she will take everything in her stride.

Now, Peter darling, here is some good news – at least I hope you will think so. Mother has decided that she is going to leave Berlin and live with her sister in Cologne which means that, for the time being at least, we can make our home here. Does that appeal to you? There is still a 30-year lease on the house so even if we stayed here for another five years (there is plenty of room for children!) we would still have a reasonable lease to sell. I do hope, darling, that you approve of this arrangement, it seems the sensible thing to do until we are in a position to make other plans for the future when peace is restored.

I had lunch at Horcher's with Lina yesterday. As always she was full of scandal and gossip which I won't bore you with but she did say that Reinhard is terribly busy with all sorts of plans involving the occupied lands in the east and that she rarely gets a chance to talk to him or to spend an evening together. He comes in very late at night and leaves before she rises in the morning. But she is never up before ten in the day, she always has breakfast in bed and makes a leisurely toilet. I know if I telephone her before nine she always sounds sleepy.

The Philharmonic now give wonderful radio concerts every Monday evening, do you have a chance to listen, can you receive their broadcasts? It would be lovely, darling, if I could think that we were listening together, it would bring you close to me...

I must hurry to catch the post now. All my deepest love, sweetheart, I think of you every moment and pray you are safe.

Ever your devoted,
Mathilde

Leutnant Peter von Vorzik
Journal entry

15th August 1940

The big battle with the RAF has begun. Adlertag, as the Führer has named it, was scheduled for the 10th but had to be postponed because of bad weather; we began the attack two days ago. Bombers and fighters from Luftflotte 2, facing south-east England, were also hampered by weather conditions but had some success in attacking naval installations at

Sheerness and the Coastal Command airfield at Eastchurch. Luftflotte 3 had major engagements yesterday. Fighters from IJG2 escorted bombers from KG54 in the morning; our first big sortie was in the afternoon. The weather cleared just after midday and we were briefed to join Emils of II JG23 to clear the path for bombers attacking targets in Hampshire and Dorset. As we took off and formed up as three Schwarme I have to admit that my heart was beating fast. I knew this was going to be a real challenge – pilots who have already had encounters with Hurricanes and Spitfires report that they are formidable opponents although our Emils appear to be superior in most respects, except in tight turns. Less than half an hour after take-off we were passing over the Isle of Wight making a direct line for the docks at Southampton which were one of the targets to be attacked by Junkers 88s of LG1. Our rendezvous, however, was further on to the north-east where another group of Ju88s was to attack the airfield at Andover. As we flew at 4,000 m over the wheat and corn fields of Hampshire, ripening in the high summer sun, there was no sign of the RAF although every pilot in the Staffel was on the *qui vive* for the enemy.

Zwemmer located the airfield and took the Staffel round in a 180° turn; as we headed south again twelve Ju88s appeared 500 m below us and began unloading their bombs. At that same moment I heard Kurt's voice on the r/t shouting that enemy fighters were attacking on the port beam. Sure enough six Hurricanes in two flights of three were diving down on the Ju88s and already one of them had peeled away with its starboard engine on fire. Zwemmer gave the order to attack and the Staffel, in turn, dived on the Hurricanes which had already broken formation. I singled out a Hurricane as a target just as he pulled away from the bomber group which was attempting to maintain a tight defensive formation. As the Hurricane climbed away it presented a fine plan-view and I pressed the firing button and observed my cannon shells registering hits on the British fighter's port wing. The enemy pilot put his aircraft into a tight turn to port and in order to follow him I used both hands to yank on the control column. Even with all my strength however, I could not turn tightly enough to get inside him and aim another burst. I glanced at my fuel gauge and saw that it registered just over a quarter full, only enough to get back to bodo – our code word for base. With Kurt nowhere in sight I realised discretion was much the better part of valour on this occasion and set course for the French coast. Flying just 100 m above me was another Emil; I called him up on the r/t and he identified himself as Leutnant Dohlmann from Staffel 2. We accompanied each other back to bodo with me flying as his Katschmarek.

We landed safely to discover that Zwemmer's Emil had sustained some minor damage from one of the Hurricanes. At the debriefing Beckmesser claimed an unconfirmed kill and I reported damage to the Hurricane I had attacked. Altogether it had been a somewhat indecisive encounter with the enemy that left me with the feeling that I should have performed better, used the superiority of my Emil to greater effect. Talking it over with Kurt who also felt he had missed a chance to record a kill, we both came to the conclusion that although the Hurricane was slower in every aspect of aerial dynamics, speed in level flight, climb and dive, and its fire-power somewhat less in destructive effect unless all eight of its machineguns could be brought to bear at one point, the aircraft's manoeuvrability and sturdiness evened up the odds. We would have to develop our tactics in order to press home the Emil's dynamic advantages, especially at higher altitudes.

News from the raids carried out by JG53 who were escorting Ju87 Stukas that attacked Warmwell aerodrome further west in Dorset indicates that they suffered losses of at least three aircraft so we seem to have fared better than they did with only minor damage to two of our Emils.

Today's attack was rather more successful. This time we escorted a Gruppe of Ju87s of StG2 whose targets were Warmwell aerodrome again and the naval base at Portland. The weather was fine and visibility good. We flew at 5,500 m, keeping station above the Stukas and throttled back to 200 kph as the bombers are really slow. Above us flew another Gruppe of Emils from JG50 manoeuvring with greater freedom; we are protecting the Stukas and they are protecting us! Once the Stukas have begun their bombing dive we, too, have more freedom to manoeuvre as we cannot follow them down but must keep a watching eye and then reform when they have climbed back for the return to base. At least, that is the plan but of course if we are attacked then the plan gets out of shape and the situation confused. And that is just what happened this afternoon.

Just before we reached the target at Portland the Stukas were attacked by a squadron of Hurricanes. Emils from JG50 pounced on the British planes while we kept station but not for long. Another Hurricane squadron appeared and I saw a Ju87 spiralling down in flames as Zwemmer gave the order to break station and engage the enemy. I saw a

Ju87 peel off and begin his bombing dive followed by a Hurricane. The Ju87 is utterly vulnerable during the dive, of course, having to maintain a constant angle of attack and before I could intervene the Hurricane had got his victim, the Ju87 suddenly changing from the fixed dive angle to a wild spiral as black smoke poured from the engine cowling. As far as I could see he had not released his bomb, slung like a great egg on a cradle beneath the fuselage; the situation was such, however, that I could not cruise around to watch the destruction of the aircraft, I was too busy in my determination to take revenge on his destroyer. The Hurricane had pulled out of his dive and was climbing back to search for another victim but I was in an advantageous position and already had him in my sights. I throttled back in a shallow dive and got in a long burst with all four guns. I don't think the British pilot had any idea of my presence; I could see my cannon shells raking the cockpit and I think he must have died instantly. The plane seemed to stand still in the air, then it stalled and went into a weird cartwheeling spin, wing tip over wing tip, totally out of control. Horrido! My first positive kill of a British fighter.

The sky was full of whirling aircraft and I still had plenty of ammunition left but, yet again, I had no recourse but to head back to bodo as the fuel indicator was below the quarter mark. Our limited range is really beginning to be a great disadvantage in this battle, even on the shortest engagements we are left with only a few minutes of potential combat period before running the risk of having to ditch in the Channel or make a forced landing in France. Last week several Emils were lost this way – and some of their pilots – when the weather deteriorated suddenly over the coast of France and our fighters could not find their home base. This afternoon I got back without any trouble but even so the needle was once more flickering on empty as I made my approach.

Reports coming in this evening indicated that it has been a hectic day for other Gruppen, and both sides seemed to have sustained heavy losses.

On a lighter note, we have been invited by Baron Achille de Montfort, a local aristocrat, to make use of his chateau as a recreation centre. It is a very magnanimous gesture much appreciated in the few hours of relaxation we are able to snatch. The Baron keeps an excellent and extensive cellar and we have enjoyed some splendid bottles of Bordeaux. Of course, we have been instructed to be on our best behaviour and although things can sometimes get a little boisterous (at a birthday celebration for one of the pilots from Staffel 2, he got thrown into the moat and was severely reprimanded) everyone is very grateful for the opportunity to enjoy such comfortable surroundings after the rigours of the airfield accommodation. Several pilots have made friends with young women from the village who are reputedly very free with their favours. Kurt seems to have fallen under the spell of one of them, Michelle, who is the daughter of the local butcher. The most obvious favour he has enjoyed has been a supply of meaty presents which, in his usual generous way, he has shared with me and which have been a most acceptable supplement to our meals in the mess. I have been very discreet in asking him about other aspects of their relationship but as his affair with the girl in Hamburg has been severed he is free to pursue any amorous intrigue. In any case, he knows that the liaison is bound to be a short one under the circumstances and I am happy that he has found some convivial companionship.

As for me, my thoughts are constantly with Mathilde and my consolation lies in her letters.

From: Gruppenführer Christian von Vorzik
116 Kaisestraße
Berlin
To: Leutnant Peter von Vorzik
III Gruppe JG233
Luftflotte 3
Northern France

18th August 1940

My Dear Peter,
We all know that you are in the thick of the great battle being fought over southern England and our hearts and prayers are with you. This great struggle in the air is of tremendous importance for the future of Germany and the successful conclusion of the war and as well as our prayers you have our pride that the young warriors of the Luftwaffe are fighting with such gallantry and dedication. We have no doubt about the final victory and we look forward to the day when we can welcome you home in triumph.

My own life and work continue on a much more mundane but, I hope, no less an important level in terms of the ultimate achievement of the

Third Reich as the leader in a New Order in Europe. The situation in the Balkans appears to be approaching a climax in which we anticipate a resolution in our favour. (The British have been conniving against us and attempting to forge some sort of alliance with Rumania.) But there are complications as Hungary and Bulgaria both have territorial claims to make on Rumania and the arguments are becoming somewhat heated. Von Ribbentrop has summoned the Hungarian and Rumanian ministers to Vienna at the end of the month, meanwhile the interior position in Rumania (as I have outlined to you previously) between the two factions of von Ribbentrop/Antonescu and Himmler/Horia Sima is coming to the boil and Heydrich wants me to continue my watching brief. This time I shall be going more or less incognito, not wearing my SS uniform. Luckily, the opera season has ended and so Frieda can accompany me – she will be very helpful in translating some of the newspaper articles, etc. Now this brings me to something of great importance to us both.

I have decided to ask Frieda to marry me. I shall propose to her during this trip and feel sure that she will accept, we are both so very happy in each other's company and, in any case, Heydrich's office encourages its officers to marry and propagate for the Party. Now that you are engaged to Mathilde I suggest that as soon as this big battle is over and I have returned from Bucharest, we should have a double wedding in Berlin. Later we could both have a second ceremony at the chapel in Adlersee, mainly for father's sake. What do you think? Is this not a good idea? Do let me know your feelings in the matter. Write as soon as you are able, address your letter to the RSHA office and they will forward it to me in Bucharest if you mark it personal.

Ever your loving brother,
Christian
Heil Hitler!

From: Fräulein Mathilde Zugmann
23 Hevelius Straße
Grunewald
To: Leutnant Peter von Vorzik
III Gruppe JG233
Luftflotte 3
Northern France

19th August 1940

My Darling Peter,

My heart beats so as I put pen to paper and wonder, even as I do so, just where you are and what is happening to you. In all the previous times when I know you have been in danger I have been torn with anxiety but nothing to compare with the terrible feelings that possess me now. I know, darling, I should not write to you in this manner but I cannot confess my innermost fears and anxieties to anyone else. Mother knows how I feel but I do not tell her just how deep it goes or how my worries are magnified by my longing to have you by my side. I know, in any case, that she would expect me to contain my emotions and not burden anyone else with them – I know she would not. But there, I am weak and lacking in self-control when I think of my own darling in danger. I hope, dearest Peter, that you will not think any the less of your fiancée because of her inability to maintain her emotional equilibrium under stress?

I spoke briefly to Edith yesterday and she, I know, shares my fears but we left them unsaid. She is very busy with her course of typing and shorthand which she is studying in parallel with her work at the Foreign Ministry where she seems to be settling in quite well although she says she feels perpetually tired and cannot wait to get home in the evening, eat and go to bed. She is still with your brother who will be arranging a small apartment for her as soon as she has completed her course, but I expect she has told you all this.

Darling, I think it would be a good idea if I, too, learnt typing and shorthand so that I might do something useful for the country – if I do not then I run the risk of being drafted into some uncongenial job in a factory or something. What do you think? It may not be for long, of course, but I should like to feel I was making a contribution to the national effort. Lina has a journalist friend working on *Die Frau* and says she would be able to find me a position on the fashion section of the magazine if I could type. That sounds interesting, doesn't it? Not that I feel particularly *au fait* with fashion but apparently the articles now concentrate on how to alter and make do with the clothes we have and Lina says – very flatteringly – that I have as much "fashion sense" as anyone on the editorial staff. Do let me know what you think about the suggestion, darling.

Although I sometimes think that Lina goes too far with her stories of gossip and scandal she is an amusing companion who is marvellous at taking one's mind off the worries of the war and for that I value her friendship. Unfortunately, I do not think it would be proper to put on paper some of the things she tells me and so, darling, they will have to wait until you are in my arms again. I pray that will be soon.

Dearest, darling Peter, write a short line to me when you can or telephone if you have the opportunity, I live for those moments when we are in contact however distant, however brief.

Keep yourself safe for me and all those who love you.

Ever your devoted,
Mathilde

Leutnant Peter von Vorzik
Journal entry

27th August 1940

It is nearly two weeks since I last made an entry in this journal. Two weeks that have been filled with momentous events, with continual fighting in the air, with some victories and some terrible losses. All of us in the Staffel – indeed, in the whole Geschwader – are battle-weary, exhausted and not a little disillusioned.

Before I recount details of the various combat missions in which I have taken part I will attempt to describe the overall picture. First, the intelligence information that we received about the numerical strength of the RAF seems to have been hopelessly wrong; day after day we have encountered squadrons of planes that sometimes even seem to outnumber us. Although their tactics are inferior to ours, less flexible, still based on flying in V-formation, the pilots are skilful and almost suicidally determined. Both the Hurricane and Spitfire are, in their different ways, formidable fighting machines; our Emils are only

113

superior in certain respects and superiority really only lies with the flying ability of the individual pilot, especially with his talent as a marksman. Nearly all our aces are pilots who, as well as flying with skill, are brilliant at using their aircraft as a gun-platform. The Emils' armament of two cannon and two machineguns can be devastating if the pilot shoots with accuracy, but the Hurricane and Spitfire have a scattergun, shotgun effect that doesn't rely so much on pinpointing the target. All this I have deduced through the experience of the last two weeks during which I have done all I can to improve my shooting ability in order to stay alive. So far I have been lucky.

We have had some dreadful losses in the Geschwader: the leader of II Gruppe, Hauptmann Heinrich Dolle, was shot down over Portland. Our Staffel has lost Ulrich Schleff, posted missing, and his brother has been given a few days' compassionate leave. Zwemmer had a bullet wound in the shoulder and was in a field hospital for four days. His place as Staffelkapitan was taken by Beckmesser by reason of his having the highest number of victories. This temporary appointment was a direct result of a conference held by Reichsmarschall Göring at Karinhall. He told Gruppenkommandeur Werner Mölders and Gruppenkommandeur Adolf Galland, the Luftwaffe's two greatest fighter aces whom he decorated with the gold pilot's badge with jewels, that he was not satisfied with the general performance of the fighter Gruppen. Göring then replaced Major Gotthardt Handrick, Kommandeur of JG26 with Galland and Major General Osterkamp, Kommandeur of JG51, with Mölders and said that all Jagdgeschwader must be led by the fighter pilots with the highest victories. These remarks have led to a great feeling of bitterness among many of the pilots who have been doing their best under great difficulties.

The bomber Geschwader have certainly suffered severe losses, particularly the Stukas which have now been withdrawn from the battle. It proved almost impossible to give them effective fighter protection. They fly so slowly that fighter escorts have to continuously weave about in order to stay with them and this leads to the fighters using up their fuel and having to return to base before the mission is completed thus leaving the Stukas unprotected and almost helpless prey to the defending fighters. Our latest orders are to concentrate on destroying the British fighter force, attacking their airfields and doing our best to destroy them in the air. As if we had not been doing that from the very beginning!

Two nights ago, British bombers attacked Berlin, apparently in retaliation for our attacks on London. Those of us with families and loved ones in the capital were in a great state of anxiety, of course. I managed to get a call through to Christian's office and the helpful Unterscharführer there later relayed a message to the Staffel office that Mathilde and Edith were safe. There have been civilian casualties, however, and many people are now saying that Göring's assurance that enemy aircraft would never be able to break through our defences has been made to appear ridiculous. Those strategists who maintained that "the bomber will always get through" have been proved right, except that, if the defences are strong enough, the bomber's losses will be too great to make it worthwhile. At the moment the losses sustained by the bombers in our daylight raids are heavy, whereas the losses during the raids carried out by night on London and other important cities have been comparatively light.

I will not try and catalogue all the sorties in which I have flown – on some days we have been involved in as many as five missions, from dawn to dusk. We sit about in the mess or, if it is sunny, in the dispersal area, waiting for that harsh voice to shout over the loudspeaker system, "Attention! Attention! Action alarm!" Sometimes we are playing cards or listening to the radio, sometimes in the middle of a meal, but whenever it is one's heart gives a leap and the adrenalin begins to rush into one's bloodstream. By the time we have reached our aircraft housed in their blast pens the mechanics are ready to help us on with our helmets, plug in the radio lead, fasten the safety harness and close the cockpit canopy. The whole process takes just six or seven minutes and the Staffel is airborne within ten.

My greatest success came just a few days ago. The morning dawned fine with some hazy high cloud. We were ordered up to 6,000 m to escort Ju88s of LG/1 (a bomber unit whose crews are mostly composed of instructors) in an attack on the naval base at Portsmouth. The Ju88 is the Luftwaffe's fastest twin-engine bomber (except for the Zerstörer that have been fitted with bomb-racks) so escorting them is easier than the Dornier 17s and Heinkel 111s. They are also used as dive bombers and they sometimes use their speed in a dive to evade attacking fighters; all in all escort duty with this type is preferable to any other, although, of course, our little Emils were not designed for this work at all. Anyway, we did not encounter any opposition until we were over the target, then we found ourselves under attack by a squadron of Spitfires and a squadron of Hurricanes.

As usual the Hurricanes went for the bombers and the Spitfires attacked us but we had a height advantage as they were still completing their intercepting climb. I selected one of three Spitfires flying 500 m or so below us on the port beam. Calling to Kurt that I was going in to the attack and to follow me down I put the Emil into a shallow dive, switched on the Revi gunsight and lined up on the leading Spitfire in the flight of three. My first burst of cannon fire caught him square amidships; the Spitfire reared up and flipped over on to its back, narrowly missing the aircraft on its starboard side, then went into an almost vertical spin, quite out of control. My instinct was to follow him down and make sure of the kill but just then Kurt yelled out a warning to me that another Spitfire was right behind me. Almost as the words left his lips I saw tracer bullets curling past my starboard wing. I yanked hard on the control column, side-slipping to the left, then pulled the Emil's nose up into a steep climb. I might still be in the British pilot's sights but I knew I could climb faster than him and in any case I needed height if I was to engage in a dogfight. I glanced over my shoulder and could see no sign of the Spitfire but about 1,000 m below, travelling at right angles to my own line of flight, I saw a Hurricane pursuing a Ju88 that was already separated from the bomber formation, its port engine stopped and obviously in grave difficulties. Once more I put the Emil into a dive, lining up the Hurricane target with quite a large amount of deflection. I held my fire until I was within about 200 m and then fired a long burst from all four guns. At first I could see no effect, then the Hurricane seemed to stall and hang on its tail before going into a flat spin. Pulling round in a wide arc in order to observe the Hurricane's final moments I saw the cockpit cover slide back and the pilot making efforts to bale out as his plane began to revolve faster and faster. Maintaining my height and keeping a watch for any attack, I saw the tiny figure fall from the cockpit and, a second or two later, his parachute billow open. His plane was destroyed but that pilot would live, perhaps, to attack us another day. I watched his descent with mixed feelings: somehow glad that he had not died and yet realising he was the enemy and I should have found satisfaction in his death.

There was no time to indulge in philosophical thoughts about war and our destinies as I saw another Spitfire flying almost parallel with me about 300 m down on the starboard side. Side-slipping to the right I lined him up in the sights and once again fired a long burst. The two wing cannon stopped firing, I was almost out of ammunition but had the satisfaction of seeing bits fly off the Spitfire, the left aileron hanging down and the plane obviously out of control. Horrido! Three victories in one afternoon, bringing my total now to eighteen kills and three probables.

Yesterday we received orders that we must regroup further up the coast and give support to Luftflotte 2. At least that means we shall be fighting over a narrower stretch of water. The Channel is referred to by pilots in a number of highly derogatory ways, the Sewer being the least vulgar! Most of us dread coming down in the sea even more than engaging a whole squadron of Spitfires single-handedly. Well, that is an exaggeration but the idea of drowning, either trapped in the cockpit of our planes (which has happened several times) or weighed down with all our flying kit, is something most pilots view with particular horror. Perhaps it is because the air is our element; if we had trained as sailors we may not have such a fear of water. Anyway, flying from bases near Calais – where I understand we are going – means we shall be faced with a mere 40 km of water rather than three times that distance. Also, joining up with Luftflotte 2 will increase the numbers with which we can attack the enemy. Perhaps now, we can achieve a decisive victory and the Wehrmacht can invade Britain and bring the war to a conclusion.

From: Edith von Vorzik
116 Kaiserstraße
Berlin
To: Leutnant Peter von Vorzik
III Gruppe JG233
Luftflotte 3
Northern France

1st September 1940

My Dearest Peter,
It is a year ago today that the war began and I remember so well receiving that short letter from you and father asking me to reply to you. So much has happened in this past twelve months, some wonderful victories, of course, but as each day passes I become more and more apprehensive about when we shall see the last victory and when peace will be restored.

I know as I write this you are involved in one of the fiercest struggles of all and there is not a moment of the day when my thoughts are not with you. It was almost something of a relief when bombs started falling on us some days ago. It must sound extremely silly but those frightening explosions at least made me feel that I was sharing the danger with you, that you and your brothers-in-arms were not the only ones carrying the burden of our efforts to overcome our enemies. Yet I do not forget, dearest, that it is your courage and your brilliance as a pilot that is defending us, while we sit passively and listen as the bombs whistle down.

I know that you made a call to Christian's office to find out if Mathilde and I were safe – as if you did not have enough worries! But now you will realise just how anxious we all have been about your safety throughout this long year.

You may congratulate me! I have passed my typing and shorthand test (though still rather slow and shaky by the standards of most secretaries here) and been attached to the staff of Dr Adam von Trott zu Solz, a charming intellectual who runs the Indian Special Bureau. Even though his department deals with the political situation in India (he is also an expert on China) I have been given the task of translating articles in British and American magazines which deal mostly with European affairs. I like the work, which is not too demanding, and the office staff are all very convivial. The canteen food is rather dreadful but at the moment I am still in Christian's apartment and my evening meals there are really delicious. Certainly, the senior members of the SS do themselves very well!

I had a call from Christian in Bucharest. I am sure you have read in the papers or heard on the radio of the dramatic events there. Christian expects to be recalled in a few days as he says that what he calls "his faction" have suffered a major political defeat and there is no longer any point in his staying on. I will be glad to have him back in Berlin and he has promised to find me an apartment of my own although I shall not enjoy the same comfort and cuisine as I have here!

Mathilde and I went to a concert by the Berliner Philharmoniker (all Brahms, the *Academic Festival Overture*, *First Piano Concerto* and *Third Symphony*) conducted by the new young protégé of maestro Furtwängler, Herbert von Karajan. His manner is very flamboyant but he certainly produced some thrilling sounds from the orchestra. The symphony, in particular, made me think of those wonderful carefree days we spent as children at Adlersee, I could see the meadows and lakes and mountains bathed in golden sunshine. Music is such a wonderful balm to the soul though I had tears in my eyes at the end of the concert. How we both wished that you had been sitting between us, dear Peter!

Let us pray that will be soon.

Ever your loving sister,
Edith

From: Gruppenführer Christian von Vorzik
116 Kaiserstraße
Berlin
To: Leutnant Peter von Vorzik
III Gruppe JG233
Luftflotte 3
Northern France

9th September 1940

Dear Peter,

As you see I am once more back in Berlin. The SS support for Horia Sima has been defeated by von Ribbentrop's personal backing for Antonescu so, for the present, our operations have been called off. In any case, Reinhard says there are more pressing problems for us to attend to in the east. I must say I was surprised that King Carol abdicated so swiftly but he obviously prefers exile in Switzerland with his Jewish mistress, Magda Lupescu, than trying to maintain his position as king in a country that does not want him. So be it. I am more concerned that the Iron Guard, with which we have such affinity, has had to go into hiding, but Reinhard says it is a temporary setback and their day will come.

Now, dear brother, I am well aware that you have been in the midst of a desperate and important battle but I had hoped that you would have found a minute to reply to the suggestion in my last letter (August 18th) that you and Mathilde, Frieda and I, have a double wedding. What do you say? Would it not be a splendid occasion? It would be one of the most important social occasions in the autumn/winter season. I know how deep your feelings are for Mathilde and, for my part, my association with Frieda has grown similarly – our recent sojourn in Bucharest was really quite idyllic. Her parents (her father is a distinguished archaeologist who has published several works on Schliemann's excavations at Hissarlik and Ithaca, her mother a delightful woman who plays the piano and sings in a very accomplished manner) were most hospitable and entertained me frequently. They seem very pleased that Frieda has consented to marry me and I have invited them to Berlin for a holiday this autumn. I will let you know when they are coming and it may be possible for you to get leave and join us. (The present battle will have been resolved by then and I am sure your unit will be deserving of a rest and refit.)

Write to me soon.

Ever yours,
Christian
Heil Hitler!

From: Leutnant Peter von Vorzik
III Gruppe JG233
Luftflotte 3
Northern France
To: Fräulein Mathilde Zugmann
23 Hevelius Straße
Grunewald

14th September 1940

My Darling Mathilde,

I am taking advantage of poor weather conditions which have kept us grounded for a few hours to write this short letter in reply to yours of almost a month ago which has only just reached me. (We have been moved again and mail has been delayed.) At the end of your letter – do you remember? – you pleaded with me to "write a short line when you can" and this is it, dearest. Short, because, as you will realise, there is little I can say that would be permissable under regulations and the rest would be repeated endearments. Is it enough, darling, that I write *I love you* and no more? You will be happy, I feel, just to know I am alive and well but am perhaps allowed to admit, in print, that I am a little weary. Do not fret, sweetheart, if my Gruppe HQ censor has blotted out that last sentence – it is really of no consequence.

Even more than weariness is my ever-present longing to be with you, to put my arms around your dear body, to find complete and utter solace in your company. During these last few weeks my greatest refuge has been in memories of our last days together. Of course I remember, in minute detail, all the things we did, the social occasions, the food, the wine, the parties, and the celebration of our engagement, but when I crawl into my narrow little bunk at night it all becomes one, a sort of miasma blanket of happiness that sends me off to sleep. I remember, in the final years at my gymnasium, we studied *Macbeth* and (although, perhaps, I should not quote from the poets of our enemy) the line "Sleep, that knits up the ravell'd sleeve of care," keeps coming back to me. How true! Sleep is my greatest luxury at present.

I am so pleased that you have dear Edith with you in Berlin and it is wonderful for her, too, to have you as a companion. I am sure she will find life in the city rather a strain at first but will soon become attuned to the pace of life there and enjoy the many advantages that the city offers. It was certainly a dreadful shock to hear that bombs had dropped on our splendid capital and those of us who have loved ones in the area were (and are) in a great state of anxiety about their safety. I am sure you will be sensible enough to take all precautions when the alarm sounds and hurry to the cellars wherever you are. I read in the paper that many customers were compelled to spend several hours in the basement of the KDW department store. I had visions of you, darling, surrounded by elegant ladies laden with shopping bags... But thank heavens you are in Grunewald, away from the city centre.

Which brings me to another point that you raise. Yes, it would be an ideal house for us in our initial years of marriage, it is a lovely location and (if your mother really has decided to move to Cologne) an ideal one in which to bring up children. I do not know what we shall do with Adlersee when, as must happen before too long, father dies, but I expect that we shall retain the Schloss as a family residence even if we (that is Christian, Edith and myself) decide to sell off part of the estate. All these questions will be resolved in a year or so when the war is behind us.

You ask if I have the chance to listen to the Berliner Philharmoniker's radio broadcasts. How I wish I could! There are several reasons why that is not possible. You see, most of my comrades much prefer to listen to popular music during those few opportunities we get to switch on the radio and even if they agreed to my request for a change of programme the general atmosphere in the mess with its chatter and clink of glasses and shouts from the card players and all sorts of general noise is hardly conducive to the appreciation of serious music. No, darling, listening to a concert is one of those wonderful pleasures I shall enjoy with you when we are together again.

I said this was to be a short letter yet I appear to have rambled on at length. My darling, let me say again how you are constantly in my thoughts – except, of course, for those brief occasions that I cannot speak of – and those thoughts invigorate my whole being and make everything I do and everything I am fighting for, worthwhile. I may not be able to write again for a while, please let Edith and Christian know that I am well and will endeavour to write to them, too, whenever I can snatch a moment.

You always enjoin me, darling, to take care of myself in these anxious times – well, now you are in danger, too, and I entreat you to do the same and take every precaution for your safety until you are once more enfolded by

Your ever loving,
Peter

Leutnant Peter von Vorzik
Journal entry

16th September 1940

Exhausted as I am I have to make an attempt to set down some impressions of yesterday, the most intense, savage and large-scale battles that we have fought so far. The whole of Luftflotte 2 and Luftflotte 3 were thrown into the fray and we were opposed by large formations of defending fighters much larger than anyone had anticipated because only a few days ago we were assured by the intelligence network that the RAF was down to its last fifty fighters. So much they know!

Our first sortie was at 11.00 hrs. Together with several other Gruppen we formed up over Calais as escorts to about 100 Dornier 17s from KG3 and KG76, flying about 1,500 m above them. Just over Maidstone we were attacked by two squadrons of Spitfires who were quickly reinforced by others, but by then we were in the thick of a huge whirling battle. The sky seemed full of fighters while the bombers continued on their mission to London with some Emils trying to stick with them. Our Gruppe was one which had received such orders but suddenly we found ourselves being attacked by a whole squadron of Spitfires and under such circumstances you simply cannot just continue along, waiting to pounce on a Hurricane or Spitfire that may be attacking a bomber. Zwemmer shouted over the r/t to break up and defend ourselves, an unnecessary instruction as most of us were already doing just that.

I glanced in the small rearview mirror placed at the top of the windscreen frame and saw a Spitfire no more than 100 m behind me. Even as I looked I saw the little flashes of flame from his eight wing guns. Surprisingly – and with great good fortune – his aim was off and I sustained no hits; I think he must have been an over-anxious novice because I must have presented him with a huge target. Once again I was lucky. At such moments one's brain is filled with the question of just what evading manoeuvre to make – the decision has to be instantaneous, of course, otherwise one is dead and this time I had two options: to bunt over into an inverted dive, a manoeuvre that is almost impossible to follow but which means losing precious height, or going into a spiralling climb, in the knowledge that the Spitfire's rate of climb is slower and at a flatter angle. I chose the latter, first because in such a confused scrap it is always best to maintain maximum altitude, and second, because the enemy pilot had already missed me when I was bang in his sights and would hardly have such a good chance again even if he did follow up.

I was right, he seemed lost in the furious fighting that was going on below and around me. To my chagrin a flaming Emil fell right across my path, the disturbed air buffeting my own little fighter. I took a deep breath and told myself to remain calm, find a bit of sky that seemed unoccupied by gyrating aircraft (as I write this I realise how silly that sounds!), make a careful observation of the scene and pick out a target or go to the help of someone in trouble. All this, although it may sound leisurely, took place in the space of a few seconds. About 1,000 m below me I spotted an Emil with a Spitfire on his tail. The Emil was twisting this way and that but each time the Spitfire turned even more sharply and seemed to get in some damaging bursts. Immediately I dived down on the British machine and opened up with all four guns; the Spitfire appeared to be hit with a thin smear of black smoke coming from under the port wing which indicated that I had damaged his oil cooler. Determined to finish him off if possible I followed him down, making sure my own superior diving speed did not carry me past him. Then, just as I lined him up in the sights, intent on making the kill, another crashing aircraft spun down in front of me, this time a Dornier 17, blazing furiously. It was a dreadful sight and I could not but feel sick at the thought of its four-man crew being incinerated. The thick pall of smoke which the flaming bomber had left in my path obscured the Spitfire for some seconds during which time he made his escape. I swore with rage and frustration and felt desperate to vent these feelings on another enemy fighter but noting that my fuel gauge was, as always, registering dangerously low if I was to make it back to bodo. Thank heavens for that narrower stretch of water!

The thing to do now was to extricate myself from the general fracas: the sky was still full of desperately skirmishing aircraft although I could not see any of the bombers we had set out with – presumably they had lumbered on to their targets in London, their protective shield of Emils peeled away by the RAF's attacking fighters. Obviously, if the plan to escort the bombers all the way to the target was to work we needed double the number of Emils we already had. In my own immediate situation I had to avoid another scrap; if I was forced into fighting I wouldn't have enough fuel to make it back.

I made, as far as possible, a 360° scrutiny of the sky through the canopy and was reassured that there was no Spitfire or Hurricane in the vicinity. I opened the throttle to maximum cruising speed and put the aircraft into a shallow dive so as to obtain speed without wasting fuel. I felt frustrated that I had registered only damaging hits on one Spitfire and still had half my ammunition left. Speeding back to base I felt as if I was running from the battle.

Back at bodo there was a tense atmosphere in the debriefing room. Reports coming in indicated that although there were many claims of Spitfires and Hurricanes being destroyed we, too, had suffered serious losses. Apparently the bombers had gone on to their targets without fighter escort and had been hunted all over London by swarms of RAF fighters, with many Do17s shot down. Worse was to come: as the afternoon wore on it became apparent that Beckmesser was missing. I had told the debriefing officer that I had seen an Emil going down in flames in front of me but had not registered the aircraft's Staffel or Gruppe markings. Perhaps it had been Beckmesser.

There was little time to dwell on the sadness of it all. Rage and frustration and despair are the worst companions for a fighter pilot and, in any case, within two hours we were in the air again, repeating the whole operation almost exactly like the morning's sortie. This time the fighting was, if anything, even more ferocious and intense. Our orders were to stick even closer to the bombers; it is all very well to give such directions but carrying them out in the heat of battle with a determined enemy pilot sitting on your tail and blasting away at you makes a great deal of difference – whatever the orders, one cannot just sit there and be shot out of the sky. But try telling that to the Staffelkommandeur who issues you with the orders who has been given them by the Gruppenkommandeur who has been given them by Sperrle or Kesselring who has been given them by the Reichsmarschall himself... Perhaps if one or two of these great men were to fly with us on a sortie they would not be so quick to demand the impossible. These are not good thoughts, I know that, but when one sees one's comrades dying in front of one it is difficult not to be bitter and cynical.

I said that this time the fighting was even more ferocious and it was; happily, for me, it was more successful than the morning had been. This time we were not the close escort but had the better position as protective cover to the escorting fighters. Somewhere over Ashford, I think it was (Zwemmer does most of the navigating for the Staffel in conjunction with the other Staffelkommandeurs, relaying our general position as we progress over enemy territory), we saw a squadron of Spitfires about 1,000 m below us, still climbing. The RAF pilots seem to have dropped their arrow formations and copied us, flying in a rough line abreast at slightly different altitudes so as to cover each other. But we had a height advantage and, as Zwemmer gave the order to attack, I don't think they had seen us. I radioed Kurt that I was lining up on the number three Spitfire on the starboard side and to do his best to stay with me at least until I had registered some hits. He gave a brief acknowledgment and I bunted over and dived on my prey.

We were approaching each other at something like 800 kph and that gave me just a few seconds to place him in my sights, allowing for some substantial deflection. To my grim satisfaction my first burst of cannon and machinegun fire hit him square on the engine cowling. The propeller shattered and flew off in tiny bits; the engine burst into flame and the aircraft spiralled down almost vertically. Horrido!

As with the first sortie that morning I decided that the time had come to make it back to bodo. Two Spitfires was not a bad bag for the day and to stay any longer with more than half my ammunition spent and the usual rapidly diminishing fuel load would be foolish. I had lost Kurt during the last scrap and hoped my faithful Katschmarek had fared as well as I had. Whenever we take off we always wave to each other and our aerial partnership is something that has become more than regulation fighter tactics: it is like a bond between brothers. My anxiety for him is as acute as any I feel for my family facing the bombing of Berlin.

I made it back to bodo in the company of an Emil from Staffel 2 who was in a bad way. I could see big bullet holes in his port wing and his port undercarriage leg was hanging down. On the r/t he told me he would have to carry out a crash landing: his hydraulics were affected and his engine was losing power. He said he hoped to reach bodo but might have to try and put the plane down somewhere before. Our airfield is only a few km inland, however, and he managed to get back but was unable to make a circuit into the wind. I watched as he attempted to land down wind; almost as soon as he touched the grass runway the Emil tipped over on its nose and burst into flames. I thought how much better it would have been if he had gained as much height as possible and baled out, but it is easy to make decisions for other people when one does not know all the details of the situation. At any rate it was a grim conclusion to my day.

Even more grim was the news we received from Abteilung 8: the Luftwaffe had had its most severe losses so far in the last month. Full details are not yet available but every Gruppe in both Luftflotte is reporting many aircraft missing. The British radio is making ridiculous claims but even if we have lost only a third of their figures it is very serious. Of course, they too, have lost many fighters but it does seem that they are still in a position to mount a strong fighter defence. Our Staffel has lost Friedrich, the youngest of the Schleff brothers. It is not known if he is alive as a prisoner of war or not; like his brother he has been posted missing and it is too terrible for the parents to have lost both their sons within a few days of each other. For the next few days, until we have new aircraft and replacement pilots, we shall be amalgamated with Staffel 2 with Zwemmer in command.

Everyone feels rather down at the moment although none of us will admit as much. But there is much less laughter in the mess and when someone makes a joke it is usually rather black humour. The battle has not gone as well as everyone had hoped and expected, we cannot claim command of the air over England and our losses, whatever the official figures might be, are undeniably heavy. Today we have some respite because the weather is generally unfavourable but no one longs for it to clear; our spirit is not broken but few, if any, of us could claim to have the same zest for battle we had a month ago. We take each day as it comes and hope we shall be alive to fly and fight tomorrow.

From: Leutnant Peter von Vorzik
III Gruppe JG233
Luftflotte 3
Northern France
To: Gruppenführer Christian von Vorzik
116 Kaiserstraße
Berlin

17th September 1940

Dear Christian,
I am snatching a few moments during a lull enforced by bad weather to reply to your last two letters. I know you will understand the reasons why I have been so lax in replying ... We do, now, seem to be passing through the climax of the battle and, either way (please God it will be victory!) I should be due for some leave.

Yes, I think that your idea of a double wedding is splendid. I have not broached the subject yet to Mathilde but I am quite confident that she will agree with me. As you know I will have to obtain permission from my Gruppenkommandeur but that, I am sure, will only be a formality. What a wonderful celebration it will be! At the moment I hardly dare think of such happiness ...

May I, dear brother, leave it to you to make all the provisional arrangements? I cannot, of course, provide you with anything like a firm date but as soon as I feel I can broach the subject to the Gruppenkommandeur I will, and will let you know immediately. There would be, I am sure, grounds for a short compassionate leave but naturally I would want to have a little longer with Mathilde than forty-eight hours. Within a week or two – even a few days – I hope to be able to be more positive.

You do not say if you have been in contact with father at all. I wonder how everything is at Adlersee – what would happen if Werner were taken ill, for instance? I know he has an iron constitution but it would be very worrying if he were unable to continue caring for father who would not accept personal attention from anyone else, I am sure. These are just

127

random thoughts but they are the sort of thing one finds oneself thinking about when events are less demanding.

It is something of a comfort to know that you are back in Berlin and able to keep a sharp eye on Edith's progress. She appears to have settled in very happily and is enjoying her work at the Foreign Ministry. It was a dreadful shock to hear that bombs had fallen on Berlin and of course I was in a great state of anxiety about Edith and Mathilde until some very pleasant young Unterscharführer in your office phoned through a message that they were both safe. If you are finding an apartment for Edith it would be as well if you could discover one away from the centre of the city although, of course, Edith would not want to have to make a long journey in to work every day. Something of a problem, I think.

I am sorry that your expedition (if that is the word) to Bucharest did not turn out in the way that you had hoped but, from a selfish point of view, it is nice to think that you are back in Berlin where, as you say, there are pressing problems to be attended to.

Anticipating an early and joyous reunion,

Ever yours,
Peter

From: Leutnant Peter von Vorzik
III Gruppe JG233
Luftflotte 3
Northern France
To: Fräulein Mathilde Zugmann
23 Hevelius Straße
Grunewald

18th September 1940

My Darling Mathilde,
Just time for a short letter while we are standing by. This time I have a reason for writing other than to express once more my deep and abiding love for you. A few weeks ago Christian wrote to me to say that he was about to propose to Frieda (I expect you have heard that news) and that he thought it would be a grand idea if we all made it a double wedding. I reacted with some enthusiasm but decided not to broach it with you at that moment, as things were – how shall I put it? – in a

state of flux and my own immediate future somewhat uncertain. Now, things have developed to the point where I can expect to have some leave granted in the not-too-distant future and it seems right that you should have the opportunity to voice your feelings about the proposal. What do you think, darling? As I have said, it sounds to me an excellent idea but you may well have another opinion; you might want the day to be ours alone and I would understand that. So think about the proposition and let me know your feelings in the matter without any persuasion from me.

Have you met Frieda lately? From my own very brief meetings I thought her a really charming young woman and Christian is obviously very much in love. If his happiness is anything to be compared to mine then he is a very fortunate man indeed! Yes, I agree with you, Lina is a very outspoken person but is certainly an amusing companion. I am glad you have her as a friend who can enliven your spirits.

I must hurry now, dearest, to catch the mail collection. I hope to be in contact soon with the news that leave has been granted.

Until then, all my love,

Peter

From: Fräulein Mathilde Zugmann
23 Hevelius Straße
Grunewald
To: Leutnant Peter von Vorzik
III Gruppe JG23
Luftflotte 3
Northern France

23rd September 1940

My Darling Peter,
Your letter arrived this morning – only three days since you posted it! I do hope my reply will reach you as quickly although I think that delivery at your end is, for obvious reasons, liable to be held up. Anyway, darling, I am hastening to answer the question you ask. Yes, I am sure it will be a lovely occasion for the four of us to be married together, a really memorable and romantic day for you and your brother, for Frieda and me. Of course, I realise that we would also have had a wonderful wedding if

129

it had been just the two of us but all that really matters is that we are together, man and wife, two people who are joyously in love. Is that not so, darling?

In fact, I have to tell you that it already looks like something of a *fait accompli*. Believe it or not, Lina has already spoken to me about it and how she has become involved, via Christian and Reinhard, in planning the event! Quite honestly, darling, the matter seems to have been taken out of our hands. It will be best if we just let everything go ahead and enjoy it all in our own way. I think there will be a number of very important people in the Party and the SS on the guest list and Lina says that there have been suggestions made for very grand premises to be lent for the reception. I do not want to give details in a letter but I am sure you will be informed very soon about some of the proposals from "official sources". As I said, darling, it will be best if we just let ourselves be swept along by it all and remember that we have each other for always, not just on the day of the ceremony. At any rate, be assured that I am deliriously happy at the prospect of being your wife.

As you may have heard on the radio we have had some "lively nights" again but here in Grunewald we feel very safe. Edith says that she makes a point of going into the cellars both at work and at Christian's apartment so please do not worry about her unduly, darling, she is a very sensible young woman and does not take risks. I am having lunch with her and Lina next Saturday (Edith cannot take much time off for lunch during the week) and you can be sure that you will figure very much in our conversations! We shall all be talking about the wedding(s) too, of course. Lina says that we should have found a prospective husband for Edith by now so that it could have been a triple event! As always she is full of gossip and amazing stories that are rather shocking to Edith but I think that she is becoming attuned to Berlin society since she started working here – I am sure you will see a difference in her when (when?!) you come on leave. Of course, darling, that is the one thought that preoccupies me every minute of the day and it is my last thought at night as I climb into bed.

I pray for your safety, darling, and for the next time you are in the arms of,

Your own,

Mathilde

PS I learnt the other day that Lina's second name is Mathilde – quite a coincidence.

Leutnant Peter von Vorzik
Journal entry

2nd October 1940

Since I last wrote, our daily attacks on England have continued (except for some days when the weather gave us a respite) although they have changed somewhat in form and composition from the sorties we were flying last month. We do not escort the heavy bombers (Heinkel 111s, Dornier 17s) any more but Zerstörer and Jabos (Messerschmitt 110s and 109s fitted with bomb-racks) and a few Junkers 88s. Apparently, the Reichsmarschall has given orders that the heavy bombers shall only operate at night. It has made things somewhat easier for us as we do not have to weave around so much and use up all our fuel but the fighting has continued to be as furious as ever and the Staffel has suffered more serious losses.

Two young replacement pilots (it is pointless to record their names as they were with us only a few days) were lost on their very first sortie which was dreadfully upsetting for all of us, of course. I have to admit that morale has suffered considerably in these last few weeks. We have to accept (although nobody says as much) that our campaign to achieve air superiority over England has not succeeded – nor do I see, at the moment, any chance of it doing so. The very fact that we are now escorting fighter-bombers instead of heavy bombers is a tacit admission that we have not been able to gain the ascendancy necessary for a successful invasion of the British Isles. We are now into October; the weather can only deteriorate, making flying much less dependable and our recent sorties would seem to have been wasteful in men and machines with very little to show for it.

Five days ago we escorted Me110 Jabos on a raid on London. Before we had crossed the Kent coast we were attacked by a squadron of Spitfires who shot down two of the Jabos before we knew they were there. During the ensuing melée I managed to damage one Spitfire before running low on fuel again; Kurt claimed to have destroyed another but without verification and altogether the Jabos lost eight from their Gruppe. It seems to have been a purposeless effort as none of the Jabos got through to London. Apparently, Ju88s of I and II KG77 missed the rendezvous with their Emil escorts and lost twelve of their aircraft before the Emils caught up with them. Such losses are difficult to make good, not only in aircraft, of course, but also in trained aircrews. Apparently, the morale of the bomber Gruppen is lower than that of the Jagdgruppen.

Two days ago JG233 joined with several other Jagdgeschwaders in a big fighter-bomber sweep towards London. Once again we were intercepted over Kent and Sussex and some ferocious battles took place. I found myself in the unnerving position of being attacked by two Spitfires and I thought my hour had come. Ever-watchful Kurt came to my rescue; he drove one off and it broke away, he says, with telltale smoke coming from beneath the engine cowling. He did not follow it down because he was anxious about me and whether I was able to cope with the other one. I was. As I so often do when I have an enemy fighter on my tail I put the Emil into a steep climb, one of the few manoeuvres which the Spitfire cannot cope with, having a slower and flatter rate of climb; that way the British pilot cannot bring his guns to bear. I kept climbing until I had reached 7,000 m when I knew I would have got well away from my pursuer. I was right, he had given up the chase and I was now in a position which afforded me a height advantage. About 1,000 m below I saw a group of Jabos making a tight defensive ring with a couple of Spitfires attempting to break them up. I put the Emil into a dive and lined up on one of the Spitfires, side-slipping to starboard in order to keep its plan-form within the graticule. At about 200 m I opened up with all four guns. The Spitfire suddenly blew up in a ball of flame and smoke and I pulled hard on the control column in order to climb out of the debris. I levelled out a few seconds later and looked around. As so often happens, one minute you seem to be in the midst of numerous aircraft, all whirling about, manoeuvring for the kill, then, after a few brief minutes of combat, you find yourself all alone with no other aircraft in sight. Where have they all gone, you wonder; all scattered, of course, duelling each other to the death over a wide area at various altitudes. Sometimes, of course, it's just the opposite, the furious carousel continues all around you and it is as much as you can do to avoid colliding with both friend and foe. Now it seemed I was alone. I put out a call on the r/t but no one answered; obviously the battle had surged away from me during that short fight. Taking another careful look around I turned sharply and headed back to bodo without any more incidents. That destruction of the Spitfire brings my total to twenty-one kills and four probables.

If the sortie had been a successful one for me it had been bad for several others. We lost three other pilots from the Gruppe, including yet another new arrival in our Staffel and Franz Steinitz has been badly wounded and will, it seems, be spending several weeks in hospital. Zwemmer says that he has sustained serious damage to his spine from bullet splinters and there is a possibility that he may suffer partial paralysis. That means, of course, his flying days are over. It is very difficult not to be despondent when confronted by such facts. Happily I still have Kurt as my Katschmarek; if anything should happen to him I would be much more than despondent. Kurt himself seems to be in good spirits. He had a letter a few days ago from Michelle, the young woman he met when we were stationed near Rouen. She has written to him in curious German with many endearments and suggested that when he has leave he might like to spend some time with her. I think Kurt would like that very much but, just as I used to be torn between spending time either at Adlersee or with Mathilde in Berlin, he feels he should go home to Hamburg and see his parents. It is a pity that Rouen and Hamburg lie in opposite directions. Kurt possesses such a marvellously even temperament, he never seems depressed even when, as now, the Geschwader has suffered such losses and many good comrades have been killed. Whatever happens he manages to maintain his good humour and his quiet confidence in our eventual victory.

We are continuing to fight with the remnants of Staffel 2 but between us we can only muster eleven serviceable aircraft and the general feeling is that the Geschwader has been so badly decimated – no, more than decimated, we have lost much more than a tenth of our strength – it can only be days now before we are pulled out of the battle for a rest and regrouping. Perhaps now is the time to ask for permission to marry.

From: Field Marshal Wilhelm Keitel
Führer's HQ, Obersalzburg
To: Field Marshal Walther von Brauchitsch, OKW
Gr. Admiral Erich Raeder
General Hans Jeschonnek

12th October 1940

Top Secret

The Führer has decided that from now until the spring, preparations for "Sea Lion" shall be continued solely for the purpose of maintaining political and military pressure on England. Should the invasion be reconsidered in the spring or early summer of 1941, orders for a renewal of operational readiness will be issued later.

Keitel

From: Gruppenführer Christian von Vorzik
116 Kaiserstraße
Berlin
To: Leutnant Peter von Vorzik
III Gruppe JG233
Luftflotte 3
Northern France

13th October 1940

Dear Peter,

I was pleased to have your letter and know that you are in agreement with the idea of a double wedding. This is to let you know that plans are proceeding quickly. I told Reinhard of our intentions and he thinks it is a great idea. I was rather surprised, however, when he told me a few days ago of the suggestions that have been put forward for the ceremony and reception. I had not expected it to involve such distinguished members of the Party but I am sure you will not object to the occasion becoming so prestigious.

I had envisaged that we would have the reception here, at my apartment, but Reinhard said that we would not possibly be able to accommodate the number of guests we shall be expecting. His own apartment is not much bigger but he mentioned the matter to the Reichsführer-SS who happened to be in conference with Goebbels who immediately said that the reception must be in his official residence at 20 Hermann Göring Straße! I feel sure that he sees the occasion as an opportunity to promote recruitment for both the Luftwaffe and the SS and I can well understand that we represent the young manhood of the Third Reich to foreign observers. Of course, the foreign press will be there and we must accept that our wedding will be made into a propaganda coup. I also suspect that if he had heard of our wedding proposals then the Reichsmarschall, too, would have suggested his residence for the reception and Goebbels wanted to get in first. Anyway, it will be a marvellous venue, Magda Goebbels has been mainly responsible for the interior decoration and she has impeccable taste which is more than can be said for some of the ministers' wives!

134

I will send you the provisional guest list in a day or so and I am sure there are names you will wish to add to it. Who will be your best man? Reinhard has offered to escort Mathilde in the absence of a father although her mother will be there, of course.

You ask about our father and I have to tell you that his mental capacity has deteriorated to a great degree since you last saw him. I drove to Adlersee last week to appraise him of our wedding plans and thinking that I might bring him back to Berlin but after only a few minutes I realised that is impossible. First, I do not think he could stand the journey, he now seems very frail, and second, he suffers from great lapses of memory. At first he recognised me and then, during dinner, to my great consternation, he asked who I was and called out to Werner that a stranger had entered the house. It is very sad, although, at other times, for a few minutes, he seems perfectly capable of rational thought. Werner says that he sleeps most of the day and eats very little. It may be that quite soon we shall have to find a nursing home for him; apparently there is an ex-soldiers' sanatorium near Starnberg where he would be comfortable and well attended but Werner says he can manage perfectly well for the time being.

We have arranged a civil ceremony at the City Hall and although I had expected that we might have a quiet private ceremony at Adlersee at some future date, mainly for father, that now seems unnecessary although, of course, you may wish to arrange something for Mathilde and yourself. As you will appreciate, neither the Reichsminister (who is a lapsed Catholic) nor the Reichsführer-SS are very favourable to the established church. There will be an SS guard of honour for Frieda and myself and a Luftwaffe guard of honour drawn from the garrison at Gatow for you and Mathilde. You see, dear brother, all the formalities are being taken care of! After the official reception there will be a cabaret and dancing, but you will be receiving a timetable and programme along with the guest list. I should have told you: there is no need for you to make a formal application for leave, the date has been set for Thursday, 31st October. Your Gruppenkommandeur has been informed.

With every good wish,

Your affectionate brother,
Christian
Heil Hitler!

From: Fräulein Mathilde Zugmann
23 Hevelius Straße
Grunewald
To: Leutnant Peter von Vorzik
III Gruppe JG233
Luftflotte 3
Northern France

15th October 1940

My Darling Peter,

I know Christian has written to you about our wedding but things are happening so fast now and it is such a short time to the day itself that I had to keep you up-to-date with the latest news. I have been expecting the telephone to ring at any moment and to hear your voice announcing that you are on your way to Berlin, but I suppose you may not be given leave until two or three days before the Great Event. I must admit that I am very excited at the prospect of such a grand occasion and keep having to pinch myself to make sure I am not dreaming it all! Who would have thought, darling, that our ceremony would be graced by so many grand people and that it would become one of the biggest social occasions of the season? To tell the truth, I am rather nervous about appearing at the centre of so many celebrities with all the press in attendance, but Lina has been very reassuring and told me just to be myself – she says they are all ordinary people beneath the finery, the decorations, uniforms and titles.

Edith and my cousin Gisela (from Cologne) will be my bridesmaids (or whatever they are called in a civil ceremony) and Frieda has two friends from the ballet who will be attending her. Lina, mother and I went shopping last week for materials and my friends will be in blue and Frieda's in pink. I have taken your dress uniform to be cleaned although, darling, it looks as if you have never worn it!

Lina very kindly offered their cottage on the island of Fehmarn (where she was born) for our honeymoon, saying that we might want to get away and be by ourselves for a few days, but she says that the weather at this time of year could be very cold except that we might not want to get out of bed, anyway! You know she makes remarks like that all the time. Christian has suggested that we all go to Paris for a few days and I must say that sounds very thrilling – I have always longed to see that city. What do you think, darling? I shall quite understand if you want to have a quiet, restful time, you have been through so much these last six weeks. But a honeymoon in Paris sounds very romantic, doesn't it?

As we will not be in church I have decided upon an ivory-coloured suit with a matching silk blouse. Mother's dressmaker has been at the house for several fittings and yesterday we went to a milliner's just off the Ku'damm and chose a hat made entirely of pale blue roses, just a little lighter than the blue that Edith and Gisela will be wearing. I realise, dearest Peter, that all this talk of clothes and hats must seem very trivial to you, but, darling, it is exciting and important to me and I feel the need to share every detail with you, however frivolous.

Much more important is that you take care of yourself. What matters to me most of all is that I have you in my arms, my own darling husband, and all the excitement of the wedding is really of no consequence so long as we are together. How I long for this war to be over, sweetheart, so that we do not have this painful separation that produces such a constant ache in my heart.

The nights have been rather noisy during this last week and mother and I spent some time in a dusty cellar the other evening as we had stayed shopping in the city rather longer than we had intended. But we know that the English cities are being bombed much more heavily and they (the British) will no doubt wish to bring all this destruction to an end soon. That is my hope.

I must close, now, darling, as mother is waiting to go to the post with letters that she has written. As always I pray for your safety and cannot wait until I see your handsome, smiling face once more. Please let me know, dearest, as soon as you have news of your leave.

Ever your own,
Mathilde

PS I have wondered, darling, how you feel about not having a church ceremony? If you feel unhappy about it of course we can arrange something for ourselves, quietly. Edith says you might want to have it in the chapel at Adlersee and that you might even want to spend our honeymoon there. Just remember, darling, I am ready to fall in with whatever you decide. M.

Edward Thorpe

Leutnant Peter von Vorzik
Journal entry

20th October 1940

I am absolutely aghast at the plans and preparations for our wedding. When Christian first made the suggestion that we make it a double wedding it seemed a charming idea, two brothers marrying on the same day, a family occasion of some note and based on a common-sense idea. After all, if we were both contemplating marriage around the same time it would seem silly to have two separate ceremonies. Now, however, the whole thing has been inflated to absurd proportions mainly, as I can gather, as a propaganda event for the foreign press.

I do not blame Christian although, through his association with Heydrich, it has almost inevitably involved a circus of Party bigwigs always ready, it would seem, to take advantage of an occasion where they can parade before the news cameras. Since I received letters from Christian and Mathilde I have been alternately furious and amused at the manner in which all the arrangements have gone ahead without any reference to me; the whole thing has been presented as a *fait accompli* as Mathilde says. She, dear darling woman, is naturally excited at the prospect of a grand occasion – I realise that a wedding day means something different to a woman – and telling me about the materials and hats they have chosen is somehow endearing. Initially, I was enraged at the way I had not been consulted but now, after a few days' thinking it over, I realise that there is no point in my being angry; the best thing I can do is accept the situation with as good grace as I can muster. Mathilde has shown the way by saying it will be best if we just let it all go ahead and enjoy it in whatever way we can and that we have all our lives together to choose what we will do without interference from anyone else. I would prefer to have a quiet honeymoon, first to be alone with my beloved and second, to get right away from the scenes of death and destruction that have been a daily part of life these last two months, but it is not difficult to see that Mathilde is very excited at the prospect of a holiday in Paris and I could not be so selfish as to deny her that. I must also admit that such a prospect is not without its attraction: it can hardly offer a quiet honeymoon but certainly a romantic one and, in its very different way, a great contrast to the recent past.

138

I must confess that I am rather relieved that it is not to be a church wedding. Christian, Edith and I were brought up in the Catholic faith but, secretly, I renounced it to myself some years ago, not just Catholicism but any form of Christianity. It took some time for me to come to terms with the disbelief that was worming away inside me, to break free from the years of indoctrination, to listen to my own questionings, to examine all the teaching and pronounce it to myself as irrational and absurd and to finally acknowledge that I had no faith. After all, what is it except to be asked to have faith in the unbelievable? For a short time I felt a great burden of guilt but that was supplanted by a wonderful sense of freedom – freedom to examine other creeds and scientific possibilities. I read some philosophy – Plato, Descartes (whom I rejected because of his proposition of a "Supreme Being"), Hegel and Kant, and a little about Mahomedanism, Hinduism and Buddhism which I found the most acceptable because it does not involve any form of deity or priesthood but imposes such a rigorous discipline of self-denial as to be impractical unless one becomes a form of hermit. In the world in which I find myself it does not, after all, take a great mind to formulate a code of morals. As for immortality, I cannot believe in a life after death, comforting though that would be. I have never discussed any of this with Christian or Edith (even setting it down somewhat incoherently seems disturbing) and, as long as I was at Adlersee, I went to Mass irregularly and kept some of the holy days purely for mother's sake as I knew how unhappy she would be if I ever confessed to her my rejection of religion. Edith, I know, retains her belief (she always writes that she is praying for me) but Christian probably feels as I do. I have never discussed the matter with Mathilde and perhaps I should have done so. It is too late now, I think, and I do not wish to precipitate a discussion that might initiate a sense of separation. I would acquiesce in any decision to have a second ceremony at Adlersee for father's sake but, according to Christian, he would hardly be aware of what was happening.

I am deeply sorry that father has apparently become senile but, if I am honest with myself, my relationship with him has been a distant one for some years. He was always a remote, forbidding figure whom I respected but again, examining my true feelings, I can hardly pretend they were founded upon love. Even so, it is very sad that he has declined so quickly during this last year and I wish he had been able to write his memoirs – I might have learned something about him that was never present in the father I knew.

Apart from the questions of the wedding and father's mental and physical health, the thoughts that have been uppermost in my mind since I last wrote in this journal have been about the poor state of the Geschwader. We have been awaiting new aircraft and replacement pilots but they have not materialised – at least, not in the numbers necessary. It seems very odd that the RAF appears able to replenish its front-line aircraft after sustaining such heavy losses but that our own Geschwader receives less than 50% of the new Emils it needs.

Low cloud has precluded any activity today but during this last week we have continued our fighter-bomber sweeps over the south of England with only moderate success. Two days ago the Geschwader (at only 60% of strength) was involved in attacks on the towns of Margate and Broadstairs while other Gruppen pressed on to London to attack the RAF fighter base at Stanmore.

As I was writing this I was called to Zwemmer's office. He informed me that I am to be granted three weeks' leave from the day after tomorrow. He congratulated me on my marriage and opened a bottle of brandy to toast my future with Mathilde. Despite this gesture I somehow had the feeling that he does not approve of my quest for marital bliss. He is unmarried himself and I suspect he thinks that marriage and – who knows? – the possibility of children are a distraction for a fighter pilot, at least while performing active duties. On the other hand, is not a family an inducement to fight for their happiness and safety?

I have asked Kurt to be my best man – who else? I probably owe my life to him protecting me in the air, it is natural that I should want him to participate in my marriage ceremony. He is, he says, both delighted and apprehensive, just as Mathilde is, at the thought of the important people who will be attending but I know he will acquit himself with his usual charm and grace. For myself, I look upon the whole occasion, now, with a certain wry amusement; all I want is to hold Mathilde in my arms and to know that she is mine for ever.

From: Edith von Vorzik
at 116 Kaiserstraße
Berlin
To: Leutnant Peter von Vorzik
III Gruppe JG233
Luftflotte 3
Northern France

21st October 1940

My Dearest Peter,

There are only eleven days to your marriage but I am writing this in the hope that it will reach you before you begin your leave. It is really only to say, dearest brother, how happy I am for you and what a wise and wonderful choice you have made in Mathilde whom I already look upon as a friend I have known for many years. Of course, I will be saying this to you when we meet but I know it is going to be such a splendid and highly organised occasion that I fear there may not be a quiet moment when I am able to express these feelings to you.

Both you and Christian have been such devoted brothers and I am so proud of you both that I find it difficult to put into words all that I feel, all that I hope and pray for you. My only regret is that mother did not live to see this happy day and that we will not all be in our little chapel at Adlersee, but that, I know, is a selfish thought and we have so much to give thanks for.

These last two weeks have been an exhausting whirl of activity. I was given a few hours off from the office in order to do some very necessary shopping (as always Mathilde has been so helpful – Lina too, although her suggestions are always so extravagant!) but there remains so much to be done and my contribution to the preparations is negligable. I have asked Mathilde what you would both like as a wedding present and she says that I should confer with you although, with the prospect of setting up house, you will need everything. I wondered, Peter, if you would like an "everyday" dinner service or cutlery? Do not forget that there is a cellarful of stuff at Adlersee which we never used but I suspect that it would seem too old-fashioned and heavy for Mathilde's taste. Please think about this suggestion and let me know when we meet.

Already parcels and packages (some of them enormous!) are arriving at Kaisestraße and Grunewald. I do not know if Mathilde has made an inventory of what there is – it may well be that someone has already anticipated my suggestion. I understand that most of the expenses will come from the Reichsminister's budget and you and Christian will only be paying for your honeymoon. Even there (I believe you are going to Paris!) it seems that the SS has commandeered some splendid accommodation that will be free. I do not know about the Luftwaffe but you will have all that information I am sure. How exciting it all is and how you must long to get away from all the dreadful events with which you have been involved these last three months.

We have had some very variable weather, rain and cloud but also some lovely late autumn days and the trees in the Tiergarten and the Unter den Linden are still ablaze with colour. I do hope, dearest Peter, that the sun will shine for you on your wedding day but if not there will be a compensating warmth in the hearts of those that love you and hold you in esteem.

None more so than

Your devoted sister,
Edith

Oberleutnant Peter von Vorzik
Journal entry

6th November 1940

Here we are in Paris and I am trying to write a few lines each day to recount the auspicious events of the last week or so. I suppose the most important news is that Mussolini's army invaded Greece just three days before our wedding. The general feeling is that this will turn out to be a major blunder, Christian says that it is common knowledge within the Party that the Führer is furious that the Duce took such a step without prior consultation. Whatever happens, one can only feel a sense of dismay that war seems to be creeping all over Europe. We must hope all turns out for the best.

Now for an account of the marriage celebrations. I cannot remember all the details of the occasion but will try and fill in the main events as I recollect them. Two days before the wedding Kurt and I were flown to Berlin in a communications Me108 Taifun. We were met at Tempelhof by an SS car and driven to Christian's apartment on Kaisestraße arriving at about 3 pm to find the household in apparent chaos with servants running to and fro, bells and telephones ringing, parcels and packages stacked in the hallway and corridors, huge bunches of flowers lying about unwrapped, little gold chairs piled in the music salon where the chandelier had been lowered for cleaning and a man was tuning the piano. Suddenly, just after we had been admitted by Hans, Christian's manservant, there came an awful crash and the sound of breaking glass from the lower floor, followed by a hubbub of angry voices. It was like the opening scene of a farce!

I showed Kurt to his room and told him he was to ring for anything he wanted; he seemed anxious and overawed by everything, just as he had been when he visited Adlersee. I retired to the bedroom that Mathilde and I had used on our previous visit, bathed and rang for a bottle of champagne and two glasses and then telephoned Grunewald to be told by Greta, Mathilde's mother, that Mathilde was already on her way. My heart began to beat faster as I anticipated her arrival but when she saw me she burst into tears and clung to me, just as she had when I proposed to her. She recovered quickly, however, and the next hour or so was one of unutterable bliss as we both surrendered to our long-suppressed desires. Afterwards, with some hesitation, she asked me if I regretted the fact that we had slept together before our marriage and I said no, not in any way. She then went on to tell me that, according to Lina, Reinhard had been cashiered from the navy, back in 1931, after refusing to marry a young woman he had made pregnant, saying he would never marry a woman who had given herself to him. I said that there were probably several differences between Reinhard and myself.

In the evening we were joined for dinner by Christian, Frieda and Edith whose appearance surprised me. She has always worn her hair in long braids encircling her head; now her hair has been cut quite short and worn loose, framing her face. She wore a long, dark blue dress with the neck cut fairly low and the effect was elegant and sophisticated. Mathilde whispered to me, "What do you think of your sister since Lina and I took her in hand?" and I smiled my approval. I noticed that Kurt, who sat opposite her, watched her covertly throughout the meal. Mathilde, I thought, looked ravishing in a pale lilac dress that had a little cape arrangement round her shoulders but the back of the dress was scooped very low showing her creamy skin. Frieda was in black with a spray of gardenias in her hair, looking very soignée. Everyone was in high spirits and the talk was all

143

about new films and plays and concerts, with no mention of the war. Neither Kurt nor I could join in the conversation very much but it was amusing to listen to the theatrical gossip that Frieda recounted.

After dinner several other people arrived, including Reinhard, Lina and Admiral Canaris, head of the intelligence service of the OKW, with his wife, Erika. They are close friends and neighbours of the Heydrichs, living in the Schlachtensee district of Grunewald and are famous for their musical soirées. In fact, we all retired to the music room where Reinhard accompanied Erika in a Mozart violin sonata. I was astonished by Reinhard's beautiful playing, by his dexterous finger-work and the expressive feeling that he put into the performance. I was even more astonished when, talking to him later in the evening, he told me he keeps his own Emil at Tempelhof and goes up on lone patrols whenever he can get away, sometimes early in the morning before he goes to his office. I knew that he is an expert horseman and fences at Olympic level, but had no idea he was also an accomplished musician and pilot. A most remarkable man.

The following evening I saw another side of Reinhard. Kurt, Christian and I had lunch at Savarin's, mainly to get away from the apartment while all the last-minute preparations were going on. During the meal Christian said that Reinhard had suggested that the three of us should join him that evening at the Salon Kitty. Apparently, this is a high-class brothel that Reinhard has been responsible for setting up and it is frequented by many of the most important Party members and the diplomatic corps. Herr von Ribbentrop and Count Ciano, the Italian Foreign Minister, have both been there. I could see that Kurt was amazed at the revelation and that Christian was somewhat embarrassed at making the suggestion. Privately, he told me that it was politic that he should fall in with Reinhard's idea. He said that perhaps I would agree to go and if the prospect did not appeal I could make some excuse and leave after we had had a few drinks by which time Reinhard would be "otherwise engaged." Reluctantly, I said yes, and would talk it over with Kurt. In fact, I was repelled by the idea. I do not think that I am a prude and must admit that, had I been unattached, I might even have found the proposition attractive but, as I was both betrothed and deeply in love, the thought of copulating with some prostitute on the eve of my wedding produced a feeling of physical nausea.

Christian said that Reinhard had the reputation of being sexually rapacious and that he always wanted to visit Salon Kitty with some subordinate – everyone on his staff dreaded the summons. Apparently, after he has finished with his chosen female he gets very drunk and likes to indulge in voyeurism. It is common knowledge that he has had the rooms wired for sound, not so much in order to listen in to the scenes of love-making but in case one of his officers makes an incautious remark about him. Thinking of our conversation of the previous evening and Reinhard's exquisite violin-playing, I could not but reflect upon what an extraordinary man the SS-Obergruppenführer is.

Kurt was both anxious and excited, I thought, about visiting Salon Kitty. After dinner at Horcher's with Christian, Reinhard and some other SS officers we were driven in three official SS cars to this louche establishment. Everyone drank champagne, there was a lot of laughter and suggestive jokes about our forthcoming marriages and I must admit that most of the women who joined in the badinage were very attractive in the vulgar manner of their profession. Kurt whispered that if I was not staying then he wanted to leave, too; I know he felt uneasy in such exalted company. At a prearranged signal, after visiting the lavatory, we both slipped away. I do not think that our desertion was noticed because everyone, including Christian, appeared deeply involved with the "hostesses" and I wondered if Christian permitted their affectionate overtures to proceed to their obvious conclusion. Neither of us has made any subsequent reference to the evening.

The day of our wedding dawned blustery and grey with dead leaves blown about in the air and low clouds the colour of gunmetal. Happily, the rain held off. I could not help wondering what the weather was like on the Channel coast and if JG233 was, even at that moment, taking off for a sweep over southern England. Kurt and I travelled in an SS car to the City Hall and Christian, and his best man, SS-Brigadeführer Walter Schellenberg, in another. Mathilde was due to come from Grunewald with her mother and Reinhard, Frieda was driving over from the Adlon Hotel with her father and mother, and Edith, Lina and the brides' attendants were all arriving in yet another car.

As we drew up at the City Hall I was surprised to see a large crowd including numerous photographers and cine cameras. As we got out of the car we were greeted by no less a person than Reichsführer-SS Heinrich Himmler himself who gave the Party salute as flashbulbs went off all around. Then, to my utter astonishment, at the top of the steps was the large, beaming figure of Reichsmarshall Göring, dressed in a long, pale blue great-coat with scarlet lapels piped in silver and with a white peaked cap. At my side I heard Kurt mutter, "My God!" We ascended the steps and gave the Luftwaffe salute, uncertain what to do. The Reichsmarshall shook hands with us and then signalled to an aide who led us into the cavernous entrance hall. On the left was a troop of SS men in steel helmets, on the right a section of Luftwaffe men in ceremonial dress. In the centre was a small dais covered in red carpet. I was positioned in the middle, Kurt was stationed in front of the Luftwaffe guard of honour. Reichsmarshall Göring strode to the dais, then the SS and Luftwaffe detachments were called to attention as Christian entered with the Reichsführer-SS and Brigadeführer Schellenberg. Behind them came Reinhard with Mathilde and her mother, and Frieda with her parents. Edith and Lina with the other attendants brought up the rear of the little procession.

There was a moment's hiatus as everyone was arranged on respective sides of the dais. I remained in my isolated, central position, wondering why I had been singled out from the others and why there had been no kind of briefing, let alone rehearsal of what appeared to be not only a formal but an official occasion. I had imagined that our respective families would assemble for a short signing ceremony that would make us two married couples, I had no idea why we were being paraded in this peculiar fashion in front of the Reichsmarschall and felt angry that Christian had not given me the slightest warning of his presence. My thoughts were interrupted by the aide calling out my name and commanding me to step forward. Bewildered, I took three paces forward which brought me to within a couple of metres of the dais. The Reichsmarschall was handed a small, open black leather case by another aide, a Hauptmann who had been standing just behind him. From the case the Reichsmarschall withdrew a scarlet, black and white ribbon from which dangled a small golden emblem. He advanced upon me with that now familiar beaming smile and in a booming voice, amplified by the hall's acoustics, announced, "By order of the Führer I hereby invest you with the addition of Oak Leaves to the Knight's Cross for outstanding services as a fighter pilot of the Third Reich." He placed the ribbon over my head and adjusted it round my neck as flashbulbs went off. He took two steps back and started to clap his white-gloved hands together, the applause taken up by the surrounding audience.

I remembered when I had first been invested by the Reichsmarschall with the Knight's Cross how nervous I had been, my legs shaking as I stood on that bleak, windswept airfield near Aachen. By contrast, in that gloomy hall, surrounded by relatives, friends and state dignitaries, I felt desperately awkward, not knowing how to respond, what was expected of me. I had anticipated it as my wedding day, not a solemn investiture, yet here were Reichsmarschall Göring and Reichsführer-SS Himmler accompanied by their retinues in whose presence I had been awarded an accolade that I felt I did not deserve, my score or so of victories insignificant when measured against the achievements of such aces as Mölders, Galland, Hartmann and Joppien. As the clapping ceased the Reichsmarschall spoke again: "As further recognition of your brilliant achievements I take great personal pleasure in promoting you to the rank of Oberleutnant," he said. "Thank you, Herr Reichsmarshall," I mumbled, quite overcome and horrified to feel myself blushing as there was another burst of applause. To my great relief the Reichsmarshall turned to his aides and said, "Let us proceed."

With the Reichsmarshall and the Reichsführer-SS leading the way, the assembled company, with the exception of the guards of honour, ascended to a large salon on the first floor. There were rows of plush-covered wooden chairs and Christian and I, Kurt and Schellenberg, were directed to one side of the front row; Mathilde and Reinhard, Frieda and her father to the other. Everyone sat facing a vast desk upon which there were several large leather-bound volumes and a big vase of white chrysanthemums. Behind the desk were two civic dignitaries, flanked by the two Reichsministers. One of the dignitaries, Lipfert I think his name was although my memory is somewhat blurred, made a short speech, a homily about the sanctity of marriage and duty to the fatherland, and then Christian and myself, Mathilde and Frieda, were called up to the desk and made to recite wedding vows after Herr Lipfert. Kurt was at my side (as my ever-watchful Katschmarek!) and presented me with the ring (which had been bought by Christian) which I placed on Mathilde's finger. I assume that Christian was doing likewise with Frieda but it was the first time that day that I had been able to look at my darling Mathilde properly and I was unaware of anything or anyone else at that moment. She looked so beautiful and elegant in the clothes she had written to me about and as we stood face to face I could see there were tears glistening in her eyes. I smiled as reassuringly as I could, anxious in case she might suddenly cling to me and cry in front of that distinguished assembly. To my relief she controlled her emotion and the rest of the brief ceremony was completed by our signing of the register. The group crowding round the desk, with the Reichsmarshall and Reichsführer-SS hovering in the background as the flashbulbs went off again, reminded me of the pictures I had seen in the newspapers a few weeks before when Herr von Ribbentrop, Count Ciano and the Japanese Ambassador, Suburo Kurusu, had signed a tripartite treaty: there were the same expressions, the serious faces of the signatories (myself included, I suppose), the smiles of the onlookers. The rather dusty surroundings, however, could hardly compete with the magnificence of the Great Hall of the Führer's Chancellery.

After the signing, Christian and Frieda, Mathilde and I, were grouped together with the Reichsmarshall and the Reichsführer-SS for more photographs, and this was repeated yet again on the steps of the building, and then more photographs of the four of us descending the steps between two rows formed by the guards of honour, making archways over our heads with ceremonial daggers. We were all seated in a fleet of cars led by the two Reichsministers in open tourers with motorcycle outriders, and driven off to Herr Goebbels's home, cheered by quite a large crowd. In the car I longed to kiss Mathilde but felt it might not be the time and place so contented myself with saying, "I love you, darling," and squeezing her hand.

I was quite unprepared for the sumptuousness of the Propaganda Minister's residence – really a small palace. Marble floors, gilded doors, huge chandeliers, pictures by Rubens, Rembrandt, Dürer, Arnold Böcklin and Caspar David Friedrich. Herr Goebbels was in the spacious hall to greet us (his wife, Magda, is in hospital expecting their sixth child at any moment) and he said that he had only moved into the residence two days before and we were the first official guests.

Moving through two large salons we were ushered into a lofty dining hall where an enormous buffet wedding-breakfast had been prepared. There were dishes of game birds, a roast boar and venison (all, apparently, from the Reichsmarshall's estate at Karinhall), salmon, a great pile of caviar in a huge silver tureen surrounded by ice, pies, cheeses, a great cornucopia of fruit, pastries and gateaux and, in the centre, a five-tier wedding-cake, the top tier surmounted by two miniature couples, back-to-back. The sides of the cake were decorated with the SS rune and the Luftwaffe eagle. There was a long top table reserved for the wedding party and dignitaries and a score or more of round tables adorned with candelabra and white lilies. Those of us at the big table were waited upon (Christian said that the waiters were also SS bodyguards) and those at the round tables had to choose their food from the buffet. Placement, of course, was by protocol which resulted in some odd contiguities: Mathilde was between me and the Reichsmarshall, Kurt was sandwiched between Frau Zugmann and Lina.

Before we began eating, Herr Goebbels made a speech of welcome that was most effusive and seemed to go on and on extolling the brilliance and valour of the Reich's armed forces and the indomitable strength of the Axis powers. It seemed a politically motivated speech for the benefit of the assembled press and ever-present photographers. Goebbels is undeniably a polished performer but there is something about him that I find very unsympathetic. Perhaps it is because of his rodent-like features, his large head, small body and club-footed, limping walk (for which, of course, he cannot be blamed), more likely his cold smile and supercilious manner, but women are supposed to find him irresistably attractive and, like Reinhard, he has the reputation of being sexually insatiable.

There were more speeches by the Reichsministers, along very similar lines followed by toasts to us, the newlyweds. Then Christian was called upon to speak. He thanked our host for the magnificence of the reception and asked us to toast the good health of the absent hostess. Then he thanked the Reichsministers for their attendance and Frieda's parents for the gift of their daughter. Then it was my turn – much the most nerve-wracking part of the day! I began by thanking the Reichsmarshall for the surprise award of the Oak Leaves which, I said, I felt I hardly deserved (he nodded and beamed at this) and thanked the Reichsministers for their encouraging words to those of us involved in the daily struggle against our enemies (I hastily added that, of course, everyone was engaged in Germany's fight for existence) while thinking to myself that Kurt and I were probably the only ones in the room who had seen any action. Then I thanked Mathilde's mother for the gift of her daughter and finally thanked Kurt for his unfailing protection as my Katschmarek and support as my best man. Schellenberg said a few words about Christian's brilliant work on Reinhard's staff and then it was poor Kurt's turn. He was in a lather of perspiration and visibly shaking but he acquitted himself well and was the only person to inject a modicum of humour into the interminable and fulsome speeches with an anecdote about how, while we were flying on patrol together, he had heard what he thought were terrible groans coming from me over the r/t only to discover, after he had anxiously enquired what was wrong, that I was singing. It was a silly story but it served very well to introduce the lieder singer who proceeded to entertain the guests with songs by Schubert and Hugo Wolf. After that two dancers from the Berlin Opera Ballet performed a duet from *The Tales of Hoffmann* and then the reception came to an end.

During the protracted leave-taking, I took the opportunity to examine some of the pictures and while I was looking at a painting by Friedrich, a Gothic cathedral that appeared to be rising from a moonlit lake, someone behind me made a comment about the picture to the effect that, had the artist been French he would have received greater renown, and I recognised Albert Speer, whose title is Architectural Inspector of the Reich. He was very affable and said that he had been responsible for the remodelling of the residence and had arranged for most of the pictures to be on loan from the Berlin National Gallery. He said that he had also included some watercolours by Emil Nolde but when the Führer had been shown around the house by Frau Goebbels he had ordered them to be taken down, calling them "impossible pictures." I had the impression that Speer's tastes did not coincide with the Führer's but he did not say so in so many words. He did say, however, that the Führer has marvellous ideas for the remodelling of Berlin after the war and if I cared to go to Speer's office any time I am on leave he would be pleased to arrange for me to see the drawings and models he is preparing. I thanked him and said I would certainly do that. I am really very interested; I have always found Berlin to be a rather forbidding city and much prefer the baroque elegance of Munich but that is probably because that city has been the background to my childhood and adolescence.

At last everyone had left. After the formal farewells to those whom Kurt calls "the grandees" we said goodbye and thanks once more to Herr Goebbels for such a splendid reception. He wished us good fortune and a happy honeymoon in Paris, having recently returned from a private visit there himself. (Afterwards, Christian said that it was generally known within the Party that Goebbels had been on an extravagant buying spree with Göring, including an Aubusson carpet for 26,000 marks for his lakeside villa at Lanke.)

Christian and Frieda, Mathilde and I and Edith and Kurt returned to Kaisestraße. The next day Kurt was travelling on to Hamburg (he had been given a week's leave which left no time to visit Michelle in Rouen) and Edith was expected back at work the very next day. At 11 pm Christian and Frieda, Mathilde and I caught the overnight sleeper to Paris.

Our two-berth compartment on the train was hardly ideal accommodation for a wedding night but we were both very tired from the day's festivities and not a little dizzy from too much champagne. We both reclined on the lower berth and held each other close in the confined space, exchanging soft kisses until we both fell asleep in our clothes. It was not the passionate climax to the day that I had envisaged but we were happy and fulfilled just to be in each other's arms. When we arrived at the Gare de l'Est it was raining heavily. We said *au revoir* to Christian and Frieda both of whom managed to look immaculate in contrast to Mathilde's and my dishevelled state. They were going to an apartment commandeered by the SS and we took a taxi to the address I had been given by a Luftwaffe liaison officer. It turned out to be a luxurious apartment on the Rue de Rivoli. There were three reception rooms, including a well-stocked library and a grand salon with a balcony, four bedrooms each with its own bathroom and dressing room, a large dining room and lavishly equipped kitchen and extensive servants' quarters on the upper floor. There was a housekeeper, a dour woman of middle-age, two maids with welcoming smiles and a tall, thin butler who stood, hands clasped and head deferentially bowed. He spoke quite good German and gave us to understand that there would be a Luftwaffe chef in attendance every day who would confer with Mathilde about the meals we wanted. The apartment was beautifully furnished with antiques, mostly in the manner of the Second Empire. The main bedroom was equipped with a huge bed with a tent-like canopy of crimson watered silk that matched the elaborately ruched curtains. The sheets were of oyster satin. I began writing this entry in my journal in the library, and Mathilde came in holding a letter that had fallen out of a little compartment in the escritoire in the salon. She had been about to write to her mother when the letter had fluttered down. "I don't usually read private correspondence," she assured me, "but I was curious to know something about the people whose home we are occupying." She handed the letter to me. It had a New York address and was dated 18th May. I have copied it down:

Dear Louise,

We have been listening on the radio to the reports of the German attack on France and the situation does seem very serious. My dear, Benny and I are very anxious about your safety, you know what terrible things the Germans did to Elsa and David and I cannot bear to think that the same might happen to you and Gerard if the Germans got to Paris. Why not join us here in New York? Benny has many contacts in the diamond business and says he would be quite prepared to go into some form of partnership with Gerard – whatever he wants. Money will be no problem and if the Germans don't get to Paris then you can always return. The only thing that matters is that you are safe from persecution. Try and bring the best jewels you have; if there is any difficulty, fly to Geneva and put them into a Swiss bank. (You might want to stay in Switzerland but, as things are, there is no knowing where the Germans will strike next.) If you have any problems taking money out of the country Benny will wire the necessary to the Credit Lyonnais in Paris to cover your travel expenses. He has been in touch with the travel bureau here and there is a Swedish ship, the *Göteborg*, leaving Marseilles on the 29th. If this does not reach you in time there are other sailings from Portugal. Dearest Louise, *do not delay*, come to us, there is a big welcome awaiting you here.

All our love,
Millie

PS Telegraph or telephone us what is happening.

I handed the letter back to Mathilde. She looked at me and said, "Peter, I don't want to stay here. I don't want you to make love to me in their bed." I understood completely how she felt and without hesitation I said that we would go to an hotel. I telephoned the Luftwaffe representative who was in charge of requisitioned accommodation and simply said that we had changed our plans and the apartment was free for anyone else to use. Then I telephoned the Crillon, the first hotel name that came into my head, I think because mother once said she had stayed there. The receptionist understood my halting French and, when I said that we were on our honeymoon, was most attentive and helpful and said that he would reserve one of the best suites for us. As soon as we arrived – the manager of the hotel attended us personally – and before we had begun to unpack, I took Mathilde by the hand, led her to the bed and began to undress her. We made passionate love for over an hour, the long-delayed celebration of our marriage, that left us both physically exhausted. While I was in the bath a waiter arrived with a gift of champagne from the management, but Mathilde wanted tea, not champagne. We seemed to have been drinking nothing but champagne for days. Ten minutes later the waiter was back with tea and tiny cakes. I telephoned Christian and told him that we had moved, saying only that Mathilde felt unhappy sleeping in someone else's bed. I did not mention the letter. He made no comment but said they were very happy where they were, another grand apartment apparently, but theirs was in the Rue Rousselet near the Bois de Boulogne.

In the evening we all had dinner at Maxim's – more champagne of course! – and went to the Casino de Paris with its cabaret of nudes. I was surprised how artistically the spectacle was presented, with lavish costuming and seductive lighting; really, one could not think it any more lascivious than a beautiful nude painting. We have also enjoyed the more usual tourist pursuits, visiting the Louvre, Versailles and Notre Dame, all of which are remarkable but I think it is the general ambience of the city that makes it all so enjoyable. The French appear to have accepted their recent defeat with remarkable equanimity, they pursue their hedonistic pleasures as if there had not been a war.

We attended a performance of *Sylvia* by the Paris Opéra Ballet (Frieda has friends in the company) and afterwards went backstage where we met the director of the company, Serge Lifar, who had also danced the hero of the ballet, Aminta. Lifar joined us for dinner and proved to be a most charming and interesting person who has led a most extraordinary life. He was born in Kiev, fought with the White Russians during the revolution, managed to audition for the great impresario Diaghilev, becoming his leading dancer and later became the director of this great French company. He seems to have known everyone of note, including members of the British Royal Family (he showed us a gold cigarette case given to him by King George VI and Queen Elizabeth when they visited Paris in 1937) and entertained Göring and Goebbels on their recent visit to Paris. Apparently he has been invited to Berlin by the Führer and intends to visit our city as soon as his many duties permit. We all agreed that that evening was the best time we had in Paris.

It has been a most wonderful honeymoon, rapturous hours with my darling Mathilde, a whirl of pleasure and enjoyment from the moment we arrived but I have to confess to having had some brief moments when my thoughts were back in the real world, as it were. Last night I found it difficult to get to sleep and my thoughts kept going round and round, coming back to two or three subjects that would not go away. Mostly they concerned JG233 and what was happening to the Staffel, particularly Kurt. Was he flying as someone else's Katschmarek, was the Geschwader still making fighter sweeps (the newspapers here give very little detail of actual operations), have the replacement aircraft arrived? Then I thought about Adlersee, where we will be spending the last weekend of my leave. How long can father remain there with Werner looking after him? What will happen to the Schloss when they leave? I must talk to Christian about it. Edith telephoned him yesterday to say that the Berlin newspapers, particularly *Der Angriff* and *Völkischer Beobachter*, had marvellous pictures of the wedding and there are excellent formal pictures, too, which both Mathilde and Frieda are anxious to see. Tonight we leave Paris and make the long and tedious train journey to Munich where we shall be staying. It would be nice for the four of us to stay at Adlersee but of course Werner could not possibly cope with so many visitors.

Christian says I must be prepared for father not to recognise me. As I said, it has been a wonderful honeymoon but I have been possessed by a nagging feeling of guilt being away from the Staffel all this time and am quite prepared to return, now, and resume my duties. The sooner the war is over, the sooner I shall be really able to enjoy married life.

Berlin

10th November

The visit to Adlersee proved a dismal occasion. The weather was bad, rain and sleet and the Schloss was cold. Werner had done his best to make us welcome but there have not been fires in the main rooms for some months and the place seemed dank and gloomy, not the house which I associate with my early years. Father looked terribly frail – it was certainly a great shock to see how he has deteriorated so rapidly. He seemed to understand that Mathilde and Frieda were his daughters-in-law, he bowed to them and clicked his heels but during lunch (prepared by Werner with some help from Frau Schuster who waited at table) he said hardly a word and when he did speak it was some *non sequitur*, a reference, as far as I could gather, to the abdication of the Kaiser. I was glad when it was over and we caught the train back to Berlin.

The wedding photographs are very good and the newspapers certainly made a big splash with a detailed account of the ceremony and numerous photographs: pictures of me receiving the Oak Leaves from the Reichsmarshall, pictures of the four of us signing the register with the Reichsministers looking on, pictures of us descending the steps of the City Hall between the guards of honour and more pictures taken at the reception. Both Mathilde and Frieda have been busy compiling scrapbooks of cuttings and photographs which they have enjoyed doing.

The current news, however, has not been good, although one has to read between the lines to understand the real significance of what is happening. The day after we returned to Berlin the RAF dealt a great blow to the Italian navy with a surprise night attack on the fleet in Taranto harbour. Apparently their torpedo planes, flying from the aircraft carrier *Illustrious* (which we had been given to understand, some weeks before, had been sunk by Luftwaffe bombers!) sank the battleship *Cavour*, seriously damaged the battleships *Littorio* and *Duilio* as well as other cruisers and destroyers. In North Africa the Italian army has also had serious setbacks with the British and Australians in Cyrenaica, and the Italian army is also suffering defeats in the Balkans, the Greeks having pushed them back into Albania. These reverses are always referred to as "strategic regrouping" but that is a euphemism for retreat. All those prognostications that Mussolini's forces would prove to be an embarrassment are coming true.

Mathilde and I are now settled in at her mother's house in Grunewald. It is comfortable and convenient but it will take me some time to think of it as home and, when the war is over, we must think in terms of establishing ourselves on a more permanent basis. I like to think it might be at Adlersee. We are both aware that this idyll is ending. I am quite ready to return to JG233 but I know Mathilde is very unhappy at my imminent departure. Just as I was writing this the mail arrived, including orders for me to rejoin the Staffel. It seems that the Geschwader is being reformed under a new Fliegerkorps Kommandeur and that we shall be receiving new aircraft. Now I am anxious to find out what is happening – above all will I still have Kurt as my Katschmarek? Nothing seems certain, the war is spreading and we must all be ready to face whatever the future holds for us. I have not said so to Mathilde but the end of the war does not yet seem to be in sight.

From: The Führer's HQ
Directive No 20
To: General Franz Halder, OKW
Reichsmarshall Hermann Göring, C-in-C Luftwaffe
Gr. Adm. Erich Raeder, C.-in-C. Navy

13th December 1940

TOP SECRET: OPERATION MARITA

In order to assist Il Duce in the fight against the Greek insurgents we shall assemble a task force of 24 divisions, assisted by a Fliegerkorps, to descend upon the Greek mainland as soon as favourable weather sets in. Preparations for Operation Marita are to begin immediately.

Adolf Hitler

From: The Führer's HQ
Directive No 21
To: General Franz Halder, OKW
Field Marshal Walther von Brauchitsch
Reichsmarshall Hermann Göring, C-in-C Luftwaffe

18th December 1940

TOP SECRET: OPERATION BARBAROSSA

The German Armed Forces must be prepared to *crush Soviet Russia in a quick campaign* before the end of the war against England. For this purpose the army will have to employ all available units with the reservation that the occupied territories will have to be safeguarded against surprise attacks.

The mass of the Russian army in western Russia is to be destroyed in daring operations by driving forward deep armoured wedges, and the retreat of intact, battle-ready troops into the wide spaces of Russia is to be prevented. The ultimate objective of the operation is to establish a defence line against Asiatic Russia from a line running from the Volga river to Archangel.

Preparations are to be completed by May 15th, 1941. Great caution has to be exercised that the intention of the attack will not be recognised.

Adolf Hitler

Book Three

War in the East

Oberleutnant Peter von Vorzik
Journal entry

19th December 1940

It is nearly eight weeks since I wrote in this journal and, once again, so many things have happened during that interval that I am hard put to it to remember all the significant details.

On my return to JG233 I received a shock and a surprise – though perhaps it would be more accurate to say two shocks. The first shock was to learn that only a few days after I went on leave Zwemmer was lost during a fighter sweep, shot down somewhere over the Thames estuary. Two pilots from the Staffel returned immediately to search the area and to provide protection for the air-sea rescue service carried out by Dornier Do18 flying boats, but without success. They saw nothing, not even a patch of oil or floating wreckage. He is posted as missing, presumed killed.

The surprise, or second shock, was to learn that in my absence I have been appointed Staffelkapitan as Zwemmer's replacement. (The main reason is that, of the remaining pilots in the Staffel, I have the highest score of victories.) The Geschwader has been withdrawn from northern France and we are in the process of being regrouped and re-equipped. Apparently we shall be operating on a flexible basis, moving from one Luftflotte to another, reinforcing units where the dictates of battle are most pressing. Great mobility has always been part of the Luftwaffe's tactical deployment and now that there are new areas of engagement in the Balkans and North Africa (mainly due to the incompetence of the Italian forces) it has been decided that JG233 must be available to fly to various operational areas at short notice. I am very grateful, now, for that short period last year when I had some experience of acting as Staffelkapitan. I shall do my best to continue the brilliant leadership and maintenance of morale that Zwemmer achieved but I feel that I shall often fall short of his standards. One thing is in my favour: we have had an intake of new young pilots and I shall be working with them from the beginning; only two pilots remain from the Staffel as it was formed during the recent battles over England (Gustav Grinke, known as GG, and Ludwig Varasch – I don't think I have mentioned them before in these accounts) and I know I shall have their support without them making unfavourable comparisons between Zwemmer and myself. But his loss is very hard to accept.

The one great and heartening fact amongst all this loss and change is that Kurt remains my Katschmarek! (He, of course, makes it three pilots from the old group.) There he was in the mess on my return, the first to congratulate me on my appointment as Staffelkapitan, his smile and handshake the greatest reassurance I could have received. We are once more on German soil, at an airfield not far outside Solingen in Bergisches Land and not far from Cologne ... I envisage more visits to the Hotel Orpheus with my darling wife. (That is, I realise, the first time I have written of Mathilde in those terms.) The airfield, thank heaven, is properly built, with concrete runways, effective drainage, solid accommodation, efficient facilities. A great relief after the various makeshift airfields we have had to operate from these last few months. The only inconvenience is, once again, inadequate provision of telephones for private calls; an hour's wait, or more, is usual if one wishes to telephone home.

We are still operating with Me109Es, some salvaged from crash landings during the recent battles. They are only for working-up with the new recruits; soon we shall be re-equipped with the new Me109Fs which is very exciting. We have had a representative from the Bayerische Flugzeugwerke demonstrating and lecturing about the new version of the Emil. (We shall have to think of a new nickname: Franz? Friedrich?) It will have a new development of the DB601 engine providing more power and greater all-round performance, faster climb and dive, greater acceleration and top speed and a faster 360° turn. Manoeuvrability is also improved and altogether the aircraft is much superior to the old Emils. The shape has been altered: the engine cowling has a more bulbous, constant curve, the spinner has been greatly enlarged, the wing tips are now elliptical instead of square-cut and the tailplane struts have been eliminated. The supercharger intake has been placed further out and the underwing radiators are wider and shallower, reducing drag. Apparently, pilots who have been lucky enough to fly them say they are a real delight to handle but unfortunately the Staffel is not scheduled to receive them until well into the new year.

Only two of the new pilots have had battle experience, both of them from the immensely successful JG26 Schlageter unit. They are Leutnant Otto Ebert and Leutnant Friedrich Gessler and it is a great help to have two such experienced pilots in the Staffel when we now have so many tyros to train. Ebert has Feldwebel Hans Zahle as his Katschmarek and Gessler has Bruno Zechlin who is close to two metres tall and finds it very difficult cramming himself into the narrow cockpit of the Emil. Like the rest of the new intake they are straight from the training school at Werneuchen and are very keen but, of course, there is nothing like first-hand combat experience to mould a pilot's instinctual fighting abilities. I have formed an intensive training programme with simulated aerial attacks with myself, Kurt, Ebert and Gessler operating as the enemy against the rest. They have also had extensive instruction in target practice. There is no doubt that the Jagdgeschwader have suffered serious losses of experienced pilots during the recent operations over England and those of us who have survived carry a heavy responsibility in making sure that these new young pilots absorb everything we have learnt during the heat of battle.

We are only a few days away from Christmas. I do not know whether I shall be able to take two or three days off from my new responsibilities but I have told Mathilde to be ready to come to Cologne at short notice. She may do that anyway so that she can see her mother and aunt even if I am stuck at base. Our honeymoon already seems a long time ago and I am anxious to have Mathilde in my arms once more.

One of our young pilots, Konrad Klepp, whose home is also in Berlin, told me that the British bombed the city last Monday hitting many shops in Tauentzienstraße and that the whole street was littered with glass. (He heard this on the phone when speaking to his mother.) Such information makes me anxious for both Edith and Mathilde, neither of whom tell me about such things. There is some consolation in that we are bombing British cities nightly and that our raids are much heavier and more concentrated than theirs. The hope is that this constant bombardment of their factories and military installations will soon bring about a capitulation. Everyone, now, is hoping for peace in 1941.

From: Mathilde von Vorzik
23 Hevelius Straße
Grunewald
To: Oberleutnant Peter von Vorzik
III Gruppe JG233
Solingen

20th December 1940

My Own Darling Peter,
Following your phone call – how marvellous it was to hear your voice! – I have booked a room at the Orpheus from the 23rd until the 2nd January. I have tried three times to reach you by phone and each time it has been unsuccessful; each time a voice said you were "unavailable" so I assumed you were bound up with your duties. I realise, darling, that with your new responsibilities you will not always be "available" when I want.

I have written to mother who, of course, is delighted that I shall be in Cologne and hopes that you will, perhaps, at least have Christmas day free and be able to enjoy lunch or dinner or both with her and Aunt Ilse and me. Of course, darling, if you do have leave, however short, you may want us to be together, just the two of us. Do let me know as soon as you can what is happening – this may only reach you a day or two before Christmas – but in any case I will not make any definite plans until I hear from you.

Dearest darling, I have some news that I wanted to keep until we were alone together but it is so marvellous, so exciting, that I cannot keep it bottled up inside me – literally! – any longer. Yes, darling, as you may have guessed, I am pregnant!! Isn't that wonderful? Ever since the doctor confirmed it last week (although I knew; women do know such things!) I have imagined whispering it in your ear as we lay in each other's arms but the news is too important to play romantic games with and, however it was communicated, I thought it was something you would be thrilled to know. So here it is, then, dearest, in pen and ink. I have not yet told another soul, not mother, not Edith, because I wanted you to be the first person to know. I am so deeply, wonderfully happy, darling, as I am sure you will be too – I cannot wait to be with you and share this happiness and talk about our future plans.

Of course, my head has been full of ideas about names and I am sure you will have definite ideas about that subject, too. If it is a boy I would like one of his names (not necessarily the first) to be Wolfgang, which, as you may remember, was my father's name. I would be very happy to have another Peter in the family. If it is a girl you may want to call her after your mother; I have always thought Renata a lovely name. But what fun it will be, darling, to discuss such things! Now I must hurry to the post so that you get this as soon as possible.

Hoping to hear from you soon, darling, and looking forward to a joyous Christmas.

Ever your own loving,
Mathilde

From: Edith von Vorzik
Apt 2, 47 Scharnhorst Straße
Berlin
To: Oberleutnant Peter von Vorzik
III Gruppe JG233
Solingen

21st December 1940

My Dear Peter,
This is mainly to let you have my new address. Christian has installed me here, a small but delightful apartment rented from one of his colleagues who has been sent to eastern Poland where he expects to be for some time. It is very much a bachelor apartment, but comfortable and equipped with a splendid gramophone and racks of records. It is within walking distance of the office and has a nice view of the River Spree, so I shall be very happy here. When you are next on leave I shall enjoy cooking supper for you and Mathilde. I had a telephone call from her today to tell me the wonderful news about her pregnancy which she said she has written to

you about. How exciting, dearest Peter – I look forward to being Aunt Edith to your first-born. Mathilde can talk of nothing else, of course, and it is ironic that the doctor confirmed her condition on the very day that she was due to have an interview with the editor of *Die Frau*, arranged by Lina. Mathilde hopes that they will be able to offer her a position after the baby has been born but that would mean having a nurse and there are many other questions to discuss.

I have made friends with a charming young woman who is attached to Adam Trott's office, Marie Vassiltchikov. She is a daughter of Prince Illarion and Princess Lydia Vassiltchikov who left Russia after the revolution. They have many connections with European aristocracy but very little money and Marie (everyone calls her Missie) and her second sister Tatiana have to work for a living. She is highly intelligent and sophisticated, has been very kind to me and we have gone to several concerts together. Unfortunately, I have been moved from Adam Trott's office and am now assistant secretary to SS-Colonel Dr Franz Stahlecker who was instrumental in getting me placed here. We do not like him for reasons I cannot elaborate upon in a letter; suffice to say he struts about the office in his uniform and high boots, carrying a whip and with a German shepherd dog in constant attendance.

I did not know what to buy you for Christmas, dear Peter, so I have sent you a parcel of little delicacies to supplement your daily rations (not easy to find everything I should have liked to send but one or two of the assistants at Horcher's are very obliging). Christian and Frieda are planning a big party on Christmas Eve (how I wish you could be there with Mathilde) and Lina has invited me to the reception she and Reinhard are giving on New Year's eve. I should like to go to Midnight Mass but do not like being out by myself after dark. Missie has kindly invited me to join her and her friends at the Christmas services they hold at the Russian church on January 7th.

This time last year we were all hoping and expecting peace in the New Year; it still seems some way off but I pray all the time that it will be soon and that you will be kept safe from harm, dearest brother. Now I wish you a happy Christmas in the hope that you will be able to spend it with Mathilde, happy in the knowledge that the coming year will bring the greatest blessing of all, a baby son or daughter.

All my love.

Ever in my thoughts,
Edith

PS Please give my regards and compliments of the season to Kurt. I know
you were wondering if he was still your Katschmarek – I do hope he is. E.

From: Gruppenführer Christian von Vorzik
116 Kaiserstraße
Berlin
To: Oberleutnant Peter von Vorzik
III Gruppe JG233
Solingen

22nd December 1940

Dear Peter,

This is just a short letter to wish you a happy Christmas and all good
fortune in the coming year. These greetings are somewhat belated and may
not reach you until after the holidays, my excuse being that here in the
RSHA office we have been frantically busy with developments in the east
and such things as seasonal festivities tend to get overlooked. Even so,
Frieda and I have arranged a little celebration for close friends and if, by
any chance, you were able to come to Berlin on leave we would naturally
be delighted to see you at any time – your room is always available whether
we are here or not. I know you now have a home in Grunewald but there
may be times when you and Mathilde prefer to be in central Berlin.

You have probably heard from Edith that I have found her a small
apartment near her office; I think she will be able to stay there for some
time during the foreseeable future as the owner, a friend of mine, has been
appointed as an aide to Dr Hans Frank, now Governor-General of eastern
Poland. I expect the appointment to be a long-term one. My own
situation here in Berlin is uncertain: Reinhard wants me close to him but
events in the Balkans demand constant attention and it may be that I shall
be returning once more to Rumania in the New Year. In that case I would
take Frieda with me but nothing is settled yet. The whole political
situation in the Balkans and the east becomes ever more complex.

I had a call from Werner yesterday to say that father is in bed with a
chill. The doctor has been in attendance and there is no need for
immediate concern but his health does seem to be as fragile as his mental

state. We must be prepared for further decline. Once more best wishes for the holiday season.

Yours ever,
Christian

From: Leutnant Claus Grüber
Erprobungsgruppe V
Rechlin am Muritzsee
To: Oberleutnant Peter von Vorzik
III Gruppe JG233
c/o Fliegerkorps HQ

23rd December 1940

Dear Peter,

Remember me? Hut 19, Werneuchen '38? I have often wondered how you have progressed since those wild and wonderful days – and nights! – at Flying Training School. And then, yesterday, someone had left a copy of *Das Schwarze Korps* in the mess (not a paper I normally see) and there was a whole page devoted to you and your brother with pictures of your double marriage ceremony. Well, many congratulations, first on your marriage and second on your decoration, received from the Reichsmarshall, no less! I am most impressed.

As you see, I am at Rechlin, seconded here after being invalided out from JG54 (bullet wounds in the knee which will never heal properly). I still manage to do a little flying now and then, but nothing of much consequence. My work here is mainly administrative but nevertheless very interesting. If you are ever in the vicinity or can get up here for a day or two it would be a splendid opportunity to do some reminiscing about old times and hearing all your news first-hand. I can promise you there is much to see which I obviously cannot refer to in a letter but which, I know, you would find absorbing. In any case, do drop me a line and let me have what personal news you can.

Here's wishing you every continued success in the coming year; the Reich is going to need pilots like you in the months to come!

Sincerely,
Claus

PS I am sending this to Fliegerkorps HQ in the expectation that they will forward it to you wherever you are. C.

Oberleutnant Peter von Vorzik
Journal entry

2nd January 1941

As I write the date on this entry it is inevitable that I find myself looking back over the past year, which has been so eventful, with as much concern as I look forward to the year to come. After our tremendous victory over the French everyone felt sure that the British would want an armistice; when they obstinately refused the olive branch offered by the Führer it seemed foregone that attacks by the Luftwaffe, preceding a land invasion, would bring about a quick and decisive victory. It was not to be: the bitter truth was that the British had a stronger air force than we reckoned with, and although their cities continue to receive a terrible pounding from the air Britain remains the proverbial thorn in our side which must be dealt with in a way that will bring about total surrender. The hope is that a winter of bombing and the shipping losses they are suffering from concentrated U-boat attacks will make them capitulate. Looking ahead, rumours abound that there will be a showdown with the Communist forces in the east. Nothing is official, of course, the Russians remain our friends since the non-aggression pact of '39, but ... Talk in the mess and conversations I had with Christian while we were in Paris suggest that, sooner or later, we shall have to have a confrontation with Stalin's menacing hordes. We have always been told that Communism is our greatest enemy and most of my colleagues are convinced the situation must be resolved. I have to confess that I view the coming year with some anxiety. The Italians have landed themselves in a fine mess, both in Greece and North Africa and doubtless we shall have to go to their aid. The war gets more and more complicated.

From a personal point of view my life could not be better. I was overjoyed to hear from Mathilde that I am going to be a father and our brief few days together at Christmas were a wonderful antidote to wartime worries. I managed to get away from the base for forty-eight hours. I took the Staffel Kübelwagen and drove in to Cologne where Mathilde was awaiting me at the Orpheus. We spent a deliriously happy Christmas Eve together, having supper in our room and retiring early... On Christmas Day we joined Mathilde's mother, Greta, and her sister, Ilse, for lunch – potato soup, fish pâté, roast pork, vanilla pudding, glacé fruits, accompanied by some excellent Rhine wines after which we walked to the cathedral where we stayed to hear an organ recital. Afterwards, Greta and Ilse attended the evening service while Mathilde and I returned to the hotel where we once again had supper in our room.

I had been very remiss in not having bought any Christmas presents (thankfully, I had taken a bottle of champagne and a bottle of brandy for Greta who had knitted me a grey-blue pullover to wear under my Tuchrock this winter) and felt very mean and guilty when Mathilde presented me with a handsome crocodile-leather wallet which she had bought while we were in Paris. Why had I not had the foresight to buy her something when we were there? I made a mental note to find her something really splendid for her birthday in February, for which I shall have to enlist the help of Edith.

Of course, lying in bed entwined in each other's arms, we talked incessantly about the baby, thinking of obscure names for the poor child. I am very happy with Mathilde's suggestions of Wolfgang or Renata and she can add any others she likes as long as they are not too bizarre! I do not think it a good idea for her to take up any offer to work on *Die Frau*, at least not for some months after the child is born, but I think Mathilde is quite keen to do so. She says that now there are very good day nurseries for working mothers.

I had to return to base the following day but managed to get away for another twenty-four hours for New Year's Eve, Mathilde having booked the room over that period for just such an eventuality. There was quite a jolly party in the small ballroom of the hotel, and at midnight the little band struck up *Deutschland über Alles* which received many cheers. We all have great hopes for the New Year but for Mathilde and me the greatest event will be the birth of little Wolfgang or Renata. At least there will be some point in continuing to write this: I said, right at the beginning, that some day it might be of interest to any children I have; at least they will have some idea of what their father was doing during these momentous times.

From: Oberleutnant Peter von Vorzik
III Gruppe JG233
Solingen
To: Leutnant Claus Grüber
Erprobungsgruppe V
Rechlin am Muritzsee

7th January 1941

Dear Claus,

Of course I remember you! How could I forget those times, both happy and anxious, at Werneuchen? Both of us were lucky to be selected for fighter training although I was very sorry indeed to learn of your wounding – that must be irksome, yet you do say you manage some flying occasionally.

Yes, I am a deliriously happy married man (I assume you are not, yet, or you would have told me) although I would not have wished our marriage to have been quite as publicised or as elaborate as it was; the result of my brother's involvement with prominent Party officials. Even so, it did result in your corresponding with me and I am delighted that we are now in touch. I will certainly take you up on your suggestion of meeting whenever the opportunity arises. At the moment I have just been appointed Staffelkapitan (replacing my old Chief who was shot down during my honeymoon, a great loss to the Gruppe, as you can imagine) and I am finding my new duties and responsibilities somewhat onerous and certainly time-consuming. I have several new recruits who must be welded into a fighting unit (not that there is any lack of keenness or *esprit de corps*) and we are awaiting re-equipment with the new F Series (which you no doubt know all about) and which has generated great excitement throughout the Gruppe.

We have a big house in Grunewald where we would always be able to accommodate you if you have some time to spare in Berlin while I am on leave (I'll keep you informed) but, of course, I would be most interested in visiting Rechlin – one hears so many extraordinary rumours of what is happening there. Enough said. So, Claus, let me say again how delighted I am to have heard from you and look forward to meeting in the not too distant future.

Yours,
Peter

Oberleutnant Peter von Vorzik
Journal entry

12th January 1941

Father is dead. He died yesterday, quietly in his sleep. The chill he had contracted turned to pneumonia and there was little that the doctor could do. Christian telephoned me last night with the news, following another call he had had from Werner who was not very coherent. Christian has left Berlin today with Edith and together they will be arranging the funeral and all the other matters attendant upon father's death. I shall not be able to attend the funeral service; I simply cannot leave the Staffel at this time with such an intense period of training and working-up in operation. Father would be the first to understand that and expect me to put my duty before personal considerations. Of course I would wish to be there in order to – well, what?

I stopped writing at this point, just as I was about to scribble some cliché about making one's final farewell but, thinking about it, my presence at the obsequies are not really very relevant except as a social formality.

In all honesty I do not, yet, feel anything very much, no real sense of grief, no great emotion of any sort, in fact. I have tried to analyse my feelings but there is a sort of numbness at the centre of my thoughts. I feel faintly guilty, of course, but I do not have any inclination to weep. Perhaps I shall experience a feeling of loss sometime later, a delayed reaction that will affect me all the more because of my current seeming indifference. In recent years father had grown progressively distant and since mother's death (which did affect me deeply) he had become even more remote, as I may have intimated in these pages. At some time in the future I will make a dutiful visit to the chapel at Adlersee and view whatever interment Christian has arranged (I know he will be buried alongside mother) and perhaps, then, I shall have the sort of deep, grieving thoughts that a son is expected to have at the death of a father. I shall certainly not be able to pray.

At present my thoughts are centred on what is happening here within the Staffel. The weather has interrupted some of the flying training and the mock combat sequences that I have devised, but that only serves to enable me to get through the awful mass of paperwork that piles up every day. I have the services of a typist/secretary from Geschwader HQ who comes in about twice a week to deal with inter-Staffel memorandums and so on but even so my in tray always seems to be overflowing with forms, messages, daily orders and information documents all of which demand immediate attention. This means I have less time for relaxation in the mess, having a drink and playing chess or cards with Kurt and the other pilots. Instead, I often retire to bed early and take some of the papers with me although I often find myself falling asleep a few minutes after starting to read them.

Sometimes I look back on those hectic days of last summer, when we were often flying as many as five sorties a day, as far less harassing than this comparatively calm period. Although we were risking our lives almost every waking hour we hardly had the chance to stop and think about it and it was only at the end of the day that we were aware that we had, perhaps, lost a comrade. Even then the reality of death was – literally – drowned in valedictory drinks and the warmth of cameraderie amongst those of us who had survived. All of us were filled with a fatalism that now, in retrospect, appears to have been less wearing on the nerves than the present constant worrying about the smooth day-to-day running of the Staffel. The truth is, like so many pilots, I am not cut out for desk work and would rather be flying.

I wrote a few moments ago about this "calm period" which, of course, is mainly due to the winter when it is often hard even to maintain daily patrols but as soon as the weather improves we all know that there will be new battles to be fought. Our main concern, therefore, is how soon we will get the new F Series which will surely give us superiority over the new variant of the Spitfire which, according to Abteilung 8, is being developed. The impulse to get into the air again and achieve final victory is like some terrible itch that cannot be assuaged or alleviated. My metaphor may not be the most elegant one but that is what it is like, a constant irritant, not on the body but in the brain.

From: Mathilde von Vorzik
23 Hevelius Straße
Grunewald
To: Oberleutnant Peter von Vorzik
III Gruppe JG233
Solingen

13th January 1941

My Darling Peter,
I have just heard from Edith that your father died yesterday. Once again I have tried to contact you by phone without success so I am writing,

darling, to offer all my love and sympathy in your sad bereavement. When my father was knocked down and killed I was only five and so have only vague, though fond, memories of him. You, however, have had your father all your life so that your feeling of loss is proportionately greater. I cannot find words that seem appropriate, only the usual clichés which, darling, I feel sure you do not need me to write down for you to know how deeply I sympathise and how I wish I could reach out and touch you, dearest one, to hold you in my arms and comfort you simply by being there. Of course, I did not know your father as well as I would have liked but in our brief meeting back in November I thought he was a marvellously chivalrous old gentleman. I do regret not having met him sooner, when he was in good health; I know I would have enjoyed listening to him reminisce about his early life. Edith says he was writing his memoirs so perhaps we can look forward to them being published?

Darling, I have begun to feel nauseous in the mornings which I cannot pretend is pleasant but it is part of being pregnant and an intimation of our baby growing. I do hope that the thought of this new life coming to us will help to lessen the loss you have suffered.

I want to post this right away. All my love as always, thinking of you day and night.

Ever your own,
Mathilde

From: Edith von Vorzik
Schloss Adlersee
Bavaria
To: Oberleutnant Peter von Vorzik
III Gruppe JG233
Solingen

17th January 1941

My Dearest Peter,
Father was buried this morning and now it is late evening and I wanted to write and let you know a few brief details about the funeral as I know how sad you must be feeling not to have been here. It was a short and simple ceremony (he said in his will that it should be so) and there were fewer people here than at mother's service; a couple from the estate, as

well as Herr Klinger and his wife; Werner, of course, with Frau Schuster and Gretl, and a few others from the village. Christian and I were the chief mourners as none of the relatives from Munich and Mannheim were able to make the journey for various reasons which I understand. They are mostly old and frail themselves now, and in any case one or two had fallen out with father years ago and could not be expected to come. Father's coffin was laid in the double sarcophagus that he had made for just this occasion many years ago – you will doubtless recall having seen it in the chapel. His name and dates of birth and death have yet to be inscribed and it will be moved to its final place of rest along the north wall. Musically it had to be very curtailed, which was a pity. Some boys from the choir at Starnberg sang parts of the plainsong Mass (the *Requiem Aeternam* and some sections of the *Dies Irae* and finally the *Libera me*.) Short as it was I found it very moving, as I am sure you would have done, dear Peter.

In his will father has left the division of the estate between Christian and yourself with a small annuity for me but Christian says that he will see that it will be divided equally between the three of us. We will see – I would not want to go against father's wishes. When you are able to get leave there is a lot we will have to discuss. At the moment Werner is staying on at Adlersee in a caretaker capacity but Christian has suggested that the SS – or the Luftwaffe – might like to have Adlersee, both the Schloss and the estate, as a convalescent home for wounded men. As none of us will be living here for the foreseeable future I think that is a good suggestion, don't you? Obviously there will be certain safeguards; the pictures and various *objets d'art* will be put into storage but we would have a nominal rental and at least the building would be inhabited and not accumulating dust and damp. Werner could stay on as general caretaker, he seems still to be fit and quite strong and of course he would have staff to assist him. And, essentially, the estate would be helping the war effort in a worthwhile way. I cannot think of a better solution, really.

There are various personal mementos that father left and you might like to select some things, including photos. Christian has taken a pocket watch that father received from the Kaiser and there is a very nice wrist-watch, Swiss I think, that mother gave him on his 60th birthday but which he never wore. It is still in its velvet case. That might be more useful to you. Shall I bring it back to Berlin for you to see? I shall be returning in a day or two – I cannot leave the office too long – although there will still be things to be settled here for some time. They will have to wait. Christian has signed cheques for outstanding local accounts and most business things are being referred to him in Berlin. Other things are being taken care of by father's solicitors in Munich so altogether we have little to worry about. I shall be glad to get back to Berlin; it seems very desolate here now and I am grateful to have Frau S as company just until I leave but she is anxious to get back to her home and family. Gretl has agreed to come up from the village once a week to see if everything is in order and do any small things, like sewing, for Werner. With mother and father both gone, you and Christian both married and Mathilde expecting a baby our world has certainly changed a lot in a little over a year; the end of an era and the beginning of another. Who knows, I might even have prospects of matrimony myself within another twelve months – I would not have thought of such a thing except that Christian brought it up. I do not think I want to consider such a possibility until this horrible war is over.

Keep well, my dearest Peter, I pray for you every night.

Ever you own sister,
Edith

From: SS-Gruppenführer Count Christian von Vorzik
116 Kaiserstraße
Berlin
To: Oberleutnant Peter von Vorzik
III Gruppe JG233
Solingen

20th January 1941

Dear Peter,

Just a short letter to add a few comments of my own following father's death. Edith said she would write to tell you about the funeral itself. I had to leave almost immediately after the ceremony as I simply could not spare more time away from the office. I would have preferred to have stayed and settled various things with the solicitors but there is no great urgency about matters that can be decided at a later date. One thing I wish to discuss with you is arranging for Edith to have a proper share of the estate. The annuity that father left her is very small indeed and she deserves generous recognition of all she did during these last eighteen months, coping with mother's illness and running things smoothly despite father's awkward ways. She is so self-effacing and does not claim credit for what she has done. Do you not agree with me? In the brief time we had together I did mention that she ought to think about marriage; there are several well-placed and well-bred young men here at the RSHA whom I could introduce her to. Since coming to work in Berlin she has lost much of her shyness and now makes a very appealing young woman. I shall enlist Lina Heydrich's help in the matter. Another thing: I mentioned to Edith that we might let the SS or some part of the armed forces have Adlersee as a convalescent home for wounded officers just for the duration of the war. Any valuables could be put in store and the building would benefit by being inhabited. Of course, we would include a clause in the agreement about regular maintenance and restoration of any damage. What do you think?

I brought back with me some of father's papers including the manuscript of his memoirs. I have given them a cursory look and after a more or less coherent, but very dull, beginning they quickly deteriorate into rambling nonsense. He spends much time analysing Hoffman's plan for the defeat of Samsonov at Tannenberg but he does not have anything new to say about the battle and his own recollections and anecdotes are too trivial and personal to be of any interest – writing pages and pages about how potato soup was prepared in the field kitchens! I begin to wonder just what part father played as a member of Ludendorff's staff – in charge of potato-peeling perhaps? Men have received the Iron Cross for less, I believe. At any rate, it is quite clear that father was suffering from senility during the last months of his life. There were a number of small things that Edith had set out as mementos, quite apart from objects mentioned in the will. I took the big pocket watch that he always said would be mine (it is really too large to carry about one's person, nowadays, so I will have it mounted on a little stand to go on my night table). There is a nice wristwatch (Chopard of Geneva, I think) that Edith thought you would like and a number of good pens, including a gold one with matching pencil. You might like that, too, I have no use for them, as Frieda gave me a beautiful platinum pen at Christmas.

The political situation, especially in the Balkans, is in such a state of ferment (one reason why we are so busy), not helped by Mussolini's blunderings that I have to hold myself in readiness to return to Rumania at a moment's notice, although I could be sent anywhere; Hungary,

Bulgaria, even Russia – as the situation is in such a state of flux and rumours circulate every day about what our foreign policy will be. The Turks, too, are playing a waiting game; they are a cunning and devious lot and both Himmler and von Ribbentrop vie with each other to have the most influence with the Führer and our developing plans in the east. Then there is the Jewish question, particularly in Poland, that still has to be settled and which preoccupies Reinhard to the exclusion of all else. But we must try and meet soon, dear brother – let me know as soon as you can when you may have leave. We have much to discuss.

With every good wish for your safety and welfare,

Ever yours,
Christian
Heil Hitler!

From: Oberleutnant Peter von Vorzik
III Gruppe JG233
Solingen
To: SS-Gruppenführer Count Christian von Vorzik
RSHA Prinz Albertstraße
Berlin

24th January 1941

Dear Christian,

Thank you for your letter; it has been a great relief to me to know you were there to cope with all the many formal details following father's death. I cannot pretend that it came as a shock – you yourself warned me in your last letter to expect a deterioration in his condition – but certainly I had not expected it so quickly. I am sure it was all for the best; he had reached a point where life gave him little pleasure. He was never one to be very demonstrative but I think mother's death was a greater blow to him than he acknowledged to us.

Yes, of course I agree that Edith should have her fair share of whatever is due after probate and the final analysis of father's will. I expect it will take some time; as I understand it these things take weeks, if not months. I am grateful, once again, that you are dealing with the solicitors. I also agree that Adlersee should be used as you suggest. We are all domiciled in Berlin now, and will be for the duration of the war and who knows how long afterwards? Assuming I survive the immediate future (one has to be practical about these things) I hope, as you know, to continue with my career in flying and do not expect Adlersee to be my home although I would like to think it was always there for us to visit. But who knows what the future holds? It could be that we might decide to sell it and build something more modern as a holiday home for our respective families. (I am thinking off the top of my head as I write; there are many possibilities.) Of course I have many happy memories of Adlersee and would always want to maintain an association with the area as I am sure you and Edith would, too.

Like you, I am continually busy; now that I am Staffelkapitan I am inundated with paperwork which is both tedious and time-consuming. We all expect a resumption of combat activity as soon as the weather improves and there is a great sense of urgency amongst everyone here, a feeling shared by all of us that we must achieve victory soon and get on with building the Greater Germany that the Führer has envisioned. It does seem, however, that the general political and military situation gets ever more complicated – as you indicate in your letter. Even so, we appear to be masters of the situation and as the year develops we might expect to see everything resolved satisfactorily. Do you not think so?

Returning to the subject of Edith: she mentioned in her letter to me that you had spoken about the prospect of marriage. I have the impression that she does not wish to contemplate such a major step while the war continues. I know that living in Berlin for a few months has made some differences in her appearance, she dresses more stylishly and seems more outgoing and assured socially, but beneath that rather more sophisticated exterior she remains the same shy, sensitive creature she has always been. I do not think we should press her too hard in this matter. She is now in a milieu where she will be meeting people with whom she could contemplate marriage; I think it best to let matters take a natural course although a little unobtrusive manipulation would not be amiss. I leave such things in your capable hands, dear brother, but timing is everything. But you are right when you say she is now a very appealing young woman.

I shall be glad, in time, to select one or two small things that belonged to father as mementos. The wristwatch would be nice for dress occasions but too delicate, I think, for everyday wear. At the moment I wear the regular heavy-duty wristwatch with which we are all issued. I have a pen which mother gave me when I joined the Luftwaffe, so that I had no excuse not to write home, as she jokingly remarked, but it tends to leak ink so father's one would be a welcome replacement. Edith says she will bring these things to Berlin and I will look at them as soon as I have leave which, at the moment, seems unlikely. Will you put in hand the offer of Adlersee to the SS or whatever organisation you think proper?

Once more, many thanks for dealing with all these burdensome duties.

Ever yours,

Peter

PS As you write that you might once more be leaving Berlin I am sending this to your RSHA office to be forwarded if necessary. P.

From: Oberleutnant Peter von Vorzik
III Gruppe JG233
Solingen
To: Mathilde von Vorzik
23 Hevelius Straße
Grunewald

25th January 1941

My Own Darling Mathilde,

It was such a joy, as always, to have your letter with your typically sweet and sensitive words of sympathy. Believe me, darling, it is thoughts of you that keep me motivated throughout every day, not just at such particular times. My career, of course, is important to me, especially now that we are involved in such a terrible struggle, but it is you, and now the advent of our baby, that forms the centre of my being, my universe. Father's death was not altogether unexpected as you know; when we saw him last he looked very frail and, mercifully, the end was swift and peaceful. He would have hated to have had to go into hospital. Losing a parent is rather traumatic and I have come to realise that however one mourns the loss of someone close and dear, one mourns even more the loss of days gone by, times past. One is beset with nostalgia for one's childhood when parents were so much closer, when they ordained so much of one's life. It is selfish to think like that, I know, dwelling upon what one has lost rather than who one has lost. In all honesty, father had become a somewhat remote person these last few years, particularly since I started flying training, so that has softened the emotional blow considerably. Now there is no one in the family at Adlersee and, together with Christian and Edith, I shall have to think of it as the past rather than the future. You, my darling, and little Wolfgang/Renata are my future. I sympathise, darling, with you, suffering your unpleasant morning symptoms of pregnancy; I do hope the nauseous feelings pass. They do, don't they? They do not last the whole nine months, I hope. I am very ignorant about such things!

It would be nice to think that I could have leave soon but I do not think that is likely. We are very busy; I have greater responsibilities now and it will be several weeks, even months, before I can expect to get home. Incidentally, it will always be difficult to phone me here. Your call comes through to a central switchboard which is dealing with a multitude of messages, most of them official and urgent, and remember, darling, this is not the only Staffel on the base. It is easier for the telephonist to say "unavailable" than to put through several subsidiary enquiries in order to find out where I am and whether I am available or not – mostly not! I only make a point of telling you this so that you will not be frustrated and disappointed. If only you could be here (how wonderful that would be!) you would see that I am only like a tiny ant in a busy anthill! It took Christian some while to reach me to tell me of father's death and he was helped by having an official – and very important – office to initiate the call. Making reverse calls to you is almost as difficult; I have to stand in line for an hour or more as there are so many pilots and ground crew and administrative staff all wanting to make calls home. Sometimes I simply cannot spare an hour from my duties – mostly wading through mountains of paperwork! – to hear the voice of my own loved one... I do think about you, darling, practically every moment of the day and even when I am engaged on some absorbing task, a training flight or trying to make returns to the Gruppe quartermaster, you are there in my subconscious — a beautiful, benign spirit urging me on to do my best at whatever it may be. Does this make sense to you, dearest?

Please promise me, darling Mathilde, that you will take cover if and when there is any danger from raids. We are not officially informed when enemy aircraft have made attacks and not knowing can be as worrying as hearing details. I know it can be very unpleasant in those airless shelters, herded in with every sort of person, but you are too precious to me to take any risks and now I have two of you to worry about! Now I must hurry to catch the collection from HQ and return to filling in forms! All my deepest love, sweetheart, please give my regards to Greta when you write.

Ever you own devoted,

Peter

From: Oberleutnant Peter von Vorzik
III Gruppe JG233
Solingen
To: Edith von Vorzik
Apt 2, 47 Scharnhorst Straße
Berlin

26th January 1941

My Dear Edith,

I was so pleased to have your letter with the details of father's funeral. Yes, I am sure it was a moving ceremony; so many memories are buried with him while, at the same time, so many memories are revived by such an occasion. From what you write I am sure he would have been pleased at the simplicity of the service. Everything he did, everything about him, always had a simplicity and directness; he liked formality but hated fuss.

Now that father has gone there is, indeed, little reason to maintain Adlersee as it was, as it has been these last few years. I fully agree with what you and Christian say about its immediate use and have written to him suggesting that he goes ahead with whatever arrangements he thinks suitable. What we should do with the Schloss in the more distant future remains to be settled. For myself, although I had an idyllic boyhood there, I retain only the faintest sentimental feeling for it. My happiest memories are centred on the grounds: the park, the lake, the farm – all the outdoor games and adventures – not so much on the stone and plasterwork. (I have been wondering if my Märklin toy railway is still packed away in one of the attics? There should also be a large model of the Emden which is propelled by hot air which was left to me by a cousin. If the SS does take over the Schloss as a convalescent home I hope these toys and any others will be brought to Berlin with the "valuables". Who knows, if Mathilde has a boy he might well obtain the same pleasure from them as I did.)

Yes, I would very much like to have father's wristwatch as a memento as well as a photograph or two – one for framing and one for my wallet, but such details can be resolved later when I have leave which will not be for some time. I do want to say how very grateful I am to you and Christian for carrying the burden that father's death has imposed and feel rather guilty that I have not contributed in any way.

Most importantly, dear Edith, as I have written to Christian, we must see that you receive a fair portion of father's estate after valuation and all the attendant taxes and dues have been paid and settled. Father belonged to a generation when all females were expected to have half-shares or none at all; times have changed – and our National Socialist government decrees that women are an important part of society so it is only right and proper that you should receive what is due to you.

I understand that Werner will be staying on at Adlersee whatever happens. He has been invaluable during this past year or so and although (I think) he is a similar age to father he seems to have a strong constitution. He is devoted to Adlersee (I think father's death will have affected him as much as any of us) and it is right that he should see out his last years there; if it does become a convalescent home there will be medical attention on the spot.

Perhaps the most important subject you mention is the possibility of your own marriage. I do not think one can force such things. Of course, it is possible to create opportunities and increase chances of meeting the right person and you have done just that by going to Berlin instead of being shut away at Adlersee. But what will be, will be. I am sure, whether you are expecting it or not, Fate will ordain that someone suitable, someone with whom you will find yourself in love, and who loves you, will suddenly be there. Think how unexpected, unplanned, was my meeting with Mathilde and Christian's with Frieda. In just the same way you will find the right person. When that happens you can start to worry whether the time is propitious or not. I just hope, dear sister, that when it occurs you will be as deliriously happy as I am to have found my own darling wife. Beware of matchmakers!

I have exhorted Mathilde to take cover whenever there is an air-raid warning and I hope you will do the same. You are even more vulnerable in central Berlin and although the raids may not be heavy (certainly not as heavy as we are bombing British cities) there is still considerable danger even from bomb-blast and flying glass. So, dear Edith, keep yourself safe for your future husband and your

Ever loving brother,
Peter

Oberleutnant Peter von Vorzik
Journal entry

2nd February 1941

Today I was involved in another death, one that affected me much more than father's. It was Hans Zahle, flying as Katschmarek to Otto Ebert. The Staffel was returning from a cross-country navigational exercise and Zahle made a careless landing, his final approach too high and too slow: his Emil stalled, nose-dived less than 20 m into the ground and flipped over on its back. Zahle was thrown clear but was terribly injured, losing an arm as he was catapulted through the cockpit canopy. He was still alive when the ground crew reached him, screaming like a trapped animal, but he died before he reached the Gruppe medical hut. It was an accident, the result of pilot error, but there is this awful feeling of being partly responsible. Perhaps I should have made a point of reminding the pilots, especially the new ones from Werneuchen, that the Me109, although it is a formidable fighting machine, is a tricky aircraft to fly, particularly at take-off and landing and unforgiving if one is careless or imprecise. Such advice would be superfluous – and even insulting – to the older, experienced pilots, of course, but perhaps the younger ones need to be reminded until their handling of the aircraft becomes almost automatic – and even that can be dangerous. A moment's inattention can be disastrous.

Some of the pilots have their wives and girlfriends in rented homes or apartments near the base, although it is officially discouraged – some of the Staffelkapitans have even forbidden it. I have been tempted to suggest to Mathilde that she might like to rent a small apartment at Solingen or even stay with her mother and aunt in Cologne, but I have decided against it. Naturally, it would be marvellous if she were nearby, to be able to enfold her in my arms after a tiring or worrying day at the base but, in reality, it could prove a desperate distraction and a drain on my physical and mental energy. Even so, it is a tantalising thought and each night as I get into my narrow little bed I indulge in fantasies before falling asleep. I hope, in the near future, to be able to take weekend leave during which Mathilde can once more join me at the Hotel Orpheus in Cologne.

The recent bad weather has hampered flying and our training exercises are behind schedule. The accident to Zahle's Emil brought the total of unserviceable aircraft in the Staffel to four; one of them is Kurt's (a constant misfire in the engine) so I have sent him on seven days' leave. He has gone to his parents in Hamburg; his affair with Michelle in Rouen seems to have reached a natural conclusion. He says that he wrote to her some weeks ago, before Christmas, but she has not replied. "Doubtless she has fallen for the charms of some young Wehrmacht officer," he remarked with a smile when I ventured to ask him about her. So far as I know he has not found any female company in Solingen although, according to gossip in the mess, there is no scarcity of young women in the town's cafés and bars who are ready to be friendly to any fighter pilot in uniform. I cannot help comparing Kurt's dutiful devotion to his family with my own rather cavalier attitude to mine during the last year or so. But then, I did have Mathilde as an irresistable inducement to stay in Berlin rather than make the long journey to Adlersee.

Now I must face the melancholy task of writing to Zahle's parents, a formal letter of sympathy in their bereavement, enclosed with his personal effects. I believe he was their only son and I cannot even make the consolatory comment that he died defending the Fatherland.

From: SS-Gruppenführer Count Christian von Vorzik
RSHA Prinz Albertstraße
Berlin
To: Oberleutnant Peter von Vorzik
III Gruppe JG233
Solingen

11th February 1941

My Dear Peter,
Thank you for your letter of January 24th. I am glad you agree with me (as I felt sure you would) about arranging for Edith to have a fair share of father's estate, and also about the future of Adlersee. I have written to the relevant departments about taking over the Schloss and in the unlikely case of anything happening to me in the next few weeks, here are the names of the men you would need to contact: Obergruppenführer Oswald Pohl of the Economic and Administrative Department; Obergruppenführer Maximilian von Herff of the Personnel Department, and Waffen-SS General Hans Jüttner, head of the Operational Department. And, of course, Reinhard is always there on a personal basis.

As I intimated in my last letter I shall be leaving Berlin almost immediately for a tour of the Balkans, gathering what information I can for both Reinhard and Walter Schellenberg (you remember, he was my best man?) of the Ausland SD. The whole area is a hell's kitchen of intrigue and the Reichsführer-SS has told Reinhard he wishes to be kept informed of developments so as to keep on level terms with von Ribbentrop's machinations.

A few days ago Field Marshal List obtained permission from the Bulgarian General Staff for our troops to pass from Rumania through Bulgaria if – as seems increasingly likely – we need to assist the Italians in Greece (how in hell could those idiots have lost Tobruk to such a tiny force of Australians?). Happily, the Bulgarians are very pro-German because they live in fear of the Russians but the Jugoslavs are proving as wily as the Turks in waiting to see what will happen and which way to jump. I understand that Prince Paul has been invited to meet the Führer at the Berghof which should hasten matters to a successful conclusion. The trouble is, that country is in turmoil with itself and von Ribbentrop thinks there will be some advantage in playing off the Croats against the Serbs. His handling of such sensitive matters, however, is usually so clumsy he only makes things worse – and to our ultimate disadvantage.

Anyway, the result of all this is that I am doing a round trip to our legations and embassies in Bucharest, Sofia and Belgrade, returning sometime next month via Vienna. Most of the time I will be incognito or ostensibly making good-will contacts but, as Reinhard has instructed, using my eyes and ears and making daily reports. All of this is very confidential so, once more, I must ask you to destroy this as soon as you have read it.

I cannot take Frieda with me on this trip but in any case she is dancing as a guest artist with the Vienna Opera Ballet for two weeks at the end of the month and I hope I shall be able to meet her in that city when I complete my tour. Lina has promised to keep an eye on both Edith and Mathilde while I am away. She (Lina) has promised to give one or two little dinner parties and musical evenings to which she will invite a number of suitable young men for Edith to meet ... the "unobtrusive manipulation" you suggest in your last letter!

It occurred to me some days ago that you might very well avail yourself of the little DKW at Adlersee for your personal transport. Werner does not need it and it is only deteriorating in the garage there. (The Maybach is under covers but I think we may as well sell it for whatever it will fetch, do you not agree?) It could be a very useful little runabout for you when other transport is not available. I am sure you are in a position to supplement the petrol ration... ? Werner would be able to drive it from Adlersee to Solingen, staying overnight en route, if necessary, and returning by train. I leave it to you to organise.

Write to me as usual at the RSHA, your letters will be forwarded with the diplomatic mail and reach me very quickly, we have a very efficient communications network!

As always, every good wish for your safety and success,

Your affectionate brother,
Christian
Heil Hitler!

PS If you do not wish to make use of the DKW we could offer it to Edith. Although she does not drive I could easily arrange for her to learn with my own chauffeur. C.

From: Oberleutnant Peter von Vorzik
III Gruppe JG233
Solingen
To: Mathilde von Vorzik
23 Hevelius Straße
Grunewald

17th February 1941

My Darling Mathilde,
Marvellous news! We are on stand-by to collect our new aircraft and I will then be stationed at Jüterbog just 50 km from Grunewald! Had I been given a choice I could scarcely have selected a closer posting! I am unable to give you an exact date but it will certainly be sometime within the coming month. Of course, most of my time will be taken up at the base but I will only be just over an hour's drive from home. I do not know how long I will be stationed so close, there are many rumoured imminent developments in the political and military situation which I cannot mention but, sweetheart, we will take advantage of the situation as often as we can.

Yesterday I had a letter from Christian in which he made the suggestion that I take over the little DKW that father bought just after the war began.

I was about to write to him and say it would be of little use to me at Solingen when the good news came at this morning's briefing which completely changes the situation. Being so close it will be marvellous to have independent transport. When I move again (I have to be realistic, I may only be at Jüterbog a month or two) Edith, or your dear self, could make use of it if you both learn to drive. Frankly, I must say I would feel uneasy thinking of you alone in the midst of Berlin traffic, especially in these coming months. But we will see. Anyway, however short my new posting will be, we must think of it as something of a holiday and make the most of it.

Hoping, darling, that you are feeling well and that this news will be a lovely surprise,

Ever you loving husband,
Peter

From: Oberleutnant Peter Von Vorzik
III Gruppe JG233
Solingen
To: Edith von Vorzik
Apt 2, 47 Scharnhorst Straße
Berlin

18th February 1941

My Dear Edith,

Before I forget (I had already forgotten until I suddenly remembered in the middle of the night!) it is Mathilde's birthday on the 27th and I rely on you to find something really special for me to give her. I do not care how much it costs I just want it to be something she will really be happy to receive. Jewellery? A fur coat? (The winter is not yet over.) An expensive handbag? An evening dress? These are random and not very imaginative suggestions, but I am sure you will think of something and Mathilde may even have seen or admired something and mentioned to you in conversation. I was very remiss in not giving her anything at Christmas (in common with the rest of the family whom I neglected!) and she had had the foresight to buy a splendid wallet for me when we were in Paris so it is imperative that I make up for it with this present.

My real news is that soon I shall be stationed at Jüterbog just 50 km to the south of Berlin so I shall be able, at least for a few weeks, to make several visits home and see you all – isn't that wonderful? Christian suggested I might make use of the DKW at Adlersee and I was on the point of saying no when this news came; now it will, indeed, be very useful. Can I make further demands on your kindness and forbearance to arrange for Werner to drive it to Berlin? It will be rather a challenging task for him but I think he may be able to do it in easy stages – Nuremberg and Leipzig seem likely overnight stops. He could stay overnight in some small Berlin hotel and return to Munich by train. Of course I will pay all his expenses and will reimburse you either through the post or as soon as I get to Berlin. I am sorry to burden you with this, dear Edith, but as you know, Christian is away.

Now I must hurry to the post.

Ever your devoted – and grateful! – brother,

Peter

Oberleutnant Peter von Vorzik
Journal entry

20th February 1941

I am filled with schoolboyish excitement. First, of course, at the news that I am going to be stationed fairly close to Grunewald; second, that we shall soon be receiving the new F Series, together with JG2 and JG26, which are stationed on the Channel coast. There has been some delay in receiving these aircraft as there were three mysterious accidents with the early production versions. Now the mystery has been resolved. As I have mentioned previously, one of the aerodynamic refinements has been the elimination of the struts supporting the tailplane and elevators. Apparently, this led to a sympathetic vibration set up at certain engine revolutions which resulted in structural failure of the tail empennage. That has now been strengthened with the application of stiffening plates and all is well. All the pilots of the Staffel are as excited as I am at the prospect of receiving the new aircraft and engaging the enemy with them, although I think there will be little immediate opportunity for that if we are at Jüterbog. Presumably, we shall be defending Berlin but as all the RAF raids are at night it is unlikely that we shall be flying on night interception missions; the Me109 is not suitable for such operational duties.

It could be that Jüterbog is just a staging post on the way east or south. Christian's letters to me have made plain that the Balkans are in a state of ferment and we have been told, with great emphasis on secrecy, that Luftwaffe units have been quietly taking over airfields in Rumania for some weeks – the ground forces, signals, administration and supply units, flak defences and construction groups, have all been there since last November, making ready for the flying units whose purpose is the defence of the Rumanian oilfields. It is thought that the British may be preparing to go to the aid of the Greeks and their mainland bases would put the oilfields at risk. Once again we have forestalled our enemies! It could even be that, were I to be sent to Rumania, I could meet up with Christian there although that is rather a fanciful idea.

From: Edith von Vorzik
Apt 2, 47 Scharnhorst Straße
Berlin
To: Oberleutnant Peter von Vorzik
III Gruppe JG233
Solingen

21st February 1941

My Dear Peter,

I hasten to reply to your letter in which you make two important requests and to let you know I have put them both in hand. First, I have spoken to Lina about a present for Mathilde as she, Lina, has such good taste and fashion sense. Our choice, based on your suggestions, has narrowed to either a piece of jewellery or a fur coat. We are waiting for your decision so, dear brother, will you reply by return of post or, if you have the opportunity, telephone me? Time is very short so if you manage to reach a telephone it would give us an extra day or two to carry out your instructions. I will probably have to leave the ultimate choice to Lina as I have very little time off to go shopping and she, I think, is glad to have something to do! Speaking for myself, I think jewellery is probably the most practical choice; good pieces always keep their price and there is something special about jewels which last the lifetime of the wearer and always remain a love-token from the giver. Alternatively, every woman loves the luxury and warmth of furs and even as I write there is a bitter wind blowing from the east and the temperature is below zero. Lina says that she knows a good furrier who has taken over what was a Jewish firm. Whatever you choose, she says she will be able to arrange a very advantageous discount through Reinhard's office.

With regard to the DKW, I managed to catch Christian before he left on his Balkan tour (he left yesterday). He said that Werner would be quite incapable of driving to Berlin; he can manage to potter around the roads at Adlersee and even venture as far as Munich but anything else is beyond him now. Christian has therefore arranged for his own driver, Walter, to collect the car while Christian is away. All being well, it should be at Grunewald by the time you arrive there yourself.

Now, dear Peter, I want to tell you something in great confidence. It is not of great importance but I would like to enlist you as an ally! Whatever can it be, I hear you asking. Well, here is the story, such as it is. Two nights ago the Heydrichs gave a small dinner party, mainly as a good-will gesture for Christian on the eve of his departure. At the reception before dinner I was introduced to a young man, Hauptsturmführer Willi Haase, who is one of Christian's aides. He was very attentive and was placed next to me at dinner. After dinner Reinhard gave one of his violin recitals and, again, Haase arranged to sit next to me. At the end of the evening Christian (who had driven with me to the Heydrichs) said he had various things to discuss with Reinhard and that Haase would take me back to my apartment. It was all so obviously contrived! He is quite an attractive young man, tall and blond – not unlike a younger version of Reinhard – but, I thought, somewhat pompous and overbearing. Anyway, after we had left Schlachtensee, instead of joining the Avus, he took a left turn on to the road that borders Lake Havel, saying it was such a beautiful night (it was frosty, with a full moon) did I mind if we took a little drive. I said I had to be in my office by nine o'clock and would rather we drove straight back to Berlin. However, he kept on driving along the borders of the lake, then stopped the car and attempted to kiss me. I resisted and there was a rather unseemly struggle. Eventually he gave up and we returned to Berlin in silence. Somewhat sulkily he apologised for his "impetuous" behaviour and said he hoped we could meet again. I replied that, under the circumstances, I thought it would be unlikely. Looking back upon the incident I can view it with some detachment – it is not without its humorous side – but I was furious at the time. Why I am telling you all this, dear Peter, is that I hope you will find some way, in the nicest and most casual way, of course, please do not make it into a drama, to let Christian know I do not want to have these introductions arranged for me, certainly not at the moment. Perhaps, when I am older and facing spinsterhood, I shall be glad of matrimonial assistance, but not now.

In haste, let me know as soon as possible your decision about Mathilde's present.

Your loving sister,
Edith

From: Mathilde von Vorzik
23 Hevelius Straße
Grunewald
To: Oberleutnant Peter von Vorzik
III Gruppe JG233
Solingen

21st February 1941

My Dearest, Darling Peter,
I could scarcely believe the marvellous news in your letter and have read it and read it over and over again just to recreate the same excitement I had when I read it for the first time. I realise, as you say, that it may only be for a short time, darling, but what a thrill it will be just to see you once more. These last few weeks have seemed an eternity, especially as the winter has been so bleak; our last meeting seeming like seven months instead of seven weeks ago. I have to admit that I feel somewhat marooned here in Grunewald, with mother in Cologne, you in Solingen, Edith busy most of the day and Lina bound up in her own social whirl. I have seen her once or twice for morning coffee and we had a little shopping expedition to the Ku'damm last week, but by myself time passes very slowly. Please don't think, darling, that I am complaining, but that is one reason why your letter was so exciting. Of course, I realise that you will be involved with your duties all day long but just to think of you so close, only an hour's drive away, does wonders for my morale.

Last week I had an examination by the gynaecologist and everything seems fine except that this nausea still persists. As yet I do not seem to have developed any of the cravings that pregnant women are said to have but be prepared to find me feasting off herrings and chocolate!

Lina has just telephoned to say she is planning a little supper party for my birthday next week and did I have anything special to request for the menu. It is very sweet of her to do this (she has done so for several years) and I will be delighted to go but hope that I will be escorted by you, my darling. Now I am hurrying to put this in the post in case you are already planning to leave for Jüterbog.

Hoping every minute to have your call, hear your voice.

Ever your own,

Mathilde

Oberleutnant Peter von Vorzik
Journal entry

2nd March 1941

Here we are – the Staffel, that is – taking delivery at long last of our new F Series, built by the Arado Aircraft Works here at Oschelsleben where the company are subcontractors to Messerschmitt. First brief flying impressions are that the aircraft is, indeed, a great improvement over the old Emil: faster overall in level flight, climb and dive, with a tighter turning circle and generally more manoeuvrable – though there are one or two new characteristics that one must take into account. For example, when diving at speeds above 400 kph the ailerons induce a turning effect which can only be countered by using both hands and, in some cases both knees as well, on the control column. There is, however, one rather controversial change that has been the subject of a lot of heated argument, and that is the alteration of the armament and its disposition. Whereas the old Emil had two cowling-mounted machineguns and two wing-mounted cannons of 20mm, the new F-2 with which we are equipped, replaces the wing cannons with a single 15mm cannon mounted between the cylinder banks of the engine and firing through the airscrew spinner. Although the new cannon has a faster rate of fire, the weight of fire is considerably less than before. The controversy does not stop there; grouping the armament in the centre of the aircraft helps manoeuvrability which is vitally important in combat but demands greater accuracy in aiming, rather than the wider spread of fire from wing-mounted guns. Apparently, Major Adolf Galland, one of our highest scoring aces and Kommodore of JG26, thinks that one cannon is quite inadequate, particularly when attacking bombers, and that the new young recruits coming from the fighter schools will not initially possess the requisite marksmanship when engaged in a dogfight with enemy fighters. On the other hand, another of our highest scoring fighter pilots, Oberstleutnant Werner Mölders, Kommodore of JG51, welcomes the new armament and considers that one centrally mounted cannon is worth two in the wings – but then he is a superb marksman! Rumour has it that Hauptmann Walter Oesau of JG1 has even refused to fly the F Series. For myself, I will wait and see how things turn out during my first encounter with the enemy in the new aircraft. Like everyone else in the Staffel I am impatient to encounter the enemy now, especially anxious to meet the new Spitfire that is coming into service, but that is unlikely while we are stationed near Berlin. I am like a child with a new toy; I go out and walk around my new aircraft, admiring its sleek new silhouette (Varasch remarked that the big spinner and bulbous cowling have a phallic profile!) and it looks resplendent in its bright new camouflage scheme: the fuselage, upper wing and tail surfaces have light green mottling over a pale grey ground, the undersurfaces remain pale blue, as before, and the nose, wing tips and rudder retain the Gruppe's recognition colour of bright blue. The spinner on my aircraft is painted white to denote that it belongs to the Staffelkapitan, as do the chevrons on the fuselage. Once again my own insignia of the flying leopard has been painted just below the cockpit. As I have remarked before, such a profusion of markings seem to negate the intention of camouflage. One other detail: my twenty-one victories have been recorded by vertical white strokes on the rudder. My earnest hope is that I shall soon be adding more.

With help and advice from Edith, ably assisted by Lina, I decided on a triple row of pearls for Mathilde's birthday. It was either that or a smallish diamond brooch, both priced around 25,000 marks including a generous discount from the jeweller, Sloninsky, arranged by Lina. Edith said she thought Mathilde would find the pearls more practical, she could wear them with a two-piece suit or with evening dress and she was sure Mathilde did not already have such a set. I had hoped there might be a chance I would get to Grunewald in time for Mathilde's birthday, but it was not to be. Edith is keeping the necklace for me to give when I do manage a visit.

Telephoning from here is much easier than it was at Solingen, I got through to Edith almost at once and was able to have a ten-minute conversation with Mathilde on her name-day although I could tell from the catch in her voice that she was near to tears. It will not be long, now, before we are together again; I long to hold her in my arms, to feel the warmth of her body against mine, to release all the pent up passion that has grown inside me each day since our last meetings in Cologne. I wonder, though, if love-making affects pregnancy? I am very ignorant of such matters and do not know whom to believe. I asked, tentatively, in the mess and got very conflicting answers. Varasch, who is unmarried but very much a ladies' man and may, he says, jokingly, have fathered several children but never waited to find out, gave it as his opinion that copulation can continue right up to the time of birth though not in the usual position! My innocent question led to some very lewd suggestions. More seriously, Kurt said he had heard that penetration, after a number of weeks, can damage the baby which seems to make sense. I am sure my darling Matilde may know and in any case there are a variety of ways in which one can obtain sexual satisfaction. All I want is to be near her.

I have made a call to Claus Grüber at Rechlin, telling him that I am going to be within fairly easy reach of him and would like to take him up on his invitation to visit the testing establishment. He was enthusiastic about my visiting him, said he had many exciting things to show me and was looking forward to a bibulous reunion. (I remember that he was always fond of beer and schnapps.) We have already had some unofficial and very secret information about a completely new fighter designed by the Focke-Wulf company which, I understand, has a superior performance even to our F Series but it is still in the development stage. I heard this from one of the Arado engineers; apparently the new aircraft is also going to be built here at Oschelsleben and the company are already tooling up for the first batch of production aircraft. He also said that they were carrying out a lot of development flying at Rechlin so no doubt I shall see the new aircraft when I visit Claus. It is all very exciting but not so stimulating to the nervous system as the contemplation of holding my darling Mathilde once more.

From: Mathilde von Vorzik
23 Hevelius Straße
Grunewald
To: Oberleutnant Peter von Vorzik
III Gruppe JG233
Jüterbog

12th March 1941

My Own Darling Peter,

It is only twenty minutes since you went and here I am, sitting in bed, wearing my lovely pearls (I will not sleep in them!) sipping a cup of hot chocolate and finding it necessary to scribble you a few lines. It is strange, but having had you close to me these last two short days, the sense of loss is more acute, now, than when we have been parted for weeks and the need to perpetuate that closeness is overwhelming. The easiest, most immediate way to do it is to put pen to paper. You will not have reached Jüterbog yet! I have nothing to say except how much I love you, how I adore your beautiful, strong, lithe body, your smile, the way you put your head slightly to one side and look up to see what effect your words have had. Did you know you do that? To me it is a particularly endearing mannerism, a look that shows you hope your words have not been too forcefully expressed or been hurtful in any way. It is a part of your naturally kind and gentle manner; the same tenderness that is there even in our most extreme moments of passion. Believe me, dearest one, I could write pages and pages enumerating all your marvellous physical, mental and emotional qualities – perhaps I will do it, just for my own secret perusal! It was typically considerate – and sweetly naive! – of you to wonder if my pregnancy precluded making love. Be assured, darling, that your comrade who said it could continue almost to the time of birth is quite correct – all other things being in order, of course. Pregnancy does bring accompanying symptoms that affect one's well-being and emotional disposition, but be assured that during the forthcoming weeks I will be waiting to give myself to you without reservation. As I always will.

Yours, for eternity,
Mathilde

From: Edith von Vorzik
Apt 2, 47 Scharnhorst Straße
Berlin
To: Oberleutnant Peter von Vorzik
III Gruppe JG233
Jüterbog

14th March 1941

My Dear Peter,

Just a line to say what a joy it was to see you on your short visit; I do hope you will be able to come again soon now that you are so close. You seemed to be in robust health and good spirits due, no doubt, to your imminent reunion with Mathilde. I know (because we have subsequently spoken on the telephone) what a wonderful tonic it was for her, too, to have you with her once again. I am no authority, of course, but I know pregnancy can often be accompanied by all sorts of physical and mental changes, including depression (particularly after the baby is born) and I am conscious that Mathilde has been feeling rather lonely these last few weeks. It would have helped if her mother had been with her at this time but it is not my place to make such suggestions. Both Lina and I try and telephone her as often as we can but with no one else in the house the time must drag very slowly for her. Perhaps, after all, it would not have been such a bad idea for her to have taken up that offer from *Die Frau*.

Anyway, the pearls have been a great success. Mathilde was thrilled with the gift, not just because they are so lovely (I am looking forward to seeing her wear them) but also she was genuinely surprised that you remembered her birthday. She said she knows just how burdensome your position as Staffelkapitan is, what a big responsibility you carry and how every moment of your day is taken up with operational duties. "It is very different from some businessman going to an office every day and perhaps forgetting his wife's birthday," she said, "Peter is involved with matters of life and death all his waking hours in a way that we simply cannot comprehend, so his remembering my name day was specially touching." I tell you this just so you know how very understanding she is.

I am trying to arrange a little evening with Mathilde, Frieda and Lina, perhaps a visit to a theatre or concert although, being the only unmarried one I might seem a little *de trop*! Frieda is leaving soon to dance with the Vienna Opera and is looking forward to meeting Christian there. She is such a nice young woman although she always seems rather shy in our company. Once, when I met her with her theatre friends, she was much livelier than I had ever seen her which, I suppose, is to be expected. I think she is intimidated by Christian's SS colleagues as, indeed, I am. One always has the feeling of being watched, as if one's behaviour and conversation is being noted down for future reference. Do you find that? I had a postcard from Christian, sent from Sofia, a picture of the new cathedral of St. Alexander which looks very Byzantine. He just said he was well and hoped we were, nothing else. Have you heard from him?

Your encouraging words about taking up Christian's offer of learning to drive under Walter's tutelage has helped me to make up my mind: yes, I will learn. As you said, it is a very useful skill to have, particularly nowadays and I am sure I will overcome my nervousness at the prospect. I can quite see how you would feel nervous at the thought of Mathilde driving about Berlin by herself but after the baby has been born it might be a good idea for her to learn, too. Perhaps I could give her lessons if I prove to be an apt pupil! Even as I write these words I see you grimacing at the thought! Anyway, I intend to start right away – with Christian away Walter will have more time to spare. If I can control his big Mercedes I should have no trouble with the DKW. Personal transport is such a luxury now; as you may have noticed, the trams in Berlin are always impossibly crowded and seem to be less and less frequent. When I make the journey to Grunewald now it takes me much longer than when I first came to Berlin just a few months ago.

Lina has just telephoned to invite me to a little soirée she is giving. I feel a bit suspicious ... another situation like the one with Haase, I wonder? Anyway, I shall go – her meals are always so delicious!

Looking forward to seeing you again soon, dearest Peter.

Ever your loving sister,
Edith

Oberleutnant Peter von Vorzik
Journal entry

21st March 1941

I have now made two visits to Grunewald to be with my darling Mathilde and I manage to telephone her almost every day. It is marvellous to be so close and have such a respite from daily duty and routine. In a totally different way I have been tremendously excited by a visit I made to Claus Grüber at Rechlin. What I saw there is absolutely fascinating and tremendously reassuring – our scientists, designers and engineers are developing such astonishing aircraft that we can be assured of technical supremacy over all our enemies and rivals for years to come. There are, of course, some things I cannot confide even to this personal and private record for fear that, somehow, it could fall into the wrong hands – however improbable that might seem – but I have been given a privileged glimpse of a future when even our new F Series and the new Focke-Wulf 190 fighter will seem obsolescent and years out-of-date.

I took the Staffel's little Taifun and made the short flight in under an hour. The airfield at Rechlin was extremely busy and I had to wait some minutes for landing permission; once on the ground I found myself surrounded by unfamiliar shapes and silhouettes, single and twin-engined aircraft of various configurations, even unfamiliar sounds from the latest engines that our new aircraft are using. Claus was amused by my schoolboyish enthusiasm. "I told you there would be much to interest you," he said, after greeting me in the operations room. He has changed very little during the last three years since we were at Werneuchen together. He looks a little gaunt in the face and walks with a noticeable limp; once or twice, while he was showing me around and negotiating the narrow gantries and walkways of the hangars and engineering shops, I saw him wince with pain. He was among the unlucky few who were wounded during the early campaign in Poland when his Emil was hit by groundfire and he had a finger shot away from his left hand. He was wounded again – his knee, the second time – during the fighting over France last summer, and invalided out of JG2. Now he does what he calls "recreational flying" and performs important work liaising between the Erprobungsstelle and the various aircraft manufacturers, mainly Messerschmitt and Focke-Wulf, as well as the engine manufacturers,

Daimler-Benz, Junkers and BMW. Other aircraft companies, such as Arado, Blohm and Voss, Dornier, Fieseler, Heinkel and Henschel, as well as their many subcontractors, are dealt with by numerous other members of the staff here. I had no idea that the Erprobungsstelle was so extensive and elaborate and, of course, this is not the only experimental and development base, there are several others around the country.

Inevitably, when we had finished discussing aviation topics, the talk turned to tactics, strategy and politics and I was astonished at some of the things that were said and the sort of inside knowledge that Claus and his colleagues seemed to have. All of them were critically contemptuous of the Italians in general and their air force, the Regia Aeronautica, in particular.

What really surprised me – well, astounded me, actually – was the general opinion that it would not be long before we would be fighting Russia. I said that, of course, the Führer and other Party leaders had always inveighed against Communism and we had always been told that the Soviet political system was a danger to our country, but that was back in the twenties when Germany was weak. Now that we had built up our strength and shown that we were invincible the Russian threat had receded entirely. There was the 1939 non-aggression pact, as well as a mutually beneficial trade agreement, and the Soviet Foreign Minister, Vyacheslav Molotov, was in Berlin only last November. Everyone looked at me and smiled indulgently, as one would at a child, as I said this. As the conversation progressed and other opinions were given, founded on facts and information of which I had no knowledge, I was made to feel very naive. Someone said that the Russians were building up huge military forces which they would ultimately use against us, that Stalin had always intended that Communism would triumph everywhere and he would not hesitate to achieve it through force of arms. The non-aggression pact was just a stalling move and only Germany could save Europe from the Communist menace. Now that we had settled things in the west we would have to do the same in the east.

I went to bed in the nice little room they had given me, befuddled by drink and bemused by the conversation.

From: SS-Gruppenführer Count Christian von Vorzik
SD HQ
Morzinplatz
Vienna
To: Oberleutnant Peter von Vorzik
III Gruppe JG233
Jüterbog

26th March 1941

My Dear Peter,

Here I am in beautiful Vienna after a most interesting and satisfactory tour of the Balkans. Our policies in this region came to fruition last night when, at a big reception at the Hofburg, the Premier and Foreign Minister of Jugoslavia joined the Tripartite Pact. The Führer was in great spirits as this agreement now allows our forces to isolate the British in Greece and fling them back into the Mediterranean. Although, as you know, the SD have their differences with Reichsminister von Ribbentrop one must allow him his due in successfully coercing the guileful Serbs and Croats into this pact – the Italians having messed things up so much by their stupid meddling.

Tonight I am going to the Staatsoper to see my dear Frieda in a revival of an old ballet, *Médée et Jason*, with music by Gluck. Afterwards we are having a little party at Sacher's. As you can imagine, I am looking forward so much to our reunion; these last three or four weeks have been somewhat irksome and Vienna seems particularly lovely after the rather drab cities of Rumania and Bulgaria. Frieda finishes her engagement at the weekend and then we shall be returning to Berlin. She has been offered a season at the Paris Opera (you remember meeting Serge Lifar there during our honeymoon visit?). She has been invited to make guest appearances in *Giselle* and she says it is an honour she cannot refuse, a great step in her career. I have to admit that I had hoped that, after our marriage, she might agree to retire from the stage but I can see, at the moment, it would be cruel to ask that, just when she is having such success. Anyway, I am happy to have an excuse to visit Paris once again!

Hoping to see you in Berlin.

Affectionately,
Christian
Heil Hitler!

Führer HQ

27th March 1941

DIRECTIVE NO 25

The military revolt in Jugoslavia has changed the political position in the Balkans. Jugoslavia, even if it makes initial professions of loyalty, must be regarded as an enemy and beaten down as quickly as possible. It is my intention to break into Jugoslavia in the general direction of Belgrade and to deal an annihilating blow to the Jugoslav forces. The extreme southern region of Jugoslavia will be cut off from the rest of the country and will be occupied as a base from which the German-Italian offensive against Greece can be continued. As soon as sufficient forces are available and the weather allows, the ground installations of the Jugoslav Air Force and the city of Belgrade will be destroyed from the air by continual day and night attack. All forces still available in Bulgaria and Rumania will be committed to the attacks which will be carried out from the Sofia area to the north-west and from the Kyustendil-Gorna Dzhumaya area to the west, with the exception that a force of about one division, with air support, must remain to protect the Rumanian oilfields. The possibility of bringing X Air Corps into action from Italian bases will be considered. The protection of convoys to Africa must however continue to be ensured. The Air Force is authorised to begin immediate discussions with the Italian and Hungarian High Commands in order to delimit the area of the air operations of the three powers. Commanders-in-Chief will inform me, through the High Command of the Armed Forces (OKW), of their plans for the operation, and of related problems.

Adolf Hitler

From: Mathilde von Vorzik
23 Hevelius Straße
Grunewald
To: Oberleutnant Peter von Vorzik
III Gruppe JG233
c/o Fliegerkorps HQ

6th April 1941

My Darling Peter,
As soon as I heard your voice on the telephone this morning I knew what you were going to say. I had already heard the early morning radio report

that our armies have crossed the borders of Greece and Jugoslavia so even when the telephone rang I knew it was you to tell me that you were being sent somewhere. When you were posted to Jüterbog you warned me that it might not be for long and so it has proved, although I did not think it would be a mere three weeks – the shortest posting you have had. As you say, darling, this is war and events move swiftly; we must be grateful for our brief moments of happiness and look forward to the day when it will all be over and my anxiety for you at an end. Of course, my one big worry, now, is where you will be sent. As I write I think of your plane taking off and flying south to the war zone, although I take comfort from your assurance that the Greeks and Jugoslavs have only small air forces and you will not be at risk in the same way as our soldiers on the ground. I just pray, dearest, that this new development will be completed soon and will hasten a conclusion to all the hostilities. The radio (which I keep on all the time) has just announced that our army in North Africa is advancing westwards and driving the British and Australians back towards Egypt. Surely with these successes the fighting will be over soon?

As you told me, I am sending this to Fliegerkorps HQ and hope it reaches you quickly. Let me know as soon as you can your new address, dearest, just a postcard will do.

Meanwhile, all my love.

Keep yourself safe for your own

Mathilde

PS As you asked, I have telephoned Edith with the news of your departure. She sends all her love and will be writing.

From: Oberleutnant Peter von Vorzik
III Gruppe JG233
Turnu-Severin
To: Mathilde von Vorzik
23 Hevelius Straße
Grunewald

9th April 1941

My Darling Mathilde,
To my astonishment your letter posted only three days ago reached me here this afternoon with the Staffel postbag, a most efficient

postal/courier service! There is not much I can tell you except that we are in modern, comfortable quarters and, at present, quite a long way from current hostilities. We shall be performing purely defensive patrols and, doubtless, boredom will be our greatest enemy. I shall have plenty of opportunity to play chess with Kurt – who always beats me. If you want to find me on the map we are close to the Danube, on a plain just south of the Carpathian mountains, about 160 km due west of Bucharest.

Yes, my dearest, my stay at Jüterbog was all too short but I am so glad we made the most of it and I had the opportunity to be with you again for those all-too-brief, ecstatically wonderful hours. I had fully anticipated that I would have been at that posting for two or three months, but it was not to be. Who could have foreseen that the political-military situation would have changed so rapidly, so totally? It was ironic that I had only just received a letter from Christian who had been celebrating a political triumph the day before! Anyway, I have every reason to suppose that we shall have restored the status quo in a very short time and I will once more find myself closer to home and your welcoming arms ...

There is no news, dearest, other than you hear on the radio and that I am in good health, well provided for, and looking forward to the time when we shall be together again. Please tell Edith and Christian that I will be writing to them as soon as I can – perhaps you will give them this new address, too?

All my love, dearest one.

Ever yours,
Peter

Oberleutnant Peter von Vorzik
Journal entry

14th April 1941

The Jugoslav army surrendered to our forces at Sarajevo yesterday although the king and his prime minister are reported to have escaped by plane to Greece where there is still fierce fighting. No planes from our Gruppe have been involved; indeed the bombing attacks on Belgrade were carried out at low level without fighter escort as the Jugoslavs had no anti-aircraft defences and a totally impotent air force. The city, according to radio reports, is in ruins. We have been carrying out uneventful patrols between our airfield here at Turnu-Severin and the oil refineries at Ploesti, about 200 km due east which is within comfortable range of our F Series at cruising speed. Were we to engage in combat over the refinery area no doubt we would be facing the same problems of short operational range as we had over southern England last summer – but then, no doubt, we would have bases closer to Ploesti.

It is all rather boring and we are all aching to use our new fighters in anger. We fly south of the Carpathian mountains which are heavily wooded and where, we are told, there are still packs of wolves and wild bears. I had been hoping that I might get leave long enough to fly to Bucharest; Christian has given me the address of Frieda's parents and other friends he has made in the city but there is no prospect of leave at the moment with the military situation in such a state of flux. None of this need have happened if that vainglorious Duce had not attacked Greece and Jugoslavia so foolishly. Everyone in the mess is convinced he was jealous of our military victories in Poland and the west and wanted to emulate them; instead he has involved us in coming to his aid in areas which are of no interest or military importance to us. It is a pity he did not use his forces to bolster his equally feeble efforts in Cyrenaica where they were being defeated by the British and Australians.

There is not much life here off base. The town is drab and the food in the cafés and restaurants unappetising. The people, too, are generally unattractive and rather boorish though friendly to us. The real problem is trying to avoid drinking too much in the mess at night, again through sheer boredom. The local wine is very pleasant and also cheap; we have ample supplies of German beer and even French brandy and champagne are available at a price. Kurt and I play chess almost every evening – I am getting better and beat him twice in succession this week and spend much time reading. Next week a troupe of dancers and singers is coming from Vienna to entertain us and there is talk of the Gruppe receiving its own cinematic equipment to be loaned out to each Staffel in rotation. The films in the local cinema are all old and the place is a real fleapit filled by the local peasantry and has been placed out of bounds to Luftwaffe personnel. According to gossip, when the airfield was being prepared by our building and maintenance units some months ago, the place was frequented by many prostitutes and there was an outbreak of venereal disease on the base. The Wehrmacht is known to have its own travelling brothels but that would not appeal to me – not now, anyway, not with my own darling Mathilde to dream and fantasise about. Varasch, of course, is already boasting about a local "conquest", a dark-haired Rumanian gypsy girl who works in one of the local taverns and who, he says, is "demandingly passionate". Some of the newer pilots drafted into the Staffel listen to his mess-room tales with avid interest but the rest of us take his lurid and lewd descriptions with a degree of scepticism.

Kurt has just come in to tell me of a news report that our new commander of Axis forces in the North African desert, General Irwin Rommel, has made rapid advances into Cyrenaica and is about to attack the British stronghold at Tobruk. Once again we have rushed to the rescue of the foolish Italians who have made a mess of things in this area, just as they did in Jugoslavia and Greece. Of course, Luftwaffe units are in close support and it seems we are the only ones without any chance of seeing action. Most frustrating! The only challenge I have is from Kurt who wants to avenge his recent defeat at chess but before I can engage him in another bout I have to make out all my state-of-equipment returns to the Staffel quartermaster. Boredom really is the most insidious enemy.

From: Edith von Vorzik
Apt 2, 47 Scharnhorst Straße
Berlin
To: Oberleutnant Peter von Vorzik
III Gruppe JG233
Turnu-Severin

17th April 1941

My Dear Peter,
Mathilde has given me your new address so I hasten to write to you as I know how much you like to receive mail, especially when you have been sent so far away once again. My life here in Berlin proceeds much the same except that I have two pieces of news that might interest you. First, I have had my first lessons in driving and Walter says I have a natural sensitivity that helps me to feel "at one with the car," as he puts it. I think that is pure flattery but I must say that after initial nerves (he made me drive straight away in the midst of Berlin traffic!) I do feel confident and actually enjoy driving very much. He is very patient with me even when

I crunch the gears but he has taught me to double-declutch and my gear changes now are quite smooth without the embarrassing jerks that I produced at first. Of course, I find that much of the traffic gives way to a Mercedes flying the SS pennant and it is amusing to see the surprise on people's faces when they observe a woman at the wheel! I shall be even more confident with the little DKW and will be able to visit Mathilde and take her for drives. Of course, dear Peter, the car will be yours when you come on leave.

The other news I have is of a personal nature. Two days after you left Jüterbog I met a most charming man at a reception at the Italian Embassy. (I had not wanted to go but Lina insisted.) He is Count Arturo Novarro-Badaelli, an aide to the military attaché here. He comes from a fine Milanese family; they have a palazzo in Lombardy and a villa near Rome, as well as a seaside villa at Riccione (his father was an aide-de-camp to Mussolini who has a villa there). He told me all this during our first meeting when we were talking about our childhoods. He said our family estates were only separated by the Alps and he knows Munich very well. Lina noticed how we spent some time talking and invited us both to one of her soirées – she is a percipient matchmaker! He plays the violin and viola and performed with Reinhard most beautifully. He has invited me to accompany him to the Italian Opera which is visiting Berlin soon. He is as tall as Reinhard and very handsome in a classically Italian way, very cultured, witty and charming. Do I sound like an infatuated schoolgirl? I have to admit I find him very attractive and look forward to meeting him again soon. He says he is anxious to meet Christian on a formal basis and gain his approval before we go to the opera together. Very correct!

Missie Vassiltchikov says her father knew Arturo's father, Count Giuliano, when he was a diplomat and they are much revered in Italy and close to King Victor Emmanuel. Arturo was a pilot in the Regia Aeronautica before the war and flew with Bruno Mussolini's squadron. He left the air force and entered the diplomatic service when his father died. Christian, I am sure, will approve of our friendship – at least Arturo has the right family background even though he is not German.

Here in Berlin we have the first glimpses of spring. The buds are bursting on the trees in the Tiergarten and the Unter den Linden and there is some real warmth in the sun when it comes out. How I do love the spring! Everyone seems in a happy mood, the restaurants are full and the cafés have their tables out again. Christian says this is going to be a decisive year and the war should be over by late autumn. By then you will have a dear little son or daughter and we must all start to rearrange our lives. Will you remain in the Luftwaffe, dear Peter, or do you think you will embark on another career in peacetime? I would very much like to go to university (you know father did not agree with that idea) although I have not made up my mind what I would like to study. Sociology, perhaps, and certainly philosophy. I should also like to take up serious musical studies although I think I lack talent in that sphere. All these wild thoughts are the result of the spring, dearest brother. Take no notice of these incoherent ramblings but always be sure that you are forever in the thoughts of

Your loving sister,
Edith

From: Oberleutnant Peter von Vorzik
III Gruppe JG233
Turnu-Severin
To: Edith von Vorzik
Apt 2, 47 Scharnhorst Straße
Berlin

19th April 1941

My Dear Edith,

I was very cheered to receive your letter as our main – only – enemy here is boredom and all mail is most welcome and read over and over again, however short. I was cheered, too, by the contents of your letter and your two pieces of good news which I will reply to in the same order in which you wrote. I am not surprised that you are a good pupil or that Walter says that you have a natural rapport with the car. You are a sensitive person and that reveals itself not only with human beings but also with inanimate objects such as pianos and motorcars! Being able to drive is, nowadays, a necessary accomplishment, even for women, and I am anxious that Mathilde should also learn but not while she is pregnant! As you say, after the big Mercedes the little DKW will be easy and light to handle and will endow you with a wonderful sense of freedom and independence.

Now, dearest Edith, I am more delighted than I can say that you have met someone whom you find attractive. I earnestly hope that everything works out well and that the relationship may develop into something more than a delightful companion to take you to the opera. However, I feel that, at the risk of sounding pompous, I must utter a word or two of brotherly caution. "Handsome, cultured, witty and charming," you call him and I can fully understand that those are qualities that would make any man attractive. But they are essentially superficial and one must look deeper, wait longer to see that he also has characteristics that are more important: honesty, fidelity, a gravitas and sensitivity to match your own – these are qualities of primal importance if you are thinking of a long-term friendship. I know you know this and will not make the mistake of yielding to a mere infatuation because of his good looks and charming ways, but it is so very easy not to heed such knowledge when you are in a captivating presence. Do take care, my dear sister, not to let your heart rule your head or your emotions lead you into any indiscretion... These words, I am sure, are superfluous and you will not take them amiss. You are eminently sensible and have a natural reserve which is a good defence mechanism; nevertheless it is very easy to find oneself behaving uncharacteristically when falling in love for the first time and reading between the lines of your letter I feel sure that is what is happening to you. So, dearest sister, beware; yet I wish you every joy and happiness in this liaison and trust it will flourish.

For myself, as I have already indicated, I have no news of any consequence as we are not in an area of operational combat and even if we were I would not be able to write about it! Like you I subsist on radio reports of what is happening in other spheres and everything seems to be going well for us. Our forces aiding the Italians (no comment!) in Greece are charging forward victoriously and no doubt there will be a quick conclusion there. Likewise in North Africa. Our bombers continue to wreak havoc on British cities – London, Manchester, Liverpool, Coventry, Bristol, Portsmouth, Southampton, Plymouth, Glasgow, Hull – there is nowhere in Britain beyond the reach of our aircraft and from the reports that you must have heard, too, the British people are about to revolt against the destruction of their homes and livelihoods. I repeat all this only to reassure you that the war is being won and before the year is out we shall surely have peace. Then, as you say, we must think about the rearrangement of our lives and look forward to a wonderful era in which Germany will be the dominant influence in Europe, if not the world.

As I wrote to Christian a year or so ago (he thought it might be opportune for me to transfer into the SS) I hope that my future will be in commercial aviation, an industry in which Germany will lead the world just as we have in military development. When the war is over new routes will be opened up everywhere and I would like to take part in pioneering them before I am relegated to some administrative position. Well, we shall see; at the moment I have to concentrate on the mundane tasks in hand, remote from all the action.

Write to me again soon, dearest Edith, and let me know how everything progresses with your "handsome, cultured, witty and charming" new acquaintance.

With deep affection,
Peter

From: SS-Gruppenführer Count Christian von Vorzik
SD HQ
Paris
To: Oberleutnant Peter von Vorzik
III Gruppe JG233
Turnu-Severin

24th April 1941

My Dear Peter,

Here we are in beautiful Paris once again and, of course, we both wish that you and Mathilde were here with us. There is no need to tell you, I am sure, that at this time of year there is no more radiant city in the world. Everyone seems in splendid spirits, food and drink are plentiful, the young women are elegant in their spring attire and it seems good to be alive. I know all this must be in considerable contrast to where you are and I refrain from saying anything about your insistence upon staying in the Luftwaffe except to remark that had you transferred to the SS as I suggested you might well be here in Paris with me ...

Last night I went to the Palais Garnier to see Frieda dance the title role in *Giselle*. I have never been a great enthusiast for the ballet but I must admit it was a most emotional experience, particularly, of course, since it was my dear wife receiving applause in this great theatre. The story is really a lot of romantic nonsense, all about a young peasant girl being betrayed by a philandering aristocrat, Albrecht, and then, after she has died from a broken heart, protecting him from the evil wilis who rise from their graves to avenge themselves upon such men. Even so, I found the second act very moving, the idea of love transcending death is, after all, an eternal truth. The role of Albrecht was taken by Serge Lifar, the director of the company. Do you remember him? He danced with great style and we dined with him afterwards. He is full of extraordinary stories of his days with Diaghilev and the Ballets Russes, as well as having a fund of anecdotes about numerous distinguished men and women in society, politics and the theatre – most entertaining! He says he was most flattered to receive the Führer, Herr Goebbels and the Reichsmarschall when they were in Paris and the Führer issued a standing invitation for him to visit Berlin.

We are staying at the Westminster Hotel as all our SS-managed accommodation is overflowing. It is smaller than the George V, Ritz or Crillon but very elegant and charming in a quiet way. The service is excellent, of course, and the staff cannot do enough for us except that, like so many Frenchmen, they manage to infer a superiority without saying or doing anything specific – most annoying! Have you managed to get to Bucharest yet? I know Frieda's parents would be only too pleased to entertain you; they are delightful people and very cultured. Do not accept their inevitable invitation to stay with them, however; I have the feeling – although I have not asked Frieda – that their resources are somewhat stretched. The cost of living is high for the population and does not buy so much as the German mark! The best place to stay, I have found, is the Athénée Palace, rather old fashioned with its Gothic columns but very comfortable. Remember me to Henri the barman who mixes a splendid champagne cocktail.

Did I tell you I have sold the Maybach? I sold it to – of all people – Obergruppenführer Kurt Daluege. He is a gross man, a real boor (a sanitary engineer by profession!) who has always been obstructive to our department but is very vain as such creatures often are and has been on the lookout for a large car for his personal use. He gave me 10,000 marks plus the expenses of having it brought from Adlersee. I shall be sending you a cheque for half that sum in due course. I have put my half of the money towards a most beautiful Talbot-Lago Coupé that I saw in a showroom here. It is a Type 15OSS (Sport Spéciale, not Schutzstaffel, but I thought it a good omen) with bodywork by Figoni et Falaschi in scarlet. The choice was between that and a Delahaye with body by Saouchik, even more elegant but not in such good condition. I am having the Talbot sent to Berlin by rail and you must drive it when you are next on leave.

The political outlook in the Balkans is now stabilised and with the British in Greece in full retreat everything in that arena is now under our control. I expect to be travelling between Berlin and Poland in the near future where Reinhard is determined that we must once and for all conclude the Jewish problem. I shall be back in Berlin next week so you can send any letters to my usual address.

Frieda joins me in sending all good wishes for your well-being and happiness.

Ever yours,
Christian
Heil Hitler!

Oberleutnant Peter von Vorzik
Journal entry

1st May 1941

Today is our national Reich holiday and I have managed to have a very short 24-hour break myself. It was possible because two days ago the Greek government capitulated, the British are trying to extricate their army from the mainland, à la Dunkirk, and the threat to the Ploesti oilfields is over.

A Ju52 was making a regular courier flight to Bucharest so I went along just to have a look at the city and what passes for civilisation in this part of the world. I did not try and make contact with Frieda's parents as Christian had suggested as my stay was so short. I did try telephoning but got no reply. I arrived just after midday and had to catch the courier plane back early the following morning. However, I did stay at the Athénée Palace, as Christian recommended, and found it very comfortable although very crowded – I was extremely fortunate to get a room on the top floor. The city is full of my compatriots, both in and out of uniform. Many are refugees from Bessarabia and Bukovina which the Russians had demanded last June, much to the rage and dismay of the Rumanians. Wehrmacht troops are everywhere and the Rumanians are confident we shall be retaking Bessarabia for them in the near future, although I do not know where they get such information from. I had a long talk with

Christian's friend, Henri the barman, who is a mine of information. Apparently, until recently, there were many English people here but they have all disappeared following the collapse of the Greek resistance. All the locals are now very pro-German whereas previously they were all very pro-British. I remember Christian saying how guileful the Balkan nations are and I can understand what he means.

I took a seat at a corner table in the bar and watched the passing show. By eight o'clock the big chandeliered room was quite full: Rumanians in operetta uniforms, Armenian salesmen, what I took to be journalists in shabby raincoats, several beautiful women accompanied by Wehrmacht officers (I was the only Luftwaffe member present) and lots of rather shifty-looking characters whose professions it was difficult to discern. Spies, perhaps? I tried to eavesdrop on conversations at nearby tables but most were in Rumanian which, of course, I do not understand. A small gypsy band wended its way between the tables playing tzigane music and there were several peddlers offering bunches of flowers to the women and their escorts. One would never see such hoi polloi in the best Parisian hotels.

A well-dressed woman in a long, dark red dress with a fur cape over her shoulders asked if she might join my table as there were no other seats available. Of course I agreed. She spoke good German and made a complimentary remark about my uniform and my looks. At once I felt suspicious: such compliments are not usually made to a complete stranger within a minute of meeting, especially if one has not been formally introduced. (At that moment I remembered how forward I thought Lina Heydrich was when I first met her at Christian's reception after my return from Poland.) This woman, who did not mention her name, said she had a Viennese mother, now dead, and she and her father had had to leave Bukovina at an hour's notice when the Russians marched in. Her father, she said, had a weak heart and was in a nursing clinic here in Bucharest. How long he could afford to stay she did not know. I offered her a drink and she asked the waiter for vodka. She was a handsome woman, in her mid-thirties I thought, with long dark hair and an oval face with regular features and large brown eyes. She wore small diamond earrings and there was a gold watch on her wrist. She said that she was so relieved that Germany had come to the aid of her country and all Rumanians were indebted to us. The Russians, she was certain, wanted to take over all the

Balkan nations and now the Germans had prevented that. Taking a gold cigarette case from her handbag she offered me a black Turkish cigarette which I declined. She lit one herself from a matching cigarette lighter, blew the smoke through her nostrils then said, smiling, "I have a bottle of Scotch whisky in my suite if you would like to join me." I sensed the implication, my suspicions had been correct! – and declined that invitation, too. I stood up, put a 1,000 lei note on the table for the drinks, clicked my heels and bowed in the best Prussian manner and left, amused that I had been singled out by what was obviously the sort of woman my mother would have called "an adventuress." I would have something to report to Varasch who, no doubt, would have accepted the invitation.

I strolled round the square to the shops in the Calea Victoriei to see if there was any little present I could buy for Mathilde but there was nothing that seemed suitable or different to anything I could buy in Berlin. I found my way to the restaurant called Capsa's, recommended by Henri. I had only just been seated by an obsequious patron when in came my adventuress accompanied by two Wehrmacht officers. They came past my table and she looked directly at me without a flicker of recognition. At least her evening was likely to prove a success after all. The meal was pleasant – quenelle of some whitefish which was probably gudgeon, veal in a lemon sauce and a bottle of Hungarian white wine – then I strolled back to the Athénée Palace. I intended to have a cognac but the bar was so crowded I went straight up to my room and enjoyed the comfort of a real bed. I had not been impressed by my brief glimpse of Bucharest but it had been a pleasant break from the dreariness of the airfield at Turnu-Severin.

Back here I was faced with another pile of forms and directives; it is astonishing what paperwork can accumulate in a mere twenty-four hours. The most significant of them indicated that the Gruppe was shortly to be withdrawn from Rumania and relocated in Poland and that all aircraft should be made serviceable at once for the imminent move. Eleven of the twelve F Series in my Staffel are operable, the twelfth with a minor hydraulic problem which is being rectified, so we are ready to move as soon as we receive the order. Poland? The reason we are being sent there has given rise to considerable conjecture in the mess. There is nothing to defend in Poland unless we are expecting trouble from the Russians which scarcely seems likely, yet that is the only logical explanation. The only aerial activity of any consequence at the moment is in western

Europe against the British. There have been reports of light raids on Berlin during the last few days but these are feeble attacks in retaliation for our devastating bombardments of British cities which the British acknowledge have done great damage to armament factories, roads and rail communications. We might have expected to be sent south, to reinforce Rommel's army in Cyrenaica or harass the British forces being withdrawn from the Greek mainland but no, we have been directed to Poland and none of us can understand why.

I amused everyone in the mess with the tale of my adventuress and as I anticipated practically everyone thought me a fool for not taking advantage of her advances. But then, none of them have my darling Mathilde to dream about.

From: Oberleutnant Peter von Vorzik
III Gruppe JG233
Turnu-Severin
To: Mathilde von Vorzik
23 Hevelius Straße
Grunewald

3rd May 1941

My Own Darling Mathilde,
This is just a short note to let you know that once more we shall be moving, this time to Poland. We shall not be leaving here for another few days, probably after you receive this, but until you hear from me again address your mail to JG HQ. Of course I am wondering if and when I may have leave again. It might be soon, it might not be for some time; the situation is very obscure although the military position is splendid, we have achieved resounding victories recently which can only reinforce the belief that the war will soon be won.

How are you, my darling? And how is little Wolfgang/Renata progressing? Not giving you any pains and nausea, I hope, yet looking at the calender I think he/she must surely be making his/her presence apparent?

We have had reports that there have been some air-raids over Berlin and that always makes me anxious for your safety, darling. Although I know the odds against your being in mortal danger are many thousands to one, I still worry. Please do not go into central Berlin unless it is really necessary. Although the raids are at night one never knows what foolhardy exploit the British might attempt by day just for a propaganda coup.

I had a letter from Christian, written from Paris, and I could not help thinking of our happy time there together. Perhaps, when our baby has arrived, we might celebrate with another visit. I did take advantage of the opportunity to spend a few hours in Bucharest which claims to be the Paris of eastern Europe but, believe me, it is nothing like the French city, but it did serve to relieve the boredom of this place for a few hours.

Now, darling, I must hurry to catch the evening mail collection. Promise to look after yourself for he who carries you in his heart,

Peter

From: Oberleutnant Peter von Vorzik
III Gruppe JG233
JG HQ
To: SS-Gruppenführer Count Christian von Vorzik
116 Kaiserstraße
Berlin

5th May 1941

Dear Christian,

As you will see from the address we are about to move again, this time to Poland. In your recent letter – which I was delighted to have – you mention the possibility of going to Poland, too; as we failed to meet in Bucharest we might succeed in Warsaw! I did make use of the opportunity to spend a bare twenty-four hours in Bucharest and was grateful for your recommendation of the Athénée Palace and the helpful barman, Henri, who sends you his greetings. I must say I was not particularly impressed with the city; it does not rival Vienna or, by all accounts, Budapest. Of course I envy you your trip to Paris; I hope I may take Mathilde there again when our baby is born. What a moving experience it must have been for you to see Frieda acclaimed by a Parisian audience – please convey to her my congratulations. I do hope, one day, to be able to see her dance. Yes, I do recall meeting Lifar although I was not impressed by him; I thought him egotistical and his manner too flamboyant, but I suppose that is commonplace amongst people of the theatre. Not a man to my taste.

I am glad you managed to sell the Maybach, it was only deteriorating at Adlersee and it is not a car either of us would want. Your description of the Talbot-Lago has certainly aroused my curiosity; it sounds very elegant and I look forward to taking a turn at the wheel. Such cars can now be obtained very cheaply; I saw a Hispano-Suiza for sale in a showroom in Bucharest, an open two-seater with yellow bodywork, very handsome if somewhat outdated now. I did not enquire about the price but I am sure it would have been a bargain.

So much has been happening in the various areas of combat, all to our advantage, and I feel very out of it here. We are all anxious to see some more action, especially with our new aircraft but our new posting hardly seems likely to provide the opportunity. Rumours abound, of course, some of them obviously absurd, and in any case I could not discuss them here but the whole Staffel – indeed the whole Gruppe – is anxious to bring the war to a conclusion. Perhaps this year we can finally defeat the British; they have suffered great reversals in Greece and North Africa. If we can only follow up our devastating attacks on the British Isles with an invasion the war would be over by Christmas, do you not think so?

I understand from Edith that she has met a charming man, Count Novarro-Badaelli. Do you know him, have you met him? I can tell by her letter she is very enamoured and of course I am delighted for her but also anxious in case she should be hurt in some way. We can be sure that she will behave with absolute circumspection but she is still emotionally vulnerable, despite her new-found sophistication. I am sure, Christian, you will keep an eye on how things develop, assuming you are still in Berlin. When do you expect to go to Poland?

We are all hoping that when we have reached our new positions in that country we shall be given leave. As you can imagine I am anxious to see my beloved Mathilde whose pregnancy must now be obvious. She has her daily cleaning woman but no other domestic help and I think that perhaps I should arrange for her to have a nurse-companion until the baby arrives. I am hopelessly ignorant about such things and I feel very helpless so far away. I would be very grateful if you could liaise with Edith over this matter and find out if there is an agency near Grunewald which could send someone on a daily visit. Of course there is room for someone to remain on a residential basis, if necessary. I know there are still four months before the baby is due but I do not want her living in the house alone. I am sorry to burden you with this but I have no one else to rely upon, dear brother, and you are a master of efficient organisation!

It is good of you to share the money from the sale of the Maybach with me, but if it is not too late could you put the money into Mathilde's account which she has set aside for the baby?

With all good wishes to you both, hoping we may meet soon.

Ever you devoted brother,

Peter

From: Edith von Vorzik
Apt 2, 47 Scharnhorst Straße
Berlin
To: Oberleutnant Peter von Vorzik
III Gruppe JG233
c/o JG HQ

9th May 1941

My Dear Peter,

Once again I have heard from Mathilde that you are moving your base, less than a month since I last wrote. I understand that you will be in Poland which does not bring you any closer to us nor, I imagine, is the posting any more enjoyable. Somewhere in France would be preferable, would it not, rather more civilised, but then you would be closer to the aerial battles we read about over northern France and the English Channel and I, certainly, would rather have you somewhere safe, dear Peter, however boring it might be.

Recent nights here have been rather noisy, more from the huge concrete flak tower that has been built near the zoo than from any bombs. I do not mind the noise so long as we are being protected by it, if you understand me. Because of the interrupted sleep, however, by the afternoon I am very sleepy, my eyelids droop and I find it necessary to read sections of my work (I am still translating foreign periodicals, mostly British and American) over and over again to make sense of it. We all drink lots of horrible ersatz coffee (whatever do they make it of? Some say acorns!) to try and combat the drowsiness but it does not seem to work.

A few nights ago I went with Arturo to the Italian Opera. (Yes, Christian gave his permission!) It was a work quite unknown to me, *Romeo and Juliet*

by Riccardo Zandonai. Have you heard of him? Apparently he is quite
prolific and still composing. It was well sung and, of course, the story is very
moving but it is not an opera I would want to see again, at least for a while.
His musical style is difficult to describe, a mixture of Verdi and Richard
Strauss! Quite apart from the opera it was a most enjoyable evening. We
dined at Horcher's and talked a great deal, about everything. Our lives to
date, our hopes for the future (Arturo wants several children, very Italian),
the war, music and art, cities we like (my list, of course, is very limited but
Arturo has travelled extensively, even to America) and discovered that we
share many tastes, from food to music. I tell you all this because, dear Peter,
you are sympathetic and understanding and more of a confidant than
anyone else in my limited sphere. I have taken note of what you said in
your last letter and am very cautious about letting my heart rule my head.
Yet Arturo is such a stimulating companion, such a gentleman in his
demeanour, that it is difficult not to respond in kind. I can assure you that
I would not countenance any impropriety – he is not like the importunate
Willi Haase! The only difficulty is that he expects to be appointed to
Count Ciano's department at the Italian Foreign Ministry very soon which
would mean his departing for Rome. We will see what transpires.

Apparently Christian had a wonderful time in Paris and was very
moved to see Frieda dancing at the Palais Garnier in *Giselle*. He is very
busy now and expects to be leaving for Poland quite soon. He would not
go into detail but when we talked he said that Reinhard had spoken to
him about a "heavy task" that the RSHA must soon undertake in the east
and inferred that something of great importance was imminent. He would
not elaborate further and told me not to repeat anything that he had said.
However, if he could say that much to me I do not see that I cannot say
that much to you. In any case everyone here ignores the General Order
No 1 which the Führer signed a year ago last January which is pasted up
in every office in the building about revealing secret information or trying
to find out what is going on; everyone repeats rumours. My own work
naturally brings me into contact with what is being said abroad and I am
constantly surprised that people accept opinions and statements which are
diametrically opposed to what we are told officially. One simply does not
know what to believe, except that much of it is just propaganda lies.

I had not meant to become so serious, do forgive me. Are you able to
hear the regular Berliner Philharmoniker concerts on the radio? I know

you have said in the past that there is so much noise going on in your mess that it was not possible, but perhaps, now, you have better facilities. I always make a point of listening, if I can, it is so refreshing to the spirit.

Ever your loving sister,
Edith

Oberleutnant Peter Von Vorzik
Journal entry

14th May 1941

We have arrived in Poland, at Siedlce, just about 45 km east of Warsaw and about the same distance from the Russian border at Brest-Litovsk. Speculation is rife that we might be defending Poland against a Russian attempt to occupy the whole country but we have heard nothing official. There have been reports on the radio that Luftwaffe aircraft have flown over Russian border territory and the Russians have protested while we have denied it. The general opinion in the mess is that of course we would want to have occasional reconnaissance to know what those wily Russkies are up to. We are the only Gruppe to have moved up here, the rest of JG233 have remained in Turnu-Severin. Just before we left, a unit of the Rumanian Air Force arrived at the airfield. They are equipped with Me109Es, but we had no opportunity to meet any of the personnel. Our flight was made in two sections with a refuelling stop at Tarnów. The airfield here is modern and comfortable, built for the Luftwaffe only a few months ago and until recently occupied by a training Gruppe. With Warsaw so close we shall have better opportunity to enjoy what leisure hours there are, although we all hope that we shall be given leave before long.

Something quite extraordinary and mysterious happened two or three days ago which has been almost the only topic of conversation since we arrived. Herr Rudolf Hess, the Führer's deputy and one of the most important members of the Party and the government, took an Me110 from its base in Augsburg and flew to Britain! It is said that he wanted to make peace overtures to the British but the official reports on the radio and in the press say that he was "in a state of hallucination". That may be true and I have always thought that he had rather wild, staring eyes, but on the other hand you have to have your wits about you to fly a Zerstörer single-handed, not to mention navigate accurately between Augsburg in southern Germany and Scotland, where he landed, or, if reports are correct, baled out. Certainly, the aircraft must have been at the extremity of its range. However mad his mission, one must acknowledge his feat of airmanship. The political situation has not changed as a result of Hess's escapade; the official view broadcast on the radio is that "it will have no effect on the continuance of the war which has been forced on Germany." It has given rise to a lot of jokes, however, such as "Göring and Goebbels are still firmly in German hands" and "The 1,000-year Reich has now become the 100-year Reich: one zero has gone." I am always slightly shocked when I hear such irreverent jokes about our leaders. It seems the British will be holding Herr Hess as a prisoner of war.

In Edith's last letter to me which I received today, she says how she and her office colleagues blithely ignore the Führer's General Order No 1 regarding secrets and the passing on of information. (I have seen the Order, too, in a score of administrative offices as well as the phrase, "Every man need only know what is going on in his own domain.") While I doubt very much that Edith and the rest of the secretarial staff at the Foreign Office Information Bureau are in possession of secrets of any great importance to the Reich, I cannot but help reflect on the difference between the shy, retiring young woman that Edith was at Adlersee and the independent, self-possessed person she has become. What a change a few months in Berlin can create! She is obviously under the spell of this Arturo and I can only hope that he is worthy of her, but it is another manifestation of her sudden maturity that she is able to command his attentions and embark on a relatively sophisticated liaison. I suppose one could wish that he was of German descent but then the aristocratic families of Europe have always intermarried even if only for political reasons. Anyway, such alliances maintain the health, if not the purity, of the stock – although I am very aware that that is not a fashionable or even patriotic opinion at the present time. At least the Italians are our allies.

New orders published today require that the Staffel patrols part of the Polish-Russian border between Siedlce and Bialystok, taking care not to overfly the border itself. We have been having instruction on recognising Russian aircraft, particularly the fat, stubby little Polikarpov 1-16 which looks like a flying barrel. The Russians used this aircraft during the Spanish Civil War and it is reputedly very manoeuvrable, but slow and with poor longitudinal stability. We are all on the qui vive to be the first to sight one of these curious little planes which have been given a variety of nicknames by the pilots who have flown them: the International Brigade in Spain called them Mosca (Fly), their Falangist opponents and our Condor Legion pilots called them Rata (Rat), and the Japanese who opposed them over the Mongolian-Manchurian border called them Abu (Gadfly). It would be interesting to know if the Russians have a name for them.

Flying up from Rumania on a direct north-south route that followed the Russian border we could see from the map what a large slice of Poland the Russians had taken when they crossed over from the east soon after we had taken offensive action from the west. Obviously they wanted to create a buffer zone between us and their own territory as well as retrieving some of the land taken from them after the World War of 1914-18. More and more we hear talk of a final showdown with the Soviets yet I cannot bring myself to believe it. When the discussion begins in the mess, which it seems to do every evening now, after our patrols, I merely ask, "What about the non-aggression pact we signed with the USSR less than two years ago? Does that count for nothing?" Everyone laughs and says that I am politically naive, just like those pilots at Rechlin – only they were too polite to actually say so in so many words. I just cannot believe, however, that a great country such as we are could break a solemn treaty-undertaking so flagrantly. There is also the military situation to consider: at the moment things are going well for us and we can look forward to final victory over Britain and her empire in a short while. I cannot think that the Führer would wish to prolong hostilities by taking on the Russians at this moment, although defending the Fatherland against Soviet aggression is another thing. Which is why, no doubt, we are here at Siedlce.

The other persistent topic at present is leave. The general feeling is that if nothing is going to happen then let us go home for a week or two to see our families, our wives and sweethearts. There is a great feeling of frustration all round. We hear of night attacks by our Kampfgeschwader against Britain (a huge incendiary raid on London four nights ago has left the city in smouldering ruins) while Jagdgeschwader in France make fighter sweeps across the English Channel by day. In North Africa the Luftwaffe is giving General Rommel wonderful support as he advances across Cyrenaica while we sit here on the Polish border doing nothing, our beautiful F Series glinting in the spring sunshine, quite impotent.

From: Oberleutnant Peter von Vorzik
III Gruppe JG233
Siedlce
To: Mathilde von Vorzik
23 Hevelius Straße
Grunewald

15th May 1941

My Own Darling Mathilde,

Our daily life here at Siedlce is interchangeable with our recent sojourn at Turnu-Severin, the outlook just the same, a bleak and featureless airfield, our daily patrols uneventful while we read of the war progressing in our favour elsewhere. Of course, we are all hoping that we shall be given leave soon although, so far, there has been no official encouragement to expect this. At the moment no-one has even had the opportunity to go so far as Warsaw. The hours drag, the days seem endless and all the pilots feel the urge of springtime!

I have asked Christian and Edith to arrange for you to have some extra help, a nurse-companion, for the next few months until the baby comes and for a period after that. I am anxious that there should be someone nearby so as to be ready for all possible eventualities, such as the baby arriving prematurely. I do realise, darling, that you may find it irksome to have someone in attendance but it will set my mind at rest to know there is a competent person on call.

Everyone was astonished to hear of Herr Hess's flight to Britain and can find no explanation for it. He must have known that the Führer's generous offer of peace was turned down by the British last year when the opportunity was favourable to them; now they have only themselves to blame as their cities are destroyed and their armies defeated yet again. Perhaps Hess thought that the British would be more amenable as they face total disaster but it was not for him to take the initiative; it is the Führer who decides policy.

I have no news for you, dearest, but I know you always like to have an assurance that I am well, in good health and spirits. Write to me soon for the reverse applies and I am anxious to hear that you and baby are thriving.

Longing, as always, to hold you in my arms again.

Ever your own devoted,

Peter

From: Oberleutnant Peter von Vorzik
111 Gruppe JG233
Siedlce
To: Edith von Vorzik
Apt 2, 47 Scharnhorst Straße
Berlin

21st May 1941

My Dear Edith,

I was so very pleased to have your letter; you always write such interesting epistles that I feel in close touch with everything that is happening in Berlin and the social world! Your visit to the opera is a case in point. No, I have never heard of Zandonai, although you say he is prolific, but then my musical education has, I am afraid, great gaps. Mozart, Haydn, Beethoven, Brahms and a little Bruckner is about the extent of my repertoire, together, of course, with some of the familiar concertos and overtures. I have very little experience of opera. I remember when we were taken to see *Hansel und Gretel* as children, I have seen *La Bohème*, *Carmen* and *Don Giovanni* and I think that is all. I have not had any opportunity to hear the Monday evening broadcasts by the Berliner Philharmoniker but your mention of them has reminded me to buy a small radio when I am next on leave and keep it in my little bunkroom which I now have as Staffelkapitan. It will certainly provide solace to the spirit. I shall also be able to listen to the news broadcasts instead of relying on hearing it second hand from the mess. We are all following the airborne attack on the British forces in Crete. Once again our Gruppe is missing out on some important action in which the Luftwaffe is playing a major role and we all feel enormously frustrated to be kicking our heels here in Poland.

Once again, dear Edith, I have need of your good offices. Will you liaise with Christian to arrange for Mathilde to have a nurse-companion for the next few months? I am anxious that she should have someone experienced in attendance until the baby is born – I have uneasy thoughts about the child being premature or something happening in the night when she is alone and unable to call for help. I realise these may be the foolish anxieties of a father-to-be but peace of mind is paramount when I cannot be there myself. I am sure you will understand.

Naturally I am happy to be your "confidant" when you wish to write about your friendship with Arturo – I hope I shall be able to meet him before long, although you mention that he may be joining Count Ciano's entourage in Rome. I do hope, for your sake, dear Edith, that the liaison will be a very happy one; as you know both Christian and I have been concerned that you should meet someone of suitable family and position and Arturo appears, from what you say, to have the right credentials. The fact that he is Italian may present some difficulties but nothing that is insurmountable. Does he have brothers and sisters, is he the eldest, are his parents alive? There are many questions to ask and I am sure you will be able to provide the answers as your friendship develops. How is your driving progressing? You have probably passed your test and received your licence by now. Christian wrote to me that he purchased a most elegant Talbot-Lago while in Paris, have you seen it? He was having it transported to Berlin by rail and has promised me that I may drive it when I am next on leave. I really must do something about purchasing a car myself and arranging for Mathilde to learn to drive although, I must admit, the prospect alarms me.

While writing this I was called to the telephone to be told that the Gruppe is to be granted leave from May 27th to June 9th! It is the news we have all been waiting for and as soon as I can I will telephone Mathilde. Just in case there is any difficulty getting through will you tell her for me as soon as you receive this in a day or two? I feel very excited myself, as you can imagine, even though it is only six weeks since I was in Berlin. The general opinion here is that our leave presages some big development in the war – or could it be peace? Perhaps the British have at last realised that they are beaten and diplomatic meetings are already under way – perhaps Herr Hess's strange departure to Britain has produced results after all. We shall see; at any rate the opportunity to see you all again is a wonderful tonic; my heart is full of the joys of spring!

All my love to you, dearest Edith.

I shall be with you soon.

Ever your devoted brother,
Peter

Oberleutnant Peter von Vorzik
Journal entry

4th June 1941

I had intended to write up this journal when I returned to Siedlce but so many notable things have happened recently that I think it best to note them down now, in the middle of my leave.

The first thing I must record are the great sea battles that have taken place in the North Atlantic, both a victory and a disaster for us. On the 22nd May our great new battleship, the *Bismarck*, the largest, fastest and most powerful warship in the world, left Bergen fjord, accompanied by the cruiser *Prinz Eugen*, and entered the North Atlantic to raid enemy shipping. On the 24th they encountered British battleships west of Iceland and engaged them; the *Bismarck*'s fifth salvo hit the magazine of the battlecruiser *Hood* which blew up and sank immediately, only three men, apparently, being saved from her complement of 400. Another British battleship, the *Prince of Wales*, was also badly damaged but managed to inflict damage on the *Bismarck* which was then pursued by several other British ships as well as aircraft from the carrier *Victorious*. The *Prinz Eugen* managed to escape to Brest but the *Bismarck* received further damage from aerial torpedoes which resulted in a loss of directional control. Many British ships homed in on the stricken giant which the Führer recently called "the pride of the German navy," and she was pounded unmercifully until, a flaming wreck, she turned over and sank, drowning 2,000 gallant sailors and her Captain, Admiral Lutjens. It was a terrible end for such a magnificent ship and the whole country has been in mourning for a week, the radio playing solemn music for hours on end.

While I am writing on naval affairs I must record another engagement which we thought to have been a victory but which now seems, to say the least, somewhat equivocal. A month or so ago the radio reported that the Italian navy had scored a great victory off Cape Matapan in southern Greece, sinking the British aircraft carrier *Formidable*. However, Edith, who sees all sorts of British and American journals and newspapers as part of her translation work at the Foreign Office, told me that the British claim to have sunk three Italian heavy cruisers, the *Pola*, *Fiume* and *Zara*, as well as inflicting serious damage on the battleship *Vittorio Veneto*. The *Formidable*, it seems, is very much afloat. If the Italian navy is anything like the Italian army and air force, then the British probably did inflict a serious naval defeat on our allies who, more and more, appear to be a dreadful liability. Much more satisfactory has been the outcome of the battle for Crete which has been decisively won by our brilliant airborne forces supported by the Luftwaffe. British and Imperial troops suffered heavy casualties as did the British navy which lost several ships trying to effect yet another evacuation of land forces. It seems that we, too, suffered heavy losses trying to land troops ferried from Greece in defenceless caiques as well as in transport aircraft, but the island is now in our hands and will prove to be an important base from which to maintain our offensive in the eastern Mediterranean.

It is all so beautifully peaceful here that it is difficult to imagine these fierce battles being waged on land, sea and in the air. I am writing this on my knee, not far from the hunting lodge at the southern end of the Grunewaldsee. The surrounding woods are in leaf, the green shoots looking almost edible; the sun shimmers on the water and the birdsong is continuous. There are many people walking their dogs and children's laughter comes from all sides. This time next year, perhaps, Mathilde and I will be wheeling little Wolfgang/Renata along the lakeside paths.

Yesterday I drove Christian's beautiful Talbot-Lago along the Avus, reaching nearly 130 kph, most exciting! The engine is a straight six of 3,994cc with a Wilson pre selector gearbox which takes some getting used to. The bodywork is a two-seater coupé with flowing lines and draws admiring glances wherever we go. Christian is very proud of it and will be sorry to leave it behind when he goes to Poland in a few weeks. He says he expects to be away for two or three months but cannot talk about his work in the east. I have never known him be so secretive. After the Talbot-Lago, the second most exciting thing that I have done this leave is to have paid a visit to the architectural studio of Albert Speer – he invited me to go any time I was in Berlin when we met at our wedding ceremony. Herr Speer was away, visiting the Führer in the Obersalzberg, but I was shown around by a most charming young woman, Annemarie Kempf, who, as Herr Speer's secretary, seemed very knowledgeable about all the plans for the rebuilding of Berlin. In a huge room downstairs I saw the amazingly detailed models of the Great Hall, which will be able to accommodate 150,000 people and the dome of which could cover St Peter's in Rome several times over; the magnificent Triumphal Arch, 125 m high, half-way down the Great Avenue, running north-south, 5 km long and 62 m wide – over 30 m wider than the Champs Elysées in Paris, and several other great buildings, including a new Chancellery, upon which work has already begun. In addition to this north-south axis there is to be an east-west axis which will open up vast new urban areas after the elimination of the Lehrter railroad station. All of this is scheduled to be completed by 1950. It is all immensely impressive but looking at the models, one does have the feeling that some of the ideas are rather megalomaniacal – the scale of the Great Hall and the Triumphal Arch will simply dwarf all human beings and make them like so many ants. The new city will be called Germania, not Berlin. Looking at some of the other numerous projects that Speer's architectural office is responsible for, including a huge new complex for the Party rallies in Nuremberg, new projects for various Gauleiters and field headquarters for the Führer and Reichsmarschall Göring, I saw several plans for Luftwaffe buildings and airfields – yes, there was Turnu-Severin and Siedlce! I had no idea that my own modest accommodation had been designed by the Führer's own architect. Of course, it may not have been designed by Speer himself, just one of his numerous staff, although Frau Kempf assured me that Speer kept a close watch on all his assignments.

By the time I arrived in Grunewald Edith had conferred with Mathilde and a charming and efficient paediatric nurse, Ursula, had been installed at the apartment. She has very little to do, at least at the moment, but her presence is very reassuring for me. Mathilde does, now, show her pregnancy and has had to buy a number of maternity clothes although she has received quite a collection from Lina which needed the minimum of alteration. Mathilde's new rotundity has not impeded our lovemaking and, indeed, she seems more passionate than ever, often initiating moments of intense sexuality even during the daytime. Naturally I respond with the same degree of intensity. It seems neither of us can assuage the physical desire we have for each other.

It has been something of a social whirl these last few days. Christian gave a large dinner party at which I was toasted as the guest of honour and, to my horror, had to give a little speech to the assembled company. At the reception before dinner I had been surprised at the number of people – Wehrmacht officers and Christian's SS colleagues – who, discussing the Weltanschauung, or World View (one hears the phrase constantly) seemed to imply that we were about to go to war with Soviet Russia. It was just the same as conversations I had had recently in the mess and I begun to wonder if I was the only person in the whole country who did not realise such a conflict was imminent. Accordingly, in my reply to the toast, I said that, as a mere Staffelkapitan in JG233, I knew that the Luftwaffe was poised in readiness for the immense tasks that faced us in the immediate future. Of course, it was vague and meaningless but I was taken aback by the noisy response my words received, shouts and banging on the table. Quite extraordinary; obviously I had touched a collective nerve.

Mathilde and I attended a concert by the Berliner Philharmoniker, Brahms' *St Anthony Chorale*, Liszt's *Piano Concerto No 1*, with Wilhelm Kempff as soloist and Beethoven's *Eroica Symphony*, conducted by the young and rather flashy Herbert von Karajan. It was all rather exciting and afterwards we had a splendid meal of lobster at Horcher's. The sirens sounded during the meal but, like most of the diners, we stayed where we were and the all clear came after about an hour. We drove home slowly in the little DKW which Edith has relinquished during my leave, and Mathilde fell asleep with her head on my shoulder. I awoke her with a kiss and we went to bed and made passionate love again, a perfect end to a blissful evening.

There are only five days of my leave left and I know from past experience how quickly the time will go. I find myself wondering more and more about the future, whether we will, in fact, find ourselves fighting the Russians, a possibility that, I must admit, fills me with foreboding... They may be weak and poorly equipped but it is such a vast country that the idea of invading such huge tracts of land is very daunting. It seems to me that we should finish off the British before we commit ourselves to fighting in the east. All the signs seem to be there, however; why else would we have been studying recognition of Russian aircraft?

From: Mathilde von Vorzik
24 Hevelius Straße
Grunewald
To: Oberleutnant Peter von Vorzik
III Gruppe JG233
Siedlce

10th June 1941

My Darling Peter,

For days after your departure I always have this utterly empty feeling inside – which is all the more desolating because I am pregnant and, physically, feeling very much fuller than usual! It is very peculiar but, of course, I know the feeling of emptiness, of being in a vacuum, comes from the brain not the stomach. Anyway, darling, it all proceeds from your absence, from having you close to me for a few precious days then snatched away. Although I did not come to the station I imagined the train at the platform, the hissing of the steam, the soldiers and airmen saying goodbye to their wives and sweethearts, the train slowly moving away and all those other women with the same empty feelings as I have. I know it was best not to be there, I know you would have hated such a sad departure, but I was there in spirit and anyway, just seeing the door close behind you, watching you from the window as you ran down the steps to the taxi, was, for me, just as emotionally draining. How I hate goodbyes!

Ursula has been a great help, not just in the house (she will not let me do a thing) but as someone to talk to, to take my mind off your absence for a few minutes. She has a fiancé in a Panzer division and he, too, has been posted to eastern Poland, so we share our anxieties and know how each of us feels although she is not married yet. She says she will not marry him until the war is over. Lina came this morning and brought a chocolate cake which we had with our coffee. She gave me some good ideas for the nursery and has offered to lend us some nursery furniture although I am looking forward to choosing things myself. But she is very kind and, having had children herself, full of practical advice. She says Reinhard has been very busy and preoccupied this last month or so and she dismissed the rumour that Stalin was ready to cede the Ukraine to us for the next 99 years. She says that conflict with Russia is inevitable but knows nothing for certain. Her comments only made me feel more anxious for you, darling; your situation in eastern Poland does seem to presage some sort of warlike action in the future, even though you tell me it is unlikely. Lina insisted that tomorrow we must both go shopping and buy a new hat! Now that clothing is rationed it is the only thing left with which we women can raise our morale! (I quote her.) I know you do not want me to go into central Berlin, but Lina says the RAF would not be so foolish as to come over in daylight and I have not bought a new hat since we were in Paris.

I also had a phone call from Frieda "just for a chat," she said, because she knew I would be depressed at your leaving. She also seems to be somewhat depressed. It looks as if Christian is going to be sent east quite soon for some considerable time and he told her if that is the case he wants her to be with him. That would mean giving up her career except, perhaps, for a few guest performances in Vienna and Budapest. "It would hardly be worth going through the gruelling physical effort of daily class," she said, "just to give half a dozen performances each season." She regards her appearance as *Giselle* in Paris as the pinnacle of her career and her success there means that she could have five years or so in leading roles. It seems she has to make a choice between continuing to dance or be a dutiful wife. "The decision is really Christian's," she admitted, "and I know he would want me with him." She also wants to have a baby and that would be recompense for abandoning her life as a dancer. But it makes her sad to think she has to give it up just as she has reached the top.

Darling Peter, my heart aches for you and I am so anxious for your safety if, as everyone seems to think, we are really going to fight the Russians. I have to admit I have never been as devout as mother but I pray for you every morning and night and hope God will keep you safe. I know you are a brilliant pilot and will not take unnecessary risks and that your loyal Katschmarek Kurt will be there to look after you but, of course, I cannot help being worried about your nearness to danger. I promise never to mention it again, dearest, I know it hardly helps you to know I am anxious about your welfare but, especially at the moment, it helps me to be able to write it – if you can understand feminine logic!

All my love and kisses,

Mathilde

The Führer and Supreme Commander of the Armed Forces
Führer Headquarters

11th June 1941

9 Copies

DIRECTIVE NO 32 (Excerpt)

(a) After the destruction of the Soviet Armed Forces, Germany and Italy will be military masters of the European Continent with the temporary exception of the Iberian Peninsula. No serious threat to Europe by land will then remain. The defence of this area, and foreseeable future offensive action, will require considerably smaller military forces than have been needed hitherto. The main efforts of the armaments industry can be diverted to the Navy and Air Force. Closer cooperation between Germany and France should and will tie down additional English forces, will eliminate the threat from the rear in the North African theatre of war, and will further restrict the movements of the British Fleet in the western Mediterranean and will protect the south-western flank of the European theatre, including the Atlantic seaboard of north and west Africa, from Anglo-Saxon attack. In the near future Spain will have to face the question of whether she is prepared to cooperate in driving the British from Gibraltar or not. The possibility of exerting strong pressure on Turkey and Iran improves the prospect of making direct or indirect use of these countries in the struggle against England.

W. Warlimont (General)
Deputy Head, Armed Forces Operations Staff

From: Edith von Vorzik
Apt 2, 47 Scharnhorst Straße
Berlin
To: Oberleutnant Peter von Vorzik
III Gruppe JG233
Siedlce

14th June 1941

Dear Peter,

By now you will be settled back with your Staffel and most likely feeling you have never been away! Mathilde told me she had written to you immediately after you returned from leave so I have waited a day or two before writing so that your mail will be staggered. I was very disappointed that, as circumstances dictated, I was not able to introduce you to Arturo. At the time I only knew that he would be away from Berlin for some days and only heard this evening, when he telephoned me from Rome, that he had been present when the Führer met Il Duce at the Brenner Pass twelve days ago. He says it was a very important meeting and involved all the Italian Foreign Office in a flurry of work. It also appears to involve the Japanese but he did not go into details on the phone. Anyway, he is returning from Rome in a few days' time but expects to be sent there permanently when he is formally appointed to Count Ciano's staff. I would so liked you to have met him, Peter, particularly as I have coerced you into being my confidant with regard to our relationship. Your impressions of him would have helped me to resolve my own equivocal feelings. Perhaps, before long...

Even as I wrote those words I realised that it may be some time before you have another opportunity to meet Arturo. All the signs are that we are about to embark on a major extension of the war and I pray it will be short and successful. Yes, everyone is talking about our situation vis-à-vis Russia and the foreign journals I read and translate every day (my English – at least my reading of it – has progressed enormously) are full of speculation about a coming conflict, as is the conversation wherever I go. You must have found that, too, while on leave? It fills me with apprehension. Russia is such a vast country and although everyone says that it is militarily weak and the administration corrupt and hopelessly inefficient, I cannot help thinking of Napoleon's debacle after Borodino. I know things are very different, now, and that our Wehrmacht is very strong – even invincible – and our wonderful Luftwaffe all-powerful, yet there is that awful feeling that invading Russia is like falling into a quicksand. Anyway, dearest brother, I must not weary you with these ignorant opinions, only implore you to take the greatest care of yourself if all this does, indeed, come to pass.

SS-Colonel Dr Stahlecker has left our office, thanks be, for I detested him. He has also gone to the east as commander of a newly-formed Task Force, Einsatzgruppe A, which will no doubt be involved with whatever hostilities there might be with Russia. Everyone here loathed him and we toasted his departure with some schnapps that someone had smuggled in! Does that shock you, dear Peter, to hear of such goings-on in a Foreign

Office department? We are a fairly convivial crowd, especially Dr Adam von Trott zu Solz and his secretary Missie Vassiltchikov, and his friend and colleague Dr Hans-Bernd von Haeften, our Chief of Personnel. They are highly intellectual and great experts on eastern culture and their talk is frequently over my head, but it is nice working with such cultured people instead of creatures like Stahlecker.

Christian told me yesterday (he looked in to the office to see how I was – he keeps a watchful eye!) that he had volunteered for one of the Einsatzgruppen but had been refused permission by Reinhard who wants Christian close to him. Reinhard apparently said that the work of the Einsatzgruppen was not right for Christian and only needed a cold heart and a strong stomach, not brains. I imagine from that that they must be some sort of advance troops, assault kommandos; if so I am glad Reinhard prevented Christian from joining.

When Mathilde telephoned in the evening she told me she had been shopping for a new hat with Lina and chosen one with a low crown and wide brim in pink, embellished with a rose in a deeper shade. She said that the hat took the eye away from her swelling stomach! We are planning to have supper together some time next week. At the moment my work load has been rather onerous, I arrive home late, cook my supper, have a bath and go straight to bed, hoping there will not be an air-raid. But it will be nice to have a meal with Mathilde, perhaps on Saturday.

I will refrain from another injunction to take care but simply send you all my love.

Edith

From: SS-Gruppenführer Count Christian von Vorzik
116 Kaiserstraße
Berlin
To: Oberleutnant Peter von Vorzik
III Gruppe JG233
JG HQ

22nd June 1941

My Dear Peter,
As I write this I know you will be part of the Third Reich's great campaign against the evils of Jewish Bolshevism which, on the Führer's

directive, began today. I salute you and all your comrades engaged in this most-important mission to destroy our greatest enemy. Of course I have had prior knowledge of this heroic endeavour and wished, many times, during your recent leave here in Berlin, that I could make you privy to such knowledge especially when I heard you, with touching naiveté, arguing against the possibility! Please forgive me if that sounds patronising but actually it reveals what admirable feelings of loyalty you have. Certainly, there have been many people in places of authority and power who also thought like you but failed to perceive just what an insidious threat Bolshevism has been to our great civilisation in the west in which Germany is foremost in defending the continuation of that culture.

The SS will be supporting our armies with Einsatzgruppen whose duties will be to root out and destroy those malignant cells which threaten to spread the poison of Communist ideology. I volunteered to lead one of these Einsatzgruppen but Reinhard insisted that I would be of greater use here within his immediate entourage. In any case he envisages that we shall be setting up SS HQ in various parts of what we intend to call Oestland as soon as our armies have completed the task of cleansing the Ukraine and areas further east.

Once again, dear brother, I salute you and wish you every success in this most important and valiant undertaking.

Ever your affectionate brother,
Christian
Heil Hitler!

Oberleutnant Peter von Vorzik
Journal entry

27th June 1941

It has been astonishing, amazing! For the last five days we have been flying five, six, even seven sorties a day across the flat, marshy plains of Russia, attacking targets on the ground just ahead of our Panzer divisions as they advance rapidly into the heart of our Bolshevik enemy. I am still in something of a mental daze at the sudden surprise and excitement of it all. When I think how dubious I was weeks, even months, ago when friends and comrades broached the subject of an inevitable conflict between the Third Reich and Soviet Russia, I am somewhat aghast at my own naiveté. But then I have never been a political person. I have rarely read political articles, never followed day-to-day changes in international relationships, except to be aware that we have defeated France, are still at war with Britain, that we have an alliance with Italy and Japan and a non-aggression treaty with Russia. Now, of course, I realise how clever our Führer has been to assuage the imperialist hunger of Communism until we were in a position to defeat the monster. So now, to my surprise, I find myself engaged in furious combat with a deadly enemy to whom I have given comparatively little thought.

For several nights before the attack we heard the distant rumble and roar of diesel engines as the tanks, armoured cars, half-tracks, gun-tractors and trucks of our Wehrmacht divisions moved into place along the Russian border. Ironically, Kurt called me outside to hear a nightingale singing on the edge of the airfield, its sweet notes clear above the menacing continuo of military motors. I remarked on the background sound and Kurt said we would soon be adding the distinctive note of our Daimler-Benz engines. How right he was!

There was a distinct sense of *déjà vu* about that early morning briefing in the Staffel operations room, the cheers that broke out when the Führer's directive for the beginning of Operation Barbarossa was announced. It was so like that first directive when we heard we were to attack Poland – even the first sortie had its similarities, taking off just as the sun rose in the east, lacquering the leading edges of our wings with gold, illuminating the whole countryside with radiant clarity. The only difference is, this time, that instead of escorting Ju87s at an altitude of around 6 or 7,000 m we have been accompanying Emil fighter-bombers at almost treetop height. Our first target was the rail junction at Kobrin where the line separates, going due east to Gomel, north-east to Minsk. Once the Emils had dropped their load we were all free to make random attacks on any target, vehicles, trains, bridges, anything that was well ahead of our advancing Panzers.

Flying as a Schwarme with Kurt, of course, as my Katschmarek, and with Gessler and Zechlin in attendance, we came across a forward Russian airfield with, unbelievably, two lines of I-16 Ratas drawn up as if for some ceremonial inspection. Have these stupid Russians never heard of dispersal? Going down almost to ground level we strafed the fat little fighters and within seconds both lines of aircraft were ablaze. We must have destroyed the equivalent of two Staffels within that short space of time. Turning sharply, with Kurt close behind, I attacked an anti-aircraft gun emplacement at the corner of the airfield. I could see the gunners clearly, some of whom appeared to be in their underwear! Gessler and Zechlin dealt with another gun crew and then, our ammunition exhausted, we turned back to our airfield at Siedlce, greeted with smiles and cheers by the ground staff and the pilots of the Emils who reported equal success with their bombing mission.

We repeated that initial operation four times in less than three hours before stopping for a quick lunch, then starting again and continuing until dusk. Each time we found plenty of random targets, meeting only sporadic opposition which was quickly silenced. Each time we flew over our advancing troops and their motorised columns we could see they had made rapid progress across country and by the end of the day were more than 50 km into Soviet territory.

That rapid progress has continued all week. Now we are in an abandoned Soviet airfield, quickly repaired by our engineers and equipped with our own mobile operations room. The fleeing Russians have destroyed everything – even the latrines! We are sharing the airfield with other F Series from JG51 and JG53, all of us part of Luftflotte 2, under the command of Feldmarschall Kesselring, supporting Army Group Centre. We shall be moving again in a day or two in order to keep up with the Wehrmacht's advance and, no doubt, find ourselves in another extremely primitive airfield. Although it is crude by comparison with the Luftwaffe's airfields, this one was obviously built within the last few months and one of our intelligence officers said that it was extraordinary how the Russians had been building new airfields so close to the border, thereby making them very vulnerable to air attack. He said all this was known to us for months past from the almost continual aerial reconnaissance we have been carrying out. We have been supplied with superbly detailed and accurate maps which have been of immense help in navigating over the rather featureless plains of the western Ukraine.

Both the Luftwaffe and the Wehrmacht are being supplied by road, rail and air. Our faithful Ju52s, the big, slow, trimotor transports affectionately christened "Auntie Ju" by Luftwaffe personnel, have been flying in ammunition, bombs, fuel, food and medical supplies ever since our offensive began. The aircraft's ability to operate from rough airstrips has meant that the vanguard of our forces has been kept supplied with all the necessities to keep up the momentum of the advance. It has been a brilliant logistic achievement by the Transport Geschwader.

This afternoon − the third sortie of the day − I had my first aerial encounter with 1-16 Ratas. This Russian fighter is much slower than our F Series but extremely manoeuvrable and, with its two 20mm ShVAK cannons and twin 7.6mm ShKAS machineguns, carries a heavier weight of armament than we do. According to intelligence reports, however, the pilots are very inexperienced, poor marksmen and seemingly unable to take advantage of their aircrafts' best features.

On the evening of the third day of Barbarossa the whole Geschwader was assembled in a bombed and blackened hangar to hear a talk by SS-Oberführer Professor Erich Meyer-Klemtau, a specialist in Soviet affairs. Using a blackboard and maps he expounded the Führer's intentions of colonising parts of eastern Europe, what he called "the master-plan for the east." The area will stretch from the newly Germanised colony of Poland, now known as the Government General, as far as the proposed line Leningrad-Lake Ladoga–Valdai Hills Briansk-bend of the River Dnieper. These areas will eventually be colonised by Germans, necessitating the resettlement of 14 million people of other races, mainly Ukrainian and Russian peasants, some of whom will be used as a labour force in Germany. These people, he said, must be considered as little better than animals. Stalin himself, the professor went on, had had no compunction in treating them as such and had allowed millions of them to starve during his agrarian policy of forcible collective farming. Our ultimate goal was to provide protection of the western world from any irruption from Asia. We must rid our hearts and minds of any sentimental feelings for these subhumans who, if allowed to thrive, would infect the blood of all those Germans brought into the resettlement areas. I have been thinking about what the professor said and have to come to the conclusion that the Führer has been proved right in all his theories and calculations.

From: Mathilde von Vorzik
23 Hevelius Straße
Grunewald
To: Oberleutnant Peter von Vorzik
III Gruppe JG233
c/o JG HQ

29th June 1941

My Darling Peter,

I have wanted to write to you from the very first day that I heard on the radio that we were at war with Russia, knowing you would be in the very forefront of the action, but thought it would be better to wait for a few days in the hope that I might get some form of communication from you. Nothing has come and I simply have to write and let you know that you are in my heart and thoughts every single moment of the day and night. Yes, I lie awake for hours thinking of you and uttering all sorts of prayers for your health and safety. My anxieties are even more intense than when you were fighting over England although the daily reports tell of our rapid advance and the weakness of the Russian forces. Yet every mile our soldiers and airmen gain in that vast country means that you are becoming farther and farther away... Oh, my dearest, I ache with anxiety for you although I know I should not tell you that. Of course, my pregnancy makes me more susceptible to worry and I know I should take consolation from the fact that you are a brilliant pilot, very experienced and more than a match for any enemy, nevertheless *my* enemy, worry, always seems to defeat me.

Everyone says that the Russians will be defeated by the end of the summer and my one hope and desire, darling, is that that will be so and you will be able to come home and greet our baby. I really am becoming very big now, impossible to hide my stomach even with voluminous maternity clothes! But I have become a very proud mother-to-be and whereas when you were last on leave I did everything to look my usual self, now I thrust my rotundity forward with pride when I am in shops or getting on the tram! Lina says I should have some snapshots taken of myself and send you evidence of my changing shape but I feel sure you would prefer our wedding picture that you say you keep with you. Lina is really most kind and helpful, often calling with some little delicacy or asking me out for a drive or just chatting on the phone. Of course, having had two sons she is able to advise me on all sorts of maternity problems. Not that I have any problems, darling, I saw the doctor two days ago and he says everything is progressing well. Of course I get tired quickly, now, heaving this precious weight about, especially in the hot weather we have been having. I can feel the baby move and wish so much that you were here to put your hands on my stomach and feel that exciting evidence of life within.

Edith phones regularly but she says she has been so very busy since the developments in the east, sometimes not getting home until ten o'clock at night. She tells me about her friendship with Arturo who writes to her regularly from Rome. Apparently he has invited her to stay with his family but she doubts if she will be able to get leave for some months but confides that she would love to go. Quite apart from seeing her paramour (should I call him that?) she longs to see Rome and all its famous antiquities. She says it would be her greatest joy to take communion in St Peter's.

I had a letter from mother to say that Aunt Ilse had been ill with pleuresy but is getting better now although feeling very weak. A nurse comes in each day to help with washing and dressing as mother cannot cope herself, Aunt Ilse being rather heavy, as you may recall. Aunt is some seven years older than mother and I do wonder if she is long for this world as she also suffers from a weak heart. If she should die it might mean mother would want to come back to Berlin to live. Anyway, darling, this is nothing to worry about now and really should not concern you at all. I only mention it in passing.

Dearest, I have very little news for you but want you to know that all is well here. Ursula is wonderful – despite her own worries over her fiancé – and insists on giving me a relaxing massage after my daily bath. Take the greatest care of yourself and, if you can, write soon to your ever-devoted wife,

Mathilde

PS Darling, I realise I said I would never write to you again about my worries – please forgive me. This really will be the last time. M.

From: *Oberleutnant Peter von Vorzik*
III Gruppe JG233
JG HQ
To: *Mathilde von Vorzik*
23 Hevelius Straße
Grunewald

6th July 1941

My Darling Mathilde,

Your letter arrived this morning and was awaiting me after I landed from the second sortie of the day. I know I have been remiss in not writing to you before this but, as you can imagine, my days have been very full. Yes, we are advancing triumphantly against our greatest enemy, one that it took me so long – too long – to recognise. The Soviet ideology is an evil one supported by enormous forces with which to subjugate the world and the Führer, in his great wisdom, realised we must destroy such a threat even before we defeat the British. I feel immensely proud to be one who has been chosen to carry out this task and I know you will share my pride at being part of our irresistible advance.

Of course, dearest one, I realise that you will worry about me and if it helps to relieve the anxiety then by all means tell me about it. I, too, am anxious about *your* welfare, how your pregnancy is progressing, if you have been subjected to air-raids (we have no news about such things but there are always rumours) and so on. We must be able to share our worries, it is part of marriage, of our love for each other. I was very perturbed that you mention getting on a tram! Please, Mathilde, do not endure the harassment of public transport in your present condition, promise to take a taxi whenever and wherever you go and promise to take Ursula with you. I am so pleased she is there to watch over you and look after you in my absence. I am also grateful to Lina for being such a helpful friend; please give her my regards when you next speak or meet.

I was very sorry to hear that Aunt Ilse had been ill but glad to know she is recovering – she is such a jolly person! If the worse should happen and your mother wish to return to Berlin, darling, she must have her house back all to herself. I am sure we can stay at Christian's for as long as necessary and there will be little difficulty in finding a new home for ourselves. There are many properties on the market now and we must think of buying a house with a larger garden for our little Wolfgang/Renata – and the other children I hope we shall have! Dearest, I hope I shall be home soon "to greet our baby," as you say, for things are progressing well. If only I could convey to you the wonderful, exhilerating feeling that possesses me as we skim over the plains of western Russia, catching glimpses of our armies thrusting ever deeper into enemy territory. I have already had some successes in destroying enemy aircraft on the ground and in the air and the whole Gruppe – the whole of Luftflotte 2 – has had magnificent triumphs that will bring peace and final victory ever closer. Everyone expects that we shall be billeted in Moscow by the autumn.

Darling, I have a small list of items which I need for personal use. Usually I can obtain them from our service canteen but now we are moving so quickly they cannot keep up with us! If you could manage to find them (I realise there may be some difficulty as certain things are getting scarce) I would be grateful but please do not put yourself to any inconvenience. Here is the list: razor blades (double edged); pocket comb (mine has broken in half); any soap, toothpaste or powder; pencils (my fountain pen has run dry but it is too dangerous to send ink, the bottle might break and spill) and writing paper and envelopes so that I can continue to write to you, dearest. I hate to burden you with such requests but minor things become disproportionately important when they are absent! Try not to worry if you do not hear from me for a week or two, as you know our time is taken up with important duties but, darling, I stress that I am in little danger as our enemy is weak and retreating in disarray. Take great care of your precious self, with all my love.

Ever your devoted husband,
Peter

PS Yes, darling, I would love any picture of yourself – the one in my wallet has become very creased.

PPS No, you should not call Arturo Edith's paramour – that means an adulterous lover!

From: Edith von Vorzik
Apt 2, 47 Scharnhorst Straße
Berlin
To: Oberleutnant Peter von Vorzik
III Gruppe JG233
c/o JG HQ

7th July 1941

My Dear Peter,

Once again I find myself writing to you at the beginning of a campaign that will affect the destiny of Europe – and perhaps the world – in which you are part of the vanguard. All those familiar anxieties that we, here at home, experienced when you were flying and fighting over Poland, France and England come surging up to the forefront of our thoughts, making it difficult to concentrate on anything else. Here in the office, where I am writing this, I am surrounded by examples of the world's press and every paper or magazine I have to translate is crammed with news items and articles examining and analysing every aspect of the great struggle in which you are taking part. So you see, dear brother, my whole working day reminds me of you, where you are, what danger you are in, what prospects are in store. My only consolation is that most commentators – including those of our enemies and potential enemies like America – seem to agree that the Russians are sure to be beaten quickly. I pray that will be so and I keep a candle lit in my apartment and pray before it every night asking the blessed Madonna to keep you safe. Already some of my colleagues are mourning the loss of friends and loved ones. Although we are advancing rapidly and winning huge battles it is not without cost. There are horrendous tales of the battles and we are told that the Russians do not honour any of the codes of war, putting up their hands to surrender and then shooting the soldiers about to take them prisoner. They have also shot at medical orderlies who have gone to help the wounded. It is all so ghastly – we are coming up to the second anniversary of the beginning of the war that we all expected would last only a few weeks.

I am sorry, Peter, to have begun this letter with such a catalogue of personal anxieties to you of all people but I know you, with your customary understanding, will make allowances. I try and call Mathilde every other day just to keep in touch and make sure everything is all right, although Ursula looks after her extremely well and does not let her undertake any unnecessary exertion although she maintains that simple exercises are helpful throughout the pregnancy. She takes Mathilde swimming at the local baths once a week – but you probably know that.

I have applied for leave from the office but do not expect to have it granted for six or seven weeks. I would so very much like to take up Arturo's invitation to visit him and his family in Rome. He tells me he is kept very busy by Count Ciano but if I go he will apply for leave too so that he may show me around. He says that he has two sisters who would love to act as duennas! Apparently young women in Italy – especially those of the middle and upper classes are far less free to go out in the city, especially after dark, than we are in Germany. In any case, he says, Rome is too insufferably hot at this time of year (several of his family are at their seaside villa in Riccione) and September or October will be ideal. It is odd, when you come to think of it, that living in southern Germany all our lives we never crossed into Italy. Arturo writes to me at least twice a week, telling me all the local news (apparently our offensive against the Russians took Mussolini and Ciano by surprise and they were upset and angry at not being taken into the Führer's confidence). Christian remarked some time ago that there is no love lost between Ciano and von Ribbentrop although they have to maintain an outward show of conviviality. Between Christian in Berlin and Arturo in Rome I get to hear all sorts of gossip about different factions! How I would love to see you, dear Peter, and tell you all this – and more – in a confidential tête-à-tête. Perhaps it will not be too long before we have you home again, the news from the eastern front is so consistently good.

Now, dearest brother, I will not reiterate all those familiar injunctions to take care of yourself, you know they are there, unspoken, unwritten, and that you are constantly in the thoughts of all your loving family, especially those of your devoted sister,

Edith

PS Is there anything I can send you? I expect you are constantly on the move so it would have to be something imperishable. Do let me know. E.

From: Leutnant Claus Grüber
Erprobungsgruppe V
Rechlin am Muritzsee
To: Oberleutnant Peter von Vorzik
III Gruppe JG233
c/o JG HQ

10th July 1941

Dear Peter,

I am sorely tempted to say "I told you so," but no, I will not! Do you remember how convinced you were last March when you visited us that there would be no conflict between the Third Reich and Russia? Now, I am sure, you find yourself in the midst of the great battles we read and hear about. Well, dear comrade, I will not labour the point except to say I am equally sure that you are acquitting yourself valiantly and making life hell for those damned Russkies.

How do you find your F Series? We have had reports that many pilots are complaining about the reduced weight of fire-power. Do you find that? If you have a moment to spare (and I realise only too well that that is unlikely!) do drop me a line and let me know your reactions to the plane under combat conditions. Things are progressing apace here and we have almost ironed out the teething troubles with the FW190. JG26 are scheduled to receive the first batch at Moorseele in Belgium where they will be reconverting from the old 109Es. We all think that the RAF are in for a shock! I have flown several aircraft from the first production lines at Warnemünde and believe me this is the best fighter in the world – although I know you are in love with your F Series!

How is your family? I remember you said that your wife was expecting a baby – when is it due or perhaps you are already a father? Anyway, I hope all is well. Do not forget that you have an open invitation to visit us here whenever you are able. I anticipate we shall have defeated Russia well before the winter.

Every good wish for your safety and success,

Yours,
Claus

Oberleutnant Peter von Vorzik
Journal entry

18th July 1941

These last three weeks have been the most hectic of my limited career as a fighter pilot. Not as dangerous or as exhausting as the battles over England last summer but simply a period of continuous flying: offensive patrols, escorting bombers, ground attack, close support, every kind of activity except the one our little fighters were designed for! There have been very few instances of aerial combat, mainly because we destroyed so many enemy aircraft on the ground during those first few days of our offensive. Even so, I have added twelve more victims to my tally making a total of thirty-four kills and four probables.

Most of the aircraft I have shot down in recent weeks were easy targets being both obsolescent and poorly flown. My score included six more of the fat little Ratas, five I-15s, the biplane fighters that preceded the Rata and a Sukhoi Su-2 light reconnaissance bomber. The Su-2 was attempting to raid our airfield along with five others. It so happened that our Staffel was returning from an early morning patrol when we came across the raiders about 5 km from bodo, flying quite low at about 1,500 m on a parallel course to ourselves. Although we had begun our descent prior to making our landing approach we still had a considerable height advantage and when I gave the order to attack we fell upon the unfortunate bombers, which were without any fighter protection, like so many eagles upon a flight of ducks!

As has been my usual practice I took the lead aircraft and, once again, my first burst of cannon fire did irreparable damage, raking the long glazed canopy and probably killing the pilot and navigator/rear gunner outright because the aircraft slewed sideways as if the pilot had slumped against the control column. It then went into a flat spin at the same time drifting first to one side then the other, a sort of grotesque aerial waltz until it hit the ground with a big explosion as its bomb load detonated. The rest of the flight were dealt with in the same decisive manner although one of the Su-2s managed to keep flying until it crashed on the perimeter of our airfield in another explosive mix of flame, smoke and earth, doing no material damage.

Although the Russkie pilots are poorly trained there is no doubting their bravery. There have been several reported instances where Russian pilots, unable to out-fly us, have attempted suicidal ramming manoeuvres. I was subjected to such treatment by one of the Ratas I shot down recently. Yet again I had dived on him from above (none of these Russians seem to fly much above 3,000 m – but then, they have open cockpits), but he managed to evade my first pass and while I was turning hard to port to come around again I found him flying straight at me on the starboard beam. Just how he got there I cannot say but those little Ratas are wonderfully manoeuvrable in the hands of someone who knows how to fly them. I saw him just in time and managed to accelerate into an almost vertical climb. He passed not more than five metres beneath me and there is no doubt about his intention. I yanked the control column over and side-slipped in a sort of skidding motion – a trick taught me by my old instructor at Werneuchen – and was soon back on his tail. He twisted and turned like a fish on a hook but I managed to stay with him and got in a long burst that registered on the fuselage and port wing. Within a few seconds he was spiralling down almost vertically with black smoke streaming behind. I followed him down to make sure of the kill and saw him hit the ground with tremendous force. He had been a resourceful and brave opponent; not one of those subhuman animals we have been told about, I thought to myself.

An even more difficult opponent to bring down proved to be one of the 1-15 biplane fighters that I encountered. He was one of a comparatively large formation – fifteen, in five flights of three – that were flying just south-east of Smolensk. I think they had been thrown into the battle as part of the Russian attempt to halt our advance in the area, as indeed they have. For any aeronautical expert our confrontation with these aircraft would have provided a perfect example of the last generation of biplane fighters in combat with our own examples of the latest high-performance low-wing monoplanes. (I must make a note to send a description of the encounter to Claus – I am sure he would be interested.) Anyway, having selected my opponent and left the rest of the Staffel to find their own victims, I found that I had no easy task on my hands. If the little Rata is considered very manoeuvrable then its predecessor is even more so. I have never encountered such a resolute and capable opponent and, had he wished, he could have escaped from me several times during our combat. Twisting and turning, rolling and side-slipping, he threw that little biplane about the sky in a way that I was quite unable to follow. Time and again I thought I would have him in my sights only to find I was looking at a patch of empty sky. I tried every trick I knew but my F Series, although much superior in speed, acceleration and climb, was just not as manoeuvrable as that little 1-15.

At one moment, as I was peering about trying to see where he was, I felt the aircraft shudder and knew I had been hit. Luckily, it seemed nothing vital had been damaged. If it had not been for his determination to shoot me down I would not have got him. He made his mistake by making another lateral pass at me from the port beam, then climbing away on the starboard side. Dragging the control column across and kicking the rudder bar I opened the throttle and there he was, just ahead and above, right in the middle of my gunsight graticule. I fired a long burst and saw large bits flying off his lower port wing. The wings on the 1-15 are made of wood and my cannon shells had almost sawn the lower wing in half. Immediately he went into a wild spin but just in case it was yet another clever manoeuvre I followed him down to about 1,000 m and watched him hit the ground with the usual spout of flame and earth. He had been a gallant opponent and because of his brilliant flying I assumed he must have been a squadron or wing commander, certainly one of the more mature pilots of the Soviet Air Force, not one of the poorly trained recruits we have been meeting. On landing I found his machineguns had made several holes near the base of the tailplane and my beloved F Series was out of service for two days. I said the Russians had halted our advance at Smolensk. They have made a stand just east of the city and it has been the scene of some bitter and bloody fighting. They have thrown in some unsuspected reserves of aircraft and tanks which came as a surprise to General Guderian's Panzer forces but the real shock has been the Russians' deployment of a devastating new weapon, a battery of rocket-propelled mortars fired in huge salvos that they call *katyusha* which, I am told, refers to a popular song. Our troops have found these assaults quite terrifying and it has been difficult to locate them and destroy them as they are mounted on some form of mobile platform and quickly change their positions. We have been searching for them in company with Jabos and Stukas but have had little success. During this same period we have also discovered that the Russian anti-aircraft batteries are surprisingly accurate and we have learned to treat them with respect – they have decimated some of the Stuka Geschwadern. I have been told that their field artillery fire is also better than the Wehrmacht's which is another nasty surprise: our intelligence information has been at fault over several aspects of the Russians' operational equipment and skills. The only welcome information is that they are short of such weapons and their tanks, such as the T26s, are inferior to our Mark IV Panzers; they burn easily and their armament is little better than peashooters. Even so, the battles around Smolensk have proved a major obstruction to our advance on Moscow.

In a recent broadcast to the Russian people their leader, Stalin, ordered them to carry out a "scorched earth" policy. This means burning and destroying everything as they retreat, not just airfields, barracks, fuel dumps and military installations but everything belonging to the civilian population as well, houses, farms, barns, wells, livestock, crops, everything they cannot move or take with them. Not only is there nothing on the land that can be used by us but also the remaining peasants – mostly women, children and old men – will have nothing for their subsistence, either. As the winter approaches they will doubtless perish through starvation and disease. Each day as I fly over the battlefields and see the burning villages, the blackened fields, the wreckage of tanks and every form of transport, I realise just what a titanic struggle is taking place across the land. Yet this is only a small section of Army Group Centre's operations; the battle line stretches several thousand km, from Army Group North fighting near the Gulf of Finland to Army Group South advancing towards the Crimea and the Black Sea, a war of unprecedented scale and importance. Every one in the Geschwader is confident of success but the early elation during the first few weeks of our attack has evaporated and been replaced by a grim determination to achieve victory as soon as possible. The Smolensk battle, however, has shown us that it may be harder and take a little longer than we originally thought.

From: Oberleutnant Peter von Vorzik
III Gruppe JG233
JG HQ/ Luftflotte 2
Eastern Front
To: Leutnant Claus Grüber
Erprobungsgruppe V
Rechlin am Müritzee

21st July 1941

Dear Claus,
Many thanks for your most welcome letter. As you know, mail is the great morale booster here and I was delighted to hear from you even if it was to

say "I told you so"! I have to confess as to having been very naive (that is what everyone calls it, kindly) about the political situation and up until the eve of the offensive I had my doubts. Anyway, they were quickly dispelled when I found myself strafing Russkie airfields at dawn just about a month ago. It was really quite extraordinary to find the Russians taken by such surprise. As you have no doubt heard, we found their aircraft lined up in rows on the airfields near the border almost inviting destruction. It has been a similar massacre in the air. With one or two exceptions their pilots are simply no match for our boys and their aircraft are quite inferior except for manoeuvrability and fire-power. Flown with some expertise and determination they can be quite formidable but the average pilot has proved to be something of an amateur. Would you believe that my most dangerous opponent proved to be a pilot in a Polikarpov I-15bis. I finally got him when he became too daring but it was pure luck. It has been much the same with the Ratas. They are devilishly manoeuvrable and one has to be pretty astute to follow them about the sky. Also they have a pretty hefty punch if they do get you in their sights. You ask about the fire-power of the F Series and, yes, speaking personally, I would like two cannons instead of the one we have but its central position does aid our own manoeuvrability which, in the circumstances, is no bad thing. As you probably know, several of our aces Mölders, Galland and Wick, have had great successes and (do not think I boast because our opponents have not been as well-equipped or as professionally polished as the RAF pilots were over England) I have made some additions to my score which now stands at thirty-four certainties.

I am pleased to hear the FW190 is about to go into service. I certainly thought it was a most impressive aircraft when I saw it under development although I have an inbred wariness about things that are complicated! I mean its motor, in particular, is a very sophisticated piece of engineering and, particularly in wartime, it seems advisable to lose a small amount of performance in order to gain in reliability and ease of servicing. Heaven knows, the F Series can be difficult enough. We have had some problems with dust infiltration. Much of the dust comes from the wheat fields which the Russians have burnt but the plains are naturally dusty in the summer and it has been very hot during the last week or two.

You ask about my wife. Thank you, she is very well and the baby is due about the middle of next month although I am told babies are in the habit of arriving sooner or later than expected! Either way, Mathilde and I are very excited at the prospect of an addition to our menage. I take it that you still remain a confirmed bachelor?

Please forgive my typing this letter (on the Staffel office machine) but the service canteen has not yet caught up with us and pens, pencils and ink are in short supply. Also my typing is not of the standard required to get me a position in any professional organisation! These small deprivations and irritations are what one notices most about being on active service; the lack of a score of little things that one simply takes for granted. The larger issues one tends to accept or ignore! On the other hand, why should one complain about the lack of ink when there seems to be a plentiful supply of French champagne and cognac? Someone has got their priorities right. Now I must try and catch the Staffel courier to post this. You would not believe how long it has taken me to type!

Best wishes, please write when you can.

Yours,

Peter

From: Mathilde von Vorzik
23 Hevelius Straße
Grunewald
To: Oberleutnant Peter von Vorzik
III Gruppe JG233
JG HQ
Eastern Front

19th July 1941

My darling Peter,

I was overjoyed to receive your letter of the sixth – it took nearly two weeks to reach me and so much has happened since then. According to the radio our forces have made wonderful advances and I look on the maps in the newspapers and wonder which part my darling is flying over. All the days seem to telescope into one, my only thoughts centred on two things: your safety and the baby. Everything else seems a blur and I have to think hard before I can recollect anything that might be of interest to you in a letter. Your safety, of course, lies in the hands of God and your own brilliant flying; the baby is not even here so, apart from saying, once again, how I pray for your safety every night and morning and how big I have become, there is no other news.

I enclose a head and shoulders photo of myself that should fit into your wallet. I could not have a picture that showed any more of me – I am huge! But I send this with all my love, darling, thinking that my picture will be in your wallet close to your heart. If only I could exchange places with that photo! Lina drove me to the portrait studio, a little place on the Ku'damm with lots of pictures in the window of soldiers and airmen. A funny little old man took the photo using one of those old-fashioned cameras which necessitated hiding his head under a velvet cloth – very threadbare and frayed. I looked at Lina and got the giggles so that is why I have a big smirk on my face that makes me look inane! Afterwards we had coffee at the Adlon which, together with Horcher's, is the only place that still serves coffee worth drinking. That has been my only outing recently. I take a short daily stroll with Ursula who says I must have some exercise but walking in the summer heat with this beloved load is now very exhausting. Otherwise, most of the day, I listen to the radio while lying on the bed to take the weight off my ankles which become very swollen after walking. I am longing for the baby to come, to see at last that little creature who has been kicking me so hard this last week or so. By the way, Lina has offered to lend us a baby carriage for the first year; the new ones are terribly expensive and now becoming rather scarce in the shops. She is such a good friend.

Although she is so busy Edith still manages to find time each evening for a short chat, which I much appreciate. Mostly we talk about you! She has been telling me about your childhood escapades, about the time you fell in the lake and nearly drowned and the model aeroplane you made that crashed into your father's study window. Why have you never told me about your boyhood? I shall have a lot of questions when I next see you, darling. There was a Furtwängler concert on the radio last night, all Beethoven, and I was so looking forward to it but fell asleep during the concerto (Fourth piano) and only woke up when they broadcast an eye-witness account from the eastern front. There were terrible sounds of gunfire and I woke in a dreadful fright, thinking it was an air-raid! I stumbled downstairs and gave Ursula a fright too, thinking I had started labour. She made me a cup of hot chocolate and put me to bed.

So, darling, that is the extent of my news. Not very enthralling for you but I know how you enjoy receiving mail and hearing of our mundane doings. Sweetest, dearest one, how I long for us to be together. I think of you constantly and tell our little unborn one all about you. Soon I will be telling him/her in reality even though he/she will not understand but I want the baby to become familiar with the sound of your name right from the very first days. Of course, I shall be saying Papa, Papa, not Peter, Peter – that is what I murmur to myself, over and over. Do I sound a little crazy? I think pregnancy makes one a little eccentric, darling, but there is surely nothing untoward in murmuring the name of one's loved one? Be assured, dearest, you have the everlasting love and devotion of your own

Mathilde

PS I have managed to get some razor blades for you which I have posted separately. M.

The Führer and Supreme Commander of the Armed Forces
Führer Headquarters

19th July 1941

DIRECTIVE NO 33 (Extract)

(b) Central Part of the Eastern Front:

After the destruction of the many pockets of enemy troops which have been surrounded and the establishment of lines of communication, Army Group Centre, while continuing to advance to Moscow with infantry formations, will use those motorised units which are not employed in the rear of the Dnieper line to cut communications between Moscow and Leningrad, and so cover the right flank of the advance on Leningrad by Army Group North.

(3) The task of the Luftwaffe is, in particular, as forces become available from the Central front, to support operations on the south-eastern front at their most important point by bringing air and anti-aircraft units into action and, if necessary, by early reinforcement or regrouping. The attack on Moscow by the bomber forces of Luftflotte 2 temporarily reinforced by bomber forces from the west will be carried out as soon as possible as reprisal for Russian attacks on Bucharest and Helsinki.

Adolf Hitler

The Chief of the High Command of the Eastern Forces
Führer Headquarters

23rd July 1941

SUPPLEMENT TO DIRECTIVE NO 33 (Extract)

(2) Central Part of the Eastern Front:

After mopping up operations around Smolensk, Army Group Centre, whose infantry formations are strong enough for the purpose, will defeat such enemy forces as remain between Smolensk and Moscow, by an advance of the left flank if possible. It will then capture Moscow.

(5) The orders given for the Luftwaffe in Directive 33 remain valid.

Keitel

Oberleutnant Peter von Vorzik
Journal entry

25th July 1941

Another unnecessary accident, destroying man and machine, for which I feel responsible. One of our youngest replacement recruits, Oberfeldwebel Friedrich Lüddecke, not long out of training school at Werneuchen, ground-rolled his F Series on take-off. When he did his conversion training he must have had it drilled into him that opening the throttle too quickly results in the powerful DB601N engine torque lifting the starboard wing before the fighter has attained flying speed. That results in the aircraft rolling upside down and smashing into the ground, which is exactly what happened. In this case the fuel tank, immediately behind the pilot's seat, ruptured and the aircraft burst into flames. The ground crew were unable to get near the conflagration and Lüddecke was incinerated. Only a few charred fragments were found, together with his skull and bones, to put into the coffin.

I feel responsible because he had only joined us recently and this was his first operational flight; I should have reminded him of take-off procedures but we were ordered into the air at short notice to support a counter-attack by our ground forces outside of Viazma and in the hurry to get airborne I omitted to mention such elementary matters in the briefing. Certainly, the experienced pilots in the Staffel would have felt insulted had I done so but I feel now that I should have had a quick private word with him on the way to the dispersal area. Kurt insists it should not have been necessary but he says that to assuage my feelings of guilt. Once again I have the sad task of writing to the parents as I did with Hans Zahle.

Yes, we are still fighting in the area east of Smolensk where the Russians continue to put up stubborn resistance. We have been flying five, six, seven sorties a day escorting Jabos and Stukas attacking ground targets, and most of the Staffel pilots are feeling the strain. It shows in short tempers in the mess, arguments over trivial matters and a tendency to drink too much in the mess bar at the end of the day. I have had to deliver a general pep talk about the maintenance of morale and had one or two pilots (I will not name them) into my makeshift office to have a quiet word of reproval in private. I hate doing this but it is necessary, otherwise things go from bad to worse in a short while. I always ask myself what Zwemmer would have done and remembering his way of reprimanding pilots who overstepped the mark in terms of behaviour in the mess (I put on record that I was never reprimanded!) I copy his example.

In their desperate defence of the so-called Stalin Line east of Smolensk the Russians have thrown in a number of their latest planes and it was something of a surprise yesterday to find ourselves faced with aircraft much superior to the Ratas. We sighted them flying towards Velikiye Luki, about 600 m below us which is much higher than Russian aircraft usually fly as we were at our regular cruising altitude of 5,000 m. I was able to identify them as MiG-3s from the extensive recognition lectures we have had in the past two months. They are very sleek low-wing monoplanes with a long nose and short fuselage. The wing-plan is somewhat similar to the British Hurricane but the tailplane and fin and rudder are distinctively pointed. Intelligence reports say that the engine is very powerful but also large and heavy – hence the long nose which affects longitudinal stability and results in relatively poor manoeuvrability. However they are very fast, particularly at high altitude and so in performance terms they are the opposite of the little Ratas. Also, they are poorly armed with just one 12.7mm UBS machinegun and two 7.62mm ShKAS machineguns mounted above the engine.

As usual I gave the order to dive on the formation of six, flying in two flights of three but they had already seen our Schwarm and scattered in several directions. I managed to get in two bursts at what had been the leading aircraft of the first flight but I do not think I registered any hits. My quarry turned to starboard in a wide circle and although I managed to turn inside him his speed was greater in the turn and, infuriatingly, I could not get him in my sights again. He headed east at full speed and I simply did not have the speed to catch him. Returning to bodo Kurt claimed to have damaged one and Gessler another but all of them escaped destruction because of their superior speed. Doubtless if they had stayed to fight it out we would have managed to destroy some of them as, apart from all-out speed, our F Series are superior in dynamics and fire-power – not to mention pilot capability! From now on we shall be on the look-out for them and try to head off any chance of escape.

There is no doubt that the Russians' stand just to the east of Smolensk has been an impediment to our victorious advance. It is on the direct route to Moscow and, apart from holding us up, the Russians have had their first opportunity to regroup their forces behind this shield. Moreover, Guderian's tanks have suffered considerable wear and tear during our advance and many are out of service which gives the Russians considerable superiority in tank numbers although their equipment, as I have said before, is inferior. But this is only a temporary hold-up; I am sure our armies will be forcing their way east again before long. One advantage of this hiatus is that our own general supplies have caught up with us. Spare parts for our aircraft, which have also suffered from constant operations, are now in plentiful supply and on a less important level we now have fresh supplies of personal items like soap, toothpaste, shoe-polish, razor blades and so on. I have built up a little reserve stock for the time when we shall be moving on again. One learns through experience!

Two nights ago we had a visit from a concert pianist, Ulrich Matthes, who gave a recital in one of our workshop hangars. He arrived in a Ju52 complete with a Steinway grand! He played Beethoven's *Hammerklavier Sonata* and Schumann's *Kinderscenen*, which was one of mother's favourites. I have to admit that the performance brought a lump to my throat and a prickling behind the eyes, but it was a wonderful respite from daily operations and a rejuvenation of the spirit. Matthes came to the mess after the concert and took a glass of champagne with us before flying back to Warsaw and thence to Berlin. According to his agent, who travelled with him, Matthes has been giving concerts to the troops in the southern sector of the front and has been received with rapture wherever he has appeared. Next week we are promised a cinema show although I do not know what the programme is. These entertainments are invaluable for maintaining morale irrespective of whether it is serious music or film comedy; it shows that someone cares about our general welfare apart from victories on land or in the air.

From: Oberleutnant Peter von Vorzik
III Gruppe JG233
JG HQ
Eastern Front
To: Mathilde von Vorzik
23 Hevelius Straße
Grunewald

26th July 1941

My Own Darling Mathilde,

As always your letter (dated 19th) did so much to boost my morale. Not that I am depressed but, as I have said so often, a letter from home lets me know that you are safe and well. And now, with the baby due so soon, you are of even greater concern to me. We are still in the same area of operations although we expect to be moving forward again soon, which is all I can say at present. No doubt you hear all the front-line news on the radio and I cannot add to that except to say that I take great care of myself under all situations.

It has been very hot these last two weeks and we have been operating in our lightweight one-piece flying suits and unlined flying helmets. After a patrol there is always a great rush to cool off in the showers! These, as you can imagine, are somewhat rudimentary. I have been wearing the pale blue silk scarf you gave me for my last birthday as it stops chafing from the neckband of the flying suit when one perspires. I think I have started a fashion for several of the Staffel have written home for coloured scarves to wear! It is against regulations, of course, but as long as we are properly dressed for formal occasions (of which there are very few during current operations!) no one seems to mind such sartorial liberties.

It has not only been very hot but the air is also very dusty. As you have no doubt heard, the Russians burned and destroyed everything as they retreated so that the air is laden with particles of soot as well as the dust from the plains. It is not until we are flying at about 3,000 m that the air becomes clear. Looking down, there is a grey pall over the earth for kilometres around as if someone had drawn a great smear across the landscape. Oily smoke rises in black columns from the thousands of Russian tanks and vehicles that are being destroyed, adding to the polluted atmosphere. From the ground the sun appears as a glowing white dot through the murk and as dusk falls the dot becomes a dull red ball. I tell you all this, darling, merely to try and sketch some idea of the scene without giving away vital information! I count myself lucky in being able to fly above the smoke and dust and feel very sorry for our soldiers who must endure the choking atmosphere.

How is Ursula? Please tell her how grateful I am that she is looking after you so well in my absence. Perhaps you could find some small gift for her and say it is from me as a token of my appreciation. Of course, I do not know what she likes: chocolates (if they are still obtainable)? Or something to wear? (I think you said hats are the only clothing not rationed.) Or perhaps something to put away for when she marries, like china or glass. I leave it to your good sense and taste, darling, but do not tire yourself looking. Perhaps the redoubtable Lina would help you? She is another stalwart friend and perhaps we should give her a present, too?

It could well be that before my next letter to you our precious Wolfgang/Renata will have arrived. I am sure you know, dearest, there is nothing in the world I would wish more than to be with you at such a time. I hate the fact that this war intervenes to separate us, and yet I realise that it is inevitable that we should be fighting our powerful enemies in order that our children should be free to grow up in a strong and victorious Reich. When the labour pains come, darling, and I am not there to hold your hand, try and think that our separation is necessary and that it will not be long before we are free to build our lives together.

Keep yourself safe and well for

Your ever loving,

Peter

PS Thank you, darling, for the razor blades which arrived just in time! Now, however, our service canteen has caught up with us and – for the present – I am able to purchase small personal items, which is why I am writing in ink again. P.

From: SS-Gruppenführer Count Christian von Vorzik
116 Kaiserstraße
Berlin
To: Oberleutnant Peter von Vorzik
III Gruppe JG233
JG HQ
Eastern Front

lst August 1941

My Dear Peter,

This is to let you know our joyous news: Frieda is expecting a baby! The child is due sometime in the spring. Of course we are delighted at the doctor's confirmation of Frieda's condition. She, because she is ready now for motherhood, having decided to give up her dancing career, and I – apart from the happy prospect of fatherhood and continuing the family line – because we in the SS must set an example in procreating strong, healthy children for the continuation of the Third Reich. At one time, when Frieda was still set upon her career, I had contemplated registering for the *Lebensborn* programme but now I can concentrate on procreating my own family. We hope to have at least four children. So, dear brother, your own little one will have a cousin of near contemporary age to play with. Reinhard threw a party to celebrate our news and the next day I accompanied him on a tour of some of the most recently formed Einsatzkommando units prior to their departure for the eastern front. We visited Pretsch, near Wittenberg (a charming baroque castle) and then moved on to the little town of Duben on the Mulde. Reinhard stressed that their task will be to eradicate the Jewish-Bolshevik units which are lurking behind the lines to organise saboteur groups and that they must be absolutely ruthless in destroying these nests of Communist ideology. He said that the Führer had given direct orders that such activists must basically be regarded as persons who, by their very existence, endanger the security of our troops and must be executed without compunction.

I must admit to you that I am glad, now, that I followed Reinhard's advice and did not join one of these units when volunteers were called for. While I am quite prepared to fight in the front-line with one of the Waffen-SS regiments I do not relish the prospect of rooting out civilians, however potentially dangerous. (I have heard some chilling accounts of the activities of the first wave of Einsatzkommandos. Reinhard was right when he said all that was needed was a cold heart and a strong stomach.) In any case he insists that I stay within his immediate entourage for there is still much to organise in making Oestland free of insidious Jewish-Bolshevik doctrine and influence. You, dear brother, are literally above this aspect of the battle but, believe me, our struggle against these subversive enemies is just as important as the immediate confrontations in which you are engaged.

Edith was at Reinhard's party and was glowing at the news that she has been granted three weeks' leave from her duties beginning in September. She plans to visit Rome and stay with the Novarro-Badaellis. This relationship appears to be developing apace, albeit by correspondence, and I suppose she could do worse as a prospective husband but I must admit I would have preferred someone of our own nationality. I did my best to introduce her to some of my SS colleagues but none of them seem to have appealed to her. Certainly Arturo has undeniable charm, very much calculated to appeal to women, and good family background. We must wait and see what develops.

Regretfully, I have had to lay up the Talbot-Lago for the present. First because my duties do not allow me the opportunity to drive it except on very rare occasions – only once since we had our little trip along the Avus – and second, because the water pump is not working and it is difficult to get a new one from France at the moment. Such pleasure must await our final victory over our enemies which will surely not be long once we have conquered the Bolsheviks. All Europe will then be ours or under our direct influence.

I trust, dear brother, that all goes well with you. Of course I receive all the news from the eastern front but on a daily basis I realise that you are often in danger. Keep well and take good care of yourself for the sake of all of us,

Especially your devoted brother,
Christian
Heil Hitler!

From: *Edith von Vorzik*
Apt 2, 47 *Scharnhorst Straße*
Berlin
To: *Oberleutnant Peter von Vorzik*
III Gruppe JG233
JG HQ
Eastern Front

6th August 1941

My Dear Peter,

You will have heard from Christian the wonderful news that Frieda is expecting a baby. That means within a year I shall be Aunt Edith to two nephews or nieces or one of each! It really is uplifting to the spirit to think of two young additions to the family amidst this daily diet of death and destruction. If only our dear mother could have lived to see her grandchildren, it would have given her so much joy.

I am allowed three weeks' leave from next month and am so excited at the prospect of accepting Arturo's invitation to visit Rome, a city that I have long longed to see. He is making all sorts of plans to show me around – his work permitting – but I am also a little nervous at the thought of meeting his mother and sisters and other members of his family. From all accounts they are accomplished in many ways. Like Arturo, his sisters both sing and play the violin (although, he says, nothing so vulgar as doing so professionally!). His young brother, Massimo, the "baby" of the family, skis at almost Olympic level. At present he is in one of the crack mountain regiments and expects to be sent to the Caucasus when the Italian 8th Army is ready to engage the Russians. Arturo's father and his mother were distinguished in Italian diplomatic society, of course. She was a celebrated hostess, particularly when her husband was stationed in Washington and now, even as a widow, from the photographs Arturo has shown me, she is still a beautiful and elegant woman. I am afraid I shall appear rather gauche in comparison with Eleanora and her daughters.

I still receive letters from Arturo twice a week and they have become more and more full of endearments. He obviously feels strongly about our relationship and I have to tell you, dearest brother, that I retain deep feelings of affection for him. I hesitate to call it love as I am unsure just

257

how that emotion feels and yet, I ask myself, what else can it be when I spend so much time thinking of Arturo, remembering details of our conversations, re-reading his letters (which I have kept), trying to formulate his features in my mind's eye. I tell you all this, Peter, in the strictest confidence, knowing that you will sympathise with my schoolgirl sentimentality and not laugh at me. Whatever they may be, my feelings are deeply engaged.

Well, enough of that! Reinhard threw a dinner party to celebrate the announcement of Frieda's expected baby – I think at the instigation of Lina. Anyway, it was a jolly occasion, I have never seen Frieda so animated. Usually she is very quiet and retiring (even more that I am!) for someone whose profession has been in the theatre, and at the party she was quite radiant in a deep pink silk dress and wearing a diamond necklace that Christian had given her. Of course Mathilde was invited but sent word that she felt too tired to come. She is quite well, however, it is just that she goes to bed very early now that the baby might come at any time. At the table I sat next to an SS-Untersturmführer, Rudolf Vedder, who is responsible for organising entertainment for the armed forces. I found him bumptious and egotistical but he was full of amusing gossip about a lot of important musicians and artists as he is also an agent. He said that he is responsible for the rivalry between Furtwängler and Karajan and that the younger man will soon be the most famous of the two. Furtwängler, apparently, is thought to be difficult to work with and somewhat out of favour with the Party, refusing to accept that politics has anything to do with music. Karajan, however, is a Party member and immensely ambitious and his concerts at the Staatsoper have received more enthusiastic reviews that Furtwängler's at the Philharmonic Hall. When one sees these great men on the podium or listens to them on the radio conducting marvellous music it is difficult to realise that they can be consumed with jealousy about each other.

Now it is time for bed, I will post this tomorrow. All my deepest love, dear brother, I always pray for you.

Ever your loving sister,
Edith

From: Oberleutnant Peter von Vorzik
III Gruppe JG233
JG HQ
Eastern Front
To: SS-Gruppenführer Count Christian von Vorzik
116 Kaiserstraße
Berlin

8th August 1941

Dear Christian,

What splendid news! My congratulations to both Frieda and yourself, you must both be very excited at the prospect of parenthood, just as Mathilde and I have been. Every day now I hope to have news that I have become a father. Like us you will no doubt be delighted with either a boy or a girl although, like me, you will be secretly hoping for a boy; you, because you write about "continuing the line," me, because I think I could be a much more interesting father to a boy, be more understanding and enthusiastic about his interests. I cannot imagine myself playing with dolls whereas I could make a son model gliders and aeroplanes.

As for the *Lebensborn* programme that you mention; I can understand the philosophy behind it and the feeling that you would want to do your duty as an SS-Gruppenführer, but it cannot give the satisfaction or joy of holding your own child in your arms. nurturing it and guiding it to maturity. After all, one is something more than a mere fertility machine, however laudable it may be to produce strong, healthy Aryan infants for the assured continuance of the Third Reich. Besides, there is nothing to stop you contributing to the programme as well, is there, if you feel it your duty to do so.

I know Mathilde will be delighted at the news and will be only too ready to advise Frieda on the problems of pregnancy. Doubtless she now considers herself an authority on the subject! Ursula will continue to assist Mathilde with our child for a while after he/she (I will not write "it") is born but then she could be of help to Frieda, should she need it. It is very gratifying to think that there will be young cousins of near contemporary age. Have you been thinking of names? As you probably know, we have decided on Wolfgang or Renata as first names. If your firstborn is a boy

259

you may wish to name him after father.

Dear brother, I sense from your letter that you have a misplaced feeling of guilt that you are not directly in the firing line in the great struggle with our enemies. You need not reassure me that your work in detecting those insidious enemies who would use every means to destroy our great country and its people is at least as important as flying with the Luftwaffe or fighting with the Waffen-SS. We both entered the service of the Reich before war began and we both continue to serve in our best capacity. How ineffective I would be in trying to do your work and how wasted you would be leading a Panzer group! I have always wanted to fly in some capacity and hope and expect to do so after the war in civilian aviation. You have always shown interest in politics and diplomacy and obviously excel at it; we both serve our country and our Führer as best we may and there is no point in making comparisons between our different ways of doing it. Be assured, Christian, I will always have the greatest admiration and respect for your achievements.

Yes, Edith is excited about going to Rome and I am sure her relationship with Arturo makes it all the more fascinating. We must be glad that she has found a very worthy object of her affections. He comes from a very distinguished family and the fact that he is not German is of little consequence. The Italian race has given the world so much that is great and noble, from classical antiquity to the flowering of the Renaissance and modern Italy is continuing in that great tradition. I would point out that you, too, have discovered a partner from beyond the borders of Greater Germany. We must hope that Edith's commitment to Arturo − if that is what it will turn out to be − is as happy as our choices have been with our own dear respective wives.

We still continue to register great military successes although the pace has slowed a little now that the initial surprise of our attack is over. Even so, I know we shall soon achieve an overwhelming victory and be reunited once more as a family. Salutations, dear brother, and once more many congratulations on your forthcoming fatherhood.

Ever your loving brother,
Peter

From: Oberleutnant Peter von Vorzik
III Gruppe JG233
JG HQ
Eastern Front
To: Edith von Vorzik
Apt 2, 47 Scharnhorst Straße
Berlin

14th August 1941

My Dear Edith,

How pleased I was to have your last letter! You always manage to give me glimpses of "normal" life back home that enable me to forget, briefly, the realities of the battlefront. In particular I was very interested to hear of your meeting with SS-Untersturmführer Vedder. Quite coincidentally I had heard his name mentioned in conversation (not very favourably) just a few days before your letter arrived. We had a very welcome visit from a concert pianist, Ulrich Matthes, travelling with his agent who had once worked with Vedder. His name came up as he is now in charge of organising concerts for the Luftwaffe and, apparently, his career has been very up and down – very up at the moment! Some years ago he was dismissed from Steinway for embezzling artists' funds. Later he was dismissed from the Reichsmusikkammer for other misdemeanours. Even so, he managed to stay out of prison and somehow become agent for such distinguished musicians as Karajan, Swarowsky, Krauss, Arrau, Fischer, Michelangeli and so on. He managed to obtain the friendship of Himmler's adjutant, Ludolf von Alvensleben, who proposed him for the SS. He even has the support of Göring! The one person he could not cajole into his net was Furtwängler, hence his antipathy to that conductor and his promotion of Karajan as a rival. However, Furtwängler has Goebbels on his side, purely to thwart Göring! Isn't all this extraordinary? And what a coincidence that you should meet Vedder about the same time that I was hearing all this gossip! You are quite right: it is difficult to understand that these distinguished and powerful people can be motivated by petty jealousies and spite.

I am only too pleased that you should continue to confide in me about your relationship with Arturo – and, indeed, about any other matter that you wish to bring up. You know, dear sister, I would never laugh at your confidences, never consider your genuine emotions as mere "schoolgirl

261

sentimentality". I think it is very likely that you are in love. It is a very perplexing emotion and I am sure it affects us all in subtly different ways. Certainly the object of one's affections stays in the mind most of one's waking hours; details of features, mannerisms, laughter are all recorded in the mind and seem to unlock themselves at regular intervals, sometimes most inconveniently! One finds oneself daydreaming when one should be on a task – even while carrying on a conversation! Anyway, these were some of my feelings when I fell in love with Mathilde and, although I have no other experience to draw upon, I feel sure that if you feel the same way about Arturo then you, too, have fallen prey to Cupid! Enjoy the emotion, dear sister, though it is rather like telling someone to enjoy a certain ache around the heart, is it not? I am sure you will have a wonderful time in Rome; it must be a splendid city and I look forward so much to hearing all about your visit. However, do not for one moment worry about meeting Arturo's family. You are a delightful person – why do you think he has singled you out for his affectionate attention? – and you need have no fear of appearing in any way inferior. Your months in Berlin have made you into a very poised young woman, in the most objective way I can call you extremely pretty, you are of good family with many connections throughout European aristocracy so I am sure Arturo will be very proud to show you off to his mother and sisters and brother. Just enjoy yourself and just be yourself.

As you will know from all the radio reports and the newspapers, we are making progress in our campaign to destroy the threat from our Communist enemy. There is a momentary hiatus here and there along the battlefront but it is a brief breathing-space before we advance again. Kurt asks to be remembered to you, he remains my ever-faithful Katschmarek and he protects me like a guardian angel! Even so, dear sister, please continue to pray for me.

Ever your loving brother,
Peter

Oberleutnant Peter von Vorzik
Journal entry

18th August 1941

By order of the Führer several Jadgeschwader have been moved from the central front to fight with the Finns approaching Leningrad and to the south-east to support our advance into the Caucasus. JG233 is remaining here, however, carrying out defensive patrols and offensive attacks against ground targets until such time as Army Group Centre is ordered to move forward again towards Moscow.

Rumour has it that there has been a great difference of opinion between the Führer and the Generals of the High Command, von Brauchitsch, Halder and von Bock, who all wanted to race on to Moscow whereas the Führer considers it more important to capture the Russian oilfields and granaries of the Caucasus and to link up with the Finns to the north. Who is to say which is the greater strategic objective? The Führer, it seems, has overruled his Generals. What is certain is that we are having an easy time of it compared to the frantic activity of the last ten weeks. There has been very little Russian air activity recently and our raids on road junctions, tank concentrations, railway centres and munitions dumps are only met with anti-aircraft fire – although I hasten to add that that is fierce and accurate. We have lost several Jabos and escorting fighters that way including one of the aces of JG53, Oberleutnant Erich Schmidt, who had been credited with forty-seven victories. Already there are horrible tales of how the Russians treat Luftwaffe aircrews who have been taken prisoner. Some have been shot out of hand, others subjected to unspeakable tortures. We have been issued with cyanide capsules, little glass phials protected by a metallic casing, to bite into should we find ourselves about to be taken prisoner; it would certainly be a preferable death to lynching by Russians troops or the Partisans who are said to infest the forest areas.

An item of news that has just filtered through is that the British Prime Minister, Winston Churchill, has sailed across the Atlantic in a British battleship to meet the American President, Theodore Roosevelt, and they have published to the world what they call the Atlantic Charter: a farrago of sanctimonious "principles" in the national policies of their respective countries, apparently meant to influence a number of important neutral nations such as Sweden, Switzerland, Turkey, Iran, Argentina and even Japan. What it does establish is that the United States is a belligerent nation only just stopping short of declaring war on us. They are already helping the British with arms and armaments and carrying out offensive patrols against our submarines in the Atlantic. What hypocrisy! Well, little do they know what risks they are taking. When I was at Rechlin Claus told me in great confidence that three of our aircraft companies, Focke-Wulf, Junkers and Messerschmitt, have received orders to develop an Amerika-bomber capable of flying to New York and back without refuelling. Just imagine what panic and destruction would ensue with even just a few bombs scattered amongst those New York skyscrapers.

Kurt had a letter from home telling him that his father had suffered a heart attack. He is out of hospital but will have to be treated as an invalid for the foreseeable future. Kurt is obviously very worried about the situation, his mother is not a strong woman and this will place an extra burden on her. I offered, in the most discreet way I could, to pay for a nurse to come in every day but he declined with profuse thanks. He also refused my suggestion that he apply for compassionate leave, saying that his duty was at my side as my Katschmarek. I said I could arrange for one of the new intake of pilots to the Staffel to take his place for two or three weeks, but he said he would not leave me in the hands of someone inexperienced. After a pause he added, "You are as important to me as any member of my family." I was so moved by that remark that I could hardly mumble my thanks.

As I write an even more emotional moment has occurred: a messenger came from the telegraph office to say that Mathilde has been safely delivered of a healthy boy – little Wolfgang! My eyes are blurred with tears of joy and excitement and I must hurry to the office and try and send a reply to my darling wife. After that a magnum of champagne in the mess to celebrate with my comrades.

From: Oberleutnant Peter von Vorzik
III Gruppe JG233
JG HQ
Eastern Front
To: Mathilde von Vorzik
23 Hevelius Straße
Grunewald

19th August 1941

My own darling Mathilde,
What happiness and relief! I wept with joy when I received the telegram to say that little Wolfchen had arrived and that you were both safe and well. I tried to get through to you by telephone, longing to hear your

voice, but it was impossible; I do hope you received my telegraphed reply? So many thoughts now clutter my head that I do not know how to put them down except as they occur to me, in a jumble, so if trivial subjects are mixed with important ones it is because I have not time to sort them out in proper order. Dearest one, my very first thought is for your health. Do not try and get up or do anything strenuous until you have completely recovered from the ordeal of the birth. I know that modern obstetrics takes a different view of postnatal activity from that which was advised for our own mothers – one of my comrades says that his sister was up and about within two days of delivery – but I would feel much happier if I could be certain that you were resting for three or four weeks. Of course I realise that you will need to do certain exercises (all my maternity information comes from friends in the mess!) to regain your figure and general health, but please do write and assure me that you will retain Ursula to look after you for the foreseeable future. I have already suggested that she might be of help to Frieda when her pregnancy is more advanced, but before Ursula leaves you we must engage a nanny or some permanent help with the baby. Is Gretchen still coming in to do the housework or has she been directed to join one of the Labour Front organisations?

I am writing to the bank manager to instruct him to double your monthly allowance so that you may have enough to draw upon for whatever you and Wolfchen may need. If this proves insufficient Christian will loan whatever you want until I am able to repay him. As soon as you are able do take little Wolfchen to the photographer's, I am longing to have a picture of him and another with you. I shall be so proud to show it to my comrades who are always displaying pictures of their wives, children and sweethearts. Does he have any hair? What colour are his eyes? Someone said all babies have blue eyes at first and then they change after a few weeks and someone else said no, that is kittens! As we both have blue eyes I expect that is what he will have, too.

My darling, every moment is filled with thoughts of you. No need to tell you how I long to take you in my arms and press my lips against yours... and to hold my own son and listen to his baby cries. It would be wrong of me to pretend that there is any chance of leave in the foreseeable future. We still have a big task in front of us to complete the total defeat of the Russians but, all being well, that should have been achieved by the autumn.

Perhaps, in another six or eight weeks my dream of seeing you and baby Wolfchen may come true. Until then I must strive to be patient. At the moment we are regrouping for the final thrust that will bring us victory.

I have met an old friend from my training days at Werneuchen. He is a pilot with a Zerstörertaffel that has been attached to us. His name is Lother Kohl and he also comes from Munich so we are able to reminisce about our childhood days and our early attempts at flying – we had the same instructors as Claus Grüber. Apart from Kurt (who sends his best wishes and congratulations to you) I have no really close friends in the Staffel; as Staffelkapitan it is best to keep one's distance so as not to appear to indulge in any favouritism, so I can be friendly with Lother without seeming to favour one pilot over another. It is strange how sometimes grown men can display schoolboyish jealousies over friendships!

Now, my darling, I must hurry this to the post so that you will know of my unbounded joy and pride at the birth of our first child and my undying love and devotion to you.

Dreaming of the moment when I am with you once more.

Ever your own,

Peter

From: Edith von Vorzik
Apt 2, 47 Scharnhorst Straße
Berlin
To: Oberleutnant Peter von Vorzik
III Gruppe JG233
JG HQ
Eastern Front

19th August 1941

My Dear Peter,

I hasten to write (typing this on the office machine) about the birth of your son as I know Mathilde may not be able to write for a day or two, simply because she is busy feeding little Wolfchen and doing all the postnatal things that women are obliged to do. Even so, she tells me that she will be sending you a letter very soon. The labour pains began about eleven at night, the day before yesterday, and after telephoning me

Ursula took Mathilde to the nursing clinic at Grunewald by taxi. All the arrangements went smoothly. Ursula has had a bag packed for the last two weeks, just in case the baby came early, and her father's brother runs a taxi service so she had primed him that there might be a call late at night. (There are few taxis to be had in Berlin these days.) As a safeguard she had arranged to call me whenever it was, day or night, and I would have driven over in the little DKW if the taxi arrangement failed, although it would have taken me the best part of an hour to get to the house. Anyway, such measures were not necessary and it was another five hours before Wolfchen made his appearance, so yesterday, 18th August, is his birthday. According to Ursula and the chief nursing sister it was an easy, straightforward birth although, of course, no birth is "easy"; all births include a lot of pain and effort but, in this case, without complications of any sort. I arrived half an hour after Wolfchen, to find Mathilde looking flushed and triumphant and Wolfchen already suckling happily!

To be honest it is not easy to say at this early stage who Wolfchen takes after, his tiny features scarcely formed, but he does have big blue eyes and a sort of light, soft down on his head which will no doubt become hair. It will be some months before we can distinguish real characteristics, it is enough that he has everything perfectly formed. I have not seen many babies in my life and each time I am astonished at their tiny hands, so exquisite, with fingernails smaller than a doll's. I know how you must be longing to see him, dear Peter; for the moment just rest assured that he has been safely born and he and his mother are in good health. Ursula has said that she will stay at least another month and will make regular visits thereafter to make sure everything is progressing well.

For my part I cannot contain my excitement now that my visit to Arturo in Rome is only two weeks away. Lina is helping me put together a wardrobe for the visit, lending me two of her evening dresses for formal occasions. The weather there will be much warmer than it is here in Berlin and I do not have many clothes for really hot weather. We are going shopping tomorrow to a new place that has opened on the Ku'damm, a sort of second-hand emporium now that clothing is rationed. Lina says she has taken clothes there and bought other things and that she has found dresses from some of the great French couture houses. I have to look smart for Arturo! I can hear you saying, "what feminine nonsense!" but you must allow me some frivolity in these harsh times. I was encouraged by your kind remarks in your last letter and feel, now, that I shall not look like a dowdy hausfrau when I meet Arturo's mother and sisters.

I have not seen very much of Christian, he has been very busy in conferences with one of von Ribbentrop's entourage, an under-secretary called Martin Luther, as Reinhard hates von R's organisation so much he cannot bring himself to collaborate personally. I understand it is all to do with forcing the Jewish community here to evacuate to the east. Christian says he hates the whole business but has to do Reinhard's bidding.

Dear brother, you are in all our thoughts even more than usual. I am so happy for you and hope it will not be long before you are able to see your beautiful son. Meanwhile I pray, as always, that God will keep you safe until you return to the loving arms of all your family;

Especially those of
your devoted sister,
Edith

From: Mathilde von Vorzik
Prinzessin Eugenie Nursing clinic
Königsallee
Grunewald
To: Oberleutnant Peter von Vorzik
III Gruppe JG233
JG HQ
Eastern Front

22nd August 1941

My Dearest Darling Peter,
Your letter arrived this morning and, as I always do, I have been reading it over and over. I think to myself: his hand held this sheet of paper, his lips sealed this envelope, and even without the words it brings me close to you. Yes, darling, we have a wonderful little baby boy, made by us, sealing our love for each other and I am deliriously happy. Only one thing detracts from that joyful state... but I project my thoughts to some day in the future and think, dream, of that moment when you are with me again. Lying here with little Wolfchen at my breast I have been thinking of so

much that has happened in these last two years, it is almost two years to the day since we met at that reception your brother gave. And, now, here I am with your child a warm little bundle at my side, your flesh made one with mine. How extraordinary life is!

I know Edith wrote to you some days ago and told you the details of Wolfchen's birth. Strangely I do not remember very much about the birth itself, those moments of pain and anxiety. I suppose it is one of nature's tricks that the actual birth pangs are soon forgotten so as not to deter one from repeating the process. I do remember hearing Wolfchen's first cries and the nursing sister calling out, "It's a boy!" Then I relapsed into a sort of dream state for a while. Edith arrived soon after and stayed with me for two hours until it was time for her to return to her office. Several friends have visited me including Lina who came with a bottle of champagne although the sister only allowed me the tiniest sip. Tomorrow I am going for a short walk in the grounds, I am anxious to regain my figure before you come on leave! Frieda also came to see me and, of course, was full of questions about the birth although, as I have told you, I found it difficult to give her any details. I think she is somewhat apprehensive as people always emphasise how painful and difficult it can be. I tried to reassure her and said I was sure that, having been a dancer, her muscles would be strong and supple and ensure an easy birth. I do not think she was convinced. She said that Christian had seemed rather morose lately, something to do with his duties which have kept him away from home a lot. I think Frieda misses the gaiety of her theatre life and friends and feels oppressed by all the formality and protocol of the diplomatic and Party circles she has to move in now. As soon as I am up and about again I will make a point of asking her for lunch and joining me on shopping excursions – although now there is less and less to shop for.

My dearest Peter, my thoughts are constantly with you. I listen avidly to all the radio reports which are encouraging but each time I hear of some battle I naturally wonder if your Staffel has been involved. You say in your letter that it may be another six or eight weeks before the Russians are defeated and although it is really only a short time in many ways it seems like an eternity. Well, it will pass and the three of us will be together at last. I comfort myself with thinking how, in some ways, time flies, how it seems, now, only a few weeks ago I was telling you in another letter that I was pregnant. Isn't it strange how time is so elastic? Sometimes it seems so slow in passing, at others it rushes by. Now, darling, I am giving this to the ward nurse to post, praying that time will rush by for us both.

Until then, all my deepest love.

Yours eternally,
Mathilde

From: SS-Gruppenführer Count Christian von Vorzik
116 Kaiserstraße
Berlin
To: Oberleutnant Peter von Vorzik
III Gruppe JG233
JG HQ
Eastern Front

23rd August 1941

My Dear Brother,

I hasten to add my congratulations on the birth of your first child. What pride and happiness you must feel! I am sure it will be an added incentive for you, in your daily fight against our enemies, to make the Third Reich safe for our families and children. Another male to carry on our lineage. I pray that I, too, will be favoured with a boy when Frieda's time comes. When you are next granted leave we must have a real celebration.

For my part I have been closely involved in a most distasteful assignment, liaising with the IVB4 office at 116 Kaiserstraße to co-ordinate the evacuation of the Jews remaining in Berlin. Reinhard has received directives from both Reichsmarschall Göring and Reichsminister Goebbels that this must be completed as an immediate priority. I have been collaborating with SS-Sturmbannführer Adolf Eichmann, a pedantic bureaucrat who has been inexplicably promoted within the ranks of the SS. Just between us, I regret the inclusion of certain people within what should be an elite organisation, creatures like Daluege, an absolute boor, and Eichmann, an unimaginative member of the petite bourgeoisie. Anyway, the assignment is completed now and Reinhard has promised that he will keep me close in his immediate entourage in future. He appreciates my loyalty to him.

Responding to Herr Goebbels's directive, it has been decided that all Jews shall wear a yellow star on their clothing for identification purposes;

they will be banned from using all forms of public transportation and they will have to turn in articles of use and luxury, such as bicycles, typewriters, gramophones, refrigerators, electric stoves, books, hand-mirrors and tobacco. They are also banned from using the services of German tradesmen. These measures may seem harsh but Goebbels is determined that what he calls "this parasitic people" should be flushed out of Germany in general and Berlin in particular. Daluege, as Chief of the Ordnungspolizei, is organising transport to take these people to Lodz, Minsk, Kovno and Riga. Incidentally, I often see Daluege riding about in our old Maybach! He really is an insufferable man – Reinhard hates him.

The situation with regard to von Ribbentrop has resolved itself, insofar that he has taken up residence in a delapidated house, Schloss Steinort, in east Prussia in order to be near the Führer in his campaign headquarters at Rastenburg. The amusing thing is, late last July von Ribbentrop had a blazing row with Hitler that ended with von R offering his resignation! Apparently, it all began because von R pestered H over some trivial question about a decoration for gallantry that von R wanted to be available for diplomats. H was irritated to be bothered with such questions when so much of his attention needed to be focused on the eastern front; one thing led to another until H had one of his rages, collapsing into a chair and accusing von R of trying to kill him! Von R later retracted his offer of resignation but retired to his bed in a darkened room for days. Apparently he has not been near Rastenburg since. Reinhard and Reichsführer-SS Himmler laughed about it for days. Frankly, I find it appalling that such scenes can occur when the whole country is engaged in a fight for survival.

I visited Mathilde in the nursing clinic and found her in splendid health and spirits. She has been walking in the grounds and looks forward to returning home with your baby son who also looks a pink bundle of health. So, dear brother, do not worry about the domestic scene, I shall keep a watching eye whenever I am able, as does Edith. The important thing is that you should take care of yourself while performing your heroic duties for the Fatherland. Let us hope that ultimate victory will be ours within a few weeks and you will be home again with your devoted family.

Ever your loving brother,
Christian

The Führer and Supreme Commander of the Armed Forces
Führer Headquarters

6th September 1941

10 Copies

DIRECTIVE NO 35 (Excerpts)

Combined with the progressive encirclement of the Leningrad area, the initial successes against the enemy forces in the area between the flanks of the Army Group south and centre have provided favourable conditions for a decisive operation against the Timoshenko Army Group which is attacking on the central front. This Army Group must be defeated and annihilated in the limited time which remains before the onset of winter weather. For this purpose it is necessary to concentrate all the forces of the Army and Air Force which can be spared on the flanks and which can be brought up in time. On the basis of the report of Commander-in-Chief Army, I issue the following orders for the preparation and execution of these operations:

2. On the central front, the operation against the Timoshenko Army Group will be planned so that the attack can begin at the earliest possible moment (end of September) with the aim of destroying enemy forces located in the area east of Smolensk by a pincer movement in the general direction of Viazma, with strong concentrations of armour on the flanks. The Air Force will support the offensive with the 2nd Air Fleet, which will be reinforced at the appropriate time, especially from the north-east area. It will concentrate on the flanks and will employ the bulk of its dive-bomber units (VIII Air Corps) in support of the motorised forces on both flanks.

4. As regards further operations, it is intended that the offensive towards Moscow by Army Group Centre should be covered by a flank guard composed of available motorised forces in the Army Group South sector and advancing in a general north-east direction, and that forces from Army Group North should be moved forward on both sides of Lake Ilmen to cover the northern flank and to maintain contact with the Finnish Karelian Army.

5. Any saving of time and consequent advance of the timetable will be to the advantage of the whole operation and its preparation.

Adolf Hitler

Oberleutnant Peter von Vorzik
Journal entry

7th September 1941

Last week was the second anniversary of the beginning of our war of survival. No one thought, then, that we would still be fighting but I think it is safe to say that the end is in sight. Our armies here on the eastern front are poised for a final assault against the Russian hordes and when they are defeated we shall be able to finish off the British at our leisure. Operational sorties have more than doubled these last two days in preparation for a new offensive by Army Group Centre that will take us to Moscow. We have been escorting Stuka and Zerstörer Staffeln attacking General Timoshenko's Army Group, bombing and strafing military convoys, ammunition dumps, troop concentrations and railway centres. We have been told, however, not to cause too much destruction to railway lines as we shall need rail communication as the major means of supplying the Army. As it is, the transport Geschwader has had to fly in fuel for our fighter and bomber bases, as well as for Guderian's tanks, because the lines of communication have become overstretched and the Russian railway system is so rickety.

During this period there has only been sporadic activity by the Russian Air Force; even so I have managed to add two more kills to my score. The first was another of those slow and vulnerable Su-2 light reconnaissance bombers which was flying alone, presumably attempting to spy on our forward positions. The other kill was rather more difficult and therefore more satisfying. Kurt and I had just taken off on one of our early morning patrols when we were alerted on the r/t that three enemy bombers had been sighted flying towards our base. It was Kurt who saw them first, about 500 m below us on the starboard beam, Petlyakov Pe-2 twin-engined machines with twin fins and rudders, very much like our Me110 Zerstörer, only slightly larger. Whoever had identified them had been very sharp-sighted, the only difference visible at a distance, especially from the ground, being the rounded wing tips of the Russian aircraft as opposed to the square tips of the Me110.

There has not been very much information available about the Pe-2 except that they are one of the latest Russian types, first seen at the May Day fly-past this year, and rumoured to be very fast – and so it proved. I assume they had not seen us as they continued flying west towards our airfield; had they turned round and flown back east I doubt that we would have caught them as I calculated their speed to be about 500 kph. It would have taken us so long to catch up that we would have been too deep into enemy territory to have had enough fuel to get back to bodo.

Although they were flying quite high, about 4,000 m, we were still above them and so, as we selected the two outer aircraft of the echelon as our targets, we attained a speed advantage as we dived down on them. As I closed in on the starboard machine I was aware of tracer bullets coming up at me from the rear gunner's position, but they went wide, over my port wing tip. At the angle of my dive I knew I was presenting a minimal target area and held my own fire until I was able to see the Pe-2 filling my gunsight, the big red stars visible on the wings, fuselage and tail empennage. Easing a little to port I lined up on the bomber's port engine nacelle and fired a long burst from all three guns. I flicked to starboard to avoid more tracer bullets then back again onto the port tack so as not to lose sight of my quarry. A thin line of black smoke issued from the port engine, the propeller blades became visible as engine revolutions dropped and flames began to flicker over the surface of the wing. As his speed slowed I was in danger of overshooting the target so I throttled back and followed him as he lost altitude, slewing first to one side, then the other. He was trying to make a 180° turn; I was able to get inside him and, as he momentarily filled the gunsight once more, I fired another short burst aiming ahead about the length of the aircraft itself. Horrido! I hit the already flaming port engine which exploded in a shower of metallic fragments and the sleek bomber went into a crazy aerial dance, falling about the sky like a piece of paper blown on the wind. There was no point in trying to follow it down, it would have been impossible to anticipate its wildly eccentric fall. I last saw the aircraft as it was swallowed up in a bank of cloud, disintegrating as it disappeared.

I was particularly pleased with this little victory although, of course, it would have been better if it had made a forced landing. Luftwaffe intelligence would have been immensely pleased to have a chance to examine one of the Russkies' latest types. As it was, at my debriefing I made the comment that if you can catch them you can destroy them. The other two managed to get away because of their great speed. What is disquieting is that with the appearance of the MiG3s and the Pe-2s the Russians are capable of designing some formidable modern aircraft in direct contradiction of everything we have been told. Thankfully they appear to have very few of them and they will not have time, now, to develop them to their full potential or produce them in sufficient numbers to affect the outcome of the war.

There is a real chill in the morning air now. Autumn is nearly here and the dreaded Russian winter will follow on quickly. We will have to reach Moscow before that happens but everyone is confident that that can be done. We have all noticed the big build-up of military material that is going on just west of the Rzhev-Bryansk line, massive concentrations of tanks, artillery and infantry divisions. We are stepping up our preliminary attacks now, daily we escort Stuka Geschwader which dive-bomb fuel and ammunition dumps behind the Russian lines, although we no longer attack bridges and railway centres. We shall need to keep open all lines of communication for Army Group Centre to be supplied on its final push to the Russian capital. Perhaps, when Moscow falls, I will get leave and be able to see my darling Mathilde and baby Wolfchen.

From: Edith von Vorzik
Palazzo Villoresi
Via della Fontana
Rome
To: Oberleutnant Peter von Vorzik
III Gruppe JG233
JG HQ
Eastern Front

16th September 1941

My Dear Peter,

I have been having such an exciting but also somewhat bewildering time! Exciting because I have been visiting all the wonderful antiquities of the city, the Colisseum, the Pantheon, above all St Peter's and the marvellous museums in the Vatican City, all arranged for me by Arturo. Bewildering because the social scene here is so different to Berlin, so elegant, so relaxed, that sometimes you would not know the country is at war – and so full of extraordinary scandal and gossip! The stories that are bandied about concerning famous people and the remarks that are made at dinner parties quite astonish me. At home one would be immediately arrested for such opinions!

Occasionally I have been aware of a certain anti-German feeling; not directed at me, not personal in any way, but I get the impression that some Italians feel that Italy has become just one of Germany's "vassal states", as they say here. For instance, there is a great amount of resentment that the Duce has allowed so many Italian works of art to be transported to Germany. But I will not continue in that vein.

I have been most generously entertained by Arturo and his family and friends and I feel so exhilarated by the experiences I have enjoyed. Arturo has been able to spend a lot of time with me as Count Ciano is in hospital with a throat infection and everything at the Italian Foreign Ministry is more or less at a standstill while he is absent. His wife, Edda, (about whom there are some extraordinarily scandalous stories which I will not repeat) is serving as a nurse on the Russian front. Very courageous, I think, and an antidote to all the malicious gossip. I am sure Lina will ply me with questions when I return!

I went to a beautiful performance of Donizetti's *Lucia di Lammermoor* (an opera I have never seen before) with Arturo, the audience very dressed up and the women bedecked with jewels. I have been very glad of the clothes that Lina lent me, otherwise I should have felt very dowdy. As I thought, Arturo's mother, Eleanora, and his sisters Elisabetta and Eloise, are very stylish but also very kind and welcoming. I have seen photographs of their young brother, Massimo, who is incredibly handsome, like a film star or, rather, like a sculpture by Donatello or Michelangelo (my head is full of Italian art!). When I remarked on Massimo's good looks Arturo said, laughingly, "I'm glad you met me before you saw him!" Massimo's regiment is about to depart for the Russian front and the family have not seen him for some weeks and are very anxious about his safety. Arturo says that the Duce has not been the same man since his son, Bruno, was killed in an aircrash last month. Such events suddenly bring home to these Romans what is happening outside their city.

The shops here seem full compared to Berlin but everything is very expensive and there is a huge black market in every sort of commodity; money and position can buy anything. Arturo has been extremely generous, buying me a beautiful silk dress (the silk garments here are fabulous and I have made some small purchases for Christmas presents) and given me a diamond and sapphire bracelet which I said I simply could not accept, but he was adamant and said it was a token of his deep affection for me and hinted that his next gift would be a ring... He said he is anxious to talk to Christian so I feel certain he is going to propose.

Dear brother, I confess I have completely lost my heart to Arturo and if he should propose I would want to say "yes". Does that surprise you? Does it seem too soon, too precipitate? I am in a great quandary but, of course, the question has not yet arisen and perhaps I am misinterpreting his intentions.

It has all been so romantic, Rome is so beautiful, the city literally glows in the evening light and the nights are still velvety warm with such starry skies. There is just one week left and I know the days will fly by, my diary (I have never had what one might call a social diary before!) is full, something every day and evening. The office will seem very drab after this marvellous holiday for which I am most grateful, a wonderful tonic for both body and spirit.

I must tell you, Arturo arranged for me to fly here from Berlin in one of the Italian courier planes, a big Savoia-Marchetti with three engines – I expect you know the type I mean. Of course it was my first experience of flying and so thrilling. Dear Peter, looking out upon the clouds I suddenly knew what you see every day of your life, I knew at once how you are permeated with the joy of flight. What a wonderful feeling of freedom it gives, flying above the earth, looking down as if from some Olympian vantage point upon mere mortals! How perfect everything seems from such heights, houses like little toys, roads and fields and rivers like a painting, my words cannot do justice to the sensation. Then I thought how terribly lonely it must seem in your single-seater until I remembered you have your faithful Katschmarek in attendance. The Alps were glorious in the sunlight although the aircraft bumped about a bit owing to the rising air currents, the steward who served me coffee and sandwiches said. A most moving and wonderful experience. I expect I shall be travelling back by train.

Here I am, dear Peter, rambling on about myself and my good fortune while you are facing dangers and horrors in distant Russia. Please believe me, you are always in my thoughts and prayers (I lit a candle for you in St Peter's) and hope it will not be too long before you can join us all again in Berlin. I must stop now, Arturo has said that this letter can go at least part of the way in the diplomatic mail.

Take great care of yourself.

Ever your loving sister,
Edith

PS Amongst the things I have bought is an exquisite little silk suit, ivory with pale blue piping, for little Wolfchen, he is too small for it yet but I know he will look adorable in it. E.

From: Oberleutnant Peter von Vorzik
III Gruppe JG233
JG HQ
Eastern Front
To: Mathilde von Vorzik
23 Hevelius Straße
Grunewald

23rd September 1941

My Darling Mathilde,

I am sending this to Grunewald as I think that by the time it reaches you you will be home again. I can picture you now in that little room we prepared for baby Wolfchen, not knowing at the time what sex our child would be. How I long to have a photo of him! I visualise a round little face with large blue eyes, a nose like a button and a little pink mouth like a doll's. I feel sure that is an accurate description as I do not think babies show any distinctive features until they are several months old, do they? Anyway, dearest, do have some pictures taken as soon as you are able. Happily, I have no difficulty in visualising you, darling, even without the aid of the last photo you sent. Your dear face is an almost ever-present image in front of me, especially in those rare moments of repose, usually when I lie in my bunk at night. I consciously conjure up memories of our times together and then I fall asleep imagining you in my arms.

Summer, such as it was, is fading fast. The early morning air is chill and we have reverted to our leather flight jerkins, gloves and boots. I had a lovely letter from Edith, full of enthusiasm for her holiday in Rome, and I envy her the warm weather she describes. It is very different to the warm weather we experienced here; as I think I told you, it was really suffocating with dust and debris from the battlefields choking the air. Darkness falls now about five o'clock (17.00 hrs in our timing) and the sunsets are lurid, scarlet, crimson and purple, long streaks of colour over the endless steppe and then the ensuing twilight is over in minutes. The onset of autumn gives us a renewed sense of purpose, of having a task to perform that will hasten the time when we are all reunited.

It is no secret that we are on the verge of completing that task, the defeat of the Russian giant that threatens Europe, and the next few weeks will surely reward us with victory. On to Moscow – and then, home by Christmas! That is the phrase one often hears in the mess; it has almost become a general salutation. My dearest, I trust all is going well with you and your recovery and that Ursula is still with you and helping with the daily tasks. Do not try and do too much too soon. One of the pilots here says his wife fell into a great state of depression soon after his baby daughter was born and the doctor told him it was a common condition following childbirth. Perhaps you and baby Wolfchen should have a holiday? How about going to visit your mother? I am sure she is longing to see her grandson and the change would do you good. You could take Ursula with you and stay in a hotel if there is not room with your mother and Aunt Ilse. Alternatively, you might ask Lina about the offer she once made of her cottage on that Baltic island but on second thought that would be too remote and doubtless rather cold at this time of year. I have distant relatives near Giessen, Schloss Gründorf in the Vogelsberg hills, lovely country; Christian and I spent holidays there as boys. Our cousins live very quietly and simply and I am sure they would make you welcome. Shall I ask Christian to arrange it?

Now, dearest, I must hurry to catch the Staffel post.

My thoughts are forever with you.

Your own,

Peter

PS Have you received notification from the bank regarding the doubling of your allowance? Please do not go short of anything, Christian will always advance you money should you need it. P.

From: Oberleutnant Peter von Vorzik
III Gruppe JG233
JG HQ
Eastern front
To: Edith von Vorzik
Apt 2, 47 Scharnhorst Straße
Berlin

28th September 1941

My Dear Edith,

It was such a tonic to receive your long letter from Rome, almost as good as having a holiday there oneself! I could picture you visiting all those architectural monuments, the sunlit city, the warm, starry nights. For a few minutes it took me into another world, away from the featureless steppes, the primitive life we have here. We are bracing ourselves for one big last push, the final few hundred kilometres to Moscow and then, who knows? I might be able to take Mathilde and baby Wolfchen to visit Rome, too.

I fully understand your quandary about Arturo. Yes, the thought of your marrying him does seem sudden. How long is it since you met him? Four months? Five? And yet, the times we are living in do speed things up, don't they? Even such things as love and marriage – and I have the strong impression that you really do love him. After all, my marriage to Mathilde was, by ordinary standards, by which I mean peacetime usages, rather quick. Normally, one would have a courtship of at least a year, perhaps two. Anything quicker would make one suspicious that the lady in question was with child! So there you are, dear Edith. Personally, I can see no impediment to your marrying him if – and only if – you are really sure you are in love, and he is, too. As you say, he has not yet formally proposed so this is all conjecture. But should that happen I would certainly be in agreement with your positive decision and I feel sure Christian would, too. His marriage to Frieda was almost equally sudden!

I have no personal news that I can write about. As I said, we anticipate a final thrust to Moscow any day now, it must come, must be over, before winter sets in. The early mornings and nights are getting cold, the only thing in common with your Roman visit is the starry sky. When the weather is clear the sky, so much further north than we are used to, is quite fantastic, just as if someone had strewn a thousand million diamonds on velvet.

Rather a cliché, I suppose, but that is really what it is like because the surrounding steppe is so flat, the horizon so low and there is no other light interference. Kurt and I spend time picking out the major constellations, Pegasus, Andromeda, Orion, Taurus, etc. While we were stargazing the other night we were quite startled by the shriek of an owl from a nearby birchwood and then there was another answering call and another. It was very eerie, somehow emphasising the vastness and loneliness of the space we inhabit. When I remarked on this to Kurt he said, "Lonely? Don't forget there are about a million men between us and Moscow!"

Thank you again for your Roman epistle. I was intrigued by what you tell me of Roman society. I do not think the Italians have the same understanding of, certainly not the commitment to, the war that we have. Their geographical position and their climate must make it all seem much more distant, less immediate, than it does to us. And, of course, their temperament is more volatile, more easily deflected than ours. You are now in a position to see both sides.

Yes, I do know the type of aeroplane you write about. I am so pleased that you have had your first flight and gained an inkling of what flying means to me. It is a wonderful feeling and I am all the more privileged in that I am in control of my machine; it sometimes feels that it is I who is flying. And no, I never feel lonely even when, on rare occasions, Kurt is not there. Alone but not lonely. So, dear sister, I must say *auf Wiedersehen* – or should it be *arrivederci*? Write to me when you are able, I am sure returning to your office will be a big bump back to reality for you.

Ever your loving brother,
Peter

Oberleutnant Peter von Vorzik
Journal entry

15th October 1941

We are on our way to Moscow! Our new offensive began just over two weeks ago and the subsequent operations for the Gruppe have been so hectic, so time-consuming, that I have not had a chance to continue this journal until now. As it is, it is late at night, 23.20 hrs, and I am writing this in my bunk by the light of a small paraffin lamp. During the last two years I have been in the vanguard of so many offensives – the attack on

Poland, the attack on France, the battles over Britain, the opening offensive on Russia and now the renewed offensive against our biggest enemy. Of course, there is more than just a sense of *déjà vu* at each briefing before a big attack, more a sense of renewed effort, another phase in an overall plan – perhaps, now, the final phase of all. With Russia kaput there can be no doubt that Britain will sue for peace. Common sense will prevail and even their aggressive Prime Minister, that posturing Churchill, will realise that his country's position is hopeless despite the help they are receiving from their Empire and America.

Once again we have been flying four, five, even six sorties a day escorting Stukas and Zerstörer during their attacks on Russian forward positions. There are streams of civilian refugees clogging the roads and tracks going east, just as they did in France last summer, adding chaos behind the enemy lines. Radio reports say that there is also a huge exodus from Moscow, real panic as our advance nears the city. When we get there we shall probably find the place quite empty! There has been very little enemy air activity during these last two weeks although between us, Kurt and I have dispatched five more Ratas, three by me, two by him. That makes my score thirty-nine certified kills and nineteen for Kurt. Other members of the Staffel have had similar successes. All five of our Ratas were easy victims flown by obviously inexperienced pilots unlike some of the fliers we encountered a month or two ago. These are novices, poorly trained, easy prey, unable to take advantage of their aircraft's capabilities, such as they are, little more than target practice for us. The Russians seem to be throwing in student pilots in a last desperate attempt to stop us.

On the ground, however, the battles have been ferocious. Several Russian divisions have been encircled in salients running north-south between Viazma and Bryansk, an area of country that the Staffel has become very familiar with during the last month. Our communiques estimate that, in attempting to break out from our encircling forces, the Russians have lost over half a million men killed, wounded or taken prisoner as well as 1,200 tanks and more than 5,000 guns.

My three Ratas were shot down while the Staffel was accompanying my friend Lother's Zerstörer Staffel from I ZG26 and in the evening I was invited over to his mess to celebrate. Lother told me he was one of the fighter pilots persuaded to join the Zerstörer Gruppen and he very much regrets it. I told him that Reichsmarschall Göring had also suggested it to me when he decorated me two years ago. Lother has been trying without success to get transferred back into a single-seat fighter Gruppe. The Me110 Zerstörer has not proved to be the superior weapon that the Reichsmarschall promised. Instead of being a fighter-destroyer paving the way for the heavy bombers its comparative slowness and lack of manoeuvrability make it in need of fighter protection itself. Trying to cheer him up, I told Lother that when I visited Rechlin I saw a sleek new aircraft, the Me210, intended as a replacement for the Me110 but Lother knew all about it as he is a friend of one of the test pilots, Flugkapitan Fritz Wendel, who had had to bale out when one of the tailplanes broke away during diving tests. Apparently the flying characteristics are so vicious that the aircraft is considered unsuitable for operational service and Messerschmitt are going to lose millions of Reichsmarks because of the delay in getting it into service. We both agreed that those test pilots risk their lives more often than we do flying on daily operations.

This evening's communique from OKW announced that General Guderian's tank forces have broken through the Viazma-Bryansk line and are within reach of Mozhaisk just 70 km from Moscow. It cannot be long now before the Führer, his Wehrmacht and his Luftwaffe will have succeeded where Napoleon and his troops failed.

From: Mathilde von Vorzik
23 Hevelius Straße
Grunewald
To: Oberleutnant Peter von Vorzik
III Gruppe JG233
JG HQ
Eastern Front

24th October 1941

My Darling Peter,
Although your lovely letter arrived nearly two weeks ago I have delayed sending this until I had the photos of Wolfchen which I know you have been longing to receive. So, here they are! I think they are very good, don't you? I took him to that same little man on the Ku'damm that I went

to before (Ursula came with me) and he took a lot of trouble with the pictures. He said small babies are less difficult to photograph than children who often cry or won't smile or cannot sit still long enough. Anyway, Wolfchen was very well behaved (I had fed him an hour before) and the only difficulty was to keep him awake. He is too young to smile yet, Ursula says he is not yet able to focus properly and what sometimes seems like a smile is only a grimace through wind! So here, darling, are the first pictures of your first child. As you see, I had some taken with me. I long for the day when we have pictures of all three of us.

We hear on the radio of the new advances and know you must be involved. It all seems to be going marvellously well but, as always, we are all apprehensive for your safety. How wonderful it will be when it is all over and we are at peace again and those anxieties are banished forever. Who would have believed that the war would last more than two years?

Now, darling, about your suggestion of taking a holiday. I really do not think it is what I need at the moment. I am feeling very well (my figure is beginning to come back I am sure you will be pleased to hear), I have a good appetite and no sign of the depression you wrote about. Rather a sense of exhilaration, in fact. I adore doing all the motherly things, feeding him and bathing him – even changing him! Wolfchen is such a good baby, hardly ever cries, has just one feed during the night and Ursula does most of the heavy work like washing and ironing. I would not want to go to Cologne (I could not bear to be alone in a hotel with memories of our visits) as mother and Ilse are not equipped to accommodate mother and baby. I have sent them copies of the photos. Nor would I want to take up your suggestion of visiting your cousins at Giessen. I am sure they are charming and hospitable people but it is quite an imposition to arrive with a new-born baby, you know. Besides, I need to be near the clinic at the moment for his monthly check-up and, again, travelling is apparently very arduous nowadays (Ursula's sister had a very tedious journey to Dresden some weeks ago). Trains are slow and very crowded and it is necessary, now, to get travel permits to visit certain areas. Lina did say again that her cottage is open to us whenever we want but, as you yourself said, the Baltic would be rather cold and remote at this time of year. As it is we have been having some lovely autumn weather; the trees have all turned into their glorious autumn colours. Whenever it is fine we take Wolfchen around the lake paths and it is almost like being in the country. We will wait, darling, until you are back with us and perhaps take a holiday then.

Lina calls once or twice a week to keep me company though she has not been quite her usual vivacious self of late. Reinhard has been in Prague for some time (he took Christian with him) and has been unable to spend much time at home. She has passed on some lovely baby clothes for Wolfchen and Edith arrived back from Rome with the most beautiful little silk suit for him. She had a wonderful time there and is obviously very much in love with Arturo. She hinted that he might be proposing to her in the near future and I am so happy for her. What an amazing change there is in her since she came to Berlin! I cannot recognise the shy retiring person I first encountered in the poised and sophisticated young woman she is now.

I must stop, darling, and get these photos to you.

Love and kisses from little Wolfchen and from

Your loving wife,
Mathilde

From: SS-Gruppenführer Count Christian von Vorzik
Lobkowitz Palace
Hradcany Castle
Prague
To: Oberleutnant Peter von Vorzik
III Gruppe JG233
JG HQ
Eastern Front

24th September 1941

My Dear Peter,
Here I am in Prague, a most beautiful city comparable, in its way, with Vienna and Paris. The Lobkowitz Palace where we are staying is quite splendid, fine pictures and tapestries, very comfortable quarters but not so well heated! My suite of rooms is very chilly now that the weather has turned cold but we are well wined and dined and attended by an army of well-trained servants. I have had little chance to view the cathedral and other architectural splendours as Reinhard has kept me extremely busy since we arrived about a week ago. All rather subjudice at the moment, R is keen to remove a leading member of the Protectorate Government whom we suspect of working with the Czech resistance movement and

the émigré Czech Government in London. No doubt you will be reading about it in the papers or hearing about it on the radio in due course.

Tomorrow we leave for Rastenburg to join Reichsführer-SS Himmler at the Führer's Wolfsschanze which is in itself rather an exciting prospect, being at the very heart of the Führer's direction of the war. Count Ciano will also be there and if I have an opportunity I will have a word with Arturo who, I am sure, will also be in attendance. I want to sound him out regarding his intentions towards Edith and I shall have a chance to form my own impressions of the man. Edith returned from Rome besotted with both her amour and the city but naturally, at her age and with her lack of experience, she is bound to be infatuated with it all. Pleased as I am that she has found someone whom she finds attractive I want to make sure that, on his part, he has integrity and prospects for the future.

Everything seems to be gathering pace, both on the political and military levels. Following the Rastenburg meeting von Ribbentrop has arranged for us to join him and Ciano at a big shoot on his estate, Schönhof, in Bohemia. Himmler does not want to go because he detests both von Ribbentrop and blood sports but the Führer has ordered him to be present. Reinhard and I are looking forward to some relaxation and will observe von Ribbentrop playing the grandiloquent host with no little amusement!

Next month we shall be back in Berlin for another big conference between the Axis foreign ministers, a celebration of the anniversary of the signing of the anti-Comintern pact, and its renewal for another five years. Perhaps, who knows, by then we shall have finally defeated Russia and the pact will be redundant. At any rate, this conference will establish the solidarity of all Europe against the threat of Communism; Bulgaria, Croatia, Denmark, Finland, Hungary, Rumania, Slovakia and Spain are all due to be signatories.

I have no doubt, dear brother, that you are once more in the midst of the new offensive, supporting our victorious troops as they advance on Moscow. It is my dearest wish to see a final victory so that you may be back from the battlefields to take your place within the family. These last few weeks have been rather trying for Frieda; just when she would have liked me to be near I have had to be away. There have been times when she might have accompanied me but now that she is pregnant we thought it best for her to take things quietly. Lina, I know, has been very helpful as she always is and I hear that Mathilde and Frieda have also visited one another. It is reassuring to know that the women in our lives give each other such support, is it not? I did warn Frieda that my work entailed much travelling about for the forseeable future but she was quite ready to accept that. Her retirement from the stage, however, has been much more difficult for her to accommodate. When the baby arrives I am sure that will be full recompense.

I will let you know in due course my feelings about Arturo.

Meanwhile, I wish you every success in your great endeavours as a pilot and may we be granted victory soon.

Ever your devoted brother,
Christian
Heil Hitler!

From: Oberleutnant Peter von Vorzik
III Gruppe JG233
JG HQ
Eastern Front
To: Mathilde von Vorzik
23 Hevelius Straße
Grunewald

3rd November 1941

My Dearest Mathilde,
Your letter and the photos of Wolfchen arrived today and seemed like a burst of brilliant sunshine in this bleak landscape! It has begun to rain here, the wind is like a knife in the face but your dear faces smiling (well, I know little Wolfchen is not smiling) from the photos have continued to cheer me up for several hours. I have looked and looked at the photos, studying every detail until they are indelibly etched on my brain and retina. You, darling, look your always adorable self, quite radiant, and I can see that motherhood has made you even more beautiful. Wolfchen is very much as I imagined him in my last letter, just a dear little round face, button nose and (in the photo of him alone) with big eyes which I know to be blue. Already I have become the mess bore showing the pictures to anyone that comes within reach! Well, I have had to endure the same treatment from my comrades for many months so now I can retaliate. Seriously, darling, it has given me such a wonderful boost to morale (not

that I am low but now the weather has changed and can only get worse one's spirit naturally gets literally dampened) that I am conscious of all those little habits that denote good humour: whistling under one's breath, walking with a bit of a swagger and so on.

Kurt sends his congratulations to you on producing such a perfect specimen! I have not been too persistent in showing him the photos because he has very little to show in return, just pictures of his frail and ageing parents. He has no fiancée or even a casual girlfriend to show off and I know (although, of course, the sentiment is unspoken) that I am his closest friend and confidant. He had a brief liaison with a girl when we were stationed in France but that, of course, died a natural death when we moved several hundred miles away. He is a rather serious undemonstrative fellow and not the type to take advantage of the girls provided by the authorities. He is one of my most reliable pilots, never goes sick, always ready to volunteer for some extra duty if others are ill and, as you know, my watchful, loyal Katschmarek. Perhaps, when we next get leave (we all hope it will be when we finally reach Moscow) I can persuade him to come to Berlin for a little while and, who knows, we might be able to produce a suitable partner for him.

I heard from Christian (for some reason his letter had been long delayed) that you had seen Frieda and that she was somewhat unhappy at his absences. He certainly seems to travel around a lot and I gather he has been staying at a grand castle in Prague. He had the cheek to complain about it being chilly! He was going on to the Führer's HQ at Rastenburg and then to enjoy himself at a shoot on von Ribbentrop's estate in Bohemia. For all that, I would not want to change places with him. Have you seen Edith since she returned from Rome? She sent me a rapturous account of her holiday there and apparently Arturo and his family entertained her lavishly. She hinted fairly strongly at possible developments in their relationship and I do hope, for her sake, it all comes to pass. I would not want her to be hurt; for all her new-found sophistication she is still an emotionally vulnerable young woman.

Rumours abound regarding enemy aerial activity over Berlin which may or may not be true but, whatever the facts may be, I entreat you to take care of yourself and our baby and only go into the city for really important reasons. Nothing frightens me in this war as much as the thought of losing you, darling.

From now on we can expect our operations to be less hectic than they have been these last few weeks; we shall be totally dependent upon the weather conditions as to how much flying we can do. At least it will afford me an opportunity to catch up on my mountains of paperwork!

All my love to you, darling, and, of course, special kisses to baby Wolfchen. I pray it will not be long before I can embrace you both and not rely on photographs.

Ever your own,
Peter

From: Oberleutnant Peter von Vorzik
III Gruppe JG233
JG HQ
Eastern Front
To: SS-Gruppenführer Count Christian von Vorzik
RSHA
Lobkowitz Palace
Hradcany Castle
Prague

9th November 1941

Dear Christian,

As always it was a pleasure to receive your letter although it seems to have taken an unusually long time to reach me. But then we have been moving from one abandoned Russian airfield to another and no doubt that is the cause for the delay. I call them airfields but not in our German sense; most of them are just crude strips of earth cut into the steppe with a few rudimentary huts scattered about. Very little drainage, primitive sanitation, nothing at all civilised. I could not suppress a wry smile when you complained about your palace quarters being cold! I hope you never have to subsist in this terrain with these living conditions. The rains have started and the weather is not only wet but penetratingly cold. The earth is beginning to turn into deep mud and vehicles of all types, including our aircraft, become bogged down. Our flying boots are encrusted with it above the ankles and we are all glad of our winter flying gear. Do not think I complain – front-line forces must expect such conditions and compared to the infantry we are privileged with our bunks heated with small wood stoves and our movements confined to walks to the mess and ablution sheds. All things are relative, are they not?

You have certainly been moving in exalted company, I look forward to hearing at first hand your impressions of Rastenburg and Schönhof. Prague is another city I would like to visit some time though having read Edith's eulogy of Rome I think that must come first on my list. At the moment such thoughts must remain mere dreams. We still have some way to go before we reach Moscow and now the weather is hampering us. I do not doubt that we shall achieve our goal but time is not on our side. We expect that when the frosts come the flying weather will be better, the ground hard for take-offs and landings and days when visibility is good.

It certainly seems that Edith is in love with Arturo and I trust that it is reciprocated. It is fortunate that you will have a chance to talk to him and assess his intentions. I cannot think that a man with his family background and position would trifle with her affections but you never know. Edith seemed quite shocked at the gossip and scandal that was discussed around the Rome dinner tables but I suppose there are factions in our own society who talk and behave in a similar way. I have been surprised at some of the things you have recounted to me in your letters regarding the rivalries and jealousies between some of our eminent leaders. Yes, it is reassuring that our womenfolk support one another especially at a time like this. Is Frieda quite alone apart from the servants? Do her theatrical friends visit her? We discussed the possibility of Mathilde's nurse-companion, Ursula, joining Frieda when her pregnancy was more advanced but Mathilde still needs her at the moment. If you are still going to be travelling around perhaps you could find someone similar to Ursula to stay with Frieda for the time being.

What is happening at Adlersee? Have the SS moved in? And have you heard how Werner is? I assume you keep in touch with the situation there; we must not allow the fabric of the Schloss to deteriorate and the furniture and pictures to be damaged. Here in this desolate place I often think of our lovely estate, the lake and meadows, the good times we enjoyed throughout our boyhood. Nostalgia is an insidious emotion, don't you think?

We had instructions today that when the weather improves all the aircraft must be serviceable for an immediate move forward, bringing us to within a few minutes' flying time of Moscow. Perhaps when I next write to you it will be from the Russian capital! We are all longing for final victory and will be straining every nerve and sinew to bring it about.

Until then, every good wish for the success of your own operations, dear brother.

Yours ever,

Peter

Oberleutnant Peter von Vorzik
Journal entry

17th November 1941

At first it was the rain, now the snow has arrived. Two weeks ago a constant deluge turned the ground into a sea of glutinous mud. Mud, not just over our ankles but up to our knees making walking almost impossible. Vehicles sank up to their axles in the ghastly slime, staff cars, trucks, fuel bowsers, all became immobilised in it. Even tractors found it difficult to move and, of course, our lovely little fighters were bogged down in the hideous stuff like so many flies caught in a monstrous web. I have seen pictures of the muddy conditions on the western front during the last war but it was nothing compared to this. We only have two tractors on the airfield and they have been employed round the clock trying to move all the other traffic that is trapped. The Wehrmacht, apparently, was suffering the same problem. All vehicular traffic was at a standstill and tanks were being used to pull gun-carriages out of the mire but even the tanks got stuck. Neither the Army or the Luftwaffe were equipped to deal with such a situation and the offensive has ground – or, rather, slithered – to a halt because of it. In the midst of this muddy hell we had reports of increased partisan activity, the blowing up of railway lines and fuel dumps, even lightning attacks on airfields. How they managed to move around with such rapidity in this all-enveloping quagmire is a mystery except that they are used to dealing with it, *Rasputitza* they call it. Sentries have been doubled and Luftwaffe Field Units have been moved in to defend the airfield and orders state that any partisans who are caught are to be summarily shot. It is thought that they operate from the vast birchwoods and swamps that stretch for miles over the steppes, moving camp continuously so that it is not possible to discover their position. Armoured cars and scout cars cannot operate in such densely wooded and swampy country and would themselves become targets for the partisans. Another frustrating enemy operation is the nuisance night-intruder bombing undertaken by obsolescent Polikarpov R-5 reconnaissance biplanes. They drone over from the front-line at treetop level, drop their small anti-personnel bombs and are gone again within a few minutes. They do little damage although some ground crew and administrative staff have been killed and wounded – but keep us awake at night wondering if a bomb will come bouncing through the door of the hut. Thankfully, the bad weather has halted these raids for the time being.

We are hoping that the colder weather will bring some clear days so that the ground will harden and our aircraft can take off and land again and afford the necessary cover and support for the Panzer divisions and infantry on the last few km to Moscow. It is so frustrating to be so near and so far. More than half the Gruppe's aircraft are out of commission, however, partly through lack of spares and partly through attrition – some Staffels have been decimated in these last few weeks. Fuel, too, is getting low; the bad flying weather and impossible landing conditions have prevented the transports from getting through with urgently needed supplies. On top of this III JG53 has been withdrawn to Germany to re-equip and II JG27 has been sent to the Mediterranean. We wait impatiently to know what will happen to III JG233. Will we be sent back to Germany as well – please God!? Or will we be part of the triumphant entry into Moscow?

As I was writing this Kurt came into the hut with a very welcome bottle of schnapps and the sad news that Major-General Ernst Udet, Chief Air Inspector General in charge of aircraft supply, has been killed while testing one of our new aircraft. I know this will be a blow to Claus who was a personal friend of his. Kurt also said that the temperature has dropped to 10° below freezing. After a couple of drinks I went to the door and looked out. I was greeted by a blast of icy air and a whirling vortex of snowflakes. Everything was blotted out in a blanket of white. Will there be a bright day tomorrow or will this blizzard continue? Will the Wehrmacht be able to batter its way on to Moscow or will we be snowed in here for another week? The next few days will determine the future.

From: Oberleutnant Peter von Vorzik
III Gruppe JG 233
JG HQ
Eastern Front
To: Leutnant Claus Grüber
Erprobungsgruppe V
Rechlin am Muritzsee

18th November 1941

Dear Claus,

I am writing to say how deeply sorry I was to hear that Major-General Ernst Udet had been killed. I know he was a personal friend of yours and that he was held in high esteem, not least for the work he had accomplished in the development of our latest fighters. His death will be a dreadful loss to the Jagdflieger in particular and the Third Reich in general.

As you probably know, we have had a small batch of FW190A-1s attached to IIJG54 who have been sharing our airfield but they have not adapted well to the rigours of the winter and most have been sent back to the maintenance units. However, we have heard excellent reports of their successes in the west, giving the new Spitfires a trouncing. In fact, there is hardly any aircraft that can stand the winter weather here! These last few weeks have been sheer hell. First we had mud practically up to our waists, everything submerged over the axles in the vile stuff, quite unable to move. Now it is snow, ice and a vicious wind that makes one feel that someone is lacerating one's body with knives. We are luckier than most in that we have our leather flying jackets and helmets, but from the waist down we are frozen stiff. Our boots are permeated with damp and go mouldy even in the hut. Fuel for the stove is severely rationed and we spend much time shivering in our bunks. It is even worse for those who do not have our flying jackets, just the comparatively thin uniforms they have been wearing all summer. Many have gone sick with frostbite; even walking to the mess makes our watering eyes freeze up! Words cannot describe the bleakness, the bitterness of it all. As for our aircraft, the guns seize up, the oil loses viscosity – even the glycol becomes frozen!

Already some of our allies have quit the front because of the terrible weather. The Hungarians have gone and so have the Slovakians; not much loss, actually, as their support was rather half-hearted and no one can pretend they were great fliers or fighters. Surprisingly, the Italians are still persevering in their little Fiat CR42 biplanes with open cockpits, would you believe it! Of course, with their air-cooled radial engines they do not have the same problems as we do with our glycol-cooled engines, but the pilots must be frozen stiff.

I hear from a friend of mine in a Zerstörer Gruppe that the Me210 has been having problems. It looked a very sleek aircraft when I saw it at Rechlin which only goes to prove that the old saying, "If it looks right it probably is right", isn't always accurate.

Did I tell you? (I think not.) I am a proud father of a baby boy! He was born on the 18th August and I have only just received photos of him. Now I am one of the mess bores showing the pictures around. My wife Mathilde is doing well and, as you can imagine, we are deliriously happy to have been so blessed. All I want now is for us to capture Moscow and perhaps have a little leave and see my son in the flesh. At the moment that seems something of a dream – the beastly weather has forestalled that victory which would surely have sealed the fate of the Russians. Leningrad, too, seems to be holding out but as it is encircled I cannot think they will be able to withstand the siege for long.

Now, Claus, how are you? How is that wounded knee of yours? Are you still able to do any flying? If I do get leave you must try and come to Berlin and visit us and give us all your news. Have you contemplated the joys of matrimony yet? I seem to remember (through a haze of alcohol!) that you thought you might be one of nature's bachelors but that the right woman could disprove that theory. Believe me, marriage can be a blissful state. Please write when you are able; now that the winter is here mail has become practically the only relief from the cold and monotony.

With best wishes and commiserations, once again, on the death of your friend Udet.

Yours,

Peter

From: *Edith von Vorzik*
Apt 2, 47 Scharnhorst Straße
Berlin
To: *Oberleutnant Peter von Vorzik*
III Gruppe JG233
JG HQ
Eastern Front

27th November 1941

My Dear Peter,

I hasten to tell you my wonderful news: Arturo has proposed marriage and I have accepted! Following my last letter I do not suppose it comes as a surprise to you but now speculation has been confirmed and we are officially engaged. Christian gave his consent after meeting Arturo in Rastenburg last month. He says he was quite impressed with the sincerity and seriousness that Arturo revealed when they had a long talk one evening. Christian has also told me that father bequeathed me a substantial sum in his will explicitly for a dowry but kept the information to himself (with the lawyer's consent) until such time as he was sure I had found a true life companion, as he puts it. Did you know about it? Christian held an engagement party for us last night, all rather hurried and informal, of course, as Arturo has to accompany Count Ciano back to Rome in a day or so (they have been here for the conference of European foreign ministers). Lina was there, and Frieda, as well as some colleagues of Christian's and Arturo's, but Mathilde decided not to come as Ursula is away for a few days (do not worry about that, she has arranged for a friend, Olga, to take her place). Mathilde would very much liked to have come but thought it best not to leave little Wolfchen for a whole evening which I quite understood. It was a happy gathering; everyone was charmed by Arturo (of course!) and congratulated me on making a splendid choice. He has given me a beautiful diamond and sapphire ring that matches the bracelet he gave me in Rome. Apparently he bought the ring at the same time but didn't want to make a formal proposal until he had an opportunity to meet and talk with Christian.

Arturo has kept me entertained with anecdotes about his visits to von Ribbentrop's estate at Schönhof and the Führer's bunker at Rastenburg. At the former he said that he and Count Ciano were amazed at the profligacy of von Ribbentrop's hospitality. At the shoot he had organised there were no less than four hundred beaters, all of them Alpine troops, which would be unheard of in wartime Italy. They bagged hundreds of pheasants and at dinner that night von Ribbentrop remarked that next year would be the first peacetime bag as both Britain and Russia will have been defeated. I hope his prophecy is true. Rastenburg was in direct contrast. Arturo says the Wolfsschanze is a bleak bunker in a dank and gloomy forest. The food is dull and monotonous and late every evening, after dinner, the Führer gives his Weltanschauung, a monologue sometimes lasting two hours which no one dares interrupt and everyone tries not to fall asleep!

We have not yet set a date for the wedding. Arturo suggests sometime next spring. In the meantime I will continue working here in my department of the Foreign Office. The ceremony will probably be in Rome or perhaps in the little church on the family estate in the Lombardy area, somewhere between Verona and Vicenza. I do hope, dear brother, when that happy day arrives, you will be able to join in the celebrations.

Life here is rather dull, especially after Rome! The daily queues get longer and longer, queues for bread and sausages, queues for trams, queues for the cinema and concerts. But I am not complaining, I am only too aware that our little inconveniences are as nothing compared to your privations. We know from the daily communiques that snow is falling on the eastern front, and some of my office colleagues tell terrible tales from friends and relatives fighting there. I continue to pray every day that the war will soon be over and you will be safely returned to us.

All my fondest love,

Ever your (deliriously happy) sister,
Edith

From: Oberleutnant Peter von Vorzik
III Gruppe JG233
JG HQ
Eastern Front
To: Edith von Vorzik
Apt 2, 47 Scharnhorst Straße
Berlin

1st December 1941

My Dear Edith,

Many congratulations! I am so very happy for you as I feel sure you have chosen a lifelong partner who will be a fine husband – and father. No, I was not really surprised by your news; even before your last letter, when you intimated that Arturo might propose, I had the feeling from your earlier accounts of meetings with him that matrimony might be possible. If I seemed hesitant in my letters to you about committing yourself, somewhat prematurely, to thoughts of marriage it was only because I was anxious that his charm and good looks, "handsome, cultured, witty and charming", you called him in your first letter about him, might turn out to be a mere facade, that his interest in you might, at best, be frivolous and, at worst, something base. I did not want you to be hurt, dear sister, because you have had so little experience of men and the ways of the world – he was, after all, your very first admirer. I am putting this very clumsily but I am sure you understand my meaning. Now we have the reassurance of his meeting with Christian and I wish you every happiness in the years to come. No, I did not know that father had made provision for your dowry but, again, I am not surprised; it is exactly the sort of prudence one would expect from him although I would not be surprised if the thought originated with mother. I certainly share your hope that I will be able to join your wedding celebrations next spring. If we can manage to defeat the Russians in the next week or two then I have no doubt that the British will at last see sense. At the moment this awful winter weather is holding up our final assault on Moscow and Leningrad; all we need is a few clear days and then, even if there is snow on the ground, we shall be able to give vital support to the Panzer divisions during their big efforts to break through the defences that ring both cities. We really are on the verge of victory.

As always I am astonished at the anecdotes you recount regarding some of our most esteemed leaders. I find it hard not to become a little cynical about the apparent fallibility of those in high places. Of course, there will always be one or two whose behaviour is, shall I say, less than perfect but from all accounts there are more than the one or two whose actions leave something to be desired. Certainly, von Ribbentrop's shoot appears rather ostentatious at a time like this and I would not have thought it necessary to try and impress the Italians in such a manner; our triumphs on the battlefield should surely be enough. If von Ribbentrop and Ciano cared to come and see for themselves what is happening here they might also question whether such extravagances were appropriate. I will not labour the point but, just between you and me, I could not but permit myself a wry thought or two when I had a letter from Christian in which he complained about his apartment in the Lobkowitz Palace being chilly! People at home have no conception of how appalling the conditions are here.

Who is this Olga you speak of as taking over from Ursula? Is she Ursula's friend or some friend of Mathilde's? Is she competent? Please make sure that Mathilde has adequate help and someone reliable to assist with Wolfchen. If necessary we must find someone with good references to stay permanently. I understand from some of my comrades here that there are now some excellent servants available from Poland and Czechoslovakia, although I would naturally prefer someone of our own nationality.

Now, dear Edith, I must hurry and get this to the mail office. Despite the difficulties it seems that our letters do get through; our reliable old Ju52s somehow manage to beat the weather that defeats our little fighters.

Once again, I wish you every happiness in the great decision you have made.

Ever your loving brother,
Peter

From: Leutnant Claus Grüber
Erprobungsgruppe V
Rechlin am Muritzsee
To: Oberleutnant Peter von Vorzik
III Gruppe JG233
JG HQ
Eastern Front

2nd December 1941

Dear Peter,

Thank you for your welcome letter, it was good to know you are still in one piece despite the worst that the Russians and their dreadful climate can do! I really do sympathise with you, I personally feel the cold very much – my knee plays up more during the winter – and I cannot imagine anything worse than the snows of the eastern front. We have seen some newsreels of the unspeakable conditions that you are enduring and be assured you and your comrades have the unstinted admiration of all of us here.

It was kind of you to remember my friendship with Udet and your message of sympathy was much appreciated. He was a good friend, very outgoing, full of the joys of life, great fun to be with and I'm afraid that that was his downfall. I tell you this in all confidence, Peter. Ernst, for all his dashing qualities, was not up to the responsibilities of his job. Quite frankly, aircraft production is in a terrible mess. Figures have been inflated, false reports circulated, contracts lost, orders unfulfilled, slackness and incompetence everywhere if not downright deceit and corruption. The showdown came at the Air Ministry a couple of weeks ago when Messerschmitt officials produced papers showing the falsification of figures and the alteration of orders. General Luftzeugmeister Erhard Milch was furious with Ernst who was humiliated before everyone. That evening there was a rather drunken party and Ernst parted from his mistress rather bitterly. Later, he telephoned her and after some words she heard a shot over the phone. She and a friend hurried over to Ernst's apartment on the Stallüponer Allee and found his body in the bedroom. There was no air accident; Ernst committed suicide. I tell you this as a friend who, I know, will understand how upsetting I find it that it ended this way. Even worse, Werner Mölders was killed in a genuine flying accident returning from the front to be a pallbearer at Ernst's funeral. What a dreadful waste of two fine men.

The sad truth is that Ernst should never have been given that job. He was temperamentally unsuited to administration, he would have been far better as the commander of a Gruppe on active service. As it is, new aircraft, especially bombers, promised for next year will not be ready until 1944, a really disastrous situation. Our big four-engined bomber, the He177 Greif, has been troubled with endless problems, not least the tendency of the DB606 coupled engines to catch fire – and now, when we need a long-range heavy bomber to attack the Russians beyond the Urals, it is not ready. Well, I do not want to burden you with our problems here at the Erprobungsgruppe, but I know you have an interest in our development plans. Yes, the FW190 was sent to the eastern front too soon, before all the difficulties with the engine had been overcome, but they have had some splendid successes over northern France against the British fighter sweeps when they attempt to shoot up trains and traffic.

We are all watching what happens on the Russian front with bated breath, knowing how much depends on a quick victory there. I have a great feeling of impotence, based here at Rechlin – not that my work isn't absorbing, you understand – but hearing about all the aerial activity in the west, the east and over the desert makes one want to be part of it. Once a fighter pilot, always a fighter pilot? Please keep writing whenever you have a chance and I shall certainly endeavour to take you up on your invitation to visit you in Berlin – which reminds me! I almost forgot to congratulate you on becoming a father! You must feel very proud and excited; please tender my congratulations to your wife when you write, I look forward to meeting her in the near future.

Until then,

Every good wish for your continuing safety and success.

Yours,
Claus

The Führer and Supreme Commander of the Armed Forces
Führer Headquarters

2nd December 1941

DIRECTIVE NO 38 (Excerpts)

1. In order to secure and extend our own positions in the Mediterranean, and to establish a focus of Axis strength in Central

Mediterranean, I order, in agreement with the Duce, that part of the German Air Force no longer required in the east to be transferred to the south Italian and North African areas, in the strength of about one Air Corps with the necessary anti-aircraft defences. Apart from the immediate effect of this movement on the war in the Mediterranean and North Africa, efforts will be made to ensure that it has a considerable effect upon further developments in the Mediterranean area as a whole.

2. I appoint Field Marshal Kesselring to command all forces employed in these operations. He is also appointed Commander-in-Chief South. His tasks are: to secure mastery of the air and sea in the area between southern Italy and North Africa in order to secure communications with Libya and Cyrenaica and, in particular, to keep Malta in subjection; to co-operate with German and Allied forces engaged in North Africa; to paralyse enemy traffic through the Mediterranean and British supplies to Tobruk and Malta, in close co-operation with the German and Italian naval forces available for this task.

3. Commander-in-Chief South will be under the orders of the Duce, whose general instructions he will receive through the Commando Supremo. In all Air Force matters Commander-in-Chief Air Force will deal direct with Commander-in-Chief South. In important matters the High Command of the Armed Forces is to be simultaneously informed.

Adolf Hitler

Oberleutnant Peter von Vorzik
Journal entry

5th December 1941

Wonderful, joyous news! Well, from a personal point of view, that is. Orders have been posted that JG233 is to be sent back to Germany to re-equip and then on to bases in southern Italy and North Africa. We shall be going from the bitter snows of Russia to the blazing heat of the desert! In the meantime it also means we shall have leave over the Christmas period and I shall at last be able to hold my baby son in my arms. I have telegraphed Mathilde and would so like to see her face when she reads it. I know she will cry with happiness and excitement.

Looking beyond this narrow view I must record that we have received a serious setback to our hopes of defeating Russia this year. Our great

Panzer divisions have rolled to a stop a mere 40 km from Moscow, their advance halted by a combination of atrocious weather and huge new reinforcements of Russian divisions brought from Siberia. Reports say that these troops are superbly equipped for fighting in sub-zero temperatures which, of course, they are used to, moving rapidly on skis and supported by new, heavily armed and armoured tanks that are impervious to our anti-tank guns. Who would have thought that the Russians would have had such equipment or been able to call on fresh divisions? It has come as a very nasty shock, not only to our infantry and motorised troops but also to our High Command and we are having to pull back to unprepared positions in the face of ferocious enemy attacks.

Those of us with serviceable aircraft (not me, unfortunately) will be taking off at dawn tomorrow and beginning the long trek home. Some personnel will go by transport aircraft, others will have to make the journey by truck with the possibility of attack from forward Russian forces. In truth, this whole situation is something of a debacle, all the more galling as we were so close to victory. My sympathies lie with the men of the Wehrmacht; they still have not received proper winter clothing and are suffering terribly from frostbite and other afflictions.

I must set down the reason why I am without my aircraft, a most frightening and hazardous incident that happened only yesterday. About 14.00 hrs Kurt and I were escorting an Me110 on reconnaissance over the Russian forward defence lines when my engine began to lose oil pressure. On the r/t I informed both Kurt and the pilot of the other plane that I would have to turn back to bodo and we decided to abort the mission. No sooner had I made a 180° turn than my engine lost all power and practically seized up. Smoke entered the cockpit and I radioed that I was going to have to make a forced landing. I put the nose down sharply, gaining speed so as not to stall and go into a spin, and looked for a likely patch where I could land with some safety. We were over heavily wooded country but through the fumes that were entering the cockpit I made out a strip of snowy ground that appeared fairly free from obstruction. Kurt radioed back that he would follow me down and mark my position. The Me110 returned to bodo unescorted. I had decided that I would make a wheels-up landing; trying to land with the undercarriage down would risk doing a ground loop, especially without power. I remembered those moments nearly two years ago when I was out of fuel and skimming the waves towards Wangerooge. Then I had had to contend with low cloud, now the weather was clear and frosty and it wasn't wavetops I had to avoid but endless treetops of birch, larch and pine. Feathering the airscrew and lowering the radiator flaps I kept the nose down to maintain flying speed. The steep glide brought the altitude down swiftly and my chosen patch grew larger with every second. I unlatched the canopy, anxious for the moment when I could inhale some fresh air; the acrid fumes in the cockpit made my eyes sting and water and brought on a fit of coughing. During these last moments before hitting the ground it was important to have visibility, to judge distances correctly while holding off the stall. The airspeed indicator registered 145 kph so I pulled the nose up a little, flattened out the glide and the leading-edge wing slots opened automatically, giving me more lift. Nearly down; I lowered the flaps, put the nose down again until I was a mere ten metres above the white expanse beneath and then, as I eased the stick back, my beloved little fighter almost floated onto the snowy surface. Violently bumping and jolting, blinded by great sprays of snow flung against the windshield, I careered along for what seemed like a kilometre before slewing sideways and coming to a stop. Undoing my harness I opened the canopy and climbed out onto the wing-root, taking in great gulps of freezing air. As I stood there, glad to find myself unhurt except for a few bruises and a trickle of blood from my nose where I had hit the Revi gunsight on impact, I heard the familiar guttural roar of a DB601 and there was Kurt, circling just a couple of hundred metres above the treetops. I waved my arms to show I was down safely, he waggled his wings in response and turned back to bodo. I knew he would report my position and I hoped I could expect rescue in a few hours.

But how? Was I behind German lines? Would they send a patrol car, maybe an Sd Kfz half-track from some local Wehrmacht position or was this Russian-held territory? Could I expect to be attacked by marauding partisans? I wiped the snow from the glazed panels of the canopy and got back into the cockpit, beginning to shiver from the icy air. I pulled the canopy back over me and within minutes the panels were steamed up and beginning to frost over. I undid my holster and drew out the Luger. I also checked I had my strychnine capsule in one of the flap pockets of my flying suit. It's a strange feeling to contemplate suicide as a final act to defeat the enemy, not through the painful process of a decision brought about by, say, despair or depression, but as a rational avoidance of a more painful death following capture. We have had numerous reports of Luftwaffe pilots suffering hideous tortures, death by disembowelling, mutilation, lynching, beating, strangulation and decapitation by Russian soldiers and partisans. The Luger would, perhaps, allow me to take one or two of the enemy with me, the strychnine a final way out. Even as I sat there in an eerie silence broken only by the soft whistling of the wind and the metallic ticking noises as the engine cooled, I imagined a Russian patrol or a group of partisans creeping up on the aircraft. With my sleeve I rubbed the condensation of the glass panels starred on the outside by frost: nothing to be seen except the white expanse of snow and the dark line of the surrounding forest. I wanted to unlatch the canopy again in order to obtain a clear all-round view but I knew if I did I would soon die from hypothermia. Bitterly cold as it was, the cockpit afforded the only protection from the elements. The light was beginning to fade; twilight lasts only a few minutes and darkness descends rapidly. Perhaps I would have to spend the whole night in the plane. Reaching behind me in the tiny space behind the protective armour plating I dragged out the survival bag we are all issued. Breaking the seal I examined the contents: a magnifying glass; a large folding knife with several blades; a thick pair of socks; a chocolate bar; hard biscuits and four tins of pressed meat; a tin-opener; a coil of rope; a water-filled bottle; a first-aid kit; a signal pistol and several coloured cartridges; a pair of binoculars. I wished I had brought a bottle of schnapps or brandy with me, several pilots do although it is strictly against regulations but in this Russian winter Staffelkapitans – including myself – ignore the practise. I opened the packet of chocolate and ate some. The thought of trying to make radio contact with bodo occurred to me but if a Russian patrol was in the vicinity they might intercept the message and home in on me with d/f equipment.

The light had almost gone. Suppose it started snowing, the plane would soon be invisible and rescue by air would be impossible until the weather cleared which might not be for days... I tried not to dwell on such daunting thoughts and concentrate instead on more positive things like going on leave; if only this damn situation hadn't happened just a few hours before my scheduled departure. But it was no use cursing fate, I had to keep alert, wait for signs of rescue, fight the growing inclination to sleep. Night had fallen but, thank heaven – literally – there was a bright three-quarter moon. After another hour or so, by which time I was shivering uncontrollably, I heard the faint drone of an aeroplane engine. Throwing back the canopy I stood up in the cockpit and listened intently. No, it was not imagination, it was getting louder. I seized the signal pistol, searched for a green cartridge, jammed it in the breech, aimed it directly overhead and fired. The moon shone on the smoky trajectory of the signal making it like a white rope to the heavens and then the cartridge burst into a glowing green ball. Even as it did so I wondered if the plane might be one of the Russian night intruders, but as the sound of the engine got louder I identified the distinct note of a Fieseler Storch's little Argus engine. That bee-like buzzing was suddenly the most beautiful sound in the world.

The Storch came in silhouetted against the dark indigo of the sky, landing in little more than its own wingspan, and taxied on its ski landing gear to within a few metres of my broken Messerschmitt. Snatching my logbook from the cockpit I slithered off the wing and stumbled through the deep snow towards my rescuers. There, within the large glazed canopy, extending an arm through the small cabin door, was Kurt, grinning triumphantly. Back at bodo we celebrated with beer, schnapps and brandy and tomorrow we leave for home. Sadly, I have to leave my lovely little F Series abandoned in the snowy wastes of Russia and travel back in a trusty old Ju52 but, thanks to Kurt (and Gerhard Fieseler's brilliant little Storch, able to land almost anywhere) I will soon be able to embrace Mathilde and little Wolfchen.

Book Four

War in the South

Oberleutnant Peter von Vorzik
Journal entry

3rd January 1942

Momentous events always seem to occur whenever I am unable, for
various reasons, to continue this journal. On the same day that I left the
bitter, icy wastes of Russia, Japanese bombers attacked the US fleet at Pearl
Harbor in Hawaii thus precipitating America's entry into the war. Within
three days the Führer had acknowledged Germany's pact with our Axis
ally by declaring war on the US and the US, in turn, declared war on us.
Italy (for what it is worth) followed suit. The only major combative
powers who have not yet declared war on each other are Russia and Japan
though that is probably only a matter of time. So, now it really is a global
war. America has been dealt a terrible blow – which she well deserves
after all her hypocritical assistance to Britain, losing four great battleships
as well as 90 other warships badly damaged. It will be a long time before
America can present a major surface fleet in the Pacific and already the
Japanese have made territorial gains among some of the islands in the area.
In addition two British battleships, the *Prince of Wales* and the *Repulse*, have
been sunk by Japanese aircraft in the South China Sea and Britain's
military and naval bases at Singapore and Hong Kong are under threat.

Despite these successes I must admit to some misgivings. We are now engaged in a life or death struggle with the British Empire, Russia and America. We must defeat them quickly, before the great production potential of America gets going. The general feeling here is that there will soon be a falling-out between Britain and America on the one side and Russia on the other. After all, they are political enemies and neither side will want to see the other as a world dominant power if Germany should lose the war. Perhaps, (someone said on the plane coming home) Britain will now sue for peace in order to let us deal with Russia while America and Japan slog it out to see who rules in the Pacific. What is certain is that the whole political and military scene has been radically changed in a few days.

The journey back from Russia was long and tedious, by plane and train. First (because I had had to leave my beloved F Series in the Russian snow) I was flown to Kiev in a Ju52, sharing the aircraft with some wounded being flown back to a military hospital in that city. From there I was bundled into an He111 being used as transport by some Wehrmacht officers on their way to Rastenburg, and the final leg of the journey was in a slow, crowded troop train (more wounded, many amputees: legs, arms, hands, feet, faces blown off or ravaged by frostbite, terrible sights). Darkness descended as I waited in a long queue for a taxi to take me to Grunewald. The taxidriver at first said he did not want to go so far, then quibbled over the fare. Finally I was on the doorstep, ringing the bell, falling into the arms of my dear Mathilde (who, of course, was in tears) and then − at last! − standing in front of the cot, looking down at the sleeping Wolfchen. Tears were in my eyes, too, realising that this tiny child was my son, created by us in a moment of joy, flesh of my flesh. What I have also realised during these few weeks is that the most rational person (which I like to think I am) is reduced to drooling sentimentality by a first child. Parenthood certainly gives meaning to one's life although it entails awesome responsibility. How will Wolfchen develop? How should we guide him, educate him? Already Mathilde and I have had long discussions about his future, what he might become, what we would like him to become (such ambitions for him!) and Wolfchen only a few weeks old.

Oh, the happiness engendered by clean sheets in a warm bed shared with my beloved! No one at home can have the remotest idea of the freezing horrors of fighting in Russia and I have not tried to inform those within the family in case I get sent back there. Christmas Day was quiet, particularly as I had developed a feverish chill. Berlin is cold but nothing compared to the east where, despite constant shivering, I remained perfectly healthy. A few days later, however, in bright sunlight, I was able to push Wolfchen in his pram around the paths surrounding the lake just as I had daydreamed of doing lying on my bunk in my frozen hut. I had no Christmas presents to give but Mathilde had knitted me a Luftwaffe-grey pullover to wear under my Tuchrok. It was her first effort at knitting and one arm was longer than the other! She said she would unpick it but I insisted that it should stay as it is; I shall cherish it more than any bought garment.

Edith arrived with a case of Bordeaux for us, fine French wine ordered through some Foreign Office friend who has contacts in Paris. Edith looks really beautiful, glowing at the prospect of marriage sometime in the spring. We took Wolfchen to a New Year's Eve party given by Christian. It was lavishly catered but we knew hardly anyone amongst a throng of SS officers and withdrew after the midnight toasts to the Führer and victory. As we raised our glasses I could not but think of all those men in Russia, unable to be with their loved ones, opening their meagre parcels from home, under imminent attack from Russian forces, while we were offered champagne and caviar, foie gras and lobster, cakes and candied fruit. Frieda is now showing her pregnancy and spent some time talking to Mathilde about Wolfchen and gazing at him, saying how she and Christian both hoped for a boy, too.

We were invited to a New Year's Day lunch given by Reinhard and Lina but declined with some excuse about the baby. We both felt tired from Christian's party and although Mathilde is very fond of Lina neither of us felt like making polite conversation with another group of SS officers we did not know. Besides, if Reinhard took up his violin as he is wont to do Wolfchen might have disgraced us by crying! The biggest surprise of the holiday was a telephone call from Kurt wishing us a happy and successful New Year and saying how he looked forward to joining me at Leipzig where we are due to take delivery of our new aircraft. I was very touched by his greeting and suspect that he is not enjoying his leave in Hamburg with only his frail parents for company. I wish he could find a nice girlfriend, worthy of his qualities of loyalty and humour. Had I thought of it I should have invited him to join us for part of his leave but then again, Mathilde may not have wanted anyone to intrude upon our time together, even someone as welcome as Kurt. My orders arrived today, together with travel documents. In two days I take the train to Leipzig to pick up my new F Series from the Erla Maschinen Werk and begin the long flight to rejoin JG233 now reforming in Catania, Sicily.

From: Oberleutnant Peter von Vorzik
III Gruppe JG233
Catania, Sicily
To: Mathilde von Vorzik
23 Hevelius Straße
Grunewald

14th January 1942

My Darling Mathilde,
Here I am, safe in Sicily! How sad I was to have to leave you and baby Wolfchen... but the blow is softened a little by being in a (relatively) warm climate. Even so, I have been grateful for my new pullover which I wear with pride. Looking from my office window I can see the snow-covered top of Mt Etna. How I wish you could be here with me to enjoy the views of this beautiful island. There are orange and lemon trees and olive groves wherever one looks. I have never seen oranges and lemons growing before, have you? The food is different but good and Kurt and I have already sampled some of the little cafés and restaurants in the nearby harbour where the fish dishes are particularly good.

This seems very much a peasant society although there are some grand estates in the hills. The old men and women are nut-brown with wrinkled faces and few teeth. There are not many young men to be seen except for the local police and, of course, military personnel. The girls are dark, plump and pretty but kept indoors and carefully chaperoned by old crones dressed in black. I think our Staffel Lothario, Varasch, will have difficulty in making his usual conquests! The narrow streets of the town are blocked by numerous ox-carts, gaily painted, carrying all sorts of merchandise from parsnips to wine barrels. (The local wine is plentiful, cheap and quite palatable.) I even saw one loaded with a grand piano.

Kurt and I hope to find time to visit some of the sites of classical antiquity. According to a little book I picked up in a tiny, dusty bookshop (written in German, published in Nuremberg in the 20's) the island has been occupied by Phoenicians, Carthaginians, Greeks, Romans, Moors, Saracens, Normans and, in more recent centuries, the Spanish and the French. The local people tend to ignore us but are quite polite when we are in their cafés and taverns.

Well, darling, that is the end of my little dissertation upon local history but, as you know, I cannot write about our daily duties here except to say we are all working hard to reform the Gruppe and are cooperating with our Italian allies in formulating various missions. Rest assured that I am in far less danger than I was in Russia and, if not exactly enjoying myself, finding life a lot less stressful than it was in the east. Do not forget to collect the developed photos we took, I am so looking forward to seeing new pictures of you both. Before I forget, darling, is there anything you particularly want for your birthday? I think the shops here are rather limited for choice but I could arrange for Edith to buy something you have had your eye on. Clothes, I know, are difficult but perhaps a new handbag (I noticed a crocodile one in a shop in the Ku'damm, but perhaps that does not appeal to you?). As always, I am sure Lina would be helpful in suggesting something. Now, duty calls, we have such a lot of work to do settling in with our new aircraft and learning new flight routines with the Regia Aeronautica.

All my deepest love, dearest, with a big kiss for yourself and baby Wolfchen.

Ever your own,
Peter

From: Mathilde von Vorzik
23 Hevelius Straße
Grunewald
To: Oberleutnant Peter von Vorzik
III Gruppe JG233
Catania, Sicily

27th January 1942

My Darling Peter,
What a joy and a relief to hear from you! Your letter took eleven days to reach us, more than the mail used to take from Russia. I took out the atlas and found that (as the crow flies) you are even further away from us than

before. Even so, I am glad you are in Sicily, not so close to the fighting and away from that terrible weather.

It has been cold here, too, with sudden flurries of snow and I have kept Wolfchen indoors as I am frightened of him catching pneumonia. Lina has gone to spend some time in Prague with Reinhard who appears to have a permanent posting there now although he made a brief return to Berlin a week or so ago for some conference or other. They have a large villa just outside Prague but Lina would much prefer to be here in Berlin – she says she only meets dreary SS wives – but does not like to leave Reinhard on his own too long; I believe he has an eye for the ladies! Christian is there, too, but Frieda has stayed here as she wants to be near her gynaecologist. I understand that there are some complications with the pregnancy but she has not volunteered any details.

The apartment seems so empty without you, darling, I hear your voice and laughter in all the rooms and I talk to Wolfchen about you all the time. Your description of Sicily makes it sound enchanting, how I would love to come and visit you there but I know that is impossible. One day... (No, I have never seen oranges and lemons growing, either.) Ursula says she cannot stay with me after next week. Poor woman, her brother was posted missing in Russia just a few days ago and she says she is needed at home. She offered to arrange for a friend to take her place but I said no, I really do not need help with Wolfchen now. As you know, darling, I am in good health and am only too happy to do everything for him myself. He does not cry in his daily bath any more, he really enjoys it, splashing with his hands and kicking his legs – I end up getting very wet! I will suggest, however that Frieda employs Ursula's friend; I think she is getting to the point when she needs someone with her.

Here are the photos, darling. As you see, some of them are very good. I especially love the one with you holding him up in the air; I am having it enlarged and framed. I have sent a copy of the three of us, the one that Edith took, to mother. She has not been too well, some germ or other and she says she has not been able to shake off a bronchial cough for some weeks. I think the time is not far off when she and Ilse will have to have someone looking after them permanently rather than Frau Gürtner coming in every day to cook and clean. Mother says that Ilse is becoming very forgetful, keeps losing things and keeps repeating herself all the time. How ghastly it must be to get old!

I will stop now, dearest, as I am anxious you should get the photos. All my love, darling, keep yourself well and safe for

Your loving wife,
Mathilde

PS I cannot think of anything I want for my birthday, darling, except, of course, to have you home with me! So do not worry about searching for something, just make sure, as I have already said, that you look after your dear self and come home safe and sound to us. M.

From: Edith von Vorzik
Apt 2, 47 Scharnhorst Straße
Berlin
To: Oberleutnant Peter von Vorzik
III Gruppe JG233
Catania, Sicily

29th January 1942

My Dear Peter,

Mathilde has given me your new address so I hasten to scribble you a note as I know how important mail is to you. We are tremendously busy now, as you can imagine, with all the new developments. I have to say that I am a little anxious to think that we are at war with America and the foreign press seems to think that we have already lost. It certainly seems we have half the world against us and some of the people here in the office are very pessimistic. (I will not mention names as it is treasonable to even think in those terms...) Perhaps all will be well, we will finally overcome the Russians and then we will have all their material resources, oil, wheat, minerals, available to us. What we may be short of, of course, is manpower. I hear (unofficially) that the casualties on the eastern front are far higher than we have been told. My friend Missie Vassiltchikov has already lost two or three close friends on the Russian front. It is all so dreadful, people fighting and dying all over the world, how I long for it to be over.

Reinhard came back to Berlin for a few days as there was a big conference at Wannsee which (so Christian told me on the phone) will decide once and for all the Jewish problem. Actually, there seem to be very few Jews left in Berlin since last autumn; they have all been resettled in the Warthegau. The nice little dressmaker, Frau Berenson (she called herself Madame Désirée) whom Mathilde introduced me to, has gone, suddenly, without notice to her clients. Christian was left in charge of the RSHA office in Prague while Reinhard was in Berlin, much to his chagrin. He doesn't like it there and would have enjoyed being back in Berlin for a few days.

Well, now for something a little less dreary! My wedding day has been set for June 14th and, as I told you, it will take place in Lombardy at a little village between Verona and Vicenza where the family have an estate. Christian hopes to get leave to escort me down the aisle and Arturo's sisters will be my bridesmaids. Of course it will be a modest affair but Arturo says we will have a grander second wedding after the war! I don't care at all, I am so happy that it is all finally decided. At first we shall be living in Rome and Arturo's mother, Eleanora, is looking for a suitable villa for us in the hills to the south of the city. I suggested an apartment nearer to the centre of the city so that it would be easier for Arturo to get to his office and all the government departments but he said it would be too hot in the summer.

Mathilde says you seem to like it in Sicily and, of course, *anywhere* must seem better after Russia! I think I may have given you a wrong impression of the Italians when I wrote to you after my Rome visit. They are certainly very different to us temperamentally, extremely volatile, gossipy, disrespectful towards authority but passionate in their beliefs. Life is much more – what shall I say? *casual*; but they are a warm-hearted, warm-blooded race and become very animated over small things. Once, when I was allowed to go shopping alone one morning on the Via Veneto I happened to ask directions from the young woman who was serving me and within minutes the whole shop was arguing about the best route I should take! However, I believe the people on the mainland look upon the Sicilians as not being proper Italians!

It would be marvellous, Peter, if you could get leave just for a day or two to come to the wedding. Do you think that might be possible? Do you think you will still be in Sicily in June? Take care of yourself, dearest brother, and try and find a moment or two to write a short letter to

Your devoted sister,
Edith

To: Oberleutnant Lother Köhl
II Gruppe ZG261
Eastern Front
From: Oberleutnant Peter von Vorzik
III Gruppe JG233
Catania, Sicily

2nd February 1942

Dear Lother,

I promised to write to you from Sicily so here I am keeping my promise! I feel somewhat guilty; first, because I was lucky enough to get Christmas leave; second, because I have a (relatively) easy posting here in Catania, and third, because you are still stationed in that freezing hell-hole called Russia! Really, I do sympathise, knowing just how terrible it is – believe me, I discovered in conversation that no one at home has any idea just how ghastly the conditions are. I suppose your only consolation is that it is even worse in the Wehrmacht than it is in the Luftwaffe. I suppose you are still snowbound which probably means fewer – if any – sorties? I know our front-line forces had to pull back (no one refers to retreat!) under the Russian attacks that began early in December. Who would have thought those bastards could have mounted a counter-offensive after such initial defeats? It was a million pities that we did not take Moscow by Christmas. I am assuming that your Staffel got away successfully. Perhaps you are with the Flotte that I hear has been sent to the Caucasus? Do write and let me know what is happening to you.

For my part I enjoyed a wonderful leave made particularly special by seeing my baby son for the first time. Nothing much has changed in Berlin; there is some superficial bomb damage and people complain about shortages of this and that but the theatres and cinemas, cafés and restaurants are still crowded, meat may be rationed but fish and shellfish are plentiful and no one goes hungry. Certainly the middle classes – not to mention Party officials! – look fat and fit.

How is your family? I think you said your home-town was Aachen? The British air-raids seem to have more nuisance value than any real threat although, of course, there have been some casualties. My wife and son, luckily, live some way from the centre of Berlin although my sister, Edith, is right there in the heart of the city. I think our anti-aircraft defences, which are improving all the time, will deter the British from attempting any increase in bombing activity.

I picked up my new F Series (complete with tropical filtration system which, of course, takes about 10 kph off performance) at the Erla works at Leipzig and made an uneventful flight via Augsburg, Bologna (skirting Switzerland – apparently they are very touchy about over-flying!) – and Naples with the aid of drop tanks, of course. Sicily is rather primitive but very beautiful – almost like a holiday after Russia! At present we are working up with the Regia Aeronautica bomber squadrons (Savoia-Marchetti SM79s) preparatory to escorting them on attacks on Malta. I wish we were attached to our own Kampfgeschwader who are equipped with Ju88s because the '79s are somewhat slow and we have to weave about to keep station just as we did over England with the He111s, Do17s, Ju87s, even – not that you need reminding! – with the Me110s! As it is, flying with drop tanks makes our own manoeuvrability rather sluggish. Active operations begin in a week or so. I am lucky to have my faithful Katschmarek, Kurt (you remember him?), still with me. All in all I am grateful to have landed this posting. So, again, write to me when you can, I am really concerned to know how you are and how your situation progresses.

All the best,

Your sincere comrade,
Peter (von Vorzik)

From: SS-Gruppenführer Count Christian von Vorzik
RSHA
Lobkowitz Palace
Hradcany Castle
Prague
To: Oberleutnant Peter von Vorzik
III Gruppe JG233
Catania, Sicily

4th February 1942

Dear Peter,

Edith gave me your address over the phone. How I envy you in the sunlit groves of Sicily whilst I shiver in the bleak midwinter of Prague! Our offices in the castle are poorly heated. Of course, Prague is rather a beautiful city in its medieval way but no doubt would have more appeal if we could be here as tourists in peacetime. Most of the Czechs resent our presence and are sullenly non-cooperative; we have to show the iron fist most of the time and in the bars, cafés and restaurants there is very little bonhomie – unlike in Paris. Reinhard had a few days away back in Berlin attending a conference at Wannsee. He returned well pleased at the outcome and says that the Jewish problem has finally been settled. They will nearly all be transported to the east (from whence many of them came) and Europe proper (by which I mean west of the Vistula) will soon be Jew-free. When that has been accomplished Reinhard has intimated that I might be sent back to Berlin. He has been sympathetic about my being separated from Frieda (especially as he now has Lina here with him in Prague) whose gynaecological problems have prevented her being here with me.

Confidentially, I must say I have some uneasiness about Edith's forthcoming marriage to Arturo. On the surface, all seems fine but his closeness to Ciano does not bode well. I hear many stories (and we have an extensive dossier) about Ciano's anti-fascist sentiments. He makes pro-British remarks at private dinners and often denigrates his father-in-law's decisions and policies. Actually, we can discount Mussolini's contribution to the war situation, the military – and political – decisions are all those of the Führer but Mussolini must remain the figurehead of Italian fascism and Ciano's attempts to undermine his authority must be countered. If I have the opportunity I will advise Arturo to keep his distance from Ciano whose political career is on the wane. I tell you all this, dear brother, so as to keep you abreast of what is happening within the Axis alliance with especial reference as to how it might affect our sister.

Walter Schellenberg visited Prague recently (you remember him, my best man at our wedding?) and we had some (very confidential) talks together. He said that he would very much like me to transfer to his foreign intelligence department but Reinhard always says that I am "indispensible" to him so such a change seems unlikely at present. Walter told me about the time when he had been sent to try and induce the Duke and Duchess of Windsor to work with the Führer towards a peace settlement with the British. It was a ridiculous fiasco but not without its amusing moments. The Duke, of course, was very favourably disposed towards Germany and deeply regretted that our countries were at war with one another. If we eventually defeat the British – or, rather, *when* – it is the Führer's intention that the Duke should be placed on the British throne.

When we were at Rastenburg everyone, from the Führer to the lowliest aide-de-camp said that this year will be decisive in terms of winning the war. We *must* defeat Russia – that is the lynchpin of our success for then we shall have all of Europe subject to the overall control of Germany with total access to essentials minerals and the road will be open for direct landlinks with Japan through the Middle East and India. The western democracies will be faced with defeat: America will retreat into isolationism again, the British Empire will collapse (Walter says that India is already on the brink of revolution against colonial rule) and the Führer's vision of a Thousand Year Reich will be fulfilled. I am full of hope that our new offensive in the east, now in preparation, will bring all this about. How petty and insignificant do our private affairs seem in comparison with our country's destiny!

I have been meaning to tell you that the economic and administrative department of the SS has declined the offer of Adlersee as a convalescent centre for the Waffen-SS. However, I have been in touch with Luftzeugmeister Milch who is quite enthusiastic about accepting it for Luftwaffe officers. Incidentally, Obergruppenführer Pohl, who put me in touch with Milch, told me that Milch had a Jewish mother but Reichsmarschall Göring arranged for her to sign an affidavit stating that Milch was the bastard son of his father and not a child of her marriage! Whatever the truth may be he is certainly an improvement on Ernst Udet who is directly responsible for our failures in aircraft production. Milch will get things done.

I have something of a favour to ask of you, dear brother. Would you permit Mathilde to undertake visits to Frieda? I know you do not like Mathilde making unnecessary visits to the city but at the moment Frieda's spirits are rather low and there is very little chance of aerial activity in daytime. The gynaecologist has specified rest, preferably in bed, and, apart from the regular staff, she sees hardly anyone on a friendly basis. Edith has managed an occasional visit but she is very busy with office affairs just now, sometimes not arriving home until quite late at night, and Lina has been once. If Mathilde could arrange a regular visit – even twice a week – it would make all the difference to Frieda's sense of loneliness, especially to talk to someone who has recently undergone the mysteries of maternity! I could arrange for Mathilde to be picked up and driven back to Grunewald by official car – my own regular driver is not with me here in Prague and has little to do. If you agree, do write a line to Mathilde and also let me know if she is willing to do this for her sister-in-law. We shall both be eternally grateful.

I trust, dear brother, that you are in good health and spirits and continuing to bring despair and devastation to our enemies.

Ever yours in the certainty of victory,
Christian

Oberleutnant Peter von Vorzik
Journal entry

9th February 1942

We have accomplished our first sortie over the Mediterranean successfully. However, after all our exercises with the Regia Aeronautica, it was decided (presumably by Field Marshal Albert Kesselring, Commander-in-Chief of Armed Forces in the area) that we should act as escorts to our own Stuka Geschwader, the Italian SM79s being escorted by Macchi C200 Saetta monoplane fighters, about the best the Italians can put into the air at the moment. They are an improvement on the Fiat CR42 biplanes but are still comparatively slow and poorly armed. We escorted the Ju87s from Stuka Geschwader 3 based at Trapani and protected them while they attacked a convoy that had almost reached Malta. We jettisoned our fuel drop tanks over the sea and prepared for fighter interception as it was reported that the carrier *Illustrious* might be with the convoy and we could expect Fairey Fulmars, large, unwieldy naval fighters or even Hurricanes to appear but nothing materialised. The Stukas claimed one medium-sized freighter sunk and two others badly damaged. Flying over the sea, expecting interception by Hurricanes and even Spitfires which we are told are based at Malta seemed like a return to the battles over southern England eighteen months ago. The expanse of the blue Mediterranean is, of course, different to the narrow grey-green waters of the English Channel but, nevertheless, the sense of *déjà vu* was quite strong. I watched as the Stukas peeled off and dived down on the convoy, meeting very little flak from the accompanying naval ships which began to put up a smokescreen. It was not long before the leading merchantman received a direct hit, capsized and sank, leaving a lot of foam and froth and a streak of oil on the surface. I could not but feel sorry for those sailors, floundering amongst the debris in the sea or, worse still, trapped below decks as the ship went down. But we had achieved our mission and celebrated in the mess afterwards. As I write, orders have been posted for another sortie tomorrow to attack the ships after they have docked at Valetta.

While on the subject of ships I must note that the vaunted British navy has suffered some devastating losses recently. Apart from the *Prince of Wales* and the *Repulse* sunk by the Japanese, our U-boats operating in the Mediterranean have sunk the aircraft carrier *Ark Royal* and the battleship *Barham*. In addition, Italian frogmen, launched from a submarine as "human torpedos", entered the harbour at Alexandria and attached explosives to the hulls of the battleships *Queen Elizabeth* and *Valiant*, putting them out of action for several months. (Kurt said that this was the first useful thing the Italians had done in the war so far.) As a result of these operations the British navy has a disastrously diminished power throughout the Mediterranean. Our bombardment of Malta is intended to put out of action this strategically placed island, half-way between Sicily and North Africa, allowing General Rommel's Afrika Korps to advance to Egypt. This is all part of the Führer's grand strategy, as we were told in a recent intelligence briefing. British forces have suffered another humiliation in the past week or so. Our own battle cruisers, *Gneisenau* and *Scharnhorst*, with the heavy cruiser *Prinz Eugen*, left the French port of Brest where they have suffered attacks from British aircraft and sailed up the English Channel unscathed, returning to their home ports in Germany, defying British torpedo planes and the long-range guns positioned at Dover. Of course they had brilliant protective coverage from our fighters all the way.

Our Staffel Lothario, Varasch, whose amorous exploits I have mentioned before, has lost no time in romancing some local beauty. However, his usual blitzkrieg tactics have been confounded by the girl's family. When he visited her house, by invitation, a toothless crone sat in the room all the time, making it impossible even to hold hands and when he invited the girl out to dine two burly brothers accompanied her! He says he is sure they are local assassins and is terrified of being knifed in some dark alley. Even worse, he says, would be to find himself compromised into marriage.

From: Oberleutnant Peter von Vorzik
III Gruppe JG233
Catania, Sicily
To: SS-Gruppenführer Count Christian von Vorzik
RSHA
Lobkowitz Palace
Hradcany Castle
Prague

12th February 1942

My Dear Christian,

Thank you for your long, interesting letter. It is always a pleasure to receive news from what seems to be another world! Yes, you are right. Sicily is warm and (fairly) welcoming, certainly something of a sinecure after the ghastliness of Russia. I am sorry your quarters are chilly although, I imagine, somewhat more munificent than our wooden huts.

I remember Schellenberg very well, we had quite a long chat during our wedding reception and he seemed a very bright, likeable person – rather more relaxed and friendly that some of your colleagues whose conversation I often find somewhat stilted. I suppose, as we belong to entirely different organisations, we have little in common except talking generalities about the war. How extraordinary that Schellenberg should have tried to persuade the Duke of Windsor to join with the Führer to create a peaceful solution to the war with Britain! I would not have thought the Duke would have carried much political weight with the British after his abdication; there was, if I remember correctly (I did not take much notice at the time) considerable public resentment against the Duchess. But then, as you have sometimes remarked, I am rather naive about political intrigues.

I must admit to being rather perturbed regarding what you say about Arturo and his closeness to Count Ciano. How is it that Ciano can voice such opinions without being dismissed as Foreign Minister? I suppose being Mussolini's son-in-law has much to do with it but I cannot imagine someone close to the Führer being allowed such licence. Do try and make your feelings known to Arturo – although he must have some inkling of Ciano's reputation. Edith is in such a state of rapture about her forthcoming marriage it would be terribly upsetting for her if Arturo's position were under threat in any way. Of course I am happy for Mathilde to visit Frieda who must be feeling very isolated with you in Prague and her parents and many of her friends in Bucharest. It would, however, be very helpful if, as you suggest, your driver could pick up Mathilde. Now that she is without Ursula it will be necessary to take Wolfchen with her and travelling with him on the trams is unthinkable and (as I have experienced) getting a taxi to and from Grunewald is difficult.

Naturally I am pleased that Milch has agreed that Adlersee may be used as a convalescent base for Luftwaffe officers; it is nice to think that our home is making some worthwhile contribution to the war effort. Father, I am sure, would have approved. Are you able to arrange for the pictures, objects, etc, to be put in store and will Milch arrange to pay for the storage? I assume that Werner will remain there and (if he is still able) play some janatorial role. We must make sure his position is recognised and, if he is now physically handicapped in any way (how old is he? Ever since I can remember I have thought of him as old!) given comfortable accommodation and care.

I understand your remarks about Udet; the tragedy was that he should never have been put in charge of aircraft production. He was a dashing, brilliant pilot and he should have been commanding one of our Jagdstaffel, or even a Flotte, not looking at reams of production figures and being fobbed off with specious reports by people he trusted. Do you remember when our governess took us to see Leni Riefenstahl in *SOS Iceberg* without father's permission? It was Udet who did all the amazing stunt flying in that picture and I think that was when I really knew I wanted to fly.

Now, duty calls. We are stepping up our attacks on Malta, as you have probably heard on the radio. The island is practically defenceless, only a few British fighters there and the anti-aircraft guns equally scarce and put out of commission by bombing. I expect we shall be making an airborne assault soon and when we are in possession of the island it will make Rommel's offensive much easier to sustain. As you say in your letter, this is the year we have to see victory.

Every good wish for your stay in Prague,

Your affectionate brother,
Peter

From: Oberleutnant Lother Köhl
II Gruppe ZG261
Eastern Front
To: Oberleutnant Peter von Vorzik
III Gruppe JG233
Catania, Sicily

27th February 1942

Dear Peter,

It was a very pleasant surprise to receive your letter. As you know, it is wonderful to receive mail but, despite the best intentions it is not always easy to find the time and opportunity to sit down and write oneself, especially with the pile of paperwork always waiting on the desk. So I do appreciate your having taken the trouble to give me your news and to inquire after mine. Actually, as you surmised, we have had more time on our hands during these last two winter months, the opportunity for flying very limited and then mainly for reconnaissance, not offensive operations. In three or four weeks we expect the thaw to begin and then we shall be back in that hideous mudbath! There has been much talk about the Gruppe being posted south to the Caucasus but we are still here at our old station just north of Bryansk, supporting the 4th Army and 2nd Panzer Army, although they are dug in the frozen ground at the moment. It is a matter of fending off the Russian attacks whenever necessary, although most of the action has been further north.

The winter, as you can imagine having seen some of it, has been absolutely horrendous; endless snowstorms, then a day or two of clear weather when we struggle to get the engines to start, the runways cleared of snow and then up for a bit of reconnaissance before the next blizzard arrives. Although we manage (mostly) to desolidify the oil and glycol we never seem to be able to thaw ourselves out. It's an agony trying to get our boots on and off (sometimes not for days!) hoping not to get frostbitten (some fellows have had their toes amputated and then returned to duty!), keeping the blood circulating, finding fuel for the stove (some partisans have left logs and branches booby-trapped) and trying to sleep while the Russkies send over those cursed nuisance bombers. As you say, however, it's worse in the Wehrmacht. Apart from all this, the truth is that the Me110 is not suitable for the jobs we have to do: too vulnerable, really, for ground attack (we lost so many aircraft last year in close support roles), too slow and sluggish, particularly with long-range drop tanks, for fighter operations, even escort duty (the Russians, believe it or not, have had occasional air superiority over certain sections of the front) and no replacement in sight; as you know, the Me210 has been a disaster. How I curse the day I was persuaded into Zerstörer! Well, enough of that, sorry to moan on at you, but the vile weather and obsolescent equipment combine to make one frustrated and bitter.

How wonderful for you to see your wife and baby son! I trust both are doing well. My family (mother and father) are fine; they do not say in their letters, of course, whether they have been troubled by enemy raids although I have heard rumours that there has been some activity in the Ruhr. My girlfriend, Hannelore (I think I showed you her photo?), writes less frequently than she did and I suspect there may be some other chap in the background although I have nothing concrete to support my suspicions but it's possible to read between the lines. Perhaps I should put a direct question? Do you think so? I miss the opportunity to have one of our serious chats. My best friend in the Staffel, Siegfried Murnau, was posted missing on reconnaissance three weeks ago. No sign of him, no r/t message, just disappeared into the snows. It was a fatal mistake to send him up without a single fighter as protection but our fuel supplies are so limited we have been forced into sending up single aircraft. I have been trying to think of something cheerful to end on! The only thing that comes to mind is that we have had a consignment of French cognac arrive recently so at least we can drown our sorrows!

Do please write again when you have a chance.

Ever your sincere comrade,
Lother

From: Oberleutnant Peter von Vorzik
III Gruppe JG233
Catania, Sicily
To: Mathilde von Vorzik
23 Hevelius Straße
Grunewald

27th February 1942

My Own Darling Mathilde,

As you can see, I am writing this on your birthday and am sure you know how I wish I could be enfolding you in my arms and smothering you in birthday kisses! But here I am, dearest one, sitting at my desk as dawn breaks, snatching a few moments before the daily operations begin to tell you how you are in my thoughts not only on your name-day but every day. But then I have told you that before, many times. Even so, today is a special day and I am hoping you are able to find some way to celebrate it. I fear you may be spending a rather lonely birthday, with Lina in Prague, Edith at work, Frieda confined to bed and your mother in Cologne. Have you made any new friends, I wonder? Are there any mothers you meet while out wheeling Wolfchen? I do hope so, darling, as friends and companionship are especially important during these times. Kurt is not only my trusted Katschmarek but also a devoted friend; his companionship is a great help while we are so far from home and our loved ones. There are no birthday cards in the local shops but I am enclosing a little hand-painted view of Mount Etna that I came across in an establishment that sells handmade writing-paper, notebooks, journals and watercolours by local artists. The view is very similar to what I see from the runway when we are taking off and I wanted to share it with you.

We are very busy now, flying every day but with minimal risk, so do not worry. Otherwise life is as good as it can be under the circumstances. We are well fed, the local wine is cheap and plentiful, the sun shines most days and the wild flowers are beginning to bloom in the fields and by the wayside. I have had letters from Christian, Edith and a friend, Lother, in a Zerstörer Geschwader, still in Russia, poor man. He has been stuck there throughout the winter and I realise how lucky I am to be posted here.

How is our darling Wolfchen? I am sure that he is growing fast and that you see a difference in him every day. I am afraid he will not know me when I am next on leave. Several of the married men in the Staffel say that when they have returned home after a long tour of duty (for instance, when we were fighting over England two summers ago) their children treated them as strangers. It was not until their leave was half over that the children would sit on their father's knee, or let the fathers join in their games or kiss them goodnight. I hope I never seem a stranger to Wolfchen. When this war is over, darling, we will have much travelling to do! Paris, to see those places we missed on our honeymoon; Prague, which Christian says is a beautiful city; Vienna, which I haven't visited since I was a boy; Munich, which I know you haven't seen and which I want to show you and, perhaps, Sicily, to see where I have been stationed. But not Russia!

Now the early morning sun is slanting across my desk as I write this and in a few minutes it will be time to join the day's first operational briefing. I do hope, darling, that you have been able to celebrate your name-day in some way and that you have not spent it alone. If only thoughts could be made tangible, visible in some way then we would be together even though thousands of miles apart.

Give Wolfchen a big kiss for me and, of course, many, many kisses for yourself from

Your ever loving husband,
Peter

From: Oberleutnant Peter von Vorzik
III Gruppe JG233
Catania, Sicily
To: Edith von Vorzik
Apt 2, 47 Scharnhorst Straße
Berlin

4th March 1942

My Dear Edith,

It is over a month since I received your welcome letter and I simply do not know where the time has gone! I try hard to keep up with my correspondence, several people are kind enough to write to me: yourself, Mathilde of course, Christian and one or two comrades in different Gruppe, but it is all I can do to find time to respond to that limited list. Our days are so very full: operations (at least from this base) begin just after dawn, we are flying an increasing number of sorties each day now, then there are routine briefings and lectures to attend, plus an ever-increasing mountain of paper work to be dealt with. In addition there are "domestic" duties, sorting out various personal problems with Staffel staff and snatching a few moments for relaxation in the mess (the occasional birthday party, some little celebration when someone has had a personal victory) and drives into town for a meal or a shopping (more like scavenging) trip. Perhaps I should resort to postcards simply to say I am safe and well rather than trying to write letters. What do you think? Had I remained in Russia (horrible thought!) I would have had more time to write (assuming my fingers were able to hold a pen in that intense cold) as I understand that flying has been severely curtailed there during the winter months.

I know you have been busy, too, since Japan and America entered the war and you must be very well informed as to what is going on in the world. A few things filter through to us via "a friend's friend's friend" who heard a rumour but the truth is very rarely verifiable and one becomes suspicious about the official communiques. According to the radio broadcasts it would certainly seem that our Japanese ally has had some amazing successes in the Pacific and South East Asia, especially the surrender of Singapore which bodes well for later this year when our new offensive in Russia begins. Here in the south we have begun a growing assault on Malta which would aid General Rommel's attack on the British and Empire forces in North Africa. As Christian said to me in his last letter, this is going to be the year in which we can expect final victory.

I began this letter by saying how quickly time flies by and, dear sister, it is now only three months to your wedding! For you, perhaps, the time will drag but I am sure you will have much to do to prepare. Of course, I would love to be with you on that day but I honestly think, as things are, it is a remote possibility. Briefings on strategy have made it plain that we will be in the forefront of an offensive that will be maintained at a high level over the next few months during which leave will be out of the question. So I will have to rely on letters and photographs to inform me about your great day. How happy I am for you, dear Edith, that you have found someone to be your lifelong partner so quickly. In that respect the three of us, yourself, myself and Christian have been very fortunate. Kurt has just come in (he sends his regards to you) to say that transport into town is leaving in ten minutes and as we want to have a meal in one of the little trattoria where they serve excellent local fish I will finish this letter by sending much love from

Your brother,
Peter

PS Please let me know what you would like for a wedding present. There is nothing suitable to send from Sicily so it will have to be something you can order for yourself from a store in Berlin. Glass, porcelain, silverware, furniture, a bed? Whatever it is I will arrange payment through my bank. P.

From: Oberleutnant Claus Grüber
Erprobungsgruppe V
Rechlin am Muritzsee
To: Oberleutnant Peter von Vorzik
III Gruppe JG233
JG HQ

12th March 1942

Dear Peter,

It is quite some time since I heard from you and I am writing in the hope that all goes well. Are you still in Russia? (I am sending this to JG HQ to forward.) I know several Jagdgeschwader have been sent south and wonder if you are amongst them. If not, I can commiserate! We have had several first-hand reports here from pilots who have returned from Russia, mostly operating with the FW190 Staffeln which, as I am sure you have heard, did not fare well in that intensely cold and tough terrain. On the other hand, they continue to achieve great success in the west, particularly against the RAF's fighter sweeps over northern France.

A development of the Mc109, the G Series, is also just going into service with various Geschwader in northern France. It has an uprated engine, the DB605N, giving greater power and increased performance including provision for nitrous oxide injection for emergencies. However, pilots tell me that modifications to the airframe which have increased all-up weight result in a deterioration in flying characteristics. I tell you this in case – wherever you are – you are about to re-equip with the 109G. Be prepared!

Here at Rechlin we have been struggling with several other types which continue to give us headaches. Would you believe it, we are still tinkering with the Me210, trying to erase those vicious handling characteristics and instability. The only reason the beastly thing has not been abandoned is that the Luftwaffe is so desperate for a replacement for the Me110 that someone (who? Udet? Milch? Göring?) at Generalluftfleigmeisteramt ordered production lines at Messerschmitt Augsburg and Regensburg and the MIAG plant at Braunschweig for 600 aircraft! Meanwhile, production of the Me110 has been reinstated. There has been an even worse headache with the Heinkel He177 Greif heavy bomber. As I think I told you the engines are two DB601s (DB606) coupled together and there have been numerous instances of these troublesome motors bursting into flames, destroying several aircraft and killing the crews. (It has earned the nickname the Luftwaffe's Lighter!) Although we know the main reasons for this combustibility (I won't go into technical details) it has been a tortuous business getting them rectified. There have been numerous other teething troubles and the aircraft is still not ready for operational duties despite the need for a long-range strategic bomber. Even when it does manage to fly without mishap the performance is below the parameters laid down by the Technischenamt.

So much for the bad news. The good news is that (highly secret) plans for the development of a revolutionary new fighter by Messerschmitt are progressing satisfactorily. I visited the development centre (somewhere in the Baltic – also secret!) and was amazed at the whole conception. I cannot write any details, suffice it to say this machine is totally unlike anything we have seen before. One of the test pilots, Heini Dittmar, is an old friend of mine (was he here when you visited us?) and has given me astonishing information about performance figures. We shall amaze our enemies yet!

As for me, I manage to get around in the old Taifun and keep my head above the flood of paperwork. On a personal level I have been seeing a very attractive widow (her husband was a bomber pilot lost over England last year) so my social life has improved and my consumption of beer and schnapps lessened somewhat. Also, as you see,

I have received a little promotion. How are your wife and baby? Have you managed to get leave to see them? I hope all is well. I hope, too, that this letter reaches you, Peter, and that you have not forgotten your old comrade,

Claus

PS I would so like it if you could manage to visit us here again, there is a lot I know would interest you. C.

From: Mathilde von Vorzik
23 Hevelius Straße
Grunewald
To: Oberleutnant Peter von Vorzik
III Gruppe JG233
Catania, Sicily

15th March 1942

My Darling Peter,

It made me so happy to receive your letter written on my birthday and to know you were thinking of me then, although we both tell each other how we think of each other all the time! But to know you were actually writing it on that day made it special. Yes, I had an enjoyable day with remembrances from mother, Edith, Frieda and some old schoolfriends. Mother sent a parcel containing a chocolate cake and some Liptauer cheese made by Aunt Ilse which she knows I adore, as well as a pair of fur-lined gloves which are too big so I will give them to the Winter Relief. Even though it is almost spring here some soldier on the eastern front (with small hands!) might be glad of them. Lina sent me (us) a charming flower picture by Adolf Ziegler. She always remembers my birthday and says she wishes she were back in Berlin. Best of all, darling, was your little water-colour of Mount Etna which I am having framed. When the framing is done I will paste your letter on the back. I think of you sitting in the cockpit of your plane looking at that view. Of all the places that you say we might visit after the war that is what I most want to see.

You ask if there are any mothers that I meet when out wheeling Wolfchen. Yes, there are two or three and we look into each other's prams and exclaim over the babies but we have not socialised yet. Maybe I should invite one or two over for coffee. (The coffee we get nowadays is horrible!)

However, wheeling Wolfchen down Hevelius Straße the other day I met Frau Kirschner, a neighbour, who was very friendly with mother – she is in her fifties. She invited me to join the local sewing circle and, what is most exciting, Frau Scholz-Klink (you probably don't know about her, darling, but she is the leader of the Women's League) is going to visit the group in two weeks. Frau Kirschner says I am welcome to take Wolfchen with me, several of the women have their small children there. She will also introduce me to the matron who runs the local crèche where Wolfchen may go when he is one. Every day I show him your photo and repeat "Papa, Papa," over and over so that he will be familiar with your face when you next see him.

I had a telephone call from Christian's office in Prague to say he has arranged for me to have a Czech girl as a household help. She will be arriving in about three weeks' time. They have sent her papers for me to sign, together with a photograph. She is just nineteen and looks very pretty. Her name is Lenka Molnik and she will help with all the cleaning work but will not have anything to do with Wolfchen. While I think of it, darling, Ernst, the gardener, has been called into the army and the garden is beginning to look rather a mess. Of course, nothing has begun to grow yet, but when it does we shall need to have someone to keep it under control or even to plant vegetables where the flower beds are. I am not very good at gardening (when I was small mother marked out a little plot for me to tend but it was never anything but a bed of weeds!) so shall I make enquiries locally about finding someone to replace Ernst?

I have enjoyed listening to the Concert Request programmes on the radio. Do you ever have the chance to listen, darling? I thought of requesting a piece of music for you and spent hours wondering what it should be. Something from *La Bohème*, the opera we saw the first time we went out together? Too sad! Zara Leander, do you like her? Schubert lieder? I realised it was unlikely you would be able to listen when it was broadcast and I would have to tell you a long time in advance that I had requested something and it all seemed too complicated. Even so, we do not need radio music to link our thoughts of each other, do we, darling? Write when you can. I realise how busy you are but cannot stop looking for the postman each morning.

All my deepest love, dear one.

Keep safe for Wolfchen and me,

Mathilde

From: Oberleutnant Peter von Vorzik
III Gruppe JG233
Catania, Sicily
To: Oberleutnant Claus Grüber
Erprobungsgruppe V
Rechlin am Muritzsee

24th March 1942

Dear Claus,

What a delightful surprise it was to receive your letter which has found me here in Sicily. Yes, you were right, our Gruppe was one of those selected to fly south and I count myself extremely lucky to have left the eastern front after only a taste of the winter. My sympathies are with all those poor devils who were left to endure it. Really, apart from being quite a long way from home, this is the most pleasant posting I have had. And although operations have become fairly hectic recently, the combat situations are less dangerous than others I have encountered. I was lucky, too, in getting leave over Christmas (prior to which I had a little adventure when my plane was forced down in the snow; rescued by my faithful Katschmarek) and being able to see my baby son for the first time. Believe me, fatherhood certainly changes one's outlook on life!

You tell me of the G Series and there has been some talk about it in the mess and some articles about it in the aviation magazines. At the moment I have a fairly new F Series which I am very happy with and have no wish to have it changed although, no doubt, at some time we will be re-equipped with the Gustavs, as I believe they are called. I only hope they prove as successful as the Friedrichs and the Emils. We have been flying as escorts to Ju87s, Ju88s and, briefly, to the Italians' SM79s. Confidentially, the reputation of the Regia Aeronautica is not very high amongst my comrades. There is no doubt the Italians' equipment is pretty poor and their combat experience seems mostly to have been confined to bombing tribesmen. Even their operations in Spain were comparatively limited, nothing like our own Condor Legion. Your description of the new Messerschmitt fighter is very exciting, even without details, and has set my imagination soaring! I have not mentioned it to any of my comrades as you stress the secrecy of the project. I feel flattered that you trusted me with the information.

Things seem to be going well for us at the moment, do they not? I really am anxious now for a final victory so that I – we – can get on with our lives and careers. I do not know whether I will stay in the Luftwaffe for a while or resign my commission and seek advancement in civilian life. I would really love to open up new air routes with Lufthansa, building on those early proving flights to South America and pioneering new ones to the Far East. With all the technological advances we have made during the last two or three years, peace will present marvellous new opportunities. I see myself as having a good ten, fifteen, even twenty years as a pilot before settling behind a desk! I was really inspired by Udet's life, you know. His death was so tragic.

Congratulations on your new amorous association! I am delighted to know you will not become a grouchy old bachelor. What is your lady's name? How did you meet? You give me tantalisingly little information – even less than that about the new Messerschmitt fighter! Of course, there is nothing I would like better than to make a second visit to Rechlin but at the moment there seems to be little likelihood of leave. We shall be well into the autumn before that happens; we are committed to a long spring and summer campaign, I think.

So, Claus, let us keep in touch. I welcome your letters and news of what is happening "behind the scenes" and wish you well in all your endeavours.

Yours,

Peter

PS Many congratulations on your promotion! P.

Oberleutnant Peter von Vorzik
Journal entry

24th March 1942

Three days ago we increased our attacks on Malta, beginning a major bombing campaign which, we are told, is the prelude to an invasion of the island which has been such a running sore on all our communications and supply systems for North Africa. Altogether, with our Italian ally, we have been flying over 300 sorties a day involving 190 long-range bombers, mostly Ju88s, plus 37 Ju87s and some SM79s. The enemy airfields and docks are our main targets. Even during the attacks on England back in '40 we never concentrated so many aircraft on a single target area so continuously.

There is very little opposition, most of Malta's anti-aircraft positions have been knocked out and there are only a handful of Spitfires to defend the island although the few that are there press home their attacks with great determination and our own losses have been quite heavy.

Yet again I am reminded of our battles over England: crossing the sea, attacking over an area about the size of Kent and Sussex, keeping a watch for Spitfires which, just as they did that summer, home in on the bombers. The Italians have suffered particularly heavily. Yesterday I watched helplessly because our brief was to protect our own bombers, as a lone Spitfire dived on a trio of SM79s. These aircraft are very vulnerable because of their poor speed and weak defensive armament. The Spitfire set one of the tri-motor bombers on fire at his first pass, turned and came up underneath a second bomber, raking the starboard engine with cannon fire. Within seconds that aircraft, too, had burst into orange flame. Both bombers rapidly lost height, trailing black smoke, and I counted just three parachutes opening and drifting towards the sea. Each SM79 carries a crew of five so that was seven men going to their deaths. I did not see any of the Italian fighters trying to protect their charges, I think they had their work cut out trying to evade the Spitfires themselves.

During that same sortie both Kurt and I managed to shoot down a Spitfire each, working together, making our kills as the British fighters were busy attacking a group of Ju87s. It was a classic surprise bounce, diving on them with the sun behind us. Kurt fired first, scoring hits on the Spitfire's fuselage and cockpit area, presumably killing the pilot as the enemy aircraft immediately went into an uncontrollable spin. Kurt followed it down until it hit the sea. My victim was, of course, immediately alerted and broke away to port with me in pursuit. I managed to get him in the gunsight and fired a long burst. Bits flew off the engine cowling and a thin line of smoke showed that my cannon had found its mark. Even so, the British pilot managed to turn inside me and get in a burst of his own. I felt the plane judder as I bunted over, knowing he could not follow. I half rolled and, peering up through the top of the canopy, found my quarry again with his engine seizing up, the propeller turning slowly. Losing speed and height rapidly, with the smoke getting thicker, the Spitfire pilot put his aircraft into a dive in a desperate attempt to get back to his base, but now he was a sitting duck. Diving after him I waited until his aircraft almost filled the gunsight graticule and gave another long burst. Suddenly, just as I climbed above him, the Spitfire blew up in a fireball, bits of debris banging and pinging against the underside of my own plane. Maybe it was his burst of cannon fire that had done the damage, maybe it was when he blew up but I could see that the engine temperature was going up and I was probably losing glycol. It would not be long before my own engine seized up. I put out a call to Kurt on the r/t and was relieved to hear his voice. "I'm 2,000 m below you and climbing," he shouted above the roar of his engine, "Try and maintain height and I'll shepherd you back to bodo."

I opened the radiator flaps and throttled back, glad that I had not had to follow the Spitfire down to confirm its destruction and was still flying at 5,000 m. With a little luck I could almost glide back to one of the bases in southern Sicily, if not to Catania. I certainly did not want a swim in the Mediterranean although there is an efficient air-sea rescue system operated by the Italians with Cant Z506B seaplanes. As it was, throttling right back and losing height very slowly I managed to regain my own airfield, watched over by the faithful Kurt. We lost three Ju87s on that raid. On landing we discovered that a cannon shell from the Spitfire had ripped a big jagged hole in the fuselage of my plane, luckily without severing any of the control cables to the tail assembly or hitting the oxygen bottles or the r/t, all of which are situated aft of the cockpit. Bits of the Spitfire itself were embedded in the oil cooler intake, which is why the engine temperature had risen, as well as the underneath of the port mainplane. Repairs took three days so I have had a chance to catch up on the everlasting paperwork that lands on my desk.

These constant attacks on Malta have depleted our supplies of fuel but, conversely, they are allowing fuel and ammunition to get through to Rommel's army in North Africa. Previously, the British, in their turn, were able to inflict great losses on our convoys to Cyrenaica but we have turned the tables. In desperate attempts to supply Malta with food and armaments the British have been sending supply convoys from both Gibraltar in the west and Alexandria in the east, losing many ships, both naval and merchant craft, in the process. Even when one or two of their ships do get through we bomb them in Valetta harbour so that there is very little left to salvage. Apart from the loss of war material we are told the islanders are near starvation level. In a few weeks an airborne landing supported by ships of the Italian navy will be possible. The general feeling in the mess is that we are poised on the verge of victory. Much depends on what our armies do in Russia this spring and summer; with the slaying of that Communist monster we shall be militarily and economically inviolable. I shall be free to forge my career in whatever way I choose and settle into a rewarding family life with my darling Mathilde and, I hope, some brothers and sisters for baby Wolfchen.

From: Edith von Vorzik
Apt 2, 47 Scharnhorst Straße
Berlin
To: Oberleutnant Peter von Vorzik
III Gruppe JG233
Catania, Sicily

28th March 1942

My Dear Peter,

Several times during the past week I have started to write to you (I write in office hours!) and each time I have been interrupted. You were right when you supposed that the general situation has kept me busy. So many newspaper and magazine articles to translate (my English is getting very good), most of which cancel out each other's opinions. The British writers are very cautious about their prognostications, only united in prophesying that it will be a long war. (It has already been a long war!) The Americans, despite their setbacks, are much more buoyant in their conviction that victory is assured, although they, too, say it will take another year or two. Frankly, I do not like reading such stuff, it is too depressing. Our own correspondents, as you probably read for yourself, are equally confident in an Axis victory, only they do not mix into the equation certain aspects of the war that the Anglo-Americans are open about. Our writers are certainly more inhibited than those of our enemies. From our point of view everything appears in our favour; from theirs certain dangers, e.g. the huge loss of shipping through the activities of our U-boats, are openly acknowledged.

Well, now, let me tell you of more verifiable matters! I snatched a few hours from office work last week and paid visits to Mathilde and Frieda. Mathilde, I must tell you, looks wonderful. She has regained her figure and seems the picture of health, while Wolfchen is adorable: a plump, smiling baby, quite alert now, registering everything around him and full of energy, his arms waving and his legs kicking. He looks just like those chubby little putti in 18th-century drawings. Mathilde is very excited about joining the local sewing circle, though she acknowledges her sewing is not up to the standard of some of the women in the group. But she feels she is making some small contribution to the war effort (they appear to be edging blankets and pillowcases for military hospitals as far as I could make out, which hardly calls for fancy stitching) and it gives her something of a social life which she would otherwise not have. By contrast Frieda looks quite ill (I tell you this in great confidence, Peter, please do not mention it when you write to Christian). Her gynaecological problems seem to have sapped all her energy, she looks pale and exhausted and spends nearly all her time in bed. She has little appetite and does not even want to read. I really think Christian should apply to return from Prague on compassionate grounds but Frieda made me promise not to write to him as she knows how bound up he is with the RSHA. The doctor visits her once a week and her bedside table was crammed with pills and medicines, tonics, mostly, she said, waving a hand at them, and I got the impression that she hardly takes any of them. I did not stay long as conversation seems to tire her. Mathilde, I know, has also visited her, picked up and taken back by Christian's chauffeur.

Yes, as you rightly surmise, I am also busy trying to prepare for my wedding. Much is being organised from Rome, of course. I sent my measurements to Eleanora who is having my wedding dress made. She says she has found a wonderful bale of champagne silk and has sent me a drawing of the pattern she is following. It is a simple dress, falling very full from the waist with a train that will be held up by Arturo's two young cousins, Ernestino and Federico, aged seven and nine, the sons of Count Paolo Gaviotti. Eleanora is also having shoes made from the same silk (I had to send a tracing of my feet!). I have a sneaking suspicion that she thinks she might otherwise have a frumpy-looking German hausfrau walking down the aisle as her daughter-in-law! Even so, I have sent some ivory lace that belonged to mother for trimming the veil. Eleanora is lending me a matching tiara and necklace of diamonds and pearls that have been in Arturo's family for generations. I also possess mother's tiara which I would have worn only I did not wish to create any controversy. I am just so very happy to be marrying Arturo, the trappings of the occasion are really not important. Arturo says he hopes that Ciano will not need him for meetings soon after the wedding as we would have to curtail or even postpone our honeymoon. As it is we shall be in a villa on Lake Como, lent by Gaviotti, so we will not be far away if Arturo is needed. Apparently, a meeting between the Führer and Mussolini has been mooted for some time but the Führer keeps putting it off as he is busy planning the spring offensive. Arturo says he dreads such meetings, there is such protocol amongst the entourages, particularly that of von Ribbentrop's, with certain members vying with each other about placings at table, who is given which hotel room and so on. It is even worse when wives (and mistresses!) are sometimes present. Arturo says that I shall have to be involved in such nonsense when we are married!

I am negotiating the sale of the lease of my apartment (I expected to be here at least another two years) and on June 5th Dr Adam Trott zu Solz, my boss, is arranging a small private farewell party for me at Horcher's. I shall miss him and Missie Vassiltchikov who has been such a charming and helpful companion in the office.

Dear Peter, many thanks for your generous offer of a wedding present. I have a list at Brüning and Pfleigers which includes a Meissen porcelain dinner service which I was so hoping someone would select. May I put your name against it? It is something I will treasure always and which will remind me of you (as if reminding were necessary!) whenever we have special guests. Of course I understand that it is unlikely that you will be able to be present at the wedding. I know that operations are increasing in the Mediterranean area. It was just that your being in Sicily seemed so near. Now I must attend to my translations, and avoid seeming to be indigent during these last few weeks. I catch myself staring into space and thinking about that villa where we shall be living in the hills above Rome.

All my love to you, dear brother.

May God go with you,
Edith

From: SS-Gruppenführer Count Christian von Vorzik
RSHA
Lobkowitz Palace
Hradcany Castle
Prague
To: Oberleutnant Peter von Vorzik
III Gruppe JG233
Catania, Sicily

5th April 1942

Dear Peter,

Thank you for your last letter.

As you see, I remain in Prague for the time being. I have had further conversations with Walter Schellenberg who made another trip to confer with Reinhard but he – Walter – feels the time is not yet right to broach the subject of my joining his Ausland SD department. Even so, things have settled down here very well during the last few months. After Reinhard managed to dispose of General Elias, who was doubtless the prime motivator behind the Czech resistance and in contact with Eduard Benes' emigré government in London, the populace has remained calm and most Czechs and Slovaks are prepared to consider themselves as second-class Germans and reap the benefit of that position. Reinhard has declared all political arrests at an end, he has raised the fat ration for over two million industrial workers, released 200,000 pairs of shoes for workers in the armaments industry and requisitioned several luxury hotels in Bohemia's spas as holiday homes as well as reorganising the Czech social security system. All these benevolent acts have convinced the people that we Germans are not the authoritarian conquerors that our enemies make out.

I had hoped that because of this general tranquillity Walter would have been able to make his request for my transfer but, as luck would have it, Reinhard had just set me an important brief which will keep me here. I am making (very surreptitious) investigations into the various industrial cartels set up under the aegis of the SS and its administration. Their ramifications are extensive and as well as concerning some very important names Reinhard is sure that there is a lot of corruption within the lower orders of these organisations.

Incidentally, here is a little anecdote that I am sure will amuse you. When Walter went to visit Reichsmarschall Göring at Karinhalle recently he was kept waiting over half an hour. Then, suddenly, the doors of the anteroom were thrown open and the Reichsmarschall appeared, clutching his marshal's baton and dressed as a Roman senator, toga, sandals and all! Later, during their conference, the Reichsmarschall sat at a table upon which was a cut-glass bowl filled with precious stones which he fingered and played with throughout their talks. Walter said he felt as if he was in the presence of the Emperor Nero!

I am most grateful to you for allowing Mathilde to visit Frieda who writes to me saying how she has enjoyed her company. Frieda tells me she is recovering her strength under the doctor's supervision although he insists upon her taking a great deal of rest so as not to endanger the baby. I long for this sojourn in Prague to be over so I can be back in Berlin with my dear wife but with Reinhard here on a permanent basis as Reich Protector of Bohemia and Moravia I think it will be some time yet. When the baby is born, of course, then Frieda will be able to join me which will make life much more enjoyable. Lina will be glad to see Frieda, too. Confidentially, she tells me that she is terribly bored here, having to entertain an endless succession of local dignitaries, members of the Prague Chamber of Commerce, the workers' associations, various guilds and minor Party officials. I tell her that compared to the Führer's HQ at Rastenberg Prague is a whirl of social gaiety!

With regard to the handing over of Adlersee to the Luftwaffe, all proceeds well. I will keep you informed as to when it is concluded. Our lawyers in Munich are negotiating financial remuneration with the Generalflugmeister's office and I am assured that it will be generous.

Write to me when you are able.

Ever your affectionate brother,
Christian

Edward Thorpe

From: Oberleutnant Peter von Vorzik
III Gruppe JG233
Catania, Sicily
To: Mathilde von Vorzik
23 Hevelius Straße
Grunewald

7th April 1942

My Darling Mathilde,

As always a great delight to have your letter, to know all is well with you and little Wolfchen and that you had a happy birthday. Next year, I hope, we shall be able to celebrate it together. I am glad you have joined Frau Kirschner's sewing circle; it is better than the position Lina proposed to find for you on the magazine *Die Frau* which would have necessitated your going into Berlin and which, in any case, would have been difficult for you with Wolfchen to look after. I read an article the other day in the *Völkische Beobachter* which proposed that all able-bodied women between the ages of 18 and 50 should register for some sort of work that would aid the war effort and that it should be compulsory, so perhaps your sewing circle will release you from such an obligation. I cannot imagine you, darling, working in some factory or driving a tram, which is what the writer of the article suggested. Anyway, it said that mothers of children under five should be exempt. Frau Scholz-Klink was even quoted as having said, "Even though our weapon is only the soup ladle its impact should be as great as other weapons." Was her visit to the sewing circle a success, and were the sewing circle ladies as excited as you to meet her?

Has your Czech girl arrived yet to help you with the domestic chores? I am pleased that you will be having help in the house. By all means find someone to look after the garden, perhaps Frau Kirschner could help you locate someone. Does she have a gardener? I think we should retain part of the garden for Wolfchen to play in but at least half of it should be for growing vegetables. I rarely hear the Concert Request programmes and I doubt if I would be free to listen if you suggested something to be played for me. Even so I spent half an hour thinking of something I would like to hear. It has to be short, does it not, a popular song or piano piece? Perhaps a Chopin étude or, yes, Zara Leander, I do like her singing.

340

We have been kept very busy lately so Kurt and I have not been able to visit some of the sites of classical antiquity around Syracuse and Messina as we had planned to do. Perhaps we will be able to visit them in a few weeks when our operational programme will be completed. If not, then it will have to be when we visit the island together, darling. Meanwhile, spring has arrived. The fields and byways are full of wild flowers and the balconies and windows of the houses are bursting with blooms. The orange and lemon trees are in flower and some are even laden with early fruit. The ones I wrote about previously were, apparently, left unharvested from last year. The snow on top of Mount Etna has almost gone and it seems almost as warm as summer in Bavaria.

I heard from Christian who tells me how pleased Frieda was to see you. I am sorry to learn from Edith, however, that Frieda seems very poorly. Did you find her so? When you next visit her do try and make sure that she is following the doctor's advice and is taking her medicines. Remind her it is for the baby's welfare as well as her own. When is the baby due? It must be quite soon, I think. Time passes so quickly when one is busy, we have already been here nearly three months. Now, darling, I have to write up my reports on the Staffel serviceability, fill out fuel and armament requisitions and so on and so on which takes up such a lot of my time. Do take care of your precious self and, of course, our darling Wolfchen. I will try and write again soon.

Ever your adoring,

Peter

From: Oberleutnant Peter von Vorzik
III Gruppe JG233
Catania, Sicily
To: Edith von Vorzik
Apt 2, 47 Scharnhorst Straße
Berlin

12th April 1942

My Dear Sister,

At last a few minutes to sit down and write to you. I was so pleased to receive your letter, really, you are the most interesting correspondent that I have, as your position in the Foreign Office provides you with insights that few of us are given. Operations have kept us extremely busy these last two or three weeks and, at the moment, are even more hectic. As you probably hear on the radio we are "softening up" the island of Malta preparatory to an airborne invasion: after that we expect the whole of the Mediterranean theatre of operations to be under our military dominance. When that happens I can begin to think of leave but it probably won't be until the autumn. As it is, and despite the workload, life here is quite pleasant, especially now that spring has arrived and it is becoming really warm.

You said in an earlier letter (I keep most of my mail from home and occasionally reread the letters) that you may have given me a wrong impression of the Italian people. I do not think so – if, indeed, the Sicilians are representative of their compatriots on the mainland. This is, I suppose, what is known as a peasant population. Life has a sort of leisureliness that is so very different from that beyond the Alps. Much to do with the climate, naturally, although the peasants seem to work hard in the fields and the local fishermen also labour long hours. It is an agrarian culture, of course, and I expect the industrial cities in the north of Italy are somewhat similar to the Ruhr. Life is less ordered than we know it and much simpler. As allies the Italians are – what shall I say? – unreliable. Militarily they are poorly equipped, which does not help them in the field, and socially and politically they are far less committed than we are, far less able to understand the threat from the east, far less concerned with the need to be amongst the leaders of the European nations. Except for the really poor they seem content with their livelihoods despite Mussolini's ambition to present them with an empire and the restoration of "the glory that was Rome." If that is achieved it will be on the back of what we, the Germans, do for them. You will have a very different view of things, dear sister, when you are launched into the much more civilised and sophisticated diplomatic scene in Rome compared to what I observe here. I look forward to your letters in a few months' time.

I am sure your wedding dress will be beautiful and you will make a ravishingly lovely bride for Arturo and his family to be proud of. How wise you are not to care too much about the accoutrements of the ceremony but to focus on your love for Arturo.

Christian does not seem too happy in Prague, especially being separated from Frieda at a time when she is pregnant and poorly. He does appreciate your visits and those of Mathilde. Thank you for your reassuring words about her and Wolfchen, I am naturally concerned about their welfare and, like Christian, wish that I could be near them. Just between us, I was amused at Mathilde's enthusiasm for her sewing circle! But you are right, it gives her something of a social life and a feeling of contributing a little towards war service.

You say your English is improving; what about your Italian? I think you will need it in the near future!

Ever you loving brother,
Peter

PS How delighted I am that you have found something that you would like as a wedding present from me. Yes, dear sister, put my name on the list. P.

From: Oberleutnant Peter von Vorzik
III Gruppe JG233
Catania, Sicily
To: SS-Obergruppenführer Count Christian von Vorzik
RSHA
Lobkowitz Palace
Hradcany Castle
Prague

17th April 1942

Dear Christian,

Many thanks for your letter. Your letters, and those of Edith, who sees and reads much of what is going on beyond our frontiers, help me to feel less uninformed and "out of things." There is no doubt that Russia remains the main focus of our struggle for survival. Even though I am eternally grateful not to have stayed in that terrible terrain throughout the winter, I feel I should be there now, supporting our armies and defending them against Russian air attacks as they are poised for the final effort to overcome the Communist monster. Even though I am sure that what we are doing here in the Mediterranean is important in the Führer's great scheme of things, I have an inward impulse to be fighting where it really matters, where the experience I have gained during these last two and a half years can do most good.

I had to smile at your anecdote about the Reichsmarschall but I must admit at being somewhat upset that he could behave in such a frivolous manner. We know he has always been flamboyant in his ways with a predeliction for spectacular uniforms, but wearing what amounts to fancy dress for a formal, serious meeting is going too far. We in the Luftwaffe have always respected him as a fighter ace in the last war and for building up our unrivalled capability in the air; now, to see him ridiculed is hard to bear.

I do not suppose you have had any opportunity to speak to Arturo. Let us hope that he has the good sense to keep his distance from Ciano and not be embroiled in any faction. I understand that you will be escorting Edith down the aisle on her wedding day; there should be ample opportunity to speak to Arturo during the ensuing festivities. I know only too well what it is to be separated from one's beloved and it must be doubly difficult for you knowing that Frieda needs the doctor's ministrations. We were lucky in that Mathilde's pregnancy was without complications – how diverse are womens' reactions to childbearing! One would think it a basic anatomical function, as relatively uncomplicated as the procreative act, but then the human body is an amazingly complex organism. Mathilde will continue seeing Frieda until the actual birth.

How pleasing it is that plans are proceeding well for the handing over of Adlersee as a convalescent hospital for Luftwaffe officers. I wonder how the various floors will be disposed? You say the remuneration will be "generous"; all we need, really, is to be assured that the objects, pictures and antique furniture will be safely stored and the fabric of the building well maintained. Also that Werner will be looked after properly. Incidentally, do we know if he has any family?

I am surprised that there should be such widespread corruption within the various cartels that you mention. How can this be in our National Socialist state? I can understand that there might be one or two corrupt individuals within any large organisation, but that there should be ramifications involving what you refer to as "some very important names" is incomprehensible. I hope your investigations are concluded swiftly and successfully so that you may be returned to Berlin and reunited with Frieda.

Ever your devoted brother,

Peter

From: Edith von Vorzik
Apt 2, 47 Scharnhorst Straße
Berlin
To: Oberleutnant Peter von Vorzik
III Gruppe JG233
Catania, Sicily

27th April 1942

My Dear Peter,

I am afraid this letter is the bearer of tragic news. Yesterday, about 4 pm, Frieda miscarried and the doctors were unable to save her or the baby. Ursula's friend, Gerda, who has been staying with Frieda as a sort of personal maid, had gone out to the Post Office. When she returned she found Frieda unconscious in a great pool of blood, lying on the bathroom floor. The ambulance took twenty-five minutes to arrive and, despite the efforts of the hospital doctors, Frieda died a half hour later and the baby – a boy – was stillborn. Just what happened after Gerda left the house we cannot tell. Whether Frieda felt labour pains, whether she passed out and fell, we have no idea. There were blood stains on the bed linen. The doctor said she haemorrhaged so badly that, had she lived, she would probably have sustained some brain damage through lack of oxygen. Gerda feels terrible, saying if only she had given the letters (including one to Christian) to a servant to post ... None of the servants heard anything. The housekeeper, cook and housemaids were in the basement, the butler was asleep in his room, the chauffeur was in the garage. It is just a dreadful tragedy and no one can be held responsible. Christian is flying back from Prague, expected tonight. I said I would write to tell you the awful news. Thank you, dear brother for your letter dated 12th April, received a few days ago. I am sure you will understand if I do not write more now, there is so much to do and Christian will need me as soon as he arrives. I telephoned the news to Mathilde who, of course, is terribly upset.

Take great care of yourself.

Ever your loving sister,
Edith

From: Oberleutnant Peter von Vorzik
III Gruppe JG233
Catania, Sicily
To: SS-Gruppenführer Count Christian von Vorzik
116 Kaiserstraße
Berlin

4th May 1942

My Dear Christian,

At a time like this words seem not only inadequate but, indeed, superfluous. Yet, as I cannot clasp your hand or hold you in a silent embrace, I must express my deepest sorrow and profoundest sympathy at your tragic loss in these few futile words. Edith's letter informing me of Frieda's death left me quite numb with shock and I cannot imagine how you must have felt receiving the dreadful news over the telephone. Dear brother, I am only too well aware that whatever I write now can only increase your unhappiness, provoke some poignant memory, add yet another gram of pain to the load you bear. Know, then, that my thoughts and feelings are constantly with you, by your side in this anguished hour.

Ever your loving brother,
Peter

PS So much may have happened since I wrote this letter – you may be back in Prague or still in Berlin, so I am sending it to your private Berlin address, they will know where to forward it. P.

From: Oberleutnant Peter von Vorzik
III Gruppe JG233
Catania, Sicily
To: Edith von Vorzik
Apt 2, 47 Scharnhorst Straße
Berlin

5th May 1942

My Dear Edith,

As you can imagine your letter informing me of Frieda's death came as a dreadful shock which remains with me. I do appreciate your writing, however, when you must have had so much to do at that hour, on that day. No doubt Frieda's funeral will be over by the time this reaches you, Christian (to whom I have written) will, perhaps, be back in Prague and you will be behind your office desk. I have tried telephoning but it is quite impossible. Our own Luftwaffe lines are not open for personal matters, however urgent, and the Sicilian/Italian telephone system does not seem to work for an insignificant German flier. All that happens is that I get some operator shouting, "Pronto? Pronto?", and then, when I begin speaking in my halting Italian, phrasebook in hand, the line goes dead. So, I must rely on the post, slow as it is. In your recent letters you refer to Frieda's – unspecified – "gynaecological problems"; might it not have been foreseen that a miscarriage could occur? Surely the doctor must have anticipated such a possibility? And might she not have been transferred to a hospital as the date of the birth drew near? Of course, it is easy to be wise in retrospect and, as you say, no one is to blame, it is just a terrible tragedy. Now, dear sister, try and put this awful thing out of your mind and concentrate on the joyful occasion awaiting you next month. How does the wedding dress progress? Will it be sent to you for a fitting? (And the shoes!?) Or will you rely on last minute adjustments when you arrive in Rome? We continue to be very active, maintaining our operations against Malta. I wonder any living thing remains on the island, we have been pounding it every day for over two months.

Now I must write to Mathilde.

Ever your loving brother,
Peter

From: Oberleutnant Peter von Vorzik
III Gruppe JG233
Catania, Sicily
To: Mathilde von Vorzik
23 Hevelius Straße
Grunewald

5th May 1942

My Own Darling Mathilde,
How dreadful it is that I should be writing this letter! By the time you receive it more than two weeks will have passed since Frieda's death and we are separated both in time and distance from a tragic occasion that

binds us all in grief. There is nothing I can say, darling, that can alleviate the loss of a dear sister-in-law but I know how dreadfully upsetting it must have been for you so close to the event. It is at times like this that one feels our separation most; how I have wished that I could be there with you and share with Christian his time of desolation. Despite the war, despite how conditioned we are to seeing and hearing of battles in which thousands are killed and maimed, the loss of a loved one far removed from national conflicts somehow affects the spirit much more. There are many questions I would ask but perhaps this is not the time to ask them. All I can think of is that there is now a great gap in Christian's life, his lovely wife and baby-to-be snatched from him by a cruel act of nature. I hope he can find the strength of will to overcome this terrible loss.

I fully expect, darling, that a letter from you will cross with this one. Never mind, it is our only means of communication at present and it helps us both to commiserate with each other. I will try and write again soon. This tragedy makes you and Wolfchen seem – if possible – even more precious to me.

Ever your own loving husband,
Peter

From: Mathilde von Vorzik
23 Hevelius Straße
Grunewald
To: Oberleutnant Peter von Vorzik
III Gruppe JG233
Catania, Sicily

6th May 1942

My Darling Peter,
Edith told me she had written to you to tell you the dreadful news. It has been a ghastly time for all of us, a trauma that has left us emotionally and physically exhausted. Of course, it is Christian who has suffered the most, a terrible loss for him, something that I fear will scar him for life. He arrived after a tiring flight from Prague, looking – so Edith told me – like a ghost, pale and drawn, his black uniform accentuating his pallor. I did not see him, he was here only two days, signing documents and forms for the hospital authorities.

There was no post-mortem. I cannot remember the clinical term that Edith said the doctor wrote on the death certificate, septicaemia something, plus massive bleeding. On the following day Christian accompanied the coffin on the train to Bucharest. Apparently, it was her parents' wish that Frieda should be buried there. I feel so sorry for them, she was their only child. After the funeral Christian caught the train back to Prague. Edith says it is much better for him to immerse himself in work rather than take leave, it would only mean he would sit around in that great big apartment and grieve. Later, perhaps, he can take a holiday somewhere, skiing in Austria or even visiting Edith and Arturo in Rome.

I had visited Frieda just an hour or two before she died. She looked very pale (but then she always did!) although she talked quite animatedly about Wolfchen, saying she hoped she would have a boy like him; she knew that was what Christian wanted although she would be very happy if it was a girl. She took two pills while I was with her and a little phial of medicine that made her grimace because she said it was very bitter. She said that the doctor said that "one of her problems" was that she was suffering from iron deficiency.

While we were talking Gerda looked in to collect a letter that Frieda had written to Christian and I left just a few minutes later so I must have been the last person to see her alive, a thought that haunts me. No one in the apartment heard anything, you know what a great big place it is, the basement where the servants are is four floors down, those huge carpeted rooms muffling any sound. No bells were rung. We think Frieda must have started bleeding, gone into the bathroom and then lost consciousness. There was blood on the bed and a trail across the carpet into the bathroom. It is all so terrible, I cannot escape the feeling that, somehow, at some moment, her death could have been avoided. If only Gerda had returned from the Post Office a little earlier! As soon as she made the terrible discovery, Gerda roused the household, the housekeeper called the ambulance and then phoned Edith's office. Edith was able to get through to the RSHA headquarters in Prague and tell Christian what had happened. At that time she did not know that Frieda had died. An hour later Christian phoned to say that he was catching the courier plane the next day. The following afternoon Edith phoned to say she would be calling in to see me. I thought at the time that it was just a social call, though something of a surprise. Edith drove over in the little DKW and broke the news, she had not wanted to tell me over the phone. Of course, I was terribly upset but it was a great comfort to have Edith there. Then, after an hour with me, she drove to Tempelhof to meet Christian's plane. It fell to her to tell Christian that Frieda had died. Edith has been quite marvellous, a tower of strength, and I had always thought of her as someone who was quite delicate herself! She has been calm and practical throughout, though obviously as deeply affected as any of us. I think it has been her Catholic faith that has sustained her. I know she has prayed for Frieda's soul. My darling, it must have been dreadful for you to receive this news alone, by letter, with no one close to talk to. I decided to write and tell you all these details as I felt sure you would want to know all that has happened. Now, life goes on. I am very well in myself and darling Wolfchen is a marvellous solace at such a time, a joy to the spirit.

Lenka, the Czech girl, arrived three days before Frieda died and it has been a great advantage to have her here in the house during this time. She is very pleasant, speaks good German and is very willing to do anything I ask. Poor girl, her mother died when she was fourteen and her father and brother have been sent to that new concentration camp at Theresienstadt. Her father is a professor of history and is considered "potentially subversive." She has not been able to contact them since they left. As you suggested I asked Frau Kirschner about a gardener and she is quite happy to share the services of her man, Friedrich. He is about 60 and has great plans for making a large vegetable garden! When you next come on leave, darling, I hope you will have fresh home-grown produce to eat.

I must hurry now to catch the post. Remember, darling,

You have the undying love of

Your own,
Mathilde

Oberleutnant Peter von Vorzik
Journal entry

12th May 1942

The shocking, lonely death of my sister-in-law, and her stillborn baby boy, has affected us all with great sadness. At this distance, with only a letter from Mathilde to give me any details, I find the whole tragedy full of unanswered questions. What exactly were Frieda's "gynaecological problems"? Could not the doctor foresee that those "problems" might presage a miscarriage? What were the pills and medicines she was prescribed? Would it not have been advisable to have had a proper nurse in attendance rather than just Ursula's friend, Gerda? Should there not have been a post-mortem? What exactly was on the death certificate? It is not for me to ask these questions, of course, and if Christian is satisfied that everything was done for Frieda during her pregnancy that could have been done, then it is not for me to interfere. But had it been my darling Mathilde – heaven forbid! – I should not have let the matter rest without more information. I grieve for Christian. To lose his wife and a baby boy, which he so much desired, is quite terrible and I feel anxious for his mental state away from his family in Prague. I hope he does not become prey to depression. I notice, incidentally, that he has long since abandoned writing Heil Hitler at the end of his letters – at least to me. However, he loses no opportunity to inform me of some absurdity relating to Party officials. His anecdote about the Reichsmarschall dressed as a Roman senator was quite upsetting.

While our private tragedy was being played out our attacks upon Malta reached a climax yesterday and the day before. The various Geschwader flew over 300 sorties each day and the air battles that took place were as wide-ranging and furiously fought as they were over Britain nearly two years ago. We suffered really severe losses, both in fighters and bombers, and today Field Marshal Kesselring gave orders to halt the attacks on the island. To our surprise, during these last two days, we were met with swarms of Spitfires. Apparently, the British have succeeded in flying in several squadrons of these aircraft from two naval carriers, their own *Eagle* and the American *Wasp*. We were warned about this at our intelligence briefing a few days ago but we underestimated just how many Spitfires there were. Four of my Staffel were lost during the two-day battles: Reichert, Fritsch, Steuben and Meurer, all young pilots who had joined us direct from Werneuchen when JG233 reassembled after Russia. Varasch was wounded in the shoulder and sent to a field hospital outside Catania and Kurt's plane was completely destroyed after a forced landing following yesterday's melée, an incident that caused me great alarm. Three hours later Kurt was back at the Staffel, bruised but safe. Never have I drunk such a heartfelt toast to comradeship as I did in the mess that evening.

From: SS-Gruppenführer Count Christian von Vorzik
RSHA HQ
Lobkowitz Palace
Hradcany Castle
Prague
To: Oberleutnant Peter von Vorzik
III Gruppe JG233
Catania, Sicily

21st May 1942

Dear Peter,

Thank you for your letter of condolence which I very much appreciate. As you say, words seem empty things at such a time, and yet, however inadequate they may be, it is comforting to know that one's grief is shared, that relatives and friends are concerned for one's welfare. It makes it worse, of course, that as a family we are scattered about Europe, that it is only through the written word that emotions can be expressed. I was immensely grateful to Edith for undertaking the drive to Tempelhof and informing me of Frieda's death. You assumed, naturally, that I had heard of it over the phone; Edith softened the blow by being there in person.

It was only after my return to Prague, as I sat alone in my rather fusty and over-furnished quarters, lit by oil lamps, that the shock of Frieda's death was borne in on me. During my brief stay in Berlin I was so taken up with formalities, with arranging for the transport of the coffin to Bucharest, that I had little time to think about my loss. Even during the funeral, a very simple affair with just Frieda's parents and one or two cousins in attendance at a small church just outside the city, I was so aware of how distraught they were, especially Frieda's mother, that I had no thought of my own grief. The memory of Frieda that keeps recurring to me is of her dancing in the second act of *Giselle*, a ghostly figure drifting about that great stage in Paris. Thinking of it now it seems almost like a premonition of her death, although I know that to be a foolish, fanciful thought. Nevertheless, it is an image that haunts me.

Reinhard and Lina have been very kind, twice asking me to dinner at Panenske-Breschen where Reinhard has his summer residence. I am grateful, too, that Reinhard had given me this investigative brief. It has kept me extremely busy and that – as Edith so sensibly said – is the best antidote to the sadness that at times engulfs me. I have certainly unearthed some astonishing information regarding various corrupt practises within the SD. Senior members of the SS and the Party have been busy building financial empires for themselves, marketing every sort of commodity from soap to shoes, cement to chemicals, under the guise of cartels secretly affiliated to the SS. Everybody, it seems, from SS-Obergruppenführers to Gauleiters, and downwards, throughout their petty dominions, has their fingers in a score of pies. I have spoken to my friend, Oswald Pohl, who is in charge of the WVHA Economic and Administrative Departments of the SS, to let him know I am investigating his subordinates; I do not want him to be suddenly confronted by Reinhard with these revelations as heads will surely roll when I put my report on Reinhard's desk in a week or two. Whether Oswald will have the good sense to act in time and root out these corrupt elements remains to be seen. But he has been warned. Many of Oswald's major executives are only nominally members of the SS and rarely wear the uniform. There is Dr Kurt May, an SS-Untersturmführer, and a furniture manufacturer from Stuttgart, now in control of the ex-Jewish Gerstel works throughout Czechoslovakia; SS-Hauptsturmführer Franz Eirenschmalz, a building tycoon controlling stone, brick and clinker works; SS-Standartenführer Hans Kammler, head of an engineering empire that builds everything from armaments works to barracks for the Waffen-SS. The more I investigate the more astonishing are the ramifications of the WVHA.

Yes, Edith's wedding will afford an excellent opportunity to speak to Arturo regarding Ciano. I look forward to the ceremony, not only for the pleasure of seeing our dear sister married but as a welcome break from routine and the emotional legacy of Frieda's death.

I hope, dear brother, that all goes well with you. The thought of the operations you are engaged in helps me to remember that there is a wider perspective to our endeavours than grieving over a personal loss, however painful that may be.

Ever your devoted brother,
Christian

From: Edith von Vorzik
Apt 2, 47 Scharnhorst Straße
Berlin
To: Oberleutnant Peter von Vorzik
III Gruppe JG233
Catania, Sicily

24th May 1942

My Dear Peter,

This may be my last letter to you as Edith von Vorzik! It is just over three weeks before I become Countess Novarro-Badaelli. There is so much to do in the intervening time but if there is little chance for me to write to you again before my wedding day you can be sure you will always be in the forefront of my thoughts.

As you can imagine, the pace of life has been hectic recently, beginning with Frieda's death. Meeting Christian at Tempelhof and having to tell him the awful news was the most difficult moment of my life. From the minute we met in the arrival hall he plied me with questions but I managed to avoid the truth until we were both in the little DKW. I took his hand in mine and said, simply, "Christian, dearest, I have to tell you that Frieda and her baby both died in the hospital." He sat for a moment or two, staring through the windscreen, without any outward show of emotion, except for gripping my hand tightly. Then he said, "I was prepared for you to tell me that." We sat in silence for a few moments before he began to ask me questions about how it had happened. I started the engine and told him all I knew as I drove slowly back to Kaiserstraße. I only saw him once again, briefly, on the morning of the next day, before he left for Bucharest. I hope he has had time to mourn, to give his emotion free reign, in the privacy of his quarters. We all deal with grief in our own way and, for Christian, I am sure it is in solitude. I spoke to him on the telephone yesterday. Apparently he has twice been to dinner with the Heydrichs. Lina was most sympathetic but all Reinhard said was, "Now you will have to find a nice young Aryan woman for yourself. Meanwhile, you must do your duty by the *Lebensborn* programme." I make no comment.

I have had several letters from Arturo, forwarded by Emilio Cecchi, the attaché at the Italian Embassy in Berlin. I give him my letters for Arturo and our correspondence goes by diplomatic bag – much quicker than the postal system! Arturo was present, with Ciano, at the meeting between the Führer and the Duce at Klessheim Castle, Salzburg, at the end of last month. He says it was the usual farrago (as he calls it), the Führer doing all the talking while the Italians listened and both entourages squabbling over protocol! In particular, the Marquis Blasco Lanza d'Aieta, Ciano's secretary, resents the high-handed way that von Ribbentrop and Bormann treat their Italian counterparts. Arturo says it is not without its comic aspect, like so many prima donnas upstaging each other. He says I will have to deal with such things when I play hostess at our dinner parties. I have told him we cannot entertain for at least six months or until I have had time to observe who's who, who likes who and who hates who! To think all this goes on while we are engaged in a frightful war!

Parcels and packing cases, all wedding presents, have been arriving; I have them sent to Christian's residence as I simply have not room for them in my little apartment. They will all have to be transported to our villa so the wedding will be over before I have seen most of them. I noticed a big packing case with the insignia of Brüning and Pfleigers on the side so I am sure that is your gift of the Meissen dinner-service, dear brother. Yes, my fittings for the wedding dress will be in Rome. The bodice of the dress is plain but, according to Eleanora, the skirt and train will be embroidered with hundreds of little seed pearls, all hand sewn, as will the shoes! Apparently Ciano has agreed to attend the wedding but will leave before the reception as he is meeting Serrano Suñer, the Spanish Foreign Minister, at Livorno the following day. There will be many other distinguished guests attending, including Prince Umberto and his wife, Princess Maria of Piedmont (I think I told you Arturo's father was a great friend of the King and the family have remained in close touch with the Royal household). Christian will be staying with his old friend SS-Standartenführer Dollmann who is now head of the SS in Rome. I feel somewhat guilty about the extravagance of it all (Arturo has told me that there have been bread riots in Venice and Matera owing to rationing. The ration is 200 grams a day with 3–400 grams for labourers). The middle and upper classes seem to have no difficulty in eating well, however, but then it is somewhat similar to Berlin, is it not? If you can afford to eat at Horcher's or Savarin's or the Adlon then there is practically nothing that you cannot have. Eleanora has sent me photographs of our villa just outside Rome. It is very modern, all white with curved metal window frames, marble floors and the very latest kitchen. There is a very large main reception room with a terrace overlooking the city, a dining room that will seat twenty, six bedrooms, three dressing rooms and three bathrooms and separate quarters for staff. Arturo has a study, there is a room that will make a library and a small round room at the corner of the terrace which Eleanora suggests I appropriate for myself. There are extensive wooded grounds that separate the villa from its neighbours and garages for three cars. I shall be very nervous playing wife and hostess but shall rely on memories of mother doing that. Eleanora, too, I am sure, will be very helpful.

Now, dear brother, I make no apology for urging you, yet again, to take the greatest care of yourself in all the operations you undertake. I thank God that at least you are not in Russia now that the summer offensive is about to begin, but I know that you are still in the midst of dangers in the area in which you are flying. Is Kurt still your Katschmarek? Ever since he rescued you from the Russian snows I have added his name to my prayers. Do not tell him so but give him my best wishes. I will try and write again before I take the train south to my new life (I am told that the journey will take 36 hours or more), but if not you know you carry with you the love and prayers of

Your devoted sister,
Edith

From: Oberleutnant Peter von Vorzik
III Gruppe JG233
Catania, Sicily
To: Mathilde von Vorzik
23 Hevelius Straße
Grunewald

27th May 1942

My Darling Mathilde,
Thank you, dearest, for writing to tell me details of Frieda's death. As you say, a terrible trauma for everyone, and a dreadful blow to Christian. It makes it worse for him being marooned in Prague. I know he is hoping, sometime, to get a transfer to Walter Schellenberg's foreign department but Reinhard keeps him busy with the RSHA and would not look kindly

on Christian leaving his entourage. Like you I was somewhat surprised that Edith coped with the situation so capably. For me, she has always been my little sister, brought up to be more or less subservient to us menfolk (that was father's view of women), made to study the piano and do needlework, not given a university education but taught by an English governess (a Miss Goadby, very prim and starchy, always quoting Shakespeare. Christian and I used to tease her unmercifully. She left us, suddenly, around summer 1936, after some scandal involving a lieder singer she met in Munich. We had a postcard from her, just before the war, sent from a sheep farm in New Zealand!). Edith has really blossomed since arriving in Berlin and working at the Foreign Office. Each time I see her I am amazed at how poised she has become. She has also written to me about Frieda and meeting Christian at Tempelhof. It was very courageous of her to face telling him the dreadful news in person.

Now, darling, my own news is that the Gruppe is moving again, this time even further from home, supporting General Rommel in the North African desert. Actually, it is not all that much further away, about an hour's flying time and really, it makes very little difference, does it, darling, whether I am 2,000 or 3,000 km from home. Either way we are separated and it is better than returning to Russia which some Gruppen are having to do. We do not know yet what our destination will be, certainly somewhere in Cyrenaica, but I will send you my address as soon as I have it. As in Russia we shall doubtless be moving forward from one airfield to another. The word is that the objective is Cairo. Meanwhile, send any mail, as usual, to JG HQ to be forwarded.

I was very pleased that your Czech girl is proving useful. In any case I was going to suggest that you try and find someone to help you in the house although I am well aware that nowadays it is difficult to get any staff. What we shall do with Adlersee when the war is over I do not know. I will talk to Christian about it when I am next on leave (Christmas?) I have happy boyhood memories of Adlersee, of course, but none of us will want to keep up such a huge rambling place in southern Germany when our lives are centred elsewhere. Perhaps we can sell it to one of the Party officials, they all seem to have a penchant for acquiring large country residences! Maybe we could keep one of the farms on the estate as a family retreat. The one I am thinking of has a lovely view of the lake and it would be less than an hour's drive from Munich. But all that is in the future.

We have been issued with tropical kit prior to arriving in Africa. I will have a photograph taken in my shorts and tunic! To think that not so long ago I was trying to keep warm in those icy wastes of Russia; now I am going to be in the broiling sun! Dearest, I must close this letter and try and write to Edith in the hope she will get it before she leaves to take up her new life in Rome. I also have a pile of work to attend to, new orders keep flooding in and the Staffel must be made ready for our flight further south.

Many kisses for yourself and baby Wolfchen.

Ever your loving husband,
Peter

PS I look forward to the produce that Friedrich is going to grow for us! P.

From: Oberleutnant Peter von Vorzik
III Gruppe JG233
Catania, Sicily
To: Edith von Vorzik
Apt 2, Scharnhorst Straße
Berlin

28th May 1942

My Dear Edith,

I was so pleased to have your letter. I am replying right away in the hope that it reaches you before you leave for Rome, otherwise it will be following you around for months. Incidentally, you did not include your Rome address; please let me have it as soon as you can. First, I want to wish you every happiness this world can bestow. If you are as happy as Mathilde and I then you will certainly be blessed. How I wish I could be present at your wedding! I am sure you will make a beautiful bride and the dress sounds exquisite. I am also sure that Arturo will be immensely proud of you as, indeed, will Christian. I am happy for him that after his dreadful loss he can participate in this joyous occasion. It was admirable of you to meet Christian and tell him the dreadful news, something I would have shrunk from doing. As it is, I have recently had to write several letters of condolence to parents and wives whose sons and husbands have been lost in battle. It is an onerous duty but nothing so daunting as that which you had to face.

I was amused by your reference to the meeting between the Führer and the Duce at Klessheim but I am no longer surprised at the behaviour of those in high places, squabbling over protocol or some such triviality when the future of the Fatherland is at stake. Christian recently told me (I think he relishes passing on such information!) how Walter Schellenberg was received by Reichsmarschall Göring dressed as a Roman senator! But then, such bizarrerie is not confined to our leaders; I expect you saw that recent newspaper photograph of the British Prime Minister holding a tommy-gun and looking like a Chicago gangster? I am sure the Führer would never allow himself to appear so undignified.

I was not surprised that the bread ration you mention was the cause of riots in Venice, 200 grams is a very small amount. Here in Sicily the (mostly) peasant population appear well fed. They seem to have enough flour for pasta and, of course, fish, fruit and vegetables are plentiful. Perhaps it is different in the big towns and cities where distribution may be difficult but I think the middle and upper classes everywhere have the means to eat well. Your villa in Rome sounds really splendid, very modern and with a fine view of the city. When the war is over I hope Mathilde and I will be able to come and stay with you. I am sure you will make a perfect hostess, as you say you have memories of mother presiding at dinner parties and you have been present at several grand receptions in Berlin and observed how it is done. What staff will you have? I imagine it is somewhat easier to find maids and housekeepers in Rome than it is in Berlin.

As Mathilde may have told you, the Gruppe is moving again, this time to North Africa where, I believe , the temperature can reach almost 50° in the shade! The last few weeks have been full of frantic activity and I anticipate it will be the same for the next couple of months. After that – who knows? Perhaps we will be due for leave. I long to see Mathilde and Wolfchen again, in two or three months it will be a year since he was born and he will probably be beginning to walk and talk. Dearest sister, I shall be thinking of you especially on 14th June and trying to visualise you walking down the aisle of the church, resplendent in your beautiful dress, attended by your bridesmaids and pages, escorted by our dear brother in his dress uniform, to be greeted at the altar by your beloved Arturo. I cannot wait to see the photos!

Once again, all my heartfelt good wishes for a lifetime of happiness

Ever your loving brother,

Peter

Oberleutnant Peter von Vorzik
Journal entry

6th June 1942

Two terrible things have happened, both touching my family. On the night of 30-31st May more than 1,000 – 1,000! – British bombers attacked Cologne, devastating the city. Three days before that, Czech partisans, probably sent from Britain, threw a grenade into Reinhard's car, mortally wounding him. He died in hospital two days ago, June 4th. According to newspaper and radio reports much of Cologne lies in ruins although, miraculously, the cathedral is still standing. I have been desperately trying to contact Mathilde by telephone, without success, to find out if she has any news of her mother and Aunt Ilse. Apparently, communication with the city, apart from official lines, is currently impossible. My only hope for them lies in the fact that they live (lived?) not far from the cathedral and as that remains untouched by the bombs perhaps the surrounding residential area has also escaped.

I am appalled at the number of bombers the British could muster over the city, almost twice the number we assembled in our greatest raids on Britain. Not only that, it is claimed that the bomber force included many of Britain's newest four-engined types, Halifaxes and Stirlings, capable of carrying huge new bombs of nearly 4,000 kg that can destroy whole streets. On the following night Essen was also attacked by over 1,000 bombers. The RAF have suffered heavy losses, we claim over 90 shot down although the British say it was just over a third of that number. Whatever the truth may be it is obvious the British are capable of breaching our defences with hundreds of machines. Moreover, they are able to put two new four-engine types into service (intelligence information refers to a third, the Lancaster, expected to appear soon) while we struggle to get the He177 operational.

On May 27th, Reinhard's assassins waited for him in a Prague suburb as he drove into the city from his summer residence. As his open car slowed down for a sharp bend on the Prague-Dresden road, one of them (there may have been two or three assassins, details are vague) lobbed a grenade into the car. Despite terrible wounds Reinhard pursued the killers on foot, firing his revolver, before collapsing. No doubt Christian will attend the funeral (thank heaven he was not travelling with Reinhard!) and I am wondering if he will be able to escort Edith at her wedding in Rome. Terrible as Reinhard's assassination is, Christian may now be free to join Schellenberg's department.

While these terrible events were taking place, General Rommel began an offensive against the British and Empire forces in Cyrenaica and is already gaining ground – or, rather, more desert! His armoured forces have broken through the lines on the British flanks and are threatening the great port and fortress of Tobruk from the south. We are preparing the Gruppe to fly out in support of this attack. Our aircraft have been painted in new camouflage colours on the upper surfaces, a sand-coloured background with olive green smudges which, I am told, merge with the desert scrub. The undersides remain pale blue. Sadly, our little fighters are being fitted with underwing bomb-racks as, we are told, we shall be used as fighter bombers attacking British armour and ground forces. That, of course, affects our performance should we need to be deployed in our proper role, either offensively or defensively, as fighters. But the whole Staffel is anxious to join the advance. Simultaneously with Rommel's attack in North Africa, the Wehrmacht has begun its summer offensive in Russia, the main thrust coming from Army Groups A and B driving towards the oil-bearing Caucasus. We have a big map in the operations room which shows, day to day, how our compatriots in the army are doing. I am sure that Lother is involved in this operation with his Zerstörer Geschwader and I must try and find time to write to him. At least, now, he will be free of the snow and ice and most likely contending with the dust and heat of summer, especially in those southern regions towards the Crimea. Looking at both maps, Russia and our new area of operations in North Africa, one can see the Führer's great strategy of carrying out a giant pincer movement, with our armies joining up somewhere in the Middle East, perhaps in Persia. What a stupendous triumph that would be!

From: Oberleutnant Peter von Vorzik
III Gruppe JG233
Martuba, Cyrenaica
To: Mathilde von Vorzik
23 Hevelius Straße, Grunewald

15th June 1942

My Darling Mathilde,

How frustrating it has been! As soon as I heard of the terrible RAF raid on Cologne I tried and tried to reach you by phone, without success. All lines, except official ones, were closed and so, once again, I am forced to rely on the slow passage of mail to communicate with you. Even slower than usual as, at that time, we were in the process of a major move for the Gruppe as you will see by my new address although that will almost certainly change any day now. Meanwhile, it is the one you should write to. I hope and trust, dearest one, that your mother and Aunt Ilse have been spared, although the raid must have been an awful experience for them. Very little news about it has filtered through to us although there have been rumours (there are always rumours!) that dreadful damage has been done to that beautiful city. According to the radio the Führer is planning retribution upon many British towns and cities. And then there was the assassination of Reinhard! I am so thankful that Christian was not in the car with him, as he could have been. If Christian had to attend the funeral, as I am sure he did, I am wondering whether he was able to get to Edith's wedding yesterday, in time? That wedding is the one bright happening amongst so many black days that we have experienced recently. I long to hear all about it and to see some of the photographs.

This town and the surrounding area is in great contrast to the Sicilian countryside which was so abundant with flowers and vegetation. Here it is extremely hot and dusty, the town only a huddle of concrete buildings, mostly built by the Italians and very cracked and run-down, with some nondescript mud-coloured native dwellings on the outskirts and a few spindly palm trees dotted about. To the north is the sea, to the south, east and west just miles of desert covered with scrub and cactus. In the far distance we can see the dim blue outline of an escarpment, otherwise the landscape is totally arid. As yet we have not done any operational flying, though that will begin in a day or two, supporting Rommel in his offensive against the British 8th Army and its colonial forces. We have been acclimatising ourselves to living in this furnace-like heat, though when the sun goes down it suddenly gets quite cold and then I am glad of the pullover you knitted me! During the day our biggest problem is avoiding dehydration as water is strictly rationed. Never mind, we have plenty of German beer flown in!

Last night, darling, there was a full moon; did you see it? I was wondering if you might be looking up at the sky at the same time as I was, the moon marking the apex of a triangle between us. When the moon rises here over the desert it seems enormous, as if it has come much closer to the earth. It begins a real golden yellow, then as it climbs up the sky it becomes first pale blue then small and silver like a little pearl. Kurt and I used to look up at the stars when we were in Russia last winter; here the constellations are switched around in the sky but they seem even more numerous, millions and millions, quite astonishing. As you can see, darling, I have very little to write about. This is merely to give you my new address and to let you know how anxious I am for news about Cologne.

Keep yourself and darling Wolfchen safe.

You are always in my thoughts,

Ever your own,
Peter

From: Oberleutnant Peter von Vorzik
III Gruppe JG233
Martuba, Cyrenaica
To: SS-Gruppenführer Count Christian von Vorzik
RSHA
Lobkowitz Palace
Hradcany Castle
Prague

17th June 1942

Dear Christian,
This is just a quick note to say how appalled I was to learn of Reinhard's assassination. I give thanks that you were not in that car with him. Even so, it must have been a great shock to you and I am wondering how it

might affect your position in the RSHA? Could you now transfer to Schellenberg's department or must you wait and see who replaces Reinhard? I also wonder if you were able to take your place at Edith's side on her wedding day as it followed quickly upon Reinhard's funeral which I am sure you had to attend. There were several photographs of it in the papers that are sent out to us with serried ranks of the SS behind the Führer and SS-Reichsminister Himmler but it was impossible to distinguish faces. There was also a picture of Lina standing with her two little boys, such a sad-looking group. Please convey my deepest sympathies to her when you either see her or write. Duty calls me, this is but to ask you to let me have all your news when you can.

Ever your loving brother,
Peter

PS You will see I have a new address; I am assuming that you will have returned to Prague for the time being. P.

From: Mathilde von Vorzik
23 Hevelius Straße
Grunewald
To: Oberleutnant Peter von Vorzik
III Gruppe JG233
Martuba, Cyrenaica

27th June 1942

My Darling Peter,

Your letter of the 15th arrived this morning and it is with a heavy heart that I must tell you that mother and Aunt Ilse were both killed in the raid on Cologne. The details are obscure but four days ago I received a letter from the Gauleiter's office in Cologne (following my letter of inquiry sent the day after the raid) to say that the whole street where mother's house was has been virtually obliterated, nothing but dust and rubble. They have not identified any bodies yet but I am told that when, if, identification is possible all bodies will be cremated and the ashes sent to relatives. I have a horror of receiving someone else's ashes by mistake! Even so, I hope they are able to identify mother (I sent a photo and description) so that I could make a final farewell. Once again Edith has been a great comfort to me, the only person I could talk to but, of course, she left for Rome a few days after. But do not worry about me, dearest, sad as I have been I have now recovered from the shock and know that I am but one amongst many thousands who have lost loved ones in this war. I find some relief in the knowledge that mother and Ilse must have died instantly, no lingering wretchedness in hospital, no life as a cripple in a wheelchair, dependent on others. Ilse's health was already giving cause for concern although mother, as you know, was still very fit and mentally alert. Wolfchen is my joy and happiness and you, darling, the one I cannot help worrying about. As long as this war lasts anxiety about your safety must be the burden I bear but then, again, it is a burden shared with thousands, millions of women. I think of Lina, widowed by an assassin's bomb, and count myself lucky.

Lina telephoned yesterday. She is in Nauen, closing down the Jagdhaus Stolphof and moving things back to Schlachtensee for the time being. She thinks she will spend the summer at Fehmarn and invited me to join her with Wolfchen if I wished. I thanked her but said I felt I should stay here in Grunewald for the present, we are far enough away from Berlin to be safe and I want to be in our home while you are away – always hoping, darling, that by some miracle you will be granted leave. Lina said the hardest task for her has been packing up Reinhard's things, his uniforms and hunting clothes, his toilet articles, hairbrush and shaving brush, everyday things that he used. There has been so much for her to do, organising the closure of the residence in Panenske-Breschen (she is glad to be leaving Czechoslovakia), the hunting lodge, the house at Schlachtensee, dealing with legal matters, answering hundreds of letters and looking after the children. She said that neither Klaus nor Heider have wept for their father, at least when she has been with them. Christian was present at Reinhard's funeral and telephoned me before he left for Rome. He sounded subdued, somewhat shaken by Reinhard's death following so quickly after the shock of Frieda's, but looking forward to Edith's wedding as something of an antidote to such dispiriting events.

I continue to do my sewing at Frau Kirschner's and it has been a form of therapy following mother's death. The other women have all been most kind and solicitous and I have visited two of them who live close by for morning coffee. They have husbands and fathers in the armed forces – one has a husband in Russia, near Leningrad, one's father is a U-boat commander, and we share our anxieties. Yes, darling, I did happen to look up and see the full moon, perhaps we were looking at it at the same time.

I've always thought of it as something romantic but now everyone says it is more likely the bombers will come! I must close now, dearest, it is Wolfchen's bedtime and I will give him a kiss for you as well as sending many kisses

From your loving wife,
Mathilde

From: SS-Gruppenführer Count Christian von Vorzik
RSHA
Lobkowitz Palace
Hradcany Castle
Prague
To: Oberleutnant Peter von Vorzik
III Gruppe JG233
Martuba, Cyrenaica

29th June 1942

Dear Peter,

I have much to tell you. First, thank you for your note expressing sympathy for Reinhard's death. It was, of course, a great shock to everyone, a vicious way to repay all the efforts Reinhard had made to reconcile the Czechs, for which they have now been subjected to ruthless punishment. As you may have read, the village of Lidice, which we strongly suspect harboured the killers, has been utterly destroyed, the male population shot, the women and children deported. Such harsh measures are the only way to deal with partisan assassins.

Reinhard's funeral was a moving and solemn affair. For two days his body was placed upon a catafalque in the forecourt of the castle here, with a ceremonial guard. Then, together with a large party of SS officials, I travelled by train to Berlin where the coffin was taken to RSHA HQ. On the 8th it was moved to the Mosaiksaal in the Reichschancellery where Reinhard again lay in state. The Führer and Reichsminister-SS appeared at 3 pm. The Führer bestowed the decoration of the German Order, the Berliner Philharmoniker, conducted by Prof Robert Heger, played the funeral march from *Götterdämmerung* and then the funeral procession wended its way to the Invaliden cemetery. Throughout it all Lina behaved with great composure and dignity, as did the two boys. Their father would have been proud of them. After the funeral I took the opportunity to have a few words with Schellenberg. He thinks this is a great opportunity for me to move to his Ausland SD department but we must wait for the right moment. For the time being Himmler is taking over Reinhard's department. I expect to be posted back to Berlin in a week or two so please address any letters to the RSHA HQ.

There was very little time for me to prepare for Edith's wedding. The day after the funeral I flew to Rome on one of our courier planes and stayed over night with SS-Standartenführer Dr Dollmann. He had arranged a car for me and the next day I undertook the long drive north to Valdagno where the Novarro–Badaellis have a large estate, not far from Lake Garda. I was one of several wedding guests who were staying with the family at their Villa Borromeo (Vincenzo Borromeo was some local hero in the 11th century who had fought in the Crusades), part medieval, part 17th and 18th century, but equipped with all modern appurtenances. I was warmly greeted by Eleanora, her youngest son, Massimo, who was on special leave from his regiment, her two daughters, Elisabetta and Eloise, and, of course, Edith, looking as I have never seen her, quite radiant. Arturo was staying at a pensione in Valdagno until the wedding day but joined us for dinner that night.

The following day, the day before the wedding, Arturo took me for a drive and we lunched at Garda. I managed to mention my reservations about Ciano (these are reinforced by Dollmann but I did not mention him) and Arturo said he knew all about the factions surrounding both Ciano and Mussolini and said he, Arturo, tried to maintain his own separate course between them and keep his own counsel. Just how successful he is in this I do not know but Dollmann thinks Arturo is a clever and intelligent man, more agreeable towards us Germans than many in Italy.

The wedding was quite splendid. The little church on the estate was packed to capacity. I felt very proud escorting Edith who looked quite ravishing in her wedding gown (the train held up by two little boys in white ruffled shirts and black velvet pantalons) and carrying a bouquet of white roses and lilies-of-the-valley. Arturo, too, looked magnificent in his white dress uniform with sword and a blue sash of some order of King Victor Emanuel III. Both Elisabetta and Eloise were in pale pink carrying bouquets of pink roses. The music was by Palestrina and Buxtehude. The reception was held in the grounds of the villa in three enormous marquees, one reserved for important guests including myself. We had lobster bisque, a soufflé, roast duck, a sorbet, roast venison, salads and all sorts of side dishes, fruit puddings and ices, champagne and red and white Italian wines, brandy and liqueurs. Ciano attended and gave a brief speech, praising Arturo and flattering Edith, then there were speeches by Arturo's *garçon d'honneur*, Count Claudio d'Arriago, Arturo and, of course, myself. (As I have only half a dozen words of Italian I stumbled through it in French.) Afterwards there was an entertainment by jugglers and acrobats, a (rather lewd) performance by a commedia dell'arte troupe which was received with great merriment, and then dancing in the ballroom. Arturo and Edith led the first dance and then, in the early evening, drove away to start their honeymoon, Edith looking very soignée in an ice-blue suit with a matching hat made entirely of feathers. For those guests staying for the evening there was another sumptuous meal followed by madrigals by Monteverdi. Altogether it was a joyous occasion accompanied by perfect weather. I do so wish, dear brother, that you could have been there.

Now the Luftwaffe's occupation of Adlersee is complete. The main bedrooms have been fitted out as wards with some of the smaller rooms, including the servants' quarters, as private rooms. The banqueting hall and the dining room both remain for that purpose for those who are ambulatory, but the kitchen has been considerably enlarged and re-equipped. Father's study is a conference room for the doctors; the library serves as a recreation room (all the books have been catalogued, as have the *objets d'art*, sculptures, busts and pictures) and the billiard room and gymnasium have both been equipped for various forms of physiotherapy. The ballroom has been sectioned off for those with special needs, such as treatment for burns and there is a proposal to pull down the stables and build a hydrotherapy pool. Werner is comfortably installed in one of the outbuildings and is looked after by one of the nursing staff. (I learned that he is 79.) I am discussing with Generalflugmeister Milch and SS-Obergruppenführer Pohl what remuneration we should receive and which I am assured will be substantial. Is it not an excellent thing that our old home should be put to such good use?

Write to me when you can.

Ever your affectionate brother,
Christian

From: Oberleutnant Peter von Vorzik
III Gruppe JG233
Martuba, Cyrenaica
To: Mathilde von Vorzik
23 Hevelius Straße
Grunewald

7th July 1942

My Darling Mathilde,

Once again I find myself writing a letter of sympathy and condolence — what a sad time it has been for us all. How very sorry I was, dearest, to have the news of the death of your mother and Aunt Ilse. I had hoped against hope that they had been spared. It is specially grievous for you not to have had the opportunity of a proper funeral, of saying a last farewell. My heart aches for you, darling, and my inability to take you in my arms and comfort you accentuates the feeling of helplessness I have in trying to assuage your grief with mere words. I have never felt our separation by distance so acutely as I do now. I know you are anxious about my safety, darling, and there is little I can say to lessen that, except that, as always, I take great care of myself and there is also my guardian angel, Kurt, to keep me from harm! Your new friends from the sewing circle have similar worries and I am sure it helps all of you to confess your fears to each other. Do they also have children? We have been flying in support of Rommel's Afrika Korps and everything is going splendidly in our favour. Our forward bases are now some way east of Martuba (if you have found it on the map) but continue to use that address for the time being. Perhaps it will not be long before you are writing to me in Alexandria or Cairo! This is necessarily a short note, my darling, as we are called upon throughout the day but I wanted to say how deeply sorry I was to receive your news and to let you know that, as always,

You are forever in the thoughts of

Your loving,
Peter

From: Oberleutnant Peter von Vorzik
III Gruppe JG233
Martuba, Cyrenaica
To: SS-Gruppenführer Count Christian von Vorzik
RSHA HQ
Prinz Albertstraße
Berlin

10th July 1942

Dear Christian,

Thank you for your long enthralling letter – I was particularly pleased to hear about Edith's wedding and to know it went so well. Edith had informed me in a previous letter that it was to be a relatively quiet affair but from your description it sounds rather grand. At any rate, I am sure it will be a day for her to remember with great joy. Now she must prepare to be a diplomatic hostess – what an extraordinary transformation our dear sister has undergone!

I do hope your expectations of being transferred to Schellenberg's department will be fulfilled, and soon. I saw some of Reinhard's state funeral on the cinema screen – or, rather, on the screen that has been rigged up in a corner of our forward airfield. It is a strange sensation looking at those shadowy images while sitting in the open air! It looked an imposing occasion and Wagner's music gave it added grandeur. The Czechs have certainly been made to pay heavily for Reinhard's death.

Yes, I am delighted that Adlersee is now functioning as a hospital, helping my fellow airmen to get back into the sky or be rehabilitated into life itself. Sometime we must discuss what we want to do with the Schloss when all this is over. I suggested to Mathilde that maybe we should sell it off altogether while keeping one of the outlying farms as a country retreat for the family. What do you think?

We have been operational again these last two weeks in close support of General (now Field Marshal!) Rommel in the attack upon and fall of Tobruk. What a great victory that has been for us! I think we are not far from destroying the British 8th Army altogether and then we shall be in control of Egypt!

Please write when you can.

Ever yours,
Peter

Oberleutnant Peter von Vorzik
Journal entry

12th July 1942

Recent family bereavements – my dear sister-in-law, Frieda, my wife's mother and aunt – as well as the assassination of my brother's superior, Heydrich, have tended to overshadow our great achievements against our enemies. The renewed offensive against Russia is making splendid headway, especially in the south towards the Caucasus and five weeks ago Field Marshal Rommel began his offensive against the British 8th Army and its allies, an offensive in which our Staffel is now taking part. After an initial setback at Bir Hakeim the Afrika Korps succeeded in taking the heavily fortified port of Tobruk, together with some 35,000 prisoners and hundreds of guns and mechanised equipment. The most important booty captured, however, was great reserves of fuel, desperately needed by the Luftwaffe and our armoured divisions. The British have been very successful in sinking many of our supply ships, the result of our failing to take the island of Malta – and much of our fuel is dependent on being supplied by air. Even some of our bomber Geschwader have been pressed into ferrying benzine. It was during the last few days of the battle for Tobruk that JG233, flying in support of JG2, entered the struggle. We are supporting JG2 because, during the latter days of the assault on Malta, the Geschwader suffered such losses that we could scarcely muster two complete Staffeln.

Our F Series have all been equipped with underwing bomb-racks and a big fuel drop tank under the centre section. Of course, these additions make our little fighters terribly unwieldy and sluggish until we have dropped the bombs and jettisoned the drop tanks and all the pilots hate these encumbrances. One of the reasons we were late in joining the battle was because we had to undergo low-level bombing training at a range near Martuba. Luckily we have encountered very little opposition from the enemy air forces (the Royal Australian, New Zealand and South African air forces are reputed to be flying alongside the RAF out here). The aircraft we have encountered have been American-built Curtiss P40 Kittyhawks, comparatively slow and poorly armed, easier prey than even the Hurricanes, some of which are armed with four 20mm cannon – a lethal armament if one is foolish enough to allow the British pilots to line you

371

up as a target. I shot down a Kittyhawk during the final attack on Tobruk. We had unloaded our bombs on the British 7th Armoured Division south of El Adem and were engaged in free-ranging attacks when our Sturm – myself with Kurt, Varasch with his new Katschmarek, Adolf Stäfel – came across a flight of six Kittyhawks of the RAF attempting to attack one of our armoured columns. They were really sitting ducks, apparently unaware of our presence above and behind them. As they began their bombing run – they are also used as fighter bombers – we dived down on them, each of us lining up one aircraft. I took the leading aircraft of the first flight of three, Kurt took the aircraft to port, Varasch the one to starboard and Stäfel took the port aircraft of the second trio. I closed up tight on my target and gave a long burst that raked the engine cowling and forward fuselage. There was a brilliant white flash of flame and the Kittyhawk plunged straight down into the desert scrub. There was a big explosion from the aircraft's underwing bombs and I pulled up into a steep climb in order to escape the debris that came up like so much flak. The other three all recorded the destruction of their targets and the remaining two Kittyhawks fled back east. They are no match for our F Series but are probably superior to the Italian Macchis and Fiats.

Now that Tobruk has fallen we are based at a forward airfield near Sidi Rezegh, doing very little except for sending up an aircraft on reconnaissance. Despite the fuel supplies captured at Tobruk there is a severe shortage. At the beginning of Rommel's attack our armoured columns were held up at Bir Hakeim for nine days due to stubborn resistance from Free French forces. During this period the fighters of JG27 and JG53, escorting the Ju87s and Ju88s of LG1 flying in from Crete, used up so much fuel that we now have very little left for offensive operations. What there is has been reserved for the Afrika Korps. They seem to be able to continue their advance without our support. There seems to be very little aerial activity on the part of the British, too. I cannot see this situation lasting for long. So far, in Poland, in France, in Russia, the war has proved that it is impossible for ground forces to advance without strong air support. So, here we are in the middle of the desert, waiting for supplies, not just for fuel but also ammunition, spares, food and water. The food is monotonous, tinned meats and hard biscuits and fresh water for drinking very scarce. Sometimes we have even had to share our shaving water! We do a lot of swimming and I have become almost as dark brown as an Arab and the sun has bleached my hair almost white. The desert conditions have played havoc with our aircraft. The sand gets everywhere, finding its way into every crack and crevice (in both men and machines!) causing problems with air intakes, filters, instruments, undercarriage mechanisms and gun ports. Every time we take off the propellers create minor sandstorms that affect following aircraft. Nature, too, creates large sandstorms that make flying impossible and life extremely uncomfortable. We have certainly experienced the whole gamut of natural forces, from the frozen hell of Russia to the blistering heat of North Africa. Personally, I think the desert heat is marginally preferable to the bitter ice and snow; at least the desert cools down at night while the below zero temperatures of the steppes are there for months on end.

During this enforced inactivity I have had several talks with Varasch. Initially it was mostly about sex – or lack of it. He joked, saying that since leaving Sicily his only lover has been his right hand. Even in Sicily he had to have recourse to the official brothels set up for military personnel, the local girl he pursued being far too closely chaperoned. There is no doubt he is highly sexed and his reputation throughout the Staffel is that of a voracious Lothario but, to my surprise, beneath this exterior of sexual braggadocio there is a serious man. He told me he envied my happy marital state and revealed himself as being very well read, able to quote from Goethe, Schiller, Voltaire, even Shakespeare. He loves music and art and had travelled widely in Europe before joining the Luftwaffe. His home is also in Bavaria, at Höchstein on the upper reaches of the Danube, and his father and grandfather were both distinguished professors of agronomy. None of this is apparent in his conversation in the mess and it has been a lesson to me not to judge men from the personality they sometimes choose to present.

From: Contessa Edith Novarro-Badaelli
Villa Sospiri
Lake Como
To: Oberleutnant Peter von Vorzik
III Gruppe JG233
Martuba, Cyrenaica

15th July 1942

My Dear Peter,

Well, now you see I am a Contessa! This last month has really been a marvellous dream. Christian promised me he would give you an account of the wedding and I trust he has done so. For me, at least, it was a joyous occasion, providing a feast of memories although, at the time, I was very nervous and so glad to see Christian and have his reassuring presence. Part of my nervousness was because everyone around me spoke in rapid Italian; Arturo's German is better than my Italian which, at the moment, is very limited but I am working hard at it with books and when we are installed in Rome I may have an Italian teacher. I had not expected so many guests and was astonished when Eleanora showed me the guest list. Half the Rome diplomatic corps seem to have been invited and Arturo has a big family of aunts, uncles and cousins. But Eleanora (of course!) had managed things beautifully, engaged more servants for the occasion, flowers everywhere, a cornucopia of food (I felt rather guilty knowing that rationing for the people is severe) and wonderful entertainment. If this was Arturo's idea of "a simple ceremony" I cannot imagine what a grand one would be!

Then, off to this heavenly place for a month. The Villa Sospiri is really beautiful, mostly 18th century, with wonderful gardens overlooking the lake. Formal gardens with an Arcadian temple, an arboretum with many exotic trees, a water garden with fountains and cascades, orchards with olives, lemons, pomegranates, apricots, nectarines and flowers and shrubs in bloom wherever one looks. We have picnicked here and taken long walks, swum in the lake, made excursions in Count Gaviotti's private motorboat. The villa's name, at least for me, has meant sighs of pleasure and contentment. The days have drifted by in a haze of happiness with only an occasional awareness of the war. We return to Rome – and reality – tomorrow. Arturo will be swept back into the whirl of diplomacy and I shall begin to learn how to be an efficient housewife and hostess.

Count Ciano attended the wedding. I cannot say I took to him although he was fulsome in his praise of me. One feels that such effusiveness is just diplomatic habit, formal flattery covering genuine thoughts and feelings although, perhaps, I am being unfair; these are first, fleeting impressions after a brief acquaintance. He left in the evening to meet Serrano Suñer at Livorno. Arturo says the Spanish are playing a waiting game (like the Turks) and the Führer is both annoyed and deeply disappointed that Franco has not joined the Axis and declared war on the British and Americans. With Spanish assistance it would have been possible to take Gibraltar and seal off the Mediterranean from the British.

Christian told me the dreadful news that Mathilde's mother and aunt were killed in the raid on Cologne and I wrote to Mathilde soon after we arrived here. And the assassination of Reinhard! I also wrote to Lina although I wasn't sure where she was. Christian said to send the letter to Schlactensee, it would be forwarded if necessary. And you, dear brother, how are you? Do not imagine that amidst all this pleasure and beauty I have forgotten you. We have scarcely listened to the radio but I know that the Afrika Korps, together with Italian forces under General Ugo Cavallero, have been advancing across Cyrenaica and that you are there, part of that force. You are always in my prayers and your photograph is illuminated each evening by a candle on my dressing-table. Arturo calls it my shrine! Now I must begin packing. The idyll is over but I count myself one of the happiest, luckiest women in the world.

Keep yourself safe for

Your loving sister,
Edith

PS My Rome address is:
Villa Frascati
Via Augusta
Rome

From: Mathilde von Vorzik
23 Hevelius Straße
Grunewald
To: Oberleutnant Peter von Vorzik
III Gruppe JG233
Martuba, Cyrenaica

17th July 1942

My Darling Peter,

Thank you, dearest, for your letter of sympathy on the death of mother and Aunt Ilse. I am only just coming to terms with the fact that mother is no longer there at the end of the telephone line. I catch myself thinking I must write to mother, I must telephone her and ask about Aunt Ilse, and then realise, with a shock once again, that they are no more. Yesterday two urns arrived (by parcel post!) containing their ashes. I trust that they are the right ones, I mean. There were formal forms enclosed giving their names and the address of the demolished house, and a receipt form to send back to the Gau office. It seems so strange that the mother I loved, the person who embraced me and talked to me, is now nothing but a pile of dust in a metal casket. But then, that is exactly what the scriptures tell us our bodies will become, do they not? Our soul survives, although I do not honestly know whether I believe that. Does that shock you, darling? We have never discussed our beliefs, have we? For myself I confess I have little belief in an afterlife. I have not decided yet what to do with the ashes; for the moment they are in a wardrobe cupboard. I think I will take a walk and scatter them along the edges of the lake, mother always loved to walk there. As for Aunt Ilse, well, I cannot go to Cologne now, and I am sure she would be happy to be by her sister.

Now, darling, let me write of something much more agreeable. Two days ago Wolfchen said, "Papa" after I had shown him your photo and said "Papa", as I always do when I put him in his crib. So his first word was for you, darling! Is that not exciting? And he will soon be walking. Holding my hand he totters two steps and then flops down. He crawls everywhere and has to be watched constantly. Lenka is very kind and adores him but I do not let her do anything special like feeding or bathing him. Those are my own precious duties. Sometimes she accompanies us on our walks and helps me carry the shopping. Incidentally, darling, it would be very helpful if I could learn to drive now. Edith no longer needs the DKW (she has left it in our garage) and sometimes it is a burden carrying all the provisions back from the shops, getting on and off the tram and so on, even with Lenka's help. Of course, there is petrol rationing but I would only use the car for those short trips. Do you think it would be possible for Christian's driver to teach me as he did Edith? Christian is back in Berlin now and his driver may not have such free time.

I miss Edith and Frieda very much. Not that I saw them very often; Edith worked long hours and only occasionally got to Grunewald and, of course, in latter weeks Frieda was mostly confined to her bed but I used to visit her, as you know, and we used to have pleasant telephone chats. Lina, too, has gone. She was such a good friend, always attentive, always suggesting some little excursion or "adventure" as she called it. Perhaps she will come back from Fehmarn when she has recovered from Reinhard's assassination.

I had a long letter from Edith who was so happy at her wedding (I expect she has written to you) and enraptured with the honeymoon villa and its gardens at Lake Como. I do hope she settles into her new life equally happily. She, too, will doubtless have moments when she feels lonely and a long way from her family, especially as she says she is not yet very conversant with the language. She says Arturo wants lots of children; I hope they are as blessed as we have been.

All my love, dearest one.

Ever your own,
Mathilde

From: SS-Gruppenführer Count Christian von Vorzik
RSHA HQ
Wilhelmstraße
Berlin
To: Oberleutnant Peter von Vorzik
III Gruppe JG233
Martuba, Cyrenaica

18th July 1942

Dear Peter,

Thank you for your last letter. Once again you find yourself in the vanguard of our advancing forces. Field Marshal Rommel appears to be making ground even faster than our forces in the east although those army groups are achieving great victories in the Don Basin and the Caucasus.

The fall of Sebastopol has opened the way to the oilfields of Baku and I think we can be confident that the war in the east and the south will be over by Christmas. Then we will be free to deal with the British and the Americans.

I did not tell you in my previous letter that, following Reinhard's funeral, Reichsführer-SS Himmler called together all the senior members of the SS and exhorted each department to work in close harmony and cooperation. He singled out both Schellenberg and myself for praise, saying that although we were the youngest men present, Reinhard had had great confidence in our abilities and he, Himmler, endorsed that confidence. Such words did not go down well with the likes of SS-Gruppenführer Müller and SS-Obergruppenführer Kaltenbrunner who were not singled out. Reinhard's death has resulted in much manoeuvring for position. Schellenberg told me in confidence that he had been considered as Reinhard's successor but that the Reichsminister thought him too young to take on the responsibility for that position. In fact, Walter would not have wanted it, considering it a poisoned chalice. He does not feel the time is yet right to broach my transference to the Ausland SD; he wants the dust to settle after Reinhard's death and all the various factions to have settled their affairs first. He is wise to be cautious.

Meanwhile, the Reichsminister had directed me to join SS-Obersturmführer Kurt Gerstein and SS-Obersturmbannführer Eichmann's second-in-command, Rolf Günther, to undertake a tour of the Jewish settlement camps in the east next month. It is a tedious duty which Himmler likes certain of his officers to undertake and appraise but it will not take long and I shall be back in Berlin before the end of August. Then I hope to take a short holiday somewhere. Perhaps I will visit Edith in Rome if it is not too soon for her to have settled in. I could stay with Dr Dollmann but that would inevitably entail conversations about colleagues in the SS and I need a rest from all that. In any case I think Rome would be too hot in August. Perhaps somewhere on the Adriatic or the Italian lakes. Edith was ecstatic about Como but then she was in a private villa. Another option is to take a riding holiday with Admiral Canaris. He has often suggested it to me and I know he was badly shaken by Reinhard's death and would be only too pleased to get away from his Abwehr duties for a while. But then, again, we could hardly refrain from discussing the work of our respective organisations and that is not what I want. A skiing holiday would be nice but at this time of year it would entail going a long way north and I want to avoid long journeys. A sailing holiday in the Greek islands has been suggested to me (a friend keeps his yacht in the harbour at Ithaca) but it is too close to operational areas for relaxation. Paris is always attractive but at the moment holds too many memories. Perhaps the south of France. I shall think of something.

I have finally heard from Luftfliegmeister Milch. His department at the Air Ministry proposed six million marks for the leasing of Adlersee for the duration of the war which I have accepted on our behalf. As it seems likely that the war in Europe will be concluded by the end of the year, certainly by next spring, it seemed to me an excellent offer. I hope you agree. I will place one half of that sum in your Berlin bank account and we might like to each make a personal gift of, say, 100,000 marks to Edith. Let me have your views.

Write when you can.

Ever yours,
Christian

From: Oberleutnant Peter von Vorzik
III Gruppe JG233
Fuka, Egypt
To: Contessa Edith Novarro-Badaelli
Villa Frascati
Via Augusta
Rome

22nd July 1942

My Dear Edith,
Here is my first letter to you as a Contessa! I was delighted to hear from Christian how splendid the wedding was and from yourself about the idyllic honeymoon. I am so happy for you, dearest sister, to know you are settled into matrimony with such contentment and prospects for the future. May it continue for the rest of your life. My only sadness is that I could not be there to witness the joyous ceremony, but between Christian and yourself I have a complete mental picture of the occasion. Christian tells me he is off on a visit to Eastern Europe to visit the new Jewish

settlements and then hopes to take a holiday, perhaps even visiting you in Rome, although he says it may be too hot in August. Do you find it so?

For myself, the hectic days of following Rommel's Afrika Korps across the desert have come to a temporary halt. We are now well inside Egypt and almost within striking distance of Alexandria and Cairo. (Ignore this address, however, and write to Martuba as before.) At present we are regrouping and awaiting fresh supplies, our lines of communication now being very long. Our great advance has been matched by our armies in Russia and looking at the map it is not too much to predict that our forces could meet up somewhere in Persia. I am sure that is the Führer's intention, a brilliant masterplan! The possibility of leave at Christmas (even, dare one say it, victory by Christmas!) is something that is in the back of all our minds out here. I so long to see my darling Mathilde and Wolfchen who will soon be one year old. How quickly the time has gone. Mathilde misses your visits and telephone chats and with Frieda's death and Lina far away in Fehmarn indefinitely, she is feeling somewhat lonely I think. She has made some friends in her sewing circle but they cannot replace family and friends of long standing.

Life here in the desert is very monotonous. The food is adequate but hardly appetising although there is a plentiful supply of dates and oranges. We barter cigarettes for wine with our Italian allies who always seem to have a good supply of Chianti! There are always shortages of small things like razor blades, toothpaste, writing paper (forgive this inelegant stationery, it is regulation issue) and ink. The sand gets everywhere despite all precautions. Then there are the scorpions and mosquitoes to contend with! Poor Kurt seems to attract the mosquitoes but I appear to have my own built-in repellent. At any rate, I am rarely bitten. Antimalaria tablets are a regular addition to our diet. I enclose a snapshot of Kurt and myself taken with his Leica (we get our films developed by friends in the photographic reconnaissance division!). We are standing by my aircraft and, as you can see, we are both very brown. Do not think my hair has gone white with worry! It has been bleached by the sun. Kurt asked me to convey to you his congratulations on your marriage.

Christian tells me Adlersee is now formally leased to the Luftwaffe for the duration of the war and has agreed a substantial sum. For some reason he has split the money between himself and me. I will be arranging for you to receive half my share. It is strange to think of our home now operating as a convalescent home, our bedrooms now wards, the banqueting hall resounding to lots of voices, the library now a doctors' conference room. But I am glad it is being used to some purpose.

Now, dear sister, I hope you are happily settling in to married life and I am sure you will cope ably with all your new responsibilities. Please write when you can, your letters are always so interesting.

My sincere regards to Arturo and

All my love to you,
Peter

PS Thank you for your prayers. I am sure the Lord has been listening. P.

From: Oberleutnant Peter von Vorzik
III Gruppe JG233
Fuka, Egypt
To: Oberleutnant Lother Köhl
II Gruppe ZG26L
Eastern Front

25th July 1942

Dear Lother,

Looking through my correspondence file I see it is several months since I heard from you and I should have replied long before this but – well, you know how it is! By now the snows will have long gone and no doubt you will be contending with the heat and dust of the steppes, if it is anything like it was this time last year. Where are you, I wonder? Are you part of the Luftflotte supporting the drive through the Caucasus as you expected? We have been receiving good reports about all our forces on the eastern front. For our part we have been racing across Cyrenaica, moving from one scruffy airfield to another and have now come to a temporary halt almost within sight of the pyramids, awaiting fresh supplies before the final push on Cairo. Much as I hated the snows of Russia I have just about had enough of desert sand! Despite all precautions it gets everywhere, in one's hair, in one's eyes and every part of the body. In one's food, in one's bed, everywhere. We have had great problems with sand in fuel lines – several forced landings because of it. I shall be very glad when we finally reach Cairo and Alexandria; I have promised myself a nice cool shower in a hotel suite and a long cool drink on the hotel verandah. We understand that the Führer's grand strategy is that our eastern and southern armies should meet up somewhere in Persia so perhaps you and I will greet each other again in the land of the Pashas!

I wonder if you have resolved the doubts you expressed in your letter regarding the fidelity of your girlfriend, Hannelore? Was there another fellow in the background? If so, perhaps it was as well that you found out about the lady's equivocal nature before your liaison progressed any further. If not, then I hope all goes well. I suppose you are still operating with the old Me110? I am still flying the F Series, ruined by having bomb-racks and long-range tanks fitted but, thankfully, the enemy types we face appear inferior, mostly American Kittyhawks although there are occasional Spitfires to contend with.

We have had a couple of sad bereavements in the family. My brother Christian's wife, Frieda, died following a miscarriage and my wife's mother and aunt were killed in the huge RAF raid on Cologne. Then my brother's superior, Heydrich, as you know, was assassinated. The one good piece of family news is that my sister, Edith, has married an aide-de-camp to Ciano and is ensconced in a new home in Rome. To be honest, my brother and I would have preferred her to have married a German but she is rapturously happy and he seems a charming man of very good family. My own family flourishes, my son now nearly a year old. Of course it is frustrating not to be able to see him growing up; I trust I shall see much more of him next year and, naturally, we plan for him to have several brothers and sisters.

Now I must stop and try to deal with the load of forms waiting on my desk. (Actually, the "desk" is a pile of ammunition boxes with some canvas thrown over it!) Is it not strange that while we wait and wait for really important supplies – fuel, ammunition, spare parts – the continuous stream of paperwork always seems to get through?

Please write when you have a chance.

Best wishes,
Peter

From: *Oberleutnant Peter von Vorzik*
III Gruppe JG233
Fuka, Egypt
To: *Mathilde von Vorzik*
23 Hevelius Straße
Grunewald

26th July 1942

My Darling Mathilde,

By the time you receive this it will be close to Wolfchen's first birthday. No need to tell you how I wish I could be there to celebrate with you. As it is I have nothing to send him as we are still located in this desert wilderness, but please give him a special kiss from me. I was thrilled to know he had said "Papa" under your tutelage and I am enclosing a snapshot, taken by Kurt, for you to show him.

We are experiencing a short hiatus while the Geschwader reforms and awaits fresh supplies before the final assault upon the British forces defending Egypt and the Suez canal. When that is completed I am sure we will be given leave but whether that means returning home to Germany remains in doubt. This has been the longest period we have been parted, darling, as I am sure you know, and for me every day now seems like an eternity. I think it is a very good idea for you to learn to drive. I dislike the thought of you struggling on and off trams with Wolfchen, even with Lenka to help you. I do not know if Christian can spare his driver to teach you (he certainly did a very good job with Edith who was much less assured than you will be) but Christian may have some helpful suggestions to make. Why not telephone him and say it is at my request? In any case the little DKW should be put to some use. I believe (at the time of writing) that Christian is visiting some Jewish settlements in the east but he will be back in Berlin before the end of the month.

How is the garden progressing? You wrote last May about the gardener growing vegetables but was that not too late to put in seeds and bulbs? Should that not have been done last October or early this year? I have very little knowledge of gardening but I seem to remember the gardeners at Adlersee preparing the ground much earlier in the year. And we had many greenhouses for nurturing young plants. Here in the desert which is sometimes covered with thin scrub and a few cactuses I miss the abundant flowers of Sicily. Every house there, however small, seemed to have geraniums, bougainvillea, oleander and hibiscus growing on balconies and window ledges.

You said in your last letter that you did not believe in an afterlife and, much as I would like to think it possible (I had a fairly strict Catholic upbringing), I have to agree with you. For various reasons I have avoided discussing the subject with anyone; it only leads to heated arguments and emotional upsets, but I am glad you have expressed a conviction similar to my own. Without mentioning it to my family I abandoned my faith soon after joining the Luftwaffe. My mother was devout, my father conformed in an unthinking way and Edith, I know, still practises her faith. Christian, I am sure, has also abandoned his faith – if he ever had it – although we have never discussed it. It would be comforting to think that some form of paradise awaited us after the strain and stress of this world, especially now in the midst of this terrible war, but rational thought only leads me to the conclusion that such an idea is simply based on wishful thinking. And yet... whenever I contemplate some natural phenomena, the stars, a flower thrusting through a crack in the concrete, I am forced into thinking where does the life-force come from? Who? What? Why? It is just that Christianity, all formal religions, insofar as I am aware of them, do not give me a satisfactory answer. So there, darling, is my non-belief. Let us take full advantage, as long as we remain in this tangible world, to develop our life together and hope that very soon you will once again be in the arms of

Your loving husband,
Peter

From: Contessa Edith Novarro-Badaelli
Villa Frascati
Via Augusta
Rome
To: Oberleutnant Peter von Vorzik
III Gruppe JG233
Martuba, Cyrenaica

5th August 1942

My Dear Peter,
I was so pleased to receive your letter and know all remains well with you. How handsome you look in that snapshot. So brown and blond! Give my

regards to Kurt and thank him for his congratulations on my wedding. Now, dear brother, first things first. It is most kind of you to apportion half your share of the Luftwaffe's payment for Adlersee to me but, really, I have no need of it. I am very well provided for; Arturo has arranged a considerable settlement in my name in case, as he says, anything should happen to him and he gives me a generous allowance for myself as well as household expenses. I also have the annuity following father's death. I would much prefer you to keep the money yourself or, perhaps, inaugurate a trust fund for little Wolfchen. Let it be my gift to him. It has been a very busy time settling in here, getting to know everything about running the house although I have plenty of assistance. The truth is, it is easier than running Adlersee during father's last few months. There is a butler, a chef, a housekeeper, two housemaids, a handyman and a gardener plus a personal maid for me (!) and a valet/chauffeur for Arturo. The last two, Maria and Franco, are a married couple and the butler and the housekeeper were previously in Eleanora's household. She says she no longer needs a large staff. I confer with the chef each day and am beginning to know several of Arturo's favourite dishes although he is not fussy about food. So far we have not entertained but with so many servants a first dinner party will not be intimidating. I have spent several happy days unpacking the wedding gifts. Your Meissen dinner service is really beautiful but will be kept for special occasions. Christian gave us four lovely silver candelabra and Eleanora a wonderful set of table linen so I am looking forward to setting the table for that first formal dinner.

Arturo had planned a great surprise for me. On the first morning after our return from Como he told me to look out of the drawing-room window and there in the driveway was a sparkling new Lancia Aprilia, his wedding gift to me. It is finished in white because Arturo says that is the best colour for a car in a hot climate as it reflects the sun rather than absorbing it like dark colours (but I expect you knew that!) with scarlet upholstery. It is a delightful car to drive, very quick and responsive after the DKW. I am so glad now that I learnt to drive. It is certainly hot in Rome at this time of year but up here in the hills we get what breeze there is and with the shutters closed the house is cool. On Thursday afternoons an elderly professor comes to instruct me in Italian but he invariably nods off to sleep in his chair and we do not progress very far! I pick up far more in conversation with the servants. Reading the papers and magazines and listening to the radio is also very helpful. As I have fairly good French I have not found it too difficult although my grammar is probably at fault. Arturo has been kept very busy since we returned, sometimes not getting home until quite late and then too tired to eat. Tomorrow he is taking me to my first diplomatic party which I am partly looking forward to and partly feel anxious about because Arturo says everyone will want to talk to me as I am "a new face." Apparently, on these occasions, one sees the same people all the time.

Well, dear brother, that is all my news. I hope so much that we shall see victory this year and you will be home with your loved ones.

All my love,
Edith

Oberleutnant Peter von Vorzik
Journal entry

18th August 1942

There are radio reports that the British have attempted a major landing on the French coast at Dieppe and have been repulsed with heavy losses with thousands killed or taken prisoner, over a hundred aircraft lost, a destroyer and thirty landing craft sunk. Whether this was meant to be a major invasion of northern France is unclear; if so it has been a disaster for the British although it seems that the majority of prisoners taken are Canadian. Here in the desert we have been subjected to day and night attacks by the RAF resulting in serious damage to our forward bases. My Staffel is down to five serviceable aircraft and the Geschwader as a whole has been seriously depleted. At the moment it seems we are heavily outnumbered in the air and it is increasingly difficult to carry out defensive patrols over the Afrika Korps, let alone attempting offensive sorties. There is no doubt the British have air superiority at the moment and it looks as if our final push into Egypt is going to be a fierce struggle.

From: *Mathilde von Vorzik*
23 Hevelius Straße
Grunewald
To: *Oberleutnant Peter von Vorzik*
III Gruppe JG233
Martuba, Cyrenaica

25th August 1942

My Darling Peter,

I have delayed sending this letter in order to wait for the development of the photos I took at Wolfchen's first birthday party. Here they are – doesn't he look wonderful? My own favourite is the one of him in the toy car. He cannot reach the pedals yet but he moves it along with his feet and manages to steer it quite well. I bought it at that big toyshop on the Ku'damm, it was very expensive but I gave it to him as a present from us both. He had two little guests at his party, small children from my new friends with whom I share coffee mornings and Lenka made a cake with one candle (you can just see it in one of the photos). Wolfchen had several other presents, a big teddy bear from Christian, a wooden train set from Edith that arrived from Rome two days after his birthday, more soft toys from his little guests and a sailor suit (too big for him yet) from Lina, sent from Fehmarn. It is typically thoughtful of her to remember his birthday despite her own troubles. When I telephoned Christian to thank him for the bear he said Edith had written to him to remind him of Wolfchen's birthday and he had arranged for one of the RSHA secretaries to buy it and have it sent to us while he was in Poland. He said the trip was extremely tiring and what with that and the turmoil following Frieda's and Reinhard's deaths he is feeling quite exhausted. Edith had mentioned to Arturo that Christian was wondering where to go on holiday and Arturo suggested he make use of the family's seaside villa at Rimini on the Adriatic, so Christian is spending three weeks there. Apparently it is a modern villa overlooking the beach, a local woman comes in to cook and clean and there is a sailing dinghy in the garage. Christian will drive himself there so his chauffeur will be free to teach me while Christian is away. Isn't that fortunate?

The garden has been transformed by Friedrich who brought plants from his own greenhouse. We have potatoes, tomatoes, beans, onions, marrows and melons growing in abundance and I will be able to give some of the produce to Frau Kirschner and the ladies at the sewing circle. Friedrich keeps chickens and often brings me fresh eggs which are such a useful addition to our cuisine now that rationing has become more severe. I have been buying fruit now that it is coming into season and Lenka has been showing me how to preserve it and make jam. I was never so domesticated before and always relied on mother to do such things. You would be quite proud of me if you could see me in the kitchen. Yesterday there was quite a contretemps at the sewing circle. One of the ladies, Mimi Gertler, was reprimanded by Frau Kirschner for wearing trousers and excessive make-up. Frau Gertler replied that she had recently read an article by Magda Goebbels which said that her husband supported the idea that German women had a duty to present themselves as examples of elegance and lightness. Frau Kirschner said that did not include trousers which were unfeminine and heavy makeup that was associated with women of easy virtue. Frau Gertler burst into tears, flung down her needles and rushed out saying she had been insulted. Frau Kirschner flushed scarlet and the rest of the afternoon passed almost in silence. I do not know whether we shall see Frau Gertler back again. I have a pair of trousers (the ones I bought in Paris, remember?) but I shall not be wearing them to the sewing circle!

I was so relieved, darling, to know you share my doubts about an after-life. I knew that Edith remains true to her Catholic upbringing and thought that you might also adhere to the faith even if you have little opportunity to worship while in the Luftwaffe. That is why I have never broached the subject between us. Mother was Lutheran but never tried to impose her belief on me, saying it was up to me to find my own way.

How pleased I was to have that lovely photo of you! Does Kurt have the negative? I would so like to have it enlarged and framed. Do let me know if it is possible. Now, darling, I want to get these pictures of Wolfchen off to you, the post to and from Africa seems to take ages.

Lots of kisses from Wolfchen and

Your ever loving wife,
Mathilde

From: *Oberleutnant Lother Köhl*
II Gruppe ZG26L
Fliegerkorps VIII
Eastern Front
To: *Oberleutnant Peter von Vorzik*
III Gruppe JG233
Martuba, Cyrenaica

26th August 1942

Dear Peter,

Your letter of 22nd July has just reached me, the envelope so covered with various operational HQ and postal redirectional stamps that my name was almost obliterated! Anyway, it was a delightful surprise to hear from you again and be brought up-to-date with your news. We hear very little of what is happening in North Africa except the odd official communique that is picked up on the radio. Everything seems to be going well with Rommel's forces, nothing but success after success and a swift advance into Egypt. I can commiserate with you over the infiltration of sand. We have had similar problems with dust, as you will remember, though nothing so bad as you describe. Since being attached to Fliegerkorps VIII we have been zig-zagging up and down the front from one "hot spot" to another. We are supposed to be the experts at coping with tactical problems – not to say crises! Last May we were sent south to the Kerch peninsular to attack the Russians holding out at Sebastopol. Then we were ordered back north as far as Voronezsh to deal with a threatened Russian breakthrough. Now we are supporting the 6h Army attacking Stalingrad. The obvious truth is the Luftwaffe has become overstretched. Unlike last year we cannot achieve air superiority over the whole front which has become so elongated. Not only have we suffered heavy losses but the blasted Russians somehow keep managing to produce more aircraft from God knows where. They also seem to have several new types operational that make life more difficult for us. The Lavochkin LAGG-3 and the Yakovlev 1 Series appear in large numbers over every section of the front, better than the old Ratas but inferior to our 109s and 190s. Our Zerstörer are vulnerable, however, and we have lost several recently, sent as escorts to Stukas as the range has become too great for single-engined fighters. Now that the 6th Army are right in Stalingrad the infantry are fighting from street to street, factory to factory, house to house, floor to floor, amidst a sea of rubble and wreckage. Whenever I fly over I thank God I am not down there in that ghastly hell's kitchen. As it is the clouds of smoke that hang over the city in a constant pall make it difficult to see the targets we have been given; we are as likely to hit our own troops as we are the Russians.

You ask about Hannelore. Yes, my suspicions were well-founded, she had met some other chap, a policeman apparently. As you said, it is as well I found out how fickle she is, not that I really blame her. I can understand how it is, someone right there rather than 2,000 km away and perhaps not coming back... I have been thinking that under the circumstances it is best for me not to have anyone I consider a fiancée, life is too indeterminate at the moment to become seriously involved. For you, of course, it is different. You made a decision at an early stage of the war and now you have a wife and little boy waiting for you at home which is wonderful. When the war is over, if I survive that long, I shall have to make a new start. I was deeply sorry to hear of your family bereavements. The raid on Cologne was apparently devastating – one of our pilots also lost two family members, a brother and a cousin, both of them in an air-raid shelter which received a direct hit. One can only hope that the losses the RAF sustained will act as a deterrent although I heard that Lübeck and Rostock also suffered extremely heavy raids with over 1,000 aircraft. Sometimes it is difficult to maintain an optimistic view about the way things are going but all one can do is plough on. I have no more news for you; we are flying three and four sorties over Stalingrad each day which leaves me exhausted. Thanks again for writing, please continue to do so whenever you can. Meanwhile

Best wishes and good luck,
Lother

From: Oberleutnant Peter von Vorzik
III Gruppe JG233
Martuba, Cyrenaica
To: SS-Gruppenführer Count Christian von Vorzik
RSHA HQ
Wilhelmstraße
Berlin

28th August 1942

Dear Christian,

Forgive me for taking so long to reply to your letter of 18th July. It is not because we have been so busy in the interim but because there has been so little of interest to write to you about. After our race across Cyrenaica into Egypt we have had to pause for breath – and supplies! – just outside this little place called Rahman, facing the British who have drawn up their defensive line at El Alamein. The supplies have been slow in coming (because of British air and naval attacks on our shipping, the supply lines stretch right back to Tripoli) and then not in the quantities we need. However, our intelligence informs us we are now poised to make our final push in a day or two when the moon is full. When I next write I hope it will be from the comfort of an hotel in Cairo or Alexandria where I finally hope to escape the sand fleas!

I wonder if, by now, Schellenberg has approached the Reichsführer-SS about your transfer to the Ausland SD? You referred to the various "manoeuvrings" for position by certain factions following Reinhard's assassination; perhaps these have now been settled and your move can be broached? It must have been gratifying for you and Walter to be commended by the Reichsführer, it suggests he will look favourably on your working together.

Where did you finally settle upon going for your holiday? (By the time this reaches you it will be over.) I know Edith would have been delighted to welcome you to their new villa; she says it is not too hot where they are in the hills overlooking Rome. According to a recent letter she appears to have plenty of servants to assist her in running the place – more than there were at Adlersee! I am so pleased that she has settled into marriage so happily. Arturo seems a perfect partner, cultured, considerate (did you know he bought her a car as a wedding present?), well-connected and, presumably, well placed to promote his career as a diplomat. It is not inconceivable that he could succeed Ciano when he finally steps down. What do you think? Edith has some trepidation about her abilities as a hostess but I am sure with a little experience she will be most successful. We have both watched, have we not, with some surprise at how she has emerged as a capable young woman, a long way from that reserved, subservient creature that she always seemed at Adlersee.

The final settlement for Adlersee was certainly munificent. Thank you for arranging everything so capably. I thought it only fair that I should share my half with Edith but she has declined, saying that she is well provided for (apparently Arturo has made a generous settlement in her name and the annuity you arranged after father's death remains untouched) and suggested I initiate a trust for Wolfchen, which I will do. I know Mathilde was going to approach you with the possibility of your chauffeur teaching her to drive at such times that you did not need him. Has she mentioned this to you? I would be so grateful if it could be arranged. At present she conducts her shopping forays via the tram (I do not like her venturing into central Berlin but there are occasions when it is necessary) and even with the girl, Lenka, to help her it is an effort, especially with Wolfchen to look after as well. In any case, the ability to drive is an asset I should like her to acquire. Incidentally, I do not think I thanked you for arranging for Mathilde to have the Czech girl's help, she has proved most satisfactory and invaluable around the house.

Now I must stop and catch the Staffel post bag which departs each day by courier plane at 14.00 hrs.

All good wishes.

Your affectionate brother,
Peter

Oberleutnant Peter von Vorzik
Journal entry

8th September 1942

We have made our final thrust against the British and failed. Now we are back where we were before, minus a considerable number of tanks, motor transport and aircraft – not to mention the dead and wounded. Rumour, rumour, rumour. One rumour has it that Rommel and Kesselring have quarrelled and Rommel has been recalled to the Führer's HQ. Another rumour is that Rommel is a sick man and has returned to Germany, while a third rumour (which I hope is true) is that III Gruppe is being taken out of the front-line and reformed. What is certain is that the whole Geschwader has suffered from constant attrition ever since we came from Sicily. The men, including the ground crews, are battle-weary and need reinvigorating. Leave in Cairo, let alone Germany, seems far away. It is all very frustrating because if we cannot dislodge the British from their position at El Alamein now it is hard to see how we can do it in the future unless we can build up our forces at a greater rate than they can. We are still in desperate need of supplies of all kinds, especially fuel, and yesterday we heard that three more of our tankers have been sunk in the Mediterranean, a disastrous loss. This situation has arisen all because of the failure to take Malta back in May when the island had been all but put out of action by our continuous bombing. An airborne assault from Sicily, then, would surely have succeeded. Now the island has regained its strength as a base for British air and naval forces which are creating havoc upon our supply lines. The general mood here is one of despondency. To be so close to Cairo and be denied the prize ... it is all too reminiscent of our failure to take Moscow last December.

We began our attack just over a week ago. According to our intelligence briefing Rommel's plan was to make his main thrust through the weakly defended southern mine belt of the British defences and then swing north to encircle them from the rear, either cutting them off against the sea or forcing them to retreat east towards Cairo. To this end our Gruppe was detailed to support the 15th and 21st Panzer divisions as they engaged the British 7th Armoured Division at Deir el Agil, due south of the Alam Haifa ridge. Equipped with underwing bombs I led what remains of the Staffel in a low level attack against the British tanks but before we could reach the enemy we were set upon by swarms of enemy fighters, Spitfires and Kittyhawks, which had the advantage of height as well as numbers. Not only were we in a bad tactical position but, of course, we were encumbered by those wretched bombs we were carrying. Not wishing to see my Staffel slaughtered I gave the order to jettison the bombs and turn and run for it back to bodo. It was a humiliating situation but we were sitting ducks, just a couple of hundred metres above the desert, outnumbered and outmanoeuvred. As it was we lost Varasch's Katschmarek, Stäfel, who was shot down together with another young pilot, Gunther Visach, who had only recently joined us.

For the first time in my experience we are consistently outnumbered in the air and also handicapped by the shortage of fuel. We are unable to support our ground forces to the extent that they need (the Stuka Geschwader have also been decimated in their recent attacks) and are forced onto the defensive even when we are attacking! If we are to be used as fighter-bombers then we need another Gruppe of fighters to cover us. Further along the coast III Gruppe JG27 under the command of our most brilliant fighter ace, Hans-Joachim Marseille, continue to take a heavy toll of the enemy but that is the only good news we have and it is unlikely that their successes will prove decisive. After our abortive attempt to attack the British tank formation they simply pulled back to the Alam Haifa ridge, heavily defended by the British 10th Armoured Division. Rommel's attacks were repulsed, as were the efforts of the Italian divisions to the north and with the Panzers consuming much of their scanty reserves of fuel over ground that had proved to be heavier going than anticipated – something of a deliberate trap – Rommel had no other recourse but to withdraw. Now we are back at Rahman, licking our wounds, awaiting new orders and still hoping for supplies. The third anniversary of the beginning of the war occurred a week ago. No one felt like raising a glass to victory, we were all too busy to notice the date and there is very little to celebrate.

From: Oberleutnant Peter von Vorzik
III Gruppe JG233
Martuba, Cyrenaica
To: Contessa Edith Novarro-Badaelli
Villa Frascati
Via Augusta
Rome

12th September 1942

Dear Edith,

I received your letter dated 5th August nearly two weeks ago and would have replied sooner but we have been kept rather busy all to little avail, I am sorry to say. I am sure you have heard of Rommel's latest thrust towards Cairo and the plain truth of the matter is, it has failed, whatever the communiques may say. So here we are, still in the desert, with little immediate prospect of moving forward. It is difficult not to be despondent, particularly after all our early successes, but it seems to be part of the recent history of the war in the desert that the respective military fortunes should flow back and forth. Let us hope that it will be our turn to seal a final victory.

Your villa sounds quite resplendent with a cohort of servants. How splendid to have a personal maid! I am delighted for you, dear Edith, that life should be so comfortable. And the car! What a marvellous present. I have seen pictures of the Lancia Aprilia in motor magazines, a very advanced car in its class, and I am sure you will have great pleasure in driving it. As you may have heard, Mathilde is now learning to drive, as you did, tutored by Christian's chauffeur, although I do not know if he has the same driver now. I have been wondering how you enjoyed that first diplomatic party in Rome and whether you have attempted your first dinner party. I have no doubt you will have been a most gracious and successful hostess. Here in the desert, where conditions are necessarily primitive, it is nice to think that there are still enclaves where civilised living is maintained. Thank you for your generous suggestion of creating a trust fund for Wolfchen with the money from Adlersee. I shall write to my bank in Munich and put it in hand. How are your Italian lessons progressing? Are you still seeing the somnolent professor? You say that reading magazines is one way of becoming familiar with the language; that apart, do you still have access to the foreign papers and periodicals you read while in the Foreign Office? It must have been interesting and informative to read the journals of our enemies and gain an insight into their ideas and attitudes about the war.

Here we have very little leisure reading available. I occasionally see a copy of the *Völkischer Beobachter* or *Das Reich* which are flown out to us but, as is to be expected, the news is always reported as being in our favour. For example, one reads about our U-boat successes (can the Allies have any shipping left?) but never about how many we may have lost. What is certain is that the Italian navy has not been able to prevent our tankers being sunk in the Mediterranean; shortage of fuel has been the bane of our operations out here.

Now, dear sister, there is very little of interest I have to write about. I am in good health and, apart from the frustration of not yet having reached Cairo, in fairly good spirits. Please do continue to write whenever you can, not only are your letters of intrinsic interest to me but they are evidence that a civilised world still exists beyond this desert!

Ever your loving brother,
Peter

From: Oberleutnant Peter von Vorzik
III Gruppe JG233
Martuba, Cyrenaica
To: Mathilde von Vorzik
23 Hevelius Straße
Grunewald

18th September 1942

My Darling Mathilde,

Your letter with the photos of Wolfchen enclosed arrived yesterday and words and pictures have done wonders to restore my morale. Yes, I have been feeling rather low at our failure, so far, to reach Cairo. Rommel's last attack, as I'm sure you have heard, was unsuccessful and it will take a month or more for us to gather sufficient forces to make another attempt. And all the while the enemy is building up his forces, too. Even our leisure time has been thwarted. For the past few weeks we have enjoyed swimming in the ocean but yesterday that pleasure was denied us by swarms of jellyfish! Some of the ground staff who ventured in for an early morning dip were badly stung on the most delicate and intimate parts of the body as they swam unprotected by any form of costume. The medical hut was besieged by men clamouring for soothing ointments amid the ribald remarks of their comrades. Luckily I was not among the swimmers as the Staffel had been detailed for an early morning patrol. Flying over the sea one could see the offending creatures as milky white streaks stretching for miles along the coast. The photos of Wolfchen are marvellous – like you, I especially like the one in the little pedal car. Of course he looks so tiny but what a difference there is from the babe-in-arms I left behind last January.

Have you begun your driving lessons and, if so, how are they progressing? How fortunate that Christian has been on holiday so that, at least, you will have had some initial tuition. The ability to drive will be a great advantage when you go shopping or even to take day trips into the country. I know petrol rationing is severe now, but the little DKW has a

396

very frugal fuel consumption and I am sure Christian will be able to find a little extra for you now and again. You say I would be proud of your domesticity, darling, but whether you are adept at jam-making, sewing or gardening I am proud of you just as you are. The contretemps, as you call it, over the trouser-wearing Frau Gertler does seem a little bit absurd in these serious times, whatever Frau Goebbels may have to say about the matter. You did not mention what sort of figure Frau Gertler has; if she is on the heavy side then trousers are, perhaps, not very becoming on her. You are slim, darling, and one of the fortunate women who look attractive is such clothes, but it is probably just as well you do not show solidarity with Frau Gertler by wearing trousers to the sewing circle.

Last night, after supper (the endless tinned meat, tinned beans and hard biscuits) Kurt and I sat by the water's edge with a bottle of schnapps he had been sent and he managed to find a Vienna radio station on his portable, relaying a concert, a Mozart concerto (No 17 in G Major I think it was) and Brahms's *Third Symphony*. As we listened the waning moon rose over the sea. It all seemed so tranquil it was hard to believe we were in the middle of the desert fighting a war. It was wonderful to hear some good music after such a long time and the illusion of peace put us both in good spirits for whatever is to come.

Let us hope, darling, that that illusion of peace will soon become a reality.

Ever your own,

Peter

From: SS-Gruppenführer Count Christian von Vorzik
116 Kaiserstraße
Berlin
To: Oberleutnant Peter von Vorzik
III Gruppe JG233
Martuba, Cyrenaica

27th September 1942

Dear Peter,

Thank you for your letter dated 28th August and received only yesterday. The regular post seems to take longer and longer. As you have probably heard by now I spent my holiday, at Arturo's invitation, at his family's seaside villa at Rimini. I arrived there in a state of almost physical and mental exhaustion although the long drive itself (I took the Talot-Lago, something of a risk but all went well) was, in its way, therapeutic. I drove by way of Leipzig and Munich (the autobahns were full of military traffic) and then across the Alps via the Brenner Pass down to Bolzano, Verona and Rimini. It took me four days and three nights. It was exactly the sort of restful holiday I needed, sunning myself beside the Adriatic, swimming and taking long walks in the pine woods. There was a five-metre dinghy available but the idea of sailing it seemed too much of an effort, especially as I have not done that sort of sailing since leaving Adlersee. At Arturo's suggestion I drove up the coast to Ravenna to see the Byzantine mosaics there and Dante's tomb, most impressive. The villa itself was simply but comfortably furnished, a woman came in every day to clean and cook, although most evenings I went out for dinner, finding some pleasant little restaurants and taverns up and down the coast.

I mentioned mental exhaustion; something of an exaggeration, perhaps, but following the shock of Frieda's death and Reinhard's assassination my tour of the camps in Poland, at the behest of the Reichsführer-SS and in the company of SS-Obersturmführer Gerstein and SS-Obersturmbannführer Günther, was traumatic in the extreme. I was totally unprepared for what we observed. For many reasons I will not describe the experience; suffice it to say I witnessed scenes of unimaginable horror, scenes such as Dante himself or Bosch could not have conceived, scenes that will haunt me for the rest of my life.

Upon my return I made a confidential report to the Reichsführer-SS and two days later was summoned to his office. He was very affable and offered me a glass of wine which I declined, knowing of his disapproval of alcohol. He told me that what I had seen was nothing untoward but was all part of a plan that would ensure that all Europe was "free from racial contamination." In fact, everything had been agreed at the conference that Reinhard had convened at Wannsee, back in January. The Reichsführer said that had I been in the field with the Einsatzgruppen (as I had once suggested to Reinhard) I would have been inured to such things. He said it was our duty to stand by the plan initiated by Reinhard in the name of the Führer and the Fatherland. Apparently, neither Gerstein nor Günther had reacted in the way that I had. While I was at Rimini I had time to reflect upon what the Reichsführer had said and that he was right. I had witnessed an aspect of our struggle against an insidious enemy and the reality of that struggle was something I was unprepared for. Now I have a greater apprehension of what that struggle entails and not all of it occurs on the battlefield.

While I was away Walter, my driver, began giving lessons to Mathilde. He is adopting the same methods he did with Edith and has started her with the big Mercedes; if she can judge distances with that car, he says, when she comes to drive the little DKW she will find it that much easier. I will make certain he is able to give her regular lessons, say twice a week, perhaps in the evenings.

No, I have not yet joined Schellenberg at the Ausland SD. The Reichsführer has still not decided who is to replace Reinhard and Schellenberg is insistent that timing is all important when dealing with Himmler. I understand Rommel is back in Germany undergoing treatment for some undisclosed illness. Even so, I trust all goes well with you and you continue in good health.

Yours affectionately,
Christian

PS For the time being I think it best if you address your letters here at Kaisestraße, not to the RSHA. C.

From: Contessa Edith Novarro-Badaelli
Hotel de Bain
Lido, Venice
To: Oberleutnant Peter von Vorzik
III Gruppe JG233
Martuba, Cyrenaica

8th October 1942

Dear Peter,

As you see, here we are in this heavenly city, La Serenissima indeed! Ciano came here for the opening of the Biennale and, a little later, Arturo decided to bring me, too. It has all been so wonderful, two weeks of splendour, banquets in private palazzi, visits to the Accademia, the Doge's palazzo, opera at La Fenice, open-air concerts on the island of San Giorgio, trips to Murano, Burano and Torcello and, of course, the Biennale itself. We were very impressed with the paintings of de Chirico who is the official Italian artist this year but thought that the Spanish Pavilion was the best. There has been something glorious for the eye and ear every moment of every day and night – I feel quite sated with the beauty of it all, most especially with Venice itself. When the war is over you must bring Mathilde here. Arturo prefers staying here on the Lido where we get the sea breezes and can swim from the hotel's private beach although the season here is over now and the visitors have gone. Last night, as we came down the Grand Canal in our private launch, there was an electric storm which lit up the facades of the palazzi and Santa Maria della Salute in the most dramatic way. As we crossed the lagoon the lightning was reflected in the water, a sort of inverted firework display.

Tomorrow we return to Rome where once again Arturo will be immersed in the Machiavellian Italian politics. Believe me, Peter, if one ever got the impression that there were various factions working against each other back in Germany (as I sometimes did, listening to conversations in the Foreign Office) there is nothing to compare with the internecine wrangles in Rome: pro-fascist-anti-monarchist-anti-Vatican-pro-monarchist-pro-Vatican-anti-fascist! The only thing that everyone seems to agree upon is a general dislike of the Germans... Everyone, of course, has been extremely, even excessively, polite to me but, even at my own dinner party (yes, I have given one!) I heard veiled anti-German remarks and epithets bandied about the table. My Italian is not yet good enough to pick up everything that is said but I caught some of it. It was made clear to me that it was nothing personal, just a resentment against certain Party members and officials about the way they treat the Italians. It is perfectly understandable, I suppose; the Italians do not have a good war record so far and senior officers like General Cavallero, in charge of the Italian forces in Africa, and General Fougier, Commander of the Regia Aeronautica, are held in contempt by their German counterparts and even some Italians! Ciano blows hot and cold, this way and that, particularly contemptuous of Göring and von Ribbentrop but ready to be obsequious when in their company, and it makes things difficult for Arturo, I know, although he rarely reveals his political opinions to me.

My first dinner party went well enough. We served bean soup, risotto with mushrooms, Parma ham, roast goose, ices and Italian cheeses with Italian and German wines (Dr Dollmann was one of the guests) Spätlese, Frascati (of course!) and Valpolicella. Arturo has begun laying down an extensive cellar. I could not have organised it without Federico, the chef, and the rest of the staff but next time I will feel a little more assured. I have now been to two diplomatic receptions in Rome, one of our own at the Palazzo Chigi and the other given by the Spanish Charge d'Affaires. Hanging on Arturo's arm I play a more or less decorative role, smiling until my face aches and murmuring platitudes in my halting Italian! I am sure it will all seem less boring when I can converse more freely (I have given up the somnolent professor) but, as Arturo's wife, I will not be able to express my opinions beyond the weather and the latest fashions we see from Paris. To my surprise I am somewhat taller than many diplomats' wives, some of them quite short and dumpy, over-madeup and wearing too much jewellery.

You ask in your letter (which arrived just before we left Rome) whether I still see foreign papers and journals. Yes, I do, because Arturo brings them home and I interpret them for him because my English is better than his. As you say, it is very instructive to get the other side of the propaganda picture and sometimes – if one believes what one reads – it is hard not to become depressed by some of the news. For example, the big naval engagements between the Japanese and the Americans in the Coral Sea and off Midway Island in the Pacific last May and June were presented to us, then, as great Japanese victories. What we were not told, and what I subsequently learnt from American newspapers and periodicals, was that in the course of these battles the Japanese lost four of their aircraft carriers, together with their complement of aircraft and highly trained crews. These losses are said to have curtailed the planned Japanese expansion in the Pacific which would have threatened both Australia and the American mainland. Of course, this information is American propaganda too, aimed at world consumption, so it is never easy to know what or whom to believe. Then, again, General Fougier told Ciano, who told Arturo, that German aircraft production is one-fifth of that of Britain and America, not counting Russia. Well, perhaps. I hope it is not true, but if it is, such knowledge could hardly be made public, could it?

Well, dear Peter, I have been rambling on again about my doings and thoughts but, in mitigation, I find myself in such a new world with such new experiences, that I cannot help writing at length about myself. How are you, dear brother? I know things have not gone too well in the last few weeks, Rommel having failed to make the final breakthrough. Each time we hear the bulletins on the radio or Arturo comes home with the latest news from the Foreign Office you are in the forefront of my thoughts. I am making up a little parcel of a few things you might like, some tinned pâtés, jams and sweets. I would send chocolate which I know you love but fear it would melt in the heat before you received it. What a pity they do not put wine in cans! Let me know if there is anything else I can send you. Goods are noticeably scarcer in the shops but seemingly not for the diplomatic corps!

Please drop me a line when you are able.

You are always in my prayers.

Ever your loving sister,
Edith

From: Mathilde von Vorzik
23 Hevelius Straße
Grunewald
To: Oberleutnant Peter von Vorzik
III Gruppe JG233
Martuba, Cyrenaica

12th October 1942

My Darling Peter,

Your letter arrived this morning and, as always, it is such a joy and relief to hear from you. I am sorry, darling, that you are feeling "low" as you put it and hope by now your spirits will have returned. I am so glad that you have been having a period of rest. Thank heavens you did not go swimming amongst the jellyfish! You joke about those poor men being stung on their intimate parts but I am sure it was very painful. Whenever I go swimming, even in the lakes around here (which I have not done for some years) I always wonder what horrid creatures might be lurking in the water. Are there sharks in the Mediterranean?

Now the summer is ending and already the leaves on the trees are beginning to turn yellow. We have had some fine days, however, and when I take Wolfchen for his daily outing around the lake he insists upon getting out of the pram and walking! Yes, he walks quite well by himself now and cries when it is time to go home and he is put back in the pram. At home he is into everything and Lenka and I have to watch him every waking moment. His great game at present is sitting on the kitchen floor, pulling all the pots and pans out of the cupboard and banging them together. I think I will have to visit the toyshop again and buy him a drum. The noise will be just as bad but at least the saucepans won't be dented and chipped.

Christian is back from his holiday now and came to visit us bringing presents of chocolate and wine. He looked very brown and seemed quite calm and relaxed. As he played with Wolfchen I guessed how he must be thinking of the baby boy he lost when Frieda died. Her death really was an awful tragedy and I am sure it will be some time yet before he recovers from it. It is very kind of Christian to arrange for his driver to teach me. I seem to be making progress although I still manage to crunch the gears which makes Walter wince! I find the clutch pedal very stiff to operate and after about twenty minutes in traffic my ankle begins to ache but of course when we get on the long straight of the Avus I am all right. I do not seem to have the same problem with the accelerator. Walter is very patient with me but I am sure I am not such an apt pupil as Edith was. I had a postcard from Edith in Venice. She said she was having a wonderful time and the picture of the Grand Canal did look beautiful. She certainly seems to be living the grand life!

A few days ago I discovered a little shop which has the razor blades you use. When I told the man you were a fighter pilot in the desert he let me have three packets. I am sending them in a separate little parcel together with some writing paper and envelopes which I know you always need. Is there anything else you would like me to send, darling? The post is so slow that only tinned food would reach you in good condition and I am sure anything else in glass would get smashed. Yet you say Kurt had a bottle of schnapps sent to him. How was that packed? You ask about Frau Gertler. She has not returned to the sewing circle although she has been seen in the street wearing trousers! She is quite a large woman but not fat. According to one of the ladies I meet for coffee (we are changing to hot chocolate which, although it is cocoa beans mixed with some unrecognisable thickening it is nicer than the horrible ersatz coffee we get) Frau Gertler is now training to be a nurse and will go to the eastern front which, I suppose, will be more useful than sewing blanket hems. We have picked our last tomatoes and beans from the garden and Friedrich is sweeping up the leaves and making a bonfire. We have to put it out before nightfall. It is beginning to get dark as I write and I must hurry to catch the last post.

Keep yourself well and safe for Wolfchen and

Your loving wife,
Mathilde

Oberleutnant Peter von Vorzik
Journal entry

18th October 1942

We have received small allocations of fuel and ammunition which allows us to fly what are called "offensive reconnaissances." We operate as four Rotte, with one aircraft equipped with cameras, the duty of the others being to defend the camera aircraft which has reduced armament. Once the reconnaissance is accomplished, three of the four Rotte are free to find any targets that present themselves: tanks, motor transport, trains, troop positions, enemy aircraft, even coastal shipping. The truth is that our Geschwader is somewhat threadbare. Only about thirty-odd aircraft are serviceable, the ground crews are overworked, patching and cannibalising aircraft to make up the semblance of three Staffeln. We are still severely rationed for fuel and ammunition and have to conserve both as best we can, making sure that they are used to maximum effect. Whenever we do meet enemy formations we are always outnumbered and it is only because our 109s have a slight edge in performance, particularly at high altitudes, over our adversaries and our pilots are often more experienced (although more and more of our veterans are being replaced by youngsters straight from flying school) that we have not been completely overwhelmed. Even so, the Fliegercorps suffered a grievous loss last month with the death of our greatest fighter ace, Hans-Joachim Marseille. With well over a hundred kills to his credit and decorated with the Luftwaffe's highest award, the Knight's Cross with diamonds, he was returning from a sortie on September 30th when his engine faltered and the cockpit filled with smoke. For a while he flew blind, guided by his Katschmarek, Oberfeldwebel Poettgen, until he shouted over the r/t that he had to get out. He put his machine on its back, the canopy flew off followed by his body. Poettgen and the rest of the Schwarme looked on in horror as the parachute failed to open and Marseille plummeted to the ground. When his body was recovered from the desert it was found that the parachute ripcord had not been pulled; Marseille had suffered a large chest wound indicating he had been hit by the tailplane of the aircraft and probably been knocked unconscious. It was a tragic ending for a young ace who had fought so valiantly and his Geschwader, JG27 – indeed the whole Luftwaffe – are in mourning for him.

Four days ago, during an offensive reconnaissance, I managed to shoot down a Martin Baltimore bomber, similar to the one I damaged back in August. We ran into the enemy bombers, protected by twice as many Spitfires, not long after we had begun our reconnaissance; in fact we were flying on an almost parallel course as they were returning from an attack on our air base at Fuka. Luckily we had a considerable height advantage as photo-reconnaissance is usually carried out above 10,000 m. I radioed that, accompanied by Kurt, I was going down to attack but that the rest of the Schwarme should continue the reconnaissance and climb even higher to stay out of any subsequent melée. With Kurt following I began the long dive down straight through the protecting Spitfires and then, levelling out, I lined up on the port Baltimore of the last flight of three, giving a long burst from all three guns. Almost immediately the bomber lost height trailing black smoke, then it suddenly stalled and spun into the ground sending up a great column of smoke, flame and debris. Horrido! Calling out to Kurt that I was climbing to starboard and turning back to bodo, we both made our escape westwards before the Spitfires had time to turn and attack us. I am sure they simply did not see us coming – we had the sun high behind us and it was all over in less than two minutes. I heard yesterday that because of this victory, which brings my score of confirmed kills to forty, I have been awarded a further accolade to my Knight's Cross. This award has been written in my paybook; the actual decoration will come sometime later.

Yesterday I received a rather odd letter from Christian in which, referring to his visit to resettlement camps in Poland, he says he observed "scenes of unimaginable horror." He also refers to "racial contamination", quoting Reichsführer-SS Himmler, so he must be referring to the Jews as this is the usual phrase used in such publications as *Der Sturmer*, *Angriff* and *Das Schwarze Korps*. I imagine Christian must have witnessed the execution of a spy or a group of partisans, in which case he is lucky to have had his sensibilities protected for so long. Now he has had a glimpse of how unpleasant war can be.

From: Oberleutnant Peter von Vorzik
III Gruppe JG233
Martuba, Cyrenaica
To: SS-Gruppenführer Count Christian von Vorzik
116 Kaiserstraße
Berlin

23rd October 1942

Dear Christian,

Thank you for your letter of 27th September. Yes, the post seems to take longer and longer each time one writes. Of course, we are not in Martuba, that is only our current HQ; the Geschwader is stationed some 300 km further east, in Egypt, so the post is collected here, taken to Martuba where, presumably, it is vetted by the censor, then on, probably to Tripoli and thence, by some devious route, onward to Berlin. What route your letters take to me I do not know, except that the final 1,000 km is probably similar, in reverse. Your letters, by the way, never show signs of attention by the censor. Do mine?

I am so glad you had a nice restful holiday at Rimini. You have suffered such emotional trauma since Frieda's death that the wonder is you did not succumb to a nervous breakdown. It certainly was a risk taking the Talbot-Lago; you could have spent all your holiday stranded in some Alpine village awaiting a gasket or a water-pump or whatever to be sent from Paris! With a car like that you could be immobilised by some small part costing no more than a few marks. As it was, however, the drive must have been delightful, controlling such beautiful machinery is a pleasure in itself and one I should have loved to have shared.

You do not elaborate upon the "unimaginable horror" you experienced in Poland, although you say it was part of a plan inaugurated by Reinhard, and I will not urge you to enlarge upon it. I can use my imagination to fill the lacuna; I have seen horrible photographs of the squalor and deprivation in some of the Jewish ghettos, for instance and I, too, have experienced ghastly moments during this war that I am sure will haunt my dreams for years to come. I have been responsible for the deaths of many men, killed by my bullets, by crashing to earth, burnt to death or drowned, but one cannot allow one's mind to dwell on such things. We are at war, fighting, as you say, for Führer and Fatherland, and war is terrible.

I am most grateful to you for organising the driving lessons for Mathilde. It will be a great advantage for her when she is finally competent and passes her test. During my last leave (ten months ago!) I discovered how difficult it is to get a taxi in Berlin and what an ordeal it is struggling onto a crowded tram. The thought of doing it with loaded shopping bags and a small child is very daunting. Mathilde said in her last letter that you had visited her and Wolfchen with presents. Edith seems to have had a glorious holiday in Venice – that is something I really envy. Marriage to Arturo has brought her into a pattern of gracious living that seems far removed from the travails of wartime existence. Long may it continue for her.

It does seem to be taking an inordinately long time to find someone to replace Reinhard. What is the difficulty? I would have thought that the position of Reich Protector of Bohemia and Moravia was an important one that needed to be filled very quickly, especially as I understood from some of your previous comments that the Czechs could be rather troublesome. Perhaps, once more, I am showing my naiveté in such matters. Do you know who is being considered for the position?

The tremendous heat of the summer has receded somewhat and the days now are really balmy apart from the occasional sandstorm which is very unpleasant and can go on for a day or two. Then we have a laborious cleaning up job to do as the sand and grit intrudes everywhere. Our food is very basic and terribly monotonous so that conversation often turns to fantasy meals. Perhaps if one is dying in the desert one has such fantasies although I think the mind would simply dwell on images of cool water. At least we are well supplied with German beer and bottles of schnapps and French brandy. The authorities obviously think that alcohol has priority over comestibles.

Now I must close and send this letter on its long journey to Berlin.

Ever your loving brother,

Peter

From: Oberleutnant Peter von Vorzik
III Gruppe JP233
Martuba, Cyrenaica
To: Contessa Edith Novarro-Badaelli
Villa Frascati
Via Augusta
Rome

27th October 1942

My Dear Edith,

Your welcome letter and the parcel of good things arrived today and I am writing this outside my tent as the sun sets in a vivid display of red, gold, pink and lilac. I must scribble quickly as the failing light does not last long; after dark I will have to write inside our tent by the dim light of a hurricane lamp turned low. The problem, then, is that the tent becomes suffocating as we must close the flap so as not to show a light to marauding enemy bombers which have been troublesome of late. You apologise unnecessarily for writing at length about your affairs. Dear Edith, what you do, who you do it with, where you go, everything that touches your life is of interest to me so please continue writing about your affairs, they constitute a window on the outside world. I must admit I was somewhat envious of your trip to Venice. From the pictures I have seen of the city it has always fascinated me because of its unique setting upon water which is such a wonderful element for reflecting the beauties of architecture. After all, we were brought up at Adlersee! Kurt reminded me that Venice was the locale for the first meeting between the Führer and the Duce.

Somehow I am not surprised by the conversations you overheard at your dinner party. The Italians have certainly not contributed much to the war so far, indeed, they have been something of a liability, having to rely on us Germans to save them from themselves as we have in Jugoslavia, Greece and North Africa, which is bound to cause resentment. I know, too, from the things that Christian has told me that there are factional rivalries amongst our own Party leaders just as there are, I am sure, within the Luftwaffe, the Wehrmacht and the SS. I think it is axiomatic that any large organisation, of whatever nationality, will have its rivalries and dissidents. When two organisations come together then the ratio of rivalry doubles. I have to say, however, that to display such factionalism in front of one's hostess seems very bad manners. Both you and Christian are in a position to witness those factions at close quarters; here, as a mere Staffelkapitan, I am aware only of the cameraderie of my compatriots.

I have shared the contents of the parcel you sent with Kurt who always shares his parcels with me. We both thank you very much for the little luxuries which have added some very needed piquancy to our rather monotonous diet. Last week we had a plague of locusts – very biblical! They flew over the airfield like a small black cloud, actually dimming the sunshine, and swarmed over everything, even our aircraft. Would you believe it, some of the Italian airmen and their mechanics who share our airfield actually scooped up and ate the creatures, frying them in a little olive oil! We looked on in amazement, declining offers to share in the feast. Our diet may be monotonous but we draw the line at such delicacies. The light has gone now and I am loath to continue this in the sweltering tent – not that I have much more of any interest to tell you. So, dear Edith, I will close with the assurance that your letters, gifts and prayers continue to sustain the good spirits of

Your loving brother,

Peter

From: Oberleutnant Peter von Vorzik
III Gruppe JG233
Martuba, Cyrenaica
To: Mathilde von Vorzik
23 Hevelius Straße
Grunewald

8th November 1942

My Darling Mathilde,
This is a hastily scribbled note to tell you that, at the moment, we are being forced to make a tactical withdrawal to the west as the British launched a very strong attack about a week ago, as you may have heard on the radio. Consequently, it may be another two or three weeks before I can write again. Do not worry, dearest one, we are in good shape and I have my faithful Katschmarek, Kurt, by my side. It is just that we shall be fairly preoccupied in the immediate future but no letter from me is not, in itself, bad news. As soon as things have quietened down and we have

dealt with the situation you can be sure I will be writing at length once more. All my love to you and Wolfchen,

Ever your loving,
Peter

PS Please let Edith and Christian know I shall not be corresponding for a while but that all is well with me. P.

Oberleutnant Peter von Vorzik
Journal entry

21st November 1942

The British and their allies have dealt us a terrible blow at El Alamein and our forces are in full retreat westwards. Kurt and I both suffered flesh wounds and are here in a field hospital at Sirte, waiting to be flown back to Germany. From a personal point of view that is, I suppose, a piece of good luck but we would both rather be in a position to hit back at our enemies and do whatever can be done to stop their advance. The British attack began almost a month ago, on October 23rd, with continuous day and night attacks on our airfields at the same time as a sustained artillery barrage upon our ground forces. Within a few days, and after fierce fighting, the armoured columns of General Montgomery's 8th Army had broken through our lines and overwhelmed our defences. All the aircraft in our Geschwader were destroyed on the ground and we were forced to join with the Afrika Korps in retreating overground – a completely new and unpleasant experience for us. Much of our motor transport had also been smashed in the aerial attacks and in a situation that had rapidly become every man for himself Kurt and I, together with Varasch and his newly appointed Katschmarek, Gregor Wolff, commandeered an Italian truck together with its driver, some cans of petrol and water, and then, amidst an enormous agglomeration of vehicles, tanks, trucks, command cars, armoured cars, kübelwagen, even tractors, took to the coast road, the only east-west road there is. Of course, this slow-moving straggling column made a perfect target and we were constantly bombed and strafed by British aircraft.

It was during one of these attacks that Kurt and I sustained our wounds. About a dozen Bristol Beaufighters, heavily armed twin-engined machines, strafed our poorly defended convoy with their cannon, hitting our truck just east of Sidi Barrani. Kurt and I, sitting in the back of the truck, were struck by metal splinters which resulted in both of us bleeding profusely, me from the upper left arm, Kurt from his right thigh. Varasch bandaged Kurt's wound with his field dressing, then because I had foolishly forgotten to pack mine, ripped his shirt to bandage my arm and make a rough sling. Without his prompt attention we might easily have bled to death. The driver of our truck had been killed outright, his body splattered all over the cab from a direct hit with a cannon shell. Varasch commandeered another vehicle, holding up the Italian driver with his Luger, then drove us as far as Bardia where we transferred to a military ambulance which took us as far as Martuba from where we were flown on to Sirte. Here we have languished for two weeks. Our wounds have healed well, leaving only small scars, and we are impatient now to be flown back to Germany where we hope JG233 will be reformed and re-equipped. We are anxious for news of Varasch and Wolff as the military situation is still confused although Rommel has been able to coordinate a semblance of a proper line of defence while still retreating.

While all this was going on the Anglo-Americans have dealt us another blow by landing a large army in Morocco and Algeria. Our forces therefore face the prospect of being squeezed from east and west. Here in the field hospital the news is slight, fuelled by the usual rumours. We do know that German forces have now occupied the so-called Free Zone of France and the Italians have occupied Nice and Corsica. The Luftwaffe is ferrying more troops into Tunisia as well as bringing over more combat aircraft. It is all so frustrating to be sitting idly by but then JG233 no longer exists as it once did. Perhaps, when we have been reformed, we shall be sent back here to north Africa or even to Russia again. Anything seems better than doing nothing. Any moment we expect the British 8th Army to renew the offensive. Apparently it is reforming and replenishing at Benghazi, less than 300 km away by road around the Gulf of Sirte and less than half an hour's flying time away. Sirte has been the target of constant attacks although our compound is marked out with large red crosses. I find it hard to believe that events have developed to our disadvantage so quickly. Only a few weeks ago we were surging towards Cairo. Now we are retreating, defeated, to the west where another big force is threatening us. How the fortunes of war change!

From: Oberleutnant Peter von Vorzik
III Gruppe JG233
Sirte, Tripolitania
To: Mathilde von Vorzik
23 Hevelius Straße
Grunewald

28th November 1942

My Darling Mathilde,

By the time this reaches you I might already be on German soil! As you will no doubt have heard, our forces are being withdrawn westward and, together with other Staffeln of our Geschwader, are waiting to be flown back to Germany to be reformed and re-equipped. There is even a possibility that I may be given leave straight away but do not anticipate it happening until you see me on the doorstep!

All my love, kisses to you and Wolfchen.

Ever your own,
Peter

Book Five

War over Germany

Hauptmann Peter von Vorzik
Journal entry

7th January 1943

Looking back over the past year, it developed triumphantly and ended in
near disaster. We so nearly reached Cairo only to be pushed back from El
Alamein all the way to the Libyan-Tunisian border. We are now fighting
on two fronts in North Africa with Rommel's army squeezed between
the British 8th Army in Libya and the British and Americans in Algeria.
The town of Sirte, where Kurt and I waited to be flown back to Europe,
was taken by the British on Christmas Day and now they are advancing
on Tripoli. At Stalingrad our 6th Army under General von Paulus is
surrounded by Russian forces and so far, Field Marshal von Manstein's
army, sent to break through the Russian ring, has failed to save the
situation and once again the terrible Russian winter has closed in on
those beleaguered men.

I wrote that we were flown back to Europe from Sirte; in fact we only
flew as far as Lecce in the heel of Italy, not far from Brindisi. We flew in
one of the big four-engined Focke-Wulf Fw 200 Condors that had been
brought from Bordeaux, where they were engaged in Atlantic
surveillance, to ferry fuel and supplies to the Afrika Korps. The aircraft was

full of badly wounded soldiers, hideously injured, like the ones I had travelled back from Russia with. It was terrible to see those poor men in close proximity, burnt, blinded, maimed, yet somehow maintaining an amazing cheerfulness that I am sure I could not sustain if it were me. After landing at Lecce we were transferred to a hospital and troop train that crawled up the whole length of Italy to the Brenner Pass, then on to Augsburg, Stuttgart and, finally for us, Mannheim. All the way the train jolted and shunted, waited in sidings, and during the 9-day journey several of the badly wounded men died. The nurses who travelled with the wounded were wonderful, administering medicines, changing blood-soaked dressings, spoon-feeding the men who had lost arms and hands, cleaning them when they soiled themselves. As our superficial wounds had healed Kurt and I were pressed into helping, washing suppurating sores, bandaging flayed flesh. There was little opportunity for us to wash, just a brackish trickle from the taps in the carriage's lavatory compartment. Rations, too, were very basic and whenever the train stopped at a station we rushed to buy whatever provisions there might be, usually stale rolls, some salami if we were lucky, and thin, sour wine. We slept, fitfully, sitting up in the fetid, smoky compartment. At Mannheim we were met by a Luftwaffe staff car and taken to our new airfield where we had the luxury of a hot bath and a cooked meal. We spent several days at Darmstadt-Griesheim, attended a number of briefings, studied new orders and directives and finally met up with the remnants of our old Geschwader including Varasch who had his own lengthy tale to tell of how he and Gregor Wolff managed to get away from the advancing British. We raised several glasses in celebration of our escape from possible captivity, or worse, and toasted missing comrades. At a small, quiet ceremony I was promoted to Hauptmann which was an excuse for more celebration. Then – leave!

I managed to obtain a lift to Berlin in a courier plane (Kurt had to face another tedious rail journey to Hamburg), one of the old faithful Ju52s, and arrived at my front door just before noon on December 23rd. Lenka opened the door to me. She began to speak and I stopped her by putting my finger to my lips. I tiptoed down the hallway into the large kitchen at the rear of the house. Mathilde called out, "Who is it, Lenka?" When she saw me grinning in the doorway she let out a shriek and dropped the spoon with which she was feeding Wolfchen in his highchair. Mathilde leapt up and ran to embrace me crying out, "Peter! Peter!" while Wolfchen, startled, began to cry. It was not until Christmas Day that he would let me hold him. After that he followed me around wherever I went. That night, as Mathilde and I undressed, she saw the bright pink scar on my otherwise brown arm and burst into tears. I reassured her that it was only a superficial wound, ironically received on the ground rather than in the air. In bed she kissed the scar and then went on to kiss every part of me in a passionate frenzy. Our love-making continued in the same fevered way, a memory that will always sustain my imagination when we are apart.

Once again I had arrived home without Christmas presents for anyone. Like last year, Mathilde had decorated a little tree with brightly painted, carved wooden fruit, candles and tinsel. The drawing room was also decorated with evergreens and more candles. Presents for Wolfchen had arrived from Christian, Edith, Lina and Mathilde's new friends at the sewing circle. Mathilde had also bought him a large ball, a drum, some building bricks and a wooden motor car to pull along. Christian had sent us a case of champagne and Edith sent a box of good things from Italy: Parma ham, salamis, pâtés, a large cake, biscuits and six bottles of Chianti, one of which was cracked and had leaked its contents over everything. Mathilde had had the foresight to send silver photograph frames to Christian, Edith and Lina.

On Christmas Day Christian gave a small dinner party for Mathilde and myself and half a dozen of his SS colleagues and their wives and lady friends, none of whom we knew. Christian sat at the head of the long mahogany dining table set with silver candelabra, a silver dining service and crystal brought from Adlersee. It was impossible not to miss the presence of Frieda who would have been sitting at the other end of the table, Christian being the only man present without an accompanying lady. I felt very proud of Mathilde who looked very soignée in a long dark green velvet dress with diamond clips at the neck and the diamond earrings I had given her as a wedding present. The food was lavish: asparagus soup, salmon, venison, truffles, meringues, ices, candied fruits, red and white wines from France, brandy and liqueurs. There were cigars for the men and French perfume for the women – Mathilde received a large bottle of Chypre. As usual at Christian's soirées Mathilde and I felt somewhat de trop and after the usual toasts we made our excuses and left.

With some trepidation we had left Wolfchen in the care of Lenka. When we reached Grunewald, however, just after midnight, all was well, Wolfchen sleeping soundly and Lenka reading by the fire. She has proved a very helpful, responsible person although, understandably, subject to moments of melancholy. She has not heard from her father or brother since they were sent to Theresienstadt. Mathilde gave her the bottle of perfume and Lenka said it was the first she had ever had.

We spent New Year's Eve quietly, opening a bottle of the champagne Christian had sent and listening to a splendid concert by the Berliner Philharmoniker on the radio. Afterwards, there were encouraging speeches by Party leaders, including Dr Goebbels and Reichsmarschall Göring. The Führer, apparently, was too busy directing the battle for Stalingrad to make a speech. After midnight and the national anthem the radio closed down and Mathilde and I went to bed, savouring every moment in each other's arms.

Throughout my leave the weather was very cold with rain, sleet and flurries of snow. I felt the cold severely after the heat of the desert but the communiques and reports from Stalingrad, where the men of the 6th Army are beleaguered by blizzards as well as the Russian shells, bombs and bullets, made me realise just how lucky I am not to be there. By trying to interpret the reality behind the communiques it does seem the 6th Army is in a difficult, not to say desperate, position. The Luftwaffe is doing all it can to fly in supplies but the weather is as much an enemy as the Russians.

Yesterday was another tearful farewell and I had a lump in my throat as I kissed Mathilde and Wolfchen goodbye on the doorstep. The taxi took me to Tempelhof and from there I had a warrant to fly to Darmstadt-Griesheim. Now, with Kurt, Varasch, Wolff and a whole contingent of raw young fighter pilots straight from flying school, we await delivery of our brand new Me109Gs. JG233 is being reborn, a Phoenix rising from the ashes of the North African desert.

From: Hauptmann Peter von Vorzik
III Gruppe JG233
Darmstadt-Griesheim
To: Contessa Edith Novarro-Badaelli
Villa Frascati
Via Augusta
Rome

12th January 1943

My Dear Edith,

At last a chance to write to you after these several busy weeks. I know
Mathilde let you know that there would be a gap in our correspondence
while I escaped from the advancing British. Their massive assault came
so suddenly that we were thrown into some confusion. How infuriating
it is that we have been pushed out of Egypt after so nearly reaching
Cairo. For a while our retreat was quite chaotic and we – Kurt and I and
other comrades – had to improvise our transport. Luckily we did not
have to rely on camels! It was particularly galling that we had to leave
our aircraft behind, all damaged by attacks on our airfield, and join in
the general exodus overland. Rommel's hurried return from Germany
at least restored a semblance of order to what was in danger of becoming
a rout. This is our first experience of retreat and I hope it will be our
last. Now here I am thankfully back on German soil for a while, re-
equipped with splendid new aircraft and anxious to resume the battle
with our enemies. Where we shall go next is, at present, unknown.
Perhaps back to Russia, perhaps to France or Italy. Wherever it is in
Europe these are the worst months for flying when the weather is so
unpredictable and, in the east, rarely favourable for more than a few
days, as our transport Geschwader are discovering at Stalingrad. Things
are pretty desperate there, I believe.

Thank you, dear sister, for the parcel of delicious things you sent to us
for Christmas (I know Mathilde is writing to you separately). They were
particularly welcome after several months of a monotonous diet and even
in Berlin such delicacies are not so easy to find as they were this time last
year. Mathilde has one or two little sources of supply who provide an
occasional luxury (mostly from France) and there are friends and contacts
who provide eggs, ham, sausages and other staples. Last year our gardener

grew quite a lot of vegetables for us and Lenka, our help from Czechoslovakia, taught Mathilde to bottle fruit. But I expect she has told you in her letters how domesticated she is becoming.

One of the many joys of being home after a year away was, of course, to see Wolfchen again. When I went away he was still a tiny baby, scarcely able to register anything or anyone around him; when I returned he was a little person, toddling around, trying to formulate words, playing with toys. At first, naturally, he was scared of me, turning his face away and crying if I held him. After a day we were great friends, he wanted me to carry him, shrieked with laughter when I lifted him high or bounced him on my knee, tottered after me from room to room. How marvellous it is when babies become children and start to develop a personality. I hope it is not another year before I see him again. And you, dear Edith. Could there be a baby in the future? Did you have an enjoyable Christmas? Have you done more formal entertaining? Write to me when you can and tell me all your news.

Best wishes to Arturo.

Ever your affectionate brother,
Peter

PS You will see I have been promoted! This is mainly because my score of enemy planes destroyed is now forty. I have also received the Oak Leaves to my Knight's Cross but I'm still a long way from the achievements of a number of other pilots. P.

From: Hauptmann Peter von Vorzik
III Gruppe JG233
Darmstadt-Griesheim
To: SS-Grüppenführer Count Christian von Vorzik
116 Kaiserstraße
Berlin

16th January 1943

Dear Christian,

Just a short letter to give you my new address and to thank you again for the case of champagne and the delightful Christmas dinner. In these increasingly fraught and anxious times your home is a haven of calm and comfort. Both Mathilde and I appreciated your lavish hospitality. I was sorry, however, that during my leave we had no opportunity to have a discussion of any length. I look to you to keep me abreast of the real state of things. In your position you are able to give an informed opinion about how the war is progressing. Not just in military terms, we know that from the daily communiques (although they are frequently imprecise) but also in so many other spheres: the home front, opinions within the Party, the situation in the occupied territories and so on. Here in the mess one hears such rumours, most of them based on third-hand knowledge, or wildly exaggerated or just plain wrong. Even our intelligence briefings can be misleading or ambiguous. What does seem certain is that so much of what we hoped and planned for at the beginning of 1942 has not happened. Sometimes it is difficult not to view the overall situation pessimistically. I forbear from asking you about your situation vis-à-vis Schellenberg; I am sure if there were any news you would have told me. It was wonderful to be with my family after such a long separation but I could not help comparing my good fortune with your own sad situation. I do hope, dear brother, that you will find some happiness during this coming year that will enable you to bury the tragic memories of 1942.

With every good wish,

Your loving brother,
Peter

From: Mathilde von Vorzik
23 Hevelius Straße
Grunewald
To: Hauptmann Peter von Vorzik
III Gruppe JG233
Darmstadt-Griesheim

21st January 1943

My Darling Peter,
Now there are two of us feeling sad at your departure. For several days after you left Wolfchen kept running into the drawing room, climbing on to the sofa by the window and, pointing to the driveway, kept repeating "Papa, Papa." At least, darling, for the time being, it is comforting to me to know that you are here in Germany. With the festivities over January is

such a bleak month and the news from the fronts does not help to foster good spirits. Friedrich called yesterday to discuss with me what vegetables we would like to grow this spring (we had a glut of tomatoes last year, more than I could give away), and after we had talked a while he suddenly burst into tears. It seems his son has been posted missing during the fighting around Stalingrad. Friedrich feels sure he is dead but his wife, Emmie, clings to the hope that he is still alive, possibly taken prisoner. Friedrich says that would be worse than death but, of course, the uncertainty is dreadful. Poor man, I gave him a glass of brandy, his son is an only child. Friedrich showed me the last letter they received. He wrote, "Thank you for the cake you sent for Christmas. All the food I have now is a small piece of bread. I never missed home more than I did today when we were singing the *Wolgalied*." I am sure the conditions there are terrible – you will be able to visualise them better than me, darling – but I cannot understand why the troops do not have enough to eat. According to the radio they are being provided with food and supplies from the air. We decided that we would plant melons instead of cucumbers this year. Friedrich also said we must trim the big linden tree in the front garden. He is too old to climb up but he knows a man who will do it, an ex-gardener from the Charlottenburg Palace.

I am having my last driving lesson tomorrow and take my driving test next week. Christian's driver says I am now quite competent. My only problem is reversing which I find difficult in the big Mercedes but much easier in the little DKW in which I shall take my test. Despite Walter's re-assurances I will be feeling nervous so, darling, wish me luck! I have had a long letter from Lina. The winter weather has been dreadful in Fehmarn but she is staying there until the spring. She says that despite the cold winds and grey seas she is glad to be away from all the machinations and manoeuvrings that go on in the SS and amongst Party officials – although she misses friends like me. I miss her, too, she has been a good friend and is always a stimulating companion. Yesterday Frau Kirschner organised a visit to the cinema for the sewing circle. (I know you do not like me visiting Berlin, darling, but I thought you would not object to this outing to a matinee performance as no one is expecting daylight raids on the city.) We saw *Münchausen*, an amazing extravaganza, with Hans Albers as the eccentric Baron. The colour was simply beautiful and the special effects quite extraordinary. I do urge you to see it if you have a chance, it is a wonderful way to forget all about the war for an hour or two. Actually, I think it runs for nearly three hours! The Sunday concerts on the radio also continue to be a great solace. With Wolfchen in bed Lenka and I listen together. We especially like the programmes given by Karajan at the new Staatsoper. Why did I not think to suggest we attend a performance there during your leave? I believe the production of *The Magic Flute* is really superb.

I have no more news for you, dearest, so will hurry and catch the last post.

All my love as always.

Ever your own,
Mathilde

From: SS-Gruppenführer Count Christian von Vorzik
116 Kaiserstraße
Berlin
To: Hauptmann Peter von Vorzik
III Gruppe JG233
Darmstadt-Griesheim

28th January 1943

Dear Peter,

Thank you for your letter with your new address and your kind wishes for the New Year. It was a great pleasure for me to see both you and Mathilde in such good health and spirits. You are right: 1942 proved to be a year of great disappointments, if not disasters, which only means we must redouble our efforts to ensure that this year brings victory. The great consensus here, in the SS and the Party, is that our overwhelming victories in Poland, Scandinavia, France and the Balkans led to a general complacency during 1940–41. We failed to eliminate Britain in 1940, which was a serious mistake, and so far we have failed to eliminate the Russians who have proved to be much stronger than we anticipated.

I understand (I will not mention the name of my informant) that Reichsminister Goebbels is forming a triumvirate with himself, State Secretary Lammers and Albert Speer (who is doing wonders now as Minister of Armaments) to persuade the Führer that the general populace must be pressed into acknowledging the need for total war. There is far too much laxity in the big cities like Berlin. There are at least a million men throughout the Reich doing very little to help the war effort and who can be conscripted into the armed forces. Women, too, can be enlisted to perform scores of tasks now being carried out by men in the factories and in the fields. In this we can follow the example of the British who have encouraged thousands of women to serve their country. The French are voluntarily providing young men to carry out various labouring work in the Reich and we can call upon an almost unlimited supply of labour from the occupied eastern territories. All this manpower is available to us to prosecute the war with much greater intensity.

Internally there is only one great stumbling block: Martin Bormann. (I tell you this in great confidence.) As head of the Party Chancellery he has inveigled himself into such a position of trust with the Führer that no one, not even senior Party members like Göring, Goebbels, von Ribbentrop, even Reichsführer-SS Himmler, can have an audience with the Führer without first approaching Bormann. It is the same with the generals: when they are summoned to Rastenburg, Vinnitsa or Berchtesgaden, wherever the Führer may be, it is Bormann who decides when and to whom an audience is given. As you can imagine, this state of affairs leads to endless manoeuvring, frustration, currying of favour, resentment, backbiting and jealousy and often hinders the making of decisions that are vital to the prosecution of the war. In the SS we are, to a certain degree, immune to Bormann's obstructiveness as we operate fairly independently, but, for example, the dilatoriness in replacing Reinhard is the result of the Reichsführer-SS being unable to obtain an early decision from the Führer because Bormann says he must not be bothered with such questions while he is so involved with the situation on the eastern front. In turn, this affects my appointment to Schellenberg's staff. Meanwhile, we are facing a tragic defeat at Stalingrad.

Here in Berlin I have very little to occupy me. I see Walter quite often, and he keeps me abreast of what is happening in the Ausland SD and I believe he has sounded out the Reichsführer's opinion regarding my transfer and received a favourable reaction but nothing can happen until Reinhard's successor is appointed. At the suggestion of the Reichsführer I have been giving some serious thought to taking part in the *Lebensborn* programme. He pointed out that it is the duty of all physically active SS officers to maintain and increase the racially pure progeny of the Reich even if they are married. I must admit that, following these months of enforced celibacy after the death of my dear Frieda I have endured a certain sexual frustration, not wanting to take advantage of such establishments as Salon Kitty. I would be accommodated with a limited degree of choice with regard to the projected partnership. Of course I would have no further contact with the young woman involved, or her child, and it would have no bearing on any other subsequent relationship. In any case I have no wish to engage in any liaison until the war is over.

Let me hear from you when you have a moment to spare.

Your affectionate brother,
Christian

From: Contessa Edith Navarro-Badaelli
Villa Frascati
Via Augusta
Rome
To: Hauptmann Peter von Vorzik
III Gruppe JG233
Darmstadt-Griesheim

4th February 1943

My Dear Peter,

It was a great relief to know you were safely back in Germany as, one way or another, the news has been rather sad and depressing. First, the family here are in mourning for Massimo, Eleanora's youngest son, who has been posted missing with the Italian 8th Army in Russia. As far as we can discover, from a letter sent by his commanding officer, his patrol was wiped out by units of the Russian 6th Army sweeping down from the north-east in their encircling movement at Stalingrad. There has been no body recovered nor any mention of him being taken prisoner. It is so dreadful to think of that handsome young man who attended my wedding, looking like a Michelangelo sculpture come to life, lying dead in the snow somewhere or blown to pieces. As you can imagine, Arturo has been devastated at the loss of his brother and feels that he, too, should have been fighting at the front. The whole debacle at Stalingrad is too terrible to contemplate. I have to say that at one or two diplomatic gatherings recently I have detected a certain *schadenfreude* amongst some of the Italians present as the Germans here have certainly been harshly critical of Italian incompetence in battle. The situation in North Africa, too, looks critical after the fall of Tripoli. Everyone says the Italians were left in the lurch by Rommel to be taken prisoner by the British.

The replacement of General Cavalerro by General Vittorio Ambrosio has not pleased the German military authorities here and the government is being criticised on all sides, especially about certain scandals associated with Mussolini. Did you know he had a mistress? Her name is Claretta (called Clara) Petacci and apparently the liaison has existed for years with the knowledge of the Duce's wife, Rachele. Many people, including Ciano and his wife, Edda, and the Princess di Gangi have urged the Duce to abandon the Petacci woman but apparently he is being blackmailed by members of her family who are all scoundrels; especially her brother Marcello, who has been in league with Signor Riccardi, the Minister of Exchange and Foreign Currency, concerning gold transactions with Spain through the diplomatic bag. There are endless ramifications with the Petacci family which would place Mussolini in an untenable position if the truth were generally known. You can imagine how shocked I have been to learn of such corruption in the highest places of the government. Even more worrying is the fact that the British and Americans have been bombing Genoa, Turin and Milan. Rome has been declared an "open city" which is some comfort.

Reichsmarschall Göring has been here, more or less privately, buying pictures and *objets d'art* and boasting how he has beaten down the dealers over prices, which hardly accords well with the news from Stalingrad. His visit has done nothing for Italo-German relations.

Last week I accompanied Eleanora, heavily veiled in mourning for Massimo, to an orphanage (Santa Maria, Our Lady of Mercy) run by an order of nuns. Eleanora has been on the board of directors for years and is involved in fund-raising for the institution. It was heartbreaking to see those lines of children, between four and fourteen, singing psalms and praying for peace. The smaller ones, particularly, looked so thin and helpless, their rations are minimal and I felt very guilty thinking of our sumptuous meals although the delicacies we enjoyed just a few weeks ago are no longer so readily available. Even so, we eat lavishly compared to those poor children. Eleanor says that after fourteen they are just pushed out into the world to fend for themselves. She says that in all the big cities there are gangs of children living by their wits, often involving prostitution, and scavenging for food. According to Arturo, Ciano has been supplying food and provisions to two actresses, Marielli Lotti and Elsa Merlini, for ages. He would be better employed in organising food for the orphanage. His reputation, both private and public, is generally poor, although there are a number who look to him as a political saviour and I am told he has the backing of the king. At the moment Arturo says he feels he is walking a tightrope, so many factions are jostling for power and position. Being German I keep my opinions very much to myself. I smile and nod agreement with anyone who is talking to me, even Arturo. Is not that the meaning of diplomacy? We have given two more dinner parties since I last wrote, both successful from the domestic point of view. I feel more assured as a hostess now, familiar with several of the local diplomats, politicians, chargés d'affaires, military and cultural attachés, etc but still very dependent on my domestic staff for everything running smoothly. During these gatherings we seem to exist in a different world; it is only next day, listening on the radio to the communiques from the various fronts, that one is jerked back to harsh reality.

No, dear brother, there is no baby expected yet in the Novarro-Badaelli household although that could happen any time and Arturo and I would be delighted. How wonderful for you to see Wolfchen again now that he is growing apace. Mathilde has sent me photographs of him and already I detect the looks of his father! In this world of war it is the children, is it not, in whom we must place our hope for the future. Even as I write these words I think of the expressions on the faces of those children in the orphanage, the look in their eyes as they were confronted with a new adult (me), hope, wariness, anxiety.

Keep well and safe, my dear brother,

You are always in my thoughts and prayers.

Edith

PS I am not exactly fluent but my Italian has improved to the point where I can converse quite well. E.

From: Hauptmann Peter von Vorzik
III Gruppe JG233
Darmstadt-Griesheim
To: Oberleutnant Lother Köhl
II Gruppe ZG26L
Fliegercorps VIII
Eastern Front

14th February 1943

Dear Lother,

We have not corresponded since the summer of last year (which I find quite extraordinary; how time flies!) although you have often been in my thoughts knowing that you were probably engaged in the struggle for Stalingrad. I trust that you have survived what seems to have been the worst battle of the war so far. At any rate, I am writing this in the hope that it will reach you. The official communiques and radio reports refer to "a glorious fight to the last breath, the last bullet," together with long excerpts from Wagner's *Rienzi*, all of which would seem to cloak the reality of a disastrous defeat – or am I being cynical? I only make that surmise because the situation had some parallels with our position in North Africa. All the reports referred to "repelling heavy British attacks," and "strategic withdrawals," when, in fact, we were retreating in headlong confusion!

Together with Kurt and several other pilots from the Staffel I managed to get away from El Alamein by the skin of my teeth (my arm, to be precise; I sustained a minor flesh wound when our truck was strafed by British aircraft). Yes, ignominiously, we had to escape overland, our aircraft destroyed on the ground. In truth we commandeered (stole!) a truck from some unfortunate Italian at gunpoint and managed to make it as far as Sirte from where we were flown to the Italian mainland and thence by rail back to Germany. Since Christmas leave (wonderful) we have been stationed here at Darmstadt waiting to be re-equipped with 109Gs. There seems to have been a hitch somewhere along the line – literally, as the British have bombed the WNF works which have the subcontract. Just where we will go when we finally receive our new aircraft is anybody's guess. I would not be surprised to find myself back in Russia as that seems to be the front in most urgent need of reinforcements. On the other hand, things look very difficult in North Africa with Rommel squeezed on two fronts; the Geschwader might well return there, having had extensive experience of desert warfare. I suppose we shall know the minute we see our 109Gs: if they have tropical supercharger intakes it means Africa! The most sanguine of my colleagues are hoping for a posting to southern France now that we have occupied the whole of the country. Personally, I think a sinecure posting somewhere on the Côte d'Azur is unlikely! I count myself to have been very lucky so far: drafted out of Russia, escaped out of Africa, I must expect a tough posting now to level things up. Maybe northern Norway or on the Leningrad front.

I said the Christmas leave was wonderful and it was. Oh, the joy of home comforts, daily baths, decent food, soft bed and the happiness engendered by a loving wife and darling baby son. Have you managed to get leave? I do hope so, the policy of keeping experienced pilots at the front for long periods must, eventually, have diminishing returns. If we had managed to get to Cairo and our Geschwader had not been decimated I would still be in Africa. So, I trust all goes well with you, Lother, even though I suspect you have had a really hard time these last six or seven months.

Write to me when you can.

Your sincere comrade,
Peter

From: Hauptmann Peter von Vorzik
III Gruppe JG233
Darmstadt-Griesheim
To: Mathilde von Vorzik
23 Hevelius Straße
Grunewald

18th February 1943

My Darling Mathilde,
Yes, it will always be sad saying goodbye even though, this time, I am not so far away. We will be staying here for a while as there is a delay in delivering our new aircraft. Then there will be a considerable working-up period while our new recruits assimilate all our combat techniques. The Geschwader lost so many fine pilots in North Africa it will take time to

achieve the same degree of efficiency and *esprit de corps* that we had before. We know it will be impossible to replace the experience that the old group had accumulated throughout so many campaigns.

I am so glad you had an enjoyable outing with the sewing circle, darling, (*Münchausen* is playing in the local cinema here with long queues to see it) but, please, do not go into Berlin any more except when it is really necessary. I know there may only be nuisance raids by daylight – the British have their new ultra-fast Mosquito bomber for such incursions – but it is simply not worth the risk of the odd stray bomb. I must tell you in all confidence that intelligence informs us that we must expect an increasing number of such raids as well as the possibility of heavy night raids such as were carried out against Cologne. Do not pass on this information to anyone in case you are accused of defeatism! The psychological climate (a phrase I read the other day) is rather poor at the moment, following Stalingrad and our position in North Africa, but it would be foolish to ignore warnings of increased enemy air activity. The plain truth is, we lost mastery of the air in Africa and the British and American bombing campaigns are increasing – Edith writes to say that major Italian cities are now being bombed.

I also read in *Das Reich* that SS-Obergruppenführer Ernst Kaltenbrunner has been appointed as Reinhard's successor, although Christian made no mention of it in his last letter. But that must mean his appointment to Schellenberg's staff can now go ahead. I do hope so; last year was dreadful for him, he desperately needs some new stimulus in his life and a move into Ausland SD could provide it. Confidentially, he tells me that he is contemplating entering the *Lebensborn* programme. I know that members of the SS are encouraged to make themselves available for this programme and I can understand the reasoning behind it but there is a part of me that recoils from the thought. It seems so (I am searching for words) mechanical, artificial, although of course it is not that. But when I think of the mutual love and happiness that produced Wolfchen then I know that I could never contemplate such a regimen myself. Perhaps if I were single and the country was in greater danger than it is now... I hope Christian is able to find some loving person before long, although he says he does not want to consider any liaison until the war is over.

I hope, dearest one, that your driving test was successful and that you are now free to drive on the roads all by yourself. I need not entreat you to take great care, I am sure, but do begin with very short journeys locally so that you become used to handling the car. I am sure you will very soon be confident. Your birthday approaches again, darling, and I wonder what you would like? Now that I am back in Germany the choice is much wider. Please let me know, maybe something you can buy for yourself.

Write again soon, dearest.

Kisses for you and Wolfchen.

Ever your own loving,

Peter

From: Hauptmann Peter von Vorzik
III Gruppe JG233
Darmstadt-Griesheim
To: Oberleutnant Claus Grüber
Erprobungsgruppe V
Rechlin am Muritzsee

23rd February 1943

Dear Claus,

Here I am, back safe and sound in Germany, having escaped the worst in North Africa. (In truth, I think the worst is yet to come.) At present JG233 is being reformed after being decimated in Africa. Myself and my Katschmarek Kurt, together with six other old hands, are being formed into a Lehr-Staffel to teach a whole new intake combat techniques and tactics. (The youngsters we are receiving appear to have learnt very little apart from how to get up and, after a fashion, get down again!) All would be well except that delivery of our new G Series (remember, you wrote to me in Sicily about the G Series?) is held up for an indeterminate time because the WNF works have been badly damaged. So, that being the case, may I take you up on your long-standing invitation to make another visit to Rechlin? I quite understand if, for various reasons, it is not convenient but as things are, I am in some need of mental stimulus − not to say how pleasant it would be to break open a bottle of schnapps with an old comrade. If you can, let me know by return of post (our switchboard here is permanently jammed ostensibly by official communications but I suspect it is the telephonists talking to their boyfriends) and I will commandeer the Staffel's Taifun for a couple of days.

Hoping to see you soon.

Best wishes,
Peter

PS Would it be permissable to bring Kurt with me? He is such a good man, he saved my life in Russia and several times in the air, and I know he would be thrilled to see what you have up your sleeve. P.

From: Mathilde von Vorzik
23 Hevelius Straße
Grunewald
To: Hauptmann Peter von Vorzik
III Gruppe JG233
Darmstadt-Griesheim

24th February 1943

My Darling Peter,

Your letter arrived this morning and it is wonderful to hear from you within days rather than weeks! I do so hope your new posting will not be too far away – or too soon! Since you left we have all had colds, including Wolfchen, who has been very unlike his usual self, fretful, pushing his food away, crying a lot, especially when I try to wipe his nose! I took him to Dr Pagoschuster, who remembers mother, and he said there was very little that I could do except to keep him warm and try and make sure he drinks plenty of fluids. Not so easy. If I thought Wolfchen was becoming feverish I was to telephone and the doctor would come and visit us. However, Wolfchen seems better today, he ate quite a good lunch and is sleeping peacefully as I write this.

Yes, darling, I will follow your advice and keep away from Berlin. However, you did ask me what I wanted for my birthday. There is nothing I really need but there is a shop on the Ku'damm that specialises in French perfume (I accompanied Lina there once) and I would like to see if they have a small bottle of Je Reviens. About two months ago I finished the large bottle you gave me when we first met although I keep the empty bottle in my underwear drawer. It would be an extravagance, an indulgence, but now I always associate the fragrance with you, with us. I am proud to say that I passed my driving test – just! The examiner (a huge fat man who could scarcely squeeze into the DKW) pointed out one or two faults; I am not very good at reversing, especially around corners, and I tend to park too far away from the kerb, but he said these were minor inaccuracies that would be corrected by practise and he passed me! I have attempted one short drive, just as far as the Schlachtensee, near Lina's home, a route I know well. I went alone and was not at all nervous. Next time I will venture a little further, maybe to the shops on the Argentinische Allee.

Edith wrote to me about Arturo's brother, Massimo. What a sad death. Of course he is but one of thousands but when it is someone you know or someone attached to the family, however distant, it brings the tragedy home to you. I do not like listening to the news now, although of course I do; the war seems to be going on an on, getting worse all the time. The awful weather we have had here, rain and high winds, does not help to keep up one's spirits. Every day I look in the garden for a snowdrop or a crocus and on the branches and twigs of the trees in the hope of seeing a bud or a new growth somewhere but winter still persists and there is no sign of spring. Christian telephoned yesterday to say that at last he has been transferred to Schellenberg's unit. He sounded so pleased and I am so happy for him. I did not mention anything about the *Lebensborn* programme. I share your feelings about it; it does seem a cold clinical way to bring a baby into the world but I suppose it is for the good of the Fatherland and if it must be done then men like Christian are the best people to do it. I am sure he looks upon it as a duty.

Wolfchen has just woken up and needs me so I will close and ask Lenka to post this. Keep well, my darling, I do so hope you stay at Darmstadt for some weeks – months? – yet.

Meanwhile, kisses from Wolfchen and

Your loving wife,
Mathilde

From: Hauptmann Peter von Vorzik
III Gruppe JG233
Darmstadt-Griesheim
To: Mathilde von Vorzik
23 Hevelius Straße
Grunewald

27th February 1943

My Darling Mathilde,
Happy birthday! I do hope this card reaches you in time, it was the only decent one I could find and I thought the flowers would help you to think it is spring! Please use the enclosed cheque to buy yourself a *large* bottle of Je Reviens.

All my love,
Peter

From: Hauptmann Peter von Vorzik
III Gruppe JG233
Darmstadt-Griesheim
To: SS-Gruppenführer Count Christian von Vorzik
116 Kaiserstraße
Berlin

28th February 1943

Dear Christian,
Thank you for your long and interesting letter. First, I hope you were not too troubled by the RAF's daylight raid last month? I gather that little damage was done and that it was more of a propaganda exploit for their new Mosquito bomber than anything else. Even so, I have asked Mathilde not to venture into the city unless it is absolutely necessary. Second, I hear from Mathilde that you have at last transferred to Schellenberg's unit. I am so happy for you, you have waited so long for this appointment it would have been galling had it been denied you for some reason. I cannot understand why such an appointment was not possible soon after Reinhard's assassination, except that the fascinating information you included in your last letter does provide an insight into the Byzantine machinations that go on behind the scenes, both in your own organisation

and within the Party. How is it that Bormann has developed such influence with the Führer, seemingly over and above such bigwigs as the Reichsmarschall and the Reichsminister-SS? Not to mention von Ribbentrop, Speer, Ley, Goebbels et al. That he should dictate which generals should have access to the Führer seems preposterous when the military situation especially in the east appears so serious.

From all sides one hears horrifying reports about what happened at Stalingrad, over and above the official communiques. Colleagues throughout the Geschwader have endless tales from friends in other Geschwader about the known impossibility of providing sufficient supplies for the 6th Army from the air, first because we lacked the necessary numbers of transports, second because of the weather conditions and third because of the lack of airfields free from attack. Everyone knows someone who has lost a son, brother, husband, cousin, friend in the battle. I am sure you know the Novarro-Badaellis are mourning the loss of Arturo's younger brother, Massimo, whom you met at Edith's wedding. What a tragedy! This year would seem to be our final chance of defeating the Russian colossus, otherwise I see little alternative to drawing back to an impregnably defensive line somewhere around the Vistula and negotiating some form of separate peace that would allow us to retain as much of what we have won as possible. After all, we have achieved almost all of our stated need for lebensraum in the east and we hold much of the rest of Europe as satraps. These, I must confess, are not my own observations but the result of conversations with various colleagues. I suppose it sounds like defeatism but I think it makes sense to look beyond the present and consider options if everything, this year, fails to go to plan as it has for the last two years. Forgive me if this sounds like naive nonsense – you know I have never had the mental capacity to understand the subtleties of politics and foreign affairs!

I do admire your willingness to consider the *lebensborn* programme, it is something I would find difficult to commit to. I realise how important it is to maintain a healthy flow of strong Aryan progeny for the state and that being in the SS makes you subject to pressure to perform that "duty". I do hope all progresses smoothly.

Write when you can, dear brother, your letters are a constant stimulus.

Yours, ever,

Peter

From: Hauptmann Peter von Vorzik
III Gruppe JG233
Darmstadt-Griesheim
To: Contessa Edith Novarro-Badaelli
Villa Frascati
Via Augusta
Rome

3rd March 1943

My Dear Edith,

Thank you, as always, for your letter although it did contain some very sad news as, indeed, so many letters do nowadays. Please convey my deepest sympathy and sincerest condolences to Arturo and his family on the loss of Massimo. So many families seem to have suffered from that battle – more of a debacle really and a terrible defeat for our aims as well as our army. It is especially grievous for the family not to have a body to bury, the opportunity for a proper funeral. Massimo's loss must act as a spur to all of us to do all we can to bring this terrible war to a successful conclusion this year.

I read in the papers and heard on the radio that Ciano had been transferred (dismissed?) from the Foreign Office to become ambassador to the Holy See. How does that affect Arturo? Will he remain part of Ciano's entourage or will he stay at the Palazzo Chigi? Why was Ciano suddenly given that posting after nearly eight years as Foreign Minister? Your revelations about Mussolini and his mistress certainly came as a surprise to me, and yet, not such a surprise as it would have been some two years ago. Since then I have received a series of surprises about the behaviour of major political figures. Both you and Christian keep me informed of the extraordinary behaviour of many of those to whom one looks for leadership, integrity, moral probity. Am I being both naive and priggish to expect better from those who direct the fortunes of our country and its allies? I find it hard to believe that the Führer would be capable of such moral laxity, yet Christian tells me of all the jockeying for position that goes on around him. Apparently, Ernst Bormann has manoeuvred himself into such a position of eminence that no one can approach the Führer except through him! That must, in itself, create a situation which produces unnecessary delays in achieving decisions.

I was somewhat premature in writing of our new aircraft in my last letter; the new aircraft have not yet arrived. I had assumed that there they would be, waiting on the airfield when we got back from leave. Well, it is we who are waiting, anxious to get on and rejoin the battle wherever we are sent. Even when we do receive the aircraft it will take some time to become operational as the Geschwader is now two-thirds composed of young recruits who, as yet, have no combat experience. It is the work of my Staffel, in particular, to instil in them the necessary technical prowess to make them a strong fighting force.

Did you happen to hear Reichsminister Dr Goebbels's speech at the Berlin Sportpalast two weeks ago? It was a most inspiring performance that had that huge audience cheering and stamping. When he concluded with the words, "Now, People, arise! and storm, break loose!" one fully expected the crowd to rush into the streets ready to do battle with the enemy then and there. I just hope that the spirit he engendered does not dissipate in the coming months which will surely be decisive for all of us. Christian says that Goebbels is actively involved in getting the Führer's approval for a much greater prosecution of the war, especially with regard to the home front where, he says, there are still untouched reserves of manpower.

Yes, the children are our future. I cannot but help comparing the images of those children you visited in the orphanage with that of my own darling Wolfchen, adored by his mother and father. It must be terrible to be orphaned, to have to rely on strangers for sustenance and sympathy. I am sure the sisters of Santa Maria are good surrogate mothers but then, as you say, being propelled into the world at fourteen, alone and unwanted, is a dreadful fate.

Please write again soon, dearest Edith.

Ever your loving brother,
Peter

From: *Oberleutnant Lother Köhl*
II Gruppe ZG26L
Fliegerkorps VIII
Eastern Front
To: Hauptmann Peter von Vorzik
III Gruppe JG233
Darmstadt-Griesheim

7th March 1943

Dear Peter,

Your letter came as a welcome surprise – most of the surprises we've had being most unwelcome! Yes, I am still here – just – still hoping for leave after what has been the worst period of my life. You were quite right in surmising that the Gruppe was involved in the disaster of Stalingrad, a disaster that should never have happened. Had the 6th Army been allowed to withdraw in time, even after the initial encirclement by the Russians, it need never have become the terrible tragedy that it was. Believe me, Peter, it was horror on a scale such as you could scarcely imagine, far, far from the "glorious fight to the last breath" that you quote. I saw thousands and thousands of men dying of dreadful wounds, dying in the snow, untended, without medicine, dying of dysentery and typhus, dying from starvation, fighting over a crust of bread, a piece of frozen flesh from the belly of a rotting horse, fighting for a place on one of the returning transports. Bleeding, frozen, starving, stinking, soiled with their own faeces, lice-ridden, covered in sores, it was total and utter human degradation.

At first the Gruppe was pressed into service escorting all manner of transports – Ju52s, Ju290s, FW200s, He111s – from bases at Rovenky, Swerewo, Schachty, Novocherkassk, Tazinskaya. and Morosovskaya to the encircled airfields at Gumrak and Pitomnik, out of range of single-engined fighters. It was a hell of a run, attacked by swarms of LAgg-3s and Mig-3s, shot at by batteries of Russian flak – we lost several transports on each flight as well as a number of 110s. Then, when we arrived at Gumrak or Pitomnik the ground staff with badly frostbitten fingers were scarcely capable of unloading two or three Staffel at a time. The runways were littered with crashed and burnt-out aircraft as well as bomb craters and shell-holes. Then the Russians overran Tazinskaya and Morosovskaya so that each sortie became longer and longer. On the 13th January I watched as a Ju290, loaded with wounded, took off from Pitomnik. The pilot attempted to climb away too steeply in order to avoid Russian flak. With its four engines screaming ineffectually at full throttle the plane stalled and crashed back on the frozen earth in a huge fireball. Apparently, with the steep angle of climb, the wounded, some on stretchers, some seated, had slid to the tail of the aircraft making it tail-heavy. I could go on and on but I won't. I just wanted you to know this was a most ghastly defeat on a gigantic scale, nothing glorious about it at all and, of course, it's the Luftwaffe being blamed for not carrying out an impossible task. I lost many friends in the Geschwader and was lucky to escape with life and limb. I have frequent nightmares about it all.

And you! I'm glad you managed to escape, too, though it begins to look as if thousands won't. It is very difficult not to feel pessimistic about the future... All I want is a couple of weeks' leave and, like you, to enjoy the comforts of home, a proper bed, proper cooking, and a rest. Through all this I have been leading a celibate life... the women in the approved brothels are (I'm told) hideous, Polish and Russian peasants, mostly. But sexual starvation has been the least of our worries. Our only relief is drink which, thank God, we seem to have a plentiful supply of. Schnapps, brandy, beer; some of the younger pilots – scarcely finished Kampfgeschwader training before being put on JU52s – have practically become alcoholics. I know of at least two pilots who managed to land at Gumrak half drunk. Well, that's my news, such as it is. We are awaiting the thaw – more mud! – and the hope of leave while the Geschwader is reformed, as yours has been. Then, who knows? I would appreciate a sunny posting!

Let us keep in touch.

All the best,
Lother

PS Congratulations on your promotion. L.

From: Oberleutnant Claus Grüber
Erprobungsgruppe V
Rechlin am Muritzsee
To: Hauptmann Peter von Vorzik
III Gruppe JG233
Darmstadt-Griesheim

12th March 1943

Dear Peter,
Forgive the delay in replying to your letter of February 23rd but I have been away on circuit, visiting Augsburg, Leipheim and Lechfeld. (I will tell you why when we meet.) Yes, yes, come whenever you can, just register your flight plan twenty-four hours before (as you know, the airfield here is always busy) and by all means bring your Katschmarek.

Looking forward to seeing you.

Yours, in haste,
Claus

Hauptmann Peter von Vorzik
Journal entry

17th March 1943

Kurt and I returned from Rechlin with heavy hangovers but with our spirits rejunvenated by what we had seen there. Our flight from Darmstadt-Griesheim in the Me108 Taifun was uneventful until we were west of Berlin when we received a call from Ground Control in the Luneberg sector to say that British fighter-bombers, thought to be Mosquitos, were reported entering the area. We kept a sharp lookout (I was glad Kurt was with me) as the 108 was the forerunner of the Me109 fighter which it superficially resembles and we did not want to run into an enemy thinking we had fighter capability. Luckily, no Mosquitos or any other RAF type materialised but we were happy to encounter two Fw190s also on their way to Rechlin so we had a fighter escort for the last 60 km. Safely down and parked on the outer eastern perimeter of the airfield, a staff car took us to Claus's office where both he and the station Commandant greeted us. After an excellent lunch for the rest of that day and the following day we were given an insight into the latest projects being developed at Rechlin and

438

other experimental bases around Germany. We watched test flights by several new aircraft as well as inspecting photographs and drawings and watching films of highly secret experimental aircraft which left us open-mouthed with astonishment and excitement.

Several of our most successful warplanes – the Do17, Ju88, Fw190 and our own Me109s – are being developed further and given new designations. Completely new types are being designed and flown by Arado, Junkers, Dornier, Heinkel and Messerschmitt. In particular we were told that the Technisches Amt of the Reichsluftfahrtministerium has issued requirements for high-altitude bombers and fighters, the former to fly above and beyond fighter interception, the latter to oppose bombers of the US Air Force which, according to intelligence information, is building up a large force in England of its B-17 Flying Fortress bombers which can operate up to 10,000 m. Claus said that our 109Gs, when we eventually get them, will probably be equipped with cockpit pressurisation to allow us to operate, with oxygen masks, at altitudes of 12,000 m or more. More exciting than all this, however, were the photographs and films we saw of the experimental aircraft being developed by Messerschmitt using totally new forms of propulsion that give speeds more than 200 kph faster than any current types. (To observe early test flights was one of the reasons Claus had visited Augsburg, Leipheim and Lechfeld.) These aircraft are simply phenomenal and place the Luftwaffe in new realms of aviation history. Of course, they are many months, even years, away from operational service, nevertheless they promise to give us absolute mastery of the air in the not-too-distant future. Referring to more mundane matters, Claus said that the He177 heavy bomber was still not satisfactory (several that were pressed into service as transports at Stalingrad were lost through technical failures rather than enemy action) but that the problems affecting the Me210 had finally been rectified and the aircraft, to obscure any failures with the 210, is now designated the 410. I hope Lother's Geschwader is equipped with this aircraft soon. I told Claus how Lother had been suffering on the eastern front and he had equally dispiriting tales to tell.

Claus seemed much older than when I saw him last; he now uses a stick to hobble about with but he still manages to pilot his own aircraft and his high spirits and enthusiasm were easily transferred to us, particularly over drinks in the mess. Back in Darmstadt, after a smooth return flight, we are still waiting for our 109Gs. This waiting becomes demoralising and takes the edge off the excitement at what we had seen at Rechlin. While we were away there had been a briefing by an intelligence officer who said almost exactly what Claus had told us, that the Americans are known to be building up a large bomber fleet in England with which they will make daylight raids on Germany. It seems that our Geschwader is one that has been selected to oppose this threat. That being so we are even more impatient to receive our new Gustavs, as they have been nicknamed.

From: Mathilde von Vorzik
23 Hevelius Straße
Grunewald
To: Hauptmann Peter von Vorzik
III Gruppe JG233
Darmstadt-Griesheim

23rd March 1943

My Darling Peter,

I cannot believe that it is nearly four weeks since I last wrote to you. With one day very like the next the days seem to drag and yet a month has flown by since I put pen to paper. Almost every day some little thing happens – usually involving Wolfchen – and I think to myself I must tell Peter that, I must put that in my next letter, yet now that I am actually writing I cannot think of any of those little anecdotes.

Thank you, darling, for your very generous cheque. I did exactly what you said and bought a large bottle of Je Reviens. (I have put a drop on this notepaper, can you smell it?) The shop on the Ku'damm has a large stock of French perfume. It is strange how everyday things are suddenly in short supply but many luxury items (mostly French!) are easily obtainable. For example, sausages are scarce but foie gras is always on offer. Safety pins (and razor blades!) are hard to find but the shelves are full of scent and face-cream. Proper coffee is like gold dust but champagne is readily available. Money can still buy most things but Reichsminister Dr Goebbels has just closed down most of Berlin's luxury restaurants, including Horcher's, which has apparently enraged Reichsmarschall Göring who enjoyed eating there. I drove to the scent shop on the Ku'damm and was back in Grunewald within the hour. Had I taken the tram it would have been twice as long. Having the DKW is really a blessing, I feel very confident with it now and have made several local shopping forays with Wolfchen and Lenka.

Last week I spent a couple of hours with Lina who was in Berlin for a few days dealing with matters arising from Reinhard's estate. I drove over to Schlachtensee with Wolfchen who behaved perfectly, I was so proud of him. He sat on Lina's knee and prattled away, mostly incomprehensibly, and she was enchanted by him. As always she had remembered my birthday and gave me a beautiful silk scarf from Paris. She was avid for news and gossip after spending the winter at Fehmarn but I had little to tell her apart from family matters. She asked whether Christian had a new liaison (she told me she had always thought him "immensely attractive") and I told her about his involvement with the *Lebensborn* programme at which she made a face and said it was a distasteful idea, typical of the Reichsführer-SS. Of course, there was never any love lost between her and Himmler. She also said she had always known about Reinhard's dalliances at Salon Kitty but it was better than him having a full-blown affair like Dr Goebbels had with Lida Baarova. Both men were sexually voracious she said, and back in 1938 Magda Goebbels had appealed to the Führer about her husband's infidelities which is why he had given up Baarova. But that has not stopped him having many affairs since.

My darling, I am wondering if your new aircraft have arrived and if that means you will be moving to another posting before long? It has been such a comfort to me knowing that you are not so far away and not involved in any fighting. Things are looking rather worrying in Tunisia, aren't they? Perhaps Rommel will yet be able to work one of his miracles and drive the British and Americans back into the sea.

At last there are signs of spring with buds on the trees and crocuses in the garden. We have had some sunny days but with cold winds and some showers, I expect you have had similar weather at Darmstadt. I was able to take Wolfchen for our favourite walk around the lake. The gardener who was at Charlottenburg came and trimmed the big linden tree; an agile man in late middle age who said he remembers when the Kaiser was in residence there. I am still doing my sewing with Frau Kirschner who says my work has "greatly improved". At times she is just like a school mistress! I take Wolfchen with me and he has his afternoon nap there, propped up on pillows. We are due there this afternoon, darling, so I must stop now, give Wolfchen his lunch and post this on the way to Frau Kirschner's.

All my love, dearest, kisses from Wolfchen and

Your devoted wife,
Mathilde

From: SS-Gruppenführer Count Christian von Vorzik
116 Kaiserstraße
Berlin
To: Hauptmann Peter von Vorzik
III Gruppe JG233
Darmstadt-Griesheim

29th March 1943

Dear Peter,

Many thanks for your letter of 28th February, forgive me for taking so long to reply. Yes, at last, I am with the Ausland SD and working closely with Walter Schellenberg, and a very extraordinary and enlightening experience it is proving to be. One sees the world from a wholly different perspective when undertaking such a move. For instance, I have learned what consternation and anger it caused when Reinhard sent me as an "observer" to Bucharest two years ago. Apparently, Schellenberg considered I was encroaching on Ausland SD territory, even though they were informed of my mission by Reinhard and the Reichsführer-SS had given his approval. They thought Reinhard was playing a double game and was trying to take over command of Ausland SD and so on. I was blissfully ignorant of all this, of course, and Walter never brought up the subject with me at any time, until now, when it is all in the past and Reinhard is dead. You wrote of your "political naiveté"; I realise I had also been politically naive during those times when I was blindly following Reinhard's dictates.

Your comments about the possibility of a careful defensive withdrawal from certain territories in the east and arranging some compromise with the western powers are not so wide of the mark but such thoughts are best not put in writing and better left unexpressed until we meet. Here in the Ausland SD I am privy to all sorts of information I did not have in the RSHA where the focus was on internal matters. Even so, I understand Herr Dr Goebbels has been rebuffed by the Führer in his attempts to lead the committee in charge of prosecuting the war on the home front with greater discipline and determination. That has now gone to a triumvirate: Bormann, of course; Hans-Heinrich Lammers, head of the Reich Chancery, and Field Marshal Wilhelm Keitel, well-known for agreeing with everything the Führer says. Goebbels feels shut out and his influence is waning. All he has personally succeeding in doing so far is shutting down Horcher's restaurant and annoying a lot of people. However, I hear it is to be reopened as a club for Luftwaffe officers on the insistence of Göring so you will still be able to eat there when you come on leave.

It is hard to say just how Bormann has acquired such influence with the Führer, except that he is constantly on hand twenty-four hours of the day and has a great knack for ameliorating the Führer's moods if things go wrong. As Hess's Chief of Staff he was well placed to step into the deputy Führer's shoes when Hess defected to Britain and, of course, he has always been in control of the Führer's private financial affairs. Their association goes back a long way and the Führer is godfather to at least one of Bormann's ten children! Himmler made a great tactical mistake last year when he approached Bormann for a loan of 80,000 Marks from Party funds in order to provide for his mistress, Hedwig Potthast, and the two children he has fathered by her. This played right into Bormann's hands so that any approach to the Führer now has to be made through B's good offices. Walter has an amusing description of the two of them: he says Himmler is like "a stork in a lily pond" and Bormann "a pig in a potato field".

Talking of Bormann's brood reminds me to tell you, briefly, about my experience within the *Lebensborn* programme. It was all over within three days. I attended a remote clinic in the country, some 60 km south of Berlin, near Cottbus overlooking the Spree, a very pleasant location. I was introduced to a young blonde woman of good appearance, a farmer's daughter she told me, from Swabia. We were conducted to a small room with a large bed and washing facilities and left to our own devices. I was not there more than an hour. She thanked me very politely, I signed various papers, including one that stipulated I had no wish to be further involved with the woman although I shall be informed as to whether the impregnation was successful. Now I am able to tell the Reichsführer-SS that I have done my duty – at least for the time being.

I agree; Stalingrad was a disaster (we have still not been told all of what happened). We must hope that the summer offensive now being planned will rectify matters on the eastern front and finally smash the Red Colossus. I think we may have to accept defeat in the North African arena, unless Rommel can pull off something brilliant, but the Anglo-Americans and their allies have numerical superiority in all materials and trying to supply our land forces via Sicily, Sardinia and Greece is a serious drain on our resources. After all, we have only been defending the Italian empire, not our own, although the grand strategy of taking Egypt and meeting up in Persia with our armies coming down through the Caucasus would have been a tremendous blow to the enemy. Now we must concentrate on defending southern Europe and the Balkans. Things would have been much more in our favour if Spain and Turkey had thrown in their lot with us.

I have been enjoying riding in the Tiergarten with the SS Riding Club. When you are next on leave you must join us. Do you still have your riding kit? If not I am sure we can fit you out. My adjutant is waiting to take my mail so I must stop writing. As always, send your letters to the Kaisestraße address.

Every good wish,

Your affectionate brother,
Christian

From: Countess Edith Novarro-Badaelli
Villa Frascati
Via Augusta
Rome
To: Hauptmann Peter von Vorzik
III Gruppe JG233
Darmstadt-Griesheim

4th April 1943

My Dear Peter,

I was so pleased to have your letter, something of a ray of sunshine in what has proved to be a rather bleak winter although the spring here now is really beautiful. On the diplomatic front here, however, everything is in a state of flux. Rumours abound and there is much coming and going at the Palazzo Chigi, the royal residence at the Villa Savoia and the Vatican. Arturo is still with

Ciano. You ask why he was dismissed as foreign minister – Arturo says it was because he has been so outspoken about Mussolini's direction of the war and how Italy is dominated by us, the Germans. Anyway, as ambassador to the Holy See Ciano has been ensconced in a grand palazzo on the Via Flaminia where he receives a constant stream of generals and admirals, cardinals and papal envoys. In particular there have been several visits from Cardinal Luigi Maglione, the papal Secretary of State. According to Arturo, who talks very little about what is going on, one of the persistent rumours is that Ciano is trying to arrange a separate peace with the British and Americans. Anfuso (who was Ciano's office favourite for years) has returned from Bucharest and says that Ciano rushes from meetings at the Vatican to Giuseppe Bottai (who has also been dismissed from the government) to General Carboni and General Castelloni, both of them known dissidents against the regime. I realise these names won't mean much to you but they have figured largely in my life this last month and I have even had to entertain them at the house! Obviously, the military situation in North Africa adds to the general feeling that events here are moving towards some sort of climax, but exactly what that is, is impossible to tell. Arturo is naturally worried; he comes home very late, exhausted, and I try not to question him.

I have made two more visits to the orphanage, once with Eleanora and once by myself to make a very small personal donation towards the appeal for the restoration of the chapel which is badly in need of repair. I find it something of a refuge from all the diplomatic talk and activity, the children representing an aspect of the real world amongst so much political theorising. Yesterday Arturo and I attended a memorial service for Massimo at St Peter's. Very sad but very impressive, wonderful singing by the double choir in Cavalli's *Requiem*, many diplomatic and army people present, Eleanora and her daughters pale behind their black veils. Eleanora is considering going to live in Switzerland with her sister who is married to a rich banker in the Italian area of Ticino. Apparently, they have a large 12-bedroom house overlooking Lake Maggiore. Eleanora says the war is getting closer and closer to Italy and with the bombing of Milan, Turin and Genoa her nerves have gone to pieces since the death of Massimo. She wants the peace and quiet – and safety – of Switzerland. There will be no difficulty in getting an extended visa, having a close relative already a resident and in any case money buys everything. I think she thinks that Eloise and Elisabetta might find rich husbands there, too!

Have you received your new aircraft yet? And do you know where you might be posted? I do hope and pray, dearest brother, that you will not be sent back to Russia.

We have acquired a goat and some chickens, all to help the domestic food situation. Provisions are not so easy to obtain as they were just a few months ago although luxury foods are still available for those who can pay for them. While I long for peace I do wonder just what lies in store for us. Arturo says Africa is lost and it is only a matter of time before the British, Americans and Russians prevail. I am sure, although he does not say so, that he agrees with Ciano and thinks we should sue for an armistice. Meanwhile, dear Peter, I know you face the obligation to do your duty in defence of the Reich and, as always, I pray for your safety and that of your loved ones.

Write when you can.

Ever your loving sister,
Edith

From: Hauptmann Peter von Vorzik
III Gruppe JG233
Darmstadt-Griesheim
To: Mathilde von Vorzik
23 Hevelius Straße
Grunewald

7th April 1943

My Darling Mathilde,
It was lovely to receive – and smell! – your letter. Je Reviens perfumed my whole bunkroom and triggered a hundred wonderful, intimate memories. Memories of our first meeting, of our times in the Hotel Orpheus in Cologne (I wonder if it survived the bombing?), of our trip to Paris and a score of other times when we have been physically close to each other.

We are promised our new aircraft any day now, they will be ferried in straight from the WNF works. There is no news about any possible posting so I presume we shall be doing all our retraining and working-up here at Darmstadt. Much depends on what is happening on the battle fronts, of course. Some units, I know, have been sent from France to Sicily and Tunisia and others are reforming on the eastern fronts. We must wait and see. We have received a whole new intake of pilots fresh from the flying schools and I begin to think of myself and the few comrades who remain from the early days of the Geschwader as old men! It will take some time and hard work to get them into shape as a fighting force, they have had a much shorter training period than I received and they will be flying much more advanced aircraft than they have been used to. We will have to cram into six weeks what, ideally, should take six months.

My darling, I do not want to sound alarmist or pessimistic but it might be as well if you arranged to clean up the cellar as an air-raid refuge. You will need to stock it with cans of food, bottles of water, a change of clothing for yourself, Wolfchen and Lenka and some basic first-aid material, bandages, iodine, ointment and a sharp knife or pair of scissors. You should also keep a bag with all important documents, ration books, birth and marriage certificates, cheque books and so on. Put an oil or electric heater down there to make it less damp (electricity might be cut off); when I went down for firewood just after Christmas I met a large toad, remember? Put down a couple of rugs, some old chairs, books and candles just to make it habitable in case there might be a heavy raid on Berlin. I think it very unlikely – the cost in planes and crews would be very high for the British – and Grunewald is very safe but just one or two bombers off course could cause local damage and it is always as well to be prepared for unforseen eventualities.

Belated congratulations, darling, for passing your driving test! I did not doubt that you could do it. However, do not venture out after dark unless it is really necessary. Driving in the blackout has many dangers with such negative visibility.

Christian seems very happy now that he is with the Ausland SD and it has given him what he calls "a wholly different perspective". With his snippets of information and the observations that Edith makes about the political situation in Italy it becomes more and more difficult not to feel cynical about some of the Axis leaders. I am so glad I never responded to Christian's suggestion that I transfer to the SS or even became an active Party member. I realise the Luftwaffe is not free of politics in its upper echelons but at Staffel level life seems quite straightforward!

Varasch has just arrived in my tiny bunkroom and, smelling the perfume, has jokingly asked if I have been entertaining a lady friend here! He has invited me to join him for a drink in the mess with some of the new recruits and reminds me that the Staffel post collection goes in three minutes. So, darling,

In haste, kisses to you and Wolfchen.

Ever your loving husband,
Peter

Hauptmann Peter von Vorzik
Journal entry

16th April 1943

Great excitement! Our new aircraft have at last arrived, proving to be Me109G-6s. No cockpit pressurisation, however, which is probably just as well, just another complication for both pilots and ground crew to deal with. Compared to our Friedrichs there are pluses and minuses. The Gustav's engine, the DB605AM, is provided with methanol/water injection to the supercharger, giving tremendous power boost and therefore extra speed for short periods but, of course, the engine is heavier than in the F Series and thus necessitates heavier engine-bearers. The all-up weight of the fighter is increased so that while the speed is greater the manoeuvrability is lesser. However, our main purpose with these machines, as explained to us in detailed briefings, is to intercept and destroy the expected American daylight bombers so that the sort of agility needed in fighter-to-fighter combat is not so important. Personally, I much prefer the F Series, a more responsive, refined aeroplane but there is no doubt the Gustav is a formidable machine. Basic armament is a single hub-firing 20mm MK108 cannon and two nose-mounted MG131 machineguns, the larger breech-blocks forming two distinctive bumps on the upper cowling. There are numerous Rustsätze kits available to vary the armament or to include a bomb load up to 500 kg, all for the purpose of increasing capability as a bomber destroyer. Our job now is to familiarise ourselves with these aircraft and their flying characteristics and develop combat tactics with the new recruits who lack air-time and have very little gunnery experience. The camouflage scheme has changed again: upper wing and tail surfaces are in a rather blurred version of the old dark-and mid-green splinter-form while the fuselage, fin and rudder are a light grey with darker grey mottling. The undersides are light blue. The Staffel emblem is painted under the cockpit, a red shield on which is superimposed a gunsight graticule, and I have had my flying leopard personal emblem painted on the cowling bumps which makes it more prominent. As Staffelkapitan the propeller boss is white and there are white chevrons on the side of the fuselage. Well, there it is. Just how successful we shall prove to be against the anticipated attacks by American bombers remains to be seen but experience has shown that daylight raids without fighter escorts are subject to unsustainable losses and the photographs and silhouettes we have seen of the Boeing B-17 Fortress and Consolidated-Vultee B-24 Liberator show them to be huge and vulnerable targets.

In Tunisia Rommel's Afrika Korps is fighting desperately to defend the city of Tunis. If the city falls then we shall have been defeated in Tunisia and the British and Americans will control all of North Africa. We have heard through intelligence reports that the Luftwaffe has lost large numbers of transport aircraft including the gigantic six-engined Me323s, all shot down by swarms of British and American fighters while attempting to keep Rommel's army supplied. It seems the enemy has air superiority through sheer weight of numbers as well as command of the sea. Continuing to defend Tunis seems a terrible waste of men and material. The loss of almost the whole of North Africa, particularly Libya, has created something of a political crisis in Italy. Mussolini seems discredited and there also seems to be a growing dissatisfaction with the Axis alliance. I glean this from Edith's letters (Ciano, too, has been demoted) and from various newspaper reports that tell of unrest within the political-military factions in Rome. Italy has proved to be something of a liability for us throughout the war and in some ways it might be to our advantage to be rid of this Fascist partner.

Our main preoccupation remains the Russian threat. It appears the Führer is planning one big final push this summer that will at last destroy the Communist giant, then we can turn all our attention to the Anglo-American enemies. We are building powerful new types of U-boat which should defeat the Atlantic convoys and, as I have seen at Rechlin, we are developing war-winning aeroplanes that will give us superiority in the air. Africa may be lost but Europe is still ours and we will make it into an impregnable fortress.

From: Mathilde von Vorzik
23 Hevelius Straße
Grunewald
To: Hauptmann Peter von Vorzik
III Gruppe JG233
Darmstadt-Griesheim

21st April 1943

My Darling Peter,

So pleased to have your letter and know you will continue to be stationed at Darmstadt for the next month or two. My greatest fear is that you will be sent back to Russia. Although I know other fronts can be just as dangerous, somehow Russia seems so much more menacing, so vast, so unfathomable, and so uncivilised. Several of my sewing circle friends have relations on the eastern front and have horrible tales to tell.

Lenka has been writing to her father and brother for months now, sending them small parcels, socks and mittens she has knitted, little cakes, bars of our terrible soap and so on, without ever having a reply. This morning she received an official notification from the Hauptamt Volkdeutsche Mittelstelle in the Warthegau, signed by the secretary to SS–Obergruppenführer Ulrich Greifelt, to say that they have been transferred from Theresienstadt to another camp for "political prisoners" called Auschwitz-Birkenau. Included in the letter was the instruction that further correspondence was forbidden. Of course, Lenka was very upset to be told that her relatives were incommunicado. She kept saying, "But they are not politically minded, let alone activists." I did not tell her but I phoned Christian to ask his advice and to see if anything could be done to obtain some form of communication, however brief. Christian was quite curt. "Don't try and pursue the matter any further," he said, and after another word or two he rang off. Later he rang back and apologised for being brusque but it had been an awkward time for him to speak. He said in any case he could not interfere in such matters, especially as he was no longer in the RSHA and that failing to conform to the notification would only make things much worse "for both parties." It is very distressing for Lenka not to be able to communicate with her relatives.

Darling, I have taken your advice and adapted the cellar as an air-raid shelter. Lenka was very helpful, especially in cleaning and sweeping out – such a mess! Quite apart from having it as a refuge, I am glad to have it cleaned up. I have put in everything you specified and I have bought one of those little portable radios to keep there so that we can listen to news bulletins. Unfortunately the reception is not too good so it is not suitable for listening to music. Wolfchen says new words every day now and sometimes even puts two words together. He is such a bright little boy, quite in advance of one or two other children who are some weeks older than he is.

I had a letter from Edith. She seems very anxious about the way things are developing in Rome, mainly because of the situation in Tunisia. Of course the Italians have lost their east African colonies and now Libya so the war has been a disaster for them. Edith made no mention of having a baby although I know she hoped and expected to be pregnant by now. Soon after she was married she wrote to me in confidence to say that Arturo was a very passionate lover, something that she found difficult to cope with at first. I got the impression that by "passionate" she meant "violent". They are both anxious to have children and I do hope she is not troubled by gynaecological problems as poor Frieda was – I cannot believe that it is almost a year to the day since she died.

Wolfchen is waiting for his lunch so I will close now and post this on our way to Frau Kirschner.

All my love, darling, kisses from us both.

Ever your own,
Mathilde

PS I only put the smallest drop of scent on my previous letter, I'm surprised that it perfumed your whole bunkroom! M.

From: Hauptmann Peter von Vorzik
III Gruppe JG233
Darmstadt-Griesheim
To: Contessa Edith Novarro-Badaelli
Villa Frascati
Via Augusta
Rome

14th May 1943

My Dear Edith,
As always such a pleasure to have your letter although I realise the situation for you in Rome must now be a difficult one. Even as I write

the radio is full of reports of how the German and Italian forces have "fought their last and most glorious battle" in Tunisia. What such words mean, of course, is that we have been thrown out of North Africa with all that that entails in the prosecution of the war. Now, the whole Axis coastline in the south is threatened and the Anglo-American forces are free to choose where they might land next, from southern France to the coast of Greece. Italy would seem the obvious target and whatever Mussolini's indiscretions might be, or whichever generals and politicians are hurrying in and out of Ciano's office, as you described in your last letter, is of little consequence. As usual it is us, the Germans, who will have to face the expected onslaught, wherever it comes.

I am so very glad, dear sister, that Rome has been declared an open city but I would not count too much on that! The British and Americans are quite capable of saying that the city is a legitimate industrial target. Is it not possible for you to go somewhere remote, such as the Italian Alps? Or perhaps go with Eleanora to Switzerland? Now it is my turn to be anxious about your welfare, although I suppose the diplomatic corps are always given a certain amount of protection. In retrospect I wonder if it was such a good idea to lease Adlersee to the Luftwaffe; the Schloss would have been a wonderful remote and safe place for all the family to go to should it be necessary. I am sure Christian knows enough people – Dr Dollmann, for example – who could arrange a transfer for Arturo, for him to become an attaché of some sort in Berlin where it is certain you would be safer than in Rome. Let me know what you think.

We are in the midst of training our new young pilots for the expected attacks by American bomber fleets operating from England which have already targeted Wilhelmshaven and Emden. This means devising a whole new combat system. There is no avoiding the reality that, whereas for the last three years our operations have been offensive, we are now having to think defensively. On most fronts we are outnumbered and in the east it is extraordinary how the Russians have been able to introduce so many new types in such numbers. Apparently, they managed to transport whole factories beyond the Urals as well as setting up new ones. This is certainly going to be a decisive year in so many areas and the final destruction of the Russian forces must be our primary aim. I think it extremely unlikely that the Anglo-Americans will ever be able to set foot in Europe successfully, but their declaration last January that they demand "total surrender" from us means that we will be fighting them to the death. Ciano's attempts to achieve a separate peace, as you suggested in your letter, will come to nothing.

I confess I was amused by your news that you have acquired a goat and some chickens! I have tried to imagine you milking the goat and plucking a chicken (not to mention wringing its neck) and found it difficult. I am sure you will leave such tasks to the servants. But it is a good idea, I might even suggest it to Mathilde. I am sure her girl, Lenka, is conversant with such bucolic ways. Your visits to the orphanage must be a stark contrast to the diplomatic milieu that you encounter every day. You always had a concern for the less fortunate – I remember you petitioning father (via mother!) for the benefit of some farm workers who you thought were underpaid and insisting on a Christmas party for the children on the estate. Do you talk to the children at the orphanage or just to the nuns?

Now I must go and attend a lecture, more intelligence information about the growing threat from the American bombers. Do not be over-anxious about such things, I have seen some amazing aircraft we have that will win the war for us.

Ever your loving brother,
Peter

From: Hauptmann Peter von Vorzik
III Gruppe JG233
Darmstadt-Griesheim
To: Oberleutnant Lother Köhl
II Gruppe ZG26L
Fliegerkorps VIII

18th May 1943

Dear Lother,
Already it is over two months since I had your welcome letter and much has happened in the interim. First, I do hope that by now you have had that long-awaited leave and rest you hoped for. You must have been soul-sick of Russia by the time your Geschwader was withdrawn from the Don front. Your harrowing account of the circumstances at Stalingrad is but one among many that I have subsequently heard, a ghastly debacle that

should never have taken place. Looking back I realise how singularly lucky I was that my Geschwader was sent to Sicily and North Africa though much good it has done us! Here at Darmstadt we are busy working-up with new recruits (with minimum training) to face the expected attacks by the American bomber fleets that we are told are assembling in England. Apparently they rely for defence on a curtain of fire from each aircraft's battery of ten or twelve heavy machineguns. It sounds formidable but on the other hand they represent a huge target and we are experimenting with all sorts of measures and tactics including rockets and (would you believe it) dropping bombs with delayed fuses into the middle of their formations! Whether such ideas will work remains to be seen. What I know for sure, after a visit to Rechlin, is that we have some sensational aircraft under development which are far in advance of anything the enemy has. I just wish they were here now! As it is, we have at last received our 109Gs. I cannot pretend I like them as much as the F Series; faster, heavier, more of an effort to fly, but no doubt they will prove themselves in the tasks we have been given.

I am wondering if you have been re-equipped with the 410s? I saw some at Rechlin and was told all (or most) of the problems that afflicted the 210s have been solved. It must have been dispiriting to have kept on flying the same machines you had three years ago. At least our 109s have been constantly developed. We are just getting in the reports on the RAF's raid on the Ruhr dams the night before last. Apparently they have created really bad floods and considerable dislocation of transport though I suppose I must not write of that. They lost more than a third of their bombers but one must acknowledge that it was a brave and daring operation cleverly accomplished. Here in Darmstadt we have been on the edge of several British raids on the Ruhr, the night-time pyrotechnics and searchlight beams clearly visible in the distance. No doubt our turn will come. Assuming you had leave, I hope you found your home in one piece and your parents safe and sound? According to reports Essen and Dortmund have been badly hit. I can well understand that you were not tempted by the Russian and Polish ladies on offer! Have you perhaps found some nice young girl to replace your unfaithful Hannelore? I count myself so fortunate to have found a darling wife, the thought of her has been a marvellous way of sustaining morale during some recent trying times, though anxiety for her welfare (and that of my son) is the reverse side of the coin. On balance I am very happy with my married state although I can understand the attitude of some of my colleagues, especially the younger ones who have just joined us, who say they will wait until the war is over before committing themselves to a permanent liaison.

Hoping that all goes well with you, do write when you can.

Ever your sincere comrade,

Peter

From: Hauptmann Peter von Vorzik
III Gruppe JG233
Darmstadt-Griesheim
To: SS-Gruppenführer Count Christian von Vorzik
116 Kaiserstraße
Berlin

28th May 1943

Dear Christian,

Once again I find myself apologising for taking nearly a month to reply to your last letter. I was very interested to hear about the background to your appointment to the Ausland SD and of the interdepartmental rivalries and antagonisms. I am sure (I know) that such things occur within the upper echelons of the Luftwaffe but as a mere Staffelkapitan I only hear of them as they filter down through the ranks weeks, months, later and then with accretions in the telling. Perhaps you will find your new position a little more – what shall I say? – relaxed? I mean one hears (more gossip and rumour!) that throughout the RSHA Reinhard was a feared taskmaster and your friendship with Walter S. must place your working relationship on a less formal basis – after all, he was best man at your wedding. I have been very fortunate in serving under Staffelkapitans and Geschwader Kommandants who were always accessible and affable however fraught the circumstances. It must be one of the acknowledged laws of anthropology that the higher one goes up the leadership scale so the degree of deviousness increases, but I think it best not to elaborate on that line of thought.

So: we have lost North Africa! A thousand pities and a terrible waste of men and material, not to mention the strategic advantage it gives our enemies. Perhaps, in the long run, it will prove a good thing, for while presenting problems it does simplify matters. Now we are free to concentrate on Europe, particularly in the east which, after all, has been our main concern. We can afford to shorten our lines, focus our forces and defeat our enemies piecemeal, first the Russians and then the Anglo-Americans. If necessary Italy is expendable. The Balkan nations are as anti-Russian as we are and will be useful as buffer states. Or am I, once again, being naive in my views? What I am sure about is that if only Spain and Turkey had had the sense and courage to come in with us we would not have been defeated in North Africa. What do you think?

Your *Lebensborn* experience appears to have been as clinical and impersonal as one supposed. I admire you for performing such a duty; personally, I do not know that I could and if I did I think I would be consumed with curiosity about the child. Incidentally, how extraordinary that Bormann has ten children! If, as you say, he is the Führer's shadow twenty-four hours a day how did he find the time to propagate so profusely? Edith appears to have become closely involved with an orphanage in Rome; she always had a very pronounced social conscience. Perhaps, if she is blessed with a child (I do not think one is expected yet) her concern with the orphanage will be deflected. Because of the political situation in Italy (again, one hears such rumours) I am concerned about her welfare in Rome. Do you think she and Arturo should make an effort to get away somewhere? I am sure he could be moved from Ciano's entourage to be, say, cultural attaché in Berlin. I understand Eleanora has plans to go to Switzerland and take her daughters with her. Could you have a word with your SS friend Dr Dollmann to keep an eye on Edith in an unobtrusive way?

I am delighted with the news that the Reichsführer has had Horcher's re-opened for Luftwaffe officers. On my next leave you must let me take you for dinner there; I have always thought it was the best food in Berlin, better even than the Eden and Adlon hotels. How splendid to be riding in the Tiergarten in this spring weather! I envy you that and will certainly take you up on your offer during my next leave although I will have to borrow some riding kit. I do not know what happened to the clothes in my dressing room when the Luftwaffe took over Adlersee, they were probably packed in trunks and now reek of mothballs!

Please write again when you are able.

Ever your affectionate brother,
Peter

From: *Hauptmann Peter von Vorzik*
III Gruppe JG233
Darmstadt-Griesheim
To: *Mathilde von Vorzik*
23 Hevelius Straße
Grunewald

7th June 1943

My Darling Mathilde,

How can it be June already and your last letter to me posted in April! Forgive me, darling, for being so tardy in replying. I try to keep up with my correspondence but Staffel affairs take up so much time and we have been so very busy training with the new young pilots, trying to cram in a few weeks what, ideally, should take months. They come to us as very raw recruits, only just able to handle the aircraft and really needing much more flying time before we try out new tactics. But there it is, we can only do so much with what we are given. As it is the weather has not helped with lots of unseasonal low cloud and there have also been some technical problems to contend with. I am very glad, darling, that you have made a refuge in the cellar. As I said in my previous letter, you may not need it but it is good to have it there if only for my peace of mind!

We have been told to be in readiness for a move within the coming week or two. I do not think it will be Russia as all our training has been towards defeating expected attacks by American bomber fleets which, as you may have heard on the radio, have raided French and Baltic coastal areas. Their area of operations is limited to the range of their accompanying fighters. It would seem likely, therefore, that we will be posted somewhere in France or within the German borders.

I am sorry for Lenka. It must be worrying for her not to be able to communicate with her relatives. However, although she says they are not "politically active", in these times the authorities cannot be too careful and her father and brother may have affiliations she is not aware of. Look what happened to Reinhard in Prague!

How I wish I could be with you and Wolfchen! These years when he is changing from a baby into a little boy are really fascinating, hearing him learn and use new words, watching him start to handle toys and objects

457

with growing competence, his character developing (I am quoting Felix Goschke, one of my ground crew, who has four children, three boys and a girl). I've always been somewhat bored when Felix has talked about his children and shown me photographs, now, as a father, I am happy to listen and even ask questions! Have you taken any new pictures of Wolfchen? Do not rely on studio portraits but use that camera of mine and take lots of snapshots. I had a brief phase of interest in photography when I was sixteen and an uncle (now deceased) gave me that Leica as a birthday present but enthusiasm soon faded. Now we must record Wolfchen's early years, especially as I am not there to see much of them. I would also like a new one of you, darling, for my wallet. The last one is now somewhat creased and torn from much perusal! Show Lenka how to use the camera so she can photograph both you and Wolfchen and both together.

You say in your last letter that Edith told you that Arturo is "passionate" in his love-making. It is surprising, then, that there is no sign of Edith being pregnant. Do you think one of them is infertile?

I will let you know our new address, darling, as soon as we are settled into our new posting. Until then, continue to write to this one which will find me.

All my love, many kisses to you both.

Ever your own,

Peter

Peter von Vorzik
Journal entry

14th June 1943

Whenever the opportunity occurs I go across to Geschwader HQ to view their large wallmaps, covered with coloured pins and flags, which show the current situation on all the battlefronts. Mostly, of course, they show the deployment of Luftwaffe units but they also indicate the fluctuating fortunes of land forces, both our own and those of our enemies and even, in some cases, naval operations including attacks on enemy convoys by our own land and sea-based aircraft as well as U-boat dispositions. In the Mediterranean the Anglo-Americans have bombarded into submission the tiny Italian island of Pantelleria – an obvious stepping-stone to Sicily. The defendants of the island received non-stop aerial attacks for six days as well as bombardment from naval guns, after which, with practically all defensive weapons destroyed, the island surrendered. From all reports the aerial bombing was even more concentrated than our attacks on Malta last year. I cannot but reflect on how circumstances have changed in a mere twelve months. Then we were subjecting Malta to constant bombardment prior to the Afrika Korps advancing across Cyrenaica towards Egypt. Now we have been driven out of North Africa altogether and the Anglo-Americans are poised to invade Sicily from where we attacked Malta! How I wish I was based in Sicily now to help defend the island, flying from that very base in Catania from which we mounted our own attacks.

In Russia, following our retaking the city of Kharkov last March, our forces are surrounding the big salient at Kursk. In the north General von Kluge's 9th Army stands ready; in the south General von Manstein has three Panzer divisions equipped with our latest Panther and Tiger tanks – superior to the Russian's T34s and KV85s. In the centre is the 2nd Army. General Jeschonnek, the Chief of the Air Staff, has massed various Luftwaffe units, including several Stuka Geschwader, around the area from Orel in the north to Belgorod in the south. And so we wait now for our third summer offensive which we hope and believe will drive the Russians back again to the Don and Volga rivers and even, perhaps, finally destroy their fighting potential.

Over Germany the RAF has made very heavy attacks on cities in the Ruhr, especially Essen, but our night fighters have taken an equally heavy toll of those intruders and while they have destroyed hundreds of homes and killed many civilians, the military targets – armament and aircraft factories, railway yards and various refineries – have escaped serious damage. Just how long the British will be able to maintain these raids while suffering such devastating losses of aircraft and aircrew remains to be seen. I understand from the intelligence personnel I sometimes talk to that many of our factories have been moved east and others situated deep underground and that production of all types of war material continues to increase. This is mainly due to the brilliant organisational ability of Albert Speer, Minister for Armaments. I remember being shown around his architectural office in Berlin and seeing the impressive plans and models he had devised for the projected redevelopment of the city. Who would have thought an architect would have proved so efficient at organising industry? Now we await the expected attacks from American

bombers which, we hope, will prove as ineffective as those of the RAF. At
sea, our U-boat flotillas, after great successes during the winter, have since
suffered terrible losses which I deduce from the numerous pins dotted
across the Atlantic, each one denoting a U-boat sunk. The pins showing
enemy ships sunk are significantly fewer. It is as if both sides are taking a
deep breath before renewed confrontation, the calm before more storms:
our offensive in the east; the Anglo-Americans attacking in the
Mediterranean; new battles in the air. This is, no doubt, a time of decision
as to who will win the war.

From: Contessa Edith Navarro-Badaelli
Villa Frascati
Via Augusta
Rome
To: Hauptmann Peter von Vorzik
III Gruppe JG233
Darmstadt-Griesheim

28th June 1943

My Dear Peter,

It was most encouraging to have your letter in these troubling times. I do
feel rather isolated here now – I mean being German in Italy. Arturo is
kept frantically busy hurrying here and there at Ciano's bidding. The city
is full of rumours and formal and informal gatherings tend to divide into
factions, pro- and anti-fascist. At a recent diplomatic reception given by
the Japanese (peculiar food!) I was approached by SS-Colonel Helfferich,
a member of General von Rintelen's staff as the German Military Attaché
here, and questioned in a very roundabout way about Ciano's reported
interest in a possible separate peace with the Anglo-Americans. Of course
I professed to have no such knowledge but it is indicative of the general
disquiet in military and political circles here when such questions are
directed at me, a relative newcomer to the diplomatic scene, from a
German official! Everybody seems suspicious of everybody else. At the
same time as Mussolini dismissed Ciano as foreign minister he also
dismissed one of Ciano's great friends, Carmine Senise, the chief of police.
But Ciano has other friends in positions of power and, Arturo says, he is
waiting for the right moment to strike, by which I presume he means

deposing Mussolini. You ask if I could not go somewhere remote from Rome while everything is in such a state of flux but I could not leave Arturo here alone to face whatever may happen. Arturo's loyalty is to Ciano (their friendship goes back decades) and mine is to Arturo so, at present, there is no question of our leaving the city. Arturo says Edda Ciano has returned from Sicily where she has been nursing the wounded and looks quite exhausted. There is very little contact between her and her husband now and she still receives her lover, Emilio Pucci, when Ciano is away. Their loyalties certainly seem divided.

Yes, dear brother, you are quite right to assume that I do not milk the goat or even gather the eggs! The goat and chickens have been a great success. From Bathsheba (the goat) the cook has made delicious cheese and the chickens provide us with a plentiful supply of eggs. The food situation has become very difficult these last few weeks since the British and Americans have been bombing cities in the north and disrupting transport. We still receive what most people would now consider luxuries: Parma ham and various cooked meats, venison and game birds, and fresh fish is always available. The orphanage, by comparison, is frugally served. They live on small amounts of pasta, a little cheese, tomatoes and fruit and when winter comes their situation will be very difficult. On my visits I sometimes manage to smuggle in a few bits and pieces, mostly leftovers from our own table when we have had a reception or dinner party – which is not often now. Yes, I try and talk to the children when they are not at their lessons or prayers but they are mostly very shy, probably because of my accent, and find it difficult to answer my questions about their backgrounds. Very few of them have recollections of mothers or fathers or elder siblings. The nuns are embarrassingly grateful for the little I do and I find myself in the position of replacing Eleanora now that she has gone to Switzerland. I have been asked to join the Board of Governors which I may do, depending on what happens here in Rome. So, that is my news, such as it is. We await developments in the military and political situation with some trepidation.

Do write when you can.

Always your loving sister,
Edith

From: Mathilde von Vorzik
23 Hevelius Straße
Grunewald
To: Hauptmann Peter von Vorzik
III Gruppe JG233
Darmstadt-Griesheim

2nd July 1943

My Darling Peter,

As it was some time since I last heard from you it was a great relief to have your letter and to know all was well. I had begun to wonder if perhaps you had had an accident during your training sessions. Please do not think, darling, that this is in any way a reproach, it is just that, as you know so well, I am always anxious for your safety. I do realise how busy you have been training your new young pilots. Here, enclosed, are the snapshots of Wolfchen and myself that you asked for. As you see, neither Lenka nor myself are very good photographers but I feel sure you will like the one that Lenka took of Wolfchen and me in the garden and the ones I took of Wolfchen carefully making a tower with his building bricks. I adore his look of concentration as he places the last one on top! Photographic materials are getting very scarce but the chemist is an old friend of mother's and let me have two rolls from his "private" stock. I told him I wanted to photograph Wolfchen for his father who is a fighter pilot and I think that is why he gave me two rolls! He was very sad to hear mother had been killed during the bombing of Cologne. He is anxious to retire but says he needs the money to look after his wife who is disabled after a stroke. Their only son is with the Wehrmacht in Norway which, he says, is a fairly safe posting.

Something very unpleasant happened at the sewing circle the other day. One of the younger women broke down in tears because her husband has been posted missing on the eastern front. She said we had lost the war and the Russians will be invading Germany at which Frau Kirschner told her to be quiet. However, she went on crying and saying we had lost the war until Frau K. sent her home. Two days later I heard that the Gestapo had taken her and her small son (he is about a year older than Wolfchen) away because Frau K. had denounced her to the People's Court as a defeatist. The atmosphere at the sewing circle is now very quiet and subdued and nobody discusses the war any more or even comments on everyday things such as where one can obtain sausages and liver off the ration. Frau K. might denounce us for buying on the black market! I must say I have never really liked Frau K., she is so school-mistressy and her smile always seems false, without warmth. I would like to find an excuse to stop attending the sewing circle and do something more useful. Now that I can drive perhaps I could drive an ambulance or something. Some women are doing it, even driving trams! What do you think, darling? I must say that although I have been friendly with some in the sewing circle, especially the women with small children, none of them have become close friends. I miss Lina very much (she is still at Fehmarn) and Edith and Frieda. Lenka has turned out to be very companionable but, of course, she is more of a servant and her conversation is limited although we both listen to the Sunday evening request concerts on the radio together. The weather has been very hot this week and the vegetables in the garden are growing apace. Lenka and I have been watering them each evening and even Wolfchen has a little watering can too (you can see it in one of the snapshots) although he gets more water over his feet than over the plants!

Now, darling, I must go and queue at the post office (there is only one clerk there now and it takes ages to be served); I am anxious you should get the snaps as soon as possible.

All our fondest love and kisses from

Mathilde and Wolfchen

From: SS-Gruppenführer Count Christian von Vorzik
116 Kaiserstraße
Berlin
To: Hauptmann Peter von Vorzik
III Gruppe JG233
Darmstadt-Griesheim

8th July 1943

Dear Peter,

Many thanks for your last letter. You were right in thinking that my work in the Ausland SD is somewhat less onerous than it was in the RSHA, for several reasons. For one thing, Walter and I have always had a great rapport and working with him is certainly very different to working with Reinhard. I always had great respect for Reinhard; he commanded the RSHA with tremendous professionalism and made it into the most efficient element of the SS but, to be honest, I always felt that there was a lack of trust on his part, that one's work was continually scrutinised for some failure to conform, some deviousness that went against his dictates. With Walter there is complete understanding, total agreement about our objectives and the means to achieve them that makes for an agreeable atmosphere within the department. Incidentally, he often asks for news of you and sends his best wishes for your continued success in the front-line, as it were. He has great admiration for everyone directly engaged in hostilities.

I, too, have some misgivings about Edith's situation in Rome. As it happens we are concerned about the activities of a certain high-ranking individual in the Abwehr (I will not mention his name at this point) who has been in suspiciously close contact with General Amé, head of the Italian Secret Service, whose commitment to continuing the war alongside Germany has been called into question. Because of this Walter has asked me to go to Rome and confer with Dr Dollmann which will give me a perfect opportunity to visit Edith and review her (and Arturo's) situation at first hand. I am leaving for Rome tomorrow and expect to be there for some days. On my return I will let you know the details of the situation. Personally, I would deem it wise for Edith to return to Berlin and I am sure arrangements could be made for Arturo to find a position here. We shall see.

As you say, Edith has always had a highly developed social conscience allied to her deep commitment to the Catholic faith so I am not surprised that she has involved herself with the orphanage that Eleanora was attached to. I just hope that they do not take advantage of her innate kindness and that she is not inveigled into parting with considerable sums of money. I know that her private income (separate from Arturo's and based on the provision from father's will) is comparatively small and she may have need of financial security in the future as far as it can be defined. I shall discuss these matters with her when we meet.

I looked upon my part in the *Lebensborn* programme purely as a necessary service to the State (and as a sop to the Reichsführer-SS) and successfully managed to submerge all emotional feelings with regard to the young woman involved and curiosity about the child. (I have since been informed that she has conceived and that her condition proceeds satisfactorily.) It was, as you say, impersonal and clinical, a duty done. I reserve my emotional involvement for such time as I shall again become a husband and, I hope, a father.

Your comments on the current situation of the war make sense. It is imperative that we finally defeat Russia this year so that we are free to deal with the Anglo-American threat. Italy may prove a running sore (has, in some ways, already done so) and if necessary we may need to lance the poison. Loyalty to allies can only be taken so far. Walter and I recently accompanied the Reichsführer-SS to the Führer's HQ at Rastenburg and although we were not present at any of the daily situation conferences I was able to talk to General Field Marshal Keitel and General Jodl, both of whom said that this summer's offensive, already raging around Kursk even as I write, will be decisive. The generals are confident that this will be the knockout blow that we have been waiting for.

Now I must prepare for my journey to Rome tomorrow.

With affectionate good wishes,
Christian

From: Oberleutnant Lother Köhl
I Gruppe Sch.Gl
Eastern Front
To: Hauptmann Peter von Vorzik
III Gruppe JG233
Darmstadt-Griesheim

9th July 1943

Dear Peter,

Thank you for your letter dated 18th May which has finally found me. Here I am, back in the hell-hole that is Russia! I had hoped (after talks with my Kommandant) that I might be transferred to one of the night-fighter Gruppen that are using Me110s back in Germany, but no, because I have so much experience here on the eastern front I have been transferred instead to a Schlachtgeschwader busily attacking Russian armour.

A dozen of us had a month's conversion course at Lippstadt flying Henschel 129Bs. They are horrible aircraft, designed especially for low-level ground assault with a cockpit so narrow and cramped that I can scarcely squeeze into it (as you know, I am not a big man) with poor visibility, sluggish flying characteristics and unreliable, French-built Gnome-Rhône engines that are highly susceptible to dust. I never thought I would hanker to get back into the cockpit of a 110 but, in retrospect, they seem highly desirable! We had a busy time attacking hordes of Russian tanks around Kursk with some success but, as you will know, our efforts did not save the day and we have had to pull back 100 km and our previous airfields are now in Russian hands. It is difficult not to feel despondent.

I certainly envy you flying the 109G, whatever its shortcomings. As I have said to you before, I bitterly regret ever volunteering to fly Zerstörer, look where it has got me! In your letter you mention sensational new aircraft being developed and I think how ironic that is as I gaze out on the airfield at my beastly, untrustworthy 189 being rearmed for another anti-tank sortie.

Well, I finally got my long-awaited leave only to arrive home and find that Aachen had had a devastating raid from the RAF and our home completely destroyed! Thankfully, my parents were in an air-raid shelter and survived in just what they were wearing. They are being temporarily housed in a school hall but they have lost everything including the bakery shop my father owned. During my leave I found accommodation with a kind neighbour two streets away who had only suffered superficial damage to roof and windows. They gave me their son's room (he is stationed in Belgium) so I did at least sleep in clean sheets. But it was not quite the leave I had planned, most of Aachen being just a pile of rubble. Even so, it was nice to see my parents again, to relax (more or less – there were other air-raid warnings but nothing materialised) for a week or two and forget about Russia. Apparently Hannelore and her mother have gone to live somewhere in the south, with a cousin, so I did not see her; neither have I found a substitute. I had a brief fling with a war widow (seven years older than me!) whose husband was killed in Africa but it was not serious for either of us and I doubt if I shall see her again although I have had two letters from her since returning from leave. I think I will wait for the war to be over before I become seriously involved with anyone.

Once again my letter to you seems to be filled with moans and complaints but, honestly, I am hard put to it to find anything to be enthusiastic about. Please continue to write when you can, your letters are a beacon of light!

Yours ever,
Lother

Hauptmann Peter von Vorzik
Journal entry

5th August 1943

Two weeks of such bad news that I am at a loss as to where to begin this sorry account. First, I suppose, I must record a succession of terrible air-raids on Hamburg by the RAF and bombers of the American 8th Air Force. The night raids by the British began on the 24th of July and continued on the 27th and 29th, with daylight raids by the Americans on the 26th and 27th. During the night of the 27th the British dropped both high explosive and incendiary bombs which created a firestorm, a holocaust so great that the city's fire services were completely overwhelmed. The bombers came back on successive days and nights to complete the devastation which, it is calculated, destroyed two-thirds of the city and killed nearly half a million people. Kurt's parents were among those killed, totally atomised by the firestorm, leaving no trace of them or their home. The poor man is distraught and says there is not even the possibility of burying a heap of bones. It is reported that two-thirds of the survivors have had to be evacuated as there is no food or water or medical supplies available for them; it is utter devastation. The general defence system that was organised some time ago by General Josef Kammhuber consisting of three zones of anti-aircraft guns and searchlight units and two radar units controlling night fighters circling a radio beam has hitherto proved immensely effective in destroying a growing percentage of intruding bombers. During these Hamburg raids, however, the enemy dropped thousands of bundles of tinfoil which, fluttering down through the night, completely confused and blinded the radar stations and rendered the whole integrated defence system inoperative.

There are many rumours, supported by Reichsminister Dr Goebbels' Ministry of Propaganda, that we have "wonder weapons" that will wreak revenge on our enemies and I presume these refer to some of the amazing aircraft I saw at Rechlin but there are no signs as yet that they are ready for operational service. Meanwhile, Dr Goebbels has issued a warning that as many women and children as possible should leave Berlin. Although Grunewald is a relatively safe suburb of the city I am anxious to find somewhere for Mathilde and Wolfchen to go that would place them completely out of harm's way. We have some distant (mostly elderly) relatives scattered about Bavaria but I do not think Mathilde would be very happy staying with them although I would be happy knowing that she and Wolfchen were safe.

In Russia our great summer offensive around the Kursk salient has been repelled and our armies are being forced to retreat. According to reports, on the 12th July the SS Panzer Corps encountered the Russians' 5th Guards Tank Army and during the ensuing battle involving over 1,200 tanks the Panzers inflicted heavy losses on the enemy despite being outnumbered. However, the offensive was apparently called off by the Führer who insisted that the 2nd SS Panzer Corps should be sent to engage the British and Americans who have landed in Sicily. Looking at the maps in Geschwader HQ and reading between the lines of the official OKW communiques it would seem that the failure to take Kursk is as significant a defeat as the debacle at Stalingrad. The Russians now appear to have the initiative all along the eastern front. Somewhere, somehow, it has become imperative that we form a strong defensive line against them.

As I write, the British and Americans are in possession of nearly all of Sicily and Field Marshal Albert Kesselring, C.-in-C. of the joint German and Italian forces in the south-west, is preparing to evacuate his troops from the island. As far as I can make out the air base at Catania from which I flew last year is already in Anglo-American hands. Their next step, obviously, will be to make a landing on the Italian mainland. The Anglo-American successes in North Africa and Sicily and the growing threat that they represent has led to an anti-fascist coup in Rome. On 24th July the Fascist Grand Council met at the Palazzo Venezia and spent many hours discussing a motion put forward by Count Dino Grandi requesting King Victor Emmanuel III to take command of the armed forces and the government, effectively deposing Mussolini as dictator. The motion was carried by nineteen votes to seven, Ciano being amongst those who voted against his father-in-law, the Duce. Mussolini was subsequently taken into custody and is being held on the small island of La Maddalena off the coast of Sardinia. The king has appointed Marshal Pietro Badoglio as prime minister and Rafaele Guariglia, previously ambassador to Spain and Turkey, as foreign minister. Badoglio has issued a statement saying that Italy remains at Germany's side and "the war continues." This political upheaval in Italy makes me anxious as to what is happening to Ciano and, by association, to Arturo as part of Ciano's entourage. Meanwhile,

American planes have bombed San Lorenzo, a suburb of Rome, killing many civilians. So much for Rome being an open city.

This, then, is the current picture: a devastating raid on Hamburg which has left the city in ruins; the failure of our Kursk offensive, handing the initiative to the Russians; the Anglo-Americans in practical control of Sicily and threatening the Italian mainland; Mussolini deposed and the Italian political scene in turmoil. If only those secret weapons we hear so much about could make their appearance and transform this depressing outlook.

From: Hauptmann Peter von Vorzik
III Gruppe JG233
Schaftstadt, Halle
To: Mathilde von Vorzik
23 Hevelius Straße
Grunewald

7th August 1943

My Darling Mathilde,
First, this is my new address. We are a lot nearer Berlin, just about 25 km south-west of Halle, nice rolling countryside with pleasant hills – not too high for easy landings! We share the airfield with IV Gruppe JG3 and continue our training, sporadically, waiting for whatever comes.

Second, how happy the new snapshots of your dear self and Wolfchen have made me. I spend hours looking at them and took them over to the operations room where they have a large magnification plate and deciphered every blurry background detail: Wolfchen's toys, which corner of the garden you were in, the light on your hair, the brooch on your dress, trying to imagine myself as part of the scene. Such pictures remind me every day how enormously lucky I am to have you and Wolfchen as my own darling family. I am not only sustained by the thought of your love but made all the more determined to fight for the world we live in. These thoughts, darling, are not only engendered by your snapshots but lead me to compare my happiness and good fortune with the wretchedness of some of my comrades. Poor Kurt who, as you know, is like a brother to me, mourns the loss of his parents in the raids on Hamburg and has no brothers or sisters of his own to share his sorrow or even a casual girlfriend to turn to for comfort. Likewise, my friend and colleague, Lother, with whom I trained at Werneuchen, has no sweetheart or wife to write to him, stuck in the wilds of Russia. Yes I, too, am thankful not to have been sent back there!

I am anxiously awaiting Christian's report back from Rome where he will have had an opportunity to talk to Edith and, I hope, Arturo, about their situation now that Mussolini has gone, with Ciano one of those who voted him out. When I suggested in a letter that Arturo might find a diplomatic position in Berlin again (or, for that matter, in Austria, Spain or Sweden), anywhere away from the turmoil that is Italy, Edith replied that her loyalty is to Arturo and his is to Ciano so it seems that for the present they are stuck in that milieu. We must just wait and see but I worry about the situation facing my sister. Both Christian and I had certain misgivings (which we concealed) about Edith marrying an Italian but she was so obviously in love and Arturo seemed socially well-placed and responsible, that we really could not voice our concern. Now events have changed the situation and although there is nothing in Arturo's character that is cause for regret (except, perhaps, his adherence to Ciano) it is the political – and, possibly, the military – position that worries us.

No, darling, I would not agree to your becoming a tram driver, whatever the "unpleasantness" that pervades the sewing circle! I am trying to think of some way in which you and Wolfchen could leave Grunewald for somewhere safer from the bombs – you know Dr Goebbels has advised women and children to leave Berlin if they can? I wish, now, that we had not given up Adlersee for the duration of the war, it would have been a perfect haven for you. I will write to Christian, perhaps we could rent a small private suite at the Schloss if the Luftwaffe do not use all the accommodation or perhaps one of the farms would have room for you, Wolfchen and Lenka. I realise you might not like immersing yourself in the countryside but during the next few months, when the course of the war will be determined, your safety is paramount. Now, darling, I must join Kurt and take our young pilots up on a training patrol. All my love, keep yourself safe and well.

Ever your own adoring,

Peter

PS I am sending you a package separately for Wolfchen's birthday. It is a model of my 109 painted in my colours, made by one of JG233's ground staff who does them to order. Put it away for him for when he is older, he is too young to appreciate it now. Will you buy a toy for him and say it is from me? P.

From: Hauptmann Peter von Vorzik
III Gruppe JG233
Schaftstadt, Halle
To: Oberleutnant Lother Köhl
I Gruppe Sch G1
Eastern Front

11th August 1943

Dear Lother,

Many thanks for your letter, I do appreciate your taking the trouble to write and tell me your news. I can certainly commiserate with you on being re-posted to Russia. I gather such postings are now looked upon as punishment for certain high-ranking officers in the Wehrmacht! As for flying the Hs129, when I was first posted to North Africa I talked to some pilots in a Schlachtflieger that was sharing our airfield and they said that their aircraft were perpetually unserviceable because of sand in the engines, all attempts at finding some effective means of filtration having been unsuccessful. They also complained, as you have, about the cramped cockpit and poor visibility.

I wonder where you are now as, looking at the marker flags on the HQ maps, our land forces appear to be pulled back to a line along the Donetz, with Luftwaffe Geschwader operating up and down between Kharkov and Taganrog. Perhaps you have been assigned to the small Gruppe defending the Crimea? For myself, our Staffel has been moved near Halle, awaiting expected attacks from American bombers. We have had a couple of months trying to get our new young pilots into shape, quite a lot of hard work as they were scarcely capable of flying our 109Gs and we had the usual crop of accidents (thankfully nothing fatal) during take-offs and landings. They certainly have not had the extensive training that we enjoyed. We have also had to train with a whole assortment of Rustsätze bits and pieces, bombs, cannon shells and rockets, practising different forms of attack which made the training very complicated. So, now we sit and wait. Meanwhile the British have done terrible damage to cities in the Ruhr and seem able to sustain their attacks despite heavy losses of machines and aircrews. Hamburg, too, I hear was ghastly, the flames of hell. Kurt, my Katschmarek, lost his parents there, their bodies and the house they lived in totally obliterated.

I am glad you found some solace with your war widow, the company of a loving woman is essential in such times as these, however transient the relationship may be. Have you replied to her letters? Well, that is the extent of my news, not very inspiring I am afraid, but we must fight on. With every day that passes it becomes more apparent that we are fighting to the death, but not, I hope, the death of Germany.

With every good wish for your safety and good health.

Ever your true comrade,

Peter

From: SS-Gruppenführer Count Christian von Vorzik
116 Kaiserstraße
Berlin
To: Hauptmann Peter von Vorzik
III Gruppe JG233
Schaftstadt, Halle

16th August 1943

Dear Peter,

As another month has passed since we last corresponded (my sojourn in Rome was longer than expected) I took the precaution of telephoning Mathilde and she gave me your new address. She sounded bright and cheerful on the 'phone and asked me to tell you she will be writing in a day or so. This is really to let you know what the situation is in Rome – or, rather, how it was when I left it a few days ago. The fact is it changes from day to day, almost hour to hour. I cannot say that the future looks good for Arturo simply because of his closeness to Ciano who, together with Edda and his children, is under house arrest at the apartment on Via Angelo Secchi. The *carabinieri* patrol the street constantly. According to Edith, Ciano's (and Arturo's) friend Count Grandi, who was also implicated in the movement to oust the Duce, has fled to Portugal. Admiral Bigliardi was prepared to smuggle Ciano out to Spain but Ciano would not leave without his family. Arturo says he will not leave Ciano and, he says, running away to Spain or Portugal would only make them look guilty of crimes against the state. Everywhere there is talk of Ciano having amassed illicit riches while working for the Fascist Party which Arturo says is not true. Edith is adamant that she will not leave Rome without Arturo so, for the moment, we are at an impasse.

I have had several conversations with Dr Dollmann who has promised he will keep a watching brief for Edith although he says he is not in a position to affect Arturo's situation; that must remain under the jurisdiction of Marshal Badoglio, at least as long as the present Italian government remains loyal to Germany. The whole political situation in Rome is in an extraordinary tangle, no one knows whom to trust and the German authorities, both political and military, are ready to act decisively if the Badoglio government shows any signs of trying to make peace with Britain and America.

My own personal mission in Rome which, as you may remember, was to investigate a suspected treacherous liaison on the part of a high-ranking member of the Abwehr, was successful inasmuch as our suspicions were confirmed with irrefutable evidence. However, for the moment the Reichsminister-SS has put my report aside for various reasons, although its contents will be disclosed to the Führer when the time is right. At the moment it is as well for our suspect to remain unaware that we know of his activities and he may yet provide us with further knowledge about his confederates. For myself, I am very sorry that the man has behaved so foolishly. I have known and liked him for some years and have frequently been a guest at his house. I must confess that working for the Ausland SD is much more interesting than the RSHA, one is afforded a world view rather than the enclosed perspective of Germany itself. In future I expect to accompany Walter, or deputise for him, on visits to Switzerland, Sweden, Turkey, France, Holland, Belgium, Spain and Portugal where we have our agents. Walter trusts me implicitly and knows I share his views on political security absolutely. Working with such a colleague makes life very pleasurable.

I will keep you posted with any news I receive from Rome.

Meanwhile, I trust all goes well with you.

Ever your affectionate brother,
Christian

Edward Thorpe

From: Mathilde von Vorzik
23 Hevelius Straße
Grunewald
To: Hauptmann Peter von Vorzik
III Gruppe JG233
Schaftstadt, Halle

18th August 1943

My Darling Peter,

It is always such a joy to see your writing on the envelope. I show your letter to Wolfchen and say, "from papa," and he repeats the words. I am glad you were happy with the snapshots, darling. As I said, neither Lenka nor I are great photographers but they will serve your purpose of having them in your wallet and when you are next on leave (when?) we must have studio portraits done, including one of the three of us.

Yesterday we heard on the radio of the American bombing raids on Schweinfurt and Regensburg and wondered if your Staffel was involved in any of the great aerial fights that were reported. According to the communiques the Americans suffered terrible losses which probably means they will not come again. We also heard that General Jeschonnek had died from a heart attack. I do not suppose his death will affect you directly but I hope whoever replaces him will be good for the fighter Geschwader. There was a lot of funereal music on the radio all day (mostly Wagner and Bruckner) and many tributes from his colleagues but no word from the Führer or the Reichsmarschall; I suppose they are too busy to go to radio stations.

The weather has been very hot and we have had daily picnics around the lake. How I wish you were here to share the occasions with us. Lots of people are swimming in the Havel and Schlachtensee but Frau Kirschner says that in the hot summer weather it is easy to catch all sorts of diseases from swimming in the lakes. I have been tempted by Lina's offer to visit Fehmarn at any time, she says it is beautiful there now, but I am put off by the journey because, apart from having to obtain special permission to make the visit I am sure it would be very tedious travelling with Wolfchen. I hear the trains are impossibly crowded nowadays and people stand for hours in the corridors. This week we had our first crop of tomatoes from the garden and the cucumbers and melons are almost

474

ready. It is so nice to have fresh vegetables and sometimes Lenka gets up very early and goes foraging in the woods for mushrooms and all sorts of leaves (that I would have considered weeds!) with which to make delicious salads. She really is a very helpful person and I am so sorry for her not hearing from her father and brother.

Two days ago Christian telephoned to ask if you had a new address and I gave it to him. He says things in Rome are in turmoil and he wishes Edith would return to Berlin but she will not leave Arturo which I can understand. Christian sounded much happier on the telephone, he says he is enjoying his new position and I hope he is recovering from Frieda's death. It occurred to me that perhaps he and Lina might get together, I know she always found him attractive. After all, he was very close to Reinhard. But perhaps she might not wish to be involved with someone who works so closely with the Reichsführer-SS whom she detests.

This is just a short letter, darling, as I have no real news for you except to say we are all well and how very relieved I am that you have not been posted back to Russia as I greatly feared. Of course I realise that wherever you are you are in danger, especially when I hear of the raids by American bombers which I know you have been training to defeat but the thought of you still in Germany and not too far away is a great recompense.

Keep yourself safe for your

Ever loving wife and baby son,
Mathilde and Wolfchen

PS I received the package with the model aeroplane safely, and put it away as you said. It is beautiful but it will be some time before Wolfchen is old enough to take proper care of it. I bought him a wooden aeroplane to pull along and told him it was from you. He plays with it all the time. Love, M.

Hauptmann Peter von Vorzik
Journal entry

22nd August 1943

Horrido! Five days ago we had our first encounter with bombers of the American 8th Air Force and gave them a bloody mauling. So bloody, in fact, that I doubt if they will be coming back. On the morning of the 17th the early warning monitoring systems reported unusual activity at the American bomber bases in England. Information received at the 1st Air

Division at Deelen predicted deep enemy penetration of central or southern Germany so that several fighter Gruppen around the North Sea coast and further inland were placed on alert. Soon after 10.00 hrs 146 American bombers, escorted by numerous Spitfires and Republic P-47 Thunderbolts, crossed the Dutch coast, then abruptly turned south. Shortly before reaching the Belgian-German border the fighter escort turned back. This was the moment our fighters had been waiting for. The bombers, flying at between 6 and 7,000 m, were attacked by Me109s and FW190s from JG11, JG26 and JG27 with great determination. The battle raged for an hour and a half, all the way to the bombers' target, the Messerschmitt factories at Regensburg, during which time the Americans lost fourteen of their huge aircraft. Expecting the raiders to return to England, one by one our fighter Staffeln were brought back to their bases, refuelled and rearmed ready for another encounter but the Americans flew on south, crossing Italy and landing in North Africa, demonstrating the enormous operational range of those B-17 Fortresses. Even so, they lost another ten aircraft to the fighters of Luftflotte 2 in Italy.

At Schaftstadt we had been kept in a state of alert all morning and then, after a quick sandwich lunch snatched under the wings of our fighters, we were ordered into the air to intercept an even larger force of 225 bombers heading south again, this time towards Schweinfurt with its all-important ball-bearing factories. We were operating alongside five Staffeln from JG11 whose 109s were equipped with 21cm rockets. My first glimpse of the bombers was from the starboard beam. They were flying in a tight, staggered formation and the black specks, growing ever larger at a closing speed of nearly 800 kph, reminded me of the cloud of locusts that descended on our airfield in North Africa. While we waited at a height of 8,000 m, the Staffel from JG11 made the first pass with their rockets, firing at the bombers from about 250 m astern. Most of the rockets fell short but two hit their targets and the bombers, still with their high-explosive load, burst into huge fireballs, their flaming fragments falling amongst surrounding aircraft. I received a prearranged signal from the Kommandant of JG11 and as his Staffel turned back to bodo to rearm and refuel it became our turn to attack. Following the tactics we have been practising these last two months or so the Staffel attacked in three waves of four, concentrating on bombers flying on the upper outer edges of the formation. This technique limits the bombers' ability to concentrate crossfire from each aircraft, the American's basic defensive arm in a formation unprotected by escorting fighters.

My leading Rotte, myself with Kurt and Varasch with his new young Katschmarek, Hugo Fingen, dived down on a B-17 flying on the rear port side of the upper tier of bombers. Our concentrated cannon shells soon had his outer port engine on fire and the inner one with its propeller only slowly rotating. As we broke away in a climbing turn I could see our victim was already losing height and speed and becoming detached from the formation, an easy target for the rest of the Staffel following behind us. Climbing back to a prearranged rendezvous height of 8,500 m and flying on a parallel course with the bombers I watched as the crippled aircraft rapidly increased its angle of descent, streaming black and grey smoke as it went. Suddenly, one, two, three black dots fell from the underside of the machine and then, like the opening of a flower, three parachutes appeared drifting and swaying slowly down. Three; according to intelligence reports these bombers have a crew of between six and ten men so several were going to their death in that flaming aircraft. Perhaps, I thought, the pilot is still at the controls, hoping to keep the aircraft steady while the rest of his crew baled out. At such times it is natural to hope that all the crew would escape until I remembered the bomber's mission and, as it disappeared from sight in a bank of silvery cumulo-nimbus cloud 3,000 m below, I realised it was still carrying its bomb load. Perhaps the brave pilot was still trying to find a target. To follow it down and finish it off might mean it crashed on some innocent civilians.

Throughout this mission the Americans were subjected to constant attacks and lost over thirty-six of their bombers during the flight to and from Schweinfurt, making their total losses for the day sixty aircraft, a terrible price to pay for their first deep penetration over Germany. More important than the loss of the aircraft was the loss of upwards of six hundred carefully trained aircrew. Inevitably, the Luftwaffe lost a number of fighters, too, including Fingen from our own Staffel. As we reassembled Varasch reported his Katschmarek missing. He neither saw nor heard anything during our initial attack but a pilot of one of the following Rotte reported seeing Fingen's 109 spinning down out of control. His plane crashed near Meiningen, his mangled body was later recovered and the coffin sent back to his home in Thuringia. He was a charming young man, not a particularly good pilot but full of enthusiasm and proud to fly as Katschmarek to Varasch who was deeply upset at his death. Despite this sad loss the Staffel celebrated its first successful encounter with the Americans with a rowdy party in the pilots' mess. Together with all the other fighter Gruppen involved we received a telegram of congratulations from the commander of the fighter arm, Lt General Adolf Galland.

From: Hauptmann Peter von Vorzik
III Gruppe JG233
Schaftstadt, Halle
To: Mathilde von Vorzik
23 Hevelius Straße
Grunewald

27th August 1943

My Darling Mathilde,

How my heart leaps when I see your writing on the envelope! Even here in Schaftstadt where I am not all that far away from you (but still too far!) a letter comes as a wonderful stimulus, a tonic, an inspiration. Daily routine seems that much easier, and life in general so much more worthwhile. Now, darling, here is an important proposition that I urge you to consider. In conversation with my comrade, Ludwig Varasch, I happened to mention that I would like you to leave Grunewald for somewhere in the country and he immediately suggested that you stay at his residence in Höchstein in Bavaria. It is on the River Aisch in the Steigerwald, fine open country far from anywhere that could conceivably be a target for bombers. He says it is a large old house, very comfortable, with no one else in residence (he has no brothers or sisters and his father and mother died in a motoring accident in Turkey a year before the war) except for a housekeeper who, he says, would be glad to have someone to look after. You could take Lenka with you as there is apparently plenty of room (seven bedrooms) and it does seem an ideal arrangement. Alternatively there are my relatives in Giessen, mother's cousins, pleasant people (although I have not seen them for years) who, I am sure, would make you welcome. Frankly, I think Ludwig's offer is the better suggestion. Most of the time you would have the house to yourself and Ludwig and I would come on leave together. I know I have mentioned him to you as the Staffel's Lothario but beneath his affected flamboyance there is a serious, cultured man. We could close up the house in Grunewald for the duration of the war (I hope it will be over this year) and you could travel down by train with Wolfchen and Lenka and I am sure I could get a few days' leave to drive down with all your luggage in the DKW.

I am really anxious that you should leave the Berlin area. Herr Dr Goebbels would not advise women and children to leave the city without good reason. I know Grunewald is some distance from the city centre but, as I have said before, a stray aircraft, particularly one that was in trouble, could still cause devastation. I am thinking of the terrible destruction in Hamburg and Cologne and the RAF are pursuing a policy of area bombing irrespective of whatever targets there may be. Let me know what you think, darling, and I will speak to Varasch and the Gruppe Kommandant about getting a few days' leave to effect the change. You were right, our Staffel was involved in attacking those American bombers. They suffered such losses that I am sure they will limit their future operations to within the range of their escorting fighters. And soon we hope to have our sensational new aircraft in the air which should stop any more daylight raids altogether.

I am still anxious for news of Edith and Arturo. Christian says that the political situation in Italy is changing from day to day and there is a general feeling that the Italians will try and make a separate peace with the British and Americans. Ciano is under house arrest and many of his closest friends have fled to Spain and Portugal. I wish Edith would return to Germany but she will not leave Arturo. So, we must just wait and see what happens.

No more now, darling, think seriously about what I have suggested, I am very anxious that you and Wolfchen should be somewhere really safe as soon as possible.

All my love as always.

Ever your own,
Peter

From: Contessa Edith Novarro-Badaelli
Villa Frascati
Via Augusta
Rome
To: Hauptmann Peter von Vorzik
III Gruppe JG233
Schaftstadt, Halle

31st August 1943

My Dear Peter,

Please forgive the scribble but my hand is shaking as I write. Yesterday, at the atrocious hour of five in the morning, several *carabinieri* arrived under Colonel Angelo Poldani (who has been a guest in our house) and arrested Arturo. He was given twenty minutes to dress and gather a small case of personal belongings before being driven away. I have spent the last twenty-four hours trying to discover where he has been taken, telephoning Carmine Senise (who has been reinstated as chief of police) without success and becoming more and more frustrated and fearful. Dr Dollmann has been very helpful and hopes to have some information for me by tomorrow. Meanwhile he has stationed an armed SS guard outside the house as protection for me though I do not think the Italian police or anyone in Badoglio's government consider me of any importance. I am just so anxious about Arturo's safety and it is not knowing where he is that makes me shake with nerves. As you may have heard, Ciano and his wife and children have fled by plane to Germany. Dr Dollmann says they were under the impression they were flying to Spain but when the plane landed at Munich it stayed there. The Führer is well-disposed to Edda as Mussolini's daughter but he dislikes and distrusts Ciano. How I wish Ciano had gone to Spain when he had the chance, Arturo could have gone with him. Now he faces heaven knows what trumped-up charges. Dr Dollmann says he could arrange a flight back to Germany for me but I feel I must stay here until the situation with Arturo is cleared up. Then perhaps we can both return to Germany as the Cianos have. It was such a joy to see Christian for a brief time, looking well and full of confidence. He was instrumental in arranging for Dr Dollmann to keep "a watching brief" (as he termed it) over me. I do so hope he can find some suitable young woman to replace Frieda; beneath his conviviality I was sure I detected a certain loneliness. He says he buries himself in work but that cannot be fulfilling in the long-term.

Well, dear brother, that is my news – I hope to be able to tell you something more positive in my next letter as I feel sure that everything will eventually be resolved satisfactorily. I find great solace in prayer. I trust all goes well with you, please write if you can spare a moment.

Ever your loving sister,
Edith

PS I heard from Christian that you would be moving soon and, after several attempts, managed to get through to Mathilde who gave me your new address. Both she and Wolfchen appear to be in good health. E.

From: Oberleutnant Claus Grüber
Erprobungsgruppe V
Rechlin am Muritzsee
To: Hauptmann Peter von Vorzik
III Gruppe JG233
Schaftstadt, Halle

1st September 1943

Dear Peter,

I happened to glance at the calendar and realised that it is four years since we both took off on that early dawn in response to the Führer's directive to attack Poland. It is also seven months since you last visited us so I thought I should write to see how you are and give you a brief progress report about some of the projects you saw last February.

Who could have foreseen that we should still be fighting (you more than me) in 1943?! And it seems we still have a lot to achieve, the news from the east and the south causing some concern. I obtained the whereabouts of JG233 from Jagdflieger HQ and surmise that you are now one of the several Gruppen charged with the task of fighting off the threat from the Americans. Those were costly raids on Regensburg and Schweinfurt, were they not? I understand your Staffel was involved and trust you came through unscathed from what must have been something of an ordeal? On the debit side I have to inform you (keep it to yourself) that the RAF recently dealt a severe blow to our establishment at Peenemünde, setting the programme back several months, mainly through the loss of important drawings and documents rather than material damage although that was fairly extensive. On the other hand, the Me262 programme is moving ahead successfully after a number of problems (of which you were aware, I think). General der Kampfflieger Galland hopes to demonstrate the 262 before the Führer in a few weeks, then it should be but a short time before the aircraft is in full production. Of course it will necessitate a very specialised training programme for the pilots. Why don't you put yourself forward? The Me163 rocket-fighter programme has many continuing problems and development has been moved from Peenemünde to Bad Zwischenahn. Maybe one day you will see one zooming over Halle! Everything is being done to get these extraordinary aircraft operational as quickly as possible but I do not think it will happen before next spring. (You would not believe how difficult it has been to get any sort of production priority agreed...)

Jeschonnek's death was a bad business. No doubt you have heard the rumours that it was not a heart attack as was officially announced? It was Udet all over again. Jeschonnek was caught between the Führer and the Fat One, having lost the support of both, and found himself taking the blame for the latter's failures with regard to production problems, etc. A bullet to the head was his way out. I can understand why the truth was suppressed but it is a thousand pities that a man's reputation was taken as well as his life. The Reichsmarschall has much to answer for. I heard all this personally from Jeschonnek's secretary, Lotte Kersten, who, poor woman, found the body. I am sorry for Generaloberst Korten who has replaced Jeschonnek as Chief of the Air Staff; at present it is a thankless task as the Luftwaffe appears outnumbered on every front. Everyone thinks Freiherr von Richtofen would have been the best man for the job but he was passed over – to his great relief, one hears.

How is your family? Well, I trust, despite the recent raids on Berlin which have, apparently, caused much damage. I remain a grumpy bachelor; the opportunity to meet anyone of the opposite sex is limited here and, in any case, what woman would want damaged goods? My knee gets gradually worse but I can still manage to kick a rudder bar although flying opportunities are few and far between nowadays – we have strict fuel rationing at present. So, dear friend, this seems to have become something of a moan and my intention was to cheer you up with a letter! Let me have your news when you can and tell me how you are getting on with your Gustav.

Ever your sincere comrade,

Claus

PS You know you are always welcome here. Regards to Kurt. C.

From: Mathilde von Vorzik
23 Hevelius Straße
Grunewald
To: Hauptmann Peter von Vorzik
III Gruppe JG233
Schaftstadt, Halle

11th September 1943

My Darling Peter,

Your letter arrived this morning having taken over two weeks to reach us as it seems the postal service has been badly disrupted. As you may have heard (although the radio reports give few details) Berlin has suffered three dreadful RAF night raids which have done terrible damage to the city. We were so very glad to have the cellar as a refuge (thanks to your foresight) and although we were on the fringe of the attacks it was quite terrifying. The noise of the bombs exploding and the sound of the anti-aircraft guns as well as the constant drone of hundreds of aircraft was nerve-wracking and we could even feel the ground shake as the bombs exploded. A stray bomb destroyed two houses not very far away and several panes of glass in our windows were shattered by blast. I have had them repaired although the glazier suggested putting in wood instead of glass. When we emerged into the daylight the sky was black with smoke from many fires and both inside and outside the house was covered in soot and grey ash. It took Lenka and me hours to clean it up and then two nights later it happened all over again!

So, darling, you can see that I am only too ready to agree to your suggestion to move away from Grunewald. Apart from the stray bomb that fell near, one of our own night-fighters also crashed nearby and I do not think my nerves will stand much more. I was all right during the first attack but on subsequent nights I was really very frightened as I lay on the little cotbed sheltering Wolfchen during the worst part of the raids which lasted nearly two hours. Water, gas and electricity have been affected and there is now a great dearth of candles in the shops as well as food shortages of all kinds. Christian has been very helpful, telephoning to see how we were and sending his driver with various supplies. He says several of the administrative offices in Prinz Albertstraße and Wilhelmstraße have been badly damaged. I think your comrade Ludwig Varasch's offer sounds wonderful – does he really mean it? Of course I would be happy to join your relatives in Giessen but I wonder how old they are? They might not be too happy to welcome a small child into their home whereas you say Ludwig's house is empty except for a housekeeper. Can you really get leave to help us move? That would be marvellous as I understand travelling by rail now is an exhausting business. I have already begun thinking of what to take for an extended stay and will probably need to buy another two suitcases. Please let me know what you can arrange, darling, and thank Ludwig for his generous offer.

I will stop now as I am anxious for you to get this.

All our fondest love.

Your own,
Mathilde and Wolfchen

PS I had a letter from Edith saying that Arturo had been arrested. Dreadful, dreadful. I have written her a long letter.

PPS What an astonishing rescue of Mussolini from that mountain fortress in the Abruzzi that was!! M.

From: Hauptmann Peter von Vorzik
III Gruppe JG233
Schaftstadt, Halle
To: Contessa Edith Novarro-Badaelli
Villa Frascati
Via Augusta
Rome

19th September 1943

My Dear Edith,

I was appalled to learn that Arturo had been arrested and trust that by now (your letter only just having reached me – the post is very bad now) he will

484

have been released. What a dreadful experience for both of you, being awakened at such an early hour and Arturo hurried away! I cannot understand why the authorities find it necessary to behave in such an uncivilised manner. I suppose they thought that Arturo might be "escaping" to Spain or Portugal as I believe Count Grandi has done. I agree with you and think it a great pity Arturo did not follow Grandi's example when he had the chance. You could have joined him wherever he was. It only goes to show Arturo's loyalty to Ciano was misplaced especially as he, too, thought he and his family were escaping to Spain and are now being kept in Germany. I am relieved to know Dr Dollmann is making sure you are safe, dear sister. I can imagine what a fraught time it has been for you. The arrest of Mussolini was a great shock and something of a propaganda triumph for our enemies but his brilliant rescue from the Abruzzi by Otto Skorzeny and his SS-Kommandos has redressed the balance. Now, however, with the establishment of the Italian Social Republic (albeit in Germany!) and Badoglio's government in Rome capitulating to the British and Americans it produces a civil-war situation. Once again it seems that German forces will have to stabilise the situation for Italy. All is not lost, dear sister, we must try and maintain our good spirits and remain resolute. Keep your courage and keep the faith that is so important to you.

Ever your loving brother,
Peter

From: Hauptmann Peter von Vorzik
III Gruppe JG233
Schaftstadt, Halle
To: Mathilde von Vorzik
23 Hevelius Straße
Grunewald

25th September 1943

My Darling Mathilde,
This is just to tell you that I have obtained permission for Ludwig Varasch and myself to take four days' leave to collect you, Wolfchen and Lenka and take you to Varasch's home in Höchstein! I will try and reach you by telephone and telegram but if I cannot (as communications are so unreliable nowadays) I am allowing this letter ten days to reach you and give you a chance to prepare for the evacuation. Contact Christian if it is

necessary to give formal information to the authorities about permission for travel and relocation. There should be no problem as Herr Dr Goebbels has advised it.

We expect to be with you about midday on 6th October. We will stay overnight then I will travel to Höchstein by train with you, Wolfchen and Lenka while Varasch drives to Höchstein with the luggage in the DKW. I will probably stay two nights so as to give Varasch the chance to arrive at Höchstein before us. He will meet us at the nearest station which I believe is Bamberg. Is that not a good plan? I will stop now, darling, and try and arrange for this to go in the courier mail. All other news when I see you.

Ever your loving husband,
Peter

PS Try and arrange for the glazier to board up all the windows after our departure. P.

From: Hauptmann Peter von Vorzik
III Gruppe JG233
Schaftstadt, Halle
To: Oberleutnant Claus Grüber
Erprobungsgruppe V
Rechlin am Muritzsee

27th September 1943

Dear Claus,

It was a very pleasant surprise to receive your letter of the 1st and you must forgive this delay in replying. First, your letter took over two weeks to get here (have you found the post to be slow nowadays?) and second, I have been closely involved in arranging for my wife and son to be evacuated from Grunewald. Not the centre of Berlin, of course (which I hear has suffered badly from RAF attention) but nevertheless close enough to be dangerous. I hope that by the time this reaches you they will be safely installed in a house at Höchstein belonging to a Staffel comrade, Ludwig Varasch. (Did you ever meet him at Verneuchen? Taller than me, blonde, good-looking, very much a ladies' man, somewhat flamboyant in manner.) It will be a great relief when they are out of harm's way.

You ask about the Gustav. It behaves well, though not as pleasant to fly as the F Series as I'm sure you know; my only combat experience with it so far was during the Americans' raid on Schweinfurt when the Staffel was successful in destroying several B-17s which have proved to be vulnerable without fighter escort. What bomber isn't? Well, yes, I suppose the Mosquito is uncatchable but that will change, will it not, when the Me262 is finally operational. I must say that from the films I saw at Rechlin it is an incredible aircraft. I can imagine how thrilled the Führer will be when it is demonstrated to him. You suggest I put myself forward as a 262 pilot which has its attractions, of course, but I do not think the Gruppe Kommandant would look upon it favourably and I would not want to leave my comrades in the Staffel – we have been through so much together. Also I think I am now a little too old to learn new tricks! Let the youngsters fresh from Verneuchen grapple with these new weapons. A pity the Me163 programme has been delayed. Now there is something really extraordinary! I acknowledge the courage of any pilot who chances their life with such a sensational concept. I could not believe it when you told me that Fräulein Hanna Reitsch was one of the test pilots! Merely to have all that unstable rocket fuel behind one is unnerving. It is certainly a different realm of flight and just how such machines may be employed in defensive tactics is difficult to see. I mean, at such speeds the target is gone in a flash and the aircraft without sufficient fuel for a second pass. But I am sure it will cause great consternation amongst our enemies when it appears. I remember telling you that I harbour hopes of flying on a commercial basis when the war is over – that is when I expect I will have to come to grips with these new means of propulsion. At the moment I am content with what I know.

Of course I would be very happy to make another visit to Rechlin, I am in need of stimulation! Things are not going too well at the moment, it seems, and Rechlin always gives one encouragement, seeing what our scientists, designers and engineers are working on. I do not see what opportunity there will be, however, at least not in the immediate future. Like you we are having to conserve fuel, training flights are cancelled and use of the Staffel's communications aircraft forbidden unless absolutely necessary. Sorry to hear you are bereft of female company, but do not despair, I am sure there is an attractive lady waiting for you somewhere – do you not get a chance for an occasional weekend in Berlin? Despite the raids, I hear (from gossip in the mess) that there are still one or two cabarets that afford entertainment and the opportunity to meet pleasant company... As for "damaged goods", a stiff knee should be no obstacle when other parts are in good working order! Now I must go and attend to those everlasting reports to the quartermaster. Please write when you can, your letters are always welcome in lieu of a visit to Rechlin.

Ever your sincere comrade,

Peter

Hauptmann Peter von Vorzik
Journal entry

10th October 1943

A mission satisfactorily completed! Not an aerial one, this time, but a civil one: transferring my loved ones from Grunewald to Varasch's home at Höchstein. All went smoothly although the rail journeys were tiring and tedious and would have been unthinkable for Mathilde, Wolfchen and Lenka had they attempted it by themselves. Varasch and I took the early morning courier flight from Schaftstadt to Berlin-Rangsdorf which meant we were in Grunewald before midday. Mathilde had everything necessary for the stay at Höchstein packed into three large suitcases which we managed to cram into the DKW's small luggage compartment and on to its back seat. After a simple lunch Varasch was on his way. He was expecting to get as far as Leipzig before dark, stay there overnight and reach Höchstein the following day which he managed to do comfortably.

I stayed at Grunewald for two nights (such bliss to hold my darling Mathilde once again!) and helped close up the house. Mathilde had told the gardener to do as he liked with the produce and arranged for the glazier to come and board up the windows the day before we left. Gas, electricity and water were turned off, the local authorities notified that the house was being closed up and then, on the third morning of my visit we took a taxi to the station. During the ride I was able to see what dreadful damage had been done to parts of the city and was very glad that my darlings were leaving. The station and the train were terribly crowded and we stood all the way to Dessau where we had to change. Mathilde took charge of Wolfchen and Lenka and I managed the luggage. It would have been physically impossible to travel with the suitcases Varasch had taken with him, there being no porters available. They have all been drafted to the eastern front Mathilde said. The station at Dessau was in turmoil, the town having been badly bombed because of the Junkers aircraft works there. We managed to find seats in a first-class compartment (it is impossible to make reservations) partly because Mathilde was carrying Wolfchen and partly, I think, because of my uniform. The train crawled along and made endless stops in the middle of the countryside for no apparent reason. We were unable to buy anything to eat during the journey, there was no restaurant car and the station buffets were besieged and had little to offer anyway, except beer and schnapps, and we soon consumed the sandwiches and cakes that Mathilde had packed. It was after midnight when we finally arrived at Bamberg but there was Varasch patiently waiting for us in his Mercedes tourer which accommodated us all easily.

The house at Höchstein is, as Varasch had said, large and comfortable, a converted farmhouse dating from the 18th century. Downstairs there is a big kitchen and an even bigger sitting room, a study lined with books, a pleasant morning room also with many bookshelves and a music room with a grand piano. Upstairs there are seven bedrooms and two bathrooms. Mathilde and I shared what Varasch said had been his parents' bedroom with a large, canopied double bed; Varasch has his own two rooms and the smaller of the two bathrooms and Lenka shared a double room with Wolfchen. Marie, the pleasant, buxom, middle-aged housekeeper who welcomed us with hot soup and freshly baked rolls on our arrival, had erected a cot for Wolfchen. She said it had been Varasch's when he was a baby and was kept in the loft. On the first night, however, as everything was strange to him, Wolfchen slept between us in the big double bed. The house stands within its own grounds with a disused dairy and stables. There is an apple orchard and a summer house on lawns that slope down to the river Aisch. I impressed on Mathilde and Lenka that they must be very vigilant with Wolfchen as he is bound to be attracted by the river. It is all really quite idyllic and although the house is only 60 km from Schweinfurt and Würzburg I am sure it is safe from marauding aircraft. I did not remark upon it but it occurred to me that I was fighting those American bombers over this countryside only a few weeks ago. We are immensely grateful to Varasch for his generosity and hospitality and I cannot think how to repay him. For his part he says he is only too delighted to have the house occupied and Marie seems genuinely pleased to have company.

Marie told us she came into Varasch's parents' employ when she was a mere girl of fourteen and Varasch himself was not even born. When she was eighteen she had had a local sweetheart who had left her for an older woman and she, Marie, has "never bothered" with men since. A pity, I thought, as I am sure she would have made a good wife and mother.

The next day, as Marie was taking Mathilde and Lenka to the local shops to register for meat and groceries, Varasch and I left to return to the Staffel. It was another tedious, interminable rail journey via Zwickau and Leipzig which took us nearly thirty-six hours but Marie had packed us plenty of food with cold chicken, homemade pies and strudel which sustained us throughout the journey as far as Halle. Back at Schaftstadt we were confronted with the bleak reality of the war which does not seem to be going very well for us. Last month the Badoglio government surrendered to the British and Americans and fled to Brindisi. Our own German forces have taken over the defence of Italy and Mussolini has been reinstated in Rome as head of the newly constituted Italian Social Republic. In various places throughout the countryside, however, civil war has broken out between loyal Fascists and Communist partisans. After much bitter fighting the British and Americans have made a successful landing at Salerno, just south of Naples which, with its port facilities, is now in the enemies' hands. The Italian fleet sailed to Malta and surrendered to the British who have also occupied the port of Taranto. The Anglo-Saxons, therefore, have succeeded in getting a foothold on the mainland of Europe. In Russia our forces have had to give ground everywhere. The Russians have retaken Smolensk and Kharkov and are threatening Kiev and our armies in the Crimea. Today they took Dnipropetrovsk. The Luftwaffe is outnumbered two-to-one on every sector of the eastern front. I think of my friend Lother and wonder where he is and if he is still alive. I must find the time to write to him soon.

From: Mathilde von Vorzik
Die Alter Scheune
Steuben Gasse
Höchstein
To: Hauptmann Peter von Vorzik
III Gruppe JG233
Schaftstadt, Halle

15th October 1943

My Darling Peter,

This is just to let you know that we are happily settled at Höchstein. Of course it takes some time to get used to being in the country after the bustle of Berlin; even Grunewald seems busy compared to the peace and tranquillity here. At night there are hardly any sounds except the murmuring of the river and an occasional owl call. We are so lucky to be free of the threat of bombs. Please thank Ludwig for us and tell him how we appreciate being here. Lenka says it reminds her of her home in Bohemia which was near the river Vltava. All the trees are in their lovely autumn colours now and the whole countryside is golden, especially the vista across the river. Both Lenka and I have heeded your warning about Wolfchen going near the water but he does not seem to have any great interest in it. His great passion at the moment is being allowed to sit up on one of the great ploughing horses owned by a local farmer. Marie took him with her to collect some eggs from the farm and they sat him up on this giant (but docile!) animal, much to Wolfchen's delight. He is enraptured by all the farm animals, goats, sheep, hens, and the farmer's wife lets him feed the chickens with some corn. I was amazed how much foodstuff is available from the farm: ham, pork, home-made sausages, eggs, cream, vegetables, all of it "by the back door" as they say here. One hardly needs to register at the shops for food supplies. Both the farmer's sons are fighting on the eastern front and he and his wife are in a constant state of worry about them. I asked if they would not have been exempt from military service working on the farm but apparently they insisted on joining the army.

I forgot to tell you that Frau Kirschner seemed very cross when I told her we were going to stay in the country. She pursed her lips and said, "Grunewald is not the city. Herr Dr Goebbels said nothing about evacuating the suburbs." I replied, "Herr Dr Goebbels is not able to decide where the bombs fall." Was that not clever of me? Her final words to me were, "Well, I hope you find some useful work to do in the country." She may have improved my sewing but I am glad not to see her any more, she had become very domineering. Speaking of self-improvement, there is such an extensive library here, all the classics - Goethe, Schiller, Heine, Voltaire, Shakespeare, Plato, Descartes, Kant, Fichte, Nietzsche, Swedenborg – that, during the winter, I intend to try and rediscover some of what we used to read at school. I doubt if I shall get very far, I always found the lessons boring but now, when I see these shelves of books, I realise how ignorant I am! I like to think I am not unintelligent, that I do have the mental capacity to absorb and appreciate what these great people wrote and thought. Anyway, that is my intention though without someone to converse with (I doubt if Lenka or Marie would care to join me in my reading programme) I shall probably give up before getting very far. Do not laugh at me, darling, your wife is taking this opportunity to try and make herself a more interesting person!

Now I must walk into the town with Wolfchen and post this to you.

Love and kisses from us both.

Ever your own,
Mathilde

From: Hauptmann Peter von Vorzik
III Gruppe JG233
Schaftstadt, Halle
To: Oberleutnant Lother Köhl
I Gruppe Sch. Gl
Eastern Front

21st October 1943

Dear Lother,

Not having had a reply to my letter of 11th August I am anxious to know that all is well with you. Please do not think that is a reproach, I know only too well how quickly time passes and how difficult it is to find some spare half hour (not to mention pen and paper!) to write and I am aware, also, how difficult it has been in recent weeks for all the Luftwaffe units on the eastern front. The loss of Smolensk, Kharkov and Kiev were great blows and

I am wondering whether you are with Fliegerkorps IV in the south or Fliegerkorps VIII in the north? Are you still flying those wretched 189s? I believe some Schlachtflieger units were being transferred to FW190s for close support work which would have brought you back in contact with single-engine fighters! I do hope so. Here in central Germany we have seen little action beyond a very successful first encounter with the Americans who, as I am sure you know, lost a large number of their B-17s when they raided Schweinfurt and Regensburg. I think we have the measure of them and they will not attempt any more deep penetration raids.

Through the generosity of a comrade in the Staffel I have been able to evacuate my wife and son to a safe area of the countryside which is a great weight off my mind. Berlin has suffered considerably from night attacks but, again, our defences have taken a heavy toll of the raiders. Well, that, briefly, is my news. I would appreciate a note from you, however short, just to let me know you are safe and well.

Ever your sincere comrade,
Peter

From: Contessa Edith Novarro-Badaelli
Villa Frascati
Via Augusta
Rome
To: Hauptmann Peter von Vorzik
III Gruppe JG233
4 Schaftstadt, Halle

27th October 1943

My Dear Peter,
This is just a short letter to let you know how things are developing here. Not too well, I am afraid. (Yes, I *am* afraid!) I finally discovered – or, rather, Dr Dollmann discovered for me – that Arturo is being held at the Scalzi prison in Verona. Ironically, I learned that this was a 16th-century Carmelite monastery converted in 1900. Most of those who voted against Mussolini in the Grand Council are incarcerated there under heavy guard. I understand that Ciano has been flown back from Germany and is imprisoned there, too, at the instigation of his one-time friend Alessandro Pavolini who is now the secretary of the new Republican Fascist Party. Last

week Dr Dollmann arranged for me to visit the prison. He provided a car and a driver and I was able to take Arturo a complete change of clothing as well as cold meats, cheese and cakes. The authorities would not let me see him but a kind officer in the *carabinieri* assured me Arturo was in good health and had been able to make contact with Ciano. I was allowed to write a message to Arturo and was assured he would receive it. I was then driven back to Rome, stopping overnight at the German consulate in Florence. It is a thousand pities that Arturo is imprisoned so far away.

I hope and pray, dearest brother, that all is well with you and your loved ones. (I had a most comforting letter from Mathilde.) I do regret involving you in my concerns but it helps to share one's anxieties and I have no close friends here, particularly now that Eleanora has moved to Switzerland.

All my love.

Ever your devoted sister,
Edith

The Führer
Führer Headquarters

3rd November 1943

27 copies

DIRECTIVE NO. 51 (Excerpts)

The hard and costly struggle against Bolshevism during the last two and a half years, which has involved the bulk of our military strength in the east, has demanded extreme exertions. The greatness of the danger and the general situation demanded it. But the situation has since changed. The danger in the east remains, but a greater danger now appears in the west: an Anglo-Saxon landing! In the east, the vast extent of the territory makes it possible for us to lose ground, even on a large scale, without a fatal blow being dealt to the nervous system of Germany.

It is very different in the west! Should the enemy succeed in breaching our defences on a wide front here, the immediate consequences would be unpredictable. Everything indicates that the enemy will launch an offensive against the western front of Europe, at the latest in the spring, perhaps even earlier.

I can therefore no longer take responsibility for further weakening in the west, in favour of other theatres of war. I have therefore decided to reinforce its defences, particularly those places from which the long-range bombardment of England will begin. For it is here that the enemy must and will attack, and it is here – unless all indications are misleading – that the decisive battle against the landing forces will be fought.

Luftwaffe.

In view of the new situation, the offensive and defensive power of formations of the Luftwaffe stationed in the west and in Denmark will be increased. Plans will be drawn up to ensure that all forces available and suitable for defensive operations will be taken from flying units and mobile anti-aircraft artillery units engaged in Home Defence, from schools and training units in the Home Defence area, and will be employed in the west, and if necessary in Denmark. Ground establishments in southern Norway, Denmark, north-western Germany and the west will be organised and supplied so that, by the largest possible degree of decentralisation, our own units are not exposed to enemy bombing at the beginning of large-scale operations, and the weight of the enemy attack will be effectively broken up. This applies particularly to our fighter forces, whose ability to go into action must be increased by the establishment of a number of emergency airfields. Particular attention will be paid to good camouflage. In this connection also I expect all possible forces to be made available for action regardless of the circumstances, by stripping less threatened areas of their troops.

SS

The Reichsführer-SS will test the preparedness of units of the Waffen-SS and police for operational, security and guard duties. Preparations will be made to raise battle-trained formations for operational and security duties from training, reserve and recuperative establishments and from schools and other units in the Home Defence area.

Commanders-in-Chief of the branches of the Armed Forces and the Reichsführer-SS will report to me by the 15th November the steps taken, and those which they propose to take. I expect all staffs concerned to exert every effort during the time which still remains in preparation for the expected decisive battle in the west. All those responsible will ensure that time and manpower are not wasted in dealing with questions of jurisdiction, but that they are employed in increasing our powers of defence and attack.

Adolf Hitler

From: Hauptmann Peter von Vorzik
III Gruppe JG233
Schaftstadt, Halle
To: Mathilde von Vorzik
Die Alter Scheune
Steuben Gasse
Höchstein

4th November 1943

My Darling Mathilde,

What a comfort it is to know that you and Wolfchen are safely settled in the countryside! I was so pleased to have your letter and I read it to Varasch who sends his greetings and says that he, too, is happy that you are settled in his home. I expect, darling, that once the novelty has worn off there will be times when you are bored with the simple routine of country life – no cinemas, no smart shops, cows and sheep instead of people – but, for the time being, it is better to be bored than bombed! It is an excellent idea of yours to take advantage of the library there and begin a reading programme of the classics although I expect you are right when you anticipate that there will be times when it is too daunting to continue. Make sure you have plenty of lighter reading, some modern novels and current magazines. Otherwise, the simple life of the countryside together with your self-imposed regime of intellectual improvement could lead to depression! And, darling, I have absolutely no need of an "improved" wife! For me, you are perfect as you are.

I am sure that, come next spring, our wonderful new aircraft and secret weapons (some of which I have seen in development) will turn the tables on our enemies and hasten the end of the war. Now that the autumn is nearly over and we are beginning a new winter our flying will be curtailed by the weather, as will the raids by enemy bombers, at least by day. Then, as I say, in the spring we can expect to achieve victory which has been so long in coming.

I received an anxious letter from Edith (who said she had received a comforting one from you) and, in turn, I am worried for her. It has been a cruel act of fate for her to have had just a few months of happily married life before having her husband snatched away through political machinations. It has all been handled badly through the best of intentions,

Arturo remaining faithful to his friend Ciano who should (like several others) have taken the obvious way out and fled to Spain or Portugal while they had the chance. It is unfortunate, too, that Eleanora went to Switzerland leaving Edith without any female company to give her support. But there it is. I will write to Christian and see if something can be done to get Arturo released. After all, he did not vote in the Grand Council and putting him in prison can only be an act of malice. Moreover, in Italy it seems that a lot can be done by the greasing of palms or by some reciprocal arrangement. Despite the setting up of the new Republican Fascist Party or whatever it is called it is we Germans who really call the tune!

No more now, I have much work to do here. All my love to you and Wolfchen, please give my regards to Marie and Lenka.

Ever your own,
Peter

PS With Christmas not so far away would it be a good idea to give Wolfchen a pony? Or is he too young? Christian and I learnt to ride at an early age. P.

From: Hauptmann Peter von Vorzik
III Gruppe JG233
Schaftstadt, Halle
To: SS-Gruppenführer Count Christian von Vorzik
116 Kaiserstraße
Berlin

8th November 1943

Dear Christian,

Since receiving your letter of the 16th August (to which I have been meaning to reply before now!) I have had two further letters from Edith keeping me informed about her situation in Rome. The imprisonment of Arturo is a bad business as I do not get the impression that he was in league with Ciano, Grandi and the others who voted Mussolini out of power. It would seem to be guilt by association, anyone working with or friendly with Ciano automatically suspect. I understand from Edith that Alessandro Pavolini, who owed much to Ciano, is now, as secretary to the new regime, exercising his power over a man who was his mentor. Anyway, I care nothing about what may happen to Ciano and, to be truthful, not very much about Arturo, only insofar as it affects our dear sister. She is my worry. How fortunate that you were able to enjoin Dr Dollmann to make sure Edith was safe from any interference or depredations from Arturo's enemies. I cannot believe that the Italians would harm a woman but they might very well try to requisition the house or something of that sort. They are not to be trusted. Can nothing be done to release Arturo? Now that the British and Americans have made a successful landing in Italy are we Germans not in political as well as military control? I begin to see why Eleanora decamped to Switzerland while she had the opportunity.

I am so relieved that Mathilde and Wolfchen are now safely in the country – thank you for all the assistance you gave them prior to leaving Berlin. Has your apartment escaped damage? From what I could see during the taxi-ride to the station parts of the city have been badly damaged despite the heavy defensive measures we employ. Perhaps, however, the British bombers are doing some of Herr Speer's demolition work for him prior to the rebuilding of the city as Germania after the war. Here at Schaftstadt flying is severely curtailed because of the persistently bad weather. Fuel is in short supply, too, which means we only fly a few standing patrols, weather permitting, so time hangs heavily. At least we do not expect the Americans to try another sortie for a while; they got so savagely beaten the last time they attempted a deep penetration raid and in any case, flying as they do at extreme heights, they need good unclouded weather. The situation in the east seems critical (I cannot believe the Russians have retaken great swathes of land over which we flew and fought two years ago) but, again, the winter weather will put a stop to large-scale operations during which time I hope we can fortify the defensive line so as to make it impregnable and, come the spring, stop the Russians in their tracks and bleed them white. I think the British and Americans must come to their senses and see the threat to western civilisation posed by the Communist hordes.

I trust your position within the Ausland SD continues to prove as satisfying as it would seem from the comments you made in your last letter. Finding satisfaction and stimulus in one's work is the basis of happiness, is it not?

All good wishes.

Ever your loving brother,
Peter

From: *Hauptmann Peter von Vorzik*
III Gruppe JG233
Schaftstadt, Halle
To: *Countess Edith Novarro-Badaelli*
Villa Frascati
Via Augusta
Rome

15th November 1943

My Dear Edith,

Naturally, since receiving your letter of the 27th I have been very concerned for you and Arturo. Surely there are good friends in high places who can plead Arturo's cause? Or have they all fled abroad or been imprisoned, too? What about Eleanora? Has she no friends or relatives who could persuade the authorities to release her son? Does she know Edda Ciano? I believe she still has influence with her father. I never really knew what Arturo's position was within Ciano's entourage – secretary, aide-de-camp, emissary? And what is the charge against him? Whatever it is Arturo does not seem to have been personally involved in the deposition of Mussolini. I suppose grudges are being paid off. I have seen and heard enough during the last two or three years about the behaviour of people in authority not to be surprised at anything. I think it particularly mean of the authorities at Scalzi not to let you see Arturo after making that long drive to Verona. How petty! What upsets me most is here I am, making my small contribution to the defence of the Reich and there you are, brutally separated from your husband, enduring anxiety about his welfare, and I am in no position to alleviate your anguish. How I wish I could be by your side, to give some comfort and support while you undergo this wretchedness. I think of you constantly, dear sister, and hope, with you, that Arturo will emerge unscathed from his ordeal.

Mathilde may have written and told you that I have arranged for her and Wolfchen to be evacuated to Höchstein through the generosity of a Staffel comrade, Ludwig Varasch? It is a great relief to me that they are away from the bombing in and around Berlin. Varasch has always had the reputation in the Staffel – indeed, throughout the Gruppe! – as being a Lothario, a woman-chaser, fostered by his own highly coloured tales of his amorous adventures, but beneath this exterior I have found him to be a man of some seriousness and sensitivity. I am most grateful to him for providing this refuge for my family. Bad weather has kept us grounded for some days now but, of course, it hinders operations by enemy aircraft, too. Travelling by train to Höchstein I saw much evidence of what the RAF night raids have done to some of our cities. Our only hope of stopping further damage is by making their losses of men and machines insupportable, and that we seem to be doing, both by night and day.

Now, dear sister, I have little I can write to you about that might raise your spirits. Keep in close contact, especially with Christian who, as you know, has many acquaintances in Berlin who could, perhaps, be instrumental in helping Arturo. Meanwhile, I am glad to hear that Dr Dollmann has been of service to you.

Everything may yet turn out well.

Ever your loving brother,
Peter

From: SS-Gruppenführer Count Christian von Vorzik
116 Kaiserstraße
Berlin
To: Hauptmann Peter von Vorzik
III Gruppe JG233
Schaftstadt, Halle

27th November 1943

Dear Peter,

Of course, like you, I am deeply concerned for Edith. Not for her own position which is secure enough but because of Arturo. The Führer is quite content that political decisions should still be an internal matter for the Duce and the resurgent Fascist Party although all military decisions are being made by Field Marshal Kesselring. Doubtless, within the Fascist Party, there are many personal vendettas being played out amongst the various factions and it was indeed very foolish of Arturo not to leave Italy when he had the chance. After all, Ciano thought he was on the way to Spain when he and his family fled Rome. He certainly was not thinking about his old comrades or members of his retinue. Now Arturo must take his chances, such as they are and, strictly between us, I do not think his future is too assured. There is nothing I can do to influence his situation. The only thing I can do is make sure Edith is personally safe; I am afraid she must face up to the possibility of losing Arturo. My own misgivings about the marriage have been confirmed. Should the worst happen I can at least make sure she has a position of some importance within one or other of our organisations. There are several situations available here within the SD, she could even be a secretary or assistant secretary to myself although I would understand if she did not want to return to Berlin. If she prefers to stay in Rome, Dr Dollmann or SS-Obersturmbannführer Wilhelm Höttl, a friend of mine who is in charge of Ausland SD interests in Italy, would be able to find a suitable position for her.

For myself I am kept extremely busy. So much is happening on the diplomatic and counterintelligence fronts. Taking an overall view of Europe today is like working on an enormous jigsaw puzzle, trying to fit thousands of pieces into place. We have agents in every country, even Russia, and their reports have to be monitored, sifted and appraised. There are tentative movements towards peace with either the Anglo-Saxons or the Russians, everyone realises it would be a serious mistake to engage our enemies on two fronts now that there is much talk of the Anglo-Saxons attempting a landing in the west. Schellenberg is busy contacting various representatives in Switzerland and Sweden with a view to stopping such a prospect, allowing us to deal unhindered with the Russians.

The difficulties are manifold: since the Anglo-Saxons made their decree at Casablanca of "unconditional surrender" they will not engage in discussions with certain Party members such as the Führer himself or the Reichsführer-SS. He, Himmler, vacillates continually, unwilling to commit himself to any plan until he sees which way the wind is blowing yet only too ready for others to attempt rapprochements and then either take the credit for whatever transpires or condemn his subordinates if the plan fails. Von Ribbentrop continues to be a thorn in the flesh, jealous and resentful of the Ausland SD, ever ready to run to the Führer with distorted tales of what we are doing or not doing while concocting absurd plans of his own, living a life of extreme luxury in that palace of his at Fuschl. (I have heard accounts of how the tapestries had to be changed four times as they were not to the liking of Frau Ribbentrop!) Kaltenbrunner and Müller are another two ever watchful for opportunities to tell malicious lies to the Führer about our department. Schellenberg has arranged for me to go and see von Papen in Turkey where the signs are that the government is leaning towards support for the Russians. We must do whatever we can to deflect that. I am not sure how long I will be away but send any letters to the Kaisestraße address.

I hope all continues to go well with you, delighted that Mathilde and Wolfchen are now safely in the countryside.

Ever your devoted brother,

Christian

PS Continue to burn all our correspondence. C.

From: Mathilde von Vorzik
Die Alter Scheune
Steuben Gasse
Höchstein
To: Hauptmann Peter von Vorzik
III Gruppe JG233
Schaftstadt, Halle

2nd December 1943

My Darling Peter,

So pleased, as always, to have your letter and to know you are safe and well. Winter is here! The days have been very cold with bitter winds and sharp frosts with the night-time temperature well below zero. I expect you have been having similar weather. The countryside certainly seems colder than the city, does it not? However, the house is very warm; we light that big wood-burning kitchen stove in the afternoon and that heats the whole house. Marie is wonderful, looking after us like a nurse, cooking delicious meals mostly from the local farm produce and she and Lenka are very companionable, almost like a mother and daughter.

Now, darling, some really important news. I am pregnant again! I do hope you will be as thrilled and happy as I am that Wolfchen is going to have a little brother or sister. I have not yet seen the local doctor or midwife but I have missed my time of the month and *I know the feelings!* Your last visit to Grunewald is what has occasioned this happy state. How blessed we are! Do tell me, darling, that you are pleased with the news even though it wasn't planned. I am not telling anyone yet except yourself, otherwise it seems to people that one is pregnant for ages. All my other news seems trivial. We make almost daily visits to the farm, mostly to please Wolfchen but Lenka and I enjoy the walk (even in this cold weather) and Frau Linder, the farmer's wife gives us little cakes warm from the oven and fresh milk straight from the cows. She and her husband had a letter from their sons which was a great relief for them although, apparently, the conditions at the front are terrible, constant attacks from the Russians and the snows beginning again.

I had a letter from Trude, one of the women I knew at the sewing circle, and she said that Frau Kirschner's house had been badly damaged in recent raids on Berlin. Frau Kirschner collapsed with the shock of it – the house next door received a direct hit – and she is moving to be with her sister in Hanover, the sewing circle now disbanded. I could not repress a smile, remembering Frau Kirschner's disapproving remarks when I told her we were moving to Höchstein! It seems that Berlin has suffered terrible damage since we left, much worse than the official communiques admit. Several of the foreign embassies in the Tiergarten have been destroyed, as well as shops and offices on the Ku'damm and Unter den Linden. Ministry buildings in Wilhelmstraße have also been badly damaged as have the Eden and Adlon hotels. There is great destruction around the zoo and many of the wild animals have been shot for fear they might escape including the crocodiles who tried to reach the River Spree! Can you imagine coming face to face with a lion or a crocodile in your garden! There were terrible fires raging everywhere, the whole city is covered with ash, the electricity is frequently cut off and water is rationed. How thankful I am we left when we did.

I do not think it a good idea to buy Wolfchen a pony for Christmas, darling, mainly because it would fall to me to look after the creature and now that I am pregnant it would become a more and more arduous undertaking. But I am sure there is somewhere locally where Wolfchen could take riding lessons. I will ask at the farm. Certainly he loves sitting up on the farmer's ploughing horses and he has no fear of the animals. I have begun reading Goethe's novel *Wilhelm Meister* which is not easy but beautiful language and I am becoming enthralled by the story about the stage-struck youth travelling the country with a theatrical company. Do you know it? Do I dare ask if there is any possibility of you having leave over Christmas? That would be so wonderful to look forward to since the news remains so depressing. Sometimes I find it hard to remain hopeful for the future.

Do write soon, darling.

Ever your own,
Mathilde and Wolfchen

Edward Thorpe

From: Oberleutnant Claus Grüber
Erprobungsgruppe V
Rechlin am Muritzsee
To: Hauptmann Peter von Vorzik
III Gruppe JG233
Schaftstadt, Halle

9th December 1943

Dear Peter,

I put pen to paper partly to send you greetings and partly to vent my feelings of rage and frustration! I expect you have heard the outcome of the demonstration of the Me262 for the Führer? If not, this is how it transpired. We all flew to an airfield at Insterburg near the Baltic coast. Cold, low grey cloud, strong cross winds – not good flying weather, at least for demonstration purposes. The Führer arrived in his Condor with an escort of FW190s then, after formal introductions and hot coffee (mine surreptitiously laced with schnapps!) the 262 was rolled out and inspected on the ground before taking off and making several low passes at high speed. All eyes are on the Führer, not the plane. After the third pass the Führer turns to Willi Messerschmitt and asks, "Can it carry bombs?" Willi, nonplussed, mutters, "Well, yes, in the last resort all aircraft can carry bombs." "So! Here at last is our blitzbomber!" says the Führer. And that is what he has decreed – one of his "intuitive decisions." The 262 is to be developed as a bomber. No matter that here is a fighter that, given the right numbers, could defeat the threat of the American daylight raiders, it must be a bomber and only a bomber.

Of course, that decision presents innumerable difficulties. The undercarriage is too slender to take the weight of bombs. The range is inadequate for bombing missions, so auxiliary tanks must be built in, adding more weight, affecting performance, displacing the centre of gravity and producing instability. No bombsight or approved method of bomb-suspension exists so the winter must be spent redesigning the aircraft and rectifying these problems instead of the factories producing hundreds of 262 fighters and the schools training hundreds of young pilots to fly them. Everyone, from Willi Messerschmitt down, is in a state of rage, frustration and despair that such an advantage should be thrown away. But there it is: the Führer has spoken, it is one of his "irrevocable resolves."

504

We face a hard winter in terms of containing our enemies. No doubt the RAF will continue its devastating night bombing and on the eastern front we must no doubt expect a winter campaign from the Russians, just as they have done the last two years. Therein lies our greatest danger for they seem to have an overwhelming advantage in numbers including tanks, aircraft and manpower. 1943 has been a bad year, has it not? We have lost the initiative everywhere and now we are faced with the possibility of fighting on two fronts. I do not think all is lost – yet; but during this coming year we will have to alter the balance somewhere, somehow, in our favour. The Reichsmarschall is a spent force. He spends his time at Karinhalle, dressing up in hunting clothes and playing with his jewels and failing to give his support to his Fliegerkorps Kommandants. He should have stood up to the Führer and insisted that the 262 be produced as a fighter.

How are you, dear comrade? Have you had any more encounters with US aircraft? I know the bombers seem to have been beaten, at least in making deep penetration attacks, but the RAF and US fighters make frequent sweeps over the English Channel but will not have penetrated so far to alert your Gruppe if you are still at Schaftstadt. I believe we are building many more fighter stations around the German frontiers ready for whatever transpires next spring. It was nice of you to suggest in your last letter that I could still attract the female sex but no moth has appeared to dance around this flickering flame! Work, work, work; that is what absorbs me at present. How is your family? Have they moved from Berlin which I hear is in a real mess. Do let me have your news when you can. Meanwhile, every good wish for the coming holiday season and let us drink a toast to final victory next year.

Ever your sincere comrade,

Claus

From: Hauptmann Peter von Vorzik
III Gruppe JG233
Schaftstadt, Halle
To: Mathilde von Vorzik
Die Alter Scheune
Steuben Gasse
Höchstein

14th December 1943

My Darling Mathilde,

What wonderful news! Yes, of course, I am overjoyed to think that you are carrying another baby for us, a brother or sister for Wolfchen. It has been a great boost to my morale and, although it is early days yet, the coming months will provide much excitement and speculation for us. Have you seen the local doctor yet? I expect Marie (have you told her?) will be able to guide you as to who are the best maternity specialists in Höchstein. More good news! At present it looks as if Varasch and I will be granted Christmas leave as we are not expecting much operational activity, at least in our sector, until well into the New Year. Our leave will not be extended into the New Year, however. The arrangement is that those of us granted leave for Christmas will return to base about the 29th to relieve others, especially those without wives and children, for the New Year festivities. I thought it best to be with you and Wolfchen over Christmas and Varasch has applied to come at the same time; after all, we will be spending the holiday in his home. No more now, darling, I wanted to reply at once to your great news and to let you have mine.

All my love.

Ever your adoring husband,
Peter

PS Can I leave it to you to buy Christmas presents for Marie, Lenka, etc. Can you find something to send Edith? Some sort of food delicacy might be most acceptable. P.

PPS No, I have not read Goethe's *Wilhelm Meister*, only *Faust*. P.

From: Hauptmann Peter von Vorzik
III Gruppe JG233
Schaftstadt, Halle
To: Contessa Edith Novarro-Badaelli
Villa Frascati
Via Augusta
Rome

12th December 1943

My Dear Edith,

I write simply to say how much you will be in our thoughts this Christmastide and to send my loving greetings together with the hope that Arturo will be restored to you early in the New Year. However, my comrade, Ludwig Varasch, has most generously said that any member of my family is welcome at Höchstein as it is a large house. So, it did occur to me that you might join us at Höchstein for a few days over the holiday period. I realise you may wish to stay in Rome in the hope of hearing good news but if not just come! Pack a bag, brave the tedious rail journey and be comforted by those close to you. I imagine you could take the Rome–Munich express and then it is a comparatively short journey via Nuremberg and Bamberg where we could meet you. I have been given a few days' leave over Christmas and it would be wonderful to see you again, even for a short time.

Do think about it.

Ever your loving brother,
Peter

From: Hauptmann Peter von Vorzik
III Gruppe JG233
Schaftstadt, Halle
To: Oberleutnant Claus Grüber
Erprobungsgruppe V
Rechlin am Muritzsee

17th December 1943

Dear Claus,

Thank you for your welcome letter, it is always a pleasure to hear from you although I confess its contents were somewhat disturbing. I refer, of

507

course, to the Führer's decision to turn the 262 into a bomber. I had not heard about the decision from any other source. I can see that, at some future date, it could be adapted as a fighter-bomber just as our 109s and 190s have been; but to ignore its potential as a war-winning fighter just when we are facing a threat from the American daylight raiders and inferiority in numbers against the Russians seems just perverse. It is difficult, of course, for anyone to defy the Führer's edict but I would have thought that he could be persuaded by men such as Generalleutnant Galland, Generaloberst Korten or even Willi Messerschmitt himself that what we need now are fighters and more fighters especially one so superior to anything the enemy possesses. Technical knowledge apart, I can understand that the Führer wishes to retain the offensive rather than move to the defensive position – that is his nature. But it cannot be denied that, at the moment, we are very much on the defensive on all fronts. It is a great pity that the Reichsmarschall has, apparently, lost all influence, not to say interest. There was a time when the Führer allowed him absolute sovereignty over all decisions affecting the Luftwaffe. Not any more, it seems, after the debacle of Stalingrad.

After our first brief but successful encounter with the Americans they have not attempted to reach as far as our sector again although I hear they are active around northern France and the Baltic, anywhere where they can have the protection of escorting fighters. Now winter weather curtails our operations and we are trying to give our young pilots greater knowledge of tactics through lectures – not as good as experience in the air. When the spring arrives I expect we will be facing more aerial battles, perhaps even earlier. I am so relieved that my family are safely ensconced in the country now that Berlin has been so relentlessly attacked. My brother, Christian, is still there, however, although he makes frequent trips abroad for the Ausland SD. At present he is in Turkey, I believe. My sister Edith remains in Rome where she is having an anxious time, her husband being imprisoned in Verona because of his association with Ciano and the faction that deposed Mussolini. For me the worst part is being unable to do anything to help matters.

Will you be going home to Göttingen for the holidays? It's fine if you can fly but I imagine an awkward journey by rail. All rail journeys are crowded and tedious these days, I have had some experience of it. How are your parents? I suppose they have heard some of the raids even if their town has not been directly targeted. Yes, dear comrade, I will be joining you over the festivities, at least in spirit, and raising a glass to our final victory in the coming year.

Sincere best wishes,

Ever yours,

Peter

From: *Contessa Edith Novarro-Badaelli*
Villa Frascati
Via Augusta
Rome
To: *Hauptmann Peter von Vorzik*
III Gruppe JG233
Schaftstadt, Halle

19th December 1943

My Dear Peter,

I am sending this letter to Höchstein as I feel sure by the time it arrives you will be on leave there. Thank you for the suggestion that I join you and please thank your comrade Ludwig Varasch for his kind offer of hospitality, but, as you surmise, I feel it necessary to remain here in Rome in the hope of hearing good news from Arturo. Dr Dollmann has said he does not think the authorities at Verona will wish to keep him imprisoned for long; there are really no reasons to charge him with actions against the state or the Fascist Party. So I wait in hope. I have decided to spend the holiday period assisting the nuns at the Santa Maria orphanage in whatever way I can. They are always short of practical helpers and I have offered to do anything, taking classes, cleaning or kitchen work, wherever I may be of help. In that way I shall keep busy and celebrate the birth of our Lord in a manner in which I hope He would approve. I have sent two small token parcels to Höchstein, one to you and Mathilde and one for Wolfchen. I hope you have a joyous and restful Christmastide with your family and trust that we shall be granted peace in the New Year.

Ever your loving sister,

Edith

Hauptmann Peter von Vorzik
Journal entry

4th January 1944

First I must record the happiest Christmas I can remember in the company of my wife and son and comrades whom I hold in deep affection. Varasch insisted on Kurt spending his Christmas leave with us at Höchstein which pleased me greatly (Kurt having no family to go to) and the three of us arrived at Bamberg station about mid-afternoon on the 23rd December having left Schaftstadt thirty-six hours before. Had I been alone it would have been a really dreary rail journey; as it was the time passed amiably enough despite a long wait at Leipzig station and another at Plauen in the middle of the night. Varasch kept us entertained with anecdotes about an eccentric aunt and risqué stories about his amorous adventures as a student at Württemberg, much of it apocryphal, I am sure. What we lacked in food we made up for in beer, brandy and schnapps; in fact, in my memory, the journey dissolves into an alcoholic haze, but we were sober enough on arrival at Höchstein, taking a taxi from Bamberg station.

On the evening of our arrival it began to snow, making the countryside wondrously beautiful, the surrounding fields and trees glittering under a full moon. Marie, Mathilde and Lenka had decorated the house with evergreens and in the hall was a large tree hung with exquisite Bohemian glass ornaments and surmounted by a star. The next morning Kurt and I made Wolfchen a large snowman and after a lunch of soup, cold meats and strudel, together with some excellent Riesling, we all went for a walk by the river which was frozen over although the ice was not thick enough to bear a man's weight. On Christmas Eve it snowed again while we gathered around the tree exchanging presents. From the Staffel quartermaster (who does a profitable private trade in luxury goods via a friend in Paris) I had managed to obtain some good cigars for Varasch and Kurt. A trip I made into Halle yielded a powder compact and scent spray in scarlet and black enamel inlaid with silver filigree for Mathilde and silk scarves for Marie and Lenka. In a dark, musty toyshop which evoked memories of my own childhood I found a box of hand-carved farm animals, horses, cows, sheep, pigs, ducks and geese for Wolfchen. I pondered over a Märklin train set but reluctantly decided he was still too young for it; I would have enjoyed setting it out for him. Mathilde had bought me a beautiful pair of soft kid gloves lined with fur which will be perfect for whatever flying we do this winter, our regulation issue gloves being much thicker and clumsier. Christian had sent us his usual case of champagne and Edith's packages included Parma ham, a large cheese, almond-flavoured biscuits and a bottle of Strega liqueur. For Wolfchen there was a silk suit in pale blue. Varasch gave me a bottle of Napoleon brandy and Kurt had assembled an album of photographs of me, himself and our aircraft in France, Russia, Sicily and North Africa. It was a very personal present which I much appreciated and passed to Mathilde for safe-keeping. Christmas Day was centred around preparations for a sumptuous evening meal: caviar, provided by Varasch who had bought it from a Wehrmacht officer returning from the Russian front; apple and parsnip soup; roast pork and goose from the farm; a chocolate pudding, *glacé* fruits from Switzerland, also courtesy of Varasch and plenty of wine and liqueurs. Afterwards we retired to the main salon and sang songs with Kurt playing the piano. I noticed Lenka watching him with admiring eyes and wondered if, perhaps, Kurt might return the interest. I shall make a point of asking him, as casually as I can. Both of them are lonely people.

I must confess we face the New Year with some trepidation. The main problem is that we have lost the initiative on all battle-fronts and, particularly in the air, are outnumbered everywhere. After his appointment as Chief of the Air Staff, replacing Jeschonnek, Generaloberst Korten devised a very necessary strategic bomber offensive against the Russians which would have impeded their advance westward. Unfortunately the plan had to be abandoned; the Russians had already advanced so far that our intended targets – rail centres and munitions factories beyond the Urals – were already out of range of the He111 while the He177 is still plagued with technical problems and in any case there are too few of them to sustain a bombing campaign. Somehow we must find a way of stopping the Russians before the Anglo-Americans try a landing somewhere across the English channel.

From: Mathilde von Vorzik
Die Alter Scheune
Steuben Gasse
Höchstein
To: Hauptmann Peter von Vorzik
III Gruppe JG233
Schaftstadt, Halle

5th January 1944

My Darling Peter,

We have all felt a depressing sense of anticlimax since you returned from leave. It was such a happy joyful time when you were here and now the house seems dark and empty after all that bonhomie, the Christmas candles, the laughter and songs and, of course, your dear, dear presence. It does not help that I have started having morning sickness again! Well, that is to be expected and in a way I welcome the reminder that I am carrying our next child. I spend hours wondering if it will be a boy or a girl and what will we call it? Of course there is plenty of time to think about such things but if it is a girl I thought perhaps we could combine the names of our two mothers. What do you think? If it is a boy I would like to include my father's name, Heinrich, though not necessarily the first. The snow has melted and it is raining now. Wolfchen was very upset when his snowman disappeared leaving only the carrot that you used for the nose! He keeps it as a sort of talisman; when it has shrivelled I will find some way to dispose of it. At the moment he carries it everywhere, even insists on it being placed on the night-table by his cot. He loves his toy farm animals and sets them out each day and has given them all names, some of which he has made up. He has such a vivid imagination.

You said you thought Lenka was attracted to Kurt and I asked her in a roundabout way what she thought of him and she blushed and said she thought he was good-looking. You might ask Kurt what he thought of Lenka and if his response is positive you could suggest that they correspond. The first letter would have to come from him. On New Year's Eve we opened a bottle of Christian's champagne and drank a toast to you and Ludwig and Kurt but it was difficult to establish a festive mood without you all here and we went to bed before midnight. How did you celebrate, darling? Was there a party in the mess? We all hope that this

New Year will bring victory and peace although the news from the fronts is not encouraging. I read recently in one of the papers that Churchill, Roosevelt and Stalin had met in Teheran last month and that we must expect an attempt by the British and Americans to try and land somewhere in northern France sometime this year. There were pictures of big guns and fortifications being built on the coast and the writer of the accompanying article said that it would be impossible to land anywhere and any invasion force would be thrown back into the sea. I do hope he is right.

I have written to Edith to thank her for her presents, it was so kind of her to think of us when she must be so worried about Arturo. I do hope he is released from prison soon. I have also written to thank Christian for the champagne. Perhaps he is back from Turkey now, if not the letter will await his return. Had you forgotten, darling, that you had asked me to find presents for Marie and Lenka? They were very pleased with the scarves you brought them and the gloves I bought for them (not as good as the ones I found for you!) will do for another time. Marie's birthday is next month. Marie is taking me to see a gynaecologist in Höchstein tomorrow. It is just a routine examination and I will be signing on his register. I will also visit the maternity home where he practises and make a provisional appointment for my confinement sometime next August. Wouldn't it be an amazing coincidence if the new baby came on Wolfchen's birthday?

Now we must wrap up against the rain and walk to the post with this. All love to you, darling, from your own

Mathilde and Wolfchen

From: Contessa Edith Novarro-Badaelli
Villa Frascati
Via Augusta
Rome
To: Hauptmann Peter von Vorzik
III Gruppe JG233
Schaftstadt, Halle

6th January 1944

My Dear Peter,
This is to tell you that my worst fears have been realised. This morning I received a communication from the Minister of the Interior, Guido

Buffarini, countersigned by Party Secretary Alessandro Pavolini, to say that Arturo had been shot "while attempting to escape." There was a rider to the effect that the jailer "who was assisting him" had also been executed. Accompanying the letter, delivered by a lieutenant in the *carabinieri*, was a cardboard box containing a metal urn within which were Arturo's ashes. A label attached gave the date of cremation as January 2nd. As you can imagine I am still numb with shock – shock at the cruel murder itself (for such I believe it to be) and shock at the crude, insensitive manner in which I was made aware of Arturo's death. I am sure he was not attempting to escape. How could he from that great prison. Even if he had suborned some jailer to assist him I do not think it would have been possible. I saw the elaborate security measures when I visited the prison last October. And why was Arturo cremated in such a hurry? Why was I not given the chance to receive the body and arrange a proper funeral? The whole foul deed reeks of collusion between men who once professed to be Arturo's friends and have now proved to be opportunist enemies. I have written to Eleanora to ask her what she would wish me to do with Arturo's ashes. It is doubly dreadful for her, one son lost in Russia with no body recovered, and now her eldest son murdered by political enemies. For myself I am not sure what my future plans will be. For the moment I am remaining here and will be in touch with you as soon as I have decided what to do.

In bitter grief but always

Your loving sister,
Edith

From: Hauptmann Peter von Vorzik
III Gruppe JG233
Schaftstadt, Halle
To: Mathilde von Vorzik
Die Alter Scheune
Steuben Gasse
Höchstein

11th January 1944

My Darling Mathilde,
Yes, it is always an anticlimax when the Christmas festivities are over and one says goodbye to loved ones. The three of us were somewhat depressed

during the rail journey back to base but we were grateful for the delicious provisions that Marie had packed for us and can you guess? – we drowned our sorrows with beer and schnapps en route. And we all of us carried memories of a very happy time. I enquired, casually, what Kurt thought of Lenka but, of course, he immediately sensed that I, we, were matchmaking! "Thank you for your interest," he said, smiling, "but I don't want to become involved with a girl until this damn war is over. I think Lenka is very nice, pretty, charming and shy, but we have seen so many comrades lost in this war and the sorrow death can bring to wives and girlfriends." Then, obviously thinking of us, he said, "Of course, you have a wonderful wife and son and it's part of my job to help keep you alive for them, but I don't have a Katschmarek!" It was said jokingly but I understood the point he was making. He has already lost his parents and Lenka has apparently lost her father and brother and he would not want anyone like Lenka mourning his death as well.

Our New Year celebration in the mess was rowdy with lots of toasts drunk to the Führer, victory and absent friends but I slipped away soon after midnight not wanting a hangover on patrol next morning. We are only doing a few regular standing patrols but as Staffel Kommandant I thought it my duty to lead the early morning flight. Weather permitting we fly a triangle between Schaftstadt, Erfurt-Bindersleben and Leutewitz contiguous with other sectors but, at the moment, flying weather has been bad and enemy activity confined to north Germany, France, Holland and Belgium.

I trust the gynaecologist's examination was satisfactory and he confirmed that we have, indeed, a new baby on the way! How often will you see him? I know your pregnancy with Wolfchen was straightforward and I presume this one will be also, darling, but do take special care of yourself during these coming months – I am haunted by the terrible thing that happened to Frieda. It is a great comfort to know you have Lenka and Marie with you. Of course you must incorporate your father's name if it is a boy and our mothers' names, too, if it is a girl. I have no special preferences just so long as the child is as beautiful and physically perfect as Wolfchen. How blessed we are. I was sorry I could not persuade Edith to join us for Christmas. I understand her feelings that she wanted to remain in Rome in the hope that she might hear some good news about Arturo but we could have consoled her for a few days and made her feel less alone in facing whatever the future brings. I have deep misgivings about the situation. You are right, I did forget that I had asked you to find presents for Lenka and Marie. When I went into Halle to look for your present I saw the scarves and thought they would be suitable. Sorry, darling, to have given you an unnecessary task. As you say, perhaps they will be useful for other occasions. I have no real news for you darling, these are dull uneventful days so I will hurry to catch the afternoon post, delivery being so slow these days.

All my love to you and Wolfchen, regards to Lenka and Marie,

Ever your adoring,

Peter

From: Hauptmann Peter von Vorzik
III Gruppe JG233
Schaftstadt, Halle
To: Contessa Edith Novarro-Badaelli
Villa Frascati
Via Augusta
Rome

14th January 1944

My Dear Edith,

I am horrified and appalled by the news of the death of Arturo and filled with anguish for you, my dear sister, suffering alone with no member of the family near you. Like you I am full of questions which, in the fullness of time, I hope will be answered. Without knowing more than the shocking events you describe in your letter it must seem a matter of personal revenge by political enemies now in power, enemies, as you point out, who masqueraded as friends. What is done is done but I sincerely hope that we may ultimately see that these evil conspirators are made to pay for Arturo's murder. News in the papers and on the radio that Ciano and five other members of the Fascist party have also been executed would seem to confirm that Arturo's death was premeditated and that you are right when you say he would not, could not, have been involved in a planned escape. Arturo was a man of integrity, faithful to his friend Ciano and, it seems, unsuspecting that others would act so treacherously. Perhaps it is an enduring trait of the Italian character? One thinks of Nero and Caligula, Brutus and Cassius, of the Borgias and Sforzas, Machiavelli and

Gonzaga, treacherous creatures, all of them. The way you were informed and the callous and indecent haste that Arturo's body was cremated points to covering up a deliberate assassination.

Dear sister, let me prevail upon you to come back to Germany, to Höchstein, where you could be at peace with Mathilde, even if, later, you wished to make some other change in your livelihood. Come back to your own country and be close to your family.

Write and let me know your plans.

> Ever your loving brother, in sorrow,
> Peter

From: Hauptmann Peter von Vorzik
III Gruppe JG233
Schaftstadt, Halle
To: Mathilde von Vorzik
Die Alter Scheune
Steuben Gasse
Höchstein

15th January 1944

My Darling Mathilde,

You may have heard from Edith. If not, she is probably relying on me to tell you the dreadful news that Arturo has been shot and killed at the Scalzi prison. The authorities there are pretending that he was shot while attempting to escape but it is safe to assume that it was judicial murder by political enemies. Of course one's thoughts are for Edith who received the news in the most callous way, his ashes sent with a brief accompanying official letter. I have written to her suggesting that she come and stay with you at Höchstein, at least for the time being. I cannot bear the thought that she is in Rome alone, with no family or friends nearby, although I know she draws comfort and strength in her great faith in the church. I am sure she would appreciate a letter from you and perhaps you could persuade her to join you at Höchstein?

In haste,

Love and kisses to your dear self and Wolfchen.

> Ever your own,
> Peter

From: Hauptmann Peter von Vorzik
III Gruppe JG233
Schaftstadt, Halle
To: SS-Gruppenführer Count Christian von Vorzik
116 Kaiserstraße
Berlin

16th January 1944

Dear Christian,

If you have returned from Turkey, I am sure you will have heard from Edith that Arturo has been callously murdered. From what Edith writes I am sure he was deliberately done to death by political enemies. As you will also doubtless know Ciano and his confrères have also been judicially executed. Because there were no grounds for a formal accusation against Arturo (after all, he was not a member of the Grand Council that voted against Mussolini) he was assassinated on some trumped-up charge by various rivals. What a treacherous, conniving lot these Italians are! I assume it is not possible to exact justice for Arturo's death at this time but when the war is over we must try and instigate a formal investigation into exactly what happened and who is responsible. We owe it to our dear sister to discover the truth. Of course it is Edith's situation that perturbs me most. I have written to her urging her to join Mathilde at Höchstein which I hope she will do. A letter from you with the same suggestion might help her to make that decision. One small blessing in this awful scenario is that there are no children involved.

No more now, write to me when you can.

Ever your loving brother,
Peter

PS I hope your trip to Turkey was successful and interesting. P.

From: Oberleutnant Lother Köhl
I Gruppe Sch.Gl
Eastern Front
To: Hauptmann Peter von Vorzik
III Gruppe JG233
Schaftstadt, Halle

18th January 1944

Dear Peter,

Where shall I begin? First, I suppose, to thank you for your letters of 11th August and 21st October which have just caught up with me! During the last three months we have led a frantic life, up and down the southern part of the front like mad things, Kursk, Belgorod, Kharkov, Stalino, Kremenchug, Krivoi Rog, Taganrog, Nikopol, there isn't a square kilometre of the southern Ukraine, right down to the Crimea, that we haven't covered. All to little purpose, it seems. The Luftwaffe is stretched to breaking point, helping the ground forces to plug gaps all along the line, losing aircraft as much through wastage, lack of servicing, lack of spares, accidents and raids by Russian ground-attack aircraft as through operational sorties. The Russian's Il-2 Shturmoviks have been particularly devastating, shooting up our airfields at low level and protected by swarms of LAGG-3s and L-a-5s. The Shturmovik is practically indestructible, at least from the ground, so heavily armoured that flak shells just bounce off it! Our own beastly 189s have been unserviceable most of the time which is, I suppose, the main reason that I am still alive!

Thankfully, we have now been withdrawn from the front-line for "rest and redevelopment" near Tarnopol which mostly means sitting out bone-aching blizzards. Winter has come almost as a solace. I have made another request for reassignment, anywhere, anything, even back to 110s, just so long as I don't have to fly the 189 again. I would be happy to retrain for nightfighting as I understand the 110s are doing well over Germany in that role. Then if I crashed it would at least be over my own country! When I look at the map and see how much ground we have given up since last summer it is very disheartening. I confess to you, Peter, that I sometimes wonder what we are fighting for. Five years ago we knew that Germany needed to resolve the injustice of the Versailles Treaty. We needed more living space for our people, we needed to help the German communities oppressed in east Prussia and Central Europe, we needed to teach a lesson to the Czechs and Poles who arrogantly breached our boundaries and we knew how to deal with the Bolshevik threat. All that was achieved by 1941. Now we find ourselves beleaguered by the British Empire, the Americans and the Russians as well as much of the rest of the world. The whole thing has got out of hand and it is difficult to see how it will end. Do you ever have these anxious feelings? Perhaps it is because I have been stuck in Russia for so long, fighting a gigantic enemy that seems to grow stronger every day, that I feel out of touch with reality. Except that is the reality!

I am glad to hear your wife and son are safe in the countryside. (What I would not give to glimpse the German countryside!) You wrote about the hell of Hamburg and every day I hear as you must do how more and more of our cities are being destroyed by the RAF's night attacks. That is one reason why I would like a transfer to a Nachtjagdgeschwader. I still receive affectionate letters from my war widow which I reply to non-committally. I am very grateful for the correspondence but do not wish to become embroiled at the moment, life seems all too precarious and she has already been widowed once. Perhaps two war-pensions would be a useful income or is that too cynical?

Please write when you can, I promise to reply as soon as I hear from you.

Ever your sincere comrade,

Lother

From: SS-Gruppenführer Count Christian von Vorzik
116 Kaiserstraße
Berlin
To: Hauptmann Peter von Vorzik
III Gruppe JG233
Schaftstadt, Halle

25th January 1944

My Dear Peter,

Yes, Edith has written to me and, indeed, it is shocking news about Arturo's death although I cannot say I am surprised. Since the deposition of Mussolini and his reinstatement as head of the newly constituted Italian Social Republic old scores are being settled through hatreds and rivalries that go back years. For some time Ciano had been acting foolishly, mouthing anti-fascist and anti-government sentiments to anyone who would listen, including political enemies. It was only to be expected that his behaviour would incite retribution if not revenge after Grandi had fled and the other traitors had been arrested. Both Arturo and Edith have been naive in their assumption that he would not be deemed part of Ciano's faction and treated accordingly. Which is not to say that I am unsympathetic towards our sister and her predicament. In my reply to her letter I made it clear that I am powerless to intervene in any way or to apply for an investigation into the circumstances of Arturo's death. We – the Germans – are in military control throughout Italy but the Führer has permitted Mussolini absolute sovereignty over interior affairs and it was he who authorised his son-in-law's execution despite pleas from Edda who, I am informed, has since escaped to Switzerland. Edith will be quite safe living quietly at her villa (both Höttl and Dollmann have promised to keep watch over her) unless the British and Americans manage to advance towards Rome in which case Edith would be advised to return to Germany. At present the Anglo-Americans do not constitute a threat to the city.

My visit to Turkey was a success insofar as I was able to gather important information from our agents there, information that came as a surprise to von Papen who was certain that the Turks intended to maintain their neutrality indefinitely. On the contrary, our agents have received incontrovertible information that they intend, by degrees, to work towards throwing in their lot with the Anglo-Americans and the Russians. This, we think, is the direct result of our enemies' recent conference in Teheran. First, the Turks will maintain their neutral stance while keeping large military forces in Thrace which tie down German divisions in Bulgaria. Meanwhile they are receiving increasing shipments of war material from America and Britain which will improve their own military preparedness while at the same time expanding their relationship with British and American military staffs. By May of this year they expect to be in a position to declare war on Germany. Such deviousness and complicity! At least we have been forewarned. Walter has told me to be prepared to accompany him to Sweden and/or Switzerland on confidential missions in the near future. His plans are constantly frustrated by von Ribbentrop, Kaltenbrunner and Müller but luckily he has the approval of Himmler in his undertakings which means our department manages to function effectively despite the machinations of other Party members.

I do not expect to be away for more than a few days so, as always, letters can be addressed here.

I trust all goes well with you and your loved ones.

Ever your loving brother,
Christian

From: Mathilde von Vorzik
Die Alter Scheune
Steuben Gasse
Höchstein
To: Hauptmann Peter von Vorzik
III Gruppe JG233
Schaftstadt, Halle

26th January 1944

My Darling Peter,
No, I had not heard from Edith so your letter of the 15th came as a terrible shock, just as I was about to reply to your one of the 11th. Poor Edith! I wonder she did not collapse at the news, particularly as it was conveyed to her in the ghastly way you describe. But, as you say, she has always had a firm belief in the Catholic faith which I am sure helps to sustain her and I have always thought there is a considerable strength of character beneath her quiet, undemonstrative manner. Even so, it must be an awful grief to bear. From her letters and conversations with me I know she was deeply in love with Arturo and to have him taken from her so soon after their marriage and in such a dreadful manner must have filled her with burdensome sorrow. Of course, on receiving your letter, I wrote to her at once and pleaded with her in the strongest terms to join us here. As yet I have not had a reply. I find it awful, as I am sure you do, that the authorities behave in such a murderous manner but I suppose it has something to do with the times we live in when human life seems so expendable.

Now, darling, to something happier. The gynaecologist confirmed my pregnancy (not that confirmation was necessary!) and said everything was proceeding normally. He has given me a diet sheet to follow (he is very keen on my eating foods that contain certain elements like iron) and forbidden me to drink alcohol. Well, as you know, I do enjoy a glass of wine but that will not be too hard to forgo for the next seven months. He has also given me exercises to do (similar to the ones I did while carrying Wolfchen) and says I must rest every afternoon with my feet up. You can imagine, I am sure, how I am being pampered by Marie who is very excited at the prospect of a baby coming.

The weather has been horrible, endless rain and high winds, so we have been staying indoors this last week or two and I have continued with my reading – I have become quite engrossed with the adventures of *Wilhelm Meister*. Wolfchen demands more and more time but both Lenka and Marie enjoy playing with him and are very happy to take him off my hands for an hour or two. I am sorry that Kurt did not respond more positively to your suggestion that he might correspond with Lenka but I understand his reasons for not wishing to become involved at this time. And he is right! It is part of his job to see no harm comes to you and for that I am immensely grateful. I expect you too have had bad weather which would have curtailed your flying. You did not say whether your Staffel was engaged in the recent raid by American bombers on Aschersleben. The radio news said that the Americans lost many planes. Whatever you do, darling, take care of your precious self for

Your loving,
Mathilde and Wolfchen

PS Fond regards to Ludwig and Kurt. M.

Hauptmann Peter von Vorzik
Journal entry

4th February 1944

I cannot eradicate from my mind the killing of my brother-in-law, Arturo, by his political enemies. I remember back in 1934, almost ten years ago, when I was still attending the gymnasium in Munich, our professor explaining to us the necessity for the summary execution of Ernst Röhm and his SA cronies who were plotting to seize power from the Führer and impose their own ideas on the National Socialist Party. That was insurrection and needed to be dealt with decisively. But Arturo was not plotting with anyone, he had merely been a loyal friend of Ciano who was

523

himself imprisoned and unable to be a threat to the state. No, this was plain murder, carried out by political opponents with no other purpose but sheer animosity. It is of course my sister for whom I feel real anguish. There is no one more gentle, loving, giving, in this world (except my wife) and it is her tragic circumstances that constantly fill my thoughts. It is frustrating to be so powerless to help, to be so far from her that I cannot give her affection and support by my physical presence. I hope she can be persuaded to join Mathilde at Höchstein.

Meanwhile the war continues to rage on all fronts despite the winter weather. On the eastern front the Russians have begun an early spring offensive pushing closer to Poland and Rumania and, it seems, they have once again trapped a large German army in a salient around the town of Korsun; almost a repetition of Stalingrad although this time the army has been given permission to fight its way out. In Italy, the British and Americans have achieved an outflanking movement by effecting a landing at Anzio, some 50 km south of Rome although they have not been able to expand their bridgehead very far. Further south-east our forces under Field Marshal Kesselring are using the dominating heights of Monte Cassino, crowned by a large monastery which the Wehrmacht has turned into a fort, to obstruct the Anglo-American advance. There is only one route past this bastion, and marshy ground around the other natural obstacle, the river Rapido, also adds to our enemies' difficulties. Each day I spend several minutes in front of our operational maps, studying the different terrains, seeing how the little flags and arrows gradually move forward towards their objectives. Rivers, mountains and marshes are as important elements of defence as are divisions, Panzer corps and Luftflotte.

On January 11th, American bombers of the 8th Army Air Force made another costly attack on central Germany, bombing the AGO aircraft works at Aschersleben. The Americans lost no less than sixty of their giant Fortresses out of a total force of 238. We lost thirty-nine fighters although some of the pilots managed to bale out. However, the most significant factor of this raid which has come as a great shock to the whole of the Luftwaffe fighter force is that the American bombers were escorted all the way to their target by North American P51 Mustang fighters. These aircraft, fitted with Rolls-Royce Merlin engines built under licence by Packard in the US, have greater speed, manoeuvrability and climb than our Me109s and FW190s and to find them capable of flying such a distance is something that has hitherto been accounted impossible. In this particular encounter the American fighters were heavily outnumbered but the fact that they were there at all is a dire threat to future confrontations. To our chagrin JG233 was not involved in the fight although we were on standby, sitting in our cockpits with engines warmed up, but doubtless we shall have an opportunity to match our wits and our machines with the Mustangs some time soon.

From: Contessa Edith Novarro-Badaelli
Villa Frascati
Via Augusta
Rome
To: Hauptmann Peter von Vorzik
III Gruppe JG233
Schaftstadt, Halle

9th February 1944

Dear Peter,

Thank you for your sweet letter of condolence. Mathilde and Christian have also written to me and your letters of support have been a great comfort. To my great surprise I have also received many letters from members of the diplomatic corps and the Vatican, several of them from people I hardly know or have never met, all of them expressing deep concern about the nature of Arturo's death. I have also heard from Eleanora who, of course, is consumed with grief at the news and she and her daughters have entered a period of deep mourning. She wrote that she has been told that, at this time, it is inadvisable for her to leave Switzerland and she has asked me if I would undertake the journey to the Borromeo estate at Valdagno and place the urn containing Arturo's ashes in the safe keeping of the *padre* at the little Byzantine church there until such time as a proper memorial service for Arturo can be arranged. Of course I have agreed to do this although it will awaken painful memories as that is where Arturo and I were married. Dr Dollmann has agreed to give me an SS man to accompany me on the journey, indeed, I expect he will be doing most of the driving. We shall be taking the little Lancia Arturo gave me. Eleanora has written to the *padre* to expect us and also told the housekeeper and her husband at Valdagno to open up two guest rooms for our stay overnight. En route we shall be staying at the German consulate in Florence as I did when I visited the Scalzi prison. In her letter Eleanora, who has always been close to Edda Ciano, said that Edda and the children, Fabrizio, Raimonda and Marzio, have managed to escape to Switzerland. The children went first, spirited across the border in the company of a man disguised as a priest and with the collusion of the Swiss police who were told that the children belonged to the Aosta branch of the royal family. Edda stayed behind and attempted to barter Ciano's life in return for his diaries apparently full of scandalous revelations about senior Nazi and Fascist Party members. According to Eleanor the whole incredible cloak and dagger episode involved Himmler, Kaltenbrunner, Goebbels, von Ribbentrop and the Führer who finally forbade any exchange. The SS thought they could find the diaries but Edda forestalled them and, like the children, managed to escape over the Swiss border with the diaries hidden under her clothes. Now everyone expects them to be published in Britain and America. There is no doubt that Edda Ciano is an exceedingly resourceful woman.

Thank you for the suggestion that I join Mathilde at Höchstein. Both Mathilde and Christian also pressed the matter in their letters, and please thank your comrade Ludwig Varasch for his offer of refuge. On returning from Valdagno I will consider my position here (the Anglo-Americans are only 70 km from Rome but appear to be stopped by Kesselring's defences) and let you know my intentions.

Thank you again, dear brother, for your concern and support. I hope all is well with you, I pray for you always.

Ever your loving sister,
Edith

From: Hauptmann Peter von Vorzik
III Gruppe JG233
Schaftstadt, Halle
To: Oberleutnant Lother Köhl
I Gruppe Sch.Gl
Eastern Front

16th February 1944

Dear Lother,

It was both a relief and a pleasure to have your letter. I was beginning to wonder if those Russian bastards or the winter weather had done you in! At least I know you are alive and in one piece despite the trials and travails you have endured. It cannot be much of a "rest" in Ternopol! Are you still there I wonder? Looking at the little flags on the operations map of the eastern front it appears as if the Russians are not far away. Korsun seems to have been another disaster with (I hear) over fifty thousand men lost in that trap as well as masses of tanks, guns and transport. How can our generals let that happen after Stalingrad? I do understand your questioning the war. You have been in the thick of the worst fighting and it must be disheartening to see the Russians regaining so much that we fought for when it seemed, a year or so ago, that we had them beaten. Perhaps we can hold them on the Vistula, perhaps they will not want any more blood-letting, perhaps the British and the Americans will see the danger the Bolsheviks present to western civilisation. Perhaps, perhaps.

Yes, my wife and baby son are safe in the countryside and, later in the year, I am to be a father again! It was unplanned but these things happen and, anyway, I am delighted that Wolfchen will have a brother or sister without too much of an age gap between them. My own sister has suffered a personal tragedy. Her husband, an Italian who was attached to Ciano's staff, was imprisoned in Verona after the reinstatement of Mussolini and then shot – murdered, really – on the pretext of trying to escape. They were married less than eighteen months ago. My brother and I always had certain misgivings about the marriage, chiefly because he was Italian, although of good family and a man of integrity. My sister remains in Rome at the moment but with the British and Americans only 70 km away we are hoping to persuade her to return to Germany.

527

I understand your reluctance to become involved with your war widow. My Katschmarck, Kurt, feels the same way, not wanting to burden some young woman with widowhood. I married at a time when it seemed the war would be over in a matter of weeks and I have been deliriously happy ever since but if I were to meet my wife now I think I would hesitate before proposing.

Bad weather has curtailed our flying these last few weeks but the American raid on Aschersleben last month brought a nasty shock – P51 Mustang fighters able to fly as far as central Germany! Apparently they are formidable opponents with a better all-round performance than our 109s and 190s, especially above 6,000 m which is where the American bombers usually operate. I expect our Gruppe will be facing the Mustangs before long.

All good wishes, Lother, look after yourself and here's hoping you get to fly something worthwhile soon.

Ever your sincere comrade,

Peter

From: Hauptmann Peter von Vorzik
III Gruppe JG233
Schaftstadt, Halle
To: Contessa Edith Novarro-Badaelli
Villa Frascati
Via Augusta
Rome

20th February 1944

Dear Edith,

This is just a brief note to say how much I admire the fortitude with which you are coping with the tragic circumstances of Arturo's death and the aftermath. It must have taken great reserves of spiritual strength to undertake that journey to Valdagno, so recently the scene of joyous memories! I hope Eleanora appreciates what you have done. What an extraordinary tale you tell of Edda Ciano's escape! She certainly is resourceful. I wonder what secrets those diaries contain. I have been progressively disillusioned about the probity and integrity of the great and powerful. Christian has recounted aspects of their lives that I find shocking and scandalous and no doubt Ciano was in a position to witness the behaviour of certain important individuals who would prefer the truth to remain hidden. I trust the journey to Valdagno and return was accomplished without mishap, I am glad you have a staunch friend in Dr Dollmann.

Hoping you will decide to join Mathilde at Höchstein.

Ever your loving brother,
Peter

From: Hauptmann Peter von Vorzik
III Gruppe JG233
Schaftstadt, Halle
To: Mathilde von Vorzik
Die Alter Scheune
Steuben Gasse
Höchstein

23rd February 1944

My Darling Mathilde,
The weather has closed in again for a few hours so I am snatching a chance to scribble you a brief note to let you know I am safe and well despite having been frantically busy as I am sure you will have heard from the daily news bulletins on the radio. More than that I cannot tell you except to say we are inflicting heavy losses on the enemy despite being outnumbered. I know it is pointless to tell you not to worry about me, darling, but remember that not only do I have much experience behind me (unlike some of our new young pilots) but also my faithful Kurt who is equally experienced at protecting me. I heard from Edith that, at the request of Eleanora, she was taking Arturo's ashes to the church at Valdagno where she was married. It must have been a mournful journey for her. I hope after she has returned to Rome she will decide to join you at Höchstein. I trust all is well with you and Wolfchen and you are not suffering too much from morning sickness. I will write at greater length, darling, when operations slow down as I feel they must do soon.

Ever your loving,
Peter

PS Regards to Marie and Lenka. P.
PPS I am sending your birthday card separately, darling, enclosing a cheque for you to buy yourself something. We have been so occupied this last week or two I have not been able to get into Halle. P.

Hauptmann Peter von Vorzik
Journal entry

2nd March 1944

Kurt, Varasch and I have survived unscathed from the biggest, bloodiest air battles of the war so far. It all began on February 20th when over nine hundred American bombers escorted by more than seven hundred British and American fighters streamed towards their targets, the various aircraft works in central Germany: ATG and Erla at Leipzig; Heiterblick and Möckau and Lutter-Miag at Brunswick and the Junkers factories at Bernberg, Halberstadt and Aschersleben. This time our Geschwader were frequently unable to get at the bombers because of the huge fighter screen and furious dogfights took place over a vast area. JG233 was in the thick of it. We were on alert from 11.45 hrs and finally took off at 12.37 hrs, climbing through thin, hazy altostratus to level out at just under 8,000 m. By the time we reached Leipzig the battle was already raging. The city was shrouded in a pall of smoke and the area was thick with P51 Mustangs, some of them shielding the bombers and others already engaged in fierce combat with 109s and 190s from Eperstedt, Eggersdorf, Volkenrode and Sachau.

We were flying in company with 109s from IV Gruppe JG3 and as we joined the melée I gave the order to my Staffel to operate as Rotte, Kurt with me, Varasch with his Katschmarek, Adolf Steubel, and Jakob Kantner with his Katschmarek, Willem Zülpich. I saw two Mustangs converging on a 190 that was already in trouble, trailing black smoke. I called to Kurt that I was going after the port Mustang and he should take the other one. If we were separated we should head back to bodo independently. The 190 was already spiralling down out of control leaving that familiar black corkscrew shape hanging in the air. My quarry had broken away, climbing to find other prey. I climbed behind and beneath him and as it became apparent he was climbing slightly faster than I was I decided to attack at a greater range than I would have liked. Even so, my guns found their target and bits began flying off the centre section and the port wing. The Mustang appeared to stall, then broke away in a side-slipping motion. I had to kick hard on the rudder bar and drag the control column across with both hands in order to follow him down. I managed to get in a second burst that tore pieces off the tailplane and this time the Mustang went into a flat spin shedding bits of metal as it went. Horrido!

Just as I was congratulating myself on a kill and looking to see if I could locate Kurt I felt the Gustav jerking from the impact of a hail of bullets. Looking back over my shoulder I made out the shadowy shape of a Mustang behind me. Unaware of what damage my aircraft had suffered I automatically rolled over into a dive knowing, as I did so, that the enemy could probably dive faster than I could. My only chance of escape was to twist and turn, roll and side-slip so as not to be in his sights for more than a split second. I remembered having to try and follow those devilishly manoeuvrable little Ratas in Russia; now it was my turn to try and be too slippery to catch. Yanking the control column, kicking the rudder bar I hoped the Gustav was not fatally damaged and would not start to break up under the stress. My tactics worked. Perhaps the American pilot had orders not to leave the bomber fleet, perhaps, because of my wild gyrations, he thought he had already made a kill; whatever the reason for giving up the pursuit I was momentarily safe and levelling out at 3,000 m in a bank of cloud I studied the instrument panel to see if there were any indications of damage sustained. Engine temperature was rising, oil pressure falling. I put out a call asking for the nearest fighter base and was rewarded with an answer from Pomssen, home base of JG27. This fighter station was east of my own but now much closer, so throttling back and turning gently to starboard I made for Pomssen.

Looking through the cockpit canopy I could see the port wing peppered with bullet holes. I guessed the Mustang pilot had hit the radiator slung beneath the wing which accounted for the rise in engine temperature and I also surmised that the inboard split flap attached to the radiator was damaged. Even if I made it to Pomssen landing would be tricky. The cockpit began to fill with fumes, the acrid smoke making me cough and my eyes water. I thought, momentarily, of baling out but, mindful of what happened to Hans-Joachim Marseille and not wanting to drift helplessly as a target for any lurking Mustang, I decided to try and make Pomssen. I throttled right back, lowered the flaps a little and practically glided down to 2,000 m. The controller at Pomssen was helpful, giving me indications of windspeed and the easiest landing run. I was through the lowest layer of cloud and, turning into wind, could see the grass-covered airfield just ahead of me. Once again I had a sense of déjà vu, of my faltering aircraft surfing the waves off Wangerooge and skimming over the snow in Russia. I pulled the electric landing gear lever on the right-hand panel and nothing happened. I was losing height rapidly and knew I would not have time to wind the wheels down with the hand lever so I was committed to another belly landing. I opened the throttle a little and raised the engine revolutions as far as I dared, hoping it would not seize up at the crucial moment, lowered the flaps fully down to hold off the stall until I was skimming over the grass. With a bone-breaking thump and a grinding of metal as the propeller blades churned into the ground I was careering along out of control but thankfully avoiding a ground loop. Clods of earth hit the windscreen. On and on I skidded, shielding my face with my arms, wondering if I might hit the perimeter fence or a building or career into a ditch. The whole landing lasted just thirty seconds or so but it seemed an eternity. At last I slewed to a stop, threw open the canopy and hauled myself out of the choking cockpit onto the starboard wing. Already a fire truck and an ambulance were racing up to me. "Primal congratulations!" the ambulance driver shouted, pleased to see me standing up in one piece.

After retrieving some personal belongings stowed behind the cockpit seat I was taken to the Pomssen operations room where I made a preliminary report including my claim of a kill. Then, after a cup of coffee and a cursory medical examination from the station medical orderly, I was driven back to Schaftstadt which I reached in the late evening. My first enquiry was for Kurt and was relieved to hear he had made it safely back to base although his aircraft was also badly shot up. I wrote out my full report and hurried to the mess for a hot meal and celebratory drinks with Kurt and Varasch. Our celebrations were tempered by several sad losses. Steubel had gone and Kantner as well as eight other pilots from the Gruppe. These young men have had such limited training, some with only 112 hours in toto with less than 40 hours on fighters. This compares with over 200 hours that I received at the A, B and C schools, the last two of which are now disbanded. In all, our combined fighter Geschwader lost more than 40 aircraft and their pilots during that day's attack while accounting for just 21 bombers from the enemy force of 941. I also learned that the pall of smoke that hung over Leipzig was from a night attack by 700 RAF bombers, 71 of which were shot down. Night bombing, without fighter escort, is more costly than day bombing with. That night, as we survivors celebrated in the mess, the RAF sent another 600 bombers to attack the aircraft factories at Stuttgart. The British and

Americans are now in a position to mount 24-hour bombing which we are powerless to stop.

Bad weather gave us a day's rest during which I received a replacement Gustav, another G6. This one came equipped with heavy ordnance, two 13mm machineguns in the top of the engine cowling, a new MK108 30mm cannon firing through the airscrew boss and two 20mm MG151 cannon in underwing gondolas. This deadly assembly of weapons was intended for destroying bombers. However, with the advent of the Mustang fighters escorting American bombers into the heart of Germany the underwing guns made the Gustav slow and lacking in manoeuvrability so I had them removed. My personal insignia was painted on the cowling bumps and the Staffelkapitan chevrons were on the fuselage. On the 22nd the Americans made another heavy daylight raid on Bernberg and Aschersleben but my Staffel was too depleted to take part on that day. Bad weather hampered the American bombers and their escort failed to rendezvous over the target area which left them vulnerable to our fighters, the Americans losing 41 out of a force of 430. On the 23rd continuing bad weather gave us a respite during which I was able to form a scratch force of myself, Kurt, Varasch with yet another young Katschmarek, Otto Heilpern, and two other pilots straight from school, Dieter Vettermann and Karel Blumberg. The 24th saw us once again engaged in furious fighting. The Americans sent over 600 bombers converging from England and Italy, 87 attacking the Daimler-Benz aero-engine works in Styria, Austria, while the larger force of bombers from England headed for Schweinfurt, Gotha, Tutow, Kreising and Posen. My little group once again supported JG3, engaging with escorting Mustangs high over Gotha, due south-east from Schaftstadt. This time we had the advantage of height, sighting a large group of twenty or so Mustangs flying behind a "box" of B-17 Fortresses. Our orders, now, are to engage the fighters, leaving the bombers to the more heavily armed G6s. I told my small group to each mark a Mustang, make one diving pass then regain height and make straight for bodo. I did not intend to lose any more young pilots by engaging in dogfights.

These tactics worked, especially having the advantage of surprise with a watery winter sun behind us. Within seconds the Mustang I targeted exploded in a ball of flame after being hit by a burst from my 30mm cannon, bits of debris floating down like autumn leaves. Kurt sent another

Mustang hurtling earthwards in flames, Varasch claimed a third and the two young pilots, Vettermann and Blumberg, both claimed to have damaged two more. As I had ordered, after our attacking dive we zoomed back up to 9,000 m, using water-methanol injection to reach just below our operational ceiling and it was with enormous relief that I saw the group land intact. For once we really had something to celebrate, three Mustangs destroyed, two damaged, without loss to ourselves. On the night of the 24th the RAF sent 700 Lancasters to batter Schweinfurt yet again, doing more terrible damage to the city although a third of the ball-bearing works there have now been dispersed. On the 25th, with fine weather prevailing right across Germany, the Americans staged yet another massive attack, two bomber streams from the 8th Army Air Force in England and the 15th Army Air Force in Italy converging on the Messerschmitt factories at Regensburg and Stuttgart. Once again our small Staffel joined with other Gruppen drawn from north and central Germany and once again we were faced with hordes of Mustangs.

I ordered the same tactics that had proved successful previously but this time, flying close to our operational ceiling, we were denied the essential element of surprise. While still some way from the bombers' target area we were bounced by numerous Mustangs free-ranging away from the bomber force and using similar tactics to those we had employed, diving on us out of the sun. In their first pass we lost Heilpern who shouted a warning to Varasch even as his plane was engulfed in flames. Varasch was lucky to escape destruction; although his Gustav was badly damaged he was able to make NGT l's night-fighter station at Fritzlar from where he was flown back to Schaftstadt yesterday. Kurt and I were both drawn into furious dogfights and it took all our experience and expertise to emerge intact. These American pilots have been well trained and what they may lack in combat experience they make up in dash and determination. In truth we were overwhelmed by sheer numbers and having fought off our attackers by dint of violent evasive manoeuvres we managed to form up together and using our emergency water-methanol injection were able to outrun our pursuers. This has been a week of unprecedented aerial battles, the Anglo-Americans making a massive assault on our fighter defences, attempting to destroy the factories and draw the various Gruppen into aerial combat. Our Gruppe is badly depleted and my Staffel is down to six pilots. Reports and directives from Generalflugmeister Milch and General der Jagdflieger Galland, whom we all revere, have outlined the dangers we face, in particular the necessity of going over and over combat tactics for the benefit of young inexperienced pilots. It is my melancholy task, now, to write to the parents of those young men of the Staffel whose burnt and broken bodies lie scattered over central Germany. How long can the British and Americans sustain the assault, how long can we hold out?

From: Mathilde von Vorzik
Die Alter Scheune
Höchstein
To: Hauptmann Peter von Vorzik
III Gruppe JG233
Schaftstadt, Halle

7th March 1944

My Darling Peter,
It was a great relief to have your letter and to know you were safe and well. Thank you, too, darling, for the pretty birthday card and the generous cheque enclosed. I am hoping to drive into Bamberg where the shops are much more extensive than Höchstein. Here in Höchstein we have been aware of the enormous amount of aerial activity that has continued since the middle of last month. We have seen and heard the great flights of bombers passing overhead day and night and once or twice we have watched the aircraft making trails in the sky. A big American bomber crashed just two km away, setting fire to some village houses and killing three people. I was told that all the men in the bomber perished. One of our own fighters (I think it was a FW190) also crashed nearby, killing the pilot. Such moments inevitably make me wonder how you are, what is happening to your Staffel. It is all so dreadful, I cannot believe that we were once told that enemy aircraft would never reach Germany when day and night we crouch in the cellar, even here in Höchstein, while fleets of bombers fill our skies and destroy our cities.

I am glad to say the morning sickness has been less of late. Marie insists on making me eat huge meals, eggs, ham and sausages from the farm and lots of milk. I would certainly not have been able to eat so well had we stayed in Grunewald. Already I am getting thick around the waist, as much from Marie's feeding as from the growing baby. Marie says she knows it is another boy! She has brought down a little wooden cradle from the attic which she says was Ludwig's. She has even shown me some of his baby clothes, beautifully preserved in tissue paper and layered with lavender bags. I think she looks upon him almost as her own son. Lenka has been very melancholy of late. There is still no news of her father and brother and she says she is sure they are dead. I say to her that if they were, no doubt she would have some official communication and that no news is good news, but she just shakes her head and her eyes fill with tears. I wish there was something I could do to find out what had happened to them but I am mindful of Christian's advice not to interfere.

Have you had news from Edith? She has not written to me and we are wondering if she has decided to join us here. I know Marie would welcome another refugee and of course it would be marvellous company for me. Marie and Lenka are very companionable but my own sister-in-law would be something special. I do hope she is not putting herself in any danger by staying in Rome, according to the radio the British and Americans are only 70 km away.

Already there are buds on the trees and the birds are singing in the morning. It seems only two or three weeks ago that we were celebrating Christmas here. What a happy time that was! I wish we could sometimes turn the clock back but I enjoy reviving those happy memories. Please scribble a line whenever you can, dearest, just a postcard will do so that I am reassured that you are safe and well.

Regards, as always, to Ludwig and Kurt,

and deepest love from,
Mathilde and Wolfchen

From: *Contessa Edith Novarro-Badaelli*
Villa Frascati
Via Augusta
Rome
To: *Hauptmann Peter von Vorzik*
III Gruppe JG233
Schaftstadt, Halle

14th March 1944

Dear Peter,

I know you may be surprised but having spent the last two weeks in prayer and contemplation I have decided to remain here in Rome. I shall be selling the house and all its appurtenances except for certain gifts that I will cherish. I am giving the whole of my estate, such as it is, including the monies and effects left to me in Arturo's will, to the orphanage. I will be living and working there as well as being a member of the board. The work will be variable, cooking, cleaning, teaching, whatever I am called upon to do. The monies will be used to repair the roof which leaks in wet weather and to generally maintain the fabric of the building. I have put all these arrangements in the hands of Arturo's solicitor who was responsible for drawing up our marriage settlement. I came to this conclusion following my sojourn at the orphanage during Christmas. I am convinced that, in His mysterious way, through trial and tribulation, God has led me to this path, on this journey. He has ordained my destiny as He does for all of us. Instead of the children that Arturo and I had hoped for I shall be helping other desperately needy children to find a beginning to their adult lives. From a practical point of view I am not concerned at the thought of the British and Americans advancing on Rome. In any case, at the moment, it seems they are unable to move beyond the Gustav line despite bombing and shelling the monastery at Monte Cassino into rubble. Even if they do ultimately capture the city I am sure they will deal with the orphanage and its inmates in a civilised manner.

As you surmised, the journey to Valdagno was a melancholy one. I spent some time in the chapel, praying with the *padre* and reliving those happy hours of our wedding celebration, which seems, now, so long ago. The weather throughout my visit was cold and wet which added to the general air of sadness. I was grateful for the presence of Joachim, the accompanying

SS-Sturmbannführer, who drove all the way there and back in an official car put at my disposal by Dr Dollmann. Now all that is past and I am ready to embrace my future. I am writing separately to Christian and Mathilde.

Ever your loving sister,
Edith

PS After the 20th March I am dropping the title Contessa and will be known simply as Signora Edith (not sister as I will not be ordained). My new address will be

Santa Maria Orfanotrofio
Campo Balbi
Rome

From: SS-Gruppenführer Count Christian von Vorzik
116 Kaiserstraße
Berlin
To: Hauptmann Peter von Vorzik
III Gruppe JG233
Schaftstadt, Halle

25th March 1944

Dear Peter,

Although I fear it may already be too late I am writing to you in the desperate hope that you may be able to persuade Edith from pursuing her preposterous plan to sell everything she possesses and give the money to the orphanage where she proposes to work. I have been in touch with our lawyer in Munich and with her legal representative in Rome and it seems that, in law, there is nothing we can do to force her to rescind her decision. The only hope is to appeal to her common sense and as I feel it may be possible that she has a closer rapport with you rather than with me, I am hoping you may be able to dissuade her from this madness. Other than the possibility that she has completely lost her wits, which I doubt, I feel certain that she has fallen under the malign influence of those damned nuns appealing to her religious susceptibilities. They have seen their opportunity to play upon her natural kindness and generosity to gain access to her estate. My greatest fear is that, as soon as they have acquired her wealth she will be pushed out to wander the streets of Rome as a vagrant without a pfennig to her name. I have alerted Dr Dollmann to the situation but there is little he can do except to offer her a refuge should my worst fears be realised. If that should happen then I can, at least, have her repatriated to Germany. How deeply I regret that we did not try and dissuade her from marrying Arturo. All this nonsense stems from that misalliance. At any other time it would be possible for me to fly to Rome and remonstrate with her; as it is Walter has deputed me to undertake an important but delicate mission to Sweden. I cannot elaborate further except to say I do not know how long I shall be away. That is why I am anxious that you should contact Edith without delay. If she has already signed papers I am informed that they may not be legally binding and we could, perhaps, prove in a court of law that she was under duress. I leave it to you to deal with the matter as you deem fit but it would be as well to emphasise that if the British and Americans manage to take Rome, which is not beyond the bounds of possibility, they will surely ransack the orphanage and the inmates, including the nuns, will be raped.

I trust all goes well with you in these hectic times.

Always your devoted brother,
Christian

From: Hauptmann Peter von Vorzik
III Gruppe JG233
Schaftstadt, Halle
To: Mathilde von Vorzik
Alter Scheune
Steuben Gasse
Höchstein

27th March 1944

My Darling Mathilde,

So pleased to have your letter. I understand very well how perturbed you must be about the aerial activity which now covers the whole of Germany. It is certainly something we never contemplated three years ago. Since then the war has escalated to a degree that I am sure even the Führer had not anticipated. It is our alliance with the Japanese that has made America our enemy and it cannot be denied that they, the Americans, have enormous material resources. All we can do is trust the Führer and his leadership and hope that our enemies, particularly the Americans and the Russians, will fall out with one another. As you well know, darling, we have been kept very busy these last few weeks, particularly since my last letter, but here I am, still safe and well, with Kurt still guarding my tail! The feeling here is that the current degree of activity cannot be sustained because both the British and Americans have suffered terrible losses, especially in aircrews. Despite the odd crashes that have occurred near you it is comforting to me to know that you and Wolfchen are not near any city or industrial area that might be targeted.

What a relief for you it must be that the morning sickness has lessened. We men certainly have the best of the bargain when it comes to creating a family! It is not just the pain of childbirth that women have to endure but all the attendant problems that are associated with maternity including several months having to heave that weight about! I suppose nature endows women with some psychological compensation, some sense of satisfaction that we men cannot know or imagine that is generally termed the maternal instinct. Otherwise the human race would have died out soon after Adam and Eve! Now I must tell you something that Ludwig confided in me. He says he feels sure that the cradle and baby clothes that Marie showed you were not his but belonged to the baby that Marie had and "lost." Do you remember she told us how, when she was eighteen, she had a relationship with a man who subsequently left her for an older woman? Ludwig says that Marie was pregnant from that relationship and that is why the man disappeared. Ludwig's parents arranged for the baby, a boy, to be adopted soon after it was born. Not long after that Ludwig himself was born and Marie transferred her affection for her own child to Ludwig. She had prepared a large layette for her baby, much of which she had made herself, and when the baby was taken away (Ludwig thinks it went to a doctor and his wife) Marie kept back some of the baby clothes. Ludwig is not sure whether he ever slept in the cradle (it was made by a local carpenter) but he is certain that it was originally intended for Marie's baby. A sad tale, is it not? This is all in confidence, of course. If Marie likes to think or pretend that the clothes and cradle were Ludwig's there is no point in contradicting her memory of events or spoiling her fantasies. She must have been anguished at the loss of her lover and her baby and sad that she never found another man to marry her.

As yet I have not heard from Edith whether she will be joining you at Höchstein.

All my love, as always.

Ever your own,
Peter

From: Hauptmann Peter von Vorzik
III Gruppe JG233
Schaftstadt, Halle
To: Signora Edith Novarro-Badaelli
Santa Maria Orfanotrofio
Campo Balbi
Rome

2nd April 1944

My Dear Edith,

Of course your letter of 14th March came as a surprise, not to say a shock, and I am finding it difficult to answer. First, let me say I respect your decision. As you say it was taken after much "prayer and contemplation", not rashly. However, I do wonder if you have really taken into consideration what your position might be if the Anglo-Americans should reach Rome? Your conjecture that they will act "in a civilised manner" may or may not be correct. We have had much evidence in this war that soldiers, of whatever nationality, can act with great brutality against both men and women and rape – even of the nuns – is a possibility. That is a risk you appear to have accepted but the reality would be horrible. Further, it could be that you may face real deprivation, starvation even, although I realise you feel you have a duty to the children you will be helping to care for. That, in itself, is noble but, again, are you confident you can face the reality? All your life, including the short period of your marriage, you have enjoyed the privilege of plenty; are you really mentally and physically equipped to face destitution?

Giving all of your estate is another act of great Christian charity. I am ready to believe that this is a decision you have reached based on the belief that you are doing God's will and not under any persuasion from the nuns. Yet I am anxious that there should be some guarantee that the orphanage will, thereafter, be able to offer you shelter and sustenance within its capability. Who is in charge? Is there a Mother Superior? Who chairs the Board of Directors? I cannot keep from you that I am writing this letter and asking these questions at the prompting of Christian who, as you may imagine, is far less ready to accept your decision than I am. He would, if it were possible, use the law to coerce you into rescinding your plans. Believe me, dear sister, in our different ways, we are both anxious for your welfare. Life has dealt you a cruel blow and we are both fearful that your reaction to the death of Arturo, together with your instinctive selflessness, may have led you into a course of action that could prove calamitous. You have lost a dear husband, just as Christian lost a beloved wife; he understands the anguish you have suffered.

From my own selfish point of view I would wish to see you in comparative safety at Höchstein with Mathilde, my whole family on German soil, able to face the future in unity. The future, of course, seems ever more uncertain. During the last month it has become clear that the Fatherland is now in mortal danger from powerful enemies. We can but do what we can. Do make sure that this momentous decision is what you really wish for yourself and that, in a few months, weeks even, you will not be assailed by regrets.

Whatever happens I shall always be

Your devoted brother,
Peter

From: Mathilde von Vorzik
Die Alter Scheune
Steuben Gasse
Höchstein
To: Hauptmann Peter von Vorzik III
Gruppe JG233
Schaftstadt, Halle

5th April 1944

My Darling Peter,
I have heard from Edith and, as she tells me she has written to you, you must be as astonished and perplexed at her news as I am. In a way I can understand her decision to give everything to the orphanage and commit herself to a life of service there because she has always had a strong sense of divine providence and her own duty to God, but I do wonder if it is a wise course to take, given that she is in a foreign country and enemy armies are not far away. Could she not devote herself to the care and teaching of children here in Germany? I am sure there would be posts open to her in the German Girls' League but then, of course, she would not have the same opportunity for religious worship within that organisation. Naturally I am deeply disappointed that she will not be joining us here at Höchstein, I had been so looking forward to her

company. You, too, darling, must be feeling great anxiety about her future as in her letter she seems positive in her decision and not to be dissuaded from it.

I have finished *Wilhelm Meister* which I enjoyed very much, and have begun *The Sorrows of Young Werther* which is so very different. Its emphasis on *Weltschmerz* and *Ichschmerz* made me think of Edith; she really has a sense of unease, both with the world and with herself, do you not think? Really, I suppose, she suffers from that sense of guilt that Catholic teaching imposes almost as if it were a crime to be alive! I was very surprised by what you said regarding Marie and the baby clothes and cradle. She talks so convincingly, so matter-of-factly, about them belonging to Ludwig but after all these years she probably has blotted out the memory of her own baby and transferred the association to Ludwig. Sad, yes, and of course I would not dream of questioning her. I have been trying very hard to take to heart what you advised in your last letter, darling, about the aerial activity not being sustained but during these last two weeks it has continued unabated and the sirens go night and day even though, as you point out, we are not near a target area. My heart pounds at such times because of the thought of you going up to engage these fleets of enemy aircraft. Thank heaven for Kurt, I think of him as your guardian angel! Give him my fond regards and also fond greetings to Ludwig.

Love and kisses from

Mathilde and Wolfchen

PS With the cheque you sent for my birthday I bought a navy maternity skirt with a scoop cut in the waistline to accommodate my growing stomach! Also two pretty nightdresses (Marie gave me some of her clothing coupons that she does not want) in flowered silk, one pink and one lilac.

PPS The scribbling at the bottom is Wolfchen's "writing" to you!

From: Oberleutnant Lother Köhl
1(F) 122
Luftflotte 6
Warsaw Okecie
To: Hauptmann Peter von Vorzik
III Gruppe JG233
Schaftstadt, Halle

9th April 1944

Dear Peter,

As you see I have at last been moved from the living hell of Russia. Not only that but I am now flying a reasonable aircraft, an Me410 A3 which we use solely for long-range reconnaissance. Your wish for me, expressed in the last part of your letter of 16th February which has just reached me, has come true. After the Hs129 it seems a superlative machine. I underwent a conversion course at Tarnowitz where I met two or three old friends from Werneuchen. Do you remember Horst Weissenberg? Matthias Gröven? Johann Schlieck? They remember you! Happy days! Anyway, the lucky devils are being posted to 2 ZG 1 at Vannes and cannot wait to lie in the sun and ogle all those French girls!

Well, I must admit, after all my protestations about not wanting a relationship until after the war I have rather fallen for a buxom dark-haired girl, Velda. I met her in a local tavern. She has grey eyes, a creamy skin and a curvaceous figure. What more could a man want? After those dreary, horrible months in Russia her company has lightened my mood somewhat. Neither of us is thinking seriously about the future, just enjoying each other's company and making life worthwhile while we can. Her father was killed during our advance on Warsaw back in '39 and she and her mother run this little tavern which the Staffel favours. I am still corresponding with my war widow! Forgive me. Here I am enthusing over this liaison when I should be writing a sympathetic message to you about the death of your brother-in-law. What a terrible shock for your sister! I do hope she is capable of coping with such a tragic situation. Have you discovered who was responsible for the murder? Is there any possibility of bringing them to justice? What treacherous bastards those Italians are! Everyone talks about the possibility of the Anglo-Americans starting a second front in the west but thanks to our Italian "allies" we already have a second front! What else are our forces doing but having to fight the British and Americans in Italy? That ties down first-class divisions, equipment, aircraft that are desperately needed in Russia.

With the 410 our reconnaissance flights are fairly safe operations. We can outrun almost anything the Russians can put in the air, especially at the altitudes at which we fly, around 6,500 m, and we have a very strong offensive-defensive armament, two 7.9mm M17 machineguns plus two MG151 20mm cannon in the nose and two rearward-firing 13mm MG131 machineguns in barbettes set into the aft fuselage. So far we haven't had any occasion to use them. I assume you have been heavily engaged with those big American raids across the length and breadth of the Fatherland? It certainly seems that there is no part of Germany that is safe now that the Americans have long-range fighters. The Mustang, which we have had lessons about in case the Americans supply them to Russia, seems a formidable fighter and they appear to have plenty of them!

Well, that is my news to date, keep writing when you can and keep away from those Mustangs!

All the very best,

Your sincere comrade,
Lother

PS Many congratulations on the expectation of another child. I hope all goes well with your wife. L.

From: Hauptmann Peter von Vorzik
III Gruppe JG233
Schaftstadt, Halle
To: Mathilde von Vorzik
Die Alter Scheune
Steuben Gasse
Höchstein

15th April 1944

My Darling Mathilde,
This is a hastily scribbled note just to let you know that I am alive and well. Yes, we have been kept frantically busy chasing those enemy bombers about the sky but our experience and *esprit de corps* have kept us out of harm's way.

Of course it was a shock to receive Edith's letter and, like you, I question the wisdom of her decision and hope she will not regret what she has done. I would have preferred it if she had continued working at the orphanage but kept her financial independence but obviously she has a religious conviction that she must sacrifice all her worldly goods and devote herself utterly to caring for those children. To me it seems unnecessarily extreme but I know nothing that I can say (beneath her quiet exterior Edith has always had something of a stubborn streak) will change her mind. Christian, of course, is very angry and would seek to use the law to change matters but that is not possible. In any case I would not want to estrange my sister; I love Edith and am ready to accept whatever she feels is the right course for her. Now, darling, I must try and catch up with my ever-growing, ever-lasting paperwork. Regards to Marie and Lenka and, as always,

Love from

Your own,
Peter

Hauptmann Peter von Vorzik
Journal entry

24th April 1944

During these last few weeks myself, Kurt and Varasch, together with his latest Katschmarek, Otto Frieling, have escaped death by the narrowest of margins. By sheer weight of numbers the Americans now have complete air superiority over the whole of Germany and no longer bother to make feinting attacks before turning to their intended targets. We have changed our defensive tactics time and again to little or no avail. A few Gruppen – III JG1 at Paderborn, II JG11 at Hustedt and I JG5 at Herzogenaurach – have been equipped with Gustavs that have a specially uprated high-altitude engine, the DB605AS, that enables them to operate up to 11,000 m. Waiting high in the sky for the escorting American fighters they dive down and pick them off before making their escape. These are tactics I have employed with my own Staffel with limited success even though we cannot achieve such speeds or altitudes, but recently, by the time we have been ordered into the air to intercept at a given point, we have still been climbing when attacked by swarms of Mustangs and the heavier radial-engined Republic P47 Thunderbolts.

It is only because of our long combat experience and a lot of luck that we have escaped destruction; that, and the occasional use of the water-methanol injection to boost the engine output for a few minutes in an emergency that helps us to outrun the enemy fighters. It is humiliating to have to turn tail and run away but when you are outnumbered three, four, sometimes five to one it is the only way to live to fight another day. As it is we have lost many of our finest fighter pilots as a well as scores of young graduates straight out of the training schools. Reichsminister Albert Speer and his departmental colleague Karl Saur have performed miracles in producing thousands of fighter aircraft; what we lack are pilots with combat experience to fly them. In one of General der Jagdflieger Adolf Galland's reports, distributed to the Jagdgeschwarder, he stated: "The ratio in which we fight today is about 1 to 7. The standard of the Americans is extraordinarily high. The day fighters have lost more than one thousand during the last four months, among them our best officers. These gaps cannot be filled. During each enemy raid we lose about fifty fighters. Things have gone so far that the danger of the collapse of our arm exists." Galland has had many conferences with Reichsmarschall Göring arguing on our behalf against the Fat One's capricious orders and defending us against his criticisms but nothing can alter the fact that we are desperately short of pilots.

In my letters home I try to minimise the dangers we face but in truth I have cheated death a dozen times recently and I often think it is only a matter of time before Mathilde is widowed and Wolfchen is fatherless. Many better pilots than I have lost their lives in these ferocious battles with an all-powerful enemy. For example: yesterday we received orders to intercept American bombers of the 8th Air Force approaching from the north and others of the 15th Air Force coming from the south, targets unknown but possibly the Messerschmitt works at Augsburg and Regensburg. Flying with aircraft from IV JG54 based at Mortitz we assembled over Gera and were flying due south, still climbing over the Fichtelgebirge area when we were bounced by a horde of Mustangs. They were everywhere, above us, diving through us, outnumbering us four to one. Within half a minute we had lost the Pfaff brothers, Dieter and Otto, both blown out of the sky before they had had a chance to fire a shot. Another new young recruit, Hans Schenken, collided with a Mustang, both aircraft locked together in a tangle of wreckage, both pilots dead.

A warning shout from Kurt over the r/t alerted me to the danger of two Mustangs approaching from behind. Shouting back at Kurt to take what evasive action he could I bunted over, then side-slipped to port, looking behind to see if I was still pursued. I was. I turned hard to starboard and could see his tracer bullets skimming over the top surface of the starboard wing. He was turning inside me. I pushed the control column right forward, almost standing the Gustav on its nose and, turning on the water-methanol injection, I began a screaming power-dive. At 3,000 m it required all my strength on the column to get the nose up again. The little plane shuddered under the G-forces and I momentarily blacked out. A second or two later, as I regained consciousness, I realised I had been successful in losing my pursuer. Looking up through the canopy I could see the whirling specks of the dogfight continuing above me. The sky was criss-crossed with white contrails and black scrawls where aircraft were falling in flames. I searched for the sight of a lone Mustang, for those square-cut wing tips and tail assembly, and was rewarded with the silhouette of one some 2 or 300 m above. Perhaps it was the very one that had chased me; at least I like to think so. Stealthily I followed his course, flying parallel some 60 or 70 m below and behind until, pulling back on the control column again, I had his plan view square in the Revi sight. I fired a long burst from all three guns, raking him from nose to tail. Bits of metal flew off the underside of the machine, flames and smoke belched from the engine cowling. Mortally wounded the Mustang hung in the air then lurched into its final death dive.

Foolishly oblivious to the danger of other Mustangs that might be targeting me I followed my victim down, anxious to record a kill until Horrido! I saw him hit a hillside somewhere near Wiesau. Turning north I managed to regain bodo safely with the fuel gauge flickering on empty. My victory, which was later confirmed, was little compensation for the loss of the Pfaff brothers, Schenken and two other pilots of the Staffel who are missing. The Staffel's once more down to seven pilots. Kurt and Varasch both made it back safely albeit via bases at Brandis and Leuterwitz where they had to refuel. We have come close to being demoralised by the constant loss of comrades. Much of my time is spent writing letters of sympathy and commiseration to the fathers, mothers and relatives of young pilots who have been shot down after only a few days of combat experience, their bodies laid to rest in the Wurstorf War Cemetery. Who, I wonder, will be writing a letter of commiseration to Mathilde about me?

From: Signora Edith Novarro-Badaelli
Santa Maria Orfanotrofio
Campo Balbi
Rome
To: Hauptmann Peter von Vorzik
III Gruppe JG233
Schaftstadt, Halle

4th May 1944

My Dear Peter,

Thank you for your letter of 2nd April. I do realise that my decision to sell most of my worldly goods and work here at the orphanage will have been a shock to you, Mathilde and Christian and I do appreciate your own understanding and forbearance in the matter. Of course it will have been more difficult for Christian to accept, he considers himself the head of the family and no doubt would have expected to have been consulted. I am sure he has genuine misgivings about my future and in any case he operates within an organisation that has little time for anything affiliated to the Catholic church. I understand his position but am glad that he cannot do anything to change matters. His reaction is one reason why I wanted to make this decision by myself after much thought and prayer. As for your own misgivings please be assured that I have considered my situation from every angle, not just from a desire to do God's will – although that is my primary motive. My legal representative here has made a binding arrangement with the Board of Directors (of which I am a member) that they shall "undertake to feed and accommodate me in accordance with the situation obtaining within the organisation." There is a Mother Superior in charge (Sister Agnes) and there is a monthly visit from a Papal representative (Monsignor Enrico d'Albo).

I cannot believe that if Rome falls to the Anglo-American forces the British and American soldiery will rape the nuns here! I know dreadful things have and are happening all over the world but I think that particular atrocity is a remote risk. If it were the Russian army advancing I would, perhaps, give the suggestion more credence. I am settled here now and have a roster of duties which include teaching music, English and German, working in the kitchen and garden and driving the orphanage van! My Italian is improving daily. I am relatively happy and have peace of mind. You write of the possibility of regrets. I suppose we all have regrets of one sort or another but I have none of any consequence. I certainly do not regret marrying Arturo; it gave me a year or so of blissful happiness and led me here to what, as I have said before, I am ready to believe was my intended destiny. Much of what happens in the outside world now passes me by. We have radio news but no newspapers, magazines or books. The Bible is our only reading. Some things I miss, concerts, opera, theatre, art galleries, but these are, ultimately, just the garnishings of life and an ambience of spirituality is ample recompense.

Do not be anxious for me, dear brother, I have found contentment after weeks of anguish. If Rome should be occupied by the British and Americans I will correspond with you via Eleanora in Switzerland. She, incidentally, has written that she applauds my decision.

I continue to pray for you every day.

With love,
Edith

PS Certain articles of value, some pictures, silver, the lovely Meissen dinner service you gave us as a wedding present and a few other things I would like to remain in the family, I am having packed up and sent to Höchstein. Dispose of them as you will. The firm transporting them is the same one who packed the *objets d'art* that Reichsmarschall Göring chose when he was last in Italy so they should arrive intact! In any case I have them insured and am sending the relevant papers by separate post. E.

From: Hauptmann Peter von Vorzik
III Gruppe JG233
Schaftstadt, Halle
To: SS-Gruppenführer Count Christian von Vorzik
116 Kaiserstraße
Berlin

14th May 1944

Dear Christian,
This is a brief letter to let you know that, as you requested, I wrote to Edith pointing out our fears for her future and the folly of signing over everything she possesses to the orphanage. Today I received a reply which, in essence, confirms her intention to act on her decision; indeed she

appears to be already in residence there. Her letter goes some way to alleviating our anxieties in that there is a legal document that binds the orphanage to providing her with accommodation and subsistence in perpetuity. She appears to accept the ascetic life she has chosen and it would seem she came to the decision alone without outside pressure or persuasion. I pointed out to her the possibility of rape and pillage should the Anglo-Americans succeed in entering Rome but she is unconvinced of the danger. I think we have to accept that she has decided upon her future and intends to abide by it. She has sent to Höchstein some valuables that she wishes to remain within the family and I will appraise you of their arrival when I hear from Mathilde. I hope your mission to Sweden was successful. As usual I am sending this to Kaisestraße to await your arrival. For myself I have been kept very busy trying to repel the almost daily incursions of the American Air Force but I fear that, at the moment, we are losing the battle. Perhaps our new V weapons will soon redress the balance.

Ever your affectionate brother,
Peter

Führer Order of 16th May 1944
REF: EMPLOYMENT OF LONG-RANGE WEAPONS AGAINST ENGLAND
Führer Headquarters, High Command of the Armed Forces

The Führer has ordered:

1. The long-range bombardment of England will begin in the middle of June. The exact date will be set by Commander-in-Chief West, who will also control the bombardment with the help of LXV Army Corps and the Third Air Fleet.

2. The following weapons will be employed:
   a) Fzg 76
   b) Fzg launched from He111
   c) Long-range artillery
   d) Bomber forces of the Third Air Fleet

3. Method:
   a) Against the main target, London.

The bombardment will open like a thunderclap by night with Fzg 76, combined with bombs (mostly incendiary) from the bomber forces, and a sudden long-range artillery attack against towns within range. It will continue with persistent harassing fire by night on London. When weather conditions make enemy air activity impossible, firing can also take place by day, This harassing fire, mingled with bombardments of varying length and intensity, will be calculated so that the supply of ammunition is always related to our capacities for production and transport. In addition, 600 Fzg 76 will be regarded as a reserve of the High Command of the Armed Forces, to be fired only with the approval of the High Command of the Armed Forces.

b) Orders will be given in due course for switching fire to other targets.

4. The orders laid down for secrecy in paragraph 7 of the order No 663082/43 for Senior Commanders will apply.

The Chief of the High Command of the Armed Forces,

Keitel

From: Mathilde von Vorzik
Die Alter Scheune
Steuben Gasse
Höchstein
To: Hauptmann Peter von Vorzik
III Gruppe JG233
Schaftstadt, Halle

17th May 1944

My Darling Peter,

Your brief letter was reassuring but, of course, so much has happened since I received it that my anxiety for your safety returns on a day-by-day basis. We have some very sad news here. Ten days ago Lenka was found drowned in the river, about a kilometre downstream. No one knows for sure whether it was suicide or an accident. The river bank there is very crumbly and it is possible if she was standing on the edge that she could have slipped in. However, as I have written before, she has been very depressed about the lack of news about her father and brother and she was convinced they were dead. She always enjoyed taking walks along the river path so there was nothing unusual about her taking that route this time. I do know she could not swim. The river bends where she was found, the water is deep and fast-flowing. The crumbly bank would have made it difficult for her to scramble out. No one saw the accident if that is what it was. There was a brief inquest at which I had to give information about her background and produce her papers and the coroner recorded a verdict of death by misadventure. That allowed for her funeral yesterday in the little local church, which I paid for. The only mourners were myself, Marie and Frau Linder from the farm. Of course Marie and I have been very upset and we miss Lenka very much. She was a kind, affectionate girl and Wolfchen keeps asking where she is. There is no one in her family I can write to. In the end we were her family. Of course Lenka was very useful in the house, doing most of the cleaning and sometimes looking after Wolfchen. Marie is happy to help me with him now and she has found a local girl, Hannelore, to do some of the rough work in the house. Now that spring is here some of the jobs are easier or not necessary; for example we do not need to chop wood for the stove but being pregnant makes it more effortful for me to do certain things. I am feeling very well, however, and we continue to get wonderful produce from the farm.

I do so hope, darling, that things go well with you. I tell myself, as the postman walks by, that no news is good news. You must be worried about Edith, I do hope she will not regret the big change in her life that she has decided upon. We heard on the radio today that the British and Americans (they also have Polish and French troops with them) are attacking the Adolf Hitler Line from Pentecorvo to Aquino which is the last line of defence before Rome. Apart from Edith's decision to give everything to the orphanage it seems foolhardy to stay in Rome with the enemy so near. If only she had come here to Höchstein, her presence would have been especially welcome now.

Please, darling, write when you can.

Ever your loving,
Mathilde and Wolfchen

From: Hauptmann Peter von Vorzik
III Gruppe JG233
Schaftstadt, Halle
To: Oberleutnant Lother Köhl
1(F) 122
Luftflotte 6
Warsaw Okecie

24th May 1944

Dear Lother,

As always it was a great pleasure to hear from you, especially as your situation appears to have improved in all respects! The tone of your letter was quite different to previous ones, especially since Stalingrad, and I am sure you feel rejuvenated having been freed from that long spell in Russia. No doubt the relief of flying the 410 has something to do with it but I suspect the lady called Velda is chiefly responsible! Despite your understandable intention of not becoming romantically involved until this horrible war is finished, when an attractive member of the opposite sex appears nature takes over... I am so pleased for you, Lother, there is nothing so effective in restoring one's equilibrium, one's sense of wellbeing as the companionship of an attractive woman. I had entertained hopes that my Katschmarek, Kurt, might have begun a friendship with the charming Czech girl, Lenka, that the authorities sent my wife to help in the house but sadly she was recently found drowned in the river near Höchstein. This was particularly upsetting for Mathilde as she had grown very fond of the young woman. Whether it was suicide or not we cannot tell. But now, you are quite a Lothario! Maintaining correspondence with your war widow gives you two strings to your bow! I mentioned this to our Staffel Lothario, Ludwig Varasch, whom I am sure I have mentioned to you (he has become a close friend who, you may remember, has generously provided a refuge for my family at Höchstein) and he said, experienced ladies' man that he is, that he had made it a rule never to try and keep two fires burning at once. Anyway, I wish you luck with both your ladies. We have been kept frantically busy with the constant daylight raids by the American 8th and 15th Air Forces. Their bombers, surrounded by swarms of fighters, are free to fly where they will over Germany and although we are sometimes able to penetrate the fighter screen most times we are engaged in a fight for our lives with the cursed Mustangs. We have lost so many good pilots as well as scores of youngsters just out of flying school that it is difficult to sustain the *esprit de corps* that is so essential during a period of high combat. Nowadays, when one of us manages to make a kill we rarely celebrate in the mess, we are more likely to raise a glass in memory of a comrade who has only been with us a week or two.

You ask about my sister Edith. Not only has she decided to stay in Rome but she has sold most of what she owns and given the money to a local orphanage where she now lives and works. Quite apart from the danger of the advancing Anglo-American armies which, as I write, have begun a new offensive toward Rome, I find it somewhat perverse to give everything away and dedicate herself to caring for Italian orphans. On the other hand, of course, some would consider it an act of Christian charity and obviously she feels she has an obligation to God to make this sacrifice.

We were all brought up in the Catholic faith but my brother Christian and I have long since abandoned our belief (we feigned adherence while my mother was alive) while Edith has remained steadfast. However, I am sure she would not have assumed this extreme position if her husband had not been politically done to death. At the moment it is impossible to seek justice; after the war we shall do all in our power to find the murderers.

Here's wishing you continued success with your amour(s) and safe flying!

Ever your sincere comrade,

Peter

From: Hauptmann Peter von Vorzik
III Gruppe JG233
Donaueschingen
To: Mathilde von Vorzik
Die Alter Scheune
Steuben Gasse
Höchstein

30th May 1944

My Darling Mathilde,
Another short letter to let you know I am well and safe and to give you my new address. If you look at a map you will see we have been moved

to the extreme south-western corner of Germany, not far from the Swiss border. The Black Forest is to the north, the city of Basel to the south-west and Lake Konstanz due east. It is a very beautiful part of the country, the Bavarian Alps are clearly visible, especially from 5,000 m, and if we should fly east I would probably be able to see Adlersee. We have to be careful not to overfly the Swiss border! We share the airfield with IV JG53 and I have met one or two old friends from Werneuchen who are serving with that Geschwader.

Darling, I was so very sad to hear of the drowning of Lenka. What a tragedy! It must have been a harrowing time for you and of course you must miss her help in the house and with Wolfchen. Please let me know how much the funeral cost and I will send a cheque to cover it right away, you must not become overdrawn at the bank. Do you think it was suicide? When do you next see your gynaecologist? Do let me know how you are, darling, and how your pregnancy progresses. You are constantly in my thoughts.

Fond regards from Kurt and Ludwig (they were both upset to hear of Lenka's death).

Kisses for you and Wolfchen from

Your adoring,
Peter

PS I do not know if Christian has returned from Sweden. Would you phone his Kaisestraße number and if he is not there give my new address to one of the servants, please? P.

From: Hauptmann Peter von Vorzik
III Gruppe JG233
Donaueschingen
To: Signora Edith Novarro-Badaelli
Santa Maria Orfanotrofio
Campo Baldi
Rome

2nd June 1944

Dear Edith,

I do not know if this letter will reach you. As I write the OKW communiques state that Kesselring's armies are desperately defending Valmontone and the Alban Hills immediately south of Rome. You must be able to hear the sound of the guns. I listen to every radio report and examine every map reference and hope that, when the inevitable happens, as it surely must, that Rome falls to the Anglo-American armies, you will be spared the horrors that I have previously written about. Just as I endeavoured to understand your reasons for staying in Rome, you will surely understand why I am so very anxious about your welfare. It is so long since I last saw you, dear sister, that I cannot help but grieve that we are not only separated by countries but also by the powers that control them. Should you read this please note my new address; the old one will suffice (via Eleanora, as you suggest) but obviously will take longer to reach me.

I leave you, confident as you are, in God's hands.

Ever your devoted brother,
Peter

Hauptmann Peter von Vorzik
Journal entry

10th June 1944

The long-expected blow from the west has fallen. Four days ago the British, American and Canadian forces effected landings on the French coast between the Cherbourg peninsular and Le Havre. Their armies are supported by a huge naval armada and thousands of aircraft. It is apparent that the British and Americans have complete air superiority which will probably prove the deciding factor in the battle. Official estimates are that the Luftwaffe fighters are outnumbered twenty to one. Weeks before the invasion force appeared the enemies' tactical air forces equipped with heavy bombers, medium bombers, fighter-bombers and fighters have been pounding the communication systems throughout northern France. Railways, roads, bridges, airfields, gun emplacements, marshalling yards, fuel and ammunition dumps, gas and electricity works have been systematically attacked day after day, night after night. The Atlantic Wall which we have been erecting for the last year has been breached. At the moment it is still uncertain whether this assault is the main thrust. We still expect that the enemy will attempt another landing, probably around the Pas de Calais area where the sea crossing is much shorter.

Our forces, under the overall command of Field Marshal Keitel, with armies under the direction of Field Marshal Runstedt and Field Marshal

Rommel, naval forces under Admiral Dönitz and the Third Air Force commanded by Field Marshal Sperrle are fighting desperately to throw the enemy back into the sea but presently they appear to have established three bridgeheads. The next week or so will surely decide the outcome of the war. If the Anglo-Americans succeed in establishing themselves on the mainland of France then we shall be unable to sustain the war on two major fronts – three if one counts Italy, which one must. We have sustained another blow. Two days before the landing in France, Anglo-American troops entered Rome. That is a major propaganda victory for our enemies but my main concern, of course, is for the safety of my sister, Edith. This situation has long been foreseen; now she is in territory occupied by the enemy and is at their mercy. Communication will be difficult and one can only hope that the conquering armies will respect the populace.

On the eastern front we have lost almost all of the Russian territories we had taken at such a huge cost in men and material. The siege of Leningrad was raised some weeks ago, we have retreated from the Crimea and now the Russian armies are poised on the frontiers of Poland, Hungary, Rumania, Bulgaria, Finland and the Baltic states of Latvia, Estonia and Lithuania. Partisans are proving a real problem in the Balkans. As for our gallant Geschwader, we have been moved south-west in an effort to defend southern Germany and the Rumanian oilfields against the sustained attacks by the American 15th Air Force flying from bases in Italy and North Africa. Our problem is that we have been so decimated during these last few weeks that it is difficult now to fly and fight as a cohesive unit. Attaching us to IV JG53 as some small appendage does not immediately create a unified force. As it is we lost one pilot, Franz Schwarzkopf, on the flight from Schaftstadt. He developed an engine problem over Ulm, became separated in a bank of cloud, tried to crash land in the Swabian hills and was killed in the process. Now we are desperately trying to train our remaining pilots in cross-country navigation, to integrate them with JG53 and the offensive-defensive tactics they have developed and to re-establish the *esprit de corps*, the inter-relationship and confidence we had several months ago. We have to acknowledge now, that Germany is ringed by her enemies and the outlook is bleak.

From: SS-Gruppenführer Count Christian von Vorzik
116 Kaiserstraße
Berlin
To: Hauptmann Peter von Vorzik
III Gruppe JG233
Donaueschingen

12th June 1944

Dear Peter,

Your letter of the 14th May was awaiting me on my return from Sweden and, fortuitously, Mathilde telephoned me yesterday evening with your new address. Thank you for doing what you could to deflect Edith from her mad decision to give everything to that orphanage. I call it mad for really I feel there is something deranged in her actions, religious mania perhaps following upon the death of Arturo. I always felt her adherence to the Catholic faith was excessive and, despite what you say to the contrary, I am sure she was subject to some subtle persuasion from someone associated with that organisation. In his latter months Ciano was ambassador to the Holy See and Arturo and Edith must have received clerics from the Vatican on a social basis. Well, what is done is done and now Edith finds herself under enemy occupation.

As you can imagine, since the Anglo-Americans landed in France, here in Berlin we are working under considerable pressure, particularly as there have been disastrous failings by the Abwehr which complicates matters for us. I cannot give you details but matters are moving towards a climax there that impose extra responsibilities on the Ausland SD. My visit to Sweden failed in its major objective (which I also cannot write about) but nevertheless I made some extremely useful contacts which may well prove productive in the future. It also served as a very pleasant change of scene after the devastation that has been wreaked on Berlin. My office has been severely damaged and I have moved into adjacent quarters. Luckily 116 is still intact.

Amongst the pile of mail awaiting my return was a communication from Adlersee to say that Werner had died at the end of May from respiratory complications and pneumonia. He has been buried in St Matthias churchyard. His death reminded me of several of our boyish escapades in which he was effective in deflecting father's wrath! Very few attended the funeral, Frau Schuster was there together with one or two of the nurses from Adlersee and a few of the older farm workers. Mathilde told me of the unfortunate death of the girl, Lenka. I offered to arrange for another Oestland worker to replace her but Mathilde says they have a local girl who is satisfactory. She also told me she is expecting another child. Congratulations!

Walter is in Switzerland which imposes extra work on me. When he returns we expect to accompany the Reichsführer-SS to report to the Führer, either at Rastenburg or the Berghof. There are many questions that need resolving and the Führer's approval but since the developments in the west it has become even more difficult to achieve an audience with him. We still maintain hopes that the Anglo-Americans can be defeated in Normandy but they may yet strike another blow further up the coast or even land somewhere in the Balkans. We can but wait upon events.

I trust all goes well with you.

Ever your affectionate brother,
Christian

From: Hauptmann Peter von Vorzik
III Gruppe JG233
Donaueschingen
To: Oberleutnant Claus Grüber
Erprobungsgruppe V
Rechlin am Muritzsee

18th June 1944

Dear Claus,

Looking through my correspondence file I see that the last time we wrote to each other was just before the New Year! I cannot believe that half a year has gone by without hearing from you (no reproach intended!) or that so much of importance to Germany's future has happened in the interim. First, then, I hope and trust that you are in good health. Second, I wonder what is happening at Rechlin that might possibly make some difference to the threatening situation we face in the west and east...? Thirdly, it would, in any case, be a boost to one's morale to hear from you.

Well, we have at long last begun our bombardment with the Fieseler Fil03 (which I understand we now refer to as Vergeltungswaffe 1, or Vl). Apparently, they are simply aimed at London and do nothing immediate to affect the Anglo-American landings in Normandy. That is where we really need some effective weapon(s) to counter the overwhelming numerical superiority our enemies have in the air. I understand that the Geschwader in the west were simply unable to get near the invasion forces. On the day of the invasion I was told that fighters of Luftflotte 3 flew only one hundred sorties compared to an announced figure of 14,600 by the enemy air forces! That gives you some idea of the enemies' strength, does it not? Where are the Me262s? The Me163s? Or the Bachem Ba349 vertical rocket interceptor that you showed me photos of during my last visit to Rechlin? Those are what we need and in their thousands if we are to succeed in repelling the Anglo-American landings. The situation looks really serious and one cannot but be anxious about what is happening on all fronts. It is the situation in the east that has me (and my comrades) really worried. Those bastard Russians are coming ever closer, Finland and the Balkan countries are preparing to abandon us, Italy has already gone inasmuch as it was ever anything but a liability – and we are constantly pounded from the air. I look to you, Claus, for words of encouragement!

Our Geschwader has suffered badly during the last two months, our new young pilots in particular being decimated, trying our best to repel the American bombers over central Germany. What is left of us has been moved south (note my new address) to intercept the Dicke Hund coming from Italian bases. The real problem has been the swarms of Mustang long-range fighters; without them we would have defeated the bombers long ago. Well, this does seem a catalogue of woe! You remember I told you that my sister's husband was imprisoned in Verona? Well, he was shot there on some trumped-up political charge. Now she has given all her money and worldly goods to a local orphanage in Rome where she also works as an all-round factotum. My brother insists she has lost her reason but I know it is because of a misplaced sense of Christian charity. She is a devout Catholic. Need I say more? Anyway, now that Rome has been occupied by the enemy she is practically incommunicado except for letters we hope to receive via her mother-in-law in Switzerland. One bright spot on this dark horizon is that my wife is pregnant again, baby expected in mid-August.

Write to me when you can, Claus, and tell me all your news.

All good wishes,

Your sincere comrade,
Peter

From: Mathilde von Vorzik
Die Alter Scheune
Steuben Gasse
Höchstein
To: Hauptmann Peter von Vorzik
III Gruppe JG233
Donaueschingen

21st June 1944

My Darling Peter,

I received your letter of 30th May yesterday. The post seems to take longer and longer to get through and, as always, I wonder (and worry) what might have happened since you wrote. We were astonished at the news of the pilotless bombs we are sending over London! What a brilliant invention, bombs without risking the loss of aircrew. I do hope they will make the British see sense and sue for peace. If only they could make pilotless fighter planes, darling, all my worries about you would be over. Otherwise the news is rather worrying. It seems the British and Americans and their allies cannot be dislodged from northern France although, according to the radio, they are stuck fast and cannot get any further while our forces blast them to pieces. The radio continues to be a great comfort to the spirit – not, I hasten to add, because of the news bulletins but I have heard some wonderful concerts recently, relayed from Berlin and Vienna, pure balm to the soul. I have also bought a recording by Deutsche Grammophon of Beethoven's *Seventh Symphony*, with von Karajan conducting the Orchestra of the Berliner Staatsoper. It is really marvellous, and they play the last movement at tremendous speed so that I want to get up and dance about the room! Except that, if you saw me now, it would be a ludicrous spectacle, I really am showing a large stomach. I am trying to get Wolfchen used to the idea of having a brother or sister. I let him pat my stomach and I say, "Baby coming for Wolfchen!" I don't know if he understands but the gynaecologist whom I saw again last week (all progresses well) said that first children frequently resent the arrival of a second child. He said we must be prepared later on for Wolfchen to start crawling again and imitating baby noises. We must make a special fuss of him for the first few weeks after the birth although, personally, I think Wolfchen will remain much more interested in the farm horses than a new baby!

I had a long talk with Christian on the phone. He would not say why he went to Sweden but said it was an enjoyable trip and a great relief to get away from Berlin and the bombing. He said he was contemplating another visit to one of the *Lebensborn* clinics. I felt like asking him if he had any female companions but did not like to broach the subject. He congratulated me on my pregnancy and I felt from the tone of his voice how he wished he had a wife who was expecting a child. He asked me if I wanted another worker from the east to replace Lenka but I said thank you, not at the moment. It would be difficult, impossible, to replace Lenka. Hannelore does very well, works hard but one has to be very specific and tell her exactly how and what one wants done. She has not got the domestic expertise that Lenka had. Thank you, darling, for the cheque which more than covered the funeral expenses. What was left over (750 Reichsmarks) I put into the savings account we started for Wolfchen.

Have you heard from Edith? I worry (as you must do) about what is happening to her in Rome under enemy occupation. If only she had come here to Höchstein! The countryside is looking so beautiful now with lovely sunny days and white clouds like bits of cotton wool – but then, darling, you know all about clouds! I will stop now and hurry to post this. Although, as you know, I am not religious, I pray every night that God, or the Gods, will keep you safe for

Your ever loving wife and son,
Mathilde and Wolfchen

PS Regards to Kurt and Ludwig. I hope they are safe, too. M.

Hauptmenn Peter von Vorzik
Journal entry

28th June 1944

Cherbourg has fallen to the Anglo-American forces and units of the German army are cut off on that peninsula. Elsewhere in northern France there is heavy fighting around the town of Caen. The enemy continues to land supplies for their ever-growing armies via two synthetic harbours at St Laurent and Arromanches. The one at St Laurent was badly damaged by a violent gale ten days ago but the other one is in operation and we have to admit this is a brilliant means of assuring consolidation of the Normandy landings and it certainly seems that we have failed in our initial endeavours to fling the enemy back into the sea. On the eastern front the Russians have launched a massive summer offensive and appear to be sweeping forward on all parts of the front, from the Finnish borders in the far north, to the Polish border in the centre to the Rumanian and Hungarian borders in the south. In Italy Field Marshal Kesselring's army is retreating northwards to the Gothic Line beyond Florence.

Late yesterday evening I was sitting with Kurt outside the operations hut watching the last rays of light in the west and listening to the eerie owl calls from the wood that borders the airfield, when he said, "You know, Peter, we have lost the war. It is only a matter of time before Germany is overwhelmed." I did not reply immediately. I found it hard to agree with him in so many words although in my heart I knew he was right. Finally I said, simply, "Yes." After a minute or two I added, "Despite everything, all you and I can do is fight on." Then it was his turn to answer monosyllabically, "Yes, that is all we can do." We both walked over to the mess where someone had a radio that was playing the overture to Johann Strauss's operetta *Der Zigeuner Baron*. The gay, lilting music seemed perversely at odds with our sombre conversation and thoughts. We drank a few glasses of schnapps and listened to the music which, together, gradually raised our spirits. It is hard, however, to maintain those spirits when faced with the reality of each dawn. During the last week or so we have been in almost continuous combat with bombers of the 15th American Air Force and its fighter escort which has been raiding the synthetic oil plants at Ploesti, Vienna, Blechhammer and Oderthal. It has been a repeat performance of our engagements further north over Leipzig and Stuttgart. The American bombers, B-17 Fortresses and B-24 Liberators, are usually protected by the familiar swarms of Mustangs, outnumbering us three to one, making it almost impossible to get through to the bombers. However, three days ago, together with Kurt, I did manage to shoot down a Dicke Hund, a Liberator, south-west of Vienna.

We had the call to warm up our motors at 11.40 hrs and remained on standby until 12.20 hrs until the target, Vienna, had been verified. Together with twenty-two Gustavs from IV JG53 we took off and headed due east expecting to make the interception somewhere north of Villach. As is so often the case we were still climbing to our preferred height of 8,000 m when we spotted the enemy formations, about two hundred bombers screened by about the same number of fighters. In one respect the lower altitude was in our favour. Although the enemy fighters had the advantage of height it also meant we could approach the bombers from beneath, their weakest defensive spot. Once we had sighted the enemy our depleted Staffel broke away from JG53 and I gave the order for the six Rotte to select a Liberator, make their attack then turn for bodo as fast as possible in order to evade the Mustangs. Taking Kurt with me I announced our target as the last bomber on the port side of the leading "box" of aircraft. Still climbing, we closed rapidly on the big machine with its fat fuselage, long narrow wings and big oval "dinner-plate" fins and rudders. I told Kurt to aim for the starboard engines and I would aim for the port ones and to hold his fire until we were within 200 m of the target. As we approached closer and closer we came under attack from the twin 0.5 inch machineguns in the rear turret. Luckily neither of us were hit as we presented a minimal target area to the gunner. When the huge aircraft filled the Revi gunsight I gave the order to fire and our 30mm cannons and 13mm machineguns raked the port and starboard engine nacelles. As we broke away to port I could see that we had both achieved hits and flames were already flickering around three of the four engines. Despite the danger from escorting fighters we circled back towards the stricken bomber which was rapidly losing height and falling away from its formation. We were anxious to confirm our kill and, if necessary, perform the *coup de grâce*. With Kurt keeping careful watch I followed the bomber down as, trailing twin columns of black smoke, it increased the angle of its dive. At 3000 m I counted seven small black specks falling from the aircraft that soon blossomed into parachutes. The Liberator, I knew, carried a crew of ten; perhaps the pilot, co-pilot and engineer were trying to crash-land the blazing aircraft, an unlikely possibility. Perhaps they were wounded, suffocating from the fumes or already dead. No more parachutes appeared and, just south of Amstetten, it hit a wooded hillside and exploded in a huge red fireball. Horrido! The death of a Dicke Hund. The pilots of JG53 claimed another two Liberators and, miraculously, everyone managed to make it back to bodo which, in itself, was something to celebrate.

From: Hauptmann Peter von Vorzik
III Gruppe JG233
Donaueschingen
To: SS-Gruppenführer Count Christian von Vorzik
116 Kaiserstraße
Berlin

8th July 1944

Dear Christian,

Many thanks for your letter. It was a forlorn hope that I might have dissuaded Edith from her chosen path. As you well know she always held an opinion with some stubborness and, with the conviction that she is doing "God's will" it was unlikely that anything that we could say would change her mind. We must hope, now, that her life will not prove too much of an ordeal under enemy occupation. In any case our family problems and considerations are of small consequence compared with the threats that confront the Fatherland, are they not? I read today that von Kluge has replaced von Runstedt as Supreme Commander in the west. I hope he will have greater success than his predecessor but with our enemies having such overwhelming command of the air I cannot see that he can work miracles.

We have been struggling to intercept the huge American air fleets that have been attacking the synthetic oil plants in the south-east. We have had some successes but in the process we continue to lose more and more pilots and our ratio of losses is disproportionate to that of the enemy who still seems able to put swarms of planes in the air where and when he chooses. Our Vergeltung pilotless bombs cannot be considered anything other than a distraction from the main issues. All they will do is cause some casualties amongst London's population and give some sense of satisfaction to the populace of our own cities that we have a technically clever means of retaliation. It will not affect the enemy armies in the east or west. This view is not defeatism, it is realism.

Yes, Mathilde is expecting another child in late August. I have mixed feelings about its arrival: of course I am delighted at the prospect of being a father again but somewhat apprehensive about the world into which the child will be born. The best that we might hope for is an honourable peace with the Anglo-Americans which would leave us free to defeat the Communist threat. I wonder that the western allies cannot see that.

Meanwhile I and my comrades continue to fight as effectively as we can. There is no other course. I was sad to hear of Werner's death. As you say he played a notable part in our childhood. He made me a marvellous kite when I was seven or eight and I think that was what initiated my interest in aerodynamic flight. Strange what influence simple things can have on the course of one's life.

Now I must try and catch the mid-day post. Please write when you can and keep me informed of all your endeavours.

Ever your affectionate brother,
Peter

PS We never did get to have that ride in the Tiergarten together. P.

From: Hauptmann Peter von Vorzik
III Gruppe JG233
Donaueschingen
To: Mathilde von Vorzik
Die Alter Scheune
Steuben Gasse
Höchstein

12th July 1944

My Darling Mathilde,

Another short letter to thank you for yours and to reassure you that I remain alive and well. Yes, the post is slow but, under the circumstances, we are lucky that it is still working. We, too, have enjoyed some beautiful summer days although the clear weather favours the enemy. We have had some success recently and the weight of the aerial attacks has been less than it was, the enemy no doubt concentrating on his efforts in northern France. We seem to be holding the Anglo-Americans there although the loss of Cherbourg was a blow. Now that your pregnancy moves into its final weeks please do take the greatest care of yourself, darling. What provision have you made if you go into labour during the night? Is Marie able to drive? Is there a local taxi service you can call on? Will the nursing clinic in Höchstein send an ambulance? Do prepare yourself for every eventuality, I am haunted by the dreadful situation that Frieda was in. I heard from Christian but he made no mention to me about the *Lebensborn* programme. I suppose he looks upon it purely as a duty that all suitable members of the SS are expected to perform. I am anxious about his safety as the British and Americans continue to make heavy raids on Berlin, even more so since we started to bombard London with our V1s. Yes, it is a brilliantly clever invention (and we have others which I hope will become operational soon) but I do not think we can drop a comparable weight of explosives on London as they can with conventional means.

I have no special news for you, darling, except to say I love you very much and send kisses to you and Wolfchen

From your adoring,

Peter

From: Signora Edith Novarro-Badaelli
Santa Maria Orfanotrofio
Campo Baldi
Rome
via Contessa Eleanora Novarro-Badaelli
Villa Brione
Via Fresne
Gordola
Switzerland

16th July 1944

Dear Peter,

By some miracle your letter of 6th July has reached me and I am hoping that a second miracle will bring this to you. I am putting it an envelope for Eleanora to post from Switzerland. Eleanora invited me to join her at Gordola in the canton of Ticino if I should find the work here too arduous. She said she would send me a rail ticket and money for the journey and could arrange the passage through the Red Cross. It is very kind of her but I made my decision to stay here and I will abide by it however difficult it becomes. Food has been scarce. I realise now just how pampered we have been in the diplomatic corps! Here we have less than the regulation 200 grams of bread a day, scarcely any flour for pasta, no meat, 50 grams of fat, 100 grams of olive oil a month – and that more often available on paper than at the market. The black market flourishes but at prices the orphanage cannot afford.

However, two days ago we had a visit from an American officer, Lt Frank Maldini, representing the Anglo-American control commission in Rome. The nuns appointed me as interpreter as I speak better English than anyone else here although the lieutenant speaks passable Italian being of Italian extraction. I told him we had very little food for the orphans and he promised to arrange a supply of flour, tinned milk, tinned meat and a strange product, powdered eggs! He also promised us basic medical supplies, bandages, aspirin, iodine and a powder to scatter that kills cockroaches, ants, lice and all manner of horrible insects that convey disease. Yesterday morning, to our astonishment, the lieutenant arrived in a truck and unloaded enough supplies for a month, we even have a problem with storage! As well as leaving papers dealing with rules under the occupation, most of which do not apply to us, such as the curfew that is in operation, the lieutenant left some American magazines and newspapers which I have not seen since I left the information office in Berlin. It is something of a revelation to read about the war from the "other side"! I will not burden you with details but suffice it to say there are aspects of the war which we Germans know nothing about, heinous crimes supposedly done in our name. Much of it is propaganda, of course, but some must have an element of truth.

I hope and trust, dear brother, that you are safe and well and that Mathilde and Wolfchen flourish at Höchstein. I pray for you all every day and if this letter reaches you please let Christian know that you have heard from me and that, ironically, my situation here has improved since the Anglo-American occupation.

Ever your loving sister,
Edith

From: Mathilde von Vorzik
Die Alter Scheune
Steuben Gasse
Höchstein
To: Hauptmann Peter von Vorzik
III Gruppe JG233
Donaueschingen

21st July 1944

My Darling Peter,

Yesterday, in the lane, I met the postman bearing your letter and he asked me if I had heard the news. I said no, and he told me of the dreadful bomb attack on the Führer. I rushed indoors and Marie and I sat listening to the radio for the rest of the day and evening. It was a great relief to hear the Führer's own voice describing his escape. What an awful conspiracy! What treachery! I cannot imagine that men in such important and responsible positions could combine to try and bring about our country's defeat. I understand the Gestapo are still searching for some of the culprits and that the conspiracy lies deep within the Party and the Wehrmacht. What angers me most is that there you are, my darling husband, risking your life every day for your country, and these wicked men would hand victory to our enemies by killing the Führer and taking control. Well, now retribution has fallen on them.

My darling, do not worry about me going into labour. The nursing clinic will send a private ambulance as soon as I feel regular contractions, even if I telephone in the middle of the night. I can take Wolfchen with me, they have nursery facilities for small children during my confinement. Marie will probably come with me. No, she does not drive. Remember, this is my second pregnancy, I know the early signs and what to expect when the labour pains begin. I have bought Wolfchen a little tricycle for his birthday. When we were shopping in Höchstein he saw a child riding one and immediately wanted it. I think at first it will be too big for him to handle but he will enjoy just pushing it! I am keeping it in the loft until the day. He has made some little friends in that row of houses just beyond the farm and I shall be asking them to join us on his birthday. Marie will bake one of her delicious apple cakes and we shall have games in the garden. How I wish, darling, that you could be there to share the day with us. I suppose there is no possibility of you obtaining leave in the near future?

You say you are anxious for Christian's safety and he is certainly at risk in Berlin. I am concerned for his general happiness. I know he still mourns the loss of Frieda and makes no mention of any other lady in his life. Of course he is kept very busy working in Schellenberg's department and it is as well that he can submerge his grief in work. I do not suppose you have heard from Edith? That is another worry for us. It must be dreadful to be under enemy occupation, cut off from one's country and family but that was her own choice which, I must say, I find difficult to understand. Christian, as you know, feels very upset about it.

Continue to do all in your power, dearest, to keep yourself safe for

Your devoted wife and son,

Mathilde and Wolfchen

PS Regards, as always, to Kurt and Ludwig. M.

PPS Darling, here are some suggested names for the new baby:

BOY

Heinrich (after my mother's brother killed in the last war)

Peter (after you!)

Wilhelm (after *Wilhelm Meister* the Goethe novel I so enjoyed)

Friedrich or

Konstantin (because I like them!)

Rudolf

GIRL

Elisabeth (after your mother)

Greta (after my mother)

Renata (as we chose before)

Emilia (because I like it)

Edward Thorpe

From: SS-Gruppenführer Count Christian von Vorzik
116 Kaiserstraße
Berlin
To: Hauptmann Peter von Vorzik
III Gruppe JG233
Donaueschingen

2nd August 1944

Dear Peter,

Thank you for your letter dated 8th July. As you can imagine, this reply
has been delayed owing to the extraordinary circumstances in which we
found ourselves following the attempted assassination of the Führer. From
the immediate confusion, not to say chaos, on 20th July, that reigned
between the OKW HQ on Bendlerstraße and the Ausland SD on Prinz
Albertstraße, to the present moment, I have scarcely had time to eat or
sleep, far less attend to personal correspondence. One good thing that has
emerged from the assassination attempt is the enhanced position of the
Reichsführer-SS and, by association, the Ausland SD. Himmler is now in
charge of the Volksturm which means he is in a position to influence what
forces are sent to the eastern and western fronts. The Führer trusts him
implicitly and has bidden him to root out the treacherous elements in the
upper echelons of the Wehrmacht. All sections of the SS are in the
ascendancy. The weakness and defeatism of the generals will be replaced
by a stronger and more determined prosecution of the war and the
defence of the Fatherland.

Kaltenbrunner is systematically working through lists of suspects who
were associated with the assassins, von Stauffenberg and von Haeften, and
these run into the hundreds. We have our own lists and Walter, his deputy
SS-Gruppenführer Otto Ohlendorf and I have spent hours examining
personal dossiers, listening to recorded telephone conversations and
interrogating agents from France, Italy, Spain, Holland and Belgium to
discover associates of the known conspirators. Believe me, the lists include
some important names within the Party and the Wehrmacht. It has been
exhausting work and it is still far from complete. The situation is
exacerbated by broadcasts from England that give lists of people they
claim have been arrested. Cleverly, these lists mix the names of innocent
people with the guilty so as to give the impression, both here and abroad,

572

that the conspiracy was more widespread than it actually was. I have to acknowledge that certain people have taken the opportunity to settle scores with old enemies by denouncing them to Dr Freisler's People's Court. That apart, there is no doubt that we are facing a very serious military situation east and west and the defeatist attitude of the generals does not help. It is the SS, both at the front and at home, that is proving to be the backbone of the country.

I wash my hands of Edith and the situation she has created for herself. At best I consider that she has succumbed to a mental aberration, at worst she has deliberately severed herself from family and Fatherland. Yes, it is a pity that we never found an opportunity to ride together in the Tiergarten. For the present all such activity has been suspended. We must put it high on our list of priorities when victory has been achieved. I hope you are well and continue to destroy those enemy bombers that are terrorising our cities. It certainly appears that the Luftwaffe is a feeble force over the battlefields.

Ever your affectionate brother,

Christian

PS It came as a shock to hear that Field Marshal Rommel had been wounded and was expected to die after his car was strafed by British fighter-bombers. Now that he appears to be making a miraculous recovery, however, Kaltenbrunner has discovered Rommel may have been in the plot to assassinate the Führer! If true it were better that he had died in his car... C.

From: Oberleutnant Claus Grüber
Erprobungsgruppe V
Rechlin am Muritzsee
To: Hauptmann Peter von Vorzik
III Gruppe JG233
Donaueschingen

9th August 1944

Dear Peter,

Delighted to get your letter and to know you are still swatting the Dicke Hunden! You know how it is these days, one hesitates to put pen to paper in case the recipient is no longer there... We have a sad catalogue of friends and comrades who have been swept away during this last summer. My parents were both killed by bombs on Göttingen, a direct hit on an air-raid shelter. The family house in the new quarter was badly damaged too. I went there to salvage what I could but there was scarcely anything worth saving. I suppose the bombers were aiming for the chemical factory but they just seem to do carpet bombing nowadays and the city, lying directly between Dortmund and Leipzig, was bound to get its share of bombs. So sorry to hear of the death of your brother-in-law. How is your sister now that Rome is in enemy hands? I suppose she finds some solace in working with the orphan children. Good news, though, about your wife's pregnancy. Life begins again amidst so much death and destruction. Germany is going to need all the young folk it can get in the next two or three decades.

I do not know if I can lift your morale, as you ask, with any other news. Certainly, we have made progress with some of our projects and the V1 is now operational. Just how successful it will prove in helping to defeat the enemy by creating panic among the London populace remains to be seen. As it seems doubtful that the weight of explosives will be more than what was dropped during the winter of '40/'41, I cannot be other than sceptical. There have already been a few encounters between Me163s flying from Rechlin and Augsburg with some success but we have only a few of them operational (and very few pilots) and they are limited by their radius of action, a mere 50 km. We need swarms of them in order to be an effective deterrent. As you know, the Me262 has been hampered by the Führer's insistence that it should be used as a bomber. No one did much to adapt it for that role and when the Führer and the Fat One found out there were terrible scenes! The idea that the 262s would be able to destroy the invasion armada didn't, couldn't, work. On June 6th we had none that could fly operationally, far less make low-level attacks on the beachheads as had been hoped. Jagdflugmeister Galland has made several attempts to persuade the Führer to allow the aircraft to be used as fighters without success. The last time he took Reichsminister Speer with him to Rastenburg to help put the case but they were dismissed by the Führer before they could speak! The Bachem 359 vertical-ramp rocket plane development proceeds at Waldsee in the Schwarzwald (not so far from where you are now) but it is plagued with many problems and so far there have only been a few pilotless launches. The Arado 234B reconnaissance bomber is near to being operational. It is a remarkable aircraft (at least it was conceived as a jet bomber!) but the simple truth regarding all these projects is, I'm afraid, that it is too little too late.

I was sorry to hear that Generaloberst Korten died as a result of the bomb attack on the Führer. He was a good man with some good ideas but, like so many others, a voice crying in the wilderness. I have my own ideas about what ought to be done now but I will refrain from putting them into words.

My knee has been playing up recently, the doctors would operate but cannot guarantee anything and it could mean that it is permanently stiff which would make me more awkward than I am now. In any case our flying has been severely curtailed owing to fuel shortage so no more weekend jaunts! You know you are always welcome here if ever you get the chance.

Write again when you can.

Ever your sincere comrade,
Claus

From: Hauptmann Peter von Vorzik
III Gruppe JG233
Donaueschingen
To: Mathilde von Vorzik
Die Alter Scheune
Steuben Gasse
Höchstein

12th August 1944

My Darling Mathilde,
Here I am, safe and well, wondering when I might hear that the new baby has arrived. Whenever I have a moment's pause (which is usually not until I climb into my narrow little bed) I envisage you beginning labour pains, calling Marie, phoning for the ambulance, the birth accomplished without complications, my dearest one holding the child (boy or girl?) to her breast. It is my way of reassuring myself that all will go smoothly. I do so hope, darling, that the birth, when it does come, (perhaps it already has!) will be as easy as in my daydreams. I realise that no birth is that easy, that the smoothest deliveries involve exhaustive effort and much pain and my dearest wish is that I could be there to encourage you. This is really to tell

you, darling, that you are constantly in my thoughts and I long to have news of you and to know we have been blessed with another child.

Life here continues much as before. We are kept busy intercepting American bombers flying from Italy and trying to bomb the hydrogenation and synthetic oil plants in southern Germany and Austria. We have had some success in that endeavour. Two or three times our sorties have taken us over the region in which Adlersee lies and I catch glimpses of the area I have known so well all my life. Of course the height at which we fly and the various cloud layers make it difficult to see any of the landscape in detail but twice I have identified the lake itself although I have not yet seen the Schloss. It is a strange feeling looking down on the land so associated with my boyhood. At other times we have flown farther west, over the Schwarzwald, which looks so beautiful and tranquil from 6,000 m.

Yes, the bomb attack on the Führer was a shock for everyone. An even greater shock was the identity of the people involved, men who one would assume had complete loyalty to the Führer. I could – just – understand it if it had been a deranged political assassin, a Czech (as with Reinhard), a Pole, a latter-day Princip, but not those from within the Party or army. The ramifications of the conspiracy extend far and wide it seems.

You ask about leave, dearest. I do not think it will be granted in the foreseeable future as at the moment we are engaged in such a struggle for the safety of the Fatherland but one can never tell in the vagaries of war. I remember your face, darling, when I arrived unexpectedly at Grunewald. How I would love to repeat that surprise! I have heard from Edith, via Eleanora, and she appears to be flourishing under the Anglo-American occupation! The Americans have unloaded food and medicines on the orphanage and, contrary to Christian's worst fears, have refrained from rape and pillage. I expect Edith will be writing to you but in any case I am sure she would like to hear from you especially after the baby has been born. Do you have Eleanora's address in Switzerland?

As for names for the baby, darling, I leave the choice entirely to you. If it is a girl I would like to incorporate my mother's name (not necessarily as the first) and if it is a boy I would like to add on Kurt to the end because I owe so much to him (including my life) and I know he would be very pleased.

Now I must stop and hurry to catch the late post. All my fondest love and hopes for a brother or sister for Wolfchen safely delivered soon.

Ever your devoted,

Peter

From: Hauptmann Peter von Vorzik
III Gruppe JG233
Donaueschingen
To: Signora Edith Novarro-Badaelli
Santa Maria Orfanotrofio
Campo Baldi
Rome
via Contessa Eleanora Novarro-Badaelli
Gordola
Switzerland

17th August 1944

Dear Edith,

The "second miracle" you hoped for has occurred and your letter of 16th July has just reached me, forwarded by Eleanora. I am sending this by the same route. It was such a relief to know you are being treated well by the occupying forces and that you have adequate supplies of food. You have been constantly in all our thoughts since the Anglo-Americans occupied the city. Thank heavens that Christian's prophecy of rape and pillage did not happen! For you, now, the war is over and in some ways I envy you. We remain locked in a deadly and bitter struggle with so many enemies and I have to admit the situation looks ever more desperate for Germany. We in the Jagdflieger have no alternative but to try and minimise the destruction of our cities from the air as best we can although the reality is that we are outnumbered everywhere and our limited forces are not always used to best advantage. We have some extraordinary new weapons in use but not enough of them to make a material difference, it seems.

You refer to "heinous crimes done in our name." What they may be I do not know and you do not elaborate. I do know that our enemies have committed heinous crimes. Have you read of the thousands of Polish officers murdered by the NKVD, their bodies found in the Katyn forest near Smolensk? I also know of ghastly atrocities committed

577

against some of our Luftwaffe pilots lost over Russia and there are also reports of American fighters shooting at our pilots after they have baled out. There are terrible things done by soldiers of all armies during war; not everyone abides by the Geneva Convention. At present I fear for our country and our culture, especially from the Russians. The possibility that we might be overrun by Asiatic hordes, primitive people who are not constrained by our conception of civilisation, is terrible to contemplate. Any day now I expect to hear from Mathilde that she has given birth to our second child. Delighted as I will be I am fearful for the world that baby will be born into.

How many orphans do you have to care for? Are you finding the work arduous? How long is the American gift of food expected to last? There are so many questions I would like to ask you, dear sister. If only we could sit down and have a proper conversation without the exigencies of time or place... It is such a long time since we last saw each other – Christmas 1941! Do you have a recent photograph of yourself? Please continue to write whenever you have the chance, mail remains the greatest boost to our morale.

With every wish for your health and happiness,

Ever your loving brother,

Peter

PS Kurt, who still protects me from our enemies, wishes to be remembered to you. P.

Hauptmann Peter von Vorzik
Journal entry

25th August 1944

One military disaster follows upon another. In the west, Paris has fallen. After furious battles around Falaise the Anglo-Americans finally succeeded in defeating our Panzer divisions that had fought so bitterly to defend the gap between Falaise and Mortain. When units of the American 3rd Army finally broke through our troops were forced into headlong retreat towards the Seine in order to avoid being surrounded. Their tanks, artillery and motorised units clogged the roads and were under constant attack from RAF fighter-bombers, particularly Hawker Typhoons armed with cannon and rockets, and suffered enormous losses of men and material. As a propaganda coup the Anglo-Americans arranged for the French division under General Leclerc to be the first to enter Paris where General von Cholitz surrendered the city. Later, General de Gaulle, the head of the so-called Free French movement, made a triumphant entry, walking down the Champs Elysées to the Notre Dame cathedral. When I heard the news I could not but help remembering Christian's and my double honeymoon with Mathilde and Frieda in Paris. How the fortunes of war change and change about!

In the east the news is equally disastrous. Russian forces are thrusting into Latvia, Estonia, Lithuania and Poland. Further south they are over-running Rumania and advancing on the Ploesti oilfields. Soon there will be no need for American bombers to raid that target. In Italy, after the fall of Rome, Kesselring's armies retreated up the west and east coasts of Italy. They made a stand at Lake Trasimeno but were dislodged by superior forces, and the Anglo-Americans, together with Canadian and Polish divisions, are moving relentlessly north towards the Gothic Line running from south of Spezia to Pesaro on the Adriatic. That defence system, however, will take some breaching. Other enemy divisions, Americans and French, have made landings in southern France, from Marseilles to Nice, and are rapidly advancing north, obviously with the intention of joining up with Anglo-American forces swinging south from Paris. This is all very disheartening. Our German armies are being overwhelmed everywhere by British, American and Russian forces which, together with their various allies, are beginning to threaten the very perimeters of the Fatherland. In our hearts we all know that ultimate defeat can only be a matter of time: months, probably, at most a year.

As I write, my darling Mathilde is about to present us with another child. Happy as I am at that prospect I can only ponder upon what sort of world our babies will have to face. What will become of us, our family, our Fatherland? My rather sanguine expectations of helping to develop new commercial air routes in a peaceful world are receding into a misty unfathomable future in which we might well have no aircraft at all! I have just this minute received a telegram from the signals office to say that Mathilde has been safely delivered of another boy, Heinrich Peter Kurt! For the moment that banishes all my melancholy musings. Whatever the military situation might be, now I have a perfect reason for a small celebration with my comrades in the mess.

From: Hauptmann Peter von Vorzik
III Gruppe JG233
Donaueschingen
To: Mathilde von Vorzik
Die Alte Scheune
Steuben Gasse
Höchstein

26th August 1944

My Darling Mathilde,

What unrestrained joy and happiness it was to receive that telegram telling me that we have another little boy! Except, of course, it did not give any details, just mother and child well. I do hope, dearest, that the delivery of little Heinrich was as straightforward as I have imagined in my daydreams and that your ordeal was not prolonged. Now I am anxious to know more. How big is he? Does he resemble Wolfchen? Does he also have blue eyes? I hope, darling, that you are staying at the nursing clinic until you have quite recovered. Do you need more money? Shall I increase the monthly allowance? I suppose one advantage of having another boy is that he can wear some of Wolfchen's early clothes, useful while rationing is in force. I remember sometimes having to wear Christian's cast-offs which I detested although mother was always good about providing my own wardrobe. Father was more thrifty and expected me to wear major items like overcoats and formal clothes that had once been my brother's. Both of us used to be sent to Herr Burgdorf, father's tailor at Burgdorf and Zander in Munich. I wonder if the company still exists? My uniforms were made in Berlin. How did Wolfchen like his tricycle? Does he try to ride it? We must try to discover what happened to the toys in the attic rooms at Adlersee, in store with the pictures and *objets d'art* probably. I have no news for you, sweetheart, except to say how happy I am at the safe arrival of Heinrich. Kiss both boys for me.

Ever your own adoring,
Peter

PS Ludwig and Kurt send their congratulations, Kurt is delighted that we have added his name to Heinrich. P.

From: Hauptmann Peter von Vorzik
III Gruppe JG233
Donaueschingen
To: SS-Gruppenführer Count Christian von Vorzik
116 Kaiserstraße
Berlin

28th August 1944

Dear Christian,

This is mainly to tell you, if you have not already heard, that Mathilde was
delivered of another baby boy, Heinrich, on the 25th. Both, I understand,
are doing well although I await the details about the birth. Of course I am
absolutely delighted to be a father again and, between you and me, glad
that it is another boy. As I may have said when Wolfchen was born, I feel
I can be a much more interesting father to a son; I could never get excited
over dolls and dollhouses. Even so, had it been a girl I am sure I would
have been equally pleased. All preferences are put aside when one holds
one's own progeny in one's arms. I just wonder what Wolfchen and Heini
will have to face when they grow up. There will be much rebuilding to
be done.

I can imagine what turmoil you faced after July 20th. The Führer
certainly had a miraculous escape and it has been a matter of astonishment
to read and hear of the ramifications of the plot against him. It is hard to
believe that Rommel, of all people, should have been implicated.

It certainly seems that the Waffen-SS divisions are proving the strongest
defence against our foes east and west. However, I do wonder about the
Reichsführer-SS's qualifications as Commander-in-Chief or whatever his
new position and title is. Has he studied strategy, tactics, fieldcraft and logistics?
Is he familiar with armour and armaments? Who are his subordinates? The
generals may have been somewhat defeatist in their approach to battlefield
problems but, after all, they have devoted their lives and careers to the study
and prosecution of warfare. They did not do so badly against Poland, France,
the Balkans and in the first year in Russia, did they? It is mainly the unmatchable
strength of our enemies that have produced the current problems.

It is difficult, dear brother, not to take exception to the final
comment in your last letter when you say, "It appears that the Luftwaffe
is a feeble force over the battlefields." The plain answer to that is that

the Luftwaffe, on all fronts, is simply overwhelmed by the numbers of the enemy. Two years ago, when the Führer was appraised of the industrial potential of the US, particularly in the production of aircraft, he dismissed the figures as utter nonsense. Now we are faced with the reality. Such pilots as we have – and many, now, are young men deficient in training and experience – are fighting as best they can against superior numbers and, in many cases, superior equipment. Our latest, most brilliant machines are too few and too late. Our lack of success in some combat areas is also attributable to misdirection from above... On-the-ground situations are frequently beyond the control of our pilots. For example, a transfer of fighter reserves to the western front unfortunately coincided with the army's headlong retreat that followed the Anglo-American breakthrough at Falaise and Avranches. This resulted in a large number of our fighters, some eight hundred in all, not getting into action at all. Worse, many were directed to airfields that had already been overrun by the enemy. At least half that number of planes and pilots were sacrificed to no purpose. The general dislocation that occurred during the retreat meant that the huge bulk of the support groups, ground staff, signals, supplies, administration, were involved in the chaos of retreat and were unable to service the fighter force. I write to you at length on this subject to explain, to some extent, why "the Luftwaffe is a feeble force over the battlefields." Meanwhile, the bulk of our fighter forces, including my own Geschwader, is desperately trying to defend our cities and factories against huge numbers of enemy bombers and their protecting fighters. You can be assured that whatever the disparities in numbers, whatever the difficulties we face, I and my comrades will continue to do our duty and defend the Fatherland to the death.

Ever your affectionate brother,

Peter

From: Hauptmann Peter von Vorzik
III Gruppe JG233
Donaueschingen
To: Signora Edith Novarro-Badaelli
Santa Maria Orfanotrofio
Campo Baldi
Rome
via Contessa Eleanora Novarro-Badaelli
Gordola
Switzerland

29th August 1944

Dear Edith,

You may not yet have received my letter of the 17th but I write now just to let you know that Mathilde bore another boy, Heinrich (after her mother's brother killed in 1917) Peter Kurt, on 25th August, just a week after Wolfchen's birthday. I have no details beyond the bald facts of the telegram, "Mother and child doing well," which is what they always say, is it not? I am, of course, delighted at the news although, as I wrote in my previous letter, at the moment the world is a harsh place to be born into. I also feel somewhat guilty in that Mathilde and I have been so blessed when Christian and yourself have been so badly served by fate although I am sure that you, dear sister, will no doubt consider it all part of God's plan. I can only hope that He is considering some compensation for you both in the near future. This is the briefest of notes just to let you know that you have another nephew but it comes, as always, with the fondest love of

Your brother,
Peter

PS As you will have guessed the addition of Kurt to Heinrich's name is in gratitude to my Katschmarek who has been my guardian angel for the last four years. He is delighted. P.

Directive 64A
The Führer

7th September 1944

SUBJECT: MILITARY POWERS OF COMMANDER-IN-CHIEF WEST

1. I confer plenary powers on Commander-in-Chief West, General Field Marshal von Runstedt:

a) To employ, in the execution of the tasks which I have entrusted to him, all available fighting forces and material of the Armed Forces and Waffen SS in his area of command, and of non-military organisations and formations. The following are excluded: crews of submarines and crews of motor torpedo boats, and nautical specialists as designated by Commander-in-Chief Navy; and operational flying personnel and specialists as designated by Commander-in-Chief Luftwaffe.

b) To take all steps necessary to restore and maintain order in his area of command. All Naval and Luftwaffe Authorities, and non-military organisations and formations, come under his orders in this respect.

2. Commander-in-Chief West may – insofar as this has not already been done by the High Command of the Armed Forces – give to the Chief of Army Equipment and the Replacement Army instructions for the distribution of protective forces along the West Wall and the western defences, which may be necessary for bringing these dispositions into conformity with the general situation in the west. The directives of Commander-in-Chief West are also valid for the Party and State authorities, when the military tasks in the western front areas are transferred to the latter.

3. Commander Armed Forces Belgium and Northern France, and Commander Armed Forces Netherlands, are fully subordinate to Commander-in-Chief West in all respects.

Adolf Hitler

From: Mathilde von Vorzik
Die Alte Scheune
Steuben Gasse
Höchstein
To: Hauptmann Peter von Vorzik
III Gruppe JG233
Donaueschingen

8th September 1944

My Darling Peter,

Back again at Höchstein where your letter of the 26th was awaiting me. The nursing clinic was most comfortable and the nursing staff quite marvellous but it is a great relief to be in the welcoming warmth of this house again and Marie pampers me dreadfully, not allowing me to do anything domestic. You ask for details of the birth, darling, and all I can say is that everything went more or less as you say you imagined it in your daydreams! I began regular contractions at about seven-thirty in the evening and the ambulance was here within half an hour. Baby Heinrich arrived just after twelve-thirty in the early morning on the 25th. Naturally, the birth itself involved considerable effort and pain but that is soon forgotten. There were no complications and it was a great joy to have Heinrich suckling at my breast. Heinrich has quite a lot of dark fluffy hair but the Head Nurse said that will probably change within a few weeks. Looking at his screwed up little face I imagine I can see a likeness to both you and Wolfchen. That is probably wishful thinking but, yes, his eyes are blue like yours. At present he wakes regularly for his night feeds and cries very little. Marie took some photographs of Heinrich in my arms an hour or two after he was born which are being developed. I have also arranged for a professional photographer in Höchstein to come to the house in a week or two to take more pictures when Heinrich will not be swaddled in blankets!

As I expected, Wolfchen is not very interested in the new baby apart from an initial curiosity and just accepts the little crib that Marie prepared for him in my room without question. His great interests remain his tricycle (he cannot yet reach the pedals but "walks" it along) and the farm horses. He does enjoy Heinrich's bathtime, however; although Heinrich usually cries when he is immersed I expect he will grow to enjoy his bath just as Wolfchen did. I mention the farm horses but tragedy has struck there. Herr Linder and his wife had a telegram to say both their sons have been posted missing. It seems they disappeared when their unit was over-run by Russian forces somewhere near Grodno. It has taken some time for the official news to come through. Of course they both cling to the thought that the brothers might not be dead just as Eleanora did with Massimo but in their hearts I think they know it is unlikely. It is terrible not knowing for certain. Herr Linder is not far from retiring age. Now, he says, there is no one to leave the farm to, it would be better to sell up and find a little country house somewhere nearby but Frau Linder cannot bear the thought of leaving the farm even if they sell off the livestock. She has a sister in Würzburg but the woman is an invalid looked after by her daughter. Her son, too, was killed on the eastern front back in 1942. Herr Linder has no family except for a distant cousin in Dresden and they have not seen each other since they were boys because of some family quarrel. I am so sorry for the Linders, their lives have been quite devastated.

I was so pleased to hear that Edith seems to be well looked after. It must be strange living under foreign occupation but I suppose the orphanage is something of a closed institution if it is run by nuns. Please send her my love when you write or if you give me Eleanora's address in Switzerland I will write to her myself.

Please say again to Ludwig how grateful we are for his hospitality. No more now, dearest, I know you are waiting to hear from me. Love and kisses from

Wolfchen, Heinrich and
Your adoring wife,
Mathilde

From: Oberleutnant Lother Köhl
1(F) 122
Luftflotte 6
Eastern Front
To: Hauptmann Peter von Vorzik
III Gruppe JG233
Jagdflieger HQ

10th September 1944

Dear Peter,

So much has happened since we corresponded last summer that I have been wondering how and where you are. We have been pushed out of Russia and almost out of France and the day cannot be far off when we are fighting on German soil. That is one thing I have envied you, you have at least been based in the Fatherland while I am still perched here in Poland. Sadly, I had to bid farewell to Velda; we both knew it was going to be a brief affair but it was fun while it lasted and good for morale. She and her family are wondering whether to abandon what they have and flee to the west or to await the arrival of the Russians and trust that a tavern will have some appeal. The Geschwader pulled out of Warsaw not long ago and have been here near Poset for nearly two weeks though for how long nobody knows. The Russian advance appears to have come to a halt but no doubt the bastards are planning a winter offensive and we shall be pulling back again. It sickens me when I look at the map and see the territories we have lost in one short year. Just how much a disaster Stalingrad was becomes more and more apparent as the months go by.

From all sides I hear talk of how our cities are being systematically destroyed and now it appears that our V1 sites have almost all been overrun and our ability to hit back is down to a minimum. The long-range bomber force is about one-fifth of what it once was. Well, we can but fight on and delay the inevitable as long as possible. I am still flying the 410 on reconnaissance when absolutely necessary but we have really suffered from a shortage of fuel, made worse now that Rumania has become an enemy and the oil from Ploesti is no longer available. Most of the aviation fuel that we do have is reserved for the Fw190 Geschwader which have replaced the Ju87s and Fs189s for ground attack but, like you, the Luftwaffe is outnumbered six-to-one on this front. We are really little more than a token force.

Enough of that. I still correspond with my war widow but I miss Velda very much – one does not have the same satisfaction going to bed with a letter! I suppose by now, your wife will have had the baby; may I offer tentative congratulations in the expectation that all went well? How is your sister faring now that Rome is occupied by the Anglo-Americans? Perhaps she decided to return to Germany after all? Religion is a strange thing, it seems people will always be ready to martyr themselves in one way or another for their religious convictions.

Well, I have no news worth reporting but writing a letter is good for the morale if only because it raises the expectation of a reply! Hoping that this reaches you and you are safe and well.

Ever your sincere comrade,
Lother

From: SS-Gruppenführer Count Christian von Vorzik
116 Kaiserstraße
Berlin
To: Hauptmann Peter von Vorzik
III Gruppe JG233
Donaueschingen

14th September 1944

Dear Peter,

First, I hasten to send my congratulations to you on becoming a father again. That is splendid news and it must give you great happiness and satisfaction. I have sent a small present for the baby direct to Mathilde at Höchstein.

Second, I can tell that you were upset by my casual comment about the performance of the Luftwaffe over the battlefields and I am sincerely sorry if I hurt your feelings and wounded your pride. To the uninitiated (and that often includes the men in the front-line) the apparent absence of our aircraft in close support operations, particularly after the successes of two or three years ago, is hard to understand. Now you have gone some way to explain the situation and I can appreciate how difficult it is to fight against overwhelming odds. Whenever I hear someone express a similar criticism (it is usually included in a criticism of the Reichsmarschall) I take it upon myself to quote you and clarify the position in which the

Luftwaffe finds itself. I meant no aspersion on the fighting spirit of the pilots.

You misunderstand the Reichsminister-SS's new appointment. He is not C.-in-C. of the army but replaces General Fromm as chief of the Replacement Army. He is responsible for recruitment and supplies, he will not be directing operations on the battlefield.

Walter was put in a most invidious position recently when he was ordered by Gruppenführer Heinrich Müller to apprehend Admiral Canaris, chief of the Abwehr, under suspicion of being involved in the plot to assassinate the Führer. Poor Walter protested that he was not an executive officer and did not want to be the one to carry out what was, in effect, an arrest. (Müller and Kaltenbrunner know that Walter had been on very friendly terms with Canaris.) Müller told Walter that if he did not do as he was ordered they would draw their own conclusions, which is that Walter was also connected with the assassination attempt. Walter went to Canaris's home in Schlachtensee and, as he had been told, accompanied Canaris to Fürstenberg where he is being held with other suspects. Canaris, whose house I visited many times with Reinhard, has been very foolish and long under suspicion. Do you remember my visit to Rome in August of last year? That was to investigate Canaris's association with General Amé, C.-in-C. of the Italian Secret Service who, at that time, was suspected of supporting the Badoglio government plotting to subvert our occupation forces in Italy. Canaris proved to be involved in that but was protected by his military chief General Keitel and the Reichsführer-SS filed the dossier for later use. Now his other treacherous activities have been discovered and his friendship with Walter and me has provided Kaltenbrunner and Müller with material with which to try and implicate us in the assassination plot. Happily we retain the goodwill and support of the Reichsführer-SS. As Canaris remarked to Walter during their drive to Fürstenberg, Kaltenbrunner and Müller are just two butchers out to extend their power by destroying others within the SS organisation. I am already suspect by reason of being a member of the aristocracy, many of whom have been expunged from the SS.

During my recent visit to Sweden I was introduced to a very pleasant young woman, Signe Oskarson, the daughter of a Swedish businessman who has been involved in import-export business with Germany. We dined together on several occasions and I have hopes of developing the relationship in the near future. I tell you this in strictest confidence. If all proceeds as I hope and plan then I shall be in a position to make a formal announcement.

With best wishes for your continued success and safety,

Ever your devoted brother,
Christian

From: Hauptmann Peter von Vorzik
III Gruppe JG233
Donaueschingen
To: Mathilde von Vorzik
Die Alter Scheune
Steuben Gasse
Höchstein

24th September 1944

My Darling Mathilde,

Wonderful news! We learnt today that the Geschwader is due for restructuring, rest and refit so that we will be given leave in about two weeks' time! It may be that we (Ludwig and Kurt will be coming with me) will arrive on the doorstep before you receive this (Ludwig is also writing to Marie so that perhaps one or other of our letters will precede us). I have tried sending a telegram but the signals office is in absolute chaos as so many of the Luftwaffe signals units have been drafted into the army by order of the Reichsmarschall that those who are left cannot cope with the volume of official communications, let alone private telegrams. I have not been able to leave the airfield these last three weeks. Anyway, sweetheart, you can imagine how my own heart beats at the thought of being with you again and holding little Heini in my arms for the first time.

No more now, I must rush to the post with this.

Ever your devoted (and excited),
Peter

From: *Hauptmann Peter von Vorzik*
III Gruppe JG233
Donaueschingen
To: *Oberleutnant Lother Köhl*
1(F) 122
Luftflotte 6
Eastern Front

11th October 1944

Dear Lother,

As always it was a pleasant surprise to receive your letter and to know you are still flourishing. You have certainly had a tough time. Two years in Russia and then a long wearisome retreat similar to that we experienced in North Africa. It is very dispiriting to look at the map and see how much we achieved and how much we have lost. To have been at the gates of Moscow and Leningrad, to have struck far into the Caucasus, to have nearly reached Cairo and now it is Germany itself that is threatened! Our so-called allies, like Finland and Rumania turn on us when times are difficult and partisans are emerging in every countryside. If only we can hold the Russians on the Vistula (or have they already crossed it?) and fight them to a standstill and perhaps do likewise with the Anglo-Americans now that they have almost reached the Rhine, all may not be lost. We simply must not give up hope however bleak the outlook.

Like you, fuel – or, rather, the lack of it – is our biggest problem since Rumania surrendered to the Russians and the Americans have concentrated on bombing the hydrogenation plants. Next comes the lack of experienced pilots. Some of the new intakes we have received have been seconded from bomber Geschwader with the minimum of conversion training. It has been very hard for them having to unlearn all they have been taught and then assimilate totally new tactics and operational codes. Here in southern Germany we have also suffered from the depletion of ground staff and signals units, drafted into the Wehrmacht on the orders of the Fat One to please the Führer, it is said. Whatever the reason, we have had problems with ground-to-air communications because of lack of trained staff just when the Americans have been attacking in strength.

Was your unit involved in the mass uprising in Warsaw? According to the reports I read there have been enormous casualties on both sides, the

591

battle somewhat reminiscent of Stalingrad, fighting house-to-house and even in the sewers. Throughout the war I have thanked my stars that I was in the Luftwaffe! It seems the Polish insurgents expected the Russians to march into Warsaw but our forces held them on the Vistula.

Sorry to hear of your parting with Velda although, as you say, it was inevitable, given the Russians' advance. But, as you leave one inamorata behind, so you draw closer to the other! It was very sensible of you to keep corresponding with your war widow. Have you any chance of leave in the near future? We are due for refitting in a few days and will be going on leave for a week or so as a result. It is rumoured that our Staffel will be attached to a Lehrgeschwader because, as a group of us belong to the old school who have managed to survive this far we will be a formal training unit although, of course, we will still fly combat operations. It will mean just so much more paperwork!

Yes, my wife was delivered of another boy, Heinrich, which has pleased us both enormously. I cannot wait to see him although, of course, I will have to bestow extra affection on the firstborn. You ask about my sister. I have heard from her, via her mother-in-law in Switzerland, and it appears she has no problems under the occupation. The orphanage is receiving food and medical supplies from the Americans. For the present, life for her seems settled. I wish it was for us, dear comrade. I have no further news for you, at least none that might raise your morale. Here's wishing you all good fortune as we appear to be reaching a climax in our endeavours to save the Reich from its enemies.

Ever yours,

Peter

From: Hauptmann Peter von Vorzik
III Gruppe JG233
Donaueschingen
To: SS-Gruppenführer Count Christian von Vorzik
116 Kaiserstraße
Berlin

13th October 1944

Dear Christian,

Many thanks for your letter. I am glad my explanation of the situation facing the Luftwaffe went some way to dispel the misapprehension over its combat efficiency. It has become a touchy subject, particularly with us fighter pilots. Despite facing overwhelming odds in the air and ever-increasing difficulties on the ground (particularly for those units on the western and eastern fronts where our land forces are in retreat and airfields are often overrun even while fighters are in the air) we have continued to do battle to the point of exhaustion while suffering enormous casualties. Even so, certain people in high places (I will mention no names) have accused us of cowardice, an accusation that has provoked much bitterness. No one, to my knowledge, has evaded combat. Rather, we have often operated beyond the call of duty when it would have been more prudent not to risk lives and aircraft to little purpose. Well, there it is. We can but do what we can. What you tell me of your own organisation leaves me dumbfounded. As I have remarked before, I find it incomprehensible that those in authority engage in such rivalries and petty jealousies.

Yes, we are overjoyed at the arrival of Heinrich. It was kind of you to send a present. Tomorrow, fortuitously, we are granted leave and within a day or so (depending on the transport situation) I shall have my first sight of him. In such times as these one's family is of incomparable value to the spirit. I have been very conscious, dear brother, of how bleak and bereft your life has been since the tragic and untimely death of Frieda. I have refrained from mentioning it in my letters to you for fear of touching upon a raw nerve, of reawakening sad thoughts, hoping, as the cliché has it, that time was healing the wound. I mention it now only in the expectation that the new liaison you tell me of will dim those memories and replace them with a new vision of happiness. Do you have a picture of Signe?

Now I must do some packing in readiness for tomorrow's journey. Train travel nowadays is not for the fainthearted!

Ever your devoted brother,
Peter

From: Signora Edith Novarro-Badaelli
Santa Maria Orfanotrofio
Campo Baldi
Rome
via Countess Eleanora Novarro-Badaelli
Gordola
Switzerland
To: Hauptmann Peter von Vorzik
III Gruppe JG233
Donaueschingen

15th October 1944

Dear Peter,

I was overjoyed to have your letter telling me that you have another son and I another nephew, Heinrich. God has certainly favoured you, dear brother, and I pray as I always do that He continues to do so. I trust that Mathilde is in good health and recovering well from childbirth. I am writing to her at the same time as I am writing this, asking Eleanora to post the letters on. The post from Switzerland seems to be very efficient. I will be sending a small gift for Heinrich separately.

We continue to live relatively well here, sustained by the American occupation services. Frank makes a weekly visit bringing food supplies, even some luxuries such as coffee, biscuits and sweets for the children. He brought me a personal gift of chocolates which I shared with the nuns. Such decadence! He is most kind and, indeed, the occupation forces are behaving extremely well towards the populace. I particularly enjoy the magazines Frank brings which give an enlightening view of life in America. Quite extraordinary! Such advances in domesticity with an array of electronic aids to make life easier for the housewife, even in these exiguous times. The advertisements are sometimes more interesting than the text which, of course, is still mainly concerned with the war, full of harrowing pictures.

And you, dear brother, how are you? I grieve that you are still bound to perform your duties in the midst of this terrible war with the Reich now surrounded by vengeful enemies. In a previous letter I mentioned heinous crimes committed in the name of Germany but, as you pointed out, I did not elaborate. That was because I did not want to burden you with more horrors and, in any case, I felt the stories were probably vile and scurrilous propaganda. However, since you raise the matter, I will be specific. In the magazines and journals that Frank has given me there are reports from London, New York and Geneva that we, the Germans, have set up camps somewhere in eastern Poland with the deliberate intention of killing thousands of Jews from all over Europe. I am sure your response will be the same as mine, disbelief, ascribing such tales as enemy propaganda of the vilest sort. However, it does appear that these assertions are from reliable and independent sources and here in Italy it is reported that the Pope has made representations to the Führer about the matter. I certainly remember Reichsminister Goebbels announcing, nearly two years ago, that Berlin was "Jew free" and that they had been sent to settlements in the east. If the reports are true and these "settlements" are something more sinister, then it is a dreadful indictment of our race and country.

I am pleased that you have added Kurt's name to Heinrich's, he has proved a valiant comrade to you. Please give him my regards, together with heartfelt wishes for your continued health and safety from

Your loving sister,

Edith

Hauptmann Peter von Vorzik
Journal entry

30th October 1944

Nine days of bliss! Of love and the warmth of comradeship, of tranquillity and peace, of food and drink, song and conviviality. Our leave began and ended, of course, with long and tedious railway journeys. From the airfield at Donaueschingen Kurt, Ludwig and I were taken by Kübelwagen to the station at Villengen and thence by train via Stuttgart and Nuremberg to Bamberg where we had the same taxidriver to take us to Höchstein as had driven the three of us last Christmas. Along the way our train hid in a tunnel while an air-raid was in progress near Stuttgart. We saw terrible evidence of bombing all along the route and the whole dismal journey waiting on dark, draughty stations, trying to doze in crowded railway compartments and corridors, failing to find edible sandwiches took over thirty-six hours. At last we reached Höchstein with Mathilde and Marie to greet us and – joy of joys! – my two small sons to hold in my arms.

I hoisted Wolfchen on my shoulders before I held Heini while Mathilde looked on, tears of happiness trickling down her cheeks. The greetings over we all sat down to a wonderful supper of mushroom soup, roast pork with potato dumplings and cabbage followed by one of Marie's delicious strudels with cream. Ludwig brought excellent wines from his extensive cellar and by ten o'clock we were all in bed, luxuriating in the calm and comfort of the house. Tired as I was I was aroused to a passionate frenzy by having my darling Mathilde beside me, our love-making reaching a series of convulsive climaxes surpassing anything I had fantasised about during these last long months of separation. Even in moments of great ardour, however, I could not help thinking of Ludwig and Kurt alone in their rooms, without the ecstasy and solace provided by wives or girlfriends. Around four o'clock I was awakened by a cry from Heini but slumbered on while Mathilde held him to her breast.

Our days were spent walking by the river, visiting the farm (where Herr Linder and his wife made a great fuss of us), gathering nuts and mushrooms from the woods and fields and flying a model aeroplane I had brought for Wolfchen. A large birch tree had fallen by the river bank and Kurt and I spent a whole day sawing and chopping the trunk and branches, then stacking the wood for the coming winter. I spent hours playing with Wolfchen, romping with him on the floor of the nursery that had once been Ludwig's, drawing pictures for him, reading stories and listening to his earnest babbling which was sometimes hard to follow as the words came tumbling out. And then there was Heini, so small, so fragile, a tiny organism unaware, unconscious of who was holding him.

In the evenings, after supper, we sang songs as Kurt played the piano. Afterwards, when Mathilde and Marie had retired, Ludwig, Kurt and I sat in the library drinking cognac and musing on the fate of the Fatherland. We talked of early days, training at Werneuchen, of comrades long gone, of past campaigns in France, Russia and North Africa. We tried to envisage what was going to happen in the weeks and months to come, how long it might be before our defences collapsed, what effect the new V2 rockets were having, how we might yet negotiate an honourable peace. All the while we talked I longed to be in the arms of Mathilde but felt bound to stay reminiscing and ruminating with my comrades. When the clock struck twelve each night I stood up and bid them both goodnight, trying not to show my eagerness to be gone. Those few idyllic days sped by and then it was tearful farewells on a misty autumnal morning and the daunting prospect of another long and tiring train journey ahead although this time we were fortified with Marie's splendid provisions.

This morning, back at base, we discovered we are to be part of a Lehrgeschwader, training new pilots (which we have been doing anyway), developing new tactics (what they can be remains to be discovered) and testing new aircraft (will we be flying the 262 jets?) The only real change, I suspect, will be in our designation.

From: Hauptmann Peter von Vorzik
I Gruppe LG294
Donaueschingen
To: Mathilde von Vorzik
Die Alte Scheune
Steuben Gasse
Höchstein

31st October 1944

My Darling Mathilde,

Just a brief note to tell you we reached base safely (note the revised address) after the usual dreary journey. What a joyous leave that was! The memory of it will stay clear and bright in my mind for weeks to come and sustain me throughout the winter that is already upon us. The weather here is bitterly cold and bad visibility, fog, frost and threatening snow preclude all flying for the moment. We are now officially a Lehrgeschwader, having been that in all but name for the past five or six months. I enjoy passing on the benefit of my several years' combat experience to the new recruits but I hear that Ludwig is the most popular instructor, no doubt seasoning his lectures with lurid tales of his amorous conquests as well as his aerial victories! We have all heard them in the mess, now he has a captive audience.

Give Marie my warmest regards and my darling sons a kiss from me and think of yourself still in the arms of

Your adoring,
Peter

From: Hauptmann Peter von Vorzik
I Gruppe LG294
Donaueschingen
To: Signora Edith Novarro-Badaelli
Santa Maria Orfanotrofio
Campo Baldi
Rome
via Countess Eleanora Novarro-Badaelli
Gordola
Switzerland

10th November 1944

My Dear Edith,

Your welcome letter was awaiting me on return from what was a joyful leave. As you say, the post via Switzerland is most efficient and Eleanora is obviously punctilious in forwarding our letters. It was wonderful to see and hold Heinrich for the first time but I must confess that tiny babies, despite being so miraculous in their perfection, are less absorbing than small children like Wolfchen. He is now so rewarding to watch playing, inventing all sorts of strange games and imaginary friends. He awakens some very distant memories of my own at that age, seeing the world in such a different way, focusing so narrowly on just a few things, his toys, his meal times and bathtime, those adults in the immediate vicinity. Everything has novelty value, awakens his curiosity, a kitchen utensil (he is fascinated by the mincer that Marie uses and has to be allowed to turn the handle), a squirrel, a wheelbarrow and, of course, every plane that flies over is "Papa's plane." We were a convivial group, Ludwig is a generous host and Kurt quite a different person away from the base as I suppose we all are. Marie mothers us all and has been marvellous to Mathilde and the children. My only wish was that you were with us, dear sister, but I am so happy that life under enemy occupation seems not to be too burdensome.

We are now a Lehrgeschwader, desperately trying to teach new recruits how to cope with combat and stay alive. The bad weather has given us some respite but on the other hand we need flying training as much as classroom lectures. Back in the summer it was so dispiriting watching young pilots, with less than half the training I had, shot out of the skies by well-trained enemies in overwhelming numbers. When the war began our

Jagdgeschwader were superior in numbers, equipment and training, now the situation is reversed. You are correct in your assumption that I view the reports of "heinous crimes" committed in our name as vile enemy propaganda. We have always been told that the Jews are enemies of the Reich so consider where those reports come from: New York, which I believe has a large Jewish population; London, which is probably the same, and Geneva, where, no doubt, many of those Swiss bankers and businessmen are Jewish. Yes, we have an announced policy of resettling the Jews in the east; after all, that is where most of them have come from, and we know the Communist party is full of Jews. For the time being I prefer to reserve judgement while acknowledging that, as I said in a previous letter, atrocities are liable to be committed by both sides in wartime.

Now, dear sister, I will bid you *auf Wiedersehen* in the hope that somehow this terrible war will draw to a satisfactory conclusion for us in the near future and that you may be reunited with

Your loving brother,

Peter

From: SS-Gruppenführer Count Christian von Vorzik
116 Kaiserstraße
Berlin
To: Hauptmann Peter von Vorzik
I Gruppe LG294
Donaueschingen

23rd November 1944

Dear Peter,

Thank you for your last letter. Mathilde phoned to thank me for the Till Eulenspiegel clown I sent for Heinrich and gave me your amended address. You comment again on the manoeuvrings and antipathies between various Party members but that is endemic in all societies. It is, of course, the basis of Nietzsche's philosophy which, in part, I adhere to. Everyone struggles to obtain mastery over his fellow-men in some way, although I do not agree with the complete abandonment of all moral precepts in the pursuit of ascendancy. Creatures like Müller and Kaltenbrunner attempt to gain power through low cunning, they are the hyenas of the human jungle, and it grieves me to see a man of Canaris's calibre fall victim to such predators. Canaris's weakness was that he lacked their ruthlessness. Walter and I know we are on their list of enemies but we are able to connive as well, if not better, than they and it will be the survival of the fittest. In your sphere it is your cunning, your expertise, your experience that defeats your enemies in the air, albeit somewhat removed from that kind of personal animosity. That is the only difference.

I learnt recently the truth about Rommel's death. Under interrogation Colonel von Hofacker implicated him in the plot against the Führer. As a result Rommel was visited by General Burgdorf at his home at Herrlingen where he was recuperating from his injuries. Acting as the Führer's emissary Burgdorf gave Rommel the choice of killing himself and receiving a funeral with full military honours or being charged with treason before the People's Court. Rommel bid farewell to his wife and son, drove some way up the road with Burgdorf and took the poison Burgdorf handed him. He died in seconds. As you no doubt heard or read the official reason for his death was given out as the result of wounds received when his car was strafed on July 17th. Such a tragic end for a great military leader.

Your previous questions about the Reichsführer-SS's competence to lead an army have become very relevant: the Führer has just appointed him C.-in-C. Army Group Upper Rhine!

Walter is planning more journeys for himself and me to Switzerland and Sweden in the near future. At this juncture of the war, diplomatic activity has become quite frenetic, the desired end result being an honourable armistice with the Anglo-Americans that would leave us free to defeat the Russians. Our efforts to this end have to contend with ever more bizarre plans by Reichsminister von Ribbentrop who even proposed that he and Walter should go to Moscow under some pretext of arranging peace and assassinate Stalin with a miniature pistol disguised as a fountain pen! The man has become quite deranged. I welcome these trips abroad, they afford some relief from the ceaseless bombing that Berlin suffers. It is not so much the bombs that keep one awake but our own flak emplacements that maintain an ear-splitting barrage. I do not go down to the cellar shelter. If I am to die I would prefer to do so in my own bed rather than be entombed underground.

I do not have a picture of Signe but she is a typically tall, blonde Swede with an attractive smile. I hope to see her during my next visit to

Stockholm; perhaps we will have a picture taken together. Now I must attend to my papers, Walter may want me to accompany him when he visits the Führer at Adlerhorst in a few days' time.

With best wishes for your continued safety,

Ever your affectionate brother,

Christian

PS I trust you destroy all my letters. C.

The Führer
Headquarters

25th November 1944

The war will decide whether the German people shall continue to exist or perish. It demands selfless exertion from every individual. Situations which have seemed hopeless have been redeemed by the courage of soldiers contemptuous of death, by the steadfast perseverance of all ranks, and by inflexible, exalted leadership. A commander is only fit to lead German troops if he daily shares, with all the powers of his mind, body and soul, the demands which he must make upon his men. Energy, willingness to take decisions, firmness of character, unshakable faith and hard, unconditional readiness for service, are the indispensable requirements for the struggle. He who does not possess them cannot be a leader and he must withdraw.

Therefore I order:

Should a commander, left to his own resources, think that he must give up the struggle, he will first ask his officers, then his non-commissioned officers, and finally his troops, if one of them is ready to carry on the task and continue the fight. If one of them will, he will hand over command to that man – regardless of his rank – and himself fall out. The new leader will then assume the command, with all its rights and duties.

Adolf Hitler

From: Mathilde von Vorzik
Die Alte Scheune
Steuben Gasse
Höchstein
To: Hauptmann Peter von Vorzik
I Gruppe LG294
Donaueschingen

25th November 1944

My Darling Peter,
So pleased to have your letter and to know you arrived safely at base. How quiet the house has seemed since the three of you departed! These are grey, dismal days and Christmas will seem very dull without you, particularly remembering what a happy time we all had last year. I suppose there is no chance of your having leave again over Christmas or New Year?

Yesterday a truck arrived with two big crates from Edith. She had told us she was sending "a few things" that were of sentimental value but we were unprepared for such a load! Marie and I spent most of yesterday and all of today unloading and unwrapping the contents of the crates and the job is far from finished. Some of the things are too heavy for us to manage (some pictures, a writing desk), what a pity they did not arrive when you, Kurt and Ludwig were here. Included in the contents was the dinner service we gave Edith and Arturo as a wedding present, all carefully wrapped in straw, paper and cardboard and as far as we can see everything intact, not a plate cracked or broken. The problem now is where to put it. Neither Marie nor I feel able to climb up into the loft with it all, in any case there is not room for it there. At the moment it is all repacked (it took us three hours!) in one of the old outhouses that Marie says was the dairy. Then there are loads of books, photograph albums and smaller pictures. All of it poses a problem of storage. Last night Marie and I spent hours looking through the photo albums. One of them contains pictures of Edith and Arturo's wedding and another includes several of you as a little boy. There is one of you (I guess at about seventeen) standing in uniform by a glider. On the back of the photo it says Schneider SG38, Moringen, 1935. Do you remember the occasion?

Packed separately was a jewel case with its key attached in a leather pouch. The box contains the diamond and sapphire bracelet and engagement ring that Arturo gave Edith, the amethyst butterfly brooch that you gave her, diamond clips and earrings and a pearl necklace. There are several unfamiliar rings, one with a ruby surrounded by diamonds, another with a large opal, a diamond brooch in the shape of a star, a cameo brooch in a gold setting, a lady's gold wrist watch with a diamond surround, and a diamond tiara. Do you recognise these pieces? Were they, perhaps, your mother's? Tomorrow I am taking it all to the bank in Höchstein where my own jewellery is kept. A big cardboard box contained Edith's wedding dress, veil and shoes, all wrapped in layers and layers of tissue. Such a sad memento! I have put it with my own best things.

Wolfchen and Heini are both well. Heini is growing visibly bigger each day. He takes notice of everything around him, particularly anything with bright colours. He is such a good baby, only wakes me once in the night now. Wolfchen seems to have a talent for drawing, I think the drawings you did for him have inspired him. He sits for hours with his pencil and crayons. I enclose a drawing he did which he says is "Papa's plane." It is very good for his age, don't you think, and really recognisable as an aeroplane. Each day we walk as far as the farm but otherwise we stay indoors as the weather has been so miserable. We do not listen to the radio much, the official communiques are so depressing. I switch on for the concert programmes but Marie is not really interested in serious music, she plays popular songs on the little gramophone in her room. Two days ago I went into Höchstein to see if the photos you took while on leave had been developed but they were not ready yet. The service is very slow these days but one is not allowed to complain!

No more now, darling, I want to catch the last post.

Ever you adoring,
Mathilde

Hauptmann Peter von Vorzik
Journal entry

3rd December 1944

We have been training our new recruits for something big although, as yet, what that may be we do not know. What we do know is that most Jagdgeschwader have been moved to airfields in the west and north. Only our Lehrstaffel remains here at Donaueschingen. Yesterday, nine of us scrambled to meet American bombers from the 15th Air Force in Italy which were attacking hydrogenation plants at Blechhammer and Floridsdorf near Vienna. We were kept warming our engines (and wasting precious fuel!) for thirty-five minutes until Operations HQ for Jagdkorps 7 decided what the targets were. When we were at last airborne we had to contend with heavy cloud formations, squally showers and generally poor visibility up to 5,000 m. It was impossible to find our quarry in such weather and we returned to base without making contact. A futile enterprise. To make matters worse one of our instructors, Leutnant Rudolf Klostermann, crash-landed his 109 somewhere near Schongau and was badly injured.

The American 8th Air Force continues to make devastating raids over Belgium, Holland and north, west and central Germany, sometimes bombing through complete cloud coverage, while British heavy bombers now frequently operate over Germany by day. Figures for Jagdkorps I operating over western and central Germany during November reveal 155 enemy aircraft shot down for the loss of 404 of our own aircraft. The figure for day-fighter pilots killed or missing, excluding accidents, was 244. The Anglo-Americans have made their first land incursion into the Fatherland, crossing the border between Belgium and Germany and taking the city of Aachen. Their attempt to capture the Lower Rhine bridge at Arnhem with a drop by British paratroopers was defeated after a bitter battle. Their plan was to receive reinforcements and to link up with a strong force of supporting troops but they suffered a succession of misfortunes – not least the fact that the 9th and 10th SS Panzer divisions were in the area – that saved the day for us. Had their daring strategy come off our major defensive line, the West Wall, would have been outflanked and the way open to Berlin. Elsewhere the Anglo-American advance appears to have come to a halt. Presumably they are consolidating their positions and strengthening their supply lines which stretch all the way back to the French ports of Cherbourg and Le Havre. They are desperately busy opening up the port of Antwerp. Bad weather has precluded them from taking advantage of their air superiority for low-level attacks on our ground forces.

Winter months are always a period of hiatus (except for the Russians who are used to mud and snow!), all sides preparing for spring offensives or, as we must acknowledge now, bolstering our defences. The Italian front remains quiet with heavy rains making movement difficult and the Anglo-Americans held in Tuscany by Kesselring's armies. However, there is still activity in the Balkans with the Jugoslav partisans making difficulties and the Russians having taken Belgrade. Their advance into Rumania and Hungary has forced us to evacuate Greece which has been occupied by the British. We await with trepidation whatever the spring will bring.

From: Hauptmann Peter von Vorzik
I Gruppe LG294
Donaueschingen
To: Claus Grüber
Erprobungsgruppe V
Rechlin am Muritzsee

12 December 1944

Dear Claus,
This letter has been long delayed but now, to my surprise, I find myself with some time on my hands! All the Geschwader have left, like a flock of migrating birds, for some big unspecified operation in the west, leaving just a few of us here to face the might of the 15th American Air Force. No doubt the next week or so will reveal all. As you see from the amended address we are a Lehrgeschwader now and I wish I had been able to go with the young recruits we have been training these last few weeks. Heaven knows, they still have a lot to learn and I fear they are being thrown into some big operational scene for which they are ill equipped. Half the intake came from Kampfgeschwader and most of them found it more difficult adjusting to fighters than the recruits fresh from basic training units, inadequate though their flying hours have been. For myself – and Kurt, who is still my Katschmarek – survival has been something of a miracle. At the moment activity is curtailed by bad weather but throughout the summer we scraped through by sheer good luck. When I read the lists of brilliant pilots who were lost between May and September I marvel that the Jagdgeschwader exist at all. We have plenty of planes, production figures are amazing considering the onslaught the factories sustained – it's pilots and fuel we lack.

As you may have heard there is considerable bitterness and animosity towards the Fat One throughout the Jagdflieger. We were labelled cowards because of the defeats we have suffered and our frequent inability to penetrate the fighter screen around the bombers. That was an unforgivable slur on men who have done their utmost, exhausted themselves and seen their comrades die in their hundreds simply because we have been, in most cases, hopelessly outnumbered. The Führer criticises us because he is misinformed; the fault lies at the door of the Fat One because of his maladministration, not because we are cowards. As you are well aware, Fliegermeister Galland has done his best for us but is continuously overruled or his advice ignored. But these moans are not what you want to hear. I know you have lost a legion of friends yourself. Apart from still being alive I must count myself blessed in so many ways. My wife was delivered of another baby boy last August and I saw him just a few weeks ago when we had leave during the refitting of the Geschwader. My sister, in Rome, appears to be quite happy under the Anglo-American occupation. At least her orphanage receives food on a regular basis and the nuns remain unmolested. My brother in the SS (Ausland SD) has frequent trips to Switzerland and Sweden which makes life bearable. Just what he goes for or why he goes there remains obscure – diplomacy covers a multitude of mysteries if not sins!

How is your knee? Not playing up too badly in this winter weather I hope. And have you found a new home after losing the one in Göttingen? Travelling to Höchstein on leave it was dreadful to see so much devastation en route. Berlin, I hear, is a shambles. I hope to hear from you soon, to know you are well and perhaps to glean some encouraging information about our latest projects. What is happening with the Amerika Bomber? Perhaps this will reach you before Christmas, if so, best wishes for the season and, whatever the Fates have in store for the Fatherland, good health and good fortune in the coming year.

Ever your sincere comrade,

Peter

From: Hauptmann Peter von Vorzik
I Gruppe LG294
Donaueschingen
To: Mathilde Von Vorzik
Die Alte Scheune
Steuben Gasse
Höchstein

15th December 1944

My Darling Mathilde,

Just received your letter of the 25th and I'm hoping that this reaches you in time to say Happy Christmas and to let you know that you, Wolfchen and Heini are constantly in my thoughts. It is impossible not to compare the present time with the same period last year – what a memorable Christmas that was! At the moment I am sustained by the more recent memories of our last time together. In my mind's eye I picture you in so many scenes: in that big kitchen, helping Marie with the baking, a smudge of flour on your face; walking by the river when it was frozen; sitting listening to records by candlelight, half of you in shadow, the other half in the glow of the candleflame and, of course, those intimate moments in the bedroom... These images are as strong as any photographs although I am looking forward to seeing those that I took. It seems that the chemicals used in processing film are scarce these days. Have you managed to find suitable presents for the children? Also Marie? Was the money I left sufficient? Do let me know if you need more. And do find something special for yourself, darling.

It was indeed a pity that Kurt, Ludwig and I were not there when those crates arrived from Edith. I, too, supposed there would be just a few small boxes. Even so, there must still have been a lot of stuff to leave or sell off for the orphanage. When I next write I will ask Edith what she bequeathed. I am sure the articles of jewellery you mention were my mother's. I remember Edith mentioning she had thought to use mother's tiara when she was married but, I think, she wore one from Eleanora instead. Eleanora was responsible for the whole of Edith's wedding ensemble, you will see it in the wedding photo album. I am sure, one day, Edith will want to reclaim these articles. Is there a storage firm in Höchstein?

All is quiet here as I write. Almost all the Jagdgeschwader have been sent to the north and west to take part in some big undisclosed operation leaving just a few of us to cope with any raids by the Americans. Actually, the weather has been so poor for the last week or so that interception has been impossible. The Americans carry on anyway, flying above the weather and dropping their bombs through the clouds. By the time we have climbed through the cloud layers and positioned ourselves the enemy has gone and we lack both the range and the fuel to pursue them.

Now, darling, renewed love and kisses to you and the children, fond regards to Marie, try and have a good festive season.

Ever your devoted,

Peter

From: Signora Edith Novarro-Badaelli
Santa Maria Orfanotrofio
Campo Baldi
Rome
via Contessa Eleanora Novarro-Badaelli
Gordola
Switzerland
To: Hauptmann Peter von Vorzik
I Gruppe LG294
Donaueschingen

22nd December 1944

Dearest Peter,

This is my fourth attempt to write this letter. I find great difficulty in expressing my feelings without appearing morbid or sentimental. The simple fact is that as we move into a new year – a year that may bring great changes – I want you to know that you are perpetually in my thoughts. I hear on the radio that our armies in the west have launched a surprise offensive that is driving the Americans back from the borders of Germany which can only intensify the death and destruction that is ravaging Europe. I feel sure that you are caught up in the struggle just as you have been during these last five terrible years which accentuates my anxiety for your safety. Nothing I can say will, I know, deter you from your course of duty to the Fatherland. Nor would I wish it to. I only ask you to take every possible care, do nothing rash or pointlessly heroic, remember that you have responsibilities to a wife and children as well as to the Reich. I confess, dear brother, that now I have lost Arturo you are my primary concern in this distraught world.

The word "confess" leads me to what, I suppose, is a humorous anecdote. We have a *padre* who comes once a week to hear our confessions. Last week Frank gave me an exotic present, a pair of stockings made not from silk but a new product made in America called nylon which looks and feels like silk but is much stronger and less prone to ladder. Of course, now I would not wear such apparel, my stockings are thick black cotton, but in the privacy of my cell I tried on the nylons. They had a sensuous feel and, briefly, I felt elegant again. Then I felt guilty and confessed this to the *padre*. He was obviously excited by my description and began asking more and more intimate questions, how high up the leg did they go, did they give rise to libidinous thoughts and if so what were they? I terminated the discussion abruptly. At our next meeting I told Frank and he said that the previous week he had encountered the *padre* as he was leaving. The *padre* first tried to sell Frank a dispensation for his sins and when Frank declined the *padre* took from under his robe a number of greasy cards that depicted semi-naked women in provocative positions! Frank said the absurd aspect of the pictures was that the women were in fashions from the turn of the century, high button boots and laced corsets, comic rather than erotic. Now, of course, my weekly confessional has an added piquancy but I am somewhat disillusioned about our local clerics. I wonder to whom the *padre* confesses his sins? Frank has invited me to accompany him to the opera. He had to obtain permission from his commanding officer as there is a fairly strict policy of non-fraternisation between the occupying forces and the general populace but in this instance he was given permission. I think the policy is devised to keep the soldiery apart from the local ladies of the evening. I have to obtain permission from Sister Agnes, our Mother Superior. My position here is different from the nuns, of course; I have not entered their order and I am a member of the board, so my request is really just a courtesy. I should very much like to go, it is Rossini's *Barber of Seville*.

I heard from Mathilde that the personal items I sent to Höchstein had arrived safely. She seemed surprised that there was "so much." The escritoire was a wedding gift to me from Eleanora, it had been her mother's. It was but a minute part of what I sold for the orphanage. There was the house itself, of course; furnishings, silverware, china and glass, chandeliers and candelabra, rococo mirrors, antique and modern pictures including two by de Chirico, one by Morandi and one by Modigliani which was a present to Arturo from Ciano who came from the same city as the artist, Livorno. There were classical sculptures and busts, carpets, tapestries and various *objets d'art*. There were two cars, my own little Aprilia and Arturo's big Alfa Romeo, a motorcycle and two bicycles. I left it all in the hands of Arturo's solicitor whom I assume is trustworthy. I believe the total sum came to several hundred million lira. I received the relevant papers and gave them to the orphanage's accountant. He has placed the money in the bank and when the winter is over we shall start repairs to the fabric of the building. When Arturo died material things seemed of no value except those few things that were precious because of the giver, or because of some family association, like mother's jewellery. I told Mathilde that she is welcome to any of it. Perhaps, someday, you will have a little girl to inherit it.

Looking through the magazines that Frank brings me it appears that Germany's Japanese allies have suffered serious defeats in south-east Asia and the Pacific. It seems there was a huge sea battle in the Gulf of Leyte in which the Americans destroyed a large part of the Japanese fleet. In Burma the Japanese attempt to invade India was defeated by the British and the Japanese army is now in retreat. They have also been forced to abandon their strongholds in many Pacific islands, and the Philippines, following the battle in Leyte, are in American hands. I tell you this as I doubt such information reaches you via the German press.

Now I must entrust this to the post and Eleanora's good offices.

May God go with you, dearest brother.

Ever your devoted sister,
Edith

PS I was terribly upset to read that my old boss at the Foreign Office, Dr Adam von Trott zu Soltz, had been implicated in the plot against the Führer, tried by the People's Court and executed. He was such a gentleman, charming, cultured, erudite. I am sure whatever he did was intended to help bring about a peaceful solution to the war. E.

From: Mathilde von Vorzik
Die Alte Scheune
Steuben Gasse
Höchstein
To: Hauptmann Peter von Vorzik
I Gruppe LG294
Donaueschingen

26th December 1944

My Darling Peter,

How we missed you this Christmas, all three of you! Such a contrast to last year but we made the most of it. Wolfchen, of course, enjoyed it all, lighting the candles on the tree, helping to hang the decorations. He was very happy with his toys, including a beautifully carved horse and cart from Herr Linder who had made it himself. Really too good to play with, I have placed it on a shelf in the nursery. The Linders came and ate with us last night. Here were we, without you, Ludwig and Kurt, and there were they, poor things, without their two sons. Nothing has been heard of them and after dinner, when we had had a few drinks, Frau Linder was overcome with grief and wept inconsolably. They brought such fine food from the farm, a goose, ready for cooking, a large ham, sausages, eggs and bottled fruit. Christian sent his usual case of champagne and a toy car for Wolfchen, one of those Mercedes racers by Schuco. It is possible to unscrew the wheel nuts and it kept Wolfchen amused for hours. There was a big blue fluffy rabbit for Heini. Christian says he thinks he is going to Switzerland early in the new year. I wonder, darling, how you spent Christmas? I do hope things were quiet for you. I listened to the radio during the holiday and the reports were all about fighting in the west where our troops have broken through the American lines. How marvellous it would be if this success could lead to peace. Of course, there are still the Russians to contend with.

I also had a letter from Edith (I wrote to her to say her things had arrived safely) who says she has sent toys for the children but they have not arrived yet. She seems happy enough in that orphanage and twice mentions an American officer called Frank who supplies the orphanage with food and medicines. He also takes her personal gifts. Do you think there is some liaison there?

611

Lina sent a card from Fehmarn, I was so pleased to hear from her. She appears happy with the quiet rural life there, after all it is her home, and is hardly aware of the war. However, she reminisces about life as it was in Berlin, the gaiety of the old days, the shopping, the theatre, the gossip!

Here, darling, at last, are the photographs from your last leave. I love the one of you with the two boys, I am having it enlarged. I also like the one of you with Kurt and Ludwig. Will you ask them if they would like copies? Now I must hurry to catch the post and end with fervent hopes that somehow peace will come at last in the new year and you will return safely to the arms of

Your loving wife,
Mathilde.

PS Kisses from me and the boys, regards to Ludwig and Kurt. M.

From: Hauptmann Peter von Vorzik
I Gruppe LG294
Donaueschingen
To: SS-Gruppenführer Count Christian von Vorzik
116 Kaiserstraße
Berlin

3rd January 1945

Dear Christian,
This is just to wish you good health and good fortune in the New Year. It is difficult to foresee the future and even more difficult to be optimistic about what changes it will bring. We are beset with numerous problems but war springs many surprises and we must assume that our leaders will find a path to ultimate victory. Von Runstedt's offensive in the Ardennes was just such a surprise and as I write we seem to have made progress towards our objective which I take to be splitting the Anglo-American forces in two and heading off their attempts to reach the Rhine. From early reports the Luftwaffe appears to have scored a great victory in its surprise attacks on Anglo-American airfields two days ago. Our Gruppe was not involved although many of the young recruits we have been training in recent weeks took part. What you told me about Rommel's death came as a shock. A terrible loss of a great general.

This was the first Christmas I have not managed to be home on leave. We had subdued celebrations in the mess, most of us simply glad to be alive. I can imagine that Stockholm seems a haven of tranquillity after Berlin. It must be delightful to see a city lit up again although I suppose Sweden is not without its manifestations of the war. Did you manage to have photos taken with Signe? I would like a new one of you to carry in my wallet.

Write to me when you can.

Ever your affectionate brother,

Peter

Hauptmann Peter von Vorzik
Journal entry

19th January 1945

Looking at the operational maps at HQ and deciphering the communiques from OKW it is obvious that von Runstedt's offensive through the Ardennes which started so well has been defeated. British troops under General Montgomery launched a tremendous counter-attack from the north at Houffalize and joined with equally forceful American armies under General Patton coming from the south. Our forces are in chaotic retreat back to the Rhine, harassed by continual attacks from the air now that the weather has improved. It also seems that our own massive air attack, code-named Baseplate, on Anglo-American airfields on New Year's Day, while destroying four hundred enemy aircraft on the ground, was not the great victory we thought it was. In fact, the Luftwaffe has, itself, suffered irreparable damage like a bee that, having used its sting, is then mortally wounded.

General der Jagdflieger, Adolf Galland, had carefully built up a large reserve of over a thousand pilots and aircraft for what he termed the Big Blow. This reserve was intended to make large-scale concentrated attack on American daylight bombers. Instead, at the instigation of the Führer, the reserve was commandeered to support von Runstedt's offensive in the Ardennes by making dawn raids on Anglo-American airfields in Holland and Belgium. Unfortunately, all our pilots had been training for high-level attacks on bomber fleets, not low-level attacks on ground targets requiring wholly different tactics. Some of the Geschwader failed to find their targets through navigational difficulties and fell prey to defending fighters. Others encountered intense flak over the target areas while many were simply disoriented by flying at hedgetop height, lost contact with their units and crashed behind enemy lines. The result was that, while the Anglo-Americans are able to replace their losses within a week or two, the Luftwaffe has lost over three hundred irreplaceable pilots as well as having depleted precious fuel stocks. Now we have no aerial forces to cover the army's retreat and even fewer pilots and aircraft with which to intercept the enemy bombers. Galland has been relieved of his command and has not, as yet, been replaced. Resentment and bitterness are rife within the Jagdgeschwader, so much so that a special meeting has been arranged at Luftwaffe HQ near Wannsee. I doubt if much will come of it. The Reichsmarschall has lost influence with the Führer and lost the confidence of his Jagdflieger commanders. Nor will he accept responsibility for the blunders of the past.

There has been a large-scale withdrawal of fighters from the western front in order to bolster our defences against the huge new offensive by Russian armies in the east which began a week ago. Marshal Koniev's army has advanced 25 km from a salient across the Vistula between Lublin and Kraców. Another Russian army under Marshal Zhukov launched surprise attacks from bridgeheads on the west of the Vistula, while to the north yet another Russian army under Marshal Rokossovski has begun an advance towards the Baltic coast. These armies have five times the men and material, seven times the artillery and seventeen times the air power of the German forces. Everywhere we are being overwhelmed. Germany is being squeezed to death from west and east while bombs continue to rain down on our cities. Now, surely, is the time for our leaders to find a path to peace.

From: Hauptmann Peter von Vorzik
I Gruppe LG294
Donaueschingen
To: Mathilde von Vorzik
Die Alter Scheune
Steuben Gasse
Höchstein

23rd January 1945

My Darling Mathilde,
So pleased to have your letter written the day after Christmas. The post takes longer and longer and then arrives in a big batch. Everyone here

subsists on mail from home. It was also a great joy to have the photographs. As always I stare at them for hours, reliving the moment they were taken and examining every detail. Yes, Kurt and Ludwig would like copies, please, all three of us like a photographic record of those happy moments. There is not much I can tell you, darling, to raise your spirits except that we continue to survive the constant raids by American bombers, sometimes achieving a small victory but mostly concentrating on staying alive to fight another day. It is no use pretending that the war is going well for us, I am just so thankful that you are in comparative safety at Höchstein. It is impossible to foretell the future but I think it unlikely that the Russians will get as far south or west as Bavaria. Should the worst happen (I am sure you will understand my meaning) I reassure myself that you are less than an hour's flight away. We all have our contingency plans for such eventualities. Bavaria could become a final redoubt around the Führer's retreat at Berchtesgaden.

Darling, how perceptive you are – female intuition? Yes, Edith makes several references to this American, Frank, who appears to pay her considerable attention. I suppose, in that all-female environment that she has so willingly embraced, the advent of any male is something to engage her attention if not her emotions. When I write I will enquire, discreetly, about the friendship.

Now, dearest, I must catch the post so that you receive this within a week or two. Keep well, kiss the boys for me and be assured that you are constantly in the thoughts of

Your ever loving,
Peter

Edward Thorpe

From: *Hauptmann Peter von Vorzik*
I Gruppe LG294
Donaueschingen
To: Signora Edith Novarro-Badaelli
Santa Maria Orfanotrofio
Campo Baldi
Rome
via Contessa Eleanora Novarro-Badaelli
Gordola
Switzerland

27th January 1945

My Dear Edith,

Many thanks for your interesting letter written before Christmas which has just reached me. It is a special pleasure to hear from you now that the vagaries of war have isolated you from the rest of the family and to be reassured that you are in good health and spirits. There could hardly be a greater indication of your sang-froid than the amusing anecdote you recount of the lascivious *padre* and his dirty postcards! I fear such behaviour is not uncharacteristic amongst the ecclesiastic fraternity. Do you remember the time when I was about fourteen and was persuaded – no, coerced – into joining the choir at St Matthias? It came about mainly through my friendship with a very devout schoolfellow, Hans-Dieter von Weisenborn, and to please mother who was very friendly with his mother. Anyway, I could tell a tale of licentiousness and perversity about two of the priests there that would no doubt shock you. Happily, I left after a month or two, mainly because of my breaking voice and also because the Hitler Jugend was more attractive. Which is not to say, of course, that all priests are subject to such frailties.

You tell me how concerned you are about my safety, as I know you have been these last five years, and I cannot keep from you that we in the Jagdflieger are hard pressed in our daily efforts to defend the Reich against the enemy bomber fleets. Here in the south we are perpetually outnumbered by the Americans who come over almost every day intent on attacking the fuel plants near Vienna. So far Kurt and I have survived these onslaughts while doing our best to thwart them and I am sure your prayers for our welfare have been heeded by the Almighty. Each day, as we take off, I am sustained by the knowledge that your thoughts fly with me while at the same time I remember your words of caution and am apprehensive of my responsibilities to family as well as Fatherland.

I do hope you managed to attend the performance of *Barber of Seville* with your new acquaintance, Frank. How can I put this delicately? Is there, perhaps, a romantic interest developing between you? Naturally, the occupying forces need female company and you, dear sister, must seem very appealing to those men. It is ironic, is it not, that you may be beguiled by an American while I am daily attempting to kill his compatriots. Do not think that I am in any way reproachful; you, of all people, are entitled to snatch whatever moments of happiness might present themselves. You have suffered terribly by the death of Arturo and your generosity towards the orphanage, the manner in which you gave up all the trappings of a privileged existence, fill me with admiration and humility.

No, I had not heard of the sea battle in the Gulf of Leyte or of any other battles the Japanese may have been engaged in. As allies they are too far away to have any bearing upon what is happening in Europe. There was a time, back in 1941, when they might have assisted us by declaring war on Russia but that did not happen. I can well believe that, after their initial successes in the Pacific and south-east Asia, the combined powers of the Americans and the British Empire are beginning to overwhelm the Japanese forces, just as we are being overwhelmed.

I will ask Mathilde to send you photos of Wolfchen and Heini that were taken during my last leave. I long for the day when we can be reunited and you may see your nephews in reality.

Meanwhile, dear sister, be assured you have the abiding love of

Your devoted brother,

Peter

From: SS-Gruppenführer Count Christian von Vorzik
German Embassy
Bern
as from 116 Kaiserstraße
Berlin
To: Hauptmann Peter von Vorzik
I Gruppe LG294
Donaueschingen

12th February 1945

Dear Peter,

Here I am in Switzerland ostensibly for discreet talks with a member of the American OSS with regard to possible peace plans with the West but also burdened with a pointless brief to keep watch upon Herr Dr Furtwängler. Furtwängler was scheduled to conduct two concerts in Berlin on the 4th and 5th of this month. On the 3rd a heavy raid by American planes destroyed the rebuilt Staatsoper on the Unter den Linden. Furtwängler sent a telegram from Vienna saying that, while out walking, he had slipped on the ice and was suffering from concussion and would be unable to conduct the two concerts scheduled for the Beethovensaal. Yet here he is in Switzerland with his second wife and stepchildren, ready to undertake a series of concerts in Zurich, Lausanne and Geneva. Alfred Rosenberg has been keeping a dossier on Furtwängler who may have been implicated in the attempted assassination of the Führer last July and is suspected of trying to find sanctuary in Switzerland. Incidentally, Dr Roland Freisler, director of the People's Court that arraigned so many of the traitors who were involved in that conspiracy, was killed during that raid on the 3rd. My own apartment suffered superficial damage (windows blown out, cracks in the walls, some pictures cut by flying glass). Luckily, I had gone with Walter to the Reichsführer-SS's new HQ. He has now been withdrawn from the Army Group Rhine to take command of the newly formed Army Group Vistula with a command post at Birkenhain, 70 km from Berlin. The Führer himself has left Adlerhorst and returned to the Chancellery in Berlin which has a bomb-proof bunker beneath.

There is a new favourite at the Führer's court, Grossadmiral Karl Dönitz, who promises great victories with his new Type XXI and Type XXIII U-boats. Unfortunately, the Führer fails to see that submarines are unlikely to stop the Russian armies that have now crossed the Oder. With the power of the SS behind him it would be possible for the Reichsführer-SS to take control of the situation but he prefers to remain uncommitted, while condoning the talks we have had with plenipotentiaries in Sweden and Switzerland with a view to concluding peace in the west. Another problem that has arisen from these talks, however, is that representatives of the West will not consider negotiations with the Reichsführer-SS even if he were disposed to engage in them. So at present it is stalemate. With the recent fall of Warsaw, Kraców and Breslau and the imminent withdrawal from Budapest, it seems that our final battles will be fought by Berlin unless the Führer decides to return to the Berghof. Because of the general uncertainty I have been making plans of my own which will probably involve another visit to Sweden. Much depends upon what our forces can achieve in the west during the next few weeks but I will keep you informed of my movements. I expect to leave Switzerland in a day or two. Continue to send your letters to the Berlin address.

   With best wishes for your own continued safety,

Your affectionate brother,
Christian

From: Mathilde von Vorzik
Die Alter Scheune
Steuben Gasse
Höchstein
To: Hauptmann Peter von Vorzik
I Gruppe LG294
Donaueschingen

19th February 1945

My Darling Peter,
Such a relief to have your letter although, as always, I cannot help wondering what has been happening since you wrote it. Of course, we are safe here but almost every day, whatever the weather, we see and hear great formations of enemy aircraft droning high overhead on their way to bomb some city or town. Occasionally we hear distant thuds and rumbles as bombs explode. Franz, the local postman (he is an old friend of Marie's and sometimes comes into the kitchen for a cup of coffee and one of Marie's

cakes), says that last week there were several terrible raids on Dresden in which thousands were killed. He said the city was practically destroyed and it was full of refugees from the east, escaping from the Russians. Those that survived are homeless in this winter weather. It is dreadful to think that our cities are being obliterated like this and what worries me more is knowing that you are daily taking off to intercept these raiders.

The toys Edith sent for Wolfchen and Heini at Christmas finally arrived, a sailing boat for Wolfchen and a velvet monkey, very realistic, for Heini. Of course Wolfchen wanted to sail his boat on the river, but I would not let him. The river is full from the winter rains and flowing fast and the boat would be swept away. I avoid the river now, anyway, as I cannot forget the tragedy of Lenka's death. I let Wolfchen play with his boat in the bath but I can see that isn't really satisfactory. The farm has a large duck-pond but at present it is much too muddy there. He can sail it in the spring and I know Herr Linder will be delighted to join in, both he and Frau Linder are very fond of Wolfchen. I have been reading Adelbert von Chamisso's *The Strange Story of Peter Schlemihl* – the name Peter on the spine of the book caught my eye! It is a sort of Faust story about a poor young man who gives his shadow to the Devil, a thin elderly man in a grey coat, for a purse of Fortunata's (we read about it at school) but his lack of a shadow makes life difficult and he becomes an outcast. The story reminds me of Richard Strauss's opera *The Woman Without a Shadow* which I saw with Lina, but that had a happy ending.

You say in your letter that you do not think the Russians will get as far as Bavaria which is a comforting thought. Do you think the Americans will advance this far? Sometimes, in the middle of the night, when I am feeding Heini, I wonder and worry about what will happen if... well, I won't say it. You reassure me when you say you are only a short flight away. If the worst should happen I would want us all to be together.

Yes, I had an "intuitive" thought about Edith and this man, Frank. Why else would she mention him twice in a letter? I am sure her emotional needs are not satisfied by either the nuns or the orphanage children. A friendly man bringing her gifts is bound to awaken romantic thoughts.

Now, darling, I must catch the post or you will not get this until March. Usual fond regards to Ludwig and Kurt and all my love to you from

Your own,
Mathilde

Hauptmann Peter von Vorzik
Journal entry

21st February 1945

We have to face the inevitable, that Germany is being crushed by her enemies and it is only a matter of time before our defences collapse. The writing has been on the wall now for over a year and we have acknowledged it in our thoughts if not in conversation. We have been hoping against hope that something, a falling-out between the Anglo-Americans and the Russians, or the advent of our V-weapons and jet aircraft would radically alter the situation. It was not to be; our enemies have remained united and our wonderful new weapons were too few and too late. All that remains now is to retain our integrity, fight to the death if need be but hope our leaders will be able to conclude a peace with honour. Two weeks ago that scheming triumvirate, Churchill, Roosevelt and Stalin, met at Yalta in the Crimea. The newspapers report that this meeting was convened to decide how to carve up a defeated Germany but they were being precipitate: Germany is not dead yet. It does not bode well for us, however; that meeting is but another indication that our defeat is a foregone conclusion.

The other evening Ludwig and I had a tentative conversation as to what we should do if there is an armistice and if we survive that long. Somehow we will make our way to Höchstein. With typical generosity Ludwig said, "That is your home for the foreseeable future." Just how we would get there depends entirely on the prevailing circumstances. We both agreed that in the final days of defeat we will face chaos; we have seen it happen to others, in Poland, France, the early days in Russia and suffered it ourselves in North Africa. Ideally, we would have our aircraft still operable but we could risk being shot down in the very last hours of the war. Ludwig has a car at the base and doubtless we could filch some fuel for it but that could place us in jeopardy from other refugees. The most likely circumstance is that we would have to walk most of the way, finding what transport we could, trucks, trains, farmcarts, anything, taking our chances with the rest of the populace. We would keep our side arms for emergencies and self-defence. Having an objective is a great stimulus for survival.

The Anglo-Americans have stepped up their bombing raids on all our major cities: Berlin, Augsburg, Hamburg, Magdeburg, Paderborn, Bielefeld, Mannheim, Stuttgart, Heilbronn, Duisburg, Düsseldorf,

Cologne, Kassel, Hamm, Münster, Vienna, Graz, Klagenfurt. Dresden was by far the worst. On the night of the 13th eight hundred British bombers rained high-explosive and incendiary bombs on that beautiful baroque city, creating a terrible firestorm. The next day, while the city was still engulfed in flames, over three hundred American bombers added further death and destruction, and then they came again the following day. It is estimated that over fifty thousand people died in those raids, many of them homeless refugees from the east. The British and the Americans lost less than 2% of their bombers, the city having very little anti-aircraft protection, the flak units moved to protect hydrogenation plants elsewhere. The humiliating aspect of the daylight raids was that our feeble forces could not reach the raiders and once again we lost young pilots through navigational inexperience.

On the 14th our Staffel was alerted to intercept American bombers of the US 8th Air Force flying from England. The range was so great that we had to refuel at Grossenhain. By the time we arrived over Dresden, blotted out by a great pall of smoke, the bombers were well on their way home. During our return to base one of our Staffel crashed near Zwickau through engine failure and another became separated in thick cloud and a hail-storm and crashed in the Fichtelgebirge mountains. The whole mission was a waste of lives and precious benzine. The only pilots likely to achieve success against these bomber fleets are those flying the Me262 jets. Back in October the first small Gruppe of 262s was formed at Achmer under Major Walter Nowotny. They had some initial successes but Nowotny was killed only a month later and the Gruppe was moved to Lechfeld for further development. Now, at last, General Galland has been appointed Kommandeur of a 262 unit based at Munich-Riem. The enemy has nothing with which to oppose these rocket-firing jets which can kill a bomber while out of range of its guns but there are only about six or seven of these fighters operational at any one time. What we needed was two thousand of them a year ago.

In the mess all is gloom and despondency. It is very difficult to maintain an *esprit de corps* under current circumstances. I hear that the meeting with the Reichsmarschall at the Haus der Flieger at Wannsee was a fiasco. The Fat One was accompanied by the Chief of the Air Staff, General Koller. The Jagddivision Kommandeure and inspectors were led by Oberst Günther Lützow who asked the Reichsmarschall not to interrupt while he placed before him the various aspects of the crisis facing the Jagdgeschwader. The Fat One flew into a monumental rage and shouted that he would have them all shot for mutiny. Lützow was relieved of his appointment and "exiled" as Kommandeur of Fighters in Italy. General Gordon Gollob has been appointed General der Jagdflieger in Galland's place. Nothing has changed.

Looking down the long lists of pilots killed, missing and injured I was deeply upset to see the name of my old friend Lother Köhl. I wrote to him last October and received no reply. Apparently his aircraft was shot down while on reconnaissance over Breslau. He spent most of the war in Russia, regretting that he had volunteered for the Reichsmarschall's vaunted Zerstörer Geschwader. Kurt has just suggested that we go to the mess and drink schnapps together. During these last two months alcohol consumption has risen over 50%. We seem to have more beer, wine and schnapps than aircraft fuel!

From: Hauptmann Peter von Vorzik
I Gruppe LG294
Donaueschingen
To: Mathilde von Vorzik
Die Alter Scheune
Höchstein

3rd March 1945

My Darling Mathilde,
So wonderful to have your letter – as I have said so often, there is nothing so effective in raising the spirits as a letter from home.

I know you must be aware of enemy air activity, our enemies are in a position to send their big bomber fleets wherever they like over the Reich, more or less with impunity. It is a terrible and humiliating admission to have to make, especially for pilots of the Jagdflieger, but it is the truth. They have been targeting transport depots and synthetic oil plants with great success and now we are gravely short of fuel.

How well-read you are becoming! I have never read anything by von Chamisso although we did read the story of Fortunata's purse when we were studying the Old German Folk-book at the Munich gymnasium. I must confess I found it extremely boring at the time. Literature, history and languages were my weakest subjects, mathematics and science my strongest. I wonder what subjects Wolfchen and Heini will excel in when they go to school? You were wise to keep Wolfchen away from the river although I understand how frustrating it must be for him not to be able to sail his boat. As small children Christian and I were always forbidden to go near Adlersee by ourselves. We were taught to swim by Werner when we were about eight and after that we were always in or on the lake. I had a canoe for my twelfth birthday and when I was fourteen father bought us a sailing dinghy between us. Christian was never as enthusiastic about it as I was and Edith would never come sailing with me. She could not bear to be hanging over the side getting wet. As far as I know the dinghy is still there, covered by a tarpaulin, in the little boathouse by the landing stage.

When I last wrote to Edith I asked her if there was any romantic association with this Frank she writes about but I have not heard from her yet, our letters have to go by such a roundabout way. Would you send her one of the photographs of Wolfchen and Heini when you have the time and opportunity, darling? This must be a short letter as I have so much paperwork to get through. It is a strange anomaly but as we do less and less flying we appear to have more and more administrative duties. New orders and directives are issued every day and often contradict what we were ordered to do the day before! It is a symptom of the times, I fear.

All my love to you, dearest, kiss the boys for me and think yourself in the embrace of

Your own,
Peter

Hauptmann Peter von Vorzik
Journal entry

17th March 1945

My heart is full of anguish, my eyes full of tears, dropping on the page and blurring the ink as I write this. My faithful Katschmarek, my loyal Kurt who rescued me from the Russian snows and saved my life countless times in the air, was shot down and killed five days ago.

At about 09.15 on the 12th our depleted Gruppe was held on standby as a large formation of US 15th Air Force bombers, shielded by hundreds of fighters, was detected approaching, anticipated target area Vienna. At 09.42 we were ordered to take off and climb to 6,000 m in the sector just north-west of Salzburg. At 10.09 we sighted the enemy, their uncamouflaged surfaces glinting silver in the morning sun. There were hundreds of them, flying in the familiar tiered boxes that give a withering wall of crossfire from each bomber group. I ordered my Staffel to climb another thousand metres as I was anxious to get above them and use the still rising sun, which was behind us, as cover. The only problem was, at that height, the canopies of our unpressurised cockpits are liable to ice over. It was a risk worth taking. I intended to employ our usual tactic, to wait until the leading group of bombers were only a km or so away then dive down on just a few selected aircraft, concentrating our fire on those targets, then climbing away and making for bodo before escorting fighters could catch us. To stay and engage in a dogfight in which we would be vastly outnumbered would be suicidal, especially for those inexperienced pilots who make up 70% of the Gruppe.

Over the r/t I announced that I had selected the leading bomber of the first group as a target for myself and Kurt and told Ludwig, Clement Schönburg and Willi Khevenmüller to make their own selection and gave the order to attack. As we dived down I could see tracer bullets streaming up from the nose and top turret of the leading B-17 but Kurt and I held our course. As the huge bomber began to fill the gun graticule I gave the order to fire and our cannon shells hit home on the nose and port inboard engine of the Dicke Hund which immediately went into a shallow dive, black smoke pouring from the big radial engine we had hit. As I started to pull out of the dive I heard Kurt's voice over the r/t: "I can't pull out, Peter, there's no response on the stick." I looked over my shoulder and could see Kurt's 109 almost on top of me. I jinked to port and throttled back, allowing his aircraft to slide alongside. I glanced at the altimetre and saw that we were just under 4,000 m and diving at an angle of about 35°. For a wild moment I thought of flying close and putting my wing tip under his to level him out. Then I realised that would most likely tip him into a spin. I could see that much of his tail empennage and the rear of his fuselage were riddled with holes.

3,000 m, 2,700, 2,500. I could see his only choice. "Kurt, you're going to have to jump for it." I tried to keep the note of anxiety out of my voice. For a few seconds there was silence over the r/t, then his voice broke in,

"I can't get the canopy open, it's jammed." His own voice sounded calm. I glanced across and could see both his arms up, struggling with the canopy. 2,000 m, 1,600... I could see the wooded hills of the Salzkammergut getting rapidly closer. If only he could level out a little, get that damned canopy open. Inexorably we continued our dive and I could feel the panic rising in my chest, my heart beating faster and faster. His voice came again, just as calm it seemed, "I've gone, Peter, I've gone." I watched grimly, helplessly, as his stricken plane fell into an ever-steeper dive. I heard my own voice calling his name, "Kurt, Kurt, Kurt!" I was almost in danger of hitting the hillside myself. I pulled back on the control column, banked a little to port to keep his plane in sight. Transfixed with horror and despair I watched as it hit the treetops, cartwheeling over and over, bits flying up as the plane disintegrated amongst the branches. Thankfully there was no fire, just a haze of dust and debris amongst which I knew my dear Kurt lay dead.

I noted the sector in which he had crashed, just south-west of Bad Ischl and put out a call to the nearest base which was Strobl. Then I pulled up into a climb and let the tears of rage and grief come unchecked. Back at bodo I sought out Ludwig and was thankful to find him safe, also claiming the destruction of a Dicke Hund, although we had also lost Khevenmüller, fallen victim to two Mustangs. Then Ludwig and I got drunk on schnapps and cognac. Kurt's body was brought from the Luftwaffenlazaretts 4/VIII at Schwarzach-St Veit to our base today and I arranged a simple military farewell for him as I have done for so many others who were less important to me. We can no longer perform the full ceremony, the Geschwader band has long since been drafted into a Luftwaffe regiment and sent to the eastern front. As Kurt's parents were killed, atomised in the raids on Hamburg, and there are no records of any other relatives, I am arranging for him to be taken to Adlersee and buried in the churchyard of St Matthias on the estate where Werner and other servants and members of my parents' household are buried. I will have a headstone erected there with Kurt's name, rank and number and a brief inscription saying he died fighting in the defence of Germany. I shall not mention his death to Mathilde or Edith, it would be too upsetting for them at this stage of the war and only increase their anxiety about me.

We heard today that that American raid on Vienna destroyed the Opera House.

From: *Hauptmann Peter von Vorzik*
I Gruppe LG294
Donaueschingen
To: *SS-Gruppenführer Count Christian von Vorzik*
116 Kaiserstraße
Berlin

21st March 1945

Dear Christian,

Thank you for your letter written from Switzerland on 12th February. It would be nice to think that the talks you mention with plenipotentiaries of the West result in peace in the near future. It may be defeatist to say it but the final collapse of our defences cannot be far away. An armistice now would allow us to salvage something from the wreckage that is our beloved country.

I can understand how irksome it must have been for you to keep a watch on Herr Dr Furtwängler. I doubt that you were following him about the streets or lurking in the corridors of the Musiksaal but when so much is at stake, when our cities are being systematically destroyed from the air, when the Russians are almost at the gates of Berlin and the Anglo-Americans crossing the Rhine, to worry over the possible defection of one man, however distinguished, seems demented. Two days ago we received the Führer's edict that everything in, on or under the land must be destroyed in case it falls into the hands of the enemy. I suppose it is similar to the scorched-earth policy adopted by the Russians after we attacked in 1941 but it has given rise to much misgiving here. We will, of course, make all our aircraft and equipment unusable if it seems likely they will be overrun by the enemy but to destroy homes, factories, utilities, farms, animals, roads, railways, bridges, every conceivable asset the country possesses would seem to be a form of mass suicide, the deliberate death of millions – *Götterdämmerung* indeed! Is that what the Führer wants?

Together with my comrade, Ludwig Varasch, I have made plans to get to his house at Höchstein where Mathilde and the babies will be if and when the end comes. Just how we will effect the journey I cannot say but thankfully we are in the southern sector of the country and it should be possible to achieve using our wits and given some good luck.

Do I infer that you plan an escape route via Scandinavia? Whatever befalls, avoid the Russians! I never thought to be writing to you in this vein but defeat has been on the horizon for over a year now although we have been forbidden to give voice to such thoughts. Now we are faced with the reality and it all comes down to every man for himself. What wounds so deeply, what gives rise to such bitterness, is the thought of the waste, the uselessness of all our efforts, the magnitude of our losses after so many victories. How could it all have been thrown away? Well, dear brother, it only remains for me to say I hope you find a way to survive the Armageddon that is about to engulf us. I know you would be welcome at Höchstein should you think it politic or possible to get there. We are facing the unknown and it is a cheering thought that we might face it together.

Please keep in touch if it is at all possible.

Ever your devoted brother,
Peter

From: Mathilde von Vorzik
Der Alter Scheune
Steuben Gasse
Höchstein
To: Hauptmann Peter von Vorzik
Luftwaffenlazaretts 3/VII
Adlersee

29th March 1945

My Darling Peter,
This morning I received the news I have been dreading every day since we were married. Ludwig managed to telephone me on a direct official line from Donaueschingen to tell me you had crashed while trying to land at Munich-Riem after your plane was hit. He said you had some nasty injuries but were expected to make a full recovery although you were still unconscious after six days. He said that the doctors said that the body needs that sort of rest after a major physical trauma and that they were expecting you to return to consciousness at any time. Of course my first instinct is to rush to be with you, darling, but that is impossible at the moment. All unofficial travel has

been suspended and in any case I could not, would not leave the children. But how I long to be at your bedside, to be there when you open your eyes, to help with the nursing, to watch over you day and night.

Ludwig says that when you are sufficiently recovered, which could take some weeks, you can be brought here by ambulance even if this part of the country is in enemy hands. (The Americans are said to be advancing towards us rapidly.) I do not know whether to believe Ludwig, whether he tells me this to help calm my anxiety. Yes, I do believe him, he is an honest man, a loyal friend and comrade. I am so thankful and relieved that he was there when you crashed. He said he followed you down and landed at Munich-Riem and was at the scene of the accident just minutes afterwards and travelled with you to Adlersee. How fortunate you have been taken there, darling, I am sure the familiar surroundings will help your recovery. Ludwig has promised to try and send me regular reports on your progress although I realise communications get more difficult as each day passes. We listen to the radio all day but the communiques are often confusing as to what is really happening. It could be that by the time you are well enough to travel, this terrible war will be over. I confess to you that I no longer care who wins or loses, I just long for peace and to have you with me for the rest of our lives. Non-believer that I have been, when Ludwig told me the awful news of your crash I offered up a prayer that your life would be spared. I asked Ludwig if he would try and communicate with Christian, I thought it would be possible to reach him at Ausland SD through official channels. I think it best not to tell Edith about it until you are well again, it would be pointless to worry and upset her now. Recover your strength, darling, and be assured that your wife and children are waiting and longing for your return.

Ever your own,
Mathilde

From: Signora Edith Novarro-Badaelli
Santa Maria Ornofotrofio
Campo Baldi
Rome
via Contessa Eleanora Novarro-Badaelli
Gordola
Switzerland
To: Hauptmann Peter von Vorzik
I Gruppe LG294
Donaueschingen

3rd April 1945

My Dear Peter,

This morning I received photographs of you with your two baby sons, sent by Mathilde. What lovely children! You have surely been blessed by God and deservedly so. I am so happy for you. I cherish the photos and will find a frame to fit them. The only pictures we are allowed to display are images of Christ but I will keep the photos among my personal possessions and look at them often. I am writing to Mathilde to thank her.

Now, I have something of great seriousness to confide in you. You have always been a helpful confidant and I shall value whatever advice you can give regarding this matter. You were most perceptive when, in your last letter, you asked if there is a romantic attachment between Frank and myself. The truth is it goes beyond the somewhat superficial interest you assume is between us. Last week Frank asked me to marry him. Not here, not now, but sometime in the future, in America. The proposal came as a shock to me as it must to you. Of course, I have not given an answer although my immediate response was to say no. However, sitting in my cell I have had plenty of time to ponder – and pray – over the matter. Frank is a very direct man, friendly, extrovert, generous, humorous, with a great deal of youthful charm. He does not have the cultured background, the poise and sophistication, the gravitas that Arturo had. But he is sincere and tells me with disarming earnestness that he is in love with me and enthuses over the life we could have together in America.

His parents emigrated from southern Italy when they were quite young. Now they own vineyards in northern California and are quite prosperous. Frank is an only child and says he will inherit his father's business when he retires in a few years' time. Frank has been brought up in the Catholic faith and says he wants children. He says that seeing me with the children here is one of the reasons he fell in love with me. As yet I do not love him but I have a deep and fond regard for his enthusiasm and general *joie de vivre* which is infectious and in such contrast to the grimness of life as it is at the moment. I could probably fall in love with him in time. At present I feel somewhat bemused by conflicting emotions. I have not yet recovered from Arturo's death and the rapidity with which this situation has developed is unsettling. Frank says he is prepared to wait for me, I am the only one for him. If I were to agree to marry him he would precede me to the US and arrange immigration papers through the state authorities in Sacramento. I asked him what his parents would think about having a German daughter-in-law, one with my previous married history, and he said they would accept anyone who made him happy. He would, of course, expect me to apply for American citizenship. The idea of taking such a momentous step is daunting and yet there is a part of me, of my brain, that responds to the prospect of starting a new life and leaving the unhappiness here behind me.

Help me, dear brother, to make a decision.

Ever your devoted sister,
Edith

Führer Order
Order of the Day

15th April 1945

Soldiers of the German eastern front! For the last time our deadly enemies the Jewish-Bolsheviks have launched their massive forces to the attack. Their aim is to reduce Germany to ruins and to exterminate our people. Many of you soldiers in the east already know the fate which threatens, above all, German women, girls and children. While the old men and children will be murdered, the women and girls will be reduced to barrack-room whores. The remainder will be marched off to Siberia.

We have foreseen this thrust, and since January have done everything possible to construct a strong front. The enemy will be greeted by massive artillery fire. Gaps in our infantry have been made good by countless new units. Our front is being strengthened by emergency units, newly raised units, and by the Volkssturm. This time the Bolshevik will meet the ancient fate of Asia – he must and shall bleed to death before the capital of the German Reich. Whoever fails in his duty at this moment behaves as a traitor to our people. The regiment or division which abandons its position acts so disgracefully that it must be ashamed before the women and children who are withstanding the terror of bombing in our cities. Above all, be on your guard against the few treacherous officers and soldiers who, in order to preserve their pitiful lives, fight against us in Russian pay, perhaps even wearing German uniform. Anyone ordering you to retreat will, unless you know him personally, be immediately arrested and, if necessary, killed on the spot, no matter what rank he may hold. If every soldier on the eastern front does his duty in the days and weeks which lie ahead, the last assault of Asia will crumple, just as the invasion in the west will finally fail, in spite of everything.

Berlin remains German, Vienna will be German again, and Europe will never be Russian.

Form yourselves into a sworn brotherhood, to defend not the empty conception of a Fatherland but your homes, your wives, your children, and, with them, our future. In these hours the whole German people look to you, my fighters in the east, and only hope that, thanks to your resolution and fanaticism, thanks to your weapons, and under your leadership, the Bolshevik assault will be choked in a bath of blood. At this moment, when Fate has removed Franklin Roosevelt from the earth, the greatest war criminal of all time, the turning point of this war will be decided.

Adolf Hitler

From: Oberleutnant Claus Grüber
Erprobungsgruppe V
Rechlin am Muritzsee
To: Hauptmann Peter von Vorzik
I Gruppe LG294
Donauaeschingen

April 21st 1945

Dear Peter,
I am writing this in the expectation that you are still in good shape and maintaining the struggle to delay the inevitable... I must apologise in

taking so long to reply to your letter received at the beginning of the year but, as you may imagine, we have been frantically busy. Most of our work here is being abandoned and to my great sorrow many secret and experimental aircraft are being deactivated or destroyed. All that wonderful work by our designers, engineers, test pilots and ground staff in ruins and to no avail.

In your letter you asked about the Amerika bomber. In two words: too late. The Junkers and Focke-Wulf projects were never accepted by the RLM and Messerschmitt's Me264 was finally abandoned in 1944 because of the scarcity of certain strategic materials. I saw the first Versuchs version at Neu-Offing back in 1942. It was a beautifully clean-looking machine with four Jumo 211 J-1 engines, a high-aspect ratio wing and twin fins and rudders. Of the other two prototypes the V2 was developed as a long-range maritime reconnaissance version and destroyed during an air-raid and the V3 never reached completion. That was the history of so many wonderful aircraft we helped develop. The situation being what it is I am making personal plans to deactivate myself! I have no intention of being hung from a lamppost or sent to Siberia so have decided to decamp west. I have managed to make a little cache of fuel and, at the earliest opportunity, probably a late afternoon, before twilight, will snatch the unit's Taifun and hedge-hop to the British lines just west of the Elbe. One of the test pilots here, Johann Limberg (did you ever meet him during one of your visits here?), will accompany me. The enterprise is not without risk, of course, but some whitewash sloshed over the markings will help anonymity or create confusion long enough to find some field or autobahn where we can land and give ourselves up. Johann hopes to be able to make his way to Frankfurt while I, who have no home, will be happy to be fed and accommodated by our captors. I expect, because of our work at Rechlin, that we will be interrogated. I have no qualms now about revealing any of our secrets to the British or Americans. So, dear comrade, wish me luck, let us hope we will be able to contact one another sometime when peace is established, although where I shall end up I cannot tell.

Wishing you and your family good fortune whatever the future may bring.

Your sincere compatriot,
Claus

From: *SS-Gruppenführer Count Christian von Vorzik*
c/o Direktör Sven Oskarson
Strandvägen 411
Stockholm
To: *Hauptmann Peter von Vorzik*
Luftwaffenlazaretts 3/VII
Adlersee

24th April 1945

Dear Peter,

Before leaving Berlin I heard from your comrade, Ludwig, that you had been shot down and were lying comatose at Adlersee. I hope that by now you will have regained consciousness and that your injuries will not prove to be too serious. How fortunate that we leased the Schloss to the Luftwaffe and that you have been taken there! I must tell you that this is the last you will hear from me for a very considerable time, maybe some years. Some days ago I left Berlin with Walter to join the Reichsführer-SS at his HQ at Hohenlychen. From thence we travelled to Plön where Walter was expecting to meet Count Bernadotte, representing the Swedish Red Cross, to expedite talks ostensibly about Scandinavian prisoners. At Plön I made my own private arrangements to take the ferry from Flensburg to Stockholm where I am staying with Signe. Signe's father, Herr Direktör Oskarson, is arranging a new identity for me with all the relevant papers. I shall shortly be sailing for Uruguay where I shall take up an appointment as his agent. I hope Signe will join me at a later date. You may wonder at these somewhat radical decisions and developments but the political and military situation demands extreme measures. I have long foreseen that, with the collapse of the Reich, senior members of the SS will be in danger of arrest by the victorious powers with the ensuing possibility of imprisonment and execution. You have but to remember what happened to Arturo to realise what can happen when there is a state of political flux. At such times I could even be in danger from certain malignant members of the SS and the Party. Walter told me that Canaris has been hanged at Flossenburg camp. I have no intention of suffering the same fate or being held to account for policies decided upon by my superiors, particularly Reinhard and the Reichsführer-SS.

You may remember I once wrote to you that, during a tour of inspection of Jewish settlements in the east, I had witnessed numerous scenes of "unimaginable horror." I never expounded upon what they were and you never asked for details. Those "settlements" were, in fact, extermination camps where Jewish men, women and children, brought from all over Europe, were systematically killed, mostly by being gassed in specially built chambers, their bodies incinerated in ovens. Others died through starvation, disease, mass shooting, torture and medical experiments carried out without anaesthetic. Their numbers run into millions. Our Einsatzgruppen (which I once volunteered to join – thank heaven Reinhard dissuaded me) entered Russia with the specific purpose of killing hundreds of thousands of ordinary civilians, political leaders, professors, priests, teachers, artisans, young and old. Germany will long be vilified for these actions and it is for these reasons that I find it necessary to adopt another identity in a distant part of the world. No doubt you will be shocked by these revelations. I have lived with this terrible knowledge for the past three years and now the time of reckoning has come. Thankfully, I do not have the prominence of men such as the Reichsführer-SS, Müller, Kaltenbrunner or a score of others I could mention. It will be easier for me to find a new life. Do not, I beg you, seek to find me or correspond with this address. Perhaps, some day, circumstances will allow us a happy reunion. Until then, best wishes for your rapid recovery. Remember me as

> Your affectionate brother,
> Christian

PS You may make up whatever story you please to tell our solicitor in Munich, that I perished in the rubble of Berlin, perhaps. I relinquish all claims to Schloss Adlersee, etc. C.

From: Hauptmann Peter von Vorzik
Luftwaffenlazaretts 3/VII
Adlersee
To: Signora Edith Novarro-Badaelli
Santa Maria Orfanotrofio
Campo Baldi
Rome
via Contessa Eleanora Novarro-Badaelli
Gordola
Switzerland

4th May 1945

My Dear Edith,

Your letter of the 3rd April arrived today with a bundle of others that had also taken a long, circuitous route. As you see, I am here at Schloss Adlersee which, as you can imagine, is a strange situation. So much is familiar and yet so much has changed. Our old rooms have been transformed into wards and surgeries. The ballroom is for physiotherapy and father's study is the director's office. The pictures and *objets d'art* have been replaced by medical apparatus, the familiar furniture, the console tables, the chandeliers, the sconces, the mirrors replaced by utilitarian tables and chairs, noticeboards and simple lamps, the velvet and damask hangings by black-out frames and coarse curtaining. Doctors and nurses and men in wheel-chairs fill the halls and passageways. Now and again I glimpse an American soldier since they occupied Bavaria some days ago. I am in what mother called the Chinese salon with the hand-painted wallpaper covered in exotic birds and with little figures crossing over bridges. Through the window I can see the lake glinting between the pine trees. So many memories keep coming back like a dream half-remembered.

Apparently, I was in a coma for over three weeks following my crash but I recall nothing beyond my attempt to land at Munich-Riem. My good friend and comrade, Ludwig, has visited me here and been most helpful in arranging certain things. In a day or so he will be making his way back to Höchstein. You will be sad to learn that Kurt was shot down and killed just eleven days before my own crash-landing. I have arranged for him to be buried in the churchyard at St Matthias. When I am able I hope to go over and view his grave.

Now, dear sister, to consider the important matter you confide in me. Yes, it was a shock to hear of Frank's proposal and yet, somehow, not a surprise. From your previous letters it was possible to discern a developing interest although I did not suppose it would reach such a conclusion so quickly. But such things do happen: love at first sight is probably more prevalent than we know. My own attachment to Mathilde was a comparatively rapid one. Frank, being American, comes from a culture that moves at a greater speed than we are used to in Europe, has less conformity to social mores, is less confined by tradition. Love itself knows no bounds. My answer to your question, then (perhaps, in the interim, you have already found the answer yourself?) is for you to say yes to Frank. Take this opportunity to begin a new life for yourself and forget the tragedy of the past. Of course, it is a big step into the unknown but trust your feelings, your own judgement. Above all think that this is possibly God's choice for you, that the devious route through Arturo, through the orphanage, is His way of leading you to happy fulfilment as a wife and mother.

Christian tells me in a final letter that he is going, incognito, to South America and asks not to be contacted. He confirms that the heinous crimes that you referred to previously which I was disposed to dismiss as enemy propaganda, did occur, even more horrible than can be imagined. Now I must confess to you that my own journey is coming to an end. Lying here at Adlersee I have been forced to consider the future, my own future and that of my wife, my children and my Fatherland and, like you, I have chosen to go into the unknown.

You have always prayed for my physical safety; pray now, dear sister, for my soul.

Ever your loving brother, in this world and the next,
Peter

From: Hauptmann Peter von Vorzik
Luftwaffenlazaretts 3/VII
Adlersee
To: Mathilde von Vorzik
Die Alter Scheune
Steuben Gasse
Höchstein

7th May 1945

My Darling Mathilde,

I am entrusting this letter to my dear friend and comrade, Ludwig, who is now making his way home to Höchstein. With luck and the cooperation of the American authorities he should be with you within two days. By the time you read this I should, figuratively speaking, have drunk the waters of Lethe and be resting in oblivion. Believe me, darling, it is not a decision I have made without difficulty and much soul-searching. Lying here in solitude I have considered the future, our future, the future of Wolfchen and Heini, from every possible angle, every conceivable perspective. At the risk of being thought cowardly (I hope my wartime service would preclude that accusation), egocentric or even cruel, I am convinced that, taking the long view, it is the best decision for all of us. I realise that, initially, you will be anguished and, possibly, angry (you have never been angry with me) but the pain of loss will lessen with time and time, I believe, will recompense you.

My own feelings of uselessness apart, I could not burden you with the responsibility of caring for a cripple for the rest of your life, you who are still young, beautiful and active, nor would I want the children to grow up pitying a father unable to share in their youthful activities. I carry with me joyful memories of our few years together, ecstatic moments snatched during troubled times. I hope, darling, that you will always remember them too, although I also hope and trust that they will be overlaid by new joys that await you. I have sent a codicil to my will to our solicitors in Munich. Ludwig returns with a copy for you, together with certain other letters and papers. The journal that I have been writing at odd moments throughout the war and which, as yet, is incomplete, will subsequently be forwarded to you with the rest of my personal effects. Dispose of them as you will.

Christian has decamped to South America and does not wish to be contacted. No doubt you will continue to correspond with Edith. I have advised her to accept the proposal of marriage from her admirer, Frank, and to seek a new life in America. It is my earnest hope that, sometime in the future, you and Ludwig may find a mutual affinity. He is a fine man, as you know, brave, loyal, generous, cultured. He would be a good influence on Wolfchen and Heini. I leave you in his capable hands at a time that will be bleak for Germany.

Farewell, my darling Mathilde, try not to think too harshly of he who was always

Your adoring and devoted,

Peter

Hauptmann Peter von Vorzik
Journal entry

8th May 1945

It is the end, it is finished. The war is over, Germany has been defeated and the Third Reich lies in ruins. According to radio reports the Führer committed suicide in his bunker beneath the Berlin Chancellery on April 30th, along with the woman he married during the last hours, Eva Braun, and together with Reichsminister Josef Goebbels, his wife Magda and their six children whom they poisoned. All the German forces throughout Europe have surrendered unconditionally and many senior members of the Party and military chiefs, including Reichsmarschall Göring, Reichsminister von Ribbentrop, Field Marshalls Jodl, Keitel, Kesselring and von Runstedt and many other Chiefs of Staff have been arrested. Germany is occupied by Anglo-American forces in the west and south and in the east, including Berlin, by the Russians. Mussolini and his mistress, Clara Petacci, have met a typically crude end, shot by Italian partisans and strung up by the feet in the main square of Milan.

My own end as a fighter pilot occurred on 23rd March. The day began with the familiar warning that bombers of the American 15th Air Force were approaching, expected target Vienna and its environs. My Staffel took off at 09.17 hrs and climbed to 6,000 m, expecting to intercept the enemy somewhere north-west of Munich. I was flying as leader of a Schwarme composed of my new replacement Katschmarek, Feldwebel

639

Josef Derner, and Ludwig with his Katschmarek, Unteroffizier Friedrich Eckermann. The weather was mostly clear with some formations of cumulo-nimbus to the south over the Bavarian Alps.

The enemy bombers were sighted in their usual box formations, heavily protected by swarms of Mustangs and Thunderbolts, looking like shoals of fish as the sun caught their silver wings and fuselages. I was about to order the attack on the leading bombers, as I had done so often before, when Ludwig's voice broke in over the r/t that we ourselves were being attacked from above and behind by a group of undetected Mustangs. Even as he spoke there was a cry from Derner and his aircraft went lurching by, almost colliding with me as it spun out of control, black smoke pouring from the engine cowling. At the same moment my own Gustav shuddered under a hail of heavy-calibre bullets that raked me from tail to propeller boss. Had they been cannon shells my aircraft would have been ripped apart. I was saved myself by the armour-plate behind the cockpit seat. Instinctively I bunted over and put the aircraft into a steep dive, looking desperately for cloud cover. There was none. Glancing over my shoulder I could see the threatening shape of my pursuer as more bullets punched holes in the starboard wing. I knew I could not out-dive the Mustang but then, just as I prepared myself for the *coup de grâce*, the enemy turned away sharply. Ludwig had had him in his sights and scored some hits with his cannon.

My Gustav, however, was mortally damaged. Leaking glycol and with the oil pressure falling and the temperature gauge rising, the engine would soon seize up or explode into flames. I put out a call to any airfield in sector Lima-Zebra and was rewarded with an answer from Munich-Riem. Throttling right back and losing height I turned south-south-west, thankful that the controls still responded and assured by Ludwig's voice saying, "I'm staying with you, Peter." Guided by the controller's voice from Riem I could see the airfield not far from the Munich-Wasserburg road. I made a long circuit to the south so as to come into the wind. As I lined up on the runway that had been specially built for the Me262s I saw that the temperature gauge was far into the red. I was already over the runway, with flaps and undercarriage down, holding off the stall when suddenly the nose dropped and I saw the concrete rushing up towards me. My last memory was desperately hauling on the stick to get the nose up again.

The doctors told me that I was in a coma for nearly three weeks. I awoke in a vaguely familiar room that I struggled to identify as I lay looking at pale yellow walls decorated with birds and begonias and little figures. There were faded patches on the walls where pictures had been. A young nurse entered the room, stared at me, hesitated, then hurried away again. Within a minute or two a doctor in a white coat appeared and began talking. I heard my own voice as if it was coming from a long way away. The doctor was asking me how I felt and I remember my distant voice saying I felt very well except that my legs were aching, especially my ankles. He pulled back the bed covers and it was then that I saw that I had no legs, just two bandaged stumps sticking out from my torso. I smiled foolishly and said to the doctor, "No legs?" He shook his head and then went on to tell me, in some detail, how my legs had been crushed to a pulp by the impact of the crash. I had been cut, unconscious, from the cockpit, given a blood transfusion and the mangled legs had been amputated. I was lucky to be alive he said, a miracle the plane had not caught fire. No legs. I have been lying in this room at Adlersee for days, thinking about the implication. A therapist has told me that I could be fitted with artificial legs when the stumps have healed properly. I could regain some mobility with the aid of the legs and crutches. Many men learn to manage very well, he said, encouragingly. Is that what I want, limited mobility? A cripple, unable to run, to play games with my boys, from time to time needing help from Mathilde. An object of pity, carefully shielded. Unable to fulfil my hopes of flying new aircraft on new routes in a peaceful world. Is that what I want? There have been brief moments when I thought I might do it, when I thought I could face a half-life. After all, the British fighter pilot, Douglas Bader, managed it. But his circumstances were different, it was wartime and he was fighting for his country. Now the war is over and I do not have that kind of courage.

My mind was made up when Ludwig arrived bringing a bundle of letters and personal effects taken from the bag kept behind the cockpit and his own good cheer. Dear Ludwig who, ironically, saved my life so that I should be faced with this decision. He wheeled me down to St Matthias so that I could see where Kurt is buried. Just a grassy mound at present but in time he will have a marble headstone. I should like to have been buried next to him but the manner of my death will preclude that. I have said in my will that I wish to be cremated and my ashes scattered in the lake. There is so much more I could write but to what purpose? I have set down all that matters and written my farewells to Mathilde and

Edith. Tonight, when the nurse has given me my tablets and my hot drink I shall reach across to the nightstand, open my toilet bag and take out the tablet of coarse soap within which I long ago hid the little metal capsule enclosing the glass ampule of strychnine, the capsule given to us when we were flying over Russia. They say death comes in a few seconds.

And so, at last, not without regret but with considerable relief I can write

FINIS